the dark FOUNDATIONS

THE LAMB AMONG THE STARS SERIES ☿ BOOK 2

TYNDALE HOUSE
PUBLISHERS, INC.,
CAROL STREAM,
ILLINOIS

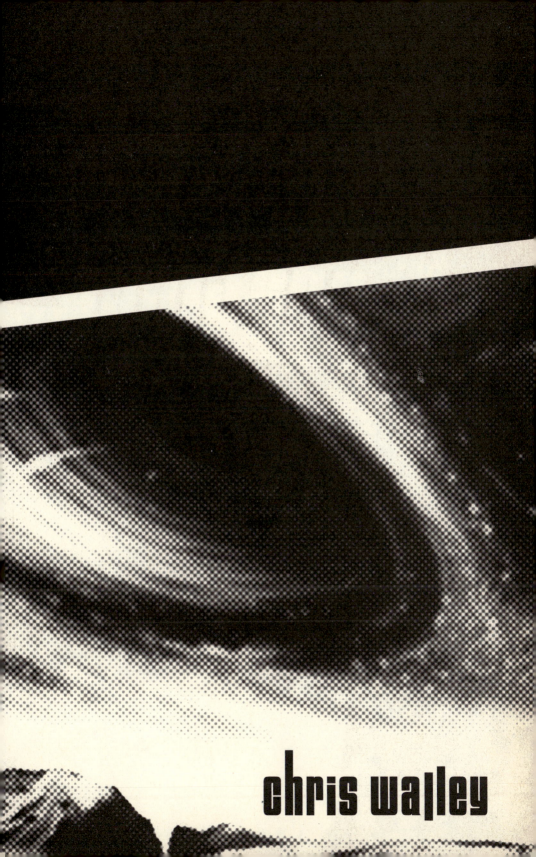

chris walley

Visit Tyndale's exciting Web site at www.tyndale.com

TYNDALE and Tyndale's quill logo are registered trademarks of Tyndale House Publishers, Inc.

The Dark Foundations

Designed by Dean H. Renninger

Edited by Linda Washington

Library of Congress Cataloging-in-Publication Data

Walley, Chris.
   The dark foundations / Chris Walley.
      p. cm. — (The lamb among the stars ; bk. 2.)
   Summary: As the Lord-Emperor of the Dominion prepares to attack Farholme, then the Assembly, Farholme's Commander Merral D'Avanos braces for war admid doubts about the planet's defenses and his own weaknesses, but then receives an offer of assistance from a most unexpected source.
   ISBN-13: 978-1-4143-0767-1 (hardcover : alk. paper)
   ISBN-10: 1-4143-0767-5 (hardcover: alk. paper)
   [1. Christian life—Fiction. 2. Science fiction.] I. Title. II. Series: Walley, Chris. Lamb among the stars ; bk. 2.
   PZ7.W159315Dar 2006
   [Fic]—dc22   2006009726

Printed in the United States of America

11 10 09 08 07 06
 7 6 5 4 3 2 1

To my many friends in the A Rocha Trust
who seek to be the faithful stewards of
the Creator by preserving his creation.
Their faith, vision, and courage are an example.

Such music (as 'tis said)
Before was never made,
But when of old the sons of morning sung,
While the Creator great
His constellations set,
And the well-balanced world on hinges hung,
And cast the dark foundations deep,
And bid the welt'ring waves their oozy channel keep.

JOHN MILTON,
ON THE MORNING OF CHRIST'S NATIVITY

ACKNOWLEDGMENTS

I would like to thank many people for help on what has been, in every sense, a long book. My wife, Alison, and the "next generation"—John (and Celia) and Mark—were continuous encouragements. As an editor, Linda Washington somehow managed to be simultaneously brave and ruthless *and* tactful and gentle.

The A Rocha Trust (www.arocha.org), to whom this book is dedicated and with whom I have had many dealings, is a Christian organization working to conserve nature. If places such as the Aammiq Wetland do survive into the future, their labors will have been a major factor.

In telling of the return of evil to the Assembly of Worlds and how Merral D'Avanos of Farholme fought against it, we have heard how the intruders came to Farholme and how their space vessel was found and destroyed at the battle of Fallambet Lake Five. Yet so far, our focus has only been on Merral and Farholme. The rest of the Assembly and the forces of the Dominion have been on only the very edges of our tale. Now though, as the field of battle opens up and the greatest of all wars looms, the scope of our tale must also broaden.

As we begin that account, we must briefly step back to just over a month before the battle at Fallambet Lake Five. For even as Merral searched for the intruder ship, his remote world was becoming the center of wider interest. At the very heart of each of the two human realms—the Dominion of Lord-Emperor Nezhuala and the Assembly of Worlds—minds and wills were turning rapidly toward Farholme.

With very different intentions.

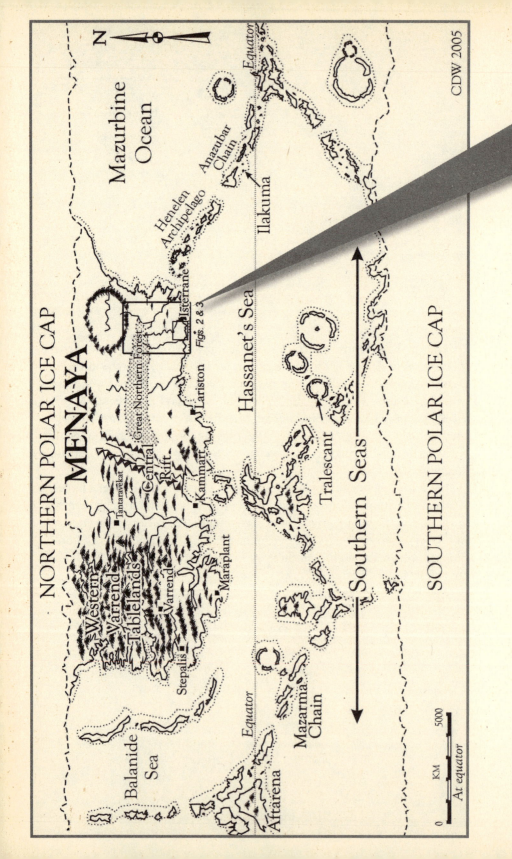

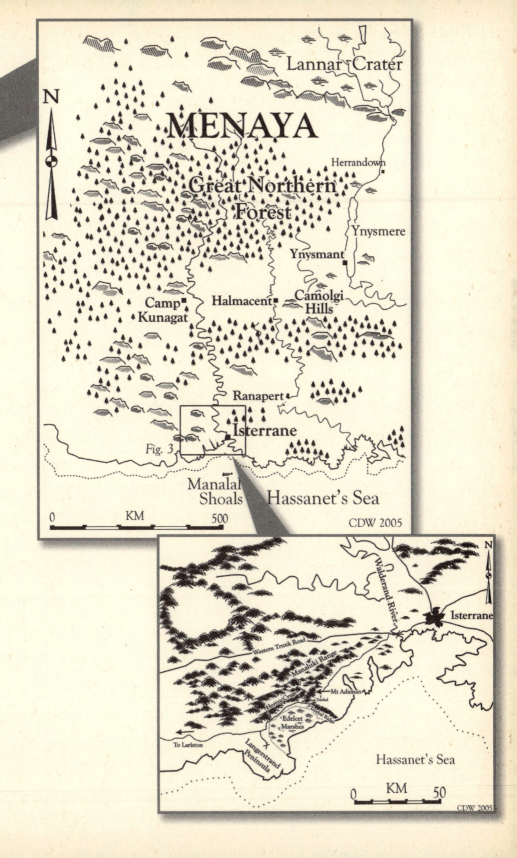

Lannar Crater

N

MENAYA

Great Northern Forest

Herrandown

Ynysmere

Ynysmant

Camolgi Hills

Camp Kunagat

Halmacent

Ranapert

Isterrane

Fig. 3

Manalai Shoals

Hassanet's Sea

0   KM   500

CDW 2005

Walderand River

N

Isterrane

Western Trunk Road

Manaluki Range

Mt Adaman

Herren Craag

Edelcet Marshes

To Lariston

Langerstrand Peninsula

Hassanet's Sea

0   KM   50

CDW 2005

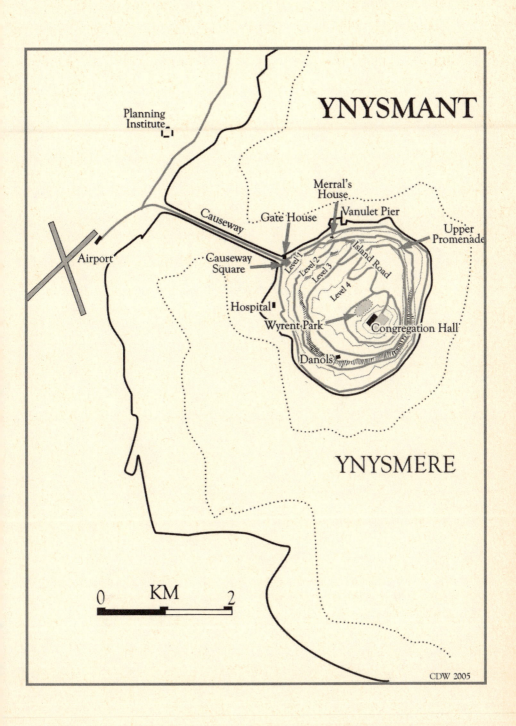

YNYSMANT

Planning
Institute

Merral's
House
Vanulet Pier
Gate House
Upper
Promenade
Causeway
Airport
Level 1
Island Road
Level 2
Causeway
Square
Level 3
Level 4
Hospital
Wyrent Park
Congregation Hall
Danols

YNYSMERE

0   KM   2

CDW 2005

Over four hundred light-years beyond Farholme, Sentius Lezaroth, Fleet-Captain of the Tenth Dominion Task Force and Margrave of Cam Nisua, scrutinized the main pilot's screen on his low-orbit lander as it entered the final moments of the descent. There was nothing for him to do—every aspect of its descent from the battleship *Strallak Ravager* through the turbulent atmosphere of Khalamaja had been handled by the planet's control center.

I hate remotely handled landings. I have no control over events. I feel vulnerable. And today, I don't even know where I'm going.

His screen showed the sprawling, dirty city of Khetelak, the planetary capital. Within moments the lander was heading toward a tiny landing pad high on the spire of what seemed to be the tallest building.

"We are landing, Admiral!" he called out, and braced himself.

The touchdown, however, was gentle. As soon as the lander was stable and all the other parameters looked normal, Lezaroth initiated the power-down procedure. *That much they allow me to do.*

He adjusted his uniform and glanced at the only other occupant of the lander, Admiral Kalartha-Har.

Kalartha-Har, a bulky man with a worn, heavy face and thinning silver hair, stared out of a window, drumming his fingers against the seat.

He's nervous. Both of us are. But then, who wouldn't be when you're suddenly called to a meeting with our elusive and mysterious Lord-Emperor Nezhuala—a man I've never met. Few of us have.

"Sir, where are we, *exactly?*"

"We are, Margrave, on the summit of the Tower of Carenas at the citadel of Kal-na-Tanamuz. In short, we are at the heart of the Dominion." The admiral's deep voice seemed studiously neutral.

Lezaroth noted that the admiral addressed him by his title rather than by his rank. *But then, as an unlanded commoner, he's probably more impressed than I am by my membership of a noble house.*

Lezaroth gazed through the cockpit glass. The Final Emblem of the Dominion, the red loop of infinity on the blackness of space, flapped energetically from a flagpole at the far end of the platform. Hundreds of meters below, the sprawl of Khetelak stretched out in the red-hued late-evening sunlight, its deep alleys and towering slums hidden by steam and smoke. To his right, the crimson orb of Sarata was setting in dust clouds over a vast salt sea.

Lezaroth turned to the small mirror above the screen that allowed the pilot a view of the four passenger seats and checked his appearance once more. *The model of a perfect Dominion warrior: a well-developed but not exaggerated musculature, the space-bronzed cheek with its small but striking scar, the broad line of significant medal ribbons, and three tiny golden rosettes on the shoulder to show I am of a high-level noble house.*

A green light flashed.

"We can disembark now, sir."

The admiral unbuckled himself and climbed stiffly out of his seat. "My muscles seem to seize up on these flights," he moaned. "I'm showing my age."

The hatch door opened. Lezaroth was struck by a cold gust of gritty, dry wind that carried a hint of sulfur. *But at least I can stand upright in it and frostbite isn't thirty seconds away.*

At the foot of the ladder, the admiral gestured Lezaroth over to his side.

Aha. He wants to say something and this is the old trick. A cooling ship emits so many other signals that it's hard for any listening device to hear what anyone is saying.

"Some advice, Margrave," the admiral said in quick, low tones. "Remember that this isn't the officers' mess of some ship of the Tenth, a hundred light-years from Sarata. Guard your tongue in the presence of the lord-emperor and pray that he hasn't heard any of your treasonable grumbling."

Lezaroth said nothing. *What you call treasonable grumbling, I call legitimate grievances. But yes, I do pray to the powers that he hasn't heard of them.*

The admiral's tired gray eyes seemed to be full of an urgent warning. "You are talented, have a good battlefield record, and are a margrave of Cam Nisua. But none of these will help you in the slightest before His Highness if he thinks you're disloyal."

"Thank you, sir."

"The lord-emperor merits the greatest respect."

"I know, sir." He paused. "But why are we here?"

"Because he asked to see us. That's all we need to know. Obey, Margrave. It is our life's purpose to serve him."

Well, Admiral, you would say that. Your loyalty to Nezhuala has paid you well. You have a family and a house on Alhama.

A green holographic arrow appeared just above the ground.

"We'd better go," the admiral hissed. "Let me do the introductions. But careful. Especially here. And at sunset."

"Why sunset?"

"Don't ask!" There was a nervous shake of the head. "There are rumors."

They walked forward, following a line of arrows toward an open hatchway.

Suddenly, Lezaroth had a feeling of alarm. *Odd. I have no gifting in extra-physical matters and have no known occult powers; but I feel that something, somewhere ahead of us, is not safe. There is danger here.*

Instinctively, Lezaroth toggled on the neuroswitch in his mind that operated his bio-augment systems. The colored biometric icons flashed on his field of view, showing no metabolic anomalies other than a slightly heightened pulse—nothing to indicate a biological reason for his unease.

He glanced at his comm systems. They were inactive; the Khetelak authorities hadn't allowed him to link up with the local net.

Upon reaching the hatchway, he toggled off the bio-augments. It was protocol to switch off all such systems in meetings with superior ranks.

His intuition of danger troubled him. *I hate this. I feel trapped. I'm without weapons, armor, comm links, or military backup. It goes against everything I have learned in ten years of warfare. I am vulnerable here.*

The hatchway revealed a steep, dark stairway. As Lezaroth and the admiral followed glowing arrows down the stairs, Lezaroth touched his chest, feeling beneath his uniform the talisman of Zahlman-Hoth, the god of soldiers. *Great Zahlman, protect me. If I must fight today, give strength to my arm and resolve to my will. If I shed blood, may you drink and enjoy it.*

Three flights down, a door slid open to reveal a large, gloomy hall. As he walked through the doorway, Lezaroth felt the hairs on the back of his neck prickle. It was a sure sign that he was in the presence of some sort of extra-physical phenomena. He looked around urgently, as tense as if he were on the battlefield, scanning for any danger and wishing again that he was armored and had weapons and backup.

The long, stone-floored hall had a high-vaulted ceiling and was full of strange, twisted statues towering twice and even three times a man's height. It was not a well-lit place and the figures cast odd shadows. In fact, the shadows dominated the room. The air was heavy and still and had an unpleasant odor.

"Fascinating," the admiral murmured. There was an edgy catch in his voice.

The statues were all totems or idols, but bigger and more impressive than the ones usually in temples. Some Lezaroth recognized. The nearest, an angular, vaguely birdlike figure with claws and jagged bill, was Naxhfulain, the god of plagues. Behind him, a stooping creature with long fangs and spidery fingers was Hamartos, the deity of miscarriage and infant death. But he had never seen so many large ones together.

The shadows caught his eye again. Did they shift or was it just his imagination?

They stood still gazing around. Lezaroth suddenly heard voices coming from somewhere, a whispering so quiet and high in pitch that it was on the very edges of audibility. As he listened, he could hear other elusive sounds: a low murmuring and a faint feverish chattering.

He felt alarmed. *This is not just a museum. There is power and hostility here. A man who strayed into this place might easily not walk out alive.*

Suddenly, the high-pitched whispering grew louder and more excited.

"He is here!" hissed the admiral.

Lezaroth looked to the far end of the hall. Between the lines of idols and their shadows, a slightly built man of medium height walked toward them. He had light brown hair and wore a long, dark jacket and matching trousers. Even at this distance Lezaroth was struck by the steady, authoritative way in which he walked. *Things wait for this man, not he for them.*

As the man came nearer, the shadows seemed to shift around him as he moved, giving the effect of light focusing on him as in a painting.

It has to be an illusion.

The noises—the whispers, murmurs, and chattering—seemed to grow louder.

A few steps away from them, the man stopped. Lezaroth noted a face that was almost entirely unremarkable apart from its extreme pallor and the dark gray, almost black, eyes that seemed to stare at him with an intensity that made him uncomfortable. There was a smooth smile on the anonymous and unblemished face.

I know that face. I have known it since childhood. It walks through my dreams. It had not changed since he first saw it on the posters that hung in every room in the nursery complex. *How old is the lord-emperor really? He has openly wielded power for fifty years. But before that, we know little. Even now, when we easily live for two or more centuries, his immunity to age is remarkable.*

The high, invisible whispering was suddenly cut short.

"Gentlemen, welcome," said Lord-Emperor Nezhuala. His voice was gentle, resonant, and utterly authoritative.

"My lord," Admiral Kalartha-Har said, and bowed swiftly and deeply.

"My lord," repeated Lezaroth the merest moment after him, and bowed in a similar manner.

The lord-emperor lifted his palms upward. His hands were covered by black gloves. "This is the great hall of Kal-na-Tanamuz—the repository of the figures of the powers."

Lezaroth was struck by the lord-emperor's conversational, even amiable tone, but warned himself again not to relax. That odd intuition of alarm was still fresh in his mind.

The admiral spoke. "Lord-Emperor, it is an honor to be received by you."

The lord-emperor made a gesture of welcome. "Admiral, it is nice to see you again. The family well? On Alhama, aren't they?"

"My lord, they are very well. And yes, it is Alhama." There was an odd hesitancy in the admiral's voice. "My lord, may I present to you Margrave Sentius Lezaroth, Fleet-Captain of the Glorious Tenth?" His words seemed hasty.

It is as if he wants to change the subject.

The lord-emperor extended a gloved hand and Lezaroth shook it. It was unresponsive, but he felt a faint sensation of energy.

"Captain, *Margrave* Lezaroth," Nezhuala began, "I am delighted to meet you. I followed your actions in the war. I know your background too. Cam Nisua is a world long loyal to me and the House of Lezaroth has always served the Freeborn well." He smiled. "I have read the commendations. You 'forcefully deployed Krallen,' 'skillfully ordered bombardments,' and 'personally donned armor and fought.'" The lord-emperor spoke in sharply truncated sentences. "Altogether splendid. The victory that we won at Tellzanur was achieved through your actions."

Lezaroth bowed. *I could honor the dead here, but I won't. They are dead and I'm alive.* "Thank you, my lord. It is my life's purpose to serve you. However many my days may be, they are all at your disposal."

They were clichés from regimental songs, but he needed something safe to say.

The lord-emperor looked at Lezaroth with that gaze of unnerving intensity.

This is a man with charisma, a man who can inspire others to sacrifice. Men will die for him and he knows it. He did not become the creator of the Dominion and the first lord-emperor for nothing.

There was something about this man that fascinated him. He tried to remember some of his many objections to the lord-emperor and found that they had somehow vanished. *How odd.*

"You are young for a margrave."

"My father died early. I had elder half-brothers, but they were killed in battle." *I will not mention that two died in family feuds.*

Nezhuala nodded. "I see. Now please, follow me. Both of you."

Nezhuala turned smoothly and walked down the hall, with the admiral and Lezaroth following at a diplomatic distance. The mysterious noises seemed to have started up again. As they walked, Lezaroth heard their feet echo oddly. Sounds seemed strange here, as if the air was somehow too thick.

The lord-emperor waved an arm at the figures. "Artists' representations of course. They look very different when you actually meet them."

He stopped suddenly and turned to Lezaroth. "Did you know that I talk to some of the powers?" His voice had a candid, almost naive tone that invited confidence.

"I had heard tales, my lord." *More than tales.* He recollected how, under torture, one renegade from Tellzanur had spat out that Nezhuala was a "witch king in league with demons." His security officer had killed the man there and then, but no one had bothered to deny the charge.

The lord-emperor's gaze seemed fixed on a carved form with holes for eyes. "It is my duty, Margrave. I do it for the Dominion. I see myself as the great intermediary—the man who stands between men and the One."

"My lord, in you we see the infinite."

Suddenly, Nezhuala tilted his head slightly as if listening to something. He nodded, as if agreeing, and whispered some inaudible words. Then he turned to Lezaroth. "Excuse me. Some of the lesser powers wanted to speak to me."

At a gap in the line of the totems the lord-emperor turned left and led the way through more shadowy figures into an open space. In the middle of the space was a weird, high-backed chair made, it seemed, out of many twisted, pale bones.

"Take the seat, Margrave."

Lezaroth, already tense, now found himself in a high state of alarm. But there was nothing to be gained by refusing, so he sat. The chair gave slightly under his weight. He was aware of a strange, unpleasant smell. A glance around showed ominous, dark stains on the floor slabs. Another glance showed that the statues all around were open-mouthed.

The alarm gave way to fear.

The admiral sat down on a stone bench not far away to his right. His hunched posture and pale, troubled face suggested a deep concern.

The lord-emperor stood before Lezaroth. "I need to talk to you, Margrave, about several things. But first . . ." He made an odd fluid movement with his hands.

In an instant, Lezaroth found himself immobilized.

Don't panic! Analyze! But terror was not far away. *A trick of extra-physical forces.* He tried to move, but his leg, back, and arm muscles were frozen solid.

"Margrave, I do not waste words. I have followed your career very closely. More closely than you think. In fact, I know everything about you." The menace in the lord-emperor's words chilled Lezaroth, and his premonitions of danger seemed to be fully justified.

He said nothing, because he didn't know what would come out. He heard the voices again and heard anticipation in their whispers and murmurs. *They are watching.*

"Supporters tell me that you say things about me. I have recordings." Nezhuala twisted his fingers and a hologram appeared just in front of Lezaroth's face. He saw himself in the weapons bay of the *Ravager* speaking loudly.

"Why does His Highness"—there was scorn in the title—"make tactical military decisions? Why does he overrule the advice of his generals? Why are there random promotions and demotions? As if on a whim? Tell me, someone!"

Another clip appeared. Lezaroth saw himself with the chief engineer, in the forward hold this time. *Oh no, not that conversation! Great Zahlman, protect me!*

"I'll tell you why this doesn't work." There was anger in Lezaroth's voice as he pounded his fist on a nonfunctional munitions lifter. "It's because it's worn out. We need a new one. And why aren't we getting one? Because all our resources are used in building this monstrous Blade of Night—a structure that no one other than the lord-emperor and his attendant demons knows what it does. Five hundred kilometers long, the mass of a sizable asteroid, yet no known purpose. Give me patience!"

A third clip. Only last week—in the ship's gym of all places.

"I don't get it. It doesn't make any sense. None at all. The war against the renegades is over—has been for months. 'The final triumph of the Dominion,' he told us. So why don't we have peace? Why haven't the battle fleets been stood down? Why haven't the Krallen factories closed? Why hasn't military conscription ended? Not a sign of any of it! The old fool at Khetelak has put the military machine into top gear. New battle fleets, new long-range ships, and Krallen production at a record high." There was a murmur from someone off camera and Lezaroth continued. "I'll tell you why! He's going to attack the Assembly and he's going to kill us all. They outnumber us twenty to one at least. It's madness!"

The holograms vanished.

"Margrave," the lord-emperor said in a cold voice, "I have more of the same. I have enough information on you for a public court-martial and the slowest of executions."

Lezaroth was as scared as he had ever been. He was more scared than at the disastrous attack at Krull's Crater and even more scared than when the deployment pod engines had failed on the descent at Nadrewai.

"My lord, I beg forgiveness and seek your mercy. I spoke rashly."

The lord-emperor took a step closer. There was a gleaming knife in his hand.

This is it. Lezaroth realized he was sweating.

The oddly twisted silver blade gently touched his throat. It was cold and seemed to be held with such extraordinary steadiness that it didn't even tremble. *He could take my life and not give it another thought.*

"I ought to kill you."

On the edge of audibility he heard the whispers reach a new intensity.

Suddenly from his right came a slight cough.

"Admiral, do you wish to say something?"

"My lord, Your Highness . . . I hardly dare." The admiral's voice was tremulous. "But the margrave is a young man. A bit rash. These statements—oh, *how* I warned him—were just words. He is a fine soldier and—for all his words—very loyal. I ask . . . for mercy."

Thank you, old man! Great Zahlman bless and protect you.

The knife at Lezaroth's throat didn't flicker. "A brave comment, Admiral. I am . . . persuaded." Nezhuala drew the knife away.

"So, Margrave, it won't happen again?"

"No, my lord. Never." *And I mean it.*

"Good." There was a flexing of the pale lips into a sort of smile. Nezhuala made another gesture and Lezaroth felt his muscles freed.

"Now, Margrave, just wait here a moment. You may leave the chair. I need to take the admiral next door. When I come back, we must talk."

Lezaroth turned to the admiral. *Thanks,* he mouthed, but there was no response. The admiral was staring at the lord-emperor with a look of intense fear and perplexity.

As the two men left, Lezaroth stood carefully and stretched his muscles. Alone among the watching statues and their shadows, he felt an almost giddy mixture of fear, relief, and gratitude.

⬡⬡⬡⬡⬡

A few minutes later Lezaroth was listening to the strange noises when he suddenly realized with a start of alarm that the lord-emperor stood before him. *I never heard him!*

"Margrave," Nezhuala began, "I did not spare you out of mercy. I despise mercy. I spared you, because I think you may be useful. But come, let us walk amid the forms."

Lezaroth followed him in silence.

"Let me explain a military paradox that I face," the lord-emperor said.

"So far, I have been able to personally supervise campaigns. But it seems that soon we will be carrying out battles a long way away."

So he is *planning war against the Assembly!*

"That will involve a new type of campaign a long way from my supervision. It may take months for messages to reach me. So I need new commanders. I need men who can act on their own initiative." Nezhuala's masklike face split into the thinnest of smiles. "I am looking for talented men who are independent thinkers, but who are also loyal. I don't want clones or mindless fanatics. And my search for such has found you. Talented, yes; independent, yes. But are you loyal enough to do my will?"

"I am, my lord." *Now.*

"Perhaps. Let me explain further. You know about what happened with the *Rahllman's Star*?"

Do I pretend that I don't know anything? No, a lie is too risky. "My lord, I pieced together more or less what happened. A group of renegades escaped from Tellzanur in the last stages of the fighting. Somehow they stole a freighter and tried to escape. They were pursued by the admiral and, in desperation it seems, headed toward the Assembly. The admiral assumed that they would be forced to stop or be destroyed by the barrier that separates them and us. But somehow they managed to pilot the ship through. The admiral followed, but lost them in the outermost inhabited system of the Assembly. He observed things for some days and then returned. Is that correct?"

"A commendable brevity. And it raised major issues. I agonized over the matter, then talked to some of my counselors." He gazed at the statues for a moment and shook his head. "It is hard work. They are full of tricks. But they confirmed my own beliefs. War with the Assembly is assured." He turned to Lezaroth. "Are you still uneasy about a war with them?"

"My lord, my words were hasty. If you think victory is possible, then it is." As he said it, Lezaroth realized that his doubtful tone undermined his statement.

"I agree, caution *is* needed. They are big, bigger than you thought. We have a mere twenty-five worlds and thirty million people. They have, we now gather, some sixteen hundred worlds and a population of a trillion."

That big!

"But there is a chance. The limited data the admiral obtained from his brief visit to the Alahir system. His distant scrutiny of the world over four hundred light-years away—Farholme they call it—suggests that these worlds are all rural. Pleasant no doubt, but rather agricultural." There was a tight smile. "They have rivers, even seas, and forests. Plants and trees produce their oxygen."

As he shook his head, Lezaroth glimpsed a strange, passionate light in his eyes. "Ah, the Assembly. It never changes. Wonderful on reforming worlds, but truly pathetic on the things that matter. Like industry. They have nothing, Margrave, like our industrial plants or our oxygen factories. Gates, gravity modification—oh, they do that, but little else. They are frightened of technology. They always were. That was the cause of the war."

He means the War of Separation, of course. Funny to think of that twelve-thousand-year-old event as the *war. We have had a thousand other wars since.*

"And no weapons. None." The lord-emperor's gaze seemed suddenly appraising. "Military comments? You did well at college, I gather."

Think! I must try and impress. The danger to me may just have been postponed. "Well, my lord, it is only the scale of the task that makes it daunting. The basic principles of combat apply. Strike fast, strike hard, and strike strategically. Go for the nerve centers before they realize what is happening."

"Good. Anything else?"

This is a test. "My lord, one big question is whether or not they know we exist. Once they start arming, we will have little chance of success."

"Good. And?"

Lezaroth thought hard. "We need more information. Much more. To strike strategically."

"Excellent. I agree. I am glad I spared you."

Nezhuala jabbed a finger toward a vast, mottled, snakelike form with red eyes and a gaping jaw. "That is Zamatouk. They worship him in the mines. Yes, as soon as I learned that the barrier was down, I immediately ordered the making of machines to build new ships. I created mechanized and robotized manufacturing systems to make more Krallen. These are now working. My goal is to have forces large enough to make just the sudden massive attack you suggest. Within half a standard year we will have that fleet ready. A fleet that will punch its way across the Assembly in well under a hundred days." Nezhuala paused and, when he spoke again, his words rang with emotion. "And take Earth."

"And take Earth!" Lezaroth echoed, unable to restrain his words. *No one has ever waged war on this scale! Or at this speed!*

There was a long silence. Was it his imagination, or had the whispering intensified?

"Yes," Nezhuala said quietly, and turned his dark eyes on him.

Lezaroth felt awed by the audacity of the lord-emperor's vision. There was something compelling in it. To take on enemies of such a size, at such a distance, and strike at their heart. *It takes warfare into a new dimension. All our wars hitherto have been petty local skirmishes. This is the great war.*

"But, Margrave, we lack the information we need. You can see the agonizing paradox. On the one hand, because we cannot win a long war with the Assembly, we must, as you say, strike soon and strike hard. Against such a foe, we will have but one chance. On the other hand, because we do not know the Assembly, we cannot risk striking at them. So what do we do?"

"A hard decision, my lord."

"Exactly." Nezhuala's lips twisted into something like a smile. "I, like you, Margrave, am cautious. It seemed an irresolvable dilemma. But now something has happened to give us a chance. We have a window of opportunity."

"We have, my lord?"

But there was no answer. The lord-emperor seemed to be listening to another voice again. Then he looked up at Lezaroth and seemed to scrutinize him. "Margrave, you are augmented?"

"The usual for frontline soldiers, my lord. Various leg, arm, and back muscles are enhanced. My eyes have been laser-collimated to the optical limits. I have supplemented anti-infectants. My nervous system has all the latest War Dep upgrades. And I have the usual neuroswitched communication and bionic systems."

"It's exciting." There was enthusiasm in Nezhuala's voice. "We are beginning to evolve beyond our mortality. Slowly—but steadily—we Freeborn are becoming more than flesh and blood. Progress, Captain. We are a long way down a road that the Assembly never took. And now the end is in sight. The long shadow of death is starting to retreat for our people. Ah, the Assembly. They resist change. Always did." Then he frowned. "Where were we? Ah yes. A window of opportunity."

He paused before a statue that looked like a great centipede with a human head and tilted his head as if to see it better. "Yes. A week ago I received a most interesting piece of news. Trying to find information, I went to the lowest depths of the Blade. My great project does have its uses, Margrave. There I talked with my counselors." He stared around the hall. "No one here. But amid all the many and useless words, they told me something interesting. It seems the crew of *Rahllman's Star* have blown up the Gate at Farholme. No more than thirty days ago."

"My lord, how can they know?"

"There is a steersman on board. They can still communicate at a very basic level with him. Do you see the significance?"

"I think so, my lord. Is it true that the Assembly still do not have Nether-Realm travel?"

There was a solemn nod. "No, just Gates. That much the admiral confirmed. It suits their cautious, rather static style."

"Then, my lord, in that case Farholme is now isolated from the Assembly."

"Indeed. Vulnerable."

"Do we have any idea why the crew did that?"

"No. The best guess is that they had been discovered. They wanted to keep themselves secret." He gazed at a statue for a moment before continuing. "So, we are planning to seize the world as soon as we can. There is a data-bank system there called the Library. The admiral found that much of their information traffic is to, or from, it. Can you imagine, Margrave, what the data repository of an open society would be like?"

"It stretches my mind, my lord."

They were near new statues now. A white ghostly form with an open mouth and slitlike eyes seemed to watch them.

"Indeed. You would have information on everything. Details of every person on every world. The location of every Gate. The operational facts on every ship. Twelve thousand years of history. Unencrypted."

"My lord, if I may speak, possessing this seems vital before the main attack."

"Exactly. So my will is this: we continue to prepare the fleet to attack the Assembly. But, in the meantime, we are going to send emissaries to Farholme. That mission will be diplomatic."

Diplomatic?

"I see your surprise."

"My lord, I had assumed . . . a military component."

"No." The smile was cruel. "Patience. We will go delicately. In Assembly culture, they think self-sacrifice is the highest virtue. If they felt they were protecting the Assembly, they would all die happily and take the Library with them. So we will go for diplomacy first. We will offer them a treaty."

"But will they accept?"

"Perhaps. We may modify our image a little." The lord-emperor gave a sudden strangled laugh. "Oh, Margrave, I like the idea of winning such a world to us. Of corrupting a part of the Assembly."

Lezaroth was aware again of the inky eyes staring at him. *I am being assessed.*

"Margrave, do you find that attractive?"

"Yes, I do, my lord."

"Good. Very good. So we will start with diplomacy. We will send a dip-lomatic vessel with two ambassadors. All being well, they will be allowed to set up a base on Farholme and be given access to this Library. We will seek to entice this world into an oath of loyalty. And if enticing doesn't work? Then we will take what we want by force. We will seize the world. And that is where I need a military leader."

Things are becoming clearer.

"There will be a military vessel along with the diplomatic ship. It will stay in the Nether-Realms. If diplomacy fails, it will immediately emerge and use all the power it has to ensure a full surrender."

"A skillful plan, my lord. May I ask, what vessel did you have in mind?"

"A full-suppression complex."

"Excellent. That ought to be convincing."

"Indeed. I intend sending the *Triumph of Sarata*."

"That's the first of the new Z class. Faster, bigger than anything else. Three-quarters of a million tons." *That would be a ship to have charge of!*

"I will be sending it fully armed," the lord-emperor continued. "And with one hundred and fifty thousand Krallen."

"Impressive." *That'd be adequate to subdue a world with weapons; for a world without, it's ridiculous overkill.*

"Do I detect that you think it is excessive, Margrave?"

"No, my lord. But I'm sure the task could be managed with fewer resources."

"Really?" The smooth voice suddenly had an unnerving chillness. "Let me warn you, Margrave. You need to respect this enemy. It is easy to mock the Assembly with its petty concerns and rustic habits. But history tells us never to underestimate them. They are dangerous."

Lezaroth tried to stop himself from shivering. "Thank you for the reminder, my lord. The texts tell us that underestimating the power of the Assembly was the mistake Jannafy made at Centauri."

The lord-emperor seemed to start. As he stepped forward, his smooth face loomed across Lezaroth's entire field of view.

He is going to strike me!

But he didn't. Instead, he hissed, "Margrave, *I* know better—far better— than the textbooks do about what happened in the War of Separation." The tone was one of barely restrained fury. "Listen! Jannafy's chief mistake was this: he misjudged his underlings. They were entrusted with making the seven ships ready to launch in time. They failed. Jannafy's main mistake was to trust fools. I have resolved not to repeat that."

"My lord, I apologize. I will revise my history." *And not speak lightly of Jannafy ever again.*

"And learn another lesson. Jannafy did indeed underestimate the Assembly, but not their power. He overlooked the way they can corrupt. I have talked of us enticing them. But be warned, my margrave, that the reverse can happen. More determined minds than yours have weakened under the impact of the Assembly and their values. The wills of many failed at Centauri because they had been weakened by the lies of the Assembly. I will not let *that* happen again. Be wary of them, Margrave. Very wary. No one is safe."

"My lord, I am listening."

There was silence. As Nezhuala stepped back, Lezaroth felt a sense of the immediate danger passing.

Now the lord-emperor spoke again. "So the man of my choosing will command the finest of ships. The pride of the fleet. He will have two tasks: the first, to bring back a copy of all the data in this Library. The second, to find *Rahllman's Star*. I want it back." There was a ring of determination in the voice. "I want to make sure its technology cannot fall into the hands of the renegades. Or the Assembly. And it has something precious on it, something I want back."

What does it have on it?

"Now, Margrave, I am a fair man. I punish failure and I reward success. He who delivers what I desire will be rewarded. He may, of course, take the *Triumph of Sarata* on with the main battle fleet to the Assembly and Earth. Or he may choose to retire. Either way, I will give him the title of Military Governor of Farholme. And as such, he may do as he likes with the world and its population."

The blank face stared at Lezaroth, the pale bloodless lips twisting into a wry smile. "Do you know that your title, margrave, is a historical curiosity? Are you aware of its origin?"

"No, my lord."

"A margrave was a military governor of a frontier province. In one of the ancient European states on Earth. Wouldn't it be appropriate—historically fitting—if you were to be such a man? A margrave in name *and* reality? I think you will find many pleasures there."

I would indeed.

Suddenly the lord-emperor paused as if listening to something. "Ah, the time draws near. But, Margrave, consider what I offer. Might and prestige with the command of the best ship in the fleet. And, if you succeed, the possibility of almost unlimited power and a world of pleasure. And above all, a key role in the greatest military venture of our time. Or any time." He waved a gloved finger for emphasis. "Not bad for a man who could be executed."

There was a pause. "So do you choose to take my offer? to serve me without any dissent? to do my will? to give me the unshakable honor I require? to love my friends and hate my enemies? Are you ready? Consider the matter."

There is a price. There is always a price. But what options have I? This opportunity may never return; the alternative may be death. I must seize it.

"My lord is generous indeed. I choose to take that offer."

"Then we shall test it."

What does that mean?

"Follow me."

The lord-emperor turned and walked down the hall. Lezaroth followed, suddenly aware that the high wordless whispering had begun again, only now there was a new note of expectancy. *It is as if the statues are talking to each other, as though they are waiting for something.*

At the far end of the room the lord-emperor motioned him through a door. As Lezaroth stepped forward a chill breeze whipped at his face, and a red waning daylight enveloped him.

He blinked and gasped.

He was on a balcony—one without railings, with an edge barely two paces away that extended above a drop of some two hundred meters. Below, a steep, strangely curved surface seemed to flow into a great disklike central platform below. On the platform, red in the light of the fiery setting sun, robed people, perhaps twenty in number, stood around a plinth.

Of course, the evening sacrifice!

Lezaroth heard the door hiss closed behind them. He looked along the balcony expecting to see only the lord-emperor, but instead saw the admiral standing between them.

There was something strange about the admiral. It took Lezaroth a second to realize that he was extraordinarily rigid. The admiral's blanched face held a look of utter terror and his gray eyes moved to meet Lezaroth's. "Help me!" they seemed to plead.

What do I do? Lezaroth looked to the lord-emperor.

Apparently heedless of the admiral, Nezhuala gazed over the scene. He sighed, as if with contentment, and as though the admiral were absent, addressed Lezaroth. "Do you know, Margrave," he said, "I like to think of this as the heart of our world."

"Indeed, my lord," was all Lezaroth could say.

"Yes, I think of this as the center, not just of this city but of this world." The lord-emperor was almost affable. "My people can be sure that, as the day ends, a sacrifice is being offered here to the powers for them."

"I see, my lord."

The lord-emperor gestured at the scene with open hands. "Here we ask the powers for their blessing on our endeavors." His smile was cold. "Do you know who is being honored today?"

"No, my lord."

"The Master Exaltzoc—the bringer of plague and disfigurement."

Far below, the robed figures, their faces indistinguishable, turned toward them. As they began a low urgent chanting, Lezaroth saw the glint of their knives. He turned to the lord-emperor, seeing the sharp, dark eyes boring into his.

"You have spotted that something is missing?" Nezhuala asked.

Lezaroth swung round to the scene below. His blood froze. *There is no sacrifice.*

"I'm afraid, Admiral, *you* are the sacrifice," Nezhuala said in a mild, apologetic tone.

I should have realized this. Lezaroth felt a mixture of horror and relief. *There* was *danger, but not for me.*

The lord-emperor turned, tilted his head slightly, and seemed to look at the admiral like a hawk evaluating a potential prey. When he spoke again, his tone was very different. It seethed with anger. "Admiral—*former* Admiral—I

was appalled at your mistakes at Tellzanur. First, you let a freighter be stolen. Then you let it escape the system. And not just any freighter, but the
Rahllman's Star. The freighter with my own grandfather's body on board:
the Great Prince Zhalatoc, a man many levels above you. We had hopes. We
thought we might restore him to the post-mortal state. We were negotiating
with the powers." His face twisted into an expression of aggrieved fury as he
leaned closer to the immobile admiral.

"Then, far too late, you headed off in pursuit. To find that, contrary to
all our experience, they could enter Assembly space. So you followed them and
watched what happened. Then, imagining that you had achieved something,
you came back. Can you imagine the damage that might have been done if
they had gone and given themselves up to the accursed Assembly?" The lord-
emperor's face was colorless with fury and Lezaroth saw spittle on his lips.

*Am I next? Great Zahlman-Hoth, god of soldiers, spare me now. Bring me
safe though this peril and I will sacrifice to you whatever you desire.*

Below, on the great lower platform, there was something oddly expect-
ant about the priests' stance. Their uplifted blades were tinged with red
sunlight.

"No, Admiral, you have failed." There was fury in the words. "So, in a
second or two, you will be on your way to the priests. They are waiting for
you. I will use my limited extra-physical powers to ensure that you stay conscious. As long as possible."

Nezhuala's hands moved in a strange position. The admiral swayed. Little
beads of sweat appeared on his face.

As the lord-emperor turned to Lezaroth, his conversational tone of voice
returned. "Margrave, this man is my enemy. Throw him off the edge."

The test! In the space of a few moments, a great argument raged in
Lezaroth's mind. At first, he resisted. *I cannot do this. I cannot repay a man
who has spoken out to serve me. I cannot harm a superior officer. I must take a
stand.* Then, a countering question came back: *Why not? The lord-emperor has
commanded it and he is master of all.* Lezaroth searched for any reason at all
that he could use to justify refusing the order. But he found nothing there: no
higher morality, no ultimate belief, no superior principle. Somehow, he felt he
ought to take a stand, but he found nothing that he could stand on.

He was about to agree to the demand when he was struck by three successive thoughts that came like hammer blows: *Do this and you cross a point
of no return. Do this and you are Nezhuala's slave. Do this and you are beyond
redemption.*

He returned the lord-emperor's gaze, his throat tight. "Whatever you
wish, my lord."

He stepped toward the admiral, took a shaking elbow with one hand and
with the other found the small of the man's rigid but quivering back.

"Oh, Admiral," the lord-emperor said, with a smile like a knife blade. "I won't forget your family."

Somehow—he had not intended it—Lezaroth found himself staring again at the admiral and seeing the desperate plea in the wide, panic-stricken eyes. He looked away and pushed.

A moment later, he looked back to see the admiral falling. He struck the curving wall with a heavy thud. Then, as rigid as a lump of wood, the heavy form slid smoothly down the concave surface toward the altar platform.

I feel dirty.

He was aware of the lord-emperor's terrible eyes watching him.

"Margrave, you pass the test. But only just. You delayed."

"My lord, I apologize for my delay."

Nezhuala turned to the scene below and sighed. "Do you know that I really don't like doing it this way? Using criminals is a cheap way of fulfilling our obligations to the powers. That's why we use ordinary people. They really prefer children. Even if they come from the underclass."

Lezaroth followed the lord-emperor's gaze and saw the great red ball of the setting sun was now just beginning to dip below a fiercely jagged horizon.

"Now, if you will excuse me for a moment, Margrave, I really ought to participate in the ceremonies. But there is more we have to discuss."

As Lezaroth bowed his head, the lord-emperor raised his right hand high. Far below there was a bustle of activity among the priests. A new chant began.

Out of the corner of his eye, Lezaroth saw Nezhuala drop his hand. The chant became urgent and savage.

The knives descended.

After a minute or so the lord-emperor said in his confiding tone, "Do you know, Margrave that there are variations on the sacrificial ritual? As to which bits they cut, in what order, and how they display them?"

"I had heard stories, my lord, but I have never studied the details. I'm a professional soldier. Culture isn't my strong point."

"I understand. But it's a fascinating subject." The lord-emperor shook his head. "Poor admiral."

There was silence and when the lord-emperor spoke again, it was in a sharper tone. "So, you have decided to serve me? Fully? Without questioning?"

"I have." *It's too late now to change my mind.*

"Then come here and bow before me."

Careful, mindful of the fitful, gusting wind and the fatal drop just a pace away, Lezaroth bowed before Nezhuala.

He glimpsed the lord-emperor taking his glove off and soon felt a cold hand on his forehead.

"Do you willingly renew your oath of allegiance to me?"

"I do."

Lezaroth felt an almost electric tingling in his forehead.

"Say it."

"I, Margrave Sentius Lezaroth, hereby resolve to serve and worship His Highness, the Lord-Emperor Nezhuala, Ruler of the Freeborn and Master of All in the Realms of the Dominion, with all that I am, and all that I have, until my death."

The lord-emperor murmured something in a strange language whose words seemed to coil and twist in the mind.

"Very good, Margrave," he said, withdrawing his hand. "You are now mine. Stand up."

Lezaroth stood.

"Now, let me give you more instructions." Nezhuala's voice was urgent and factual now. "I appoint you to the rank and pay of fleet-commander. You will leave in eight days' time. Because of the urgency, you and the ambassadors will travel very deep and fast in the Nether-Realms."

"My lord, isn't that dangerous?" There were horror stories of ships that went too deep.

There was a look of rebuke. "Oh, my margrave, don't dissent now. . . . But I am negotiating with the powers. You will have a cargo that will stop the ship from being molested."

"A cargo, my lord?"

"All being well, a baziliarch will go with you."

A terrible vision of vast yellow, iridescent eyes, blackness, wings, and claws filled Lezaroth's mind.

"On *my* ship? One of the seven?"

"Don't be alarmed, Margrave. It will be dormant for the trip. You'll be given an intermediary. Baziliarchs can be tricky, but they're wonderful weapons. As I found out on Tellzanur. They have that ability to tear information out of minds, which you may find useful. And nothing is going to tangle with a convoy with a baziliarch. Even in the deepest Nether-Realms."

"My lord . . . I bow to your wisdom. And as for crew, may I choose my own?"

"Yes, with one exception. Your second-in-command will be Lucretor Hanax."

Blank your expression. Hide your dismay. "My lord, is that . . . ?"

"Is that *wise* you were going to say?"

Hanax is pushy and overconfident, and we hate each other. But how do I say that?

"Well, my lord, he has risen rather rapidly through the ranks. I had thought . . . that a period of consolidation might be appropriate. It is tradition."

"My margrave, I know your background. You are of an old family and he comes from nowhere. I know the objections to Hanax—that he rises too fast and he hates the noble families. I know everything. But his record is excellent."

"If it is your will, my lord . . ."

"But it *is* my will." There was an irresistible force in the voice. "Work with him. The powers have told me that he will play a great role."

That may be, but on my ship, he will know his place.

"Very well, my lord."

The chant changed as the last sliver of Sarata dipped below the horizon. Below in the congealing gloom, Lezaroth could see that the priests were leaving. Something soft, wet, and red—no, several things—were arranged on the plinth.

Apparently catching his gaze, Nezhuala pointed down. "Notice how swiftly they leave, Margrave. They summon The Master Exaltzoc, but they do not stay for his appearing." Then, as if listening to his private voices, he shook his head and fell silent.

It came to Lezaroth that he needed to clarify his orders or he might end up like the admiral. "My lord, how much force may I use?"

Nezhuala smiled. "As much as is needed. But I would prefer some captives. The powers grow hungry at the base of the Blade and some fresh flesh would be very well received. Men and women and, especially, children from the Assembly would be welcome. And we need tissue samples at least of the best specimens. We may strip their genes of the best code and add it to ours. As for force: once you get me the Library data intact, the *Rahllman's Star,* and the DNA, you can kill them all as far as I am concerned." Nezhuala smiled again. "Set an example. But spare the world itself. It would be a shame to wreck it. It looked rather . . . nice. . . . I might stop and inspect it on my way to Earth."

"Whatever you will, my lord."

"A few more things, Fleet-Commander." Suddenly, for the first time, the lord-emperor seemed to be slightly ill at ease. "What do you know of the tale—the myth—of the great adversary?"

I need to be careful here. "I heard of it from the captives at Tellzanur. It is the belief that the rise of the Dominion will be threatened by a man who will come close to defeating it."

"Or?"

"Well, of course they saw him as actually defeating it. We treated it with scorn."

"Quite so." The lord-emperor was silent for some time, apparently gripped by thoughts. "But it is a far older belief," he said at last. "The powers have mentioned it to me. They know of it. It is the idea that, in the last battles, there will be a single warrior who will stand in our way. Of course, we succeed; we cannot fail. But this being opposes us. Or so the myth says." A slight spasm seemed to run through the lord-emperor's body. "They mention a name in connection with this great adversary." His voice sounded strained. "Can you guess whose name it is?"

"In the accounts of the War of Separation, the blame for our loss is attributed to one man—Lucas Ringell."

"Yes!" The word came out like a hiss. "It is a matter of history that, without him, the outcome of the War of Separation would have been very different."

"He killed Jannafy."

The lord-emperor stared at the ground. "Ah well, I remember that. But yes, it is Ringell's name that is whispered among the powers. There is babble of him 'returning soon,' but what that means is unclear to me. And, I think, to them." The lord-emperor looked up. "My guess—no more than that—is that they speak of another warrior. One who will be like Lucas Ringell and who will stand in the way of the final triumph of we who are the Freeborn."

A new gust of wind whipped across the balcony. Lezaroth tried not to shiver. In the night sky, stars were appearing.

"I mention the matter, my margrave, for one reason: I want you to watch out for this man. He may be on Earth. But he may be on Farholme. And if he is there, I want him found."

Lezaroth heard anger in Nezhuala's voice now, and perhaps also fear.

"I want him brought to me. Or at least destroyed. Whatever the cost. If you lose a thousand Krallen to kill him, then do it."

Could the lord-emperor be afraid of a myth?

"My lord, if he is there, I will take him or slay him."

The lord-emperor seemed to stare at the embers of the sunset. Through the dusty and contaminated atmosphere Lezaroth could make out the distant gleams of the domes on the slopes above Khetelak that gave the nobles and their families some protection from both the city's pollution and the planet's wildly fluctuating temperatures.

Suddenly, Lezaroth felt again the prickling of the hairs on the back of his neck. He glanced down to the shadowy platform below and had to struggle to restrain a gasp. There around the plinth something prowled, something more solid than smoke and less solid than flesh, something indescribable, but with four legs and a head that bent to snuffle and lick.

"It's all due to topology, my margrave."

Topology—the science of surfaces. But how?

"That being below us is, of course, The Master Exaltzoc. I am told that such sacrifices—rightly done—make a temporary and local adjustment in the topology of the boundary surface between the Nether-Realms and normal space. For a brief moment, the powers can appear in our world. Do you understand?"

"Yes. Of course, my lord." Lezaroth knew his voice sounded numb and mechanical. *I have glimpsed such things in the gray shadows of the deep Nether-Realms. I have seen steersmen and caught sight of a baziliarch. But never, however briefly, have I seen a power walking around freely on our worlds.*

"Ah, Margrave, they long to be liberated. To move unfettered through the worlds of men. That is their great wish. The powers will give anything to the one who aids them in this."

"I'm sure, my lord." Lezaroth knew that what the lord-emperor was saying must be of the greatest significance. But somehow the sight of a power prowling around a few hundred meters away was so astonishing, his words barely registered.

As the figure slowly faded away, the lord-emperor said, "Come, it is time for you to leave. You have preparations to make. Follow me."

The door at the back of the balcony opened.

"Stay close to me, Margrave, through the hall. After sunset . . . with the blood . . ."

They walked back through the hall. It seemed darker now, as if the shadows had solidified, and the whisperings and murmurings seemed clearer and more audible. *This is my life from now on—protected from the powers by the lord-emperor.*

But as they left the hall and climbed the stairs another truth came to him. *Admiral Kalartha-Har is dead and I am alive. And isn't that, after all, all that counts?*

As they emerged onto the topmost platform, Lezaroth saw that the stars were out.

"Stay," the lord-emperor said. "Look up."

Lezaroth followed his outstretched hand to where, above the dirty air, a tiny line of silver light cut the darkness.

The Blade of Night.

"You were wrong on that, my margrave," Nezhuala said. "The Blade of Night is of greatest value. And it will be even more so. You have landed at the access station?"

"Twice, my lord. Once on exercise, once when delivering the condemned." *And the entire crew breathed a sigh of relief when we blasted off. It's a haunted monstrosity. Enough extra-physical phenomena to drive the sanest man mad.*

The lord-emperor continued to gaze upward. "It is a remarkable structure. I have journeyed down to the lower levels," he said, in a voice that was so strangely detached that it sounded like it belonged to someone else. "The very lowest depths. There are things that you would not believe."

Then suddenly he seemed to shake himself free of whatever extraordinary vision possessed him. Lezaroth found it hard to read his expression in the darkness, but felt certain of a strange, burning urgency in his eyes. *This man is driven by what happens there. I had assumed that these meetings with the powers were incidental to his life, but they are central.*

"These are extraordinary times, Margrave. We are on the verge of great changes. I cannot explain now about the true uniting of the realms that we seek, but it is coming. Very soon. And I am glad that you are willing to serve me."

The lord-emperor walked to the lander hatchway and stood by as Lezaroth opened it. "Tell them at the *Ravager* that I have detained the admiral on business."

Lezaroth climbed on board. "Yes, my lord."

"A question. Did you enjoy pushing the admiral to his doom?"

"You ordered it, my lord."

"Ah, Margrave, I need more." A glove was raised in reprimand. "I don't like my men to be too cool. I like hatred. Indeed I expect it. The admiral was my enemy: to destroy such people should give you pleasure." The voice was sterner now. "As you face the Assembly, you must learn to hate them. Do not go coolly to attack them. You must enjoy their defeat; you must delight in their fear and pain. Hate energizes!"

"My lord, I appreciate your candor. I will follow your advice."

"Oh, Margrave. Seven days from today is the Feast of Zahlman-Hoth, the god of all who fight. It would be appropriate for you to join me here again to invoke the great Zahlman's blessing on your venture. Of course, he needs an offering. So, I am having the admiral's wife and children brought to Khetelak. I would like you to meet them at the port and escort them here. It will be good practice."

"Whatever you will, my lord. It is my life's purpose to serve you."

"Thank you." Nezhuala paused. "Smile, my margrave. It's an order: smile."

The door closed and Lezaroth sat back in his seat. Suddenly, he broke out in uncontrollable shivering. *What have I done? What have I become?*

Then Lezaroth caught a glimpse of himself in the mirror and gasped in horror.

He *was* smiling.

2

At almost the same time but over seven hundred light-years away, Doctor Ethan Malunal, Chairman of the Council of High Stewards, leaned on the balcony rail of the wooden guesthouse, gazing at the endless dark green-blue lines of the ancient cedar forest of Lebanon toward the Mediterranean Sea.

It was late in May. Although there were still thick patches of snow under the shade of the trees, spring was fast turning to summer. He breathed in deeply, enjoying the sharp tang of the great trees, feeling the early afternoon sun on his face and hearing the chorus of birdsong. *Here, I could almost persuade myself that all is well with me and the worlds. But it's not.*

He sighed. *It is the burden of history. Tomorrow I will lead the emergency meeting of the full Congregation of Stewards as we make the most serious decision the Assembly has had to make for twelve thousand years. In all those years we have debated little more grave than the speed at which we colonize the stars. Now we are face-to-face with an appalling crisis that has come from nowhere, and we who are charged with making decisions for the Assembly must act decisively. From tomorrow, all that we have ever been will change. We who have known only peace for innumerable generations, will be effectively at war.*

His eyes tracked an eagle as it cruised over the forest.

And if I must start the matter, I want no part of it beyond that.

Ethan looked at his pale, veined, and wrinkled hands. *I feel my age—all my seventy-five years. Would my attitude be different if Anna were still alive?*

His troubled thoughts were interrupted by the gentle hum of a gravity-modifying sled winding its way up the steep road. His guests were here and on time.

Ethan walked over to greet them. A study in contrasts, he thought. Eliza

Majweske, the current president of the Sentinel Council, was a well-built woman in her midfifties, with dark brown skin, tight-coiled hair of black and silver, an easy manner, and a broad, comforting smile. On her blouse, Ethan could see the sentinel emblem of a stone tower rising up against a blue sky surrounded by a gold circle.

Professor Andreas Hmong, Senior Elder of the Custodians of the Faith, a man in his sixties, was a slighter figure. He was balding, with a long beard and a face that showed his Asiatic genes, with alert green eyes that spoke of intelligence.

"Friends, welcome!" Ethan said, and hugged them both in turn.

Having established that they had eaten en route from Jerusalem, Ethan gestured to where, at the end of a wooden patio, a table stood just below the outstretched branches of a large cedar.

"Drinks are in the kitchen. Help yourself and then let's gather outside."

A few minutes later, amid the recounting of the doings of families and children, they pulled up chairs around the table under the shade of the great tree.

"Have you been here long, Eeth?" Eliza asked in her deep, melodic voice. Ethan noticed how her brown eyes somehow conveyed not just a relaxed gentleness but also shrewdness.

"I caught the rail to Sidon three days ago and got Forestry to bring me up. I came up with just a bag and box of food. I've been alone with my thoughts and my prayers. Have you been here before?"

"Years ago."

"You, Andreas?"

"I'm afraid not. I count it a grave omission. I love the air and the fresh tang of the trees." Andreas looked slowly around as if examining everything. "And all the history! Solomon was here and the old authors spoke highly of these forests and their wildlife. There are some fine poems." He paused, the intense look on his face suggesting he was mentally repeating some stanza. When he spoke again, his voice had acquired a dreamy quality. "And Assembly poets have made much of their restoration to something of their former glory."

He gazed around again, his green eyes softening. "I fancy more might be written. Of the diffuse shade through such trees, the light glinting off the needles, the scent of the resin, the wind whispering in the ancient boughs . . ." Suddenly embarrassed, he stopped.

Ethan smiled and caught the laughter in Eliza's eyes.

Andreas made a dismissive gesture with his hands. "My apologies," he said, with a self-conscious smile. "This is hardly relevant, is it? After all, this meeting is to do with the crisis."

Eliza laughed gently. "It is a great work of grace that we can, even now, still think of poetry. I'm glad that our senior elder is still a literary man."

Ethan remembered that one reason why Andreas had been chosen to lead the custodians was because he was a poet and the new hymnbook had been in preparation. He felt a sudden pang of nostalgia for a world where the biggest theological issue had been over song lyrics.

"And I'm glad we can laugh," Ethan added. "And when this crisis is over, you must come up and stay here. It's tiny, but an excellent place for thought and prayer—and poetry." There were smiles all around. "But to business. Friends, it is good of you to come at such short notice. Tomorrow's meeting of the entire Congregation of Stewards has raised three issues in my mind on which I need help. And you are not only the leaders of the custodians and the sentinels but also trusted friends."

"It's our privilege, friend Ethan," muttered Andreas.

"Yes," Eliza agreed with a quiet emphasis.

"Thank you. As you know, tomorrow I will put forward to all the stewards the recommendations of the Council of High Stewards on how we should respond to the events at Farholme. Every world will be represented."

"Even Farholme?" Andreas asked.

"Yes, their steward was offworld when the Gate loss occurred. And, as you also know, it seems certain that these . . . momentous proposals will be approved."

Eliza shook her head and Andreas nodded slightly; yet both gestures expressed a common concern. "And because they *are* so awesome, I want to talk through some of them with you. But first, let's pray."

And so, lit by the dappled yellow sunlight filtering through the vast spreading branches, they prayed for wisdom and guidance.

When they had ended their prayers, Ethan sat back in his seat. "Perhaps there is a blessing in the way perilous times force us to rely on the one who is the true head of the Assembly." There were sounds of assent. "Now, my friends, my first issue is this. If, as seems almost certain, the recommendations I put forward are accepted, then everything we are as the Assembly changes— now and for the foreseeable future. So, in view of the momentous nature of my statement, can I be totally sure of the ground on which I stand?"

"*Momentous* is a word that is often overused, but not in this case," murmured Andreas.

Eliza said nothing. Somewhere in the woods a woodpecker drummed.

Ethan continued. "As you know, my background is engineering: a notoriously focused and perhaps narrow-minded discipline. I need wise friends like you to help me see more than I can." He picked up a folder from beside his chair, took out three small pieces of paper, and distributed them.

"Three dozen words apparently from a man whom only Eliza has ever met, on a world that is—or *was*—a byword for remoteness."

"Farholme," Eliza said and shook her head in an expression of disbelief.

"And transmitted by a method few of us understand," Andreas added. Eliza grunted agreement.

"I'm only a little wiser on this matter of quantum-linked photons," Ethan said, "but it seems to have worked. Now, I know you know every word by heart, but let me read this again. 'Farholme Gate destruction not an accident but sabotage by non-Assembly forces. Evidence of genetically modified humans, superior technology, and hostile intent. Intruder presence associated with a corrupting spiritual evil. Arm the Assembly! Verofaza Laertes Enand, Sentinel.'"

There was an uneasy silence. Andreas creased his brow and knit his fingers together. Eliza stared at the paper, her face inscrutable.

Ethan continued. "You know the story. It was apparently transmitted by a Dr. Gerrana Anna Habbentz on Farholme to Dr. Amin Ferraldo Ryhan on Tahmolan. We believe it was sent mere days after the Gate was destroyed. And, of course, we have no way of communicating with Farholme to confirm its truth, except through transmissions at light speed and that of course means decades of waiting. Any dissent on that background?"

Andreas shook his head. "Not from me."

"No," said Eliza. "Incidentally, Eeth, there is a typically sentinel take on this. This is either a genuine message about the return of evil, or it is a fake. If it is a fake, it is so malicious that it demonstrates that evil has indeed returned."

"I'm glad you are here, Eliza. My brain is strictly linear," Ethan replied. "But a dozen teams have studied this and all conclude that this is an authentic message of a genuine threat. So I must act on it." Ethan sipped his drink and then looked in turn at his guests.

"But there is other evidence," Eliza said with a quiet insistence.

She seems uneasy. "Yes," Ethan answered. "Engineering. There is a vast interchange of data between any two Gates when a ship passes between them. So the Bannermene Gate received detailed data from the Farholme Gate in the minutes before it exploded. That data has been analyzed. The consensus of the experts is—let me quote from memory—the situation it reveals 'could not have occurred naturally, but is, in all probability, the product of sabotage.' I can also reveal that they have identified a sabotage method and last week tested it on an old Gate near Eridani. They got within thirty seconds of a class four failure. So, Eliza, you are right; it is not just Verofaza's report."

"Eeth," Eliza said, "the sentinels have looked at this backward, forward, and sideways. We really believe this is genuine. Verofaza Laertes Enand was the sentinel sent to Farholme, because our man there felt there was a threat. But . . ."

"You have doubts?"

She shrugged. "Verofaza—I only briefly met him—is bright and skeptical. But we would like more information than we have. As would you." She hesitated and seemed to stare into the distance, before looking back at Ethan. "Try and see this from our point of view. If this alarm is right, then the sentinels have justified their existence. At last, we did what Moshe Adlen created us for. We sounded an alarm. But otherwise . . ."

"Yes. I know," said Andreas. "Otherwise. That is, if this is some mistake or hoax, then the sentinels are finished. You will be closed down."

For a poet and a theologian, his words can be cutting.

"Be closed down?" Eliza shook her head. "No, we will close ourselves down. But, Eeth, listen to me. We believe that there is a genuine peril, and we still believe that the recommendations are, sadly, necessary."

"I am reassured. But no further ideas where this evil is from?"

"Some, but nothing firm. There's no mention of aliens, only 'modified humans.' That 'superior technology' comment implies habitable worlds."

"True," Ethan added. "Or something like our cities-in-space. But, most likely, *worlds.* That's why there is a science team scanning with the best scopes we have for habitable worlds beyond Farholme. We have rushed a scope out to Bannermene. We're checking for oxygen, water, the right orbit, right sun type, and signs of civilization, such as electromagnetic radiation emissions. That sort of thing."

"And so far?" Andreas asked, although his attention seemed to be elsewhere, his eyes apparently following a large butterfly.

"Too early to say. The science team has only just started and all we can say is that there are possibilities. They may just be slime worlds: worlds with no more than bacteria or algae. But what we can say—I think—is that if there are any civilizations around, they are at least as far away from Farholme as we are. Say, three hundred light-years. But, Eliza, any other thoughts from your people?"

"Only one more. And it's an odd one. We are wondering if anything survived the Rebellion."

"Surely not," Andreas said, turning his eyes quickly to her. "Evil was purged then. Nothing could have survived. Could it, Ethan?"

"Andreas, we have also considered it as a possibility. But a massive weapon was used then. Even today, the debris at Centauri is highly radioactive. Nothing could have survived."

Andreas grunted softly. "It was spiritual surgery of the toughest sort."

Eliza frowned. "Andreas, it was all done very quickly." She exhaled heavily. "In hindsight, possibly too quickly. Anyway, we are looking at it again—reading all the old data, searching files that have not been opened for centuries. It's ongoing." She looked away, as if staring at something beyond the trees.

"How interesting," Andreas replied.

"Now, Professor Andreas, can you add anything from the Custodians of the Faith? I read your report, of course."

Andreas shifted on his chair and toyed with his glass. "We theologians are perplexed. The references in the message to a range of evils are chilling. But they are consistent; in the old books evils rarely came singly."

"What about this idea of a corrupting spiritual evil?"

"I have a team of research theologians working on it. The early suggestions are worrying. The Assembly is like a house built on pillars. Two of those pillars are trust and honesty. For instance, the three of us trust each other so much that we can be honest with each other. We take that for granted. But imagine if we weren't either trusting or honest here today?"

"Exactly," Eliza muttered, with a frown.

Ethan struggled with the idea of having conversations with people he couldn't trust and found the idea just too perplexing.

"Friend Ethan the engineer," said Andreas, "think of it like this. Consider Assembly society as being like a high tower. Strong winds from outside may bring it down—that's your direct enemy attack. But so may corrosion from within."

Ethan nodded. "And the quickest way to destruction may be both at once."

A silence fell. The air was now chillier.

Andreas was evidently listening to something. At length he spoke. "The noises here are wonderful. It's as if there are layers of sound: there are birds singing, insects buzzing, and wind in the needles of the trees. And beneath that there is a deep and total silence." A look of regret crossed his face. "Another time, maybe."

" 'Fraid so," Eliza said softly. "Eeth is seeking reassurance that he is doing the right thing. As I would if I had to do what he's got to do tomorrow."

"True," Andreas answered. "Very well, what else can I add? Only this: we have had a number of reports of dreams and visions of a growing evil."

"Since when?" Ethan asked.

"In most cases, after this message became public knowledge—" Andreas gestured at the sheet of paper—"but in some cases, before. And, in one or two cases, even before the Farholme Gate went. We are looking into all of them, but some seem credible." He looked at Eliza. "Have your people heard anything like this?"

"Yes. The sentinels have always been alert for such things. After all, we were set up to watch for any evidence for the return of evil. We have tended to be skeptical, but in the last few weeks we have found these dreams and visions convincing and alarming."

Ethan sensed a hint of defensiveness in Eliza's answer, as if she felt that the sentinels should have more clearly foreseen the crisis coming. He caught her eye. "What do you take them to mean?"

"It's hard to pin down. But we feel there is . . . how can I put it? A sense of a shadow falling."

Andreas looked upward as if searching the sky for something. "A shadow falling? Do I agree? Yes and no. A shadow is neutral; a mere passive absence of light." He shook his head. "I think, Eliza, among some of the custodians, there is a growing mood—a feeling—that what we face is an active force: a moving, living darkness up there, a darkness that hates us all."

"I see," Ethan said slowly. He was almost getting used to the idea that he was quite out of his depth. "So what are you doing about it?"

"We are looking into how a return of evil might occur and how it might manifest itself." Andreas tapped the table. When he turned back to Ethan, his eyes seemed perturbed. "And how it might best be countered and contained before it spreads." Then, as if embarrassed, he looked away. "The theology of evil and sin is a neglected one these days."

There was a new silence. In it, Ethan suddenly had all the reassurance he needed.

"Thank you. So, neither the sentinels nor the Custodians of the Faith feel that they want to change their advice? Very well. Tomorrow I will do all I can to persuade the entire Congregation of Stewards to accept the proposals."

"They will vote in favor," Eliza said, her voice full of certainty.

"Yes. Technically, the Congregation could reject a recommendation of the Council of High Stewards, but in reality, it is unlikely. In fact, I have already booked studio time for three-thirty to record a message for the worlds. I have been preparing that here."

"An unenviable task," Andreas said in a thoughtful tone. "What note to strike? Elegiac? Comforting? A stirring call to arms perhaps? You have my prayers."

"Thank you," Ethan said. "First issue resolved, then. Now my second issue is less clear. The way beyond the vote is dark; it is an uncharted path. I feel sure it is full of pitfalls. What can your eyes see on it that mine cannot?"

Andreas seemed to stare at the trees again. "Tomorrow, as you say, everything changes. The Assembly will turn on its axis. It will be a date in the history books." He turned back to Ethan. "You will call a day of prayer and fasting?"

"Of course," Ethan replied. "That was an easy decision. But the practical steps have preoccupied me. The first decisions are sketched out. Any further expansion of the Assembly will be frozen. All existing Seeding projects will be put on minimum or maintenance mode. All our energies will be devoted to the creation of a fleet, weapons, and defenses." His voice conveyed sadness. "We need to revisit research programs that were frozen a dozen millennia ago.

We have to create a fighting force out of people who know war only from images or museums."

He soon saw sympathy in Eliza's eyes. "You scared, Eeth?" she asked.

"Yes, Eliza. But oddly enough, I am more scared of taking a wrong step than of the enemy—whoever they are."

"Best way to be. The Lord can take care of our enemies. But we've got to take care of ourselves."

"I hang on to that."

Ethan caught a sharp glance from Andreas. "Let me offer you this half-digested thought. I think there is a danger that you—we—may falter. If we agree that this threat is genuine, then we have no option but to respond to it with all we have. I do not see how we can go at this in a halfhearted manner."

"Agreed. We cannot delay," Eliza said. "We've lost weeks debating the matter and making plans. But we had no option. It would've been folly to rush in without checking everything. But we've got to make up for lost time." She shivered. "Say, Eeth, is there any chance of a walk? I guess my blood is thin. I'm getting cold sitting down. There must be forest tracks here. We can talk as we go."

Andreas agreed and they were soon walking up a pathway toward the crest of the ridge. Ethan led and Eliza walked beside him while Andreas followed close behind.

"Have you any specific plans for the defense?" Eliza asked.

"Teams are already working on it," Ethan answered. "But the best ideas so far are to create more fighting ships and make polyvalent fusion weapons."

To their right, something—a deer of some sort, he thought—bounded away through the undergrowth. After a pause, he continued. "It's a tactical guess that any enemy will attack in a straight line toward us here on Earth. So, we will try and clear those worlds that are in the way. There are about a dozen."

"Is evacuating entire worlds really feasible?"

"Hardly. Even with say three or four thousand-seater ships landing and leaving every day you'd barely clear a million people in a year. But we can get off the vulnerable."

"How soon can we make warcraft?" Andreas asked.

"It will take time. But within a few months, we will produce some military vessels. And given our resources, the engineers think we will soon double our fighting capacity every two months. But that's just engineering."

"'Just engineering,' Eeth?"

Ethan smiled. "Engineering is just making things. It's the social issues that are the real unknowns. For instance, we are going to have to move to production-line technology—endless lines of people and machines. It maximizes output, but at the expense of human satisfaction."

"No one will like that."

"No. There are other issues. Can you take a peaceful people and make them warriors?"

"Good question. I can see that."

A few moments later Eliza spoke again. "I have a concern. Are we going to have conscription?"

Of course. She has two sons of a suitable age. And Andreas and I have grandchildren.

"No. Full-scale conscription is unlikely at this stage. We'll ask for volunteers. And there will be probably be some training for everyone on what will be called civil defense. But we'll see."

"I asked you whether you were afraid earlier," Eliza said, "because I am."

"What of? Our unknown enemies somewhere beyond the stars?"

"No, of what will happen to us. I don't like the sound of a warrior Assembly."

"Me neither," Andreas said.

"I know." Ethan paused for breath. "By the grace of God, the Assembly has worked well for over eleven thousand years. Now we have to change it. But can our systems and structures handle those changes?"

"Good point. But what I fear is more than that." Eliza shook her head. There was frustration in the gesture. "But I can't express it. Not yet. Not in words. In one way we remain sinners, of course! But in another we have become, I suppose, innocent of evil. No, perhaps a better word is *naive*. We have forgotten the perils of evil." Her eyes seemed to cloud with anxiety. "Eeth, I just feel we need to be very careful. Very careful indeed. As the Word says 'watch and pray.'"

I must mark her words.

The path grew steeper. They fell silent, saving their breath.

As they climbed Ethan thought about history and how everything would change tomorrow with his words. *But that is the wrong way to think about it. I do not turn history: the Almighty God does that. He is the Lord of history. It is just that I happen to be at the place and time when it changes. I ought to think of it as a privilege.*

Increasingly as they ascended, Ethan gasped for breath and soon asked that they stop.

"You okay, Eeth? I didn't really ask about you." Eliza sounded concerned.

"I'm okay-ish. It's been a tough year with Anna's death." He hung his head, letting the air get into his lungs. "Fifty odd years ago—I would have bounded up this path."

"You've had a medical exam recently?" Andreas asked.

"Yes. My health is good, but not outstanding. No obvious risk of imminent death." Ethan wiped sweat off his forehead and took more deep breaths. "This is the third of the issues I mentioned. I am seventy-five. Recently widowed." He kept his sentences short to stabilize his breathing. "I've reached an age where custom decrees we ease off at work. I'm tempted to resign very soon. The day after tomorrow in fact. Lead the meeting, announce the verdict, and then slip away quietly."

Eliza and Andreas exchanged glances.

Ethan took another deep breath. "You see, my job will change. As Chairman of the Council of High Stewards, my position will become effectively that of the leader of a trillion people at war, steering a vast wartime economy. The pressures will be enormous. So, I say to myself, 'Would it not be better to let a younger man or woman take it?'"

As he could have predicted, there was no rush for words, no flurry of easy answers—just a long, sympathetic silence.

"Eeth, we understand." Eliza's words were soft. "No one would blame you. It's going to be a tough job. It's bad enough doing such a thing for a world like Earth with a billion people to lead. But to do it for the whole Assembly is going to be . . . well, challenging."

"I agree," Andreas said. "Do you mind if I put my cold, analytical, theologian's hat on?"

"Please. Let's walk on though. The view is worth it. But be gentle."

"Okay. Now, Ethan, aren't there two issues here? Isn't it a matter of—shall we say—professional competence and personal comfort?"

Eliza drew her breath in sharply.

"Go on," Ethan said, feeling sure that Andreas was going to strike a nerve.

"Do you wish to resign because you feel that you will not be competent for the job? Or do you wish to resign because you feel the job will affect you personally in a way you don't like?"

"Hey, that hurt, Andreas," Eliza protested.

Ethan shook his head. "That's a blunt way of expressing it, but I value it nonetheless. The answer, Andreas, is that I'm not sure."

After another quarter of an hour of walking up the path, they began to crest the hill. The snow under the trees was thicker now, although everywhere it was melting and there was the constant sound of running water. The cedars were smaller and more twisted and had tiny red cyclamens and crocuses amid their roots.

To the east was a high mountain with snow draped around the summit like a cloak.

"Mount Hermon—Jebel esh Sheik in the old language," Ethan said, his words broken up by little gasps.

They walked farther on until they stood on the ridge itself. There as they caught their breath, they took in the gnarled line of the Anti-Lebanon range, the icy heights of Hermon, and the long intervening plain of the Bekaa Valley below them. The air was clear and the flat valley floor was a dazzling mosaic of livid green patches of fresh vegetation and gleaming silver expanses of open water. Flocks of white birds could be seen below, some flying, some roosting in the trees.

"Storks," Ethan said. "They're nesting at the Aammiq Wetland."

Andreas nodded. "Evocative. How does it go in the psalms? 'The Lord's trees are well watered—the cedars of Lebanon that he planted. The birds build their nests there, and the storks have their homes in the pine trees.'" He fell silent.

Ethan looked down the valley, following the traces of disused roads. In places there were ancient ruins and in others, modern buildings could be seen. He gestured east. "At night, you can just see the lights of Damascus, one of the oldest of cities."

"All our past laid out before us," Andreas said, toying with his beard. "Here, beauty and history meet." After gazing at it a while, he turned and looked north along the ridge.

Ethan watched a line of buzzards migrating north, as he thought about his choices. *If I were to stay on as chairman, when would I come back here or anywhere like it? I would face endless deadlines and meetings. The best I can expect will be snatched hours in parks and gardens between meetings.* The thought appalled him.

"Eeth, I sympathize," Eliza said. She stood near him. "I can guess your thoughts. You didn't sign up for what your job is about to become. Becoming chairman was a known quantity when you took it on. Starting tomorrow it's all different."

"I could do the job, I think, or at least as well as anyone can."

"I agree."

"Andreas is right though. There is a lot to do with my personal comfort. Oh, I will have helpers and secretaries, but it will squeeze me badly." He paused and stared across the great valley. "And, Eliza, I say to God, isn't it enough to set it going? Haven't I done all I need to do? The last month has been bad enough and it's going to get worse. Can't I be spared?"

"I can't answer that. You *can* do the job. God will support you, if you let him." She shrugged. "But these are easy words to say."

Nothing more was spoken between them for some time. The hum of insects, the whisper of the wind in the trees, and the calls of birds were heard, but there were no other sounds.

"Odd," Andreas suddenly said, his voice clear in the stillness. "Very odd."

"What?" Eliza called out. "What do you see?"

"The ground here. It's not natural. See this ditch?" He gestured toward a long, rough linear depression broken up by trees. "These are man-made features."

Ethan noted the structure he was referring to and glimpsed something half buried at the near end. He walked over, wondering what might have once been there. A summer palace? Some ancient biblical feature?

The object that caught his eye was next to a cluster of crimson cyclamens. It was just a slab of stone. Or was it?

Ethan bent down and peered at the crumbling, rotting rock, then picked up a fragment and held it up to the light.

"What is it?" Eliza asked.

"Concrete. Badly weathered. Very old." He looked at the view ahead, feeling a sudden sharp pang of realization. *Of course. How appropriate.*

He called Andreas over.

"I'm afraid all this is the remains of a fortification. Twentieth to mid-twenty-first century. We have ramparts, a trench, and a concrete bunker. A strategic site."

Andreas's face twisted up as if he had just smelled something disagreeable.

"There were many wars here," Eliza said, as if to herself.

Ethan watched as Andreas wandered slowly around the floor of the ditch, shaking his head. He stopped to peer over the ruined ramparts, then walked back and squatted on the slab near Ethan and propped his thin face between his hands.

Eventually, Andreas spoke in a voice thick with emotion. "It is surely no accident we are here this day. This, Ethan and Eliza, is what we want to bring back." He tapped the concrete lightly as if he found it contaminating. "No, I do not seek to dissuade you. It must be done. But I can see this as it was." His voice became quieter and taut. "I see ghosts."

Ethan saw Eliza's face tighten as Andreas continued. "I can see them now: scared, pale-faced boys from farms firing bullets or lasers at other scared, pale-faced boys from farms." Andreas motioned with his hand along the ditch. "All those thousands and thousands of years ago, lined up behind these bulwarks with camouflage jackets and body armor. All waiting for death to strike them at any moment. I can hear the firing, the screams, and hear the orders. I can see the wounded being attended, see the ground wet with blood as red as that cyclamen. I can smell the smoke, the burned flesh, and the fear. I can feel the hate."

Andreas stood. His face was blanched. "Friend Ethan, this has been a great help. There is a problem with language. We glibly use words without seeing their real meaning. We talk about war and we think about deaths and maybe injuries. But it's more than just death. If it were that, it would be bad, but it would be manageable. After all, we all will die. But it isn't just simply death, it is all the other bits—the blood, the torn flesh, and all the hatred and fear that goes with it."

Has he changed his mind? "So, Andreas, you are advising me not to put the Assembly on a war footing?"

The answer was slow in coming. "No, that's not what I'm saying. Ethan, war is like a very hot object—if you handle it for more than the briefest time, you will be burned. It corrupts. So, if we have to have a war, let's do it as quickly as we can. We should make it our goal to win and end any conflict as fast as possible. War is so horrid a business that we must do all we can to cut it short."

"Thank you," Ethan said.

Silence fell.

They're waiting for me.

"I too have learned more here than I thought."

He caught Eliza staring at him, dark eyebrows raised in inquiry. "Yes. Professor Andreas's ghosts have been helpful. They've solved my third issue."

"How so, Eeth?"

Ethan gestured at the eroded trench. "I can hardly ask for a sacrifice from others if I am not prepared for it myself. It would be selfish. No, I will stay in office as long as it is helpful. Whatever it costs."

"Well said, Eeth."

"Good point."

"Friends," Ethan said. "I think it's time to walk back."

He looked at his diary adjunct. "Nearly four. By this time tomorrow, our world will have changed."

He sighed and turned his back on the valley, the mountain, and the trees. "And I must be a part of it."

3

Verofaza Enand bounded down the sunlit steps of Western Isterrane Main Hospital. He tried to ignore the stares of the people clustered at the entrance as he ran over to the small two-seater transport parked by the gate.

A woman with short, auburn hair sitting in the driver's seat looked up, her gray-blue eyes registering alarmed inquiry.

"M-Merral's in q-quarantine, P-P-Perena! For a w-week!" Vero blurted out. He hated the stammer in his voice. *It's the stress.*

"But is he okay?" Perena Lewitz asked.

"Yes. I talked to him through a comms link."

He suddenly noted the direction of Perena's eyes, and turned to see that people continued to stare at him.

"Get in," she said, sliding the door open.

Vero sat in the passenger seat and closed the door. "They're watching me." *And I don't like it.*

"Your skin marks you out as an offworlder." Her voice was calm, analytical even. "And now that Farholme has been turned upside down, people are suddenly sensitive to anything different. Don't forget many of those people are waiting for news of casualties."

Yes, it's just curiosity, driven by anxiety. But I don't like being the center of attention.

Perena pressed the motor switch. The transporter glided away. "So what happened?" she asked. "Merral was okay yesterday. You talked to him. And Anya . . ." Her words hinted at awkwardness as she mentioned her sister. *I must try and find out what has happened between Merral and Anya.*

"It was Corradon's speech yesterday and his mention of Merral 'hero-ically entering the intruder ship.' The medical authorities suddenly realized they had broken every guideline on biohazard containment and that Merral could be incubating all sorts of plagues and diseases. So they rushed him into a sterile isolation unit. A classic case of locking the stable door after the horse has bolted."

"The horse has what?" She smiled suddenly. "Oh. I get it."

"He'll be there for forty-eight hours while they investigate him in detail and then, all being well, they plan to move him to a disease isolation unit for five days—no guests."

"Best thing for him." Now her smile seemed tired. "Look, where do you want to go? I'm just driving around at the moment."

"Perena, I need time to think. Badly. I was hoping to sound some ideas off Merral, but I can't do it with a ward of technicians listening in. Somewhere quiet, please."

"I know a quiet park. I often run there."

She turned off along an avenue lined by high trees.

Almost Earthlike. He regretted the thought, because it made him homesick.

"The thing is, P.—" Vero paused, wondering if she would object to the contraction but she didn't—"I looked no further than the encounter with the ship. I rather hoped, I suppose, that whatever happened there would sort things out."

Perena shrugged. "What else could you have done? No one knew what we would find."

"Thanks for that reassurance. But now there's a new threat. And we have to produce an expanded Defense Force f-for an attack that might come any day. I don't know where to begin. Well, I do, but it's s-staggering."

Perena nodded slightly, her eyes never leaving the road.

Funny to be driven around town at forty kilometers an hour by a spaceship pilot more used to speeds a thousand times that.

"I face a similar problem," Perena said, in her quiet, understated way.

Does she ever lose her temper? ever panic? She must be very soothing to live with. "How so?" he asked.

"Corradon promised a defense capacity with a 'range out to the system's edge.' It was a great line. Very reassuring. But I don't think the representative had thought it through. A planetary system is 3-D, not flat like the maps on walls. And the volumes get horrendous when you have what is effectively a sphere with a radius of six billion kilometers."

"Ah. You mean we're wide open to attack?"

"Near enough. We can't defend Farholme with the dozen deep-space vessels we have."

So there is no real protection. That makes things a whole lot harder.

"Is that why you play chess the old way?" he asked.

"Rather than the 3-D versions? That's a part of it. The mind can just about handle five moves ahead on a flat board. But if you add an extra dimension, it gets too overwhelming."

Vero stared out of the window. "There's so much to think about. Vehicles, accommodation, structure, communications, and a dozen other things. I have tons of ideas, but they all need to be thought through."

"You can't do it all on your own, you know."

He smiled at the concern in her voice. "I know I can't, P. I just have to try to set up a system that will enable us to get started on building Farholme's defenses. Get the ball rolling. I am making a list of what I need. Of course, the basis will be the existing Farholme Defense Unit."

Perena pulled through gates into broad rolling parkland studded with copses and avenues of trees. Despite the sunny afternoon, it appeared largely empty. There were small knots of people, some deep in conversation, and a few families, but otherwise the park had a deserted air.

"There is too much news to digest," Perena said as they overtook a bus with just three passengers on board.

She stopped the vehicle under some large, spreading trees. Vero waited until she climbed out, then indicated a direction in which to walk.

"I find the sun bright these days, P. But this is fine." He looked around. "Nice trees. Merral would know what these are."

"You can always read the labels," Perena said, pointing to one nearby with a slight smile.

"I'd be no wiser." Vero sat down heavily under the tree and sighed. "So, the FDU becomes the *FDF:* the Farholme Defense Force. Where do we begin? Communications, I suppose."

Perena sat silently next to him.

"Maria Dalphey was working on a secure system. I must contact her."

"Yes. There wasn't time to develop it before the battle."

"Was it really just the day before yesterday? It seems like months ago."

"In a way, it was years ago," she said softly. "It was another time, Vero. It occurred in another world."

A couple with a young child between them walked past, wariness in their faces. Each parent had tight hold of a tiny hand.

"They watch their children now," Vero said.

"This used to be a carefree world. It's only hours since the speech. And it's sinking in that we have been attacked and we could be attacked again. We have enemies."

In the long silence that followed Vero thought about his father. *I long to see him again.* He sighed. *There's no time for such thoughts. I must think of the practicalities: There's work to do here.*

"I am going to live at Brenito Camsar's cottage near Isterrane, P. You must come. There's a lot of space artifacts."

"But why there? Other than that nice setting on the headland."

"Because it's off the beaten track, and it will allow me the freedom to come and go at will. I want to stay out of the way. Keep a low profile. And if I have any spare time I also want to start something of a research project on all Brenito's material. I live in hope that there might be something there that can help us."

He leaned back, looking at the shafts of light coming through the leaves. "And Merral is going to write a detailed account of what happened on the ship. *Everything*—every last fragment may be of value to us."

"Are you terribly upset that it was destroyed?"

He noted how delicately she asked the question. "Yes and no. The idea that we could have taken a working vessel and navigated it all those light-years back to the Assembly was always unrealistic. And who was to say that I might have been on it? The ship would have had limited space and there are lots of people with more pressing reasons to return to Earth than me. So, I suppose I was prepared for the worse." *Was I really?*

"I like your attitude. I can sympathize with that."

"Thanks, Perena. I really value your friendship." *I really do—more than I dare say.* Yet the words came out. "I'm a long way from home. And, as of yesterday, it doesn't look like I'm going back any day soon. It's a pity . . . I'd have liked you to meet my family. I'm pretty certain my father isn't going to be around in fifty years—or fifty months."

"That sounds like an offer," Perena said with such an out-of-the-ordinary tone of voice that Vero felt a pang of some deep and turbulent emotion. "Is it?"

Is it? "No—well, yes. I mean—*no*."

A succession of thoughts tumbled through his mind. *I admire Perena and respect her. I am fond of her . . . maybe more than fond. I would like to pursue that possibility.*

"Is it or isn't it, Verofaza?" Perena's smile was inviting.

There's nothing to be lost and everything to gain. Take the initiative! "Er, yes. I mean, *definitely*."

Perena touched his hand, then sighed as she withdrew hers. "Normally, I would be delighted to explore that offer of a deeper friendship between us. But now?" She exhaled heavily and her face acquired an expression in which conern and hope seemed mixed. "Do you mind if I walk on my own? I want to think about what you just said."

This is going wrong. Vero felt near despair. *I shouldn't have said it. Wrong place, wrong time. Probably wrong planet.*

"I'm sorry," he said. "I didn't mean to say anything. I'm just overwhelmed by things. I know that's not a very good reason for expressing an interest." He stared at a tree trunk. "It's probably the worst reason there can be." *I dug myself into a hole and I need to dig myself out.*

"Don't, Vero," Perena said gently. "Don't apologize. There are far worse reasons. But in the meantime, I need to think and pray."

"You're right. And I too."

He watched her slim, lithe frame walk away with a brisk and steady pace. Then he put his head in his hands and asked for wisdom, clarity, and courage for them both. But he knew that beneath his words, he really asked for what he desired to be granted. *I'm giving God orders.* He rebuked himself. But he kept praying and as he did, he slowly saw beyond his own wishes. Soon the answer was plain.

"I'd better get back to work," he said aloud. Taking out his diary, he began making notes on matters to do with organization and structure for the FDF.

Twenty minutes later, he looked up and Perena was there. With a single fluid motion, she sat on the grass next to him.

"So, have you saved the world yet, Vero?" she asked. Her levity seemed artificial. Indeed, she looked as if she had been crying.

"Not yet, Miss P. I have other things on my mind." Face-to-face with her, he felt his resolve slipping.

Perena gave a tiny nod. "Vero—," she began.

"No, let me," he interrupted, wanting to get the words out before he could think the better of them. "I'm not sure the time is right for . . . anything more between us." *There! I've said it!*

He saw the relief on her face.

"Ah," she said slowly. "My conclusion, most reluctantly, was the same— that we should just be good friends. The best of friends . . . but no more. For the moment."

"This just isn't my day, is it? Nor the last *two* days. First, I lose my lift home, and now I get my hopes dashed." He knew his attempts at humor seemed artificial. The sadness was too near the surface. "But I'm not going to argue. It's what I felt. I'm lonely and—to be honest—I'm scared and a relationship with you would brighten my life. But that's not the right reason, is it?"

"No," she said. "But a pity. I was hoping you would argue me into it." But in her eyes he saw a warning: *Don't try!*

Perena took a deep breath and leaned forward, hugging her knees. "I think we have to bear in mind that our world is now unstable. Sin has crept back and relationships are being distorted. I don't really understand what happened with my sister and Merral. In some ways I don't want to know. That's their business. But it indicates the way things are going. If what happened can happen to them, then it can happen between us. We never used to worry about such things; we assumed it would all work out. We need to be careful. Do I make myself plain?"

"Yes."

"There's something else. The day before yesterday, perhaps twenty-five people died to seize that ship. We thought its destruction was the end; we now know it may be the beginning of problems to come." She breathed deeply, as if in pain. "Vero, they made a sacrifice. I don't know if I'm expressing this well, but . . . but we may have to do the same. We must be realistic. If there is an attack—a proper attack—then we pilots will bear the brunt of it. We can maybe muster a dozen ships that might be used in any space defense. And twenty, maybe thirty pilots."

With no armor—and so far—no weapons.

"And if that is what lies ahead," she went on, "then it's going to be hard, because I love life. But if I was committed to someone, it might be almost impossible to do what I might have to do."

Vero looked at the grass. *It's a good way of hiding your feelings.*

"One of the things . . . ," he began, then realized that the words he started to say bore little resemblance to the painful intensity of what he felt. "Let's start again. One of the things that I really like about you, Perena, is your ability to see beyond surface things."

"And I admire your ingenuity."

"It's a dangerous gift." He paused. *I have to respond to what she has said.* "P., Perena, the only problem is . . . the way you've said it and the way that you've handled things has increased, rather than decreased, the attraction I feel for you."

"Sorry."

"But when it's all over, can we reconsider?"

"When it's all over?" She smiled. "Yes. But not until. . . . We might be old by then."

Or dead. Vero sat back against the tree. *Work is a good cure for a frustrated love affair, and I've got plenty of work.*

"Okay," he said. "Let's put it behind us."

"Agreed. But not without sadness."

There was a protracted silence that seem filled with regret.

Finally, Perena shook herself. "To work. Do you have any bright ideas about saving us from further intruders?"

"I'm hoping for some clues from the various reports—Merral's especially. But we need an army, P." He hesitated. "It's not easy to make one of those. So, you think more intruders will get through any defenses that we can come up with in space?"

"More than likely. We might take out 5 percent of an attack force if we're lucky. But no more."

"So they'll end up in orbit around us. Is it possible that they'll just blast us into dust using nuclear weapons or even a polyvalent fusion bomb?"

Perena gazed eastward across the greenery of the park before answering. "It's possible. We know so little about them. And from the nastiness on the ship Merral hinted at, we can't rule it out. But I don't think it's likely. It's a hunch, that's all."

"Explain."

"We've scanned the worlds beyond ours. There is no other star system that has any indication of anything other than a trace of water. Not for at least three hundred light-years. At that point we lose resolution. This place—" she gestured to the trees and the grass—"is valuable. Good planets are hard to find."

"So they might try and occupy us?"

"The most likely scenario."

Occupation. A word I have met in many documents having to do with war. Occupation, though, was sometimes defeated by resistance. I must do some studying fast.

Vero became aware that Perena was watching him. "Thanks, P. You've helped me."

"I can't see how."

As he rose, she followed, carefully brushing a few strands of grass off her clothes.

"P., can you take me to Planetary Affairs? I need to start some things going. Gather my aides. But the first step is to see Corradon in his office. There is work to do."

"Of course."

"I gather there are offices already being made ready for Merral and the FDF. But I need some space. Preferably private. . . . Yes, hidden. Somewhere in the city. Any ideas?"

"What's wrong with the Walderand water project site you used before?"

"It's too far and it's an obvious target."

"How many people are you thinking of?"

"Maybe a hundred."

"Talk to the city engineers." Perena gestured toward the buildings that were the heart of Isterrane. "This is the first city. Do you understand what that means?"

"Only that it was here that the first settlement on the planet was founded. But what does that have to do with anything?"

"Oh, Earther—" he heard amusement in her voice—"you people don't understand the Made Worlds, do you?"

"Explain."

"When Farholme was settled, oh, around three thousand years ago, it was so inhospitable that, as with all Made Worlds, the first city was built underground. And then, as the stabilization of Farholme progressed, a new city was built on top of the first one."

"You mean there is an old city beneath this one?" *It sounds too good to be true.*

"Well, maybe a lot of old tunnels and chambers. That's all I know. Every few years there are trips down to the foundations for the curious. I've never been."

"Right. I'll get a guided tour. Thanks for the information."

As they walked slowly on to the vehicle Vero said, "Talking of defense, I worry about Merral."

"He seems able to take care of himself. But why?"

"It seems he only went on that ship because the envoy told him to. But it was very dangerous. And the point is he has become a hero. He was a hero to his soldiers the day before yesterday. They're already talking as if he single-handedly destroyed the ship. And after Corradon's speech, he is now a hero to the whole planet."

"Yes, that's true. A world that needs a hero has found one in Merral."

"In the last war, the Assembly forces had Lucas Ringell. We have Merral D'Avanos."

"That puts him under awful pressure. We must pray for him," Perena said with a shake of the head that conveyed both concern and unease. "Incidentally, I think we ought to try and see if we can sort out whatever happened with Anya. It's a complication we can do without. They need to be able to work together. I'll talk to her; you talk to him."

"I will. But look, to get back to his safety, the fact is that we can't afford to lose him. He is absolutely invaluable as a leader. And, also, we need to protect him from the crowds of people who are now going to want to see him."

There were at the vehicle now, but Perena showed no signs of wanting to open the door. "Why do I feel that this is the preamble to one of Verofaza Enand's cunning schemes?"

"Well, someone has to come up with the ideas."

Perena looked doubtful, but said nothing.

"Anyway, to take the pressure off him and to reduce the risk, I'm thinking that he needs a bodyguard."

"A *what?*"

"It doesn't really have an equivalent in Communal. It would be, well, someone who would be with him to protect him. Watch over him."

"Merral won't like it."

"I think you're right. I'll have to disguise it as something else."

Perena leaned against the side of the vehicle, sighing. "Oh, Vero, I don't like our world now. I don't like the way all our best desires are frustrated. And I don't like that it's produced a climate in which all the worst things in us thrive. We now scheme against our friends."

"It's not scheming. It's in his best interest."

"Of course." There was the faintest hint of irony.

"But I agree. It's unfortunate we were born for such a troubled time and place."

Perena smiled ruefully. "Do you know, when I first started pilot training, I once wished that I had been alive at the time of the Rebellion and flown for the Assembly?" She drummed her fingers on the roof. "I thought it was heroic, epic." Her eyes brightened but her smile was tinged with a deep melancholy. "And now my wishes have been granted. We again live in such days. And we must serve our Lord in ways that we thought were long gone."

"Truly said."

She opened the doors. "Come on, Vero. Let's leave this sunlit park and go our ways. Let me take you to see Corradon so you can raise your army. And I must go to the simulators and revive maneuvers we long felt were ancient history."

She sounds determined. "I suppose so."

"Rejoice, Vero. It's not just Merral. We're going to be heroes too."

"But P., I don't want to be a hero."

"That's what makes one."

4

Sitting on his bed in the spotless, white-walled room of the disease isolation unit, Merral D'Avanos looked up at the wall clock. It was five to nine. The morning's sun streamed in past the trees. The only noise he could hear was that of sparrows squabbling on the balcony.

In five minutes, Vero will be here. And now, a week after the battle at Fallambet, my new life as Commander of the Farholme Defense Force will begin.

Merral sighed with an intensity that made him aware of his still-healing ribs. Although he had protested when the doctors ordered him into quarantine, his time in the unit had been a blessing. His injuries had had the chance to heal and he had been isolated from the furor that erupted in the wake of Corradon's announcement of the intruders and the battle.

In the seclusion of the unit, Merral had written a full report on the battle from his own point of view, penned personal letters to the next of kin of the casualties, and a formal letter of resignation from his Forestry post at the Planning Institute. He had answered a selected number of messages from Corradon asking for his opinion. But above all, he had thought and prayed through what he had to do.

His few possessions were packed, but there was one more matter remaining. From a small dark wood box on the dressing table he carefully drew out an identity disk. The scratched titanium caught the morning sunlight.

For some time, he stared at the ancient circle of metal. *Do I wear it— Lucas Ringell's identity tag, a testimony now to wars both ancient and modern?* He gazed at himself in the mirror, seeing new lines on his face and feeling that he had aged. *If I put this on, I take on the role of defender of the Assembly.* A range of emotions—inadequacy, guilt, fear, and more—passed through his mind. He bowed his head and prayed, and as he did he realized that he had no choice.

"I will not take it off until the war is over," he said softly as he placed the chain around his neck and tucked it beneath his shirt. "So help me God."

ロ○ロ○ロ

Vero was waiting for him outside the isolation unit next to a small, blue two-seater transport with the letters *FDF* freshly painted on the sides.

Merral was surprised to see that his friend wore very dark glasses. Also his clothes hung loosely on him. *It is as if events are melting him away.*

They embraced and exchanged concerned inquiries about each other's health.

"Are your eyes all right?" Merral asked, as he took his seat. "It's still early morning."

"Fine. I just prefer wearing these glasses."

"Is it an Ancient Earth thing? It's rare to wear them so dark here, even when it's bright. They conceal the eyes."

"Just so," Vero replied. He slid the glasses down his nose, revealing his brown eyes, and smiled before sliding them back up and starting the engine. "I was told you wanted to go to the airport."

"Yes. I have things to sort out at Ynysmant. I need to see my parents . . . and Isabella."

"Of course."

"There are . . . things to sort out. I'll be back tomorrow night."

"Good."

"And I need to talk to Jorgio."

"I have had a thought there," Vero said as they pulled away. "I've moved into Brenito's place, but I haven't had a chance to do anything with the garden. It's starting to look a mess. So I was wondering if you could persuade Jorgio to come and live with me and help out."

"I can ask. I know he doesn't like traveling though. I presume you're not just concerned about getting a gardener."

"No. I'd like him near us in case he has any more of his insights. And he's easier to protect here than in Ynysmant."

"A good idea. I'll ask him to come."

Vero turned the vehicle onto the road leading to Isterrane. "My friend, we have a lot to talk about. But where to begin? Well, for a start there's a new diary for you in the back."

As he turned to look at Merral, the vehicle swung from side to side. "Sorry . . . It has a new encrypted mode on it that's supposed to be impossible to break. Maria Dalphey came up with it. I assumed she was staying on as a communications officer. Your friends and family will have a direct link to you; everyone else goes through the Farholme Defense Force office. You've had about a thousand calls so far. Okay?"

An inevitable innovation. Merral nodded.

As they overtook a crowded bus, Merral noted eyes turning toward them.

"The FDF is the focus of attention," Vero commented. "I was thinking of getting tinted glass fitted on these vehicles."

"But I *like* looking out."

"That's not the point. It stops people looking *in*." As Vero turned to Merral again, the car wandered nervously before the steering correction circuit adjusted it.

"Why not put it on autosteer?"

"Good idea." Vero pressed a switch, then took off his dark glasses and tucked them in his shirt pocket. Turning back to Merral, he said, "But you do know you're now a major figure? a celebrity?"

"Oh dear. I wish Corradon had kept my name secret."

"He had his reasons. But I thought I'd warn you. Anyway, we've had to make a lot of decisions in your absence. Some you've been informed of; others have been made for you. We could've talked them through with you, but we felt it best that you be given quiet to recover. Anyway Zak Larraine's been acting commander. He's taken to it like a fish to water. We have started to recruit three regiments. Each—"

"Regiments?" Merral interrupted, sensing another long-buried military word being revived from the history files.

"A decent-sized army unit—about a thousand soldiers each. Men and women this time. And another thousand for reserves. We've started work on weapons and gear for them all. It's just as well the planet has spare manufacturing capacity. There's a folder in the back for you on this and other matters."

Merral stared out of the window at the woodland they were passing. The trees—dwarf oaks and a fine clump of Neyther's pines—seemed to clamor for his attention. He pushed them out of his mind. *Three thousand soldiers? On the one hand, an army; on the other, an utterly inadequate force.* He turned back to face his friend. "Vero, I hate all this."

"I know you do. But it has to be done. Now, on weapons, your account of your traverse of the ship has thrown a spanner into the works."

"A spanner? But—"

"Remember how your cutter gun went dead? And your diary?"

"Yes."

"And both returned when the steersman was slain. And we had a diary blockage on Carson's Sill when we first hunted the intruders. So we must assume they have some sort of ability to suppress electronics, perhaps by these steersmen. You see the military significance?"

"Ah. I can guess."

"We can't rely on weapons using electronics. That's why we've started looking at other weapons—rifles that fire rockets or bullets. Weapons that can't be jammed. Older weapons. And they are lighter, so they can be carried by women."

"I hadn't thought of that, but yes, it makes sense."

There are too many unknowns . . . unknown enemies in unknown numbers with unknown powers.

There was a long silence.

"Vero, I'm now a commander. I have an army and I'm a celebrity. I can't get used to the way my life has changed."

"I'm sorry. You will find that it's all a very different kettle of fish now."

"A what?"

Vero shrugged. "That's what they said in the past. I've read it recently. I presume it was a cooking method."

"In a *kettle*?"

"Hmm." Vero frowned. "Maybe that's how they caught them. Oh well. Anyway, it's all changing."

"How's everyone else?"

"Under the circumstances, fine. Corradon is going round Farholme making speeches and boosting morale. Doctor Clemant sits in his office and keeps things going in his absence. Perena is busy on space defenses."

"And Anya?"

"Ah, *Anya*," There was a significant pause. Vero's brown eyes tightened. "Anya's fine, or as fine as anyone can be when they are dissecting the corpses of cockroach-beasts and ape-creatures we killed at Fallambet. We wish we had some of those Krallen. They're the things that really worry us. We have read and reread that section of your report. You really think we will meet them again?"

"The envoy implied as much," Merral said, "and on the assumption he is an angelic being, I trust him." He stared out of the window, seeing the woodland pass into bleached stony scrub, and tried not to think of the cold malice of the Krallen pack he had encountered on the ship.

"There is one other thing," Vero said, interrupting Merral's troubled memories. "Well, one *major* thing. I decided we needed to create irregular units—a potential guerrilla force."

Merral stared at him. "Two new words for me there: *irregular* and *guerrilla*. For the commander of the Farholme Defense Force, my education is rather inadequate."

Vero grinned at him. "*Inadequate* is an overused word at the moment.

Everything on every front is inadequate. Anyway the fact is that, despite Corradon's words, any attackers will easily get into Farholme orbit. Perena alerted me to the problem and Gerry Habbentz has confirmed it. And if that happens, we have an issue with our three regiments."

"Go on."

"They are both too small and too visible to resist any occupation."

"I can see that. So what's the answer?"

"An irregular force. We train and arm ordinary people wherever they live. They have no uniforms, no barracks, no machines of war. They are just ordinary people in ordinary jobs. But when the enemy lands, they use surprise and their knowledge of the terrain to make sudden attacks. So for instance, imagine we are occupying forces. See that woman there?" He pointed to a woman sitting at a bus stop. "She just picks an explosive charge out of her bag and throws it at us, and then disappears into the crowds. Eventually, such attacks—guerrilla attacks—would wear down the much more powerful attacking power. Does that make sense?"

"Yes . . . I suppose . . . ," Merral said as he wrestled with the idea. "The occupier finds that everyone is a potential enemy. But it doesn't sound very, well, *fair*."

Vero laughed. "Oh, Merral, war isn't a Team-Ball tournament. The point is that if they attack civilians, then the civilians have a right to attack back."

"I suppose so—on those terms. But these irregulars—where will we have them?"

"Everywhere. Every settlement across the planet." Vero seemed enthusiastic. "We just supply them with secret bases, weapons, training, and communications."

"So, what do you want me to do?"

"Ah. Well, the irregulars are already being set up. And we'd like your approval." He shrugged. "But if you really don't like them . . . well, we can always restrict them."

Merral considered the matter in silence as the traffic grew heavier and the first orchards of Isterrane came into sight.

"I think I approve," he said finally. "I need to think about it though. But who would head it up?"

"Ultimately, you, of course. The regulars and the irregulars have to work together. But the irregulars will have a separate chain of command and a heavy involvement from Intelligence."

"In other words, *you*."

Vero looked uneasy. "Well, yes. It's a natural extension of what I have been doing."

"And you've started working on them?"

"Yes. We couldn't wait. We are funneling anybody we don't take for the regulars into the irregs. There were fifty groups planned as of last night."

"I'll give you my answer soon. But I can't foresee disagreeing with you."

They were silent until they reached the edge of the city. Then Vero began to speak in a hesitant way, betraying his unease. "My friend . . . I am aware this is personal, but can I ask what exactly is going on between you and Isabella and Anya? I know a bit and can guess a bit more, but I think I ought to know more." He paused. "I mean in one sense, it's none of my business, but in another, it is. We have enough problems to face without difficulties between you and Anya. We need to work together."

Merral stared at Vero. *He's embarrassed.* "Yes, Vero, you are right. And anyway maybe you can help me. You remember that my parents—and Isabella's—were reluctant to allow us to proceed to commitment?"

"Yes, you told me about it soon after we met. It seems like years ago. You were going to wait—keep the relationship as something open and nonexclusive."

"Yes. Well, that's what I thought. But just before we walked north looking for the intruders, Isabella persuaded me to agree to something. I wasn't paying attention, so I agreed. But ever since, she has said—or implied—that we agreed to be committed to each other."

"Without parental consent?" Vero frowned.

"Yes."

"So—let's get this right—*she* sees you as committed to her and therefore on the way to engagement and marriage. But *you* don't."

"Exactly."

"And so you got involved with someone else—"

"No! Put like that, you make me sound utterly immoral!"

Vero winced. "S-sorry. Look, you tell it your way."

"Oh, the apology is mine. I didn't mean to snap. To be honest, I feel terrible about the whole business. But it's weird. I was happy with Isabella. I really didn't mind the idea of commitment and marriage to her. Yet I started having these feelings for Anya."

"Ah. But why didn't you just tell Anya that you were already, well . . ." Vero paused. "At least, in some sense, committed?"

"There's the heart of the matter." Merral turned back to the passing landscape, seeing the bladelike structure of the Planetary Administration building rising above the Isterrane skyline.

"I suppose," he said slowly, "I felt that it wasn't a real commitment. And it all happened so suddenly. It's no excuse, I know."

"So, what do you propose to do?"

"Well, I have to see Isabella and call it all off. After all, not even engagements are unbreakable."

"True. But it's rare and by mutual consent. Or at least I should say, hitherto it has been rare. But everything is changing." Vero shook his head mournfully. "Everything." A moment later he spoke again. "Incidentally, you may not be surprised to know that you're not alone. Other similar problems have been reported. Clemant, that careful observer of social detail, is most concerned. Delastro made a big thing of it in his speech the other night."

"Delastro?"

"Of course, you have been out of it. Balthazar Delastro has been designated prebendant by the Farholme congregations three . . . no . . . four days ago."

"What's a prebendant?"

"I'm not sure. It's a role dug out for the crisis. But he has authority. Technically, the rather frail Octavio Jenat is still the president of the congregations. But Delastro is making the speeches." Vero looked pensive. "You—we—may need to watch this man. So far the congregations have not been an issue. After all, when the loss of the Gate was presumed to be a technical failure, it wasn't their business. But now that they all know there are intruders and that evil is spreading, the crisis is very much their business. Anyway, there is a new factor: Prebendant Balthazar Delastro. But you were saying? About your . . . well . . . relational difficulties."

"Yes. Well, I need to see Anya too . . . to apologize again and ask that our relationship go back to being just friends. So the aim with both is the same: to put the clock back. For the duration."

"The duration?" Vero's expression seemed almost agonized. "I wonder what that means. Part of me wonders if it will be forever." Vero gestured at the vehicle's rear mirror. "The past, the Assembly, all our old values: all seem to be like what I see here—an image rapidly receding. Some nights I wake up and wonder if it was all a dream."

Merral turned away, embarrassed by the intensity of the sadness that had been revealed. "I can understand that," he answered. "But, Vero, do you think I can do it—turn everything back?"

"Ah, my friend, I have read much more pre-Intervention literature than you. I now read almost nothing else. You'll find your situation described there. Look up *love triangle* in the Library. As for your chances . . . well, I wish I was more confident. But in his wisdom the Lord of All didn't make us like machines. It's not easy to turn things back—there are no cogs we can turn, no buttons to press to reset the mechanisms of the heart. But I wish you well, and I'll pray you can do it. I'll also do what I can do to explain things to Anya."

"Thanks."

Emboldened and feeling almost a sense of release, Merral said, "While we are on the topic can I ask about you and Perena?"

"You can ask, but there is nothing to say. That's all 'on hold' as they say." Vero shrugged. "I hope you notice the perverse symmetry to our lives, my friend. You have two relationships where you should have one. I have none where perhaps I should have one." He sighed. "Welcome to the new world."

Silence returned as they curved round the center of Isterrane on the airport road. Vero spoke at last. "Oh, one last thing, Merral. We decided that you needed some s-support. So I have taken the liberty to recruit Lloyd Enomoto as your aide."

"Enomoto? Do I know him?"

"Maybe not. Lloyd used to be an agricultural student. He came late into the FDU reserves but he arrived at Fallambet in time to kill a cockroach-beast at the ship. Zak promoted him to sergeant in the FDF. He's a big guy, nearly too big to fit in a ship."

"But an aide? How does that work?"

"He helps you, gets whatever you need." Vero seemed cautious. "Carries your bags, goes places with you—that sort of thing. Anyway, I figured that Lloyd would go with you to Ynysmant."

"Vero, I hardly think I need an aide in my hometown."

"Well, Lloyd would manage communications too. So, if I need you, I'll call him."

"Hmm. So Lloyd goes around with me? Everywhere?"

"Not *absolutely* everywhere, of course."

"So, what about when I talk with Isabella?"

"He'd sit outside the door, out of earshot. We've discussed all this. And he's sworn to secrecy, of course."

"Sworn?"

"I mean he'll be totally confidential."

"I'm uneasy about it—very."

"We think it's useful. We'd feel happier if he went with you."

Merral wondered who "we" were, but didn't ask. "I'm not sure about this."

"He's at the airport. We'll decide there."

Vero switched off the autosteer circuit and drove the vehicle to the main terminal building, stopping in the parking area marked *Airport Staff Only, Please*.

"But we aren't—," Merral began.

Vero wagged a slender finger. "Three letters, my friend: *F-D-F*. We take priority." He put his dark glasses on.

Merral was still pondering the issues that "priority" raised as they walked to the entrance. Suddenly, he looked up to see dozens of faces at the windows staring intently at him. He turned, expecting to see someone behind him. There was no one.

"Vero, why is everyone looking at us?"

Vero's mouth twitched as if he was trying to stifle his amusement. "Because, Commander, one of us is a very famous person. And it isn't me."

"You mean—"

"Welcome, Commander!" came a shout from a window. Merral looked up to see people waving at him.

"Vero," Merral said, his voice bristling with agitation, "this is appalling!"

"Relax!" Vero hissed with a firm intensity. "It goes with the job."

"But what do I do?"

"I suggest, Commander D'Avanos, that as ever, you play the part. Just raise your right hand as a relaxed and informal acknowledgment."

Merral hesitated.

"Go on!"

Merral lifted his right hand rather stiffly.

"Not bad. . . . No, not too high. You don't want to encourage them. Now give them a little smile, please."

"It's a farce," Merral whispered between clenched teeth. "An utter farce. I'm encouraging the creation of some sort of celebrity culture. It's unethical."

"Perhaps," Vero murmured. "But remember, these are scared people. They need all the reassurance you can give them. And not to give it definitely would be unethical."

Upon entering the building, Merral found himself nodding and giving more waves of acknowledgment.

As they passed the ticketing booth, Vero nodded toward it. "Remember too, that from now on, you have priority here as well. If you want a seat on a flight and it's full, you have the authority to throw someone off."

"Throw them off?"

"Not, of course, literally. Uh, take their seat . . . have them take a later flight."

"That doesn't sound very polite."

Vero took off his glasses, folded them into his shirt pocket, and then glanced around to make sure no one was in earshot before giving Merral a severe look. "Commander," he said in a low and impassioned voice, "I see our job as saving Farholme and, maybe, the Assembly. On that basis, courtesy and politeness are now, sadly, optional extras. So let's go and meet Sergeant Enomoto."

They found Lloyd Enomoto sitting alone in a small room off the main lounge, reading something on his diary with a look of determined intensity. He was indeed a big man. Even wearing a casual, loose-fitting, gray suit, you could sense his muscles. In fact, Merral decided that Lloyd didn't so much sit on the chair, as sit *over* it. His face was tanned and rugged, his eyes small and blue, and his eyebrows and close-cropped hair were so blond as to be almost white.

Lloyd rose, gave them a warm lazy smile, and saluted.

Merral stared up him, realizing that his eyes only came to Lloyd's chin. He decided to ignore the salute and shook hands instead.

"Good to see you, sir," Lloyd said in a leisurely voice that was almost a drawl, and Merral noted the twang of the southern islands. "Last time I saw you, you were hanging on to that undercarriage and heading off over the lake. I was really pleased to hear you made it. Glad you're well."

"Thanks, Sergeant. Remind me where you are from? Bailor?"

"Not quite, sir, Tralescant—next island west."

Merral noticed that Lloyd had two bags, a backpack with shoulder straps and a small brown bag with an odd, elongated shape.

"Preparing for a trip, eh?"

"Yup. My own stuff and . . ." Lloyd gestured to the brown bag. "Well, my . . . gear." His voice had a note of awkwardness that caught Merral's attention.

"Gear? What sort of gear?"

A look passed between Vero and Lloyd.

"The usual stuff, sir," Lloyd said, looking away.

"T-the Commander doesn't really want—," Vero began.

"Oh, I do. I really do. What's in there?" Merral nodded to the brown bag.

Vero shrugged. "Better open it, Sergeant."

As soon as Lloyd opened the bag, Merral peered in, seeing a diagnostic medical unit. He pushed the DMU aside and found a familiar object with a dull gray tube and a long grip.

"A cutter gun," Merral said. He looked deeper. "And a bush knife. And some other things . . . explosives." He paused. "Excuse me, Sergeant. Could you leave us alone for a few minutes?"

"Yes, sir," Lloyd said and left the room.

"Okay, Vero. Explain. An aide—with weaponry?"

Vero cast the unhappiest of expressions at the bag. "W-well, it's like this. I didn't want to alarm you. B-but we have no idea whether we killed all the inhabitants of that ship. We have no inventory, no passenger list to check them off. We don't know whether, somewhere out there, there are still cockroach-beasts, another Krallen pack, or another winged dragon thing."

"I see. I had, well, assumed, that we had got them all." Merral sighed. "No, you're right. But surely Ynysmant is safe? There are places farther north. Herrandown, Wilamall's Farm, other settlements."

Vero shook his head wearily. "No longer. Last week the decision was

made to close down Herrandown immediately. The inhabitants—your uncle
and his family included—are now in Ynysmant. And Wilamall's Farm is being
wound down. And the others."

"I didn't know that." Merral found himself oddly shaken by the news.
Yet another pillar of his old familiar world had been brought down.

"The images of the dragon thing scared everyone. Clemant and Corradon
decided to close down the settlements almost as soon as the battle was over.
After all, with the ship destroyed, any surviving creatures have nowhere to go.
And yes, there are teams out there scouring the countryside. So far they have
found nothing. There is a ten-man rapid-response team armed and sitting in
a hangar out there." He gestured out of a small window. "They're waiting to
go at five minutes' notice. But there *is* a risk. Anyway, the sad reality is that
Wilamall's Farm and Herrandown are just a burden to Farholme now."

"No!" Merral said, defiance ringing in his voice. "They are a vital part of
making this a habitable world—like all the Forestry projects, the land reclama-
tion, the stabilization of the coasts. It is a continuation of the more than ten
thousand years of work here since the Seeding."

"My friend, it's all been put on hold for a generation. You need to
understand. The battle—and the news that there may be further ships on the
way—has changed everything. *Everything.* It's a whole new ball game. All the
resources of this planet that can be spared are being redirected to defense.
Expansion is over. When the Gate went, we went into maintenance mode.
After Fallambet, we shifted into defense mode."

"I see," Merral said, feeling angry but not knowing whom, or what, he
was angry with. He stabbed a finger toward the bag. "But I don't need one
of these men. He's not just an aide. What is he in reality?"

"A bodyguard."

"I don't need a bodyguard in my hometown. I'll go alone."

Vero grimaced. "I'm not sure it's wise."

"I'll risk it. It's my life."

A look of hard resolution suddenly crossed Vero's face. "I-is it?" He
clenched his fists. "I'm sorry to argue with you again, but I'm not sure it is.
You now have a public duty. This is a shaken world. I've been out there. I
know. The Gate explosion was bad enough, but people handled it. Now the
news of the intruders has been too much. An isolated world facing unseen
enemies? No one is prepared for that."

"God should be their hope."

"He is. But they look to a visible and human expression of that, and
that person is *you*. You are the hero of two encounters with the intruders."
Vero's voice was full of agitation. "Merral, you led the attack. You entered the
ship and came out alive. You stopped the ship escaping. They need you and
you can't disappoint them. It's *not* your life at all. Not any more. It's *theirs*."

Vero paused, as if to draw breath. "And that applies to Ynysmant, most of all. Those people look north every evening and wonder what may be creeping or slithering through the forest toward them. Their town is at the very edge of inhabited Menaya and they know it. They are on the front line. Ynysmant is probably the most scared place on the planet. They need a hero. Your job, *Commander*, is to steady their nerves. You gotta play ball."

"You want me to act? to play a part like Corradon?"

"And what if he does 'play a part'? He's no fool. My friend, the representative knows—as Clemant does—that we face two enemies: the intruders and ourselves. We have the potential for self-destruction. If our morale holds, Farholme may have a chance against an enemy. If we lose our nerve, we have had it. Maybe even before another vessel of this Dominion—if indeed that vessel belonged to them—is sighted. Merral, get real!"

Unable to respond Merral turned, took a few paces away. Realizing his position was indefensible, he turned back toward Vero. "I see," he said softly, feeling chastened and humbled. "You're right. But where does Lloyd fit in?"

"Lloyd is my attempt to help you. Lloyd's job is to make your hard tasks a little easier; to assist you, free you up, keep the crowds at a distance, and—maybe—even defend you. We need you too."

"Oh, dear. What a mess we are in." Merral threw his hands up in the air. "Oh, very well. You leave me little option. I'll take him. But I don't have to like it."

Two hours later, Merral and Lloyd were on the short-haul passenger flier heading west. From the moment he joined the queue for the flier, Merral had been aware of the stares, glances, and whispers focused on him. Trying to distract himself, he turned to Lloyd, who was sitting in the aisle seat, scrolling through something on his diary.

"What are you reading, Lloyd?"

"It's something Mr. V. found me—"

"Mr. *V.?*"

"Mr. Vero, sir. It's his nickname. Sorry."

"I see. Go on."

"It's for my job. *The Bodyguard's Handbook*, 2023 edition. There were later editions apparently, but this is the latest we have. Very interesting, sir. Hard to read though. You keep thinking they can't really mean that. But they do."

Suddenly a man in the aisle peered around Lloyd's bulk to catch Merral's eye.

"Excuse me, Commander," he said apologetically. "We've never met, but I was wondering—we all were—what you could tell us . . . about the situation."

Suddenly every head swiveled toward them.

Lloyd leaned over and whispered in Merral's ear. "Sir, do you want me to move him on? Gently, of course. Mr. V. says it's okay. Part of the job."

"No. No, thanks," Merral replied. "I have a public duty." He squeezed past Lloyd and stood in the aisle. "Hands up anybody here who *doesn't* know who I am."

There was no movement.

"I was afraid of that," Merral said, trying—and failing—to smile. "Well, I don't want to talk about the battle. I heard the representative's speech as you did and I don't really want to add to what he said. We've had intruders. We stumbled upon them, and they destroyed the Gate. We then raised the first Assembly armed force for twelve thousand years. By the grace of God, we defeated the intruders. We had hoped to seize their ship, but failed. At least we destroyed it. As far as we know, they are now gone. I don't want to say any more. It was very unpleasant. We lost some very good men—" he paused, remembering the loss of the diplomatic team—"and a fine woman. I can guess a bit about how you feel. All I can say at the moment is to reassure you that there is no existing threat to Farholme that we know about. But we are taking precautions. Just do your jobs, and pray for our world and us. Thank you."

As he sat down, there was a round of applause.

Ten minutes later, a young woman in the seat in front of Merral's leaned over the back of her seat.

"Commander, I'm from Ynysmant. Can I be naughty and ask you a personal question? It's not about the fighting or anything like that."

"Have we met?"

"I don't think so. It's just that I know Isabella Danol's family."

Merral suddenly had an uncomfortable feeling, rather as if a large insect were creeping down his spine.

"Ah, *Isabella*. Yes, we are good friends."

"So I heard. Anyway I was going to ask . . ." The woman paused and gave him a rather sheepish look. "Is it true that you two are going to announce your commitment?"

merral stared at the woman, utterly lost for words. The thought came to him that life was now like Vero's guerrilla warfare, full of vicious attacks that came out of nowhere.

"A commitment?" he said at last. His smile was one that he didn't feel. "You can see that you've taken me by surprise. It's . . . well . . . a personal matter. I hope you don't mind me saying that."

The cabin juddered and the warning lights flashed. From the speakers came a warm, soprano voice. "Captain Hamandri here. Better return to your seats. We're hitting a a regional dust storm with some associated turbulence, I'm afraid."

The young woman shrugged apologetically and slid down into her seat.

As the flier bounced and swayed through the turbulence, Merral's premonition of trouble grew.

◌◌◌◌◌

It was just after midday local time when, amid buffeting winds, they landed on the runway at Ynysmant. The flier had only just stopped when the captain came aft to Merral. "Commander, can you disembark first?" she said. "Warden Enatus is waiting to greet you."

Further troubled, Merral made his way to the passenger door and stared out into the thick gritty daylight.

"Oh," he said. It wasn't just the warden waiting for him; half the town seemed to be with him. And they were all clapping.

Stunned, Merral gazed at the sight, noticing a strange long strip of orange carpet at the foot of the steps and the terminal building with a large flapping poster—hanging at the oddest of angles—bearing the words *Ynysmant welcomes home COMMANDER D'AVANOS*. Far away beyond the causeway, flags were flying on the flagpoles, towers, and spires of Ynysmant. *What are they celebrating?* With a shock he realized he was the reason.

At the bottom of the steps stood the small, stocky figure of Warden Enatus. He wore a black formal suit with the emblem of Ynysmant emblazoned on the breast pocket. His round, red mustachioed face bore a broad smile and his bald head seemed almost polished.

I must play ball. Merral walked carefully down the steps, feeling the wind ruffle his hair.

Ahead, people in dark red blazers with musical instruments moved into position in a flurry of confusion. After a fervent wave of the conductor's arm, the band began to play the Ynysmant anthem, "Amid the Lake We Stand."

"Welcome back!" shouted Enatus, struggling to make his voice heard over the wind, the band, and the dying rumble of the turbines. Eagerly extending a stubby hand, he stepped forward off the carpet. As he did, the wind caught its edge and in a moment, the entire line of orange fabric took to the air. It buckled sideways, and then in a long drawn-out process of utter inevitability, slapped forcibly into the neat ranks of the band.

The music ground to a halt in a series of discords. Amid the crowd's whoops of laughter, the band tried to retain their balance and hold on to hats and instruments.

"Oh," said Enatus, with an expression of surprised embarrassment. He looked up at Merral with bright blue eyes and said out of the corner of his mouth, "To tell you the whole truth, that wasn't supposed to happen." He stroked his expansive black mustache briefly and then shook Merral's hand with great enthusiasm. "Well done. Very well done."

He returned his gaze to where the band and the strip of carpet were being disentangled from each other. "Hmm. A bad idea that." He turned to Merral. "We wanted a long red carpet, but there was only this orange one around."

"It doesn't matter, Warden," Merral said, trying not to laugh at the combination of the chaotic sight and the sheer pleasure of being home. "It's just good to be back."

Amid cheers and clapping, shouts of greeting, and the sounds of the band starting up again, Merral was led through an increasingly disorganized crowd to where his mother and father stood. *It's unreal . . . as if I won the Inter-System Team-Ball Cup for Farholme.*

As his parents were pushed forward, and kissed and hugged him, he wished that the casing on his healing ribs was a bit thicker.

"Oh, Merral," said his mother, tears filling her eyes. "Oh, I *wish* I had known. I'd have sent you off with some *more* clothes."

His father, his neatly trimmed beard contrasting with the wildness of his windswept hair, clapped him on the shoulders. "Well, Son, I always said you would do something special, but this beats what I had in mind."

And suddenly there was Isabella, with her dark eyes glistening. As she threw her arms around him, there was a new round of applause and whistles.

"Oh, Merral," she said in his ear. "I wish you had told me. But well done."

"Isabella," he answered, not daring to say more. One part of him wanted to weep for joy at being back and another wanted to run back to the flier.

Then he was off shaking hands and clutching arms. In the midst of it all he saw his Uncle Barrand and Aunt Zennia and with them his cousins Elana, Lenia, Debora, and Thomas, all waving madly.

He fought his way over to them. They in turn kissed and hugged him.

In the end, helped by Lloyd, who seemed to have a flair for parting crowds, they made it to an open-backed transporter and drove slowly away off the strip between two tangled lines of cheering people. They came to the causeway where the gusting wind buffeted the white spray off the lake around them. As they did the dirty clouds parted and a shaft of dusty golden sunlight came down on the town, and Merral thought he had never seen it look so lovely.

Yet as they drove between more applauding crowds he suddenly decided that beneath the exuberance there was something else, something that he had never known before in a crowd. *They need something to celebrate. I'm all they have.* Like a cold blast of wind, it came to him that, underneath it all, they were scared.

◯◯◯◯◯

Merral's parents welcomed Lloyd to their house and gave him one of the empty attic bedrooms at the very top of the house that had once belonged to one of Merral's sisters. Yet despite their welcome, Merral was certain that they felt his aide was an intrusion.

As Lloyd was shown upstairs, Merral looked around the general room sensing an unusual neatness. The ornaments on the shelves seemed precisely placed, the pictures aligned perfectly, the curtains were drawn with a careful symmetry, and there was not the slightest trace of dust anywhere.

Merral felt disappointed. He had arrived hoping that he would feel that he had returned home. But now he felt like a stranger. *This may be my home, but it doesn't feel like home.*

His mother hugged him again, then stepped back. "Let's look at you. . . . Merral dear, that jacket . . . those trousers. Where *did* you get them?"

"The hospital. In Isterrane."

She shook her head. "They are a *terrible* fit. They might have given you a proper uniform of some sort. And what's *this* under your jacket?"

"It's the cast. I broke some ribs," Merral said, realizing that he sounded apologetic. "But they're almost fine now."

He had expected his mother to commiserate. Instead, she shook her head again as if reproving him. "Oh, *typical* of the men of this house! Both of you are in *constant* trouble. *Always.* Your sisters have never *ever* given me anything like the same problems."

On the edge of his vision, Merral saw his father, who had been standing rather awkwardly in a corner of the general room, beginning to slide toward the kitchen.

His mother followed Merral's gaze. "Stefan," she said, in an almost triumphant tone, "where are *you* off to?"

His father turned toward them, a hunted expression on his face.

"Sorry, Lena," he said, looking up at her with troubled eyes. "I was just going to check on something in my workroom. The model I'm— "

"In your best *clothes?* I think not. Take them *off* and hang them up neatly. *Now.* I don't want you getting one of your messes on it. Glue, *varnish*, paint. And when you've changed, I don't want you *sneaking* off to 'be with your mates.' There's work to be done here *now*. We have an *extra* guest." She put her hands on her hips. "And Stefan," she said in a tone of great weariness, "do *trim* your hair. I noticed it was *all* over the place at airport. Remember, your *son* is now a commander."

"It was the wind," his father offered in a pathetic tone. With his head slumped over his chest, he walked slowly upstairs.

Before his mother could speak again, there was a knock on the door. She left to answer it.

Troubled by his parents' conversation, Merral slipped away to his room.

As he entered his bedroom, he stopped and looked around, aware that there was something unfamiliar about it. There was a curious odor, a faint tang of engineering oil and machinery—a smell he always associated with his father. Merral glanced around, sensing other oddities: the bed slightly askew, books out of place, a mirror at an odd angle.

Mystified, Merral went to the wardrobe for some of his clothes, only to find one of his father's work overalls hanging up. As he changed, he puzzled over the matter. Could it really be that his father had been sleeping here and not sharing a bed with his mother? It was a disturbing thought and as Merral sat on the bed to try and think it through, his foot struck the edge of something. He reached down and picked up a dusty, thick blue book: *Prifysgol Geiriadur Cymraeg.* Underneath that title—far more comprehensibly—were the words *Welsh Language Dictionary, Finalized Grammar Version, AD 12450.* Merral wiped it clean with the care that one gave bound books.

The book gave him the excuse he needed. He went to his parents' room, feeling sure his father would be there, knocked, and entered.

His father sat at the bedside table in front of the mirror with a pair of scissors in his hands, examining his hair with a sullen expression.

"Father, I found this under my bed," Merral said, holding out the heavy book. "Had you lost it?"

His father made a noise that might have been a sniff. "Oh, *that.* I did wonder where it was." His voice held no interest or enthusiasm over the book's discovery. "I must have left it there when I was studying."

"How's the Historic going?"

His father's mouth creased as if he had eaten something bitter. "It's not. And before you blame me, it's not just me. The other Welsh speakers are the same and I've heard it's the same for the other Historics. No one can get enthusiastic about the old languages anymore. Not now." He glanced at the book. "Look what it says on the front. *Finalized Grammar Version.* The grammar is now fixed. Oh, we can add the odd word, but we can't change how we use them. Let's be honest, Son—it's a dead language. It was only ever a little living language and now it's a little dead one fit for the scrap heap. Why speak it now?"

Pushing to one side the uneasy thought that, apart from the deciphering the debased English of the military manuals, he had done nothing with his own Historics, Merral dug deep for forgotten classroom arguments.

"Well, Father, the principle behind the Historics is that these languages are worth keeping alive because they represent once-living cultures and contain things of beauty and nobility. And the Historics prevent a uniformity that an Assembly based only on the Communal language could have." He paused and then remembered something else. "Oh, and a great principle of the Assembly has always been that, as we have the forward vision to press onward to make worlds, so we must look back to preserve the past."

His father shook his head. "Oh, it's all changed here, Son. Or maybe you have been too busy to notice. All the great principles of the Assembly are in trouble here. The forward vision *and* looking back? We don't have forward vision. Not anymore. Herrandown, Wilamall's Farm, and a dozen other settlements are closed."

There was an unusual clarity and brevity to his father's arguments. "Who has been saying this, Father? It's not just you, is it?"

"There's a group of us meet together—my mates from work and a few others. We play a few games, have a drink or two, and chat. . . . No, Son, survival is all we can hope for now. In the meantime, the 'great principles' are put back in the cupboard." He took the book from Merral.

"Father, can I ask you another question?"

"Yes, but we better watch it. I need to help your mother with supper. If I'm not down soon, she'll be furious. She gets like that now. 'Tidy this, Stefan, tidy that.'"

"You've been sleeping in my room, haven't you?"

His father stared blankly at Merral. "Yes, well . . ." He gave a tragic little shrug. "It's not easy here, Son," he muttered in a low whisper. "Not at all." He turned to the mirror again, scissors in hand.

Merral, saddened beyond words, slipped out of the room.

Outside, he hesitated and then walked up the stairs to the bedroom Lloyd had been allocated. He knocked on the door and walked in.

Lloyd, his blond head nearly touching the sloping roof, turned to face Merral with an uncomfortable look on his face. He stood in front of a mirror with his right hand deep inside the left side of his jacket.

"Sergeant, what *are* you doing?"

"Uh, practicing, sir," came the answer as, keeping his left hand hidden, Lloyd nodded at his diary, which lay on a table. "As suggested by the handbook."

"So, what's in your hand?"

With reluctance Lloyd pulled out his hand to reveal a bush knife with an unextended blade.

Merral suddenly felt he had endured almost more than he could handle. "Can you explain?" he said.

Lloyd extended the blade. "Sir, it's like this. You can't have an unarmed bodyguard. And so far all we have in small weapons are these things. I mean you wouldn't want me to carry a cutter gun around under my jacket, would you? Not here. And the handbook says you need to practice to make sure you can use your weapon rapidly when needed. For defense, you see. So, I've been practicing to see how fast I can pull out the knife and extend the blade. Do you want to see how fast—?"

"No! Categorically, utterly, no!" *I sound like my mother,* Merral realized with alarm. "So, you intend to wander around my town with a lethal weapon?"

"Well, Mr. V. said to guard you. It's my job." A note of fixed resolve rang out in the voice.

Merral gestured to the windows with their view over the ranks of rooftops down to the lake. "But, Lloyd, this is the quietest town in the world—perhaps in all the worlds."

"Sir, I shouldn't argue, but I have to say that . . . well . . . it may have been that once, but this is getting to be a very strange world."

"Nonsen—"

"Stefan! Where *are* you?" The harsh cry echoed up the stairwell. "There's people at the door and I need help in the kitchen. Now!"

Lloyd raised a pale eyebrow.

"Point taken," Merral said. "Let's go and offer to help."

ↀↀↀↀↀ

Merral was excused from helping. Lloyd, however, was given the task of answering the door and telling the many well-wishers that the D'Avanos family were very busy at the moment, but they could leave messages. And the callers—and there were many of them—would look up at Lloyd almost entirely filling the doorway and decide to leave their message and depart. At one point, the frequency of visitors wanting to see Merral or his parents was so great that Lloyd found it easiest to sit by the door on a creaking chair and read his diary.

As they gathered round the table for the meal and bowed their heads to ask a blessing, Merral silently added an extra clause: *Lord, please don't let there be a row.*

Whether it was the prayer or the presence of Lloyd, who periodically had to get up to answer the door, there was no row. It was, Merral felt, a very near thing.

As they were eating the first course, his mother said "I was ever so *surprised* during the representative's broadcast when he said, 'Merral D'Avanos,' and showed *that* picture." She pointed to a photograph of Merral on a bookshelf. "I said to Stefan, 'That's the name of *our* son and he even *looks* like him.' And Stefan said 'That's because it *is* our son.' Only your father *could* have been more polite about what he *called* me."

"The heat of the moment, my dear," his father said calmly, tenderly stroking the newly trimmed fringe above his right ear as if it were a fresh wound. "I have the very highest respect for your intelligence. I always ha—"

"But the *shock*, Merral dear. Your sisters called and I didn't *know* what to say to them *or* to the neighbors. Not at all. . . . I *do* think you should have told us; I really do. We are your *family*. Don't you agree, Lloyd?"

Lloyd looked thoughtful. "Well, Mrs. D'Avanos, it was a secret operation."

"Secret? Well, Merral, you could have *told* us it was secret. You could have said 'I'm on a secret mission to *find* this ship.'"

"In which case . . . ," his father began to protest. "Oh, never mind."

"Still we *are* honored," his mother began again. "And the representative mentioned your name *three* times. I couldn't believe it *really*. Nothing like this has happened to *my* family before. But your *father* had a great-uncle who was given the Silver Globe medal for rescuing a *canoe* with children in it. Isn't that right, Stefan? Oh, you're dribbling into that beard *again*."

"Sorry, dear," his father said, dabbing at his lips with a napkin, "but that business with Gregory was . . . well . . . a little different." He turned to Merral. "Now, Son, as commander—I have a job to get my mind around that title—you will have to brush up on new machines. You'll be making new ships, I suppose. Make sure you get some good engineers and make very sure they design ships that have long service intervals. Take it from me, you don't want to be in dock having your turbines lubed when the enemy appears. And from personal experience—not of course with such things—you really can't have too many backup systems. Have backups for backups, I say—"

"Oh Stefan, there you go *again* about your machines. You've become a *bore*. Our son doesn't want to hear about all *that*. He's got advisors for that. But what I want to say, Merral dear, is that you need to be sure there are *uniforms*. Properly tailored ones. It's *good* for morale."

The conversation continued in this way as the meal progressed. The evening light filtering through the window began to fade. Merral, discouraged and alarmed, felt very much marginalized. He decided not to intervene and soon discovered that if, every so often, he uttered a meaningless phrase such as "That's a good idea," "Possibly," or "I ought to think about that," the dialogue continued without him. The fact that he was effectively distanced from the conversation gave Merral a chance to analyze what he was seeing in his family. He was dismayed that his parents and their relationship seemed to have developed into savage caricatures of what they once were. *My mother always could say silly things. But they were limited, and her sanity and grace outweighed them all. Now it's as if everything is overturned and only an unchecked silliness prevails. And my father's long-windedness has lost the amiability that once excused it. My mother, sadly, is right: he's now a bore. And it's not just them that's the problem. Their only partially successful pretense at maintaining the illusion of marital friendliness is worrying.*

At the meal's conclusion, Lloyd thanked Merral's parents profusely and offered to continue his role as doorman so that they could "have a family conversation." With a nod at Merral, which seemed to suggest both disquiet and sympathy, he went out into the hall.

As they sat down in the general room, Merral threw up a prayer for grace, patience, and guidance. He knew that the matter of Isabella was going to be raised and feared the worst.

"Well, Son," his father said, "this *is* a change in events. You are commander of this Farholme Defense Force. It's hard to take in. You'll be based in Isterrane, I suppose."

"They're giving me an office there."

"To be expected. There are good facilities there. Excellent workshops at the airport. And the port. A very fine dry dock, one of the bes—"

"I was hoping you could stay here," his mother interrupted. "We need a commander here this close to the forest and those things that may be in it."

His father frowned, cast a furtive glance northward, and nodded as his mother continued. "And there's spare office space around. You'd be close to Isabella. That's important now."

And so here we are. Merral braced himself, trying not to reveal anything by his expression. "Why now, Mother?"

A look passed between his mother and father, almost that of coconspirators, Merral decided.

"Well," she said, with a slight awkwardness, "we were going to tell you that . . . that we approved your commitment to Isabella last week."

"Oh," Merral said, trying—and failing—to keep his tone neutral.

"You don't seem very pleased." His mother's tone was sharp.

"I'm sorry. But what happened?" *Let them talk. It's safer.* Merral struggled to control his anger.

"Just after the broadcast the Danols came round," his mother replied. "They reminded us—very nicely—that we had agreed to *review* things after six months and it was nearly that. And they pointed out—what we knew—that now you were a commander, *everything* was changed. They felt it seemed a bit *silly* to withhold parental approval to someone who was *leading* our world as a commander does. We would have been embarrassed. And we felt that you would need all the *support* that you could get and that a wife would be an *excellent* thing."

"And it wasn't just you that changed, Son," his father added quickly. "Things are now different for Isabella. She is now what they are calling a crisis counselor to Warden Enatus."

"That's impressive, isn't it, Merral?" his mother said. "A crisis counselor to the warden. We've never had one of *those* before."

"That's because we've never had a crisis," his father mumbled in an acid tone and was rewarded by a glare.

"Your father has taken to *muttering*. I tell him not to do it, but he persists. Anyway, the Danols *persuaded* us . . . no, we agreed *together* that we should approve a commitment, *immediately*."

"I wish you had asked me," Merral said, struggling to keep his anger out of his voice. "So, who else knows about this?"

"Well, your sisters. And your uncles and aunts. And the Danols, of *course*. And their family."

The whole town and beyond. He suddenly remembered the woman from the flier. "I see," he said slowly.

"But isn't it what you wanted?" his mother asked. "We assumed that you *wished* it. I mean, we only did it for *you*." Her tone was defensive.

They've been manipulated by the Danols. Had the idea come from them? Ultimately, had Isabella been the instigator? He had his suspicions.

He suddenly realized that his parents were looking at him as if waiting for a response. After some thought he said, "You're right that a lot has changed since we discussed the matter at Nativity. And there are things that Isabella and I need to talk over."

"She's a nice girl," his father said, rather mechanically.

"Very well thought of. A *crisis* counselor now."

Again they looked expectantly at Merral, but he said nothing.

"Oh, Merral dear, it will work out all right. Marriages *do*."

They did once. Merral tried to bottle up all the boundless resentment that he felt. He shrugged and said nothing.

A long silence that followed was soon ended by his mother. "Anyway, about tomorrow, Merral. I don't know what you are intending to do, but there are things planned."

"I have to see Isabella. There are . . . matters that need sorting out. And I have other things to do. But what else is scheduled?"

"No need to sound so suspicious. You are among family here. There's a party in Wyrent Park. Warden Enatus has arranged it in your honor."

"That's kind of him."

"And there's going to be a presentation there."

"What sort of presentation?"

"Of a medal. And the *whole* town will be there. Well, *most* of it. And you'll have to give a *speech*."

Suddenly, Merral felt that he had had as much as he could stand. He got to his feet. "I need a walk. Some fresh air."

His mother frowned. "It's late. And you have a big day tomorrow."

"I need some exercise."

"Are you all right, Merral dear?" His mother peered at him.

"I just need some exercise—doctor's orders." As soon as he had said it, Merral realized that he had lied and the only shock he felt was the realization that he *wasn't* shocked.

"The sun's set," his mother said.

"What's wrong with going for a walk at night?"

His parents exchanged uneasy glances. "It's been, well, *rowdy* at night lately," his father said.

"Rowdy?"

"Noisy, uncomfortable. That sort of thing."

"In *Ynysmant?*"

His parents looked at each other with expressions of perplexity.

"I'll take Lloyd."

◌◌◌◌◌

As they stepped onto the darkened street, Merral noted that although Lloyd left his bag behind, his jacket seemed to have acquired an odd bulge. He considered inquiring about the cause, but decided not to. The conversation with his parents had given him enough to worry about.

The afternoon's wind had died down to little more than a gentle breeze. The air was dry, warm, and dusty, and the sky had cleared to give a view of hazy stars. From out of the open windows and the people sitting on balconies came the slow buzz of conversation.

"I apologize for my parents. They're not always like this. Did Vero mention the social and psychological trends we're seeing?"

"Yup. I guess that's one reason why I'm here. Mr. V. hinted that things were moving rapidly, back to a sort of bad pre-Intervention state. That's why he gave me the handbook and suggested I watched a lot of really old films." Lloyd paused and when he spoke again there was a puzzled tone in his voice. "But, sir, I don't understand *why* things are changing."

"Why?" Merral echoed, as he looked up, seeing the ruggedness of Lloyd's face highlighted by the streetlights. "We don't know."

"Well, something's happening, sir. If I had read the stuff in *The Bodyguard's Handbook* a few months ago, I'd have either laughed or fallen asleep. But when I read it now, it's like it all seems familiar territory, if you understand me."

"That's a worrying comment," Merral said. He gestured to an alley. "Let's go up here. We get up to one of the best vantage points this way."

"The handbook says it's a good idea to always know where you are for escape routes," Lloyd said. "But, sir, I have to say I find this place a bit confusing."

"Ynysmant *is* confusing, especially in the dark. People who have lived here for months can easily take a wrong turning. There are five levels—only they aren't very level—with more or less circular roads that we call circles. The main road—Island Road—runs up from the Gate House to Congregation Square on the summit and links them. But there are lots of small side roads that run off. Like this."

"It's interesting. Pretty."

"Thanks. But it's all steep, Lloyd. And having all these three and four-story terraced houses makes it seem even steeper. They say the design deliberately echoes some of the old strongholds—fortified towns—on Ancient Earth."

They continued up the street.

"Sir, I'm surprised how few people there are out. Is that normal?"

"No." Merral paused. "It's odd."

At a street corner, a poster on a wall caught Merral's eye.

"What's this?" he said and read the headline aloud. "'Unhappy with the shape you are? Join our Slimming Classes.'" He looked at his aide. "Make any sense to you, Lloyd?"

"Not at all, sir. I mean, our shape's a thing that the Most High gives us, isn't it? So why be unhappy about it?"

"Exactly. And posters? We never had them before. It's ugly."

Lloyd shrugged. "Beats me."

They walked on upward and soon encountered more posters. One declared that Renato's was *the finest bakery in Ynysmant*; another, a few steps further on, proclaimed that *Carig's Bakery gives* fresher *bread*. It was almost, Merral thought with some puzzlement, as if they were in competition with each other.

As they walked on, they saw other posters. Merral continued to note the trend toward competition. Against an announcement of a concert at the Lakeside Center was another for Forestview Hall, which proclaimed in larger letters that, on the same night, their music played *longer, later, and louder*.

Merral frowned. "Lloyd, I know this town. At least, I *knew* it. I roamed every street as a kid. But now? It's like being in a different town altogether."

Lloyd murmured his sympathies.

They walked under an ivy-draped archway, their footsteps making an echoing clatter.

"What's that?" Merral said, hearing new noises.

From some distance away came the sound of shouting, strident laughter, and running feet. Clearly, Merral decided, some sort of boisterous party was coming their way.

To his right, a door shut with a firm click. To his left, a sash window slid closed. Above him, a balcony was quietly vacated. All around, lights flicked off.

As the noise grew, it seemed to indicate a group of teens.

Lloyd gently grabbed Merral's shoulder. "Sir," he said, gesturing to a side alley, "I think we ought to get out of the way."

A panic-stricken cat flashed past them, a flying pebble bouncing after it over the cobblestones.

"No!" said Merral sharply, pulling Lloyd's hand off his shoulder. "This is *my* town and I'm not running away from some kids."

"The handbook advises that it is far better to avoid confrontation."

The footsteps were louder now. The youths almost in sight.

"Sergeant, I'm supposed to be the commander of the Farholme Defense Force. I am *not* going to run from some noisy adolescents!"

"Very well, sir. But I'll stand here." Lloyd gestured to a nearby recess in a wall that was hidden in darkness. "If there's trouble, I have the advantage of surprise."

"Go ahead. But I'm not moving."

Ahead, the group rounded the corner. Merral stared at them, straining his eyes to try to make out who they were. There were six of them, all under twenty. All wore almost identical light gray clothing.

The group came to a ragged halt a few paces in front of Merral. Peering at them, he saw that they all had dark paint daubs on their faces.

"So who's this then?" said the leading youth in an aggressive tone.

"Let's say I'm a visitor," Merral said, irritated, alarmed, and—he now realized—a little frightened.

"We don't like visitors, do we?" rasped the leader, moving his face uncomfortably close to Merral's.

"Nah!" chorused the others.

"They bring diseases!" another lad hooted, as if it were the funniest joke he had ever heard. There was more hooting and laughter and Merral was aware of an unsettling odor of sweat and hormones.

"Lads," Merral said, trying to adopt a soothing tone of voice, "it's late and you're a bit noisy. Why not head off home?"

"Giving orders are we?" the leader said, once more sticking his face so close to Merral that Merral could smell his sour breath. "We don't like that, do we, boys?"

There was a roar of agreement.

This is crazy! This is my *town!* "It was just a suggestion," he answered, still trying to lower the tension.

"Same thing," said the leader, moving even closer.

As he did, a large form, distorted by the streetlights into something even larger, emerged from the darkness, reached out, and in a single swift move, lifted the youth into the air.

"Let me down!" he yelped as his feet swung off the ground.

"I think it's bedtime." Lloyd's voice was a slow drawl.

"Okay, okay!" the wriggling figure replied. "It was just a joke!"

There was a new noise now, the sound of a motorized vehicle rattling and bouncing over the cobbles.

"Police! Time to go!" The other youths fled down the passageway with wild yells. Lloyd dropped the lad he was holding and swung out hard with his foot as the boy turned to run. There was a yelp and the teen hobbled away, rubbing his bottom.

"I hope you didn't object to my interference, sir," Lloyd said. "Mr. V. authorized all reasonable force. And the handbook would have suggested more drastic measures. It's part of the job."

"No . . . thanks. It was an appropriate response, I suppose. But what's this?"

The two-seater came to a stop just in front of them, a blue light on the roof flashing brightly. Blinking in the glare, Merral saw two men emerge with long sticks and handlights.

"Ynysmant Police. Names and addresses," the taller of the two said in a curt tone.

"Good grief," Merral muttered. He stepped forward, gesturing Lloyd back. He could now see that the men wore uniforms.

"Merral Stefan D'Avanos," he replied, then added, as an afterthought, "Commander."

The handlight flashed on his face.

"Indeed."

"So it is," the shorter man added.

"Sorry, sir," the taller man said. "We knew you were in town. Of course. There's a gang of kids from down Hanston Road roaming around. Being very troublesome, they are. Were they a nuisance?"

"They weren't as friendly as they might have been."

"One way of putting it. This town's the devil to police. Too many alleys."

"They run through the gardens," the shorter man said.

"What would you have done if you had caught them?" Merral asked.

"Just warned them. We have no power yet. In a month though, they say, we will. Powers of arrest and detention. Lockups, magistrates."

"And a penal code," said the shorter policeman.

"I wasn't aware of this," Merral said.

"It's brand-new. And who is this with you, sir?"

Lloyd made as if to speak, but Merral gestured him to be silent. "A friend," he said.

"Your name please?" the taller policeman said, staring up at Lloyd.

"Why do you need it?" Merral asked.

"Orders from Isterrane. We have to make full reports of any incidents."

"With names," added the shorter man.

"Ah," said Merral, feeling irritated and alarmed for the second time in five minutes. "I'm afraid my friend here is on FDF business with me. I can't reveal his name."

The two men walked back to the vehicle, consulted with each other, and then came back.

"It's all very irregular," the taller man said, "but we can't argue. Anyway, off you go. But watch yourself on these streets." And with that they got into the vehicle and reversed away.

Merral turned to Lloyd. "Forget the walk. I want to go to bed. I've had as much as I can take today."

n the morning, Merral left for Isabella's with Lloyd, whose jacket again bulged oddly. The Danols lived on the other side of town and the easiest route would have been a more or less direct walk through the parks at the foot of the low cliffs that here formed the base of the third circle. Instead Merral chose to take a longer route. This took him round the upper promenade, a roadway that overlooked, and in places, almost overhung, Ynysmere Lake.

As they walked, Merral found himself the focus of attention for many people and spent a lot of time exchanging greetings or acknowledging the waved and shouted good wishes. But behind all the goodwill, Merral felt the same hunger for reassurance he had felt at the airport.

At a craggy point where the promenade turned to the southeast, Merral stopped and looked over the low wall. Below, the steep cliff face fell sharply down to tiered houses, and a hundred meters below, the lake, its waters gleaming pale in the morning light.

To the left, beyond the narrow two-kilometer string of the causeway, the land rose toward the green haze of the Great Northern Forest.

He stared at it moodily. *The word* forest *used to refer to something pleasant and delightful, a place where children played and couples walked. Now it has become something dark and fearsome. Our world has become haunted.*

High above them, the bell on the tower of Congregation Hall tolled nine.

"Well, Sergeant, we must go. Battle looms."

"Battle, sir? I thought you were seeing this Isabella."

"Lloyd, the words *battle* and *Isabella* are, sadly, not mutually exclusive."

❁❁❁❁

Merral's knock at the door of the Danols' house was quickly answered by Isabella. He had the briefest impression of a very smart blue summer dress before she clutched him in a tight hug.

"Oh, Merral!" she said with a little cry of pleasure. But she seemed to stiffen as Lloyd stepped from behind Merral.

"Let me introduce you," Merral said, untangling himself from her grasp. "My aide, Sergeant Lloyd Enomoto. Lloyd, Isabella Danol."

"Pleased to meet you, Lloyd," she said, but her tone hinted otherwise.

"And you, Isabella," came the response.

Isabella stared at the big man and then turned to Merral with a look of inquiry.

"Lloyd goes with me everywhere," Merral explained hastily. "But he'll just take a seat here downstairs."

"I have plenty of work to do," Lloyd added.

"That's fine," Isabella said, her tone rather too crisp. "You can use the general room on the ground floor. My sisters are out with my parents. Merral, let's go upstairs."

As they climbed to the top floor, Isabella turned to Merral and said in a half whisper, "What's *he* for?"

Here we go, the start of the penetrating questions. Remember, whatever she says and however sweetly she says it, don't relax.

"It's quite simple. Vero is—rather unreasonably in my view—still worried about security. He believes there's still a risk and is concerned that I might be the focus of that risk."

"So, is Lloyd a bodyguard?"

He looked at her, noticing that she had take a great deal of care over her dress and appearance. There was not a hair out of place and her clothes had sharp creases in all the right places. "Yes. I'm impressed you know the word. I didn't."

He walked to the window of the upper room, his eyes drawn to the panorama over the lake.

"Then he's hardly needed here," Isabella said, moving quietly beside him. "Sleepy Ynysmant—the town at the end of Worlds' End." Her voice lacked affection and her right hand made a faintly dismissive gesture.

"'Sleepy'? I would have agreed until we met the kids from Hanston Road yesterday."

"Oh, *them*." She gave a condescending smile. "With the face paint? Same gray clothes? I hear the stories. I think it's overrated. High spirits on one side and fear on the other. Since Corradon's speech, people have been very jumpy. . . . Would you like a coffee?"

"No thanks. Too soon after breakfast. . . . But the police took them seriously. What do you think of them?"

"Ah, the police. If I had still been in my old job, I might have been troubled. In my new role—have you heard?—of crisis counselor to Enatus, I find them intriguing, and potentially useful."

"Useful?"

"Why, Merral," she said, with a lift of her fine eyebrows, "you don't think my job is just to tabulate incidents, do you? It is to define policy and, increasingly, to carry out that policy. And Lucian's police provide me—us—with a potentially useful tool."

With a stab of concern, Merral realized that he had completely failed to appreciate Isabella's position and authority. He had been aware that the crisis and her own resolve had elevated her to a position of importance, but he had overlooked how high that position was.

"Lucian?" he said, struck belatedly by the name.

"Dr. Lucian Clemant—the advisor to Representative Corradon. I presume you report to him too?"

"Yes. Of course. Corradon too. Sorry. I just hadn't realized you were on first-name terms."

"Inevitably." She gave Merral a bemused look. "He's the crisis advisor for Farholme, and I, effectively, have the same role for Ynysmant. So, we are talking. Not that frequently so far, but it happens."

The completely unexpected—but perfectly logical—link with Clemant was something Merral found troubling in a way that he couldn't immediately express.

"Anyway," Isabella said, "enough of that. Where shall we sit?"

"Out on the balcony?" he suggested, thinking that it might be safer to be somewhere where people could see them.

"That's not very romantic," she said with a slight smile. "We would be overlooked. Besides, people can hear whatever you say. And you're famous now. Let's stay inside." She gestured to the sofa. "Come and sit next to me."

"Do you mind if I sit opposite?" Merral said, painfully reminded that the mess he now found himself in with Isabella was the result of exactly such a seating arrangement.

"Well, if you must," she replied, with a fleeting look of sour puzzlement.

"A lot has happened," Merral said, sitting down, looking at the abstract paintings on the walls and the neatly laid out pottery items on the shelves.

"Indeed."

"The last time we met, it all went wrong."

"You apologized for it and the apology was accepted. It's past. You were under a lot of stress." Her voice was now very gentle and sweet.

It was when she spoke like this that Merral realized he needed to be especially wary. Yet the fact that he could think such a thing made him feel guilty. "Thank you," he said.

"We need to move on."

"Indeed."

There was silence for a moment.

"You've changed," she said, leaning back in the chair.

She's very pretty. He felt some of his resolve waning.

"And so have you," he replied. As he said it, he knew that the creation of the new, hard-edged Isabella who sat before him was not something he wanted to comment on. It was far safer to talk about himself. "Yes," he said, "a lot has happened to me."

"Tell me all," Isabella said, her voice at its most alluring.

Merral had expected such a question and had already mentally rehearsed a version of the story of the confrontation with the intruders that omitted a number of awkward elements. So maneuvering delicately around such matters as the presence of the envoy and the dreadful, doom-laden message of the steersman, he told her what had happened from the moment he left Isterrane in the *Emilia Kay* to when, injured and half frozen, he was pulled out of Fallambet Lake Five.

"And the next thing I knew," he concluded, "I was a celebrity."

Isabella beamed at him. "I am very proud of you. You're a *hero.*"

"I don't see myself as a hero. Not at all. I could have done better."

"Well, that's what you say. You're very modest." A shadow crossed her face. "But, Merral, I just wish I had known more. I thought you trusted me. After all, lots of people knew. Several hundred people at least, from what I gather. I must admit that when I heard the broadcast, I was torn between awe at what you had done and irritation that I hadn't been told. Of course, everyone assumed that I knew all about what was going on. It was *so* embarrassing. I mean, I had to pretend that I had known."

"Of course. We just couldn't risk it. I'm sorry."

Isabella gently touched her fine black hair as if to check whether it was still neatly in place.

On one level, I still find her attractive; on another, she scares me.

"Anyway, that's past," she said. "But did your parents tell you the news?" Her expression was one of anticipation.

"Yes. It was . . . well . . . most interesting."

"They approved our commitment! Isn't that good news?"

"To be honest, it's taken me a bit by surprise. I wish there had been time to discuss it."

"What's to discuss?" Isabella said, her voice suddenly sharp. "We wanted to be committed. We made our private commitment, and now the door has opened for us to be publicly committed. To be honest, the way my parents feel about you, we could even announce a wedding date."

The word *wedding* injected a new and appalling note of anxiety into Merral's mind. "I gather," he said, after a long moment of silence, "that your parents took the initiative?"

"Oh yes," she said. "They looked at the situation and realized that now you're a commander, everything had changed. It would seem a bit silly to withhold parental approval to someone who was in charge of defending our world. It would have been embarrassing. And there were the positives. In this new job, you will need all the support you could get."

As he recognized the arguments—the same ones his mother had used—Merral's suspicion that Isabella had manipulated her parents into making the decision was confirmed.

"It could be a lonely and dangerous job," he protested. "I nearly didn't come back from the Fallambet."

"I understand that. I hope I would be supportive."

"There's more to it than that," he said, realizing as he spoke how feeble his words sounded.

"Oh, I know. There's a lot still to be sorted out."

"I see." To gain time he asked the question he had already asked his mother. "So who knows about it?"

Isabella thought for a moment. "It's not been formally announced, but a lot of people suspect it's coming. So there'll be a reference to it in Malhan's speech tonight."

"I'm sorry?"

"Warden Enatus! His first name is Malhan."

"Oh yes . . . but the speech?"

"Tonight at the reception, when Malhan gives you a medal—the Ynysmant Heroism Medal. Incidentally, I helped design it. And as he gives the speech, he will say . . . wait." She picked up some sheets of paper from the table. "Yes, here we are. He says, 'I also gather that you are going to be giving us some long-expected news about the status of a relationship between you and a certain young lady.' Then he ends with this: 'Ladies and gentlemen, will you join with me in a round of applause for Merral Stefan D'Avanos, Commander of the Farholme Defense Force, and the first hero of Ynysmant.' All will applaud and you will then respond."

Merral, almost physically stunned by her words, was speechless. As anger battled with confusion in his mind, he briefly—but very seriously—considered walking out of the room, getting the next flier to Isterrane, and never coming back.

"I see," he said eventually in as measured a tone as he could manage. "Uh, how do you know what's in the speech?"

"I wrote it. There are bits earlier about heroism that you'll like. 'Cometh the hour, cometh the man.' 'Never in the field of Assembly history have so many owed' and so on." She smiled with what appeared to be contented satisfaction. "Some great words. I did a lot of work researching them. . . . You look surprised. Malhan is a cute little man. He's just out of his depth on this sort of epic speech. He'd be the first to admit it."

"I see."

"Don't keep repeating yourself. Your father does that."

"Sorry. Look, do you really want to go ahead, Isabella?"

"Yes." Her voice held a rocklike determination. "I think that a commitment—and all it leads to—will be good for us."

Merral took a deep breath. It was time to stop the nonsense. *Remember you are a commander.*

"Isabella, I do not feel this is right." He was pleased that his voice sounded firm.

"Why not?" Her face paled.

"I think we've grown apart."

"We *have* changed, true. But I think it will work out. I am resolved that it will."

"I am far less sure."

Her expression held a flicker of alarm. "Is there anybody else?"

"The issue is simple—I just want to end this!" *Indeed, even if Anya did not exist, I would not want to be married to the person this woman has become.*

"Are you serious?" Isabella exclaimed. The bite in her words made him aware that anger bubbled just below the surface.

"Yes."

"But you can't go back now!" Her voice sounded as taut as a stretched wire. "The town is expecting the announcement. Everyone knows. It's common knowledge. That's why it's in the speech."

Merral hesitated. *Think tactically. Outmaneuver her.* "Look, marriage between us just won't work."

"We will have to *make* it work, won't we?"

Merral took a long deep breath. "Isabella, let me say this. I might wed you in the ceremony, we might share a house and even a bed, but there would be no real love between us. You can't force that. Our marriage would be a cold disaster. Why would you want that?"

"I think . . ." She swallowed. "We could make it work. I know we could."

Why would anyone want a loveless marriage? Wouldn't celibacy be better?

"And if we couldn't?" he asked, sensing that he now had the advantage.

"I would just have to pretend that everything was fine." Isabella hesitated. "I would occupy myself with all that being a commander's wife in Isterrane involved."

A commander's wife in Isterrane? A light broke into Merral's mind. *Of course. I'm no longer a forester in remote Ynysmant. I'm a commander in the capital. Isabella might find the escape from Ynysmant and the position of power an adequate compensation for being in a counterfeit marriage.*

"You hate being here, don't you?" he asked.

She smiled, but the action seemed more like baring her neat white teeth. "This place is slow, dull, and narrow-minded. I could do better. I *will* do better."

"Look, it's over."

She gave him a rueful smile. "It's a bit late now."

"I will tell them there is no commitment."

"Then our world will know that *Commander* Merral D'Avanos doesn't keep his promises." The sarcasm was like a blade.

"You wouldn't do that." But as he said the words, he realized that she would. Ignoring a strong temptation to storm out, Merral waved a finger at the papers on the table. "Can you remove that passage?"

"If I wished to."

"Then *please,* will you remove it?"

"No." In the look she gave him, he saw defiance and control.

Suddenly, a solution came to Merral and it was all he could do to avoid breaking out in a smile. It was a solution that was fitting and satisfying and one that would give her a taste of her own medicine. Isabella had manipulated people to get what she wanted from him. He would turn the tables on her. Nevertheless, it was only fair to warn her.

"Isabella, if you don't remove that phrase about us, I promise you that you'll regret it."

"Is that a threat?" She gave him a cold look.

"Let's call it a statement of cause and effect." He rose. "I'm sorry it's come to this. But let me repeat myself. If Enatus says that tonight, you will regret it."

Isabella stood, her expression a mixture of anger, fear, and puzzlement.

He turned his back on her and walked down the stairs.

"Lloyd," Merral said as he forcefully closed the door of the Danols' house behind him, "are you committed or engaged?"

"No, sir."

"Don't be in a hurry."

"You sound pretty sour, sir. If I may say so."

"Lloyd, I *am* sour. *Very* sour. Let's go back to our house."

7

Upon returning home, Merral retired to his room, saying that he had some work to do. There he sat with Vero's report on guerrilla warfare and tried to focus on what was in it. But he had not been there long when his mother knocked, entered, and closed the door crisply behind her.

"Merral dear," she said in the lowest of voices. "I do hope you had a good meeting with Isabella. I won't ask what happened. That's *private*. But I wanted to say something about our decision. I'm so *sorry* we didn't consult you. I did think about it, but . . . well . . . your father was *desperately* keen." She gave a rueful and disapproving shake of the head. "He really wants to see you settle *down*. He'd like grandchildren nearby. The *girls* are too far away. It's all *very* sad."

As she ran her fingers through her hair, Merral could see a lot more silver there than there had been. "And, of course, I didn't want to *oppose* him. It would be quite wrong to publicly disagree with your spouse. But I'm sorry now, that I *didn't* take a stand. Very sorry."

She made an excuse, then quietly left.

Merral sighed. *Now what?*

Unable to return his mind to the report, he decided to sort out some of the things he wanted to take to Isterrane. He felt certain that he was not going to be back in Ynysmant for some time and there were things that he wanted with him. He picked up the silver egg of his castle tree simulation; he had invested too much time and energy on that to leave it behind. As he packed it into a travel bag, he realized how much he looked forward to spending time inside the simulation of the massive life form that he had created.

"It's a simpler and saner world in there," he said under his breath and was surprised—and a little alarmed—at his words.

As he packed some shirts into his travel case there was a quiet knock on the door. His father entered and closed the door softly behind him.

"Son, I need to say this to you, while she is busy." He gestured down toward the kitchen.

"I'm sorry about Isabella," he said in a voice that was barely more than a whisper. "It was your mother's idea to agree with the Danols. She couldn't bear the idea of being made to look stupid. But please don't blame me. *Please.* It wasn't my idea."

And before Merral could say anything, he had gone.

◯◯◯◯◯

After a lunch in which Merral tried—and largely succeeded—in leading the conversation away from Isabella, he decided to take Lloyd to find Jorgio.

A diary call to Daoud, the old man's brother, revealed that the stable hand was now staying at the Planning Institute. Somewhat puzzled by this change of address, Merral walked with Lloyd over the causeway to the Institute. As they approached, Merral found himself mystified at the way the extensive complex was now crowded with men, animals, and machinery until it came to him that he was seeing the results of the sudden closure of Wilamall's Farm. Resisting the desire to visit his old office—what good would it do?—he made inquiries as to where he might find Jorgio. Eventually, they were directed up a flight of steps to an attic above the stables.

Merral peered through the open doorway. The long room was lined by rafters and beams and lit by shafts of dusty sunlight from four skylights.

Halfway along it, an older man with a twisted body sat on a battered sofa, unpacking crockery from a box.

Merral knocked. "Jorgio, my old friend!" he called out.

Jorgio looked up and rose awkwardly to greet them, bending to avoid a low wooden beam.

"Mr. Merral," Jorgio replied, rubbing his rough hands on his faded green suit and shaking his head. "I might have known as it would be you."

Merral was struck by an odd tone in his voice—a note of regret or even irritation.

"Why, I could almost imagine you weren't happy to see me," Merral answered, aware of the noises and smells of animals drifting through the open door.

"Oh, I'm happy to see *you*," Jorgio said, hugging him. "But there's more to you turning up than just *you*. Mr. Merral, I reckon as you bring more than a guest with you."

"That's a riddle, my old friend. But this is Lloyd Enomoto. My aide."

"An aide?" Jorgio asked, with a sharp glance at Merral as he shook hands with Lloyd. "That's a fancy word for a fighting man. And with something under his jacket."

Merral and Lloyd looked at each other. "I should have warned you, Sergeant, that Jorgio is full of surprises. He will probably tell you your future."

"*His* future?" Jorgio said with a troubled pout. "*Tut*. I reckon as I have enough bother with my own. But, Mr. Lloyd, take your jacket off. You'll be too hot. Come, both of you, and have some tea."

Lloyd hung his jacket on a nail, revealing a bush knife handle protruding from an inside pocket, then helped Merral pull another old sofa closer.

Jorgio's mood and his ambivalent welcome had put Merral somewhat on edge. He looked around the room, noting a pot of red carnations, the half-opened trunk, stacked rolls of carpet, and dust motes drifting through the beams of light.

"So what are you doing here, my old friend?" Merral asked. "I thought you were staying with Daoud."

As Jorgio turned to reply, Merral was suddenly struck anew by the way one amber eye was higher than the other.

"*Tut*. That was temporary that was. A great mercy too. Ynysmant is an odd town now. There were children making fun of me the other day. *That* never happened before."

"I'm appalled," Merral said, but realized that he was not surprised. *It is just another symptom of the spiritual disease that has affected us.*

"Anyway, when they moved all the animals down here last week they realized as they needed someone to look after them. So they found me. And then there was this attic, so I asked for it, and they said why not? So, here I am. It needs work—a bit of paint at least—and I'll need some heating for winter, but I reckon as it could be cozy. And there's a bit of a garden outside I can work on."

"I'm delighted. So you are here to stay?"

A look of profound emotion crossed Jorgio's face as he rubbed a stubbly cheek with a finger. "Tea'll be brewed by now. Let me pour it and you can tell me about the fighting you were in. Then I'll tell you what's happened to me."

So, as they drank tea, Merral recounted the tale of the battle of Fallambet Lake Five for the second time that day. *At least with Jorgio I'm able to be a little more open about what happened.*

As Jorgio listened, he slurped his tea and made low *tut-tut* noises. When

Merral described his encounter with the Krallen pack, the old man looked uneasy and his hands shook so much that tea slopped over the edge of his mug.

"Four legs, hard skin, and teeth, you say?" he interrupted, his eyes seeming to focus a long way away. "So what have we? Something a bit like lions or dogs?"

"A bit. Or big lizards. In a pack. But they were machines. . . . Why do you ask?"

"Never you mind. Not now, at least."

Merral resumed his account. When he had finished, there was a hush.

"Well, thank you," Jorgio said. "Thank you, indeed. I knew as there was a real nastiness on that ship, but I didn't know *what*. And I reckon there was more that went on there than you have said. But there's such a thing as privacy. Anyway the Lord, bless his name, was as gracious as ever."

He gave a rough, enigmatic snort and looked at Merral with his strange eyes. "You do know as this isn't the end of the fighting?"

"Yes. We assume there will soon be other ships. Vero and the others are already making plans for the defense of Farholme. I will be taking charge the day after tomorrow."

Jorgio nodded, sipped his tea noisily, and seemed to stare into a dark corner of the room for some time. Finally, he turned uneasy eyes to Merral. "That's good that is, because trouble is on its way."

"What do you know?"

Jorgio put his mug down slowly. "See, Mr. Merral, I have been dreaming again. Not good dreams, they are."

"What are they about?"

"Not much. Mostly just . . . well . . . shadows. Lots of them. All moving. It's all dark and I just hears footsteps."

"Footsteps? You mean human footsteps?"

"No. Not human." Jorgio screwed his face up. "Too small, too light, too many. I wasn't sure at first, as it was such a quiet sound. But I am now."

"Two legs or four? Or even more?"

Jorgio's face twisted. "Four, I'd say. But there are so many of them. So very many."

"Animals?"

"I don't know. I've worked with animals all my life and I don't reckon these are animals. Like them maybe. . . ."

"You think they might be these Krallen?"

Jorgio nodded stiffly. "I reckon."

"What else?"

"Something big. Something that rattles when it moves. Something that brings night with it."

"Rattles?"

"Like dry sticks." His shoulders shuddered.

Jorgio is afraid, Merral realized with a shock of alarm.

"Where are they from?" Merral asked. "The north?"

Jorgio rubbed his bent nose with a heavy finger. "No. It's like . . . I don't know. . . . It's like someone has opened a door beyond the stars and all these things have come out and are running across the roof of the world." He made a grimace. "Like rats. And then I usually wake up and pray to the Lord of All Power and the noises go away. But then, the next night they come back, only this time, it's a bit noisier . . . as if they've got a bit nearer."

"What makes the sounds?" Merral inquired softly, noticing that Lloyd's blue eyes were wide. "Can you see them?"

"No, it's all dark. But whatever they are there are so many of them that they blot out the stars." Jorgio bared his irregular teeth and made a face. "And they are on their way here." Another shiver passed through the big frame. "I don't mind saying, Mr. Merral—and you, Mr. Lloyd—I'm scared."

"I understand. Any idea when they will get here?"

"Don't know. I really don't. I wish it weren't in my lifetime." He looked at the roof as if trying to see the creatures. "But it will be."

"I see. Weeks? A few months? Longer?"

"Weeks." The word was no more than a rough whisper.

"Has anything else happened?"

"Yes." There was a long pause. "I've been given a choice."

"What sort of a choice?"

"I've had a conversation."

"With who?"

"With the King."

"Ah," Merral said. "Is it private?"

"'Tis and 'tisn't."

Jorgio tilted his big bald head, a gesture that seemed to make it even more distorted. "Two days ago. No, maybe it was three. First night I was here anyway. I was lying in my bed." He waved a large hand toward a bed tucked under the eaves. "And I was just praising the Most High for him giving me this place when I was aware of him being with me.

"'Jorgio Aneld Serter,' he says.

"'Sir,' I answers back.

"'Do you like this place?' he says, and I can see as he is looking around. He was standing there."

Jorgio pointed to the floor in the center of the attic and continued. "'It's *very* nice, Your Majesty,' I says. 'Ideal for me. A bit of room, a patch of garden, the animals. Everything as I want and I'm very grateful, sir.' And then, because I reckon there's no harm in asking, I says, 'I confess, sir, I'm hoping as I can keep it.'

"'Are you?' he says, and he looks at me, and I can feel his eyes searching me through and through. 'Well, I have come to tell you that you will soon face a choice. The great battle is beginning. I would like you to fight for me elsewhere.'

"'Elsewhere?' I says, not liking the sound of that one bit." He fell silent for a moment as if pondering something. "And then what he says is this: 'Jorgio, there is a task I have in mind for you. If I asked you to leave Ynysmant, to travel and fight at the heart of the battle, what would you say?'

"'I would say . . . ,' I says and then I stops. 'I would say, sir, if I may, that I am no soldier. I'm an old man with a little strength, but no speed or skill.'

"'Jorgio, I know my servants. I never ask them to do what they cannot. I do, however, often ask them to do what they do not want to do.'"

There was another pause and Merral sensed the old man grappling with what he had experienced.

"And then I says—I hope you two don't think badly of me for saying it as I don't have a lot of courage, least of all against the sort of thing as the enemy is. I says, 'Indeed, to be honest, sir, I'm frightened by them.'

"He looks at me and he says, 'Remember, Jorgio, there is only the thinnest line between fear and lack of faith.'"

Jorgio picked up his mug of tea again and sipped it, looking thoughtfully at the ceiling. "So I says, 'Sir, would I get to come back here?' But all he says is this: 'I make no such promise. In fact, all I can promise you is—'" He broke off, his eyes seeming far away, his broad brow rippled into a frown. He shook his head. "No, that's private that is—what I saw. And it was what I glimpsed, not what he said.

"'The request will come in a few days,' he says. 'You will know it when it comes.' And then he was gone."

There was a long silence in which Merral could hear the sound of flies buzzing in the warm still air and noise of the animals outside.

"My old friend," Merral said slowly. "You may as well know . . . I came here to ask you to come to Isterrane with us."

A succession of intense emotions showed on the jowled face. "When?"

"The four o'clock flight tomorrow."

"Isterrane? I've never been there."

"Sentinel Vero has a house—Brenito's old house—that needs some gardening. It's by the sea. You'd be out in the country. We need you nearby. Your visions confirm that."

"Are there any horses?"

"That," said Merral, with a smile, "can be arranged."

Jorgio rose awkwardly to his feet and walked to the nearest skylight, his lurching gait seemingly more evident than ever. There, his head just peering over the frame, he stared out over the Institute grounds. Finally, he turned round and a single, heavy tear dribbled down a cheek.

"I'll come with you," he said, his words drawn out with reluctance. "I had to choose. And I've made my choice. I don't come happily. The King has offered me a long dark road. But I'll start on it at least."

◌◌◌◌◌

That evening Merral went with his family and Lloyd to the reception that Warden Enatus had arranged at Wyrent Park, a broad area of spreading trees, grass, and fountains near the civic offices high on Ynysmant.

It was a typical warm summer's evening. The gritty feel to the air was only slightly allayed by the humidity that rose from the lake. All around the crowds mingled under the trees, ate the food, or just listened to the music.

Enatus had invited everyone who was a relative or friend of Merral, a condition that a surprisingly large number of people seem to feel they fulfilled. Merral didn't mind the numbers; after all, being among several hundred people meant that no one expected him to be with Isabella all the time. In fact, they said very little to each other—mainly forced pleasantries spoken with fixed smiles.

We are both acting a part. That unhappy thought merely strengthened his resolve to make sure the matter between them ended.

Lloyd, still wearing his jacket and sweating slightly, took up a position under a clump of chestnut trees a few meters away from where Merral stood and tried to look relaxed.

Merral talked with a seemingly endless stream of people before his uncle Barrand came over and embraced him heartily. Feeling encouraged by his uncle's apparent high spirits, Merral expressed his sympathy about the closure of Herrandown.

Barrand shrugged. "Oh, 'the Lord gives and the Lord takes away; blessed be his name.' No, Nephew, it was a decision that had to be made. But it was made swiftly and done well. So, here we all are. We have a house, praise be. They have even found room nearby for my parents."

"What are you going to be doing?"

"Me? For the next week or so, putting all the equipment from Herrandown in storage. And then?" A smile crossed his ruddy face. "Ho! We will see what the Lord sends us."

"I have to say, Uncle, I'm delighted to see you in good heart. The last few times I vis—"

"Ah yes, *that*." Barrand frowned and moved closer as if to ensure that no one overheard his words. "An odd business that. *Most* odd. And I need to apologize to you. I really do. I have now come to realize that something evil came upon us." He ran his fingers through the curls of his black beard. "Ho! It took me a long time to realize what was happening. Then I saw that I—*we*—had given in to evil and listened to the lies of the enemy of our souls. So, I fasted and prayed." He breathed out heavily. "*Ha*. What a battle. But in the end, the mist lifted. And I saw we had been tricked. So I decided to fight against it." He shook his head. "I wish I had known that evening when the meteor fell . . . the meteor that was really the intruders' ship. Instead, I lied to you."

"So I gathered. And the rest of the family?"

Barrand stroked his beard. "Ah, well, Elana understands what has happened. The others . . ." His face clouded. "Not so far. But we pray on. Ah, here is Elana now. I know *she* wants to talk to you. But before she does, let me say something." He edged closer to Merral. "This 'commander' business you are about now. With a 'Defense Force,' whatever that looks like. Count me in, if you need people. I may not be the most agile man around, and I doubt I'll ever fit into any spacesuit if you want to attack them up there, but I do have a respectable experience with explosives and cutters. Most respectable." He gave a hard smile that displayed teeth. "And oh, I have some scores to settle."

Merral clasped his arm. "Uncle, this is one of the best pieces of news I have heard for days. Fight on. And if we can use you, be assured, we will."

Barrand gave him a broad wink and slapped him heartily on the back before walking away.

As he saw Elana coming over, her curly blonde hair bobbing as she moved, Merral nervously drew in his breath and felt his hands clench as he remembered their troubling encounter at Herrandown.

As Lloyd suddenly stiffened in response, Merral gestured him to relax.

Elana looked up at Merral with a strained face, and then quickly stared at her feet, her cheeks flushed. "Merral," she said in a barely audible voice, "can I apologize?"

"Apologies are due on both sides," he said slowly. He knew that he blushed as well.

She shook her head. "You did nothing wrong. I just want to say how sorry I am. I don't know what came over me. I was desperate. It was wrong. And that's what I wanted to say."

She lifted her head and Merral saw a look of release in her blue eyes.

"Thanks," said Merral, "I admire your courage. It was . . . well . . . awkward. . . . Oh, I don't have the words for it."

Elana colored again, swept a strand of blonde hair from her forehead in embarrassment, and nodded slightly.

"Anyway," Merral said, "apology accepted. The matter is forgotten."

"There's something *wrong* in our world, isn't there?"

He nodded.

"More than the Gate going and the intruders coming?"

"Yes, more than that."

"I think . . . I think it's like an invisible fungus—an evil, slimy fungus that sneaks into your life."

"That's a fair way of putting it."

"And it has spores—we did spores in school last month—and they spread and hatch. And it makes you stop praying, takes your eyes off Jesus and makes you want to do what's wrong." She stopped and seemed to consider something before looking at him with widened pale blue eyes. "Actually that's not right. It doesn't *make* you. *You* do the wrong things. It's a thing that just encourages you to do wrong. It whispers in your ear and you listen."

"Ah, that is an excellent statement of the way things are."

"And we have to fight it." As she said the words, she seemed to bounce on her feet almost as if she wanted to stamp on this invisible fungus. "And, Merral, that's what I shall try and do. My father has realized it too."

"I know. Fight on, Elana."

"I will. Thanks." She smiled and Merral felt that the young girl was back. Then she glanced around, leaned forward on tiptoe, and whispered in his ear. "You aren't going to marry Isabella, are you?"

"Would I tell *you*?"

"No," she admitted with a smile. "But don't. She's got the fungus. Real bad."

Then, with all the agility and awkwardness of her age, she slipped away.

◌◌◌◌◌

After an hour—and what seemed like a hundred conversations—Merral saw Enatus making his way through the crowds toward him.

"Merral," the little man said, wiping his shiny red forehead and looking at his watch. "Time for our little presentation. It's being imaged so that the whole town will see it. I hope you like the speech. Isabella played a big part in its writing. I was so grateful."

In the gloom, Merral noticed the sheaf of papers sticking out of the warden's pocket and was suddenly and powerfully struck with a thought. *I could simply ask if the troubling passage is still there and have Enatus delete it.* He considered the idea for a moment before rejecting it. *What I intend will be much more effective and it will teach Isabella a badly needed lesson.*

Enatus led him onto a small platform in a corner of the grounds. Merral glanced around, seeing the crowds gathering and Lloyd standing at the extreme left-hand side of the platform where he could watch the crowd.

Suddenly he glimpsed Isabella, her face pale and taut under the lights. *She's close to the steps so she can come up on the platform if invited.*

Enatus tilted his head toward Merral. "To tell you the whole truth, I'm a bit nervous," he said, in a confiding aside. "I've never done one of these before. We worked hours on the speech. It's hard—very hard—to get the tone just right." He adjusted his suit, stroked his mustache, mopped his forehead, and stepped into the circle of light and began speaking.

Merral, who had always rather liked Enatus, soon found the speech eroded his goodwill. It was too long, overwritten, and there was far too much in it of one man's "heroism" and too little of the courage and sacrifice of others. Merral felt sure that even if the speech had been in praise of someone else, he would still have loathed it. Nevertheless, as Enatus turned over what seemed to be an interminable succession of pages, he tried to maintain a look of polite if gently embarrassed interest.

Finally, the warden reached the last page and then paused.

Merral held his breath. *Is the passage in?*

Beaming, Enatus turned to face him. "We also gather that you are going to be giving us some long-expected and welcome news about the relationship between you and a certain young lady."

Merral struggled to contain his anger, as amid applause and whistles, Enatus beckoned him forward.

"Ladies and gentlemen, citizens of our noble town, will you join with me in a round of applause for Merral Stefan D'Avanos, Commander of the Farholme Defense Force and the first hero of Ynysmant."

The band gave a drumroll. There were wild cheers and waves of clapping. Merral counted to ten, then walked over and embraced Enatus as if they were the oldest and best of friends, before stepping in his turn into the circle of light.

Enatus took the medal, a heavy bronze disk with blue and yellow stripes on the ribbon, and pinned it to his chest. "Hope you like it," he whispered with his usual confiding geniality. "We got it off a history file. From the Zulu Wars—whatever they were."

Merral shook hands and stepped forward, raising a hand to still the crowd. He had memorized his words and felt strangely calm. "Friends, relatives, citizens of my hometown, I have little to say tonight. Although I thank Warden Enatus for his fine words, he was overgenerous. As I heard his description of me, I did wonder who he was referring to." There was easy laughter. "But seriously, all who were at Fallambet Lake Five that day deserve medals and some—sadly—are not alive to receive them."

Merral paused, letting his words sink in. "In view of what was said about me, I would like to quote the words of the writer of a psalm. In an age when war was usual, rather than unprecedented, he wrote, 'Do not put your trust in princes, in mortal men, who cannot save. . . . Blessed is he whose help is the God of Jacob, whose hope is in the Lord, his God.'" He took a breath. "Were he here today, the psalm writer would, no doubt, have added 'Don't put your trust in commanders either.' To think too much of people like myself is to slip into idolatry. Our great—and *only*—defense is the Lord of the Assembly."

There was a quiet mutter of agreement as Merral continued. "Remember, too, that the war may not be over. We need to raise an army and we may yet have to fight wars. Further sacrifices may still be needed. Evil is still present and we need vigilance and discipline."

A deathly silence fell. They hadn't wanted to be reminded of this, Merral discerned. Some glanced uneasily northward.

"Finally," he said, relishing every word he was about to say, "let me end with a personal comment. I was intrigued by our good warden's comments about a personal relationship. Here I need to say something. I have been asked by the representatives to build up and command the defense force that will seek to protect our world. This is a task of such magnitude that, regardless of my own feelings and desires, I have resolved to put aside *all* such relationships until such a time as we can be assured of peace and stability. So can I end all such rumors? As the Word says, 'There is a time for everything, and a season for every activity under heaven . . . a time to love, and a time to hate; a time for war, and a time for peace.' We have unfinished business to complete. In view of that, I hope you will understand that everything else must wait."

Merral took a breath, hearing murmurings of approval in the crowd. "Ladies and gentlemen, I commend you to the grace of our Lord. Thank you and good night."

Amid cheers, he stepped out of the light. "Game over, Isabella," he whispered to himself.

◁○◁○◁

That night, something woke Merral. He lay in bed, staring upward in the darkness of his room, realizing that he was unsure whether that *something* was a sound, a vibration, or even a change in temperature. But he knew that something in his room had changed.

Perturbed, Merral peered around, noting from the pale digits of the wall clock that it was not yet midnight.

His muscles suddenly stiffened.

In the deep blackness of the far corner sat a figure. The form was that of a large man. For a brief moment, Merral tried to tell himself that it was Lloyd. But that idea died as fast as it formed. The shape was all wrong. This man was thinner and Merral heard no sound of breathing.

Merral shivered and swallowed, now able to make out that the figure was draped in a long dark coat and wore some sort of dark hat. And, most unnervingly, whoever it was seemed to stare at him.

In an instant, Merral knew who was in the room and in another instant, he knew what the topic of conversation was going to be.

"Man, time passes. The darkness has fallen and the war spreads."

At the sound of that voice—neither human nor mechanical—the last lingering doubts about the figure's identity fled. Aware of the envoy's scrutiny, Merral sat upright, drawing the sheet around him.

"You!" There was fear in his voice.

"Indeed." There was an intense pause. "So, you are no longer a captain but a *commander* now? You humans love your titles." The tone was sad rather than scornful.

"Envoy, those titles were given me. I did not seek them."

"Good. Remember, the King considers them as nothing and beware that you do not count them as something."

"I know that. I was only saying tonight tha—"

"Fool!" The word stung like a slap in the face. "The King knows what you said. That is why I have been sent. You abused the position you were called to. You spoke noble words about serving the King simply to try to settle matters with Isabella. What a monstrous act! Were the King not merciful, you would have been destined to be a brief moment's play for a Krallen."

Merral felt his throat constrict. With trembling fingers, he gripped the sheet tight. "I was simply reacting, in the best way I could, to what Isabella had done."

"*Retaliating* would be a more honest word. Is that the way of grace? And to hide such a deed under a veneer of goodness and sacrifice? To wrap it in the words of Scripture to give it weight?"

Merral stared at the envoy. Here, as on the terrible intruder ship, it was difficult to focus on the figure, almost as if his visitor were an optical illusion. Yet to think of an "illusion" was a thoroughly misleading idea. There was an awesome solidity to the envoy, almost as if he was the reality and Merral and his world were illusionary. This being, he realized with an awe that bordered on terror, was there before the cosmos was created. He watched the stars being made.

Yet as he tried to focus on the fearsome darkness-made-solid that confronted him, Merral sensed that it was not just the impression of vast power, age, and privilege that overwhelmed him. It was something else, something that in his fear he struggled to define, until the word *holiness* came to his mind. That was it, he realized, and in that moment, he understood all the passages in the Word that talked about people falling down in awe and terror before that which was holy.

"I'm sorry," whispered Merral, a hairbreadth from utter terror, as the wrongness of all he had done was suddenly visible to him. Yet even here, he felt an irresistible urge to say something in his defense. "But what else could I do? She manipulated everything."

The dark figure leaned toward him. "What Isabella did is a matter between her and the King. *You* were not asked to be her judge. And there was a way out given you. Had you spoken to the warden, he would have removed the words."

"I'm sorry," Merral said, this time meaning it.

A strange silence seemed to fill the room, a brooding quiet only broken when the envoy spoke again. "I am to tell you that the Most High accepts your repentance and you are spared the judgment, but not the consequences. Your action was not just wrong, it was also unwise. You have made yourself an enemy and you will pay a price for today's words."

Merral was silent for a moment before curiosity got the better of him. "How?" he asked.

"I have not been told. You have repented for what has happened, but you will also come to regret it bitterly. And let this be a lesson to you. You have been given a demanding task. You must walk the narrowest of paths. You must be brave but not reckless, resolute but not cruel. Above all, you must lead with confidence yet also follow the King with obedience. You must be shepherd and sheep; leader and servant."

"Envoy, can no one else do this? I can't do it."

"You have been chosen. And those the Most High calls, he equips. Remember, to abandon your task is to fail."

Merral wiped sweat off his brow. "I will not abandon it. I will do my best."

"Good. Now pay attention. The victory at the lake has gained you a brief reprieve. Although evil is still working through your world, it can be resisted by those who choose to fight it. You have met such already. But the time of peace is short. The enemy approaches with powerful forces. Now rise and see what I have been told to show you."

With a strange reluctance, Merral left his bed and stood in the middle of the room. The envoy rose from his chair and stood by him. Merral flinched at his presence, painfully aware of an awesome gulf between the envoy and himself—a great gap that made him think of how dirty he felt. And yet the envoy was only a servant of the great Three-in-One. But the thought only increased his unease.

The envoy moved his hand in a deliberate gesture. In an instant, the far wall of the room where Merral's wardrobe stood noiselessly faded away and was replaced by a night sky.

Merral gasped and looked down. While his bare feet remained on the carpet, just a step in front of him was a patch of bare, sharp-edged rock lit only by starlight. Beyond that the ground fell away sharply to a great and gloomy plain whose features were hidden in the darkness.

I am on top of a cliff somewhere. Merral looked around, trying to recognize where he was. A cluster of lights to his left caught his eye: a village, perhaps a small town, only a few kilometers away.

"Watch!"

High above, a point of brightness flared into a cone of oily, yellow light, the haze around it smearing the stars. The light grew and above it Merral could make out the dark mass of a ship sliding across the constellations. As he heard the deep rumble of the engine, he trembled with foreboding. The ship descended, the lurid brilliance of its exhaust highlighting the roughness of the landscape. With a final bubbling of radiance, the vessel landed on a rise of ground to his right. For a moment, darkness returned, only to be broken again within seconds as a vertical slit of white light grew at the base of the ship.

Out of the slit something emerged, something that poured on the ground like liquid. Merral held his breath. Unable to interpret what he was seeing, he watched as the fluid, glinting oddly in the gloom, began to move down the hill with an ominous increase of speed. The lobe of fluid moved toward him and as it did, he heard the sound of its motion: a weird, insistent, rapid drumming.

"What is this?" he asked in a scared whisper, but there was no answer. As he was about to repeat his question, the lobe crested a rise, and in a moment of stark terror, he realized that what he saw was not a liquid. It was an army of regimented creatures speeding across the ground in perfect synchronization.

"Krallen!"

"Indeed," said the envoy in his unearthly voice.

There must be thousands of them! Merral watched them flow with an unstoppable energy around and over the landscape. As they came nearer, the drumming resolved itself into the sound of thousands of feet pounding the ground. Now Merral saw things flying above them: dark whip-tailed creatures that moved with an extraordinary rippling motion of sail-like wings—the same as the appalling winged creature he had faced—and slain—in the intruder ship. His stomach writhed.

Below the scarp upon which he stood, the Krallen raced faster than a man could run, the starlight gleaming on their backs. Standing close by, Merral could hear the eerie whistling and hooting tones they made. The sounds chilled his blood. Where were they going with this relentless purpose? Yet no sooner had he raised the question than he knew the terrible answer.

They were heading toward a settlement.

In less than a minute, they reached the outer buildings. Merral watched horror-struck as the vast army broke upon the homes like a great tidal wave. Far away, Merral could hear high screams of terror, which rose and then were abruptly stilled. One by one, the lights of the settlement died until all was darkness.

Sickened, Merral watched the Krallen forces with their escort of dragon creatures regroup and then move under the faint starlight. And as he gazed at them, he saw another cone of light and then another appear in the heavens.

"God have mercy," he said softly, realizing that he was shaking.

The scene faded and he was suddenly back in his room. He sat on the bed, wiped sweaty hands on his night-suit, and stared at the envoy.

"That . . . ," he said, waving a hand at his wardrobe, "that hasn't happened, has it?"

"No. Not yet."

"Thank God. Is that what *will* happen?"

"I do not know whether that will occur here. But such things—and worse—have happened on the worlds beyond the Assembly."

"So it may not happen?"

"Only the Most High knows the future. It is for the best. If you knew that it would happen, you might despair; and if you knew it would not, you might relax. Instead, be warned and prepare."

Suddenly, Merral's fear and shock turned to anger. He wanted to protest against the fact that he had been singled out to be responsible for defending his world against such forces. But he fought with the resentment, realizing it could do no good. And anyway, he reminded himself, anger had already betrayed him once that day.

"Thank you for letting me see the vision." Merral paused, his mind made up. "I will do all I can to defend my world." He was surprised at the resolve in his voice. "I shall make it my business to ensure that no settlement falls without a fight."

"Well said. May your deeds match your words." The envoy shifted his long coat in a way that seemed a prelude to his leaving.

"But," Merral began, his head now filled with urgent questions, "how can we resist enemies who can destroy cities so effortlessly?"

The envoy turned his head to stare at him. "At such a time, you will find a way of defense offered to you. But be warned. It will be a costly way, one that only the very bravest will take." He lifted his head as if hearing a far-off summons. "I must go. But I have some advice for you. First, you do well to take Jorgio to Isterrane. Guard him well: his time is coming. Second, let me repeat what you have already sensed: this world, and the Assembly, are being tested. That testing comes both from beyond your world and also from within it. You will find that much you have taken for granted will fail you. In particular, do not presume upon the unity that has long governed the worlds of the Lord's Assembly. Thus far, those in your world have worked together; they may not do so for much longer. Be careful who you trust."

The envoy leaned forward as if gazing into Merral's soul. "Above all, watch yourself."

He shook his head as his form slowly dissolved, his darkness passing into the less solid darkness of the room.

"Wait! How much time do we have?"

"Very little," came the answer, the words already fading away. "Before summer ends in Ynysmant, war will come to Farholme."

8

"Three months." Vero nudged the accelerator lever a fraction. "We have only three months before we are at war. That's my reading of what the envoy said."

Merral glanced over his shoulder to reassure himself that the two-seater Lloyd drove still followed them. Vero had met them at the airport and after dropping Jorgio off at Brenito's old home, they now headed back into the main part of Isterrane.

The sun set behind torn clouds, tinting everything orange.

"I agree, but I wish he'd been more explicit," Merral replied. "We always consider summer at an end when the schools restart. Say twelve weeks away. By any standards we don't have much time."

"Very little. And the envoy just vanished?"

"Not a trace. No one else in the house heard anything."

"Hmm."

"In hindsight there's a lot I wish I'd asked him. But I was stunned—no, *appalled*—by the vision he showed me. Anyway, what I saw and heard confirmed your decision about the irregular forces. You have my full support."

"Good. But the time scale is now desperately short. I had hoped for at least a year."

"Can the work on the defenses be speeded up?"

Vero frowned. "We'll do what we can. But your account of what the envoy said has a detail that alarms me. 'Be careful who you trust.' I don't like that at all."

"Me neither. How do we guard against that?"

"A good question. We can start by being careful of what we say and who we say it to. We must always ask now, 'Do they need to know this?'"

"But, Vero, every principle of the Assembly centers on openness."

"Ah." The word was drawn out. "But that was the past."

There was another long and absorbed silence. A glance out of the window showed the Gardens of Querantal. Merral breathed in to catch the famous scent of the orange blossoms. The fragrance reminded him painfully of the innocent and tranquil world he had once known that now seemed to be lost forever.

"Incidentally, my friend," Vero commented, "the presentation of that medal to you was seen everywhere."

"You're joking! That was a local affair."

"Perhaps, but you are a global personality now. Everyone saw it. There is an extraordinary interest in you. Your final comments have been much praised."

"Oh, dear. I'm afraid I said too much. They were a mistake. I was rebuked."

Vero stared at him, his eyes gleaming faintly. "Ah. I felt there was more to the envoy's appearing than you said. And how did Isabella take it?"

"Very badly. We were at a meeting this morning. Every time our eyes met I saw she was glaring at me."

"'Looking daggers' I believe they once called it."

"A phrase I now understand. Anyway, I have written her an apology, but I fear the damage is done."

"Ah." Vero gave a sigh of unhappy resignation.

"Yes. Lloyd did a good job of protecting me from others. I should have warned him that I needed protecting from myself."

ＯＣＯＣＯ

Not long after, they entered what Merral considered the educational area of Isterrane. Vero pulled off onto a gravel driveway and stopped the vehicle before a single-floor structure tucked between two taller administrative buildings.

Lloyd pulled alongside and together they walked to the door.

"This," Vero said, as he tucked his dark glasses in his shirt pocket, "is where you're going to be living. Narreza Tower is too public." There was a pause, and Merral wondered if it was too close to Anya.

"This is the Kolbjorn Suite—an apartment unit for visiting off-world scholars." After finding a key Vero opened the door. "Sorry about the lock. Security is now important."

As they walked in, Merral glanced around. The suite was a large, four-bedroom apartment recently refurbished. There was a smell of new paint.

Vero pointed to a front room. "I suggest that Lloyd take this room by the door and you take an inner bedroom. It's more secure."

Lloyd nodded.

Again we use the words secure *and* security. *Am I irritated or alarmed?*

He trailed behind as Vero strode through the apartment and threw open the rear door. Lights came on to reveal a small, enclosed courtyard with a single palm tree, a few seats, and a small ornamental pond stocked with goldfish.

Vero stood beside Merral. "One of the big attractions is that it's not over-looked. You can sit here and no one will know whether you're here or not."

"Does that matter?"

Vero's smile seemed pained. "My friend, the days when you could sit on an open balcony in full view of everybody are gone. At best, you are going to have a lot of unwelcome attention and at worst . . ." Vero shrugged and motioned Merral back inside. "You can look around here later. It's late, and I'm afraid I have a lot to do. Your encounter with the envoy only adds more urgency to my tasks. But I have one more thing to show you."

Vero led them down a side corridor, stopping in front of a full-length mirror.

"Watch," he said, pressing two tiny silver buttons at the side of the frame.

The mirror swung noiselessly and smoothly outward to reveal a narrow, poorly illuminated vertical shaft with a metal ladder at the rear.

"What is this?" Merral asked, suddenly aware of the smell of fresh dust and powdered stone.

"The Kolbjorn Suite is close to the center of the city and lies above one of the main utility passageways. I had a link put in last week."

"Fascinating," Merral said, beginning to uneasily formulate a guess at why the link had been made.

Vero pointed down. "It seemed too good an opportunity to miss. This is a way of entering and leaving the building without being seen. Twenty meters down is a passageway that leads to the Planetary Administration building. That's about a ten-minute walk away. I'll teach Lloyd the route soon. It may be useful as an emergency escape. And it allows me to visit you."

"Aha," said Lloyd, with a knowing glance at Merral. "Nice one, Mr. V."

"I'm glad someone appreciates its value," Vero said with a hint of frustration. He raised a finger in caution. "And don't reveal the existence of the route to anyone."

"Why not? What else is down there?"

Vero's smile was pinched. "Oh, just the foundations. That's all." He looked at his watch. "Now, I'm afraid I have work to do." He raised his hand in a half-jesting salute. "Welcome back, Commander. Remember, you're down to see Corradon tomorrow at eight, and I expect you'll see Clemant afterward. So, when you are free, I will take you to your office."

With a surprisingly nimble motion Vero grasped the ladder and lowered himself into the gloomy depths.

"Where are you off to?"

"Ah, it's a secret. We now live in a world of secrets. Good night to you both."

And with that Vero disappeared from sight.

ᢙᢙᢙᢙᢙ

The next morning, Lloyd and Merral drove to the Planetary Administration building. As he entered, Merral was again made painfully conscious of curious faces turning toward him. *Can I ever be anonymous again?*

After sending Lloyd to look for the new FDF offices, Merral made his way to Corradon's office and was shown in immediately.

He found the representative jacketless and with an open-necked shirt, stooping over a pot of yellow anemones on a corner table. As Corradon looked up and smiled, Merral wondered whether the smile revealed welcome or relief.

"Ah, Merral," he said, walking over to shake hands. "Good to see you. You are recovered?"

"Largely, sir." Merral couldn't bring himself to call the representative by his first name. "I should have the chest cast off this week. Then I can start gentle exercise. But I'm to avoid too much stressful physical activity for a bit."

As Corradon slowly nodded, Merral looked at the representative carefully, trying to read his mood. *He seems dignified and unruffled, but I must remember that with this man, surface appearances cannot be relied on. Here, in this public office, he wears his public face.*

"First time you've been here?" Corradon asked, waving a big hand around.

Merral nodded, looking about. The room was fuller and much less formal than he had imagined it would be. There were numerous books, statuettes, and plants on the shelves and the walls bore a series of maps, paintings, and family images. On the desk was an untidy pile of paper and datapaks and a small painting of a woman whom Merral recognized as Corradon's wife, Victoria. The single large window looked south to the sunlit sea, and on the floor were a number of large potted plants.

"I like the plants," the representative observed in a melancholy voice, evidently catching Merral's gaze. "Increasingly, in fact. They are much less trouble to manage than people." He gestured for Merral to sit on one of the two easy chairs in front of the desk.

"I saw your speech," Corradon said, sitting heavily in the other chair. "Well done. Fine words."

Merral considered confessing that it had been a bad mistake, but refrained. *I like Corradon, but I feel reluctant to trust a man who seems to be two separate people.* "Sir," he said, "if I'd known it was to go out globally, I would have thought more about what I said. But I gather you have been giving a lot of speeches too."

In an instant Corradon's look of dignified control dissolved into one of sad weariness. "Ah. Too many. A dozen speeches in five days. I have traveled a long way." Corradon stared stiffly out of the window, then turned with a forlorn look on his face. His large frame seemed to sag. "And, of course, I had to see the bereaved. Widows, orphans, mothers, fathers. That's my job too."

"How was that?"

"It was . . ." For a moment, Corradon seemed unable to speak, seemingly wrestling with his emotions. "Somber? Moving? Inspiring? All of these; there was courage also." The words rang with affirmation, but the tired blue eyes told another story.

"I ought to meet them."

"They will be here for the memorial service in ten days' time." Corradon shook his head gloomily. "But there were too many, Merral. Too many."

"I'm sorry."

"No, you misunderstand me." He leaned forward and brushed the leaf of an aspidistra by his feet. "I wasn't blaming you. I just found the losses . . . well, let's say I *felt* them—every single one of them." He shook himself as if trying to free himself from something, and then turned to Merral. "Now, I suppose we'd better turn to business. You are happy with Sentinel Enand's irregulars?"

"Yes. I had more or less made up my mind on that when I had an unexpected visitor in Ynysmant who confirmed my decision."

"Who?"

"The envoy."

"Ah." Corradon closed his eyes for a moment as if in pain. "Our angelic visitant. Who said . . . ?"

In as few words as possible, Merral told Corradon those things the envoy had said that he considered relevant. He omitted the specific warnings, considering them of relevance only to himself. As he spoke, he noticed how the representative's face lost its color.

When Merral finished, Corradon rubbed his face wearily and frowned. "You are making a habit of this. Just when I begin to hope, you present me with new bad news. 'War will come to Farholme.'" He sighed heavily. "War. Casualties. More bereavements."

He paused as if considering the matter and then shook his head. "Yet perhaps, just perhaps, it may not be so. Perhaps the danger may pass." He paused again and his next words were little more than a whispered prayer. "Please, God, may it be so."

"Amen."

Tapping a finger nervously on his knee, Corradon stared at Merral. "So, given that we have so little time, you think Sentinel Enand's approach is wise?"

"Yes."

"Good. I was uneasy about it, but I felt there was no option."

"What did Dr. Clemant say?"

"Lucian approved. Although I prefer not to go against his advice, I would have done on this." Corradon stared out of the window. "It is strange, Merral, how this crisis has affected us differently. I always used to find him easy to work with. . . ." His voice was distant and distracted. Then, as if awakening from a daydream, he turned to Merral. "Yes, he approved. But you'd better go and see him."

He rose stiffly from his chair.

"One other thing," Corradon added, his face suggesting a vague unease. "Prebendant Balthazar Delastro. Dr. Clemant wants to him to be chaplain-in-chief of the Farholme Defense Force. On consideration, I approve. But it's your decision."

"But I don't know him," Merral answered. "And it was a post that I had assumed Luke Tenerelt would fill."

"No. Luke is too young. Delastro is a senior figure and Lucian makes the valid point that to have Delastro on board might help us get support from the local congregations. Frankly, I am reluctant to cross Lucian on this. I think you'd better meet with the prebendant."

"Very well."

"I think that's all for the moment. You will just be downstairs. So, if you need anything . . ." Corradon's voice trailed off as he bent over a dwarf orange bush.

Merral realized the meeting was over. As he left the office, he glanced back to catch a glimpse of Corradon peering at the leaves and shaking his head sadly.

◌Ο◌Ο◌

"Commander," Clemant said, rising stiffly from behind his large, bare desk as Merral was shown in. "Thank you for coming. It is splendid to see you up and about."

They shook hands.

"Please, take a seat," Clemant said with a gentle formality as he lowered himself back onto his high-backed chair.

The advisor looked tired, Merral decided. There were bags under his eyes and he seemed to have put on weight.

Merral sat down and looked around, realizing that he could have predicted that Clemant's office would look like this. The room was no bigger than Corradon's, but the far fewer furnishings made it seem larger. There was a polished black desk, some cabinets and shelves, and the only painting in the room was a large abstract made up of neat geometrical slivers of grays and whites.

The main feature of the room was a large floor-to-ceiling wallscreen, subdivided into a dozen smaller panels, each of which displayed some sort of map, chart, or image, on a sidewall. Merral glanced at it, feeling almost overwhelmed by the quantity of information it revealed. *Clemant must feel that he can monitor all Farholme with this.*

The view out of the window provided some compensation. It consisted of a mosaic of houses, fields, and orchards to the north.

"So," Clemant asked, as Merral turned to face him, "how was Ynysmant?"

Merral sensed Clemant's dark gray eyes scrutinizing him. "Interesting," he answered, feeling oddly wary. "There are changes taking place."

"I know. I gather you and Sergeant Enomoto made contact with some unruly elements?"

"Your information is accurate, Dr. Clemant," Merral said, noting without surprise that his aide's name had been discovered and forwarded. "Your police presumably told you."

"Hardly *my* police, Commander." Clemant's lips moved in a feeble attempt at a smile. "Although they do report to me. Oh, and I saw the broadcast of the medal ceremony by the way. You made a good speech, but—if I may make a suggestion—you could have been longer." There was an expressive pause. "Anwar—" he gestured with his head toward the representative's office—"has done a good job on his tour, but people want to hear you. You reassure them."

"I don't like this public role."

"I understand; you are a reluctant leader. It is commendable. But your reluctance is a luxury. Incidentally, I haven't commended you for the battle at the lake. Well done."

"We failed to take the ship and we lost a lot of men."

Clemant's round face showed a renewed attempt at a smile. "Oh, come, Commander. You destroyed the ship and the casualty figures—while unfortunate—were, by historical standards, not excessive. You lost barely 20 percent of your total attack force. Against overwhelming odds, that is a creditable performance."

Merral shrugged. "Forgive me if I just don't see it in those terms."

"I understand, but in what lies ahead, we will need strong leadership." Merral heard an odd but significant stress in the words. For a fraction of a second, Clemant's eyes slid in the direction of Corradon's office.

"I hardly see that as my task. I'm a man who has been entrusted with being in charge of a military force. I'm not a civil administrator."

Clemant's gaze seemed faintly appraising. "Ah, Commander, we're entering uncharted waters. Who knows what any of us will be called on to do?"

"Indeed."

The advisor steepled his hands and perched his chin on them. "So, you support Sentinel Enand's most interesting proposal?"

"Yes."

"Indeed?" Clemant's tone and expression were scrupulously neutral.

"Yes, my decision was already made when we had a new piece of data."

"Namely?"

Merral paused, suddenly remembering the skepticism that Clemant had shown when Perena reported the first appearance of the envoy and wondered how the report of the new appearance would be received. "The envoy has appeared again."

Clemant's dark eyes widened. "Aha. The *envoy*. And what did *he* say?"

Merral told him what he had told Corradon. As he did, Clemant listened carefully and said nothing, his face showing little expression. He rose and paced slowly to the window and back, tapping his chin with a finger.

"An extraordinary experience, Commander. When Captain Lewitz said she had such an encounter, I was, perhaps, a little skeptical. I am much less so now. The cumulative evidence of a sudden irruption into our world of the supernatural on scale unparalleled in Assembly history is now so extensive, that it seems hard to deny it. So, how long do we have?"

"A maximum of twelve weeks. Possibly less."

"I see." Clemant fell silent.

"I think we need to prepare to defend the towns as a matter of urgency. Where we can, with regular forces; where we can't, with irregulars."

Clemant nodded and then, apparently deep in thought, sat and stared abstractedly at the vast wallscreen. After several moments, he turned to Merral with a quite unreadable expression.

"Defend the towns, yes, but how? In what way? All of them? What about the smaller settlements?"

"We will come up with some ideas."

"It will not be easy." Clemant gestured at the screen. "Let me show you some disturbing data."

He tapped a digital pad at his desk. The maps and charts vanished and were replaced by a single large map of Farholme showing all the main cities and larger settlements.

"Something very unpleasant has come into our world, Commander. Let me show you what I have found. Remember, if you please, that my expertise is in social matters. I now have a team of people compiling and categorizing all reports of social, psychological, or spiritual anomalies. Now, although we know that oddities occurred as early as Nativity at Herrandown, our earliest significant data is from about ten weeks ago. Watch."

A cluster of tiny red lights flickered on the map. Merral recognized Herrandown, Ynysmant, and Larrenport.

"This is ten weeks ago. Now watch as we jump week by week." He tapped the button again.

The lights grew and spread as if they were red ants moving out from a nest. Lights spread all along the southern coast of Menaya from Isterrane to Lariston, around the mouth of the rift, and then round the edge of the Varrend Tablelands.

"Last week." More points of light appeared in new locations.

"This week, compiled this morning." New lights glowed almost everywhere. It seemed as if there were new cases across the planet.

"How many cases have you reported in total?"

"There have been 8,731 definite and 15,232 probables. And as one of the tasks of the police force is to record these things, we can soon expect an increase. But that data is yet to come in. Are you surprised at this map?"

Merral again noted Clemant's probing gaze. "I'd need to look a lot more closely at the data. I suppose I'm not surprised, but I am alarmed. What sort of things are you recording as events?"

"Now? All sort of things. Fights, negligence, a school protest, graffiti—"

"What's that?"

"You may well ask. Graffiti is writing or painting slogans on walls, defacing property. What else? Petty theft—someone stole someone else's garden plants in Ganarat. Increasing sexual incidents. We had a rape the other day."

"Are you serious? *Here?*"

"I'm afraid so."

"It's appalling!"

"I agree."

Merral stared at the map again. "Wait. Can you go back a bit, please?" he asked. "A few weeks. There, the cluster on the Anuzabar Chain. That's Ilakuma, is it?"

"Yes."

"The legal disputes?"

"It's now worse. There was a brawl there the other day. Windows smashed, an arm broken."

"It's odd. The other cases seem to spread out from points of contact with the intruders: Herrandown, Larrenport, Ynysmant, and so on. But what's the link with Ilakuma?"

"We have no idea." Clemant paused. "My theory is that in the early days there needed to be some contact for this contagion to spread." His face showed perplexity. "But now it seems different. Even the remotest places—isolated survey bases, remote mountain communities—are affected. And despite the destruction of the intruder ship a week ago, it is continuing to spread."

"So it seems."

"In light of this data and despite deep reservations, I have also backed our sentinel's suggestion that we create an irregular defense force. Your news just reinforces my belief."

"Can you explain your reasoning?"

"Very well. As Sentinel Enand points out, creating a large armed force would take years to put into action. But based on the trends that this map shows, we don't have that time. Our social fabric is beginning to disintegrate, Commander." His eyes were intense, troubled pools of darkness. "I foresee anarchy." Beneath any pretense at detachment, the advisor seemed afraid.

"I see."

"We have no option; we never did. And certainly not after yesterday's warning. But I have some conditions on defending the towns."

"Which are?"

"However you—*we*—prepare our defenses we must tread carefully. Very carefully. Can you imagine what will happen if people start building—I don't know—forts and walls? In this state, they will panic." There was a heavy stress on the word *panic*.

"So what do we do?"

"I don't know, but you need to find a way to do it without causing a fuss. And I want what the envoy said—and what you saw—to be kept totally secret. This world is too volatile for any rumors of doom to be allowed to circulate." He shuddered.

"Very well."

"Now let me say some things about the defense strategy. First, these irregulars are part of the Farholme Defense Force. I want you to be in ultimate charge of them."

"I gather that's what's planned."

"Good. Second, I don't want them interfering with the police. We'll draw up some protocols as to who does what. Liaison officers for each district—that sort of thing."

"Seems reasonable. I agree, again."

"And third, I'd like to look at the possibility of putting some defenses up in space. Once these enemy forces are on the ground, it may be too late. Can you talk to Professor Habbentz about that?"

"Gerry?" Merral thought for a moment. "Very well. I will set up a meeting with her."

"Thank you. And finally, do you know Prebendant Balthazar Delastro?"

"Only by name."

"The prebendant is a remarkable man. His expertise is not mine, but I believe he will strengthen our hand. I would think he would make an excellent chaplain-in-chief. Of course, it is your decision."

"Thank you." Merral rose to his feet. "I have a lot of work to do."

"As do we all. But let me summon Sentinel Enand. I gather that he wants to take you to your office."

Clemant spoke into a desk phone briefly and then walked to the front of his desk.

"I gather Captain Larraine has done a good job in your absence. What will you do with him?"

"I haven't decided where to put Zak. Training, perhaps?"

"A good choice. I have been impressed by his attitude." Clemant paused. "I look forward to working with you, Commander. These are challenging times." He paused again, his pale face grave.

There was a knock at the door. "Ah, here is our sentinel and chief of intelligence. Come up and see me if you have any problems. Our offices are very close."

ᴏᴑᴏᴑᴏ

Merral hadn't gone far down the corridor with Vero before his friend stopped him. "A moment," he said with a quiet urgency. "Let's talk."

"Very well. It seems like the irregulars have universal support. Clemant is backing them, but has conditions."

Vero closed his eyes for a moment. "I'm very glad to hear of his support. What conditions though?"

Merral explained.

"Delastro as chaplain-in-chief?" Vero asked.

"He will be under my command. But it was an interesting conversation with Clemant. There was a lot that was unsaid."

Vero nodded in agreement. "We are seeing conversations drift back to a pre-Intervention style—less trusting, less open, and more ambiguous. It would be fascinating were it not so frightening. But I'm not surprised that your meeting with Clemant was interesting."

"Why?"

"My friend, let me tell you something that I suspect has not occurred to you."

"Go on."

"You and Clemant are now the two most powerful men on this planet."

"Oh, Vero, come on!" Merral laughed. "What about Corradon, the other representatives, or the president of the congregations, Octavio Jenat? I could name many others. And when has power ever been an issue?"

"True. The representatives have delegated responsibility to Corradon. But he is weak and increasingly a figurehead who is reliant on Clemant. And there lies the real power. With his creation of a police force—I do wish he had consulted us—our advisor is now very important."

"Yes. But is it wise that Clemant has so much power? Shouldn't the representatives be in charge?"

"Maybe, but I think we can work with him."

"I hope so. But this police business. I'm half-minded to challenge him on that."

Vero shook his head urgently. "Don't! *Please.*"

"Why not? I think these police of his need to be accountable to someone else."

"Look, he has his police; we have the irregulars. If they keep him happy and don't get in our way, then fine. Please leave him, Merral . . . for now."

Merral sighed heavily. "Very well. But these are scary days."

"I'm glad you noticed. We talk of the Assembly being tested but we *are* the Assembly; *we* are being tested. Now as for these urban defenses, I have a new suggestion: we set up a central team here—an architect, a planner, a historian—immediately, to advise on what is needed. They can tell us about siege warfare. They put together guidelines in a few days and then we get them sent to every town to be implemented by a small team."

"Agreed. Can you find me such people?"

"Yes. I'll make it a priority. Can you meet with them this afternoon?"

"That soon? Of course."

"Good. Anyway, your office awaits."

ero led Merral down a flight of stairs and along a corridor to a set of doors above which a maintenance worker fixed a sign with the words *Farholme Defense Force.*

"It used to be the Office for Inter-World Exchange Visits," Vero said as an aside. "As that is now a redundant body, we have been given it."

He weaved his way under the ladder, through the doors, and along a line of opened cartons and boxes. Merral followed him, seeing people filling shelves and moving furniture. He was increasingly aware of eyes following him.

They entered a large room of tightly packed tables, desks, and deskscreens. More faces swiveled toward him. Some Merral recognized: Lucia Dmitri and Maria Dalphey were in a corner; Luke Tenerelt rose from behind a desk.

"The commander is here!" hissed a voice from a nearby doorway.

"Relax, everyone!" Merral called out, trying to inject some confidence and enthusiasm into his voice.

The next few minutes were taken up with handshakes, hugs, and introductions. Eventually, Merral disentangled himself and was led by Vero toward a door at the end of the room.

"Morning, sir," said a cheery voice, and Merral looked round to see a big man sitting at a desk by the door, a brown bag on the floor at his feet.

"Sorry, Lloyd, I didn't notice you." Indeed, Merral noted, for all of Lloyd's bulk there was something oddly unobtrusive about him.

Vero touched Merral's elbow. "I'll leave you here," he said, gesturing to a nearby door. "My office is there—well, one of my offices. I have work. You may—or may not—be able to find me there. But you can always get me on the secure diary link anytime." He quickly departed.

At the desk in his office, Merral found a tall, muscular man with short, wavy blond hair wearing a green uniform. Zak Larraine.

"Welcome, Commander, sir," Zak said with genial enthusiasm as he leaped to his feet. Merral reached out to shake hands and then, as Zak gave him a sharp, precise salute, withdrew his hand and responded in a similar fashion.

Zak was wearing a matching shirt and trousers in a dark olive green, like the combat uniform they had worn but smarter and better fitting.

"What are you wearing, Zak?"

"It's the new uniform, sir. For the office. Once we get your measurements, we will get you one."

"But we aren't fighting."

"Sir, we are soldiers, and we dress like soldiers."

Merral found the idea of wearing a uniform on a daily basis once more a troubling one.

Zak grabbed a folder and his diary from the desk and snapped upright again. "Sir, your desk." The words were crisp and formal. "I hereby relinquish it. You are now in charge of the Farholme Defense Force."

"Thank you," Merral said, wondering if he ought to respond with a similar formality.

"Sir, you'll be wanting me to show you what I have done." He gestured to a tall, neat, pile of folders.

"Yes. Of course. Take a seat Zak, uh, *Captain*. Tell me everything."

ananan

With breaks for other tasks, Merral worked with Zak for the next few hours as Zak explained how the recruiting was going and introduced him to various new FDF members.

Merral found Zak's unremitting eagerness not only wearisome but also troubling. Despite having seen heavy fighting at Fallambet—a man either side of him had been killed—he had not lost any enthusiasm for warfare. In fact, the fighting seemed to have intensified his zeal. Merral also realized that Zak's earnestness for the FDF challenged his own commitment. *Although I will work as hard as I can at this awful business of warfare and weapons, I do it with reluctance. Not a minute passes without me wishing it was over. Yet for Zak there is no such lack of enthusiasm.*

Yet Merral could only approve of what Zak had done over the previous week. He had pushed the development of the FDF forward with energy and insight. But when Zak explained that he had invited those who had been in the old Farholme Defense Unit to join the new force, Merral asked whether that invitation had been universal.

Zak hesitated, his keen blue eyes evasive. "In two cases, no." He paused. "Elihami and Xu panicked at the lake. They're a liability, sir. We could have had a court-martial, but it seemed best just to have them dropped from the force."

Court-martial? Merral tried to remember what the term meant. "Give me the details," he said after a moment. "Perhaps we can use them somewhere else. Maybe in the irregulars."

A frown appeared on Zak's smooth face. "Sir, these guys failed under pressure. That is *not* good. They froze."

"Did they run away?"

"Not exactly."

"Let me see the reports, Captain. I'm inclined to be merciful. Fallambet was a tough place." At Zak's silence, he asked, "You disagree?"

"Sir . . ." Zak seemed to struggle for words. "I reckon mercy is God's business. But in army affairs, I think it's a dangerous policy."

"Perhaps. I'm less inclined to reject it. I have needed it a bit myself. And anyway Zak—*Captain*—someone who fails on a strange battlefield may be very different when he or she is defending their home. "

"Sir, it's your decision."

"It is. Reinstate them with a warning."

ꗊꗊꗊꗊ

By midafternoon, Merral had acquired an administrative assistant and a pair of researchers and had already started compiling memos, organizing meetings, and chasing up facts.

His labors were interrupted by the arrival of Frankie Thuron, whom he had last seen at the Fallambet battle. Frankie looked pale. He also wore a large dressing where his left hand had been.

They hugged each other.

"Sorry to hear about your hand," Merral said.

"Yes, it was one of those Krallen things." Frankie grimaced. "It was about to strike again—I thought I was dead, then suddenly it turned and ran back to the ship. But it was a clean cut—those claws are like razors. They're fixing me with a prosthetic one. It's not the same, but I reckon I got off lightly. Better than some." He fell silent and his brown eyes seemed filled with sadness.

He's remembering Lorrin Venn, Merral decided. *Neither of us will ever forget that death.*

"So you decided to stay on?" Merral asked quietly.

"I hope that's all right, sir. I was going to ask you." Frankie looked hopeful.

"What do you want to do?"

"Whatever I can. The dressings will be off soon; the prosthetic's ready. Zak was suggesting a desk job." The look on his face communicated undisguised disappointment.

"Frankie, I'm looking for people to command these regiments. I'd prefer people who have fought. Would you like a command position? You don't have to say yes."

Frankie's smile slowly warmed. "You mean that? That'd suit me fine, sir. It really would. I mean, would that be okay?"

"See me tomorrow."

"Yes, sir!"

ɔOɔOɔ

By four, Merral had had enough. He had met with what was already being called the Urban Defense Planning Team and sent them away with a request for some feasible ways of defending towns and settlements. He had signed orders for more—and lighter—cutter guns and prototypes of more advanced guns. In addition to confirming Frankie Thuron as colonel and head of the Eastern Regiment, Merral also interviewed and appointed two other veterans of Fallambet—Leroy Makunga and Leopold Lanier—as the heads of the Western and the Central Regiments respectively. Zak Larraine was promoted to colonel as well and put in charge of training.

His head reeling with names of people, administrative charts, and weapons specifications, Merral left his office to look for Vero. The office door—marked simply *Chief, Intelligence*—was closed. Finding the room unlocked, Merral entered. Apart from a desk, a chair, and a large cabinet stuck against the wall, the windowless room was bare.

He walked outside to the nearest desk. "Anybody seen Vero?"

A crop-haired woman setting up a deskscreen looked blank.

"Thin, dark-skinned guy? Sunglasses in his breast pocket?" said Merral.

"Oh Mr. V.? He comes and goes."

"Did you see him go?"

She shrugged. "Sorry, sir. I didn't see him leave. But he's very quiet."

Suddenly seized by an idea, Merral walked back into the room and went over to the cabinet. The doors didn't open. An examination and a push revealed that it was not just flush to the wall, but also securely attached to it. Suspicion mounting, he looked around for a catch or a key slot, but found nothing.

Merral left the room and went back to the woman at the desk outside.

"Let me guess. Were there people working in this room last week? Drilling, banging?"

She frowned. "Yes, sir. There *was* a lot of dust. Why do you ask?"

"Just forget I asked the question."

Merral walked back to his office. He considered calling Vero, but instead, with a heady mixture of emotions, decided to call Anya instead.

For at least a dozen seconds, there was no answer from her diary, and it crossed Merral's mind that she was going to refuse to answer him. Just as he was about to give up, her face appeared on screen. She was dressed in a lab coat. Even with her red hair tied up under a white cap, he thought she looked both weary and beautiful.

"So, the commander of the Farholme Defense Force calls," she said, in the driest of tones. "I thought I'd better answer."

"Hi, Anya," he said slowly.

She gave him a grimace. "I'm in the middle of chopping up dead bodies and I get a call from you. How *very* appropriate." He felt the humor was labored.

"I want to talk to you about your work. Can I visit?"

She gave a long weary sigh. "Very well. In half an hour. The end lab. You can't miss it as there's a guard at the door. A professional meeting, right?" She bared her teeth. "And I'm wielding a remote electro-scalpel, so don't mess me around."

✿✿✿✿

At the lab, Merral left Lloyd with the guard and went in though a series of doors marked with lurid biohazard signs.

Anya, still wearing her white lab coat, came out of a room at the end of a corridor. Merral could see no trace of the electro-scalpel, but noticed that the coat was creased and grubby.

"Over here."

Merral followed her through doors that closed behind him with sucking noises into a large, brilliantly lit room full of steel drawers and tables and reeking of disinfectant. Through a glass panel on the wall he glimpsed something red and moist stretched out on a table with a fearsome apparatus of glittering steel blades hanging over it. He averted his eyes and looked at Anya.

"I've come to find out about your research," he said. His voice sounded flat. "And to say sorry again. And to ask that, if at all possible, we can go back to being friends and colleagues. And—"

She raised a hand to interrupt him. "Let's take it bit by bit, shall we? My research. Yes, let's talk about that. You saying 'sorry' . . ." She paused. "Do you mean it?"

"Yes," he said, staring at the ground. "I do mean it. What happened was bad and wrong. I can make excuses, but it would be wrong to do so. I apologize unreservedly."

Anya stared at him, as if trying to decide whether she believed him.

"May I?" Merral asked as he sat on a lab stool.

Anya pulled up another stool and sat facing him. Their eyes met.

"I accept that apology," she said in very quiet voice. "But I don't do it lightly. It's been a hard time for me. I had built so much on what you said."

She paused, her face a picture of turmoil, then gave a little shake as if trying to throw something off. She took a deep breath. "I watched your speech," she said.

He was struck by how the lighting here accentuated her freckles and pushed the thought out of his mind. *Stay focused!* "So then you heard what I said. Another bad move on my part, but I felt I had to say it."

But as he said the words, he realized that now—this close to Anya—he wished he hadn't said what he had. *By ending everything with Isabella that way, I have also ended the possibility of anything with Anya.*

"Did you mean it?" Anya flushed slightly as if embarrassed. "Sorry, we never used to ask such things. But now . . ."

"But now, people lie."

Anya did not correct his completion of her sentence.

"Yes, I meant it," he went on, "for the foreseeable future."

Anya open her mouth to speak and then closed it. "Very well," she said eventually. "Let's try and work something out on that basis."

"We can try. . . ."

Merral was aware that in the reflections in the glass partitions he could still see an out-of-focus moist redness that made him uncomfortable.

"You heard that your guess about predators was correct?"

"The Krallen? I read your report." She shook her head. "I was only partly correct. I failed to realize that these intruders might go beyond biology to make artificial predators."

"An understandable oversight. But it's a pity we don't have one to dissect or dismantle. We killed these things—" Merral gestured toward the corpse in the other room without looking at it—"but the Krallen seem to be in a different league. They seem almost invulnerable. I gather they resisted everything the men could throw at them."

Anya frowned. After a pause, she said, "So, let me tell you about my research. I haven't done a great deal, because there were changes that needed to be made to this lab to make it more biosecure. And my team and I have gone slowly; we don't know what we face. I have done one AC and one CB.

Sorry, code: one ape-creature and one cockroach-beast. And I checked some things on other specimens."

She gestured to the chamber beyond the glass. "Almost all of the work is done by remote, of course. It reduces the contamination risk and any others. As we guessed, they are clones bioengineered for tasks. They have a limited life span and reduced neural circuitry." She toyed thoughtfully with a strand of hair. "Yet, the most interesting thing is not what we learn about the beasts, but what we learn about the makers."

"Go on."

"I'd better show you our biggest puzzle."

Anya opened a steel drawer, pulled out something in a small clear box with the label *DANGER!* pasted over it, and handed it carefully to Merral. "Don't open it—it could kill you."

With great care, he held it up and stared at it, seeing nothing more than a small gray disk the size of a large coat button from which six tapering arms extended, giving the object an approximate resemblance to a small starfish.

"What is it?"

"We found it on the upper chest of both ACs and CBs. The arms are linked to blood vessels. They all seem to have them. We call it the spider circuit."

"What does it do?"

Anya shrugged. "Frankly, we don't know. There are circuits at the heart of it and something that may pick up an electromagnetic signal. But it dispenses a rather nasty neurotoxin that would be rapidly fatal."

"Internally? That makes no sense."

"None." She shrugged again and he sensed more irritation. *Is it me, or is she angry with the world? She was once full of energy and life; now she seems drained and tired.*

Merral handed the box back. "I suppose it gives whoever is in charge of these things the power to kill them."

"True. Two other facts by the way. All the spider circuits we have looked at secrete toxin. Extrapolating back from their current rates of flow, it looks like they started issuing poison a day or so after the creatures died."

"That definitely makes no sense. Why poison a dead crew?"

Anya gave another tired shrug. "I was hoping *you* could tell *me*."

"I'm sorry, Anya. I can't see any sense in this. But it's evil."

"Tell me something new."

A strange stillness fell between them. Merral caught a glimpse of some deep emotion in Anya's eyes. Aware that he was on the edge of difficult matters, he spoke suddenly. "So, are you planning to work longer on these creatures?"

"No. Vero called me today. He wants me to shift my emphasis to the Krallen."

"Ah. But I see two problems. First, they are synthetic—biomechanicals to use your word—and you are a biologist."

"Are you doubting—?" she began and then stopped. "Sorry. I'm just fed up with things these days."

"Is it me?"

She gave a faint semblance of a smile. "You haven't helped. But it's more than that. It's everything." She sighed. "Anyway, these Krallen imitate animals and even adopt animal behavior, so I may be able to predict some things. Remember, I predicted, however partially, the existence of specialist predators."

"True."

"What was your second objection?"

"Simply that we have none to study."

"True. But although we haven't any specimens we can try to make guesses from your account and from what the others have reported."

"I wish you well. But you are right to focus on them."

Suddenly, Merral realized that he ought to leave. This meeting had gone better than he had any right to expect and he had no wish to jeopardize things by staying longer. "I'd better go."

"Yes," she replied with an odd intensity and for a second he glimpsed longing in her eyes. He felt an almost overpowering desire to hug her, but knew he had to resist. It was all over.

He suddenly realized how much he had lost. "I'm sorry," he said, his voice thick with emotion. He moved toward the door, his feet feeling as if they were weighted down. "Good-bye. And thanks."

ꝏꝏꝏ

"You okay, sir?" Lloyd asked as he drove Merral back from the lab. "You seem, well—preoccupied."

"Sorry. I am. Meeting with Anya gave me a lot to think about."

"I expect seeing those things cut up would do."

"Yes," Merral said slowly, catching a reflection of his wan face in the window. "Dead things upset me."

10

On the following day, after Merral had spent the morning in meetings, Luke Tenerelt arrived in his office at lunchtime with some sandwiches. During the training at Tanaris, Merral had grown to both like and respect the chaplain even though most people found Luke a rather off-putting figure initially. His tall frame, bony face, and intense dark eyes made him look rather intimidating, an impression heightened by his booming voice and sharp intellect. Yet anyone who spent any time at all with Luke knew that he was a wise, gentle, and caring man.

They went up to the roof of the building. There was no one else around. They found some shade to sit under at the edge of the emergency landing pad and ate their lunch.

"Luke," Merral asked after a while, "this whole thing—the return of evil, the intruders. Is this the end?"

"You mean are we on the edge of the Lord's return and the Great Remaking?"

"Yes."

"I don't know. Maybe, maybe not. I've heard arguments both ways. In one sense, it isn't an important question."

"*Not* important? How can you say that?"

"Where we are in the great timetable has no real bearing on matters of right and wrong. Every day we're given choices and every day we have to make the right decisions. If I knew the King was returning tomorrow or in ten thousand years' time, it wouldn't alter my choice. And, Merral, that's what counts. We just battle evil until the whistle blows—whenever that is." Luke looked sharply at Merral. "You agree?"

"Put like that, yes."

Merral paused, then said, "Here's a tricky one, Luke: I was going to ask you to be chaplain-in-chief. But I have been asked to consider Prebendant Delastro instead."

Luke slowly wiped a crumb from his mouth. "That rumor reached me. Look, not being chaplain-in-chief doesn't grieve me."

"I thought you'd like it."

Luke's thin face wrinkled into a smile. "No. When I was an engineer, I always preferred getting my hands dirty with machines to sitting at a desk." He stared into the distance as if deep in thought. "I would prefer to be with the men and women in the ranks. That's where the needs will be."

"Regimental chaplain then? We need three."

"Thanks. It'd be an honor. But if I may, I'd like to stay close to you. Do you believe in accountability?"

Merral hesitated for a fraction of a second. "Yes, I do."

"It's a wise idea, Merral."

"Of course."

"So, you agree that I can ask you any question, anytime?"

"Well . . ."

"So, you *don't* believe in accountability?"

Merral laughed. "Okay, Luke, you win. I am utterly outmaneuvered. I give you the right to ask me any question, anytime."

"Thanks. It may not be necessary, but you *are* vulnerable." Luke put his hand on Merral's shoulder. "A lot rides on you. And I'm sure the devil knows that."

"Thanks for that encouragement. Look, this Delastro, what do you know about him?"

"Not much. I took a class he taught: Issues in Early Assembly Theology. He's different from the ordinary sort of teacher in the congregation colleges. I reckon I knew him much less than almost any other of my lecturers. He'd just walk in, teach, and leave. Very bright in a dry sort of way; has a fine way with words. But . . ." Luke seemed to slowly chew over something in his mind before nodding. "Distant. Dry. Academic in the worst sense of the word. Didn't seem to warm to students much. A tough grader too. But you must make your own assessment."

"You seem cautious."

Luke squinted into the distance before answering. "Merral, our world is changing. A few months ago I would have been happy to say this will work. Now . . ." He rubbed an ear. "Now? I'm not sure. My idea of a chaplain is someone you can sit down with over a coffee and open your heart to. Balthazar Delastro isn't that sort of man." He shrugged. "But we're talking about military chaplains here. Maybe he's what we need. I'm afraid it has to be your decision."

"Thanks," Merral said, glancing at his watch. There was another meeting he had to chair. "I just wanted to ask your opinion. I have to meet him this afternoon."

⬡⬡⬡⬡

It was late in the afternoon before Merral got a chance to meet the prebendant. Delastro had an office at a congregation leaders' training campus—a cluster of red-roofed buildings set in woods on a low ridge, just north of Isterrane.

After seeking directions from several people, eventually Merral and Lloyd were shown into a large, high-walled garden where sharp-edged gravel paths marked a neat geometric array of plants, lawns, and pruned trees. Merral decided that he didn't like the garden; it was too artificial and regimented for his tastes.

There were just three people there: two young men in pale brown suits standing against the far wall and a tall, older black-suited man walking with rapid steps along the gravel. Merral knew he had to be the prebendant.

As the man in the black suit walked toward him, there was something about him—the rigid back, the thin, long-limbed frame, the stiff-legged gait perhaps—that reminded Merral of a bird. His face was triangular, narrowing from a broad, lined forehead to a sharp chin. He had a wild rim of almost colorless gray hair. Merral found his age hard to assess, concluding that he was over sixty but under eighty.

Even at a distance, the prebendant radiated authority and self-control. Merral felt strangely certain that he could be either a tremendous asset or a great hindrance.

Prebendant Delastro came to a stop just in front of Merral and appeared to observe him with a strange, inquiring tilt of the head. His eyes, hard and searching, were an odd shade of dark green. With his dusty, pale complexion and the almost colorless hair, they were the only point of color on him.

The prebendant smiled thinly. "Why, Commander," he said, his voice light, confident, and somehow full of approval.

Merral made a slight bow of acknowledgment. "Prebendant Delastro?"

"In person." The bow was returned.

"Is this is a convenient time to talk?" Merral asked, somewhat ill at ease.

The prebendant's expression turned to one of cool, knowing amusement and he threw thin, gnarled hands wide open in a gesture of self-deprecation. "The commander of the defense forces—the leader of the Lord's armies—asks me if it is 'convenient'?"

Merral, made self-conscious by the address, noticed the way that the words rose and fell in a singsong cadence.

"I accept the first title; the second goes too far."

"I have no such doubts. Please, would you be so good as to walk round with me?" Delastro looked at Lloyd. "And do leave your man at the gate."

He gestured to the two men. "My assistants."

Merral was struck by the style of the suits that all three wore, particularly the oddly stiff, high-shouldered jackets. Among the extraordinary diversity of clothes that people wore, these seemed to stand out. *It's as if they were a uniform.*

Delastro was already walking away, his sandaled feet crunching on the gravel, and Merral, after a quick word to Lloyd, had to stride to catch up with him.

"Commander," he said, "I'm delighted to meet you. I have heard about your exploits at Fallambet Lake Five and I believe that the Most High has chosen you for this time. You have struck down his enemies and crushed them utterly."

"I confess, Prebendant, that I find it hard to respond to such words. I consider myself to be, at best, an unfaithful servant."

"As do we all, but I sense that you are the man we have been sent for this hour of trial."

"I . . uh . . . I appreciate your perspective." Merral felt troubled by the words.

Delastro threw him a sharp glance. "Do you want to know how I see the situation?"

"Well, yes. . . ."

"We face not just a crisis, Commander, but *the* great crisis of our age—perhaps of any age in the entire Assembly." The harshly melodic way he made his announcement seemed to highlight the gravity of the situation. "The enemy seeks to stretch his hand over the worlds of the Most High. I have no doubt that the devil, our ancient adversary, the great serpent, wants to destroy us. We must resist, Commander. Resist! The Ancient of Days has chosen us from among our generation to defy him and turn him back at the very boundary of the Assembly."

He gave Merral the sternest of looks. "This is an honor and yet a most terrifying responsibility. We must not fall short."

Merral found himself agreeing with Luke that this was not a man you would want to sit down with about a personal problem.

"I understand your interpretation, Prebendant. So how would you advise me to proceed?"

"With rigor, Commander. With *utter* rigor and with holy rigor. You must be tough with the soldiers and tougher still with the enemy. Our soldiers must appreciate what they face. This is not some local sports tournament." His tone was scathing and Merral, who rather enjoyed sports tournaments, felt uncomfortable. "Yes, we must prepare for the harder struggle: for losses, for great sacrifices. We must use whatever resources we have. We must be prepared to wage war with all that the Most High has given us. *Total* war." His voice resounded across the garden.

"I am hardly going to disagree," Merral said quietly, trusting that his lack of enthusiasm might go undetected.

To his surprise, Delastro clapped a skeletal hand tightly on his shoulder. "Commander, I saw you give your speech at Ynysmant. I knew you and I were kindred spirits. You demonstrated the very meaning of sacrifice."

Merral squirmed inwardly.

"Your noble words of sacrifice showed me that you see the only road to victory is the hard one. We must make sacrifices." Delastro stared into the distance. "We cannot be less than 100 percent committed. Does it not say in the Word 'He that does not despise father, mother, children, family for my sake is not worthy of the Lord'?"

Despite being troubled, not just at a text that seemed to have come adrift from its moorings, but at the whole tone of the conversation, Merral simply nodded. This was not a man he wanted to argue with. He was wondering how he could walk away and tell Clemant and Corradon that there was no way he could work with this man when Delastro turned to him, tilted his head in his odd way, and gave him a sharp look. "I gather you want me to be chaplain-in-chief?"

Merral, suddenly wrong-footed, stuttered, "W-well . . . I certainly wanted to talk to you about the situation."

Delastro looked away and Merral was reminded how much like a skull the fleshless face was. "It is the highest calling. The highest. I wouldn't dare to accept it unless I felt that it was the will of the Most High. But now, on the verge of the hour of destiny, is not the time to prevaricate." Delastro turned back to Merral. "Commander, I accept."

Merral suddenly realized that he had been outmaneuvered. *Just like with Isabella.* The thought was bitter. Another thought came to him: the post of chaplain-in-chief might not be that critical. Luke was probably right in thinking that it would be a desk job and Delastro might not have a great deal of influence. But some things had to be made plain.

"Prebendant, you realize that this post would be under my authority?"

"Commander, I respect authority."

"Good. And you know that the regimental chaplains would have a large measure of autonomy?"

"I understand the constraints. But I want to be part of the great battle of our age. I believe that all my life has been in preparation for this."

It was impossible to argue with a man who felt so certain that God and destiny were on his side.

Suddenly Merral was aware of another sharp glance from the prebendant. "I have a question for you, Commander. I have heard you met with an angelic being—one of those who serve the Lord of the armies of heaven."

"Well . . . yes."

"How do you contact him?" Delastro's green eyes flashed with inquiry and his voice was sharp.

"I don't. The meetings have been at his bidding, not mine."

"Had you fasted? devoted yourself to prayer? recited scripture? claimed promises?"

Merral stared at the prebendant. "Mostly, I failed."

Delastro gave him a look of incomprehension. "I see. Do you know his name?"

"Is that important?"

"According to the old authorities, if we knew his name, we could make him back our cause."

"I don't think it works like that."

"Commander, these beings are our servants, you know. They serve the elect."

"I'm sure they do. But I don't think we order them around."

Delastro's faint smile seemed condescending, as if Merral were a student who had given a very wrong answer. "A common misunderstanding. It's not 'ordering them around,' it's using our spiritual authority as the chosen of the Lord."

"I see. But I don't know his name."

They had almost completed the circuit of the garden when the prebendant suddenly stopped. "Very well." He sighed, a small gesture almost of impatience. "But do let me know when he turns up. I would like to meet him."

As he folded his hands to his chest, Merral suddenly knew that the interview was over.

Later that evening, Perena came round to see Merral at his apartment. She took a look round it and then shook her head. "Merral, let's get outside. I think there's going to be a good sunset and I don't want to miss it."

As the evening light turned red, Lloyd drove them in a four-seater to a small cove that formed one of the minor indentations of the great curve of Isterrane Bay. There as Lloyd sat watchfully by the vehicle and the sun set in a flaming glow of reds and yellows, Merral and Perena walked together across the sands.

Perena seemed in a strange frame of mind. Much of the time she was pensive and her shoulders would sag as if under a burden of care and she would seem much older than she was. Yet there were moments when the burden would suddenly lift somehow and she would seem to be filled with an otherworldly and almost childlike joy. One minute they were talking about the problems of modifying the *Emilia Kay* to give it more armor and the next she was slipping her shoes off, throwing them to Merral to hold, and running off to paddle in the warm waters.

It was in one of those moments that she stopped in midstep, pirouetted in the sand, and then stood silently. Merral watched her gaze move from the forested cliffs to the waves that were tinged red by the sunset.

"Ah," she sighed appreciatively. "It's lovely. You know Merral, our crisis has many perils and vices, but I think that one of the most serious is that we have squeezed out the time to stand and stare at the creation."

"I stand rebuked," Merral said, feeling a new longing for home and woods. "The challenges I face seem to drive all this away."

"Make time, Merral. Make time." She looked up. "The first star!" she cried, with all the eagerness of a child.

"You have not lost your sense of wonder?" Merral said, puzzling again at how poet and pilot coexisted in the same person.

As Perena looked at him, he sensed pain in her eyes. "Not yet," she said. "Amid all this talk of wars and armies, I have to struggle to keep joy and wonder—and praise—in my own life. Daily."

They walked on and Merral described as much as he felt was relevant of his encounter with the envoy at Ynysmant. Perena, who had slipped back into her introspective mode, listened attentively.

"I asked him," Merral said, "about defending Farholme from an attack from space and he said, 'At such a time you will find a way of defense offered to you. But be warned. It will be a costly way, one that only the very bravest will take.'"

Perena repeated the words to herself in a low, almost fearful, voice and then fell into a deep silence.

After a minute or so, Merral asked, "Do his words help you?"

"Yes and no. I find them an encouragement against a fear that has troubled me. There is reassurance. It is not hopeless: 'you will find a way.' But they are dark words, Merral. And the challenge they make scares me." Silence engulfed her again.

"I have an appointment with Gerry tomorrow," Merral said after some time. "I'll see if she has any ideas."

"She may. She works on her own and has not shared her thoughts with me. We're very different people and this crisis seems to heighten such differences."

Her mood seemed to lift and she bounced along, making patterns with her bare feet and stopping to snatch up shells.

Suddenly she turned to Merral. "What do you most fear?"

"I fear . . ." The words came slowly. "I fear what Corradon fears: more deaths, more suffering. I saw Lorrin Venn die. I don't want to see others."

"Do you fear your own death?"

"Six months ago, I would have smiled at that question, as we all would. Now . . ." Merral paused. "I'm less sure. But no. Not yet." He turned to her. "And you? What do you fear?"

Perena's answer was long in coming. "I fear doing the wrong thing."

They walked back across the darkening sands to the vehicle in silence.

ㅇㅇㅇㅇ

The next morning Professor Gerry Habbentz swept into Merral's office on a wave of energy.

"Hey, Commander," she said, tossing her wavy black hair over her shoulders. "It's great to see you. I've been following *all* your exploits."

Merral, who had been working his way through an interminable list of supplies to be requisitioned, grinned. Simply being in the presence of Gerry was invigorating.

She asked him for some details of the battle at Fallambet and as Merral recounted something of what had happened, he sensed a deep anger in her dark brown eyes. The hatred of the intruders who had separated her from the man she loved still seemed to burn as fiercely as ever.

"So, Gerry, any progress on how the intruders got here?"

She scratched a dark eyebrow. "Yeah. Team opinion is hardening that they used some sort of autonomous Below-Space system. You have a ship that can inject itself into Below-Space, travel in it at many times light-speed and then reemerge into Normal-Space. Technically feasible. Give me five years and a lot of resources and we might be able to do it."

"Five years? That's bad news. What about weapons? You come up with anything?"

"We kicked around the theory of using the few nukes we have sitting out near the asteroid belt for mining, but we can't get excited."

"Why not?"

"No delivery system. And they'd be too little to destroy a fleet. Probably just make them mad, like wasps. See, Merral, what we really need is something big enough to take them all out in an instant. A one-shot destruction of a fleet."

"What about a polyvalent fusion bomb—the sort that ended the Rebellion?"

"We looked at that, too. But there's a string of problems. Technically, it's hard to make, and even one of those might not be big enough if an incoming fleet was dispersed. And you'd have to deliver it a long way out in order not to soak Farholme with hard X-rays. And they'd see it coming."

She pointed at Merral with a long finger. "The really neat weapon I reckon would be to use a Below-Space delivery system to put a polyvalent fusion bomb in the middle of them. That'd be the trick. It would just appear from nowhere. Nothing and then *boom!*"

Something about her excitement troubled Merral, but he was more struck by the practical problems. "So, you want a bomb we can't make, mounted on a delivery system we can't imagine?"

"Okay, okay. A lady can dream, right?"

"How long to make the bomb on its own?"

"Eighteen months."

"I'm afraid we don't have that time."

Gerry suddenly leaned forward. "You know something, don't you? What?"

"This is confidential. Three days ago, I had a visit from a being—an angelic being we call the envoy."

"You're serious?" Gerry said, incredulity stamped on every syllable. "I'd heard rumors, but I'd assumed it was, well . . . nerves."

"No. There have been four known appearances. The first to Perena Lewitz. The rest to me."

Gerry rose and paced the length of the office, her large but graceful form full of barely suppressed agitation. "The captain, huh? No kidding?"

"Not at all."

"Weird. You specially favored or something?"

"No. I seem to need his advice more than most."

As she stood in a corner looking at him, her gaze seemed skeptical. "I find all this hard to believe."

"Is it really so improbable? We're seeing the return of evil. Is it improbable that good may respond in a similar way?"

"Weeelllll . . ." The word was drawn out to an almost impossible length. Gerry shrugged. "Okay, let me buy in on that for the moment. So what did this angel say?"

"He said, in effect, that we have barely three months before we have a visit—"

"Three months?" There was alarm on her face. "We can't do a thing in that time! We'd be an open target!"

"I asked him about defending ourselves from orbiting vessels."

"And?"

"His response was this: 'At such a time, you will find a way of defense offered to you. But be warned. It will be a costly way, one that only the very bravest will take.'"

"That's all?"

"Sorry."

"That's awful vague. No magic formula for a big, bad bomb?"

"No."

"'A costly way, one that only the very bravest will take.' The exact words, right?"

Merral nodded and looked up at the clock. He had another meeting. He always did.

Gerry stared at him. "And what does it mean?"

"I'm hoping you can find out. You have under eighty days to find out."

Gerry gave a loud theatrical sigh. "Okay, we'll work on it. But don't hold out too much hope."

◌◯◌◯◌

Merral had not seen Vero for two days and was relieved when, that afternoon, he had a message from him saying that he would meet him that night at the apartment.

Just after nine, the mirror in the corridor opened and Vero appeared. He gave an exaggerated bow. "Like Alice through the looking glass." Seeing the blank stares, he shrugged. "Oh, never mind. Lloyd, can you fix me a coffee? Long and strong?"

After the coffee had been made, Merral and Vero pulled up chairs in the warm dark seclusion of the courtyard and shared news.

Vero frowned at Merral's assessment of Delastro. "I hope he can do no harm," he muttered. "I try—desperately hard—to manage things but it's like herding cats—"

"Herding cats?"

"Meaning, I think, nothing quite goes to plan. Look, give Delastro paperwork. Get him to write speeches. Have him produce a working paper on the nature of evil. But let me know if he causes trouble. Now there are other issues." Vero took a large sip of coffee. "My friend, we have a problem. We are developing an army of sorts, but we can't keep anything secret."

"We can't?"

"No. Everything we do is filed on the Admin-Net. Everything we research is recorded by the Library. If an intruder logged on to the Admin-

Net, they could find out what the factories had made and where they had shipped the supplies. They could find out where every vehicle, every sea or space vessel is. If they logged on to the Library, they could see who consulted what files, where, and when. Any secrecy, and hence any defense, is almost impossible."

"I see. Assembly transparency works against us. So what do you propose?"

"A drastic but simple solution. Encrypt the entire Library and Admin-Net with a molecular key and whenever the intruders appear, we switch off the decryption. They couldn't be used without the key. The computer theorists tell me that it could take a thousand years with the fastest computers to crack such a code."

"Close *both* the Admin-Net and the Library? Could we survive?"

"With the Library, yes—if people were told to download what they needed in advance. And with the Admin-Net? Probably. You'd have to create a separate subnetwork of basic data on such things as power, electricity, and water. You'd migrate users to that before locking it down."

"Is it feasible?"

"I have some people working on that. We think so. But I wanted to warn you this is what we're thinking of."

"I would be interested in what Corradon and Clemant would say."

Vero shook his head. "Please don't. Not yet."

"Why not?"

Vero looked away. "I'm saying that they don't need to know yet. We have to be cautious."

"With both of *them*? But aren't we answerable to them?"

"Ultimately, but . . . 'Be careful who you trust,' the envoy said."

"But if we can't trust them . . ." Merral let the words trail off.

"I don't mistrust them. I-it's just that Clemant has his own agenda. And Corradon is so weak that when trouble comes, he may crumble."

With a rueful shrug, he downed the last of his coffee and left Merral alone with his troubled thoughts.

ꙨꙨꙨꙨꙨ

Over the next few days Merral found himself immersed in a ceaseless and wearying blur of meetings, reviewing reports, and approving decisions. He found it easy to be depressed by all the difficulties he faced. Nevertheless, within days he could see progress being made.

The three regiments acquired bases, recruitment grew, and training pro-grams began. Some weapons and equipment were already being made and others tested. As far as Merral could tell, Vero was making progress with the irregulars, but was rarely seen. When he appeared, he volunteered little information.

The Urban Defense Planning Team came up with their suggestions: all settlements should make the most of natural attributes such as rivers or cliffs to create defensive barriers. Where these did not exist, plans should be drawn up so that, within days, excavators could create encircling pairs of ditches and ramparts. Every settlement should prepare designs for walls and gateways to make attacks harder.

The team also made recommendations on the issue of refuges. As part of standard Made World practice, all Farholme settlements had one or more refuges designed to give protection from volcanic eruptions, tidal waves, ice storms, hurricanes, and the like. The team advocated the expansion and restocking of all refuges and suggested an ominous novelty: a way of sealing the refuge doors shut from the inside.

After a long meeting on the eve of the Lord's Day the plans were approved, and confidential guidelines for every warden and community leader prepared. Every settlement was to prepare a defensive strategy that could be implemented in no more than forty-eight hours. Refuges were to be checked, restocked, and made secure from the inside. All earthmoving machinery, both robotic and manned, was to be overhauled and placed at locations for rapid deployment. Where defense was deemed impractical, plans for evacuation were to be drawn up.

Merral read the guidelines through one last time and then gave orders for their distribution to every settlement at the start of the working week.

ㅁㅇㅁㅇㅁ

Merral did his best to relax on the Lord's Day but found it hard; he had so many concerns. The next morning, as he sat at his desk, Merral noticed calls already flooding in from wardens and leaders in the Henelen Archipelago and the Anuzabar Chain. He wondered how soon it would he before he heard from Isabella.

She called just after nine, her face framed by her perfect hair. *Impressive. She has seen the document within an hour of it arriving on Enatus's desk.*

"Merral," she said, "these defense guidelines. What's going on?" Beneath the very polite tone of her voice Merral sensed the faintest ugly note. She seemed to glare at him from the diary screen.

Merral chose his words carefully. "Well, what do *you* think?"

"I know what *I* think. I want *you* to tell me."

"I want to know what you think, Isabella," he said firmly, struck by how smartly she was dressed for a day in the office.

"You want us to be prepared for attack. A powerful ground attack."

"True."

"But I want to know more. I *need* to know more. By what? When? What numbers?"

"If we knew any more, we would have expanded the guidelines."

A look of irritation crossed her face. "What can you tell me? Privately. This is your town."

"Nothing."

"Nothing?"

"It wouldn't be fair. I can have no favorites."

"But *I'm* asking you."

"It makes no difference."

"So it's like that, is it? This town . . . us . . . nothing of our past counts for anything?"

"Isabella, it's not that. But I can't—and I won't—bend rules for you or anybody."

She glared at him. "Very well, if you won't help me, then I'll just have to help myself. Thanks—for nothing!"

Merral stared at the blank screen for some moments. Then, sighing deeply, he tried to concentrate on other matters.

11

The following day Merral was invited to Anya's office in the Planetary Ecology Center. He found her slumped in her chair with her feet on the table, staring at a diagram.

"Welcome, Commander Tree Man," Anya said with a tired voice. "Excuse the mess. Too many hours. Blame the Krallen."

Merral looked around, remembering his first visit. The office had seemed full then; it now seemed even more so. In fact, it was much more untidy than it had been then. There were unstable piles of books and datapaks on the desks, dirty mugs on shelves, and a discarded lab coat draped carelessly over the model of the giant sloth. The animal smell common to all biology offices seemed even stronger.

Anya put the diagram down and rose to meet him. She gave him a formal, almost halfhearted embrace and closed the door behind him. As she did, Merral glimpsed a lock. *Here too.*

"Thanks for coming," she said.

They sat heavily in opposite chairs and stared at each other in silence for a moment. From the far corner came the chatter of tree hamsters in their cage.

She looks weary and in need of a break, exercise, and some sunlight. But then we all do. He was struck too by the carelessness in her dress. Her blouse had seen better days and her trousers had a stain on them. Her hair needed combing. *How odd. Isabella now dresses up. Anya now dresses down. The changes in our world affect people in different ways.*

"So, what's new?" he asked, dragging himself to the present.

"We're coming to the end of what we can do on the Krallen project. As the only man to get a really good look at the things, I want you to check the reconstructions."

She pressed a button on the desk and the blinds closed. She touched her diary and a gray, four-legged, holographic form floated just above the floor.

"Ugh," Merral said with a shudder.

"Good, we got close enough to elicit a response of disgust," Anya observed drily. "Now look it over and I will adjust the model."

Merral took a breath. "Okay. Rotate it around a vertical axis. . . . Stop. It's too doglike. Make the head a bit bigger."

After half an hour of reshaping everything from teeth to tail, Merral was satisfied. He walked round the image one more time. "Close enough. Can you make it move?"

"Watch."

The model Krallen began moving in a slow lope.

"Good," Merral said. "A bit more fluid. More flexing at the knee joints. And when I saw them, they moved more on the tips of their toes than on the soles of their feet. They move lightly, not like machines at all."

Anya nodded and jotted down some notes. "I'll work on that. And you say they climb too?"

"Very agile. Some hung upside down in the ship. They have opposing claws on their feet."

She made a further note, but said nothing.

"Any bright ideas?" he asked.

"On how to defeat them?" Anya shook her head in a forlorn way. "They have replaceable tiles of armored skin, are tireless, fast, superbly agile, have claws and teeth, and work in perfectly coordinated packs. They're the perfect weapon. The best way to defeat them is to nuke them before they land."

"That's what everyone says."

She shrugged. "We are worried about the accounts from those who fought them at Fallambet. Much of the energy of cutter gun blasts seems to have been absorbed by this skin. Some kind of bullet might penetrate the skin, but the engineers suggest that all these angled surfaces may mean that bullets just skim off. But in the absence of real specimens, we just don't know. " Anya stared glumly at the holographic model. "Sorry."

"It's not your fault," he said, feeling pity—and more—for her.

"How much time have we got? Twelve, thirteen weeks?"

"Twelve maximum. Maybe less."

Anya shook her head in silence.

"What'll you do next?" he asked.

"Look at pack behavior. There are animal analogues that may throw some light on how they operate. It may give us a clue. Help defenses."

Anya gazed unhappily at the holograph and then tabbed the diary. The model of the Krallen vanished. She turned back to Merral. "So, how are you?"

"Surviving on a diet of meetings and decisions. I worry about both my enemies and my friends. But what about you?"

There was a moment's silence. "I still hurt," she said in a low sad voice and looked away into the corner where the hamsters scuttled noisily around their cage. She looked at Merral, seeming to blink a tear away, and sighed. "But I tell myself that I must forgive."

"I appreciate that."

"If I don't forgive you, then *I* suffer. The evil multiplies. And we—*I*—can't afford that."

"I know. But I appreciate the forgiveness. I really do."

She shrugged and looked away again. "It's the least I can do."

He rose, then on impulse, walked over and kissed her gently on the forehead as one might a child. She made no response and as he left the room, he glimpsed her staring blankly at the hamsters.

ΩΩΩΩΩ

On the day before the memorial service after a rehearsal at Isterrane's Great Congregation Hall, Merral fell into a quiet conversation with Luke Tenerelt, who was now chaplain of the Central Regiment.

Luke told him that the organization had been problematic. Delastro had managed to get on the organizing committee and had wanted to rewrite Jenat's speech and other parts of the service, but his counsel had been rejected.

"How did he want to change it?" Merral asked.

"He wanted more emphasis on the war we face, on the struggle against evil, and on the need to resist the devil."

"All good things, but it's a memorial service. There will be time enough for that."

"I know."

"But are you happy with the service now?"

"I have my reservations," Luke said, glancing around as if concerned about who might be in earshot.

"Namely?"

"It's too downbeat, Merral. Ends confidently but quietly. A hushed *amen* and then, in reflective spirit, we all walk quietly out into the sunlight."

"You want something else?"

Luke gave Merral a vaguely perplexed look. "I don't know. I think Delastro is wrong, but I feel this format is wrong too. Call it pastor's intuition." He shrugged. "But, oh, it may just be me."

⌀⌀⌀⌀

The morning of the memorial service brought a surprise in the form of a mist that moved inland in the early hours and soon enveloped the city in a dense white cloak.

The service had been scheduled to start at ten. When Merral arrived at the great plaza in front of the Great Congregation Hall at half past nine, the mist was still thick. Figures moved in and out of the mist trying to find others with calls and cries. Feeling awkward in his dress uniform, Merral made his way to where everyone who had either fought at Fallambet or been part of that venture was assembling. Lloyd followed him.

Whether Lloyd should act as a bodyguard during the service had been much discussed. The conclusion had been that he could, as long as any weapons he bore remained concealed. Lloyd, who had developed what Merral felt was an unhealthy interest in weapons, had responded by acquiring the prototype of a new pistol-sized cutter gun that he could conceal under a suit jacket.

Vero suddenly emerged from the mist, and walked over to Merral. He wore the same gray suit with the sentinel's badge of a gold encircled tower against a blue sky that he had worn at Nativity, an event that now seemed centuries ago.

They exchanged muted greetings as Lloyd drifted tactfully to one side.

"I don't like this," Vero said, looking around. "It makes everything seem so gloomy. Depresses me."

"Me too. It's most unexpected. It should have burned itself off by now. Beware the weather—"

"—in the Made Worlds? Yes. But I find it odd. Almost sinister." Vero frowned, then slipped away.

As other people arrived, Merral considered the weather. It *was* strange. The mist was heavy and clammy, giving a weird, drab light that cast no shadows and seemed to give everything an oddly drained quality. *How suitable for when we commemorate the dead.*

Still thinking about losses and endings, Merral allowed himself to be shepherded by the marshals to the front of the long line of men and women. He would lead the procession into the hall with the veterans following behind in pairs alphabetically. A gap would be left to represent a man who perished.

Merral glimpsed Delastro, looking severe in a black suit and a strange angular cap, taking his place. He carried a bronze-tipped black staff.

"Everyone ready? A minute to go," said the marshal.

Merral suddenly shivered.

Luke, who stood behind, leaned forward. "You okay?" he whispered.

"No, not really Luke," Merral whispered back. "I'll be glad when this is over."

Another sheet of mist drifted in front of them. Above, the great bells began their slow tolling, the sound pulsating through the heavy air.

Merral began to walk forward, his pace as measured as the tolling of the bells, the long line of men following him. As he entered under the great archway, the drums thudded out a muffled beat, the sound echoing and reechoing in the vast space so that the whole building quivered with their solemn throb.

Only vaguely aware of the thousands on either side of the aisle, Merral walked on until, at the very end of the strangely dark hall, an usher guided him to his place in the front row. As the others filed into their seats beside and behind him, Merral numbly bowed and committed himself to the Lord. Thoughts of death and loss seemed to fill his mind. What had the ancients called something similar? A *requiem*, that was it—a service of mourning and loss.

He looked around, seeing to his left the bank of choir and orchestra half hidden by their score screens. Not far away from them, Lloyd moved his head around in a slow, careful scrutiny of the congregation.

Merral looked to his right, seeing Delastro, seated on a slightly elevated chair. His hands were clasped together and the way he leaned forward made Merral think of an eagle perched on a crag. Ahead, President Jenat and Representative Corradon took their seats on the platform.

Merral glanced behind, seeing the vast columns, the splendid archways, the high balconies, and the ribbons and flowers. He was struck by how dark the hall seemed. The lighting was on, but somehow the gloom seemed to overpower it.

Suddenly, the bells and drums stopped, the reverberations dying into an intense hush. President Jenat, a slight, elderly figure with wispy white hair, rose, stepped to the reading stand, and in a frail, silvery voice, intoned, "Blessed are they that mourn: for they shall be comforted."

Ahead, the vast screen, three storys high, displayed the face of Lee Allane and the dates AD 13830 to 13852. A single great bell tolled.

"They that sow in tears shall reap in joy." The screen changed, revealing another smiling, youthful—too youthful—face. *Twenty-two more names to go.*

As the verses, the images, and the tolling bell continued, Merral found himself slowly crushed into the depths. The words that should have had so much meaning brought him little comfort.

It's a requiem, he thought miserably. *For them, for us, for Farholme.*

The twenty-third name was that of Lorrin Venn.

Tears sprang to Merral's eyes. *He was an only child.*

The last face vanished off the screen and the service moved on through hymns and readings. Yet as it did, Merral stayed mired in his dark mood, feeling as if he watched everything through thick glass.

As Jenat began his sermon, Merral, seeing for a moment beyond his own preoccupations, noticed that the light, already dull, was fading further. Pale mist crept into the hall along the floor. Merral shivered again and received a concerned glance from Luke next to him.

"We mourn, but we are not broken," Jenat said. "We are not alone. We have hope."

Do we? Do I have hope?

The idea seemed an empty joke. Merral looked around again, aware now that the light through the great windows had become even more dimmed. Indeed, it was almost as though the mist was a sort of negative force, something that sucked away both light and hope.

Jenat's words seemed distant. *What was the man saying? Did it even matter?*

A new tongue of mist crept round the corner of the seats as if heading for his feet. *Almost like an animal.*

The darkness in his mind was deeper now. *It's not just a funeral for Farholme but for the entire Assembly.* The remembrance of a cold and alien voice came back to him. *We will win. We are your inheritors. The uniting of the realms will take place. The end of the Assembly has come.*

It's a lie! Merral felt shaken at his remembrance of the steersman's words, but in the next breath, he wondered if it really was a lie.

Beyond the depths of his own concerns, Merral soon realized Luke's restlessness. His tall frame twisted in his seat as he looked this way and that. Finally, Luke tilted his head to Merral. "This is more than a mist," he whispered, an urgent tremor of alarm in his voice.

Shaking himself free from his introspection, Merral glanced sharply around. Luke was right. There was something purposeful in the gray mist, something that was not of pure physics or meteorology. As he watched, a strand seemed to move across the aisle, heading with an extraordinary deliberateness toward Jenat.

Merral sensed a growing restlessness among the congregation; he heard other whispers, glimpsed others looking around. He exchanged a look with Lloyd, reading alarm there.

Yes, he too has sensed it.

He stared at the mist, seeing in it shapes solidifying out of the vapor, sensing as much as seeing heads, bodies, and tails. Just beyond his feet strands of mist seemed to coalesce so that they formed a face from whose depths a pair of dark red eyes peered out. *Like Krallen.* He blinked in alarm and the staring eyes vanished.

Suddenly, Jenat's voice faltered in midsentence. The old man looked around, shook his head, blinked, and began again.

"Pray!" Luke hissed.

He's right. Merral closed his eyes. "Father of lights, lighten our darkness," he whispered. "Lift the darkness that has come upon us and our hearts. For Jesus' sake."

Like a candle blown out by a gale, the words seemed to vanish into the darkness. Merral opened his eyes to see that the mist like rising floodwater was up to his ankles and he could no longer see his feet. He glanced to the right, seeing Delastro muttering and waving his staff at the sea of turbulent, hostile fog that swirled around his feet. Something like a snake of vapor seemed to coil up the staff and then slither off.

All of a sudden, there were noises to Merral's left. He turned to see that the score screens in front of the orchestra and singers had flickered into pale light. There were looks of perplexity across the faces of the musicians.

"Something's going on," Luke muttered in a puzzled whisper.

Jenat hesitated again, looked around in utter consternation, tried to start, and then stopped dead, frozen at the reading stand.

Lloyd was sitting bolt upright, his eyes scanning the congregation, his right hand sliding under his suit jacket. Suddenly, his head swung up, as he seemed to focus on something high up on the right side of the hall.

Merral followed the direction of his gaze. Deep in the shadows of an access balcony, a tall, black-clad, and hatted figure stood, his hand raised.

Suddenly, Merral knew with a strange certainty what was going to happen. He suddenly felt like smiling. "Luke, take over. It's all right. We're all going to sing like we've never sung before. Go!"

"Take over?" Luke gazed at Merral, then opened and closed his mouth. He rose and strode rapidly through the knee-deep lake of mist to the platform.

How like the Steersman chamber. Merral realized the similarity was no accident.

To his left, the choir rose. He was aware of fevered action in the orchestra as trumpeters unscrewed mutes, the organist pressed buttons, and the percussionists changed drumsticks.

Like the preparations for battle. The image was fitting.

Luke bounded onto the platform and walked round an aide who helped the dumbstruck Jenat away. "So," he said, his voice slightly quavering, "in conclusion, we all need faithful endurance. And now there is a change in the program. We shall all rise to sing . . ." He gestured behind him.

On cue, the enormous screen came alive with two lines of text:

We praise you, O God: we acknowledge you to be the Lord.

All the worlds worship you, the Father everlasting.

Luke turned to it. ". . . the *Te Deum*. And may we sing and play with all that we have."

With a great clatter of sound, everyone rose, mist eddying around their feet. The silence returned. Then the music director raised her baton and brought it down sharply.

There was a vast crescendo of music as above the organ's thunder and the awesome rumble of drums, trumpets blazed, horns clamored, and strings and woodwind sang together. And then, just as it seemed the deafening roar of sound could get no louder, every voice sang, "We praise you, O God! We acknowledge you to be the Lord!"

And Merral sang with them, giving all he had to the ancient words, aware of a defiant and exuberant joy cascading into every space in that vast hall. His thoughts were with the words and their meaning, but beyond that he sensed that what he was participating in was more than music—it was a united act of defiance against evil.

Perhaps too, it was more than that. The accounts of those who were there were never in total agreement, but there were many who claimed that at the words "*To you, all angels cry aloud: the heavens and all the powers therein; to you, cherubim and seraphim continually do cry, Holy, Holy, Holy: Lord God of the armies of heaven,*" other voices—not of flesh and blood—could be heard singing too. Indeed, there were those who claimed to have seen flames of fire dancing with high-spirited joy among the vast vaulted expanse of the roof.

But what was undeniable—for the whole of Farholme saw it—was that as the congregation sang the words "*You are the King of Glory, O Christ*" an extraordinary thing happened, so extraordinary that even in the midst of singing with all they had, men and women gasped with joy.

The mist parted and through the great south windows, bathing all in a glorious dazzling golden light, shone the sun.

ᎧᎧᎧᎧᎧ

As soon as he could after the end of the service, Merral broke away from the animated crowds and found the access doorway at the side of the hall. He left Lloyd sitting in a seat nearby and climbed up the long spiral stairway to the service balcony. He felt lighthearted, as if a heavy burden had been lifted off him and he could hardly now remember the gloom he had experienced minutes earlier.

He expected to find no one in the balcony and was not surprised to find that it was empty. He stood there, gazing down at the floor of the hall far below.

Suddenly he knew he was not alone and turned to see, on the very edge of his vision, a tall dark form. He didn't even bother to try to focus on the figure; he knew it was the envoy and that the effort would be worthless.

"Thank you," he said.

"Thank him who sent me," came the reply. Here in this vast echoing chamber the absence of any resonance in the envoy's voice seemed even more striking.

"You altered the order of service."

"I make no apology. The enemy loathes praise and joy."

"What happened?"

"For long centuries, the Lord's Assembly has been spared the worst attentions of the enemy. But now, in his wisdom, the Highest has lifted his hand of protection and for an allotted time, the enemy is unchained. From now on the power of the enemy will be felt both here and across the Assembly. Today, the great serpent chose to move against you. He saw an opportunity to crush your spirits, but in his haste and hate, he overstepped the bounds set for him by the Most High. And, as he breached such limits, I was allowed to intervene. I can only do what is permitted."

"The enemy is affecting the rest of the Assembly?"

"From now on, yes. Those who have so far only known the summer of God's grace must now stand and face the bitter winds of winter. They will feel the enemy's hatred and power in many ways."

"But why?"

"Why?" There was a sting of rebuke in the word. "All must be tested. That is why. And your duty, Man, lies not in guessing your Lord's purposes but in doing his will. Now listen." Here his voice seemed gentler. "For the appointed time, the enemy is moving against the Assembly. He finds much that will serve him: wind and mist, sea and air, bird and beast, and increasingly, men and women. Yet even now, his authority is limited."

"I see. What would have happened if you had not intervened?"

"You would have been defeated before war came. Remember, the enemy doesn't seek to destroy you utterly."

"I thought he did."

"No, he prefers your corruption. He seeks to win men and women to himself, to have them yield to his power and will. His goal is the entire Assembly turned to his ends and the creation of a dark empire whose emblem would not be the Slain Lamb among the Stars but the serpent triumphant over them. Now, return to your work. I have already been sent to counsel you to watch, stand firm, and hope. I now add to it a new command: fight."

"Thank you." Seeing that the envoy was about to leave, he asked on impulse, "Do you like music?" As the words came out, he marveled at his folly.

"Do *I* like music?" For the first time, Merral sensed bemusement in the envoy's tone. There was a pause. "Yes."

Merral turned to the figure, seeing the vague, out-of-focus image of a long black coat and a head half hidden under a strange black broad-brimmed hat. Yet somehow in the face Merral sensed delight. "Where I come from," the envoy said in his bloodless voice, "there is always music and joy, as you know."

"So we read," Merral said, his heart seized with a wild longing.

"Indeed and it is so. And, remember this: in eternity, neither music, nor joy, nor anything else of worth can exist outside the presence of the Most High. That is the awesome choice that all of your race must make: whether to sing the music of the Lord that will never end or to scream in the clamor that can never be silenced."

A gloved hand rose to the brim of the hat as if in a salute; then, in a silent moment, reality seemed to flicker and the figure was gone.

ⲟⲟⲟⲟⲟ

Merral descended the stairs in high spirits. He opened the door at the bottom and found Delastro waiting for him, with an irritated tilt to his head.

"Commander, what were you doing up there?"

Merral sighed. "I met with the envoy. I saw him there. He organized everything."

Out of the corner of his eye, Merral saw Lloyd lean forward, his posture perhaps suggestive of a man in prayer, but his sharp blue eyes watched Delastro.

"I see. And you had nothing to do with what happened? Nothing?" There was barely suppressed exasperation in Delastro's voice.

"You credit me with too much power, Prebendant."

"I saw you order Tenerelt over to the platform."

"Someone had to take charge."

Merral sensed a strange expression on the prebendant's face. *Of course. He feels that task should have fallen to him.*

"And what did this envoy say about what happened?"

"That the enemy tried to crush us, but overstepped the limits set for him."

"And did you try and bind this envoy of our Lord? bind him to your will?"

"*Bind* him?"

"Order him to aid us by the Lamb, by the shed blood, by the eternal covenant."

Andreas and Eliza looked at each other, and then nodded. "Were you surprised, Eeth?" Eliza asked.

Ethan saw sympathy in her rich brown eyes. "Yes," he said. "I am bemused and alarmed by this development. We have a common enemy and a common crisis. I had assumed that we would all pull together." He gestured at the document. "But now, on world after world, we find some form of dissent."

He opened the booklet and began reading aloud. "'With this strategy of the Stewards we don't need intruders to destroy us—we will do it ourselves.' Another quote: 'We do not know whether the new weapons will destroy the enemy, but we do know that they have destroyed our dreams.' And still another: 'We gave all we had to build worlds; we now find we must throw away all we have in the name of defense.'" He put the booklet down, took a sip of water, and waited for comments.

"Have a sense of perspective, Eeth. These are a handful of voices in a trillion."

"Perhaps. But they hurt, Eliza. . . . Andreas, what do you think?"

The senior elder of the Custodians of the Faith ran his fingers through his beard and frowned. "Well, it is rare for me to dissent from Eliza's judgment, but I do so here. Friend Ethan, these voices, these samples, are a sign of something. And although few, they are growing. It is naive to believe that stress automatically brings people together. It can also push them apart." He paused and his green eyes seem to focus on the distance. He shook his head. "No, you are right to be worried."

From outside the room, Ethan heard the manic screams of the swifts as they darted above the roofs. For a moment he envied their ignorance and freedom. "Please continue, Andreas," he said.

"Very well. At the moment, these voices you quote are merely a nuisance. No one actively opposes what we are doing in creating ships and armies. Yet there *is* concern among the Custodians of the Faith."

"In what way?"

"They feel it is a sign that evil is once more among us in power. Didn't the message we were sent speak of 'a corrupting spiritual evil'? And isn't this what we are seeing? Today we see dissent. But will not tomorrow bring disagreement? And will not the day after division?"

Eliza nodded, looking unhappy.

"I see it within the Custodians of the Faith," Andreas continued. "We are all drifting apart. We were a convoy of ships sailing together; now we are vessels that go in different directions. There are new views and antagonistic views, but there is no certainty and no direction. And underneath it all is a tension, even a bitterness, that there never was before. And, Friend Ethan, it grows." He flicked through the booklet. "There is a warning here for us."

"Perhaps so," murmured Eliza.

"I'm not at all sure that would have been a good idea." Merral paused, and vaguely aware that his euphoria made him reckless, smiled. "But I did ask him about music."

The prebendant gave an impatient tap on the ground with his staff. "Commander, your attitude borders on folly."

"I'm sorry. My question to the envoy was an innocent one."

As the dry colorless face turned toward him, Merral read anger in the eyes. "If it was all so innocent, then why did you lock this door?"

Merral quickly swung the door open. "You must be mistaken. There is no lock."

As the prebendant bent to peer at the door, Merral made a hasty apology and began to leave.

"Commander," Delastro called after him, "beware that you are not out of your depth."

We all are out of our depth. But he said nothing.

As he walked through the lofty doors to the sunlit plaza where the crowds mingled, he was aware of a large form striding beside him. "So, Lloyd, did the prebendant try the door?"

"Funny that, sir. He did, several times. But it wouldn't open."

"And if he had opened it and gone up, what would you have done?"

"I'd have followed and taken any appropriate action. I have orders to protect you."

"You are no respecter of persons, are you, Sergeant?"

There was a pause. "It's my job, sir. That takes priority."

"But he's a leader of a congregation—a cleric."

Lloyd shrugged. "Sir, as I've said before, this is getting to be one very strange world."

12

On Ancient Earth shortly afterward, Chairman Ethan Malunal met once more with Eliza Majweske and Andreas Hmong, this time in the southern part of the land that had once been known as France not far from the ancient city of Avignon.

They sat around a plain table of time-darkened oak in a small, bare, and ancient stonewalled room. It was midafternoon on a blazing hot summer's day and rather than have the air conditioning on, Ethan had thrown open the shuttered windows and the door to the balcony.

Through the open doorway Ethan could see red-tiled roofs, the heavy silver coils of the Rhône, and beyond them both the dusty green roughness of the vineyards on the slopes beyond the river.

Despite the open shutters, the room was still warm. But there was a heaviness in the air that seemed to lower his spirits.

Over a long lunch and coffee they discussed the state of the Assembly's preparations for war. Nearly two months had passed since the Assembly had been put on a war footing, Although it had taken weeks for the vast manufacturing potential of the Assembly to switch to military demands, it had now done so. On a thousand worlds weapons were in production and ships of war were assembled in a dozen orbiting factories. Across the vast height and breadth of the Assembly the recruitment and training of armies were under way. Encouragement for the new military programs had been given by the preliminary—and still unofficial—results of the deep space observation satellite at Bannermene that had identified a cluster of apparently modified and industrialized worlds far beyond Farholme.

Finally, Ethan steered them to the matter that most troubled him. He tapped the thin red-covered booklet before him. "You've read this?"

"So, Andreas, what do you suggest I do about it? We can't stop people saying these things."

Andreas tilted his head. "No, but we should create an environment where such things aren't said."

"How?"

"I think this sort of dissent reflects the confusion of the moment. People are pulling in different directions."

"There is something in that, Andreas," Eliza said. "But please, what should Ethan do about it?"

Andreas bit his lip. "This may sound a criticism, but I need to say it. Ethan, we need strong, affirmative leadership. Our people need direction."

"So, you want me to be a stronger leader?"

"You need to steer a course. You need to challenge the critics to support you or stay silent. Point out the issues at stake. Remind them that we are in a spiritual battle for the very heart and soul of the Assembly. They must submit to authority."

"But Andreas, that's not my style."

Andreas's shrug suggested irritation. "Ethan, let me urge you to make it your style. You're too gentle, too much of a committeeman."

"Also, there is the constitution. I am merely a chairman. And these people—" Ethan tapped the booklet—"have a right to speak."

Andreas shook his head vigorously. "The chair's role is flexible. In a crisis the constitution allows for emergency actions."

Ethan made no answer, but instead stared out beyond the balcony, wrestling with his thoughts. "No," he said, his voice ringing with determination. "I will lead as chairman, not as anything else. And I will let there be dissent."

Andreas shook his head again. "Ethan, old friend, consider the matter again soon. Swift action may head these matters off, but any delay . . ." He let the words hang menacingly in the air.

Somewhere a bell chimed. Andreas gave a start, checked the time, and then with an apology and an explanation that he had another meeting, he quickly left.

After the door closed behind him, there was a long silence.

Ethan walked across the warm stone floor to the balcony and watched as Andreas strode away energetically down the shadowed canyons of the streets.

"Is he right?" he asked when Eliza joined him at the balcony.

"He may be, Eeth. Or at least he has a point, even if he is too blunt." She sighed. "We have seen and heard what he reports. There *is* an unprecedented turbulence in Assembly society. And I, too, worry about the leadership issue."

"But I don't wish to be a leader in that sense."

"I know. But I have a greater concern."

"Which is?"

"The lack of harmony between the three of us. I worry that we are a mirror of the Assembly." Her voice held immeasurable sadness.

Ethan stared out across the shimmering landscape. "Eliza, if we are, then we are in the very deepest of troubles."

ⴲⴲⴲⴲⴲ

A hundred light-years away from Farholme, Fleet-Commander Lezaroth rubbed his eyes and stared wearily at the shapeless gray thing like a dirty cloth that was sliding across the command console of the *Triumph of Sarata*. *Another ghost slug*. He used a pen to flick it into a vacuum bin. *We've never had so many of them on a trip.*

Lezaroth glanced around the bridge, seeing the all-gray world of a ship in the Nether-Realms. The screens, the seats, the decking, even Hanax's red hair all were a colorless gray.

He gazed at the man foisted on him as his second-in-command. Hanax, a mere twenty-eight, his face still unlined, slumped in his seat staring at the screen ahead of him.

I hate him. The thought was a matter of routine.

More extra-physical phenomena soon caught his attention. A ghostly tendril snaked disrespectfully around the lord-emperor's image while a blob like a large jellyfish slithered across the floor between the vacant weapons officer's couch and the shrine to Hatathaz-Thal, the god of dangerous travel.

The lord-emperor had—of course—been right. The baziliarch, even while dormant, had deterred the really nasty and more striking extra-physical manifestations of deep Nether-Realms flight. There had been nothing like the giant man-sized crab forms or the twisted human corpses that Lezaroth had seen on other trips. Instead though, there had been a vast number of the smaller creatures such as those that were currently present on the bridge. Lezaroth knew that these creatures, the lower forms of the largely uncatalogued and mostly appalling beings that dwelt in the Nether-Realms, were merely nuisances. But the baziliarch's presence had caused another and more serious problem.

There had been psychological disturbances, the worst that Lezaroth, or any of the human crew, had ever known. The most drastic effect was that proper sleep had become almost impossible. Whenever you lay down and drifted toward sleep, you always sensed a dread, clawed something ready to slip into your mind—something that, if you managed to glimpse its form, had great black wings and huge, yellow iridescent eyes. And when you felt *that* circling hungrily on the edge of your mind, you fought to stay awake.

The eighteen human crew members of the full-suppression complex and the twenty-four members of the ground attack team all reported the same phenomenon and all knew the creature that stole their sleep: the baziliarch stored away in dormancy—whatever that meant—in Aft-Hold 12. So no one slept and after seven weeks in the Nether-Realms the crew walked around as if they were half dead.

Lezaroth stared at a now yawning Hanax and wondered what to do. *We all need sleep. We're well below the very minimum state of efficiency that I would be happy with in battle.*

As he pondered the matter, a gray light flashed on the internal systems screen. It was the steersman handler. Lezaroth tapped the response button and the image of a gaunt, hairless, corpse-pale face came on screen.

"Sir," the handler said, his voice the usual mumble, "the steersman isn't happy. He's restless, thrashing about on the couch."

Lezaroth glanced at Hanax and decided that he was probably out of earshot. But taking no chances, he swung his chair around to deprive his colleague of the chance of lip reading.

"What is it, Handler?" he said quietly. "Is the baziliarch affecting it?"

"I don't think so." There were more mumbles. "But I can't tell. As you know, I can't enter the room while it is navigating."

"But we *are* on course?"

"As far as I can tell."

Dealing with steersmen over a long time destroyed your powers of speech and Lezaroth felt that the handler's mumbling testified to it. "But you aren't sure, are you?"

The handler looked uneasy. "I *think* we are on course . . . so far."

By the powers, I don't need this! An erring steersman could take us anywhere at this speed. And with two other ships tagging along behind, a lot hinges on him getting it right.

Clearly they needed to go to Standard-Space. He could use such an occasion to sort out a number of issues. *Including whether it is me or the ambassadors who are really running this operation.*

"That isn't good enough, Handler. Not for this trip. . . . Let me take the ship up into Standard-Space and I'll have our position checked. As soon as we emerge, you interrogate the steersman and find out what's wrong. Feed it something."

He paused, staring at the deathly pale face. "And remember, Handler, report only to me. Or else."

He noted the handler's look of dread.

He's afraid of me. He knows that failing handlers are traditionally fed to their steersmen. And he knows that I am now the sort of man who would do that without a second thought. All fear me now, even the security officer. Once I wanted respect and admiration from my crew, but I now have only fear. Well, that will suffice.

The screen went blank.

Lezaroth squinted at the gray figures on the navigation screen. All being well, they were between systems.

Hanax, now tossing and turning in his seat, caught his attention.

I hate that man. He comes from a no-good family on a third-rate world. I hate the way he has climbed up the ladder. And I hate the way he wants to work with me, not under me.

"Hanax!" he yelled.

Hanax sat bolt upright and rubbed his face. "Sir?"

"Wake up, man! I'm going aft. Mind the bridge." *And don't do a thing,* Lezaroth added as a mental postscript.

"Yes, sir," came the reply and with it a forced smile close to a snarl.

Lezaroth walked down the aft corridor, kicking a ghost slug away as he did. *I hate Hanax but I also fear him. I have no doubt he wants to replace me. Fortunately, like the rest of the crew, he is life-bonded to me. I need fear no assassination attempt.* He slid open the door at the end. Deltathree, the *Triumph's* Allenix unit, sat staring at six screens of what appeared to be pure electrical noise. She swung her head smoothly toward him and stared at him with dark glassy eyes. With her normal green color turned to gray, she looked more like a dog than ever.

"Deltathree," he said, "I'm planning to surface. Are you picking up anything local?"

The inhuman eyes stared at him. "Nothing, sir." The voice was light, precise, and devoid of emotion. "Down here, as you know, signals are distorted. But there is no indication of transmissions from any ship or civilization within a hundred light-years. The nearest source to us now is our destination, Farholme."

Typical machine certainty. "Very well, but as we start to surface, intensify your scan. I don't want to bump into anything."

"As you wish, sir."

I dislike machines as a rule. But the Allenix have their virtues: constant alertness, ability to scan a dozen channels, and, unlike us, they aren't troubled by the Nether-Realms. Of course, you need to have them life-bonded if they are to be reliable. But she at least hasn't lost any sleep with the baziliarch's presence.

Back in the corridor Lezaroth paused. He knew tradition demanded that he consult with the ship's priest, but decided not to bother. He would risk having him as an enemy. But there was one man he would consult. He knocked on the door marked *Weapons Officer* and walked in.

The man on the couch lurched upright and glared at him with icy eyes. "What the—Oh, it's you. Sorry, Cap'n."

Lezaroth closed the door behind him. Wepps was a veteran now close to retirement. They had been together on three campaigns and survived some bad moments. If he trusted anyone on the ship, it was Wepps.

"Wepps, I want to surface and check our precise location. Got any objections?"

"Depends where we are, Cap'n." Wepps rose, cursed, ran a hand through cropped hair, and peered at a screen. "Looks okay to me. Middle of nowhere. Any reason?"

"I want to get some sleep."

"Fair reason enough, I suppose. Wouldn't mind some myself."

"I'll see you get it. Oh, and as we surface, I am going to run a full attack drill. Any objections to that?"

Wepps rolled his cold eyes. "Not from me, Cap'n. The crew won't like it. And the results will be poor, I can tell you. And because it ain't textbook, Hanax won't like it either."

"Another reason for doing it."

Wepps leered. "You really don't like the guy, do you, Cap'n?"

"No, I don't. He's a nothing."

"But he wants to be something."

"That's the problem." *And if he thinks this trip is going to be another inevitable step up the ladder for him—it isn't.* "Better prepare for the drill, Wepps."

"Yes, Cap'n. On my way to the bridge now."

On the bridge Lezaroth walked over to Hanax as Wepps took up position on his couch. "Under-Captain, we are surfacing."

"Surfacing?" Hanax's face showed disbelief.

"That's what I said."

Hanax's look was one in which irritation and curiosity were mixed.

Hanax doesn't fear me. He thinks being the lord-emperor's appointee protects him. He hated Hanax even more because he didn't fear him.

"It's my decision," Lezaroth said.

Hanax tapped the screen with fast fingers. "There's nothing here," he said.

"That's why we are surfacing." Hanax's irritation satisfied him. *He feels he ought to have been consulted on such a major maneuver and he's right. Another little provocation.*

"Warn the *Dove*," Lezaroth ordered after a suitable pause. "Make sure it stays at least ten kilometers away. We don't want them to dirty their pretty white paintwork, do we? Then signal the *Comet*. That robopilot shouldn't need any such warning."

"Yes, sir. Any other message?"

"Yes. Tell them I'm coming over to see the ambassadors and Captain Benek-Hal."

"Is anything wrong?" Hanax asked, his dark eyes searching for answers.

"No, Under-Captain." *I love that prefix* under. *It reminds him who he is.* "Nothing is wrong. It is just that as commander of this little flotilla I have made a decision."

"I just wondered. I mean, this is a major maneuver. Standard operating procedure is that both the captain and his deputy must agree on it."

By the powers! What was Nezhuala thinking of when he sent me this man? "Under-Captain, you will probably find I wrote the manual on standard operating procedure when you were still playing with toys. But do you disagree with my decision?"

Hanax's tired eyes were filled with protest. "I *do* need to know the basis for your decision, sir."

Patience! "Very well. Carrying the baziliarch has put a heavy strain on my men. I want to surface to Standard-Space for twenty hours or so and cleanse this ship of this extra-physical trash." As he spoke, he saw another smokelike tendril coagulating into a solid existence by the emergency hatchway. "We can all get some uninterrupted sleep. And, as a long-term solution, while we are in Standard-Space, I want to transfer the baziliarch to the *Dove* for the rest of the voyage. Those, Under-Captain, are my reasons. Do you disagree now?"

"No, sir."

"Very good. Now carry out my orders."

"Sir!"

Lezaroth waited until Hanax made the calls, then pressed a button that, in a world of color, would have been bright red.

A siren echoed throughout the ship.

"Hear this all crew!" Lezaroth snapped, feeling the thrill of power that issuing such orders always gave him. "We will start to surface to Standard-Space in a minute's time. We'll be fully visible in twenty minutes. I do not anticipate any threat, but we are coming out ready for it. On my word, I want all crew to attack positions at orange alert wearing full anti-rad suits and high-G gear. I want all defense missiles primed. Have grappling and arresting gear ready, the laser cannon charged, the blast doors sealed, and Krallen deployment pods ready for launch—now!"

He pressed another button and a new siren rang out.

A robotic voice spoke. "Ship ascending to Standard-Space. Emergence in twenty minutes."

As they began the ascent Lezaroth turned to Hanax. "When we surface and have the all-clear, I want to run some drills—a full series of timed, target-acquisition drills. You will give them coordinates."

Hanax controlled a grimace. "Yes, sir."

"Have the men do ten drills and I want the figures for accuracy and speed immediately. Are you happy with that?"

"Well . . . sir, it's not standard policy. The manuals state that you should rest a tired crew before running drills."

"Under-Captain, maybe they omitted to tell you in college that war doesn't wait until we have had a good night's sleep. We must always be prepared to fight."

"Sir, I merely point out that it's not policy. And it's not good for morale. The men will be unhappy."

"Hanax, I don't care. And I have a security officer to take care of complainers. We will do the target drills."

Lezaroth turned sharply to the screens to watch his crewmen slipping on suits, moving to attack positions, and strapping themselves into the seats of the firing consoles. For all their haste, there was a wearied clumsiness about their actions that annoyed him. *They are too slow!*

As the minutes passed, color seeped back into the ship. Grays became blues, reds, and yellows. No one—at least no one Lezaroth knew—fully understood why color vanished in the Nether-Realms, but everybody who'd ever traveled the depths knew the lifting of the spirits that came on the ascent when color came back. And as color returned, the extra-physical phenomena vanished.

As they rose, Lezaroth maintained his vigilance on the wealth of output data running across the screen, listening to the noises of the ship as he did. He could hear the bustle of activity now: the thud-thud of machinery, the pumping of hydraulics, and the hiss of pressure valves. Everything seemed in order. *This is my ship and I control it.*

"Fleet-Commander Lezaroth!"

He turned to see the night-blue robed figure of the ship's priest, offended pride and anger in the tattooed face and in the drug-heightened blackness of the eyes.

"Yes?"

"We are surfacing! I should have been consulted."

"I'm sorry. Operational necessity."

"We need to make a sacrifice as we surface to celebrate color and starlight and to seek safe passage."

"Do so. You have sacrifices?"

"Chilled. Not the same as live. The blood is too thick."

"A pity. But use them with my blessing."

"As captain, it would be appropriate if you joined us."

"Priest, I am busy. And I trust Zahlman-Hoth." Lezaroth clutched the talisman through his shirt. "He is a power who understands a warrior's needs and does not expect such sacrifices."

The priest's black eyes tightened. Lezaroth knew that ships' priests were always negative about Zahlman-Hoth, because he required so few sacrifices.

"Have Under-Captain Hanax help you. I'm busy."

The priest shook his head, muttered something, and slunk toward Hanax.

Lezaroth ordered the opening of portholes that had been sealed shut to reduce the extra-physical phenomena in the deep Nether-Realms. Here, close to the surface of the Nether-Realms, it was safe to look out without the risk of madness. He took his position at his command console and soon saw through the portholes stars appearing as faint points of light in a sea of pearly mist.

"Entering Standard-Space now," the robotic voice said.

The mist suddenly cleared and they were in the starry blackness of space.

"Wepps, give me an assessment," Lezaroth ordered.

Since the weapons officer was the only crewman Lezaroth allowed to link into his bio-augment circuits, he soon heard the answer directly into his head. "Data still coming in, Cap'n, but we are on our own. Nothing here, but I'm picking up perturbations to port. Two sets. Looks like the other ships emerging."

Lezaroth targeted a camera on the anomalies and was rewarded by the sight of the smooth white form of the *Dove of Dawn* popping up like an ancient sea creature through the distant blackness. He watched the brilliant blue lines tracing manic paths around it as the energies were balanced. *The ambassadors' ship.* He scorned it and all it stood for.

Behind it, the dull titanium gray bulk of the star series freighter hauled its way into the starlight. It was the *Nanmaxat's Comet,* a last-minute addition to the fleet at Lezaroth's insistence. His reasoning had been that because the *Dove* traveled light and the *Triumph* was full of military equipment, they needed a third ship to carry supplies and—assuming all went well—captives back to the lord-emperor. Lezaroth had been in campaigns where warships had been forced to transport captives and didn't care for the practice.

"We are clear," he announced to Hanax. "Run the drills. I'm going aft. And when you have finished, get me a shuttle ready."

Round the corner he called the chief engineer. "We will be here no more than twenty-four hours. I suggest you put a couple of probes up to check the outside of the ship. Have the chimpies and the bug boys deployed on routine inspection inside."

"Sir, it's hardly . . ." The engineer hesitated, then said, "As you will, sir."

My will must prevail on this ship. I must have an automatic and instant obedience before we reach Farholme.

Lezaroth walked the half kilometer along the ship to the steersman chamber, overriding the closed blast doors as he went. He strode past humming laser cannon positions with their tang of ozone, ducked around the murmuring silver bulbs of the particle guns, passed the dozen vast columns of kinetic energy weapons, and walked between the whispering cylinders of the forward Krallen deployment pods. Everywhere he heard sounds of activity, but saw none of his crew. All eighteen were at their posts.

When he arrived at the steersman chamber, the handler was there. He had clearly only just come out of the chamber and stood by the door mopping the sweat off his white face with a towel.

Lezaroth suddenly remembered that handlers rarely lived long due to the stress of dealing with steersmen. He didn't think this one would last long.

"Sir!" the man said with a start. His hands visibly trembled. "I wasn't expecting . . ."

"I wanted to find out what the problem was. Personally."

"It's bad." The man nodded toward the chamber. "He's scared."

"Why?"

The handler dabbed nervously at his brow with the towel. "You know steersmen retain some sort of link with each other?" The words blurred into each other.

"Yes."

He nodded toward the chamber again. "He found out that the steersman of the *Rahllman's Star* was killed."

His words were so slurred, it took Lezaroth some seconds to work out what had been said. *Killed? I wish I knew more about these creatures.* "You mean his body was destroyed?"

"No, sir. In that case he would have continued as a spirit. It is worse. He was destroyed—utterly."

"At this Farholme?"

"Apparently. Steersmen are not easy to get information from, sir." *Don't blame me,* his eyes pleaded. "Not when they are disturbed like this. You can only get bits and pieces out of them."

Lezaroth's mind raced. *This is significant, even worrying.* "But, Handler, *how* can they be killed? Some sort of accident?"

"No. Even if we hit a star, he'd survive as a spirit. No, it must have been deliberate. And you'd need the knowledge. Probably power as well."

"Power?"

"Extra-physical. Something like a wizard or a mage."

"I see. So, something—or someone—very potent attacked this steersman in his chamber?"

"Must be. They never leave them."

This raises a lot of issues, an awful lot. "Handler, does this mean the *Rahllman's Star* is destroyed?"

"I don't know. . . . Maybe. . . . Not necessarily. . . . Sorry, sir."

"And when did this happen?"

"Hard to tell. They are vague on time. Some weeks ago is my guess."

"Can we find out more?"

"Sorry, sir. Not now. He's eating a bug boy. . . . Soothes them."

"I need more information, Handler."

"I understand, sir. You could talk to him yourself. They like captains. Honors them."

"You think that would work?"

"Sir, it's the best. He's uneasy about going on. You may have to make him promises."

"What sort of promises?"

The handler clicked a screen on a wall nearby. Lezaroth saw a bizarre, straw-colored figure like the empty shell of a man bent over a wriggling brown form with a skin like a cockroach, but with strangely humanoid arms and legs.

"Better food." The handler's words were a quiet mutter.

"I'll be back. I have a visit to make," Lezaroth said. "Tell no one." He caught the man's tired eyes and nodded toward the screen. "You really wouldn't want to be that better food, would you?"

The handler took a step back and touched the wall as if for reassurance. He shook his head rapidly.

"Good." Lezaroth turned and walked to the spine of the ship where he took a transport pod that whisked him back to the bridge. There he checked the ship's position—they were where they ought to be—frowned at the appalling results from the timed target acquisition drills, and checked on the state of the baziliarch. After a moment's deliberation about what to wear on his visit, he put on his battlefield armored jacket and leggings. He ordered the crew (apart from Hanax) to stand down and get some sleep. Then, after having given the under-captain specific—and very limited—authority, he boarded the shuttle.

⬡⬡⬡⬡⬡

For much of the ten-minute flight to the *Dove of Dawn,* Lezaroth, fighting tiredness, reviewed on screen the specifics of the *Rahllman's Star.* Like the *Nanmaxat's Comet* it was—or had been—a star series freighter with the fairly standard pattern of a large and clumsy main master unit coupled with a smaller more streamlined slave unit capable of planetary landing. He reasoned that if the *Rahllman's Star* had remained in space, then the steersman would have been in the master unit. On the other hand if—as was most likely—they had landed on Farholme, then it would have been in the smaller steersman compartment of the slave unit. This suggested that at least one, or possibly both, elements of the *Rahllman's Star* had fallen into Assembly hands.

The lord-emperor isn't going to like that.

He also recognized something else, something very troubling. Intelligence had suggested that as many as thirty renegades might have been on the *Rahllman's Star*. Lezaroth had no sympathy for them, but by any reckoning, they were brave, tough, and innovative men. And they had not been defenseless. In addition to their own arms, the *Rahllman's Star* as a freighter in a war zone carried some weapons and a Krallen pack. Yet, for all this, something had gone badly wrong. Somehow unarmed people from a peaceful planet had managed to slay a steersman. That meant someone had entered the ship either on Farholme, or in space, got past all the defenses, and done something very remarkable.

The lord-emperor's warning was wise. The Assembly is not to be treated lightly. He wondered what to tell the ambassadors, but decided that the steersman's information was a card he might better play with more profit at another time. For now he would tell them nothing.

⬡⬡⬡⬡⬡

Through the glass of the airlock of the *Dove*, Lezaroth saw Captain Benek-Hal waiting for him. Although he had not been on board the *Dove* before, Lezaroth had met Benek-Hal before and knew him to be a long-haul convoy pilot with no frontline experience. He understood why the man had been chosen; the lord-emperor wanted someone who would fit with the civilian profile of the ambassadors' mission. *Well, there are no civilians in our war society. But a freight-hauling pilot might pass as one.*

As the door slid open, Benek-Hal seemed to start at Lezaroth's armored jacket and leggings. He visibly paled.

As I intended. I want them to know I mean business.

The captain, clean-shaven and well groomed in an immaculate white uniform, saluted with precision. "Welcome to the *Dove of Dawn*, sir," he said in a deferential tone and motioned Lezaroth to a small anteroom.

Lezaroth was surprised at how light and airy the *Dove* was. There was white paint everywhere and the ship smelled almost medicinal in its sterility.

"It's an honor to have you, sir," Captain Benek-Hal added.

"Thanks." *Let's not waste time.* "Captain, I've come to tell you that we will be shifting the baziliarch over in two hours' time."

"Over where?" Benek-Hal's neck wobbled nervously.

"Here. More specifically, your forward hold."

"Sir . . . was this agreed?" Benek-Hal's voice registered unease and his brown eyes held fear.

"Not at this stage in the voyage, true, but an earlier transfer has become a military necessity."

"How so?"

"The thing's affecting crew performance. I just ran a drill on my men. Fifteen seconds average for targeting. A mere 92 percent accuracy. Quite unacceptable, Captain. If we do run into trouble in the Farholme system, we need to do better than that."

"What about putting him on the *Comet*?"

"No. A baziliarch needs managing. We will send you the intermediary as well."

"Sir, I'm unhappy about all this."

Lezaroth took the man's arm in a gesture that could be interpreted as one of friendship or threat.

"Captain," he said in a low, insistent tone that he often found himself using these days, "you don't want me as an enemy, do you?"

Benek-Hal paused, then looked away. "No, sir."

Suddenly a wallscreen blinked on. A pale face, puffy on one side and heavily bandaged on the other, appeared. Only a single, bloodshot gray eye was visible. Lezaroth glimpsed medical tubes behind the face.

"Ah, Margrave!" It was a man's voice, light, smooth, and polite. "What seems to be the problem?"

"I don't think we have been introduced."

"No, we haven't. You may call me . . .." He paused as if remembering something. "Ambassador Hazderzal. My colleague, who is also undergoing a little reconstruction, is Ambassador Tinternli."

Not their real names of course. I'll never know those. They are no doubt people from the lord-emperor's trusted inner circle.

"Ambassador Hazderzal, a pleasure." Lezaroth bowed. "I'm sorry that our hasty departure prevented us from meeting earlier."

"A sad necessity. But this surfacing? And your visit? There is no problem, I trust."

"I just came over to inform you that there has been a slight change of plan. From now on you are taking the baziliarch."

A glimmer of fear shone in the single eye. "No. The agreement was the transfer would take place just outside the system. I refuse." His defiance seemed hollow.

I was afraid of this. The ambassadors no doubt see themselves as in control of this trip. That is an issue of principle that needs dealing with firmly and now. "I think we need to talk personally," he said, then switched the screen off. "Take me to them, Captain."

Benek-Hal looked unhappy. "Sir, they are in a sterile setting—flesh sculpting. The doctor will not allow a visit."

Lezaroth leaned toward him. "Captain," he said with a deliberate slowness, "just take me."

"Very well." Benek-Hal looked away again. "This way."

Lezaroth was led down a series of corridors. As they walked, he found himself struck by the differences between the *Dove* and the *Triumph*. It wasn't just the white paint and greater illumination; there were other things. Particularly striking was the absence of shrines or images. Some of the alcoves where there would have normally been statues of gods or powers were empty; others had other statues or even vases of flowers. He saw only one image of Lord-Emperor Nezhuala.

On one wall was a mural of trees and woods. Lezaroth paused to read the caption: *The forests of central Narazdov.*

Someone has a grim sense of humor. Central Narazdov is so radiation blasted that it glows at night.

Finally the captain led the way through tightly sealed doors to a room with two beds and a multitude of medical equipment. The air was cool and sanitized.

As the doors opened, an angry man in a white coat strode forward with determined steps. "This is impossible! It's a breach of—" He stopped and seemed to take in Lezaroth's armor and badges of rank. "My apologies, sir," the doctor added, his face emptying of color. He stepped back awkwardly.

"Thank you." Lezaroth turned to the captain. "I like a man who knows his place in the great scheme of things."

On the left-hand bed lay a still figure covered in bandages and with tubing entering and exiting at various points. Only the fact that the chest rose and fell gently indicated life. To the right, a figure slowly rose from the bed with inflexible movements.

Lezaroth strode over. "Ambassador Hazderzal," he said, hearing the mockery in his voice, "please don't feel you have to get up."

The bandaged figure slumped back onto the bed.

Lezaroth pulled up a chair and sat down. "I thought that you and I should talk face-to-face."

"I think it is unnecessary. You should keep the baziliarch," the ambassador quavered.

Lezaroth glanced at a large diagram on the wall labeled *Ambassador Hazderzal* that had a series of summary tissue-sculpting diagrams underneath. In one corner was a picture of a man with a short, neatly pointed gray beard and a lean face with soft gray-brown eyes and wispy white hair.

"Ah, what you will be. The acceptable face of the Dominion. . . . Tissue grafts, new cheekbones, new eyes. Very nice."

"Margrave—Fleet-Commander—" A bandaged jaw opened to reveal a half-completed array of teeth. "I really would prefer that the baziliarch remain on your ship. You have the space."

"Ambassador, we need to get one thing straight. This operation is fundamentally a military one. It has a diplomatic preamble that may—or may not—succeed. But the chances are that we will use the full-suppression complex that I command. So, my task is to make sure my men are at peak efficiency. And in order to maintain that efficiency, I have made the decision to transfer the baziliarch to this ship."

"I still disagree."

"Oh, dear." Lezaroth looked slowly and deliberately around at the half dozen tubes running into the man's body. "You know, Ambassador, tissue programming and flesh sculpture always carries risks." He suddenly grasped a tube with red fluid in it. "On a ship, it is riskier still." His fingers tightened around the tube. "And in the Nether-Realms, it's *very* risky. No colors to guide you in surgery. Accidents do happen."

The ambassador's head twisted around, as if he looked for help. But the doctor and Captain Benek-Hal had vanished. "You wouldn't dare, Lezaroth!" His voice seethed with hatred.

"Margrave or Fleet-Commander, if you please. . . . Oh, I would. We only need one ambassador really. She will do fine. And the doctor would sign the death certificate."

"Margrave, if you as much as touch me, the lord-emperor will send you to the far end of the Blade of Night. There are things there that can keep you in torment forever."

"Ambassador, if we mess up this mission, we will all get sent down the Blade together. My job is to make it succeed. Trust me. My men need to be fighting fit. Take the baziliarch."

The ambassador's jaw opened and closed. "Very well. We will take the baziliarch. But don't think the lord-emperor won't hear about your threats."

"What threats? Do I bear a gun? Ambassador, since we have to work together, we need some working rules. So learn a rule: *I'm* in charge. Agreed?"

He tweaked the tube.

"Agreed." The word was a gasp.

"Good-bye. The baziliarch will be on his way soon. We will be en route in twenty hours or so. See you and the lady ambassador in a month's time." He leaned close to the ambassador's face. "Sweet dreams."

ㅁㅁㅁㅁㅁ

Back on the *Triumph*, Lezaroth ordered the transfer of the baziliarch with Hanax supervising, ostensibly because it required a senior officer. In reality, if anything went wrong, he could blame it on the under-captain.

The creature, in its dormant state, was housed in a syn-crystal container the size of a large room that could be transferred by robotic tugs.

Steeling himself, he returned to the steersman chamber.

I hate talking to steersmen. But I have no option. I need to get everything I can out of this creature about what happened on Farholme. I must ask the right questions.

The handler let him into the chamber. As the door slid shut behind him, Lezaroth blinked, trying to force his eyes to see in the gloom. A chill vapor wrapped around his feet and a foul smell struck his nostrils. He looked up, seeing on the high ceiling the spheres that represented the local stars. He stepped forward, his feet crunching on bones.

As Lezaroth walked toward the seat where the steersman sat, he gazed at the floor. *I do not wish to look at this being.* Finally, he looked up, seeing a tall, thin, hollow form, resembling a man.

He tried to reassure himself. *I must remember that while I can hear him, he cannot read my mind. Only a baziliarch can do that.*

In a few paces, he stood in front of the dimensional column, with its six sides carved with the great incantations that only the Wielders of the Powers knew. Behind it sat the steersman. Lezaroth saw the light glinting on the metal crown and below it the empty voids of the eye sockets. With a rustling sound, the being rose up with an uncoordinated motion, a distorted parody of the human form—the epitome of emptiness.

Who are you? said the voice in Lezaroth's mind.

"I am Margrave Sentius Lezaroth, Fleet-Commander by personal appointment of the Lord-Emperor Nezhuala, Dynast of the House of Carenas."

The captain himself.

"Indeed. It is an honor to be received by you. We value your services." Lezaroth saw that the being's strange fingers looked like dry twigs and were stained with drying blood.

I do not wish to go to Farholme.

"Why not?"

Something happened there.

"What?"

A kinsman of mine was killed there. Destroyed. There was fear in the words.

"I'm sorry. How was he destroyed?"

A man did it.

"On his own?"

Yes.

"Tell me about it."

I felt fear. My kinsman was very afraid. There was a man. A man destroyed him.

There was a silence.

"We will protect you," Lezaroth said. "This ship is bigger. We are well armed. We travel with a powerful ally from the Nether-Realms."

The husklike figure tilted forward.

Yes. One of the seven is with us. I feel his presence. But I am afraid.

"We will find this man and kill him. You will get revenge."

I want revenge.

Despite the cold, Lezaroth realized he was sweating. "If we go to Farholme, you will get revenge." He heard the shakiness in his voice.

What else?

"You will have new flesh. Women. Children."

Good. Do you promise?

"Yes."

You know what happens if you cheat me?

"Yes. Just get us all to Farholme fast."

Revenge and children?

"Yes. It's a promise."

The fingers clicked as if in agreement.

A promise then.

As Lezaroth turned to go, suddenly a thought struck him. "Did you get the name of the man?"

A name? Yes, there was a name mentioned.

"Can you tell me that name?"

Perhaps.

"Please."

Ringell. Lucas Ringell.

ᗧᗤᗧᗤᗧ

Lezaroth did not return to the bridge as he had intended. Instead, with his tired mind reeling, he took the elevator to the summit of the dorsal spine of the *Triumph* and headed to a small chamber with wide views fore and aft over the ship. An apemorph—"a chimpie"—was checking panels inside but, at his entry, the creature made an urgent grunt, bowed, and fled.

Lezaroth walked to the curved glass window and looked out. As his eyes adjusted to a scene lit only by starlight and some stray illumination from the ship, he was able to make out the robotic tugs towing away a crystal box that gleamed with a faint blue light under the stars.

The baziliarch was on his way.

Lucas Ringell—that name again. The lord-emperor said that Ringell's name had been mentioned among the powers. Whoever has taken on that name is the great adversary. And the lord-emperor wants him dead at all costs. What will he reward the one who slays this man?

Lezaroth stared at the enormous mass of the ship that projected far ahead of him and blotted out the stars. *Funny. When the lord-emperor mentioned the name Ringell, I thought it some sort of a fantasy. But hearing it just now from the steersman, I believe it.*

He looked at the immense number of stars that enveloped the ship. Around one of those pinpricks of cold light ahead was Farholme. The lord-emperor's enemy—*his* enemy—was there. A man who had killed a steersman.

For the briefest moment, Lezaroth felt fear. He looked again at the ship before him with its stark proud array of weapon turrets, its forests of surveillance antennae, its arrays of gaping missile tubes, and the proud ensign of the Final Emblem of the Dominion on its hull. And as he did, any trace of his fear fled. *I command the latest and greatest full-suppression complex—three-quarters of a million tons and the most formidable accumulation of weapons the human race has ever built. I have enough sheer power at my command here to erase an entire mountain chain in a second and enough range to obliterate a city from a hundred thousand kilometers. And I have more than just brute power too. I have enough Krallen to cleanse an entire planet of its population within a few weeks.*

He felt reassured. *There is no threat. On the contrary, my enemy is there and trapped. Within weeks we will be face-to-face and I will destroy him and the lord-emperor will be delighted.*

He caught a glimpse of his tired, troubled face reflected in the glass. *But I must be careful. I must be sure that I alone take the glory. Neither Hanax nor the ambassadors must do that.*

He smiled. *How strange. My biggest fear is not of the Assembly, but of those on my own side.*

13

After the memorial service, Merral's life slipped into a routine. Every day except the Lord's Day, he would rise at six, pray, and read his Bible, and then go for a twenty-minute run. Although Lloyd could move fast when the need arose, he was no runner and arranged for two young soldiers to accompany Merral, each carrying the new pocket-sized cutter guns hidden beneath loose running tops. After the run, Merral would shower, eat breakfast, and then be driven to the Planetary Administration building, where around half past seven, he would start his long day. Typically, what followed then was a succession of meetings, both real and virtual, interrupted at times by a trip to observe some piece of new equipment or oversee a new maneuver. Sometime after six, he would return with Lloyd to the Kolbjorn Suite where they would take turns cooking supper. After eating, Merral would work until late in the night, looking at papers, assessing plans, or reading reports. It was, he knew, an unsustainable pace, but he consoled himself with the fact that it didn't have to be sustainable. He only had to keep it up for weeks.

But how many weeks? Merral kept a calendar chart on his wall on which he crossed off each day. It was a necessary evil, he decided, but the unrelenting reduction in the days left to the end of summer increasingly came to haunt him. Soon only sixty, and then fifty, days were left. And that, he grimly reminded himself, was the maximum.

Yet at first slowly, and then with an encouraging pace, the Farholme Defense Force grew. The regular forces were recruited, trained under programs devised and often supervised by Zak, and then assigned to units. The three regiments were dispersed to new bases across Menaya: the Eastern Regiment to a new site just west of Halmacent, the Central Regiment to a landing strip at the southern end of the rift, and the Western to just outside

Varrend on the Tablelands. In order to provide some cover across the vast distances of the islands of the southern hemisphere, six mobile brigades, each 150 men strong, were raised and posted to six different islands.

Farholme became used to the sight of green-uniformed soldiers transiting through its airports and driving along its roads.

And in the lowest levels of the Planetary Administration building, a basement was cleared out, equipped to refuge standards, and given communication links and lockable doors. Merral was troubled by the name it became known by but knew of none better: the *war room*.

◁◁◁◁◁

Merral tried to ensure that he had at least one undisturbed meeting a week with Vero.

Late one still and humid afternoon, three weeks after the memorial service, Merral met with Vero. On a whim, Merral arranged for Lloyd to take the two of them out on a small sailing vessel in Isterrane Bay. As Lloyd struggled to use the faint breezes to take them around the bay, Merral and Vero talked in the shade of a low awning by the prow.

"So, what's the progress with the irregulars?" Merral asked.

Vero peered over his dark glasses. "It's good and bad, my friend."

"Tell me about the good first."

"By now almost every settlement has a core group."

"Whose task is to recruit others."

"Right. That seems easy enough. Everyone wants to join. But in most of the large settlements, we have now issued a small cache of weapons and at least some explosives. There are a lot of people like your uncle Barrand tutoring the irregs in the handling of explosives. And there is the promise of guns as soon as enough are available."

"So how many irregulars are there? Clemant asked me that the other day."

Vero shrugged slightly. "He would. About twenty thousand. We have issued that number of the brown jerkins and berets. But there are more irregs than uniforms."

"You can't be more precise?"

Vero gave a wry smile tinged with concern. "My friend, let me tell you a secret." He lowered his voice. "One of the positive features of the irregulars was that the enemy would never be able to know who they were. I now realize that this has a negative side."

"You don't either?"

There was a little awkward laugh. "Well, it's getting that way."

"Vero, that's all very . . ."

"Irregular?"

Merral gazed across the bay where the haze of the sky met the silvery sea. "Vero, I have mixed feelings about them. Clemant is uneasy. And the prebendant too."

"That goes without saying, Merral. I try to avoid Delastro. But look—what's the alternative? Take the southern islands. There are a lot of people down there. Can you cover them all?"

"No."

"Or even the main towns of Menaya?"

Merral sighed. "No."

"There we are. And it's good for morale. The public will see the irregs and think they are being protected, which they may be."

"I thought the irregulars were secret?"

"You can't hide training people with weapons and explosives."

"I suppose not."

Vero took a drink. "And your own plans. How are they progressing?"

"Well enough, I suppose. But how can I say when I have nothing to measure them against? The new cutter guns seem to be well liked—more power, less weight. But can we trust them?" He hesitated.

"I don't think we can rely on cutter guns either. We are issuing chemical fuses for explosives to the irregs." He gestured to where Lloyd stood at the helm of the yacht. "I see that connoisseur of weapons Lloyd is carrying an XQ gun in his bag."

"I hadn't noticed. I've given up looking inside. It scares me."

"I think he's a success."

"Vero, he is definitely one of your very best ideas. I'm just made uneasy by the way he experiments with bits of weaponry. And his reading material is violent. And those ancient films . . ."

"Oh, *those*." Vero sounded embarrassed.

"He says they were your idea. I watched bits and what I saw was either absurd or violent."

"They are odd, aren't they? I just thought he might find them, well, useful. Get some hints. That sort of thing. My friend, I think he'll be useful."

"I wish I thought you were wrong."

There was silence and then Vero spoke again. "These XQ guns—are you pleased with them?"

"Yes. No electronics, just rocket-propelled bullets. An early twenty-first century design we found in the Library. It's the best thing we have. The rounds are tungsten-tipped and will go through a wall. We've ordered ten thousand."

Vero raised an eyebrow. "You don't sound enthusiastic."

"Vero, they raise issues typical of all the problems we face. For a start, we don't know if they'll work against Krallen. We know those things have angled hard surfaces so our bullets may just glance off them. But in the last few days, we've found a second problem."

"Oh, dear."

"Anya has been simulating Krallen attacks. We'd been thinking of head-on attacks. But she raised the question of what would happen when some Krallen forced their way into a unit of soldiers." Merral pushed the fingers of his right hand deep into his left palm. "As happened at the lake. If the soldiers keep firing at them, they will soon be pumping ricocheting armor-piercing rounds into each other. In close-quarter fighting, weapons like that may be worse than useless."

"I see." Vero's brow furrowed. "I hadn't thought of that."

"Nor had we." Merral thumped his hand against the hull. "You see, Vero, we are so naive. We don't know about our enemies, and we don't know how to fight. At times . . ." He paused, trying to recover his composure. "At times, I don't think we can do it."

Vero rubbed his head. "We must pray and trust, my friend. But you—we—are making progress. I watch and I hear. . . . The long-barreled sniper's rifle for instance. Are the rumors true?"

"Yes. The women are taking that up. They like it. All the regiments will have female sniper units." Merral stared out to sea. "Amazing, isn't it, how we can discuss weapons so easily now, eh, Vero? I had a conversation the other day with a materials engineer about the new blades that will replace the bush knives. 'We can molecularly tune the edges to cut better against flesh,' he said. What a world we live in."

A long silence followed in which only the creak of the boat and the gentle lapping of the waves against the hull could be heard.

"My friend, we need better weapons on a large scale." Vero's voice was thick with worry.

"Yes. We examined the two vortex blasters we have in orbit. They were built to give planners and foresters a last-resort capability to sterilize large tracts of land. I can't remember when they were last used. Anyway, they might be effective against large concentrations of enemy, but . . ."

"There is always a 'but' these days."

"Indeed. But they're slow to aim and each have only five firing charges. There are no replacement charges. We have ten shots, maybe. And I okayed the production of thirty artillery cannons that can fire shells a dozen kilometers."

"Will they be ready?"

"We don't know. And finally we have a handful of fliers that were designed for low-speed dispersal of plant seeds and fertilizer. We're modifying them to carry weaponloads of bombs and flares."

"Well, I suppose the good point is that we're not tempted to put our trust in our weapons."

"A limited consolation."

"What we need is to stop them up there before they land," Vero said, gesturing skyward. "That's where they are vulnerable. Any progress there?"

"Vero, in a word, no. I talked to Gerry—always an enjoyable experience. She's pursuing her work on space weapons, but all I saw were formulas, graphs, and speculations. 'Not enough time,' she said. 'Not enough resources.' She has taken a hint from the envoy's words and is broadening her vision 'to look at bold and brave ideas.'"

"Such as?"

"She was vague. Or I didn't understand the physics. But she's been talking about using a Below-Space delivery system to deliver a polyvalent fusion bomb. When I saw her last, she got quite animated. 'There are some extraordinary possibilities for doing *really* serious harm. We could fry them all.'"

"I can hear her voice."

"It's great, but it's all theory in almost every area."

"By the way," Vero asked, "how's Zak doing? I hear stories."

Merral read caution in his friend's eyes. "Ah, Zak. Vero, I'm very ambivalent about Colonel Zachary Larraine. He's undeniably a very gifted organizer and a talented strategist with an extraordinary flair for military matters. But his attitude to discipline borders on the brutal."

"Really?"

"There was one case where Zak apparently pushed a soldier out of a hovering rotorcraft. The guy broke a leg. There was another where he is alleged to have denied medical treatment to heat-exhausted soldiers. I talked to him about them."

"What did he say?"

"He was defiant. He always is. 'Sir, I figured we don't need cowards or weaklings.' So I warned him. But Clemant backs him. 'Perhaps his toughness balances your tenderness.' That was his comment."

Vero looked thoughtful. "Actually, there may be something in that."

"You really think so?"

"Maybe."

Just then Lloyd yelled, "I feel a breeze!"

The sails filled and the boat sawed swiftly through the water.

"Better take us back, Lloyd, I've a lot to do!" Merral called out.

He turned to his friend. "Vero, what else is happening? What do you see that I might have missed?"

Vero shook his head. "Our world continues to change. Farholme society is unraveling." He pulled his diary off his belt. "Let me tell you what's happened these last few days. In Kanamusa, there was a riot at a concert when a band failed to turn up. Hutertooth College—ah yes; two students cheated on their exams. Lewi Island: reports of gambling. In Marinoff Town the warden has refused to stand down at the end of his term of office. Numerous fistfights. Sound familiar?"

"Depressingly so. I saw a man the other day angrily protesting that all the military pilots were women and demanding to know why he couldn't undergo flight training."

"I heard about that. But look at this." Vero tapped the diary screen and handed it to Merral. The image was that of another poster advertising a meeting. At the top of the sheet, written in a large and angry black font, were two phrases:

Ruling Farholme after the Gate has gone.
Toward a better way!

"This was found on the High Street in Clanmannera yesterday," Vero said.

"I don't understand its significance. Is it all that alarming?"

"Oh yes," Vero said with a wag of a finger. "You see, Farholme has now got politics."

ᢒᢒᢒᢒᢒ

The subtle changes taking place across Farholme made Merral's task even worse. The universal and automatic trust that he had always taken for granted seemed to be fading away. Increasingly, he wondered at people's motives and even questioned their judgment.

Corradon was a case in point. The representative was increasingly valued as an inspirational speaker and a general soother of frayed nerves in troubled times and seemed to view this as his main role. He took to giving a weekly state-of-the-world address in which he spoke with eloquence, dignity, and confidence. The broadcasts soon acquired a large following and Merral was fascinated to hear how often people would later quote something he had said. And between these Corradon continued his habit of visiting major towns to speak publicly, shake hands, listen solicitously, and generally be seen. And every time he spoke, the feedback from the hearers was always the same: "We are reassured by his confidence and encouraged by his hope." Yet Merral sensed that Corradon found the speaking an excuse to avoid the hard issues resulting from the crisis. Although he had been given overall charge of affairs by the Council of Representatives his supervision seemed perfunctory.

Whenever Merral met with Corradon to get forms signed, he would generally find the representative either fine-tuning a speech or tending his plants. They would sit down together and Corradon would ask some questions about "how things were going." He seemed to listen with apparent care, sometimes jotting down facts or a phrase that might be useful for a speech, before losing interest and gazing out of the window. Eventually, Merral would hand him the relevant forms and he would stare at the paper, grimace, and then, with a despairing shake of his head, sign them with his florid signature. Merral wondered how outrageous his requests would have to be before they were rejected.

But it wasn't just Corradon's inattentiveness that worried Merral.

"Merral," the representative said one day as he signed an order for more weapons, "I have to be optimistic, but I really don't know whether we can win against another attack by the intruders. Can you reassure me?"

Merral, seeing the worry etched in Corradon's eyes, agonized for a moment. "No," he said. "I can't. Not honestly."

"So what do I *do*?"

"Do what you can to reassure the people. Maintain a tone of cautious optimism. Encourage them to put their hope in the Lord of the Assembly."

"Fine words," Corradon said, massaging his nose. "Very fine words. But I begin to worry if I can carry this off. Some of these people—perhaps many of them—are going to die. Aren't I lying?"

Merral didn't immediately answer, but eventually said, "I don't think so. You have to give them hope."

He left the representative's office with troubling questions ringing in his mind: *How long can Corradon maintain this act? And what happens when it fails?*

ᘓᘐᘐᘐᘓ

Clemant, with whom Merral had dealings with on almost a daily basis, was very different, but no less worrying. With Corradon's frequent absences and increasing detachment, the advisor made most of the day-to-day decisions in Planetary Administration. He never seemed to leave his austere office and relentlessly scrutinized the details of every order or initiative. Merral soon found Clemant's desire to know exactly what was happening and manage it both irritating and perturbing.

The advisor's attempt to create an effective police force, however, met a check. Although small in number—there were barely a thousand across the entire planet—the police proved to be singularly disliked. The reason was simple: both the regular and irregular wings of the FDF were accepted as being a necessary defense to counter a mysterious and dangerous threat from outside. But the police, especially once they were equipped with powers of arrest, were seen as having no such justification and the assumption grew that their sole purpose was to make the lives of ordinary citizens hard. Farholme being the world it was, the protests were muted and, in general, expressed in nothing more than restrained grumbles and dark looks. But the police got the message and took to staying inside their new offices and memorizing the new Farholme Penal Code. And Merral noticed that every time the word *police* was mentioned in his hearing, Clemant seemed to scowl.

Very soon, Clemant suggested that, far from hiding what was going on, Merral ought to allow at least some publicity for the FDF. Merral resisted; he had, by now, seen many old films of parades and displays and had found almost all of them objectionable in their celebration of military force. Clemant, though, was persistent.

"Commander," he said in his deep voice as he leaned forward over his desk, "the people need reassuring. We need to make some broadcasts. We can film some training exercises, show them the transports, the new guns. And you, of course. You should be seen there personally—the man in charge."

"Isn't that Representative Corradon?"

Clemant gave him a sharp but inscrutable look. "Oh, of course. But it doesn't hurt to have two such public leaders. After all, you never know. . . ." And his voice tailed away into an expressive silence.

So, reluctantly, Merral became used to being filmed standing among the troops, surveying freshly reconditioned vessels, and examining new weapons. He hated it, but he played the part and even took some pleasure in the messages of appreciation that came in. "It's necessary," he told himself but that gave him little reassurance.

On most matters Merral found the advisor helpful. Yet the irregulars caused frequent problems. Although he had approved their formation, Clemant was obviously suspicious of them. Merral felt certain these suspicions centered on the fact that the irregulars were outside the advisor's control. With that suspicion of the irregulars came disquiet and even suspicion about Vero, something that the sentinel's increasingly elusive habits only served to worsen.

At one private meeting with Clemant, a matter to do with the irregulars emerged. The advisor leaned back in his chair, his eyes on Merral. "Commander," he said, "do *you* know where Sentinel Enand is right now?"

"Well, no. Not at this exact moment."

A look of irritation crossed Clemant's smooth face. "No one ever does. What's going on with these irregulars, Commander? Do *you* really know?"

"I have a fairly good idea."

"'A fairly good idea'? Is that all? Where is Vero based?"

Trying to conceal his unease, Merral gestured with a thumb. "He has a room next to mine."

"Technically. But he's never there."

"He has an office in Petersen Square."

"He is rarely there either."

"There are other places he could be."

"I have tried them. But he isn't there. We are pouring resources into his organization, but see little of him. He's a rather shadowy figure." He gazed sternly at Merral. "It's not satisfactory, not at all."

αΟαΟα

If Clemant felt uneasy about Vero, Merral felt much the same about Prebendant Delastro. When he went out among regulars he did much that was good and Merral felt that his talks on the importance of prayer, sacrifice, and resisting evil were a useful counterbalance to the rather mechanical and unspiritual business of soldiering.

However there were some emphases that troubled Merral. Delastro would often talk to the troops about a "holy war" and his preaching often seemed to draw its inspiration from the bloodier passages of the Old Covenant wars. He also seemed obsessed with the envoy. Vero (who seemed to know these things) mentioned that the prebendant was researching the matter of angels in the Library. Also, like Clemant, the prebendant seemed increasingly dubious about Vero.

About a month after the memorial service Merral and Delastro met by accident in a corridor of the Planetary Administration building, just outside of Delastro's office.

His assistants quietly moved out of earshot.

"Your sentinel friend seems to go out of his way to avoid me," the prebendant complained.

"Well, I don't see much of him either."

"Let me ask you a question," the prebendant said, his green eyes narrowing and his voice dropping to a whisper. "How much do we know about this Vero—this mysterious Mr. V.?"

"What do you mean?"

Delastro's long fingers tapped his staff. "We must consider all possibilities. We must be as 'wise as serpents.' When did he first arrive on Farholme?"

"Two, three days before I met him on Nativity's Eve."

"Hmm. Had you heard of him before?"

"No. Of course not. But Brenito had."

"Brenito is dead. Rather convenient that. And remind me, Commander, when did this intruder ship land?"

"Two days before Nativity."

"Hmm. The *same* time." Delastro stared at Merral as if inviting him to make a connection. He then turned on his heel, summoned his followers with an imperious gesture of the fingers, and walked rapidly on.

αΩαΩα

Two days later Vero delivered his proposal to lock down the Library and the Admin-Net in the event of the arrival of more intruders. Merral reviewed it, decided it made good sense, and summoned a meeting with Corradon and Clemant. There, Vero made his case, pointing out the need to shut down both systems instantly and demonstrating a model of the system that would be employed.

"W-we encrypt the data in the Library so it cannot be physically seized. So from now on anyone accessing the Library gets the data through an invisible decryption process. Once we detect an intrusion, the decryption system is switched off. If there is a serious attempt to get into the Library, we destroy the decryption unit and the Library data is locked."

Vero pulled a matte gray wafer out of his pocket and held it up. "This key holds the decryption files so that the system will only be unlocked by its being physically inserted into the mechanism. And because the decryption is based on a code at the molecular level, it is utterly unique. There is no possibility of making a duplicate or of finding it by trial and error."

Corradon frowned and looked at his advisor as if asking for guidance.

Clemant, who had been staring at the key, shifted his gaze to Vero. "And who, Sentinel, would hold this key?" There was an almost combative edge to his words. Merral was reminded that some expression of tension between them now occurred at almost every meeting.

For a few seconds, Vero returned Clemant's gaze, as if trying to prove he was not intimidated, then turned to Corradon. "W-why, the representative, of course."

"And if, despite all that, they try to force their way into the system?"

"It wouldn't help them, even if they could. But I suggest, reluctantly, that we would destroy the Library files to be safe."

"Destroy them? Are you serious?" There was incredulity in Clemant's voice.

"That does, well . . . seem rather severe," Corradon added.

"I am utterly serious."

Clemant shook his head. "Sentinel, that would be an act of madness. I refuse to consider it."

Vero leaned back in his chair. "B-but look at it another way. If the enemy seizes the Library, they would know everything about the Assembly. They would have vital strategic information. In fact, *not* to destroy the Library would be to b-betray the Assembly."

A long, heavy silence followed and as it continued, Merral knew that Vero had won his point. That was confirmed when, a week after the discussion,

Corradon announced in one of his weekly talks that a temporary loss of the Library in the future could not be ruled out and that people might want to prepare for that eventuality.

Reflecting on it later, Merral decided that while Vero had won, it was apparently a painful victory. Afterward he avoided direct confrontation, seeming instead to work even more behind the scenes than he had hitherto. His appearances became increasingly rare and erratic and the watchwords of his lifestyle seemed to be secrecy and unpredictability.

ᘓᘓᘓᘓᘓ

During this time Merral saw very little of his other friends. Perena always seemed to be away flying and Anya was busy at the Ecology Center, still apparently hoping for a breakthrough on the Krallen.

But shortly after the decision about the Library, Merral attended a meeting where Anya was present. At a coffee break they drifted apart from the crowd and stared at each other.

"Any progress on Krallen behavior?" he asked, trying to find a safe topic. *We have so many issues—so much to fear, so much to hope for. But do I dare to hope?*

"In theory."

"I hear the word *theory* too much. But go on."

"Your evidence, and that of the soldiers at Fallambet, is that there was a pack of twelve. If they operate in twelves as a rule, that's very suggestive."

"It is?"

"Twelve gives them multiple attack options. They can split up into sixes and attack from two points of the compass, into fours and attack from three directions, or into threes and attack from all four sides."

"Thanks," Merral said, suppressing a shudder. "I hope that information stays theoretical. Anything else?"

"Yes. They are regimented. And while that is effective, there is a price to be paid."

"Which is?"

"Initiative. They have no imagination; they operate on formulas. And the need to operate in groups probably slows them down. In a battle they may need to constantly regroup." She shrugged her shoulders. "But that's theory too."

There was an awkward pause between them.

"Have you seen your sister recently?" Merral asked, trying to start a new conversation.

"Last time I met her, she was in orbit." She shook her head, looking puzzled.

"I hadn't heard that."

"It's a joke, Commander Tree Man. I mean that she was in her own little world."

"I see." Merral paused. "Do you understand her?"

"Me?" Anya seemed to stare into the distance before focusing her sky blue eyes on him. "No. We are very different. And you know, what worries me is that I never used to find those differences an issue. But I do now. I get irritated with her, because I don't understand her."

She sighed. "Everything's changing, Merral. You, me, our world. And I don't like it."

◯◯◯◯◯

Merral found that the tensions in relationships that Anya had remarked on were heartbreakingly displayed in his family. He tried to keep in touch with his three sisters, all of whom lived some distance from either Ynysmant or Isterrane, but they now seemed increasingly preoccupied with their own worlds of children and friends. It was as if faced with a crisis of this magnitude, all they could do was turn their back on it and retreat into a familiar world.

He kept more closely in touch with his mother and father, although he found the widening gulf between them all too evident. They took to calling him separately and informing him about their spouse's shortcomings (and in his mother's case, those of her daughters as well). After these conversations Merral often found himself close to tears, but whether with grief or frustration, he could not tell.

His relationship—or lack of it—with Isabella also proved a continuing trial. He had little direct contact with her, but they did meet at a conference for wardens held in Isterrane. She had come with Enatus and sat next to him at the table. Merral noticed how often during the discussions the warden would tilt his head to her with a worried look and mutter something that was obviously a question. Isabella would lean toward him, whisper in his ear, and he would nod agreement.

For some time, she and Enatus were preoccupied by a speaker and Merral was able to watch her unobserved. As he did he felt a faint pang of his old affection. It came to him as an intriguing thought that, if this crisis could be resolved, perhaps things might be put right between them. However, when they met at the reception later that evening, he realized that she had still not forgiven him.

Isabella, wearing a blue suit of intimidating elegance, curved her lips into a facsimile of a smile, put stiff arms around Merral's shoulders, and gave him an icy kiss on the cheek.

"How lovely to see you again," she whispered through clenched teeth. "We do miss our hero in his hometown."

"Nice to see you, Isabella," he replied and unable to stop himself, added, "I hear it's in good hands."

She stepped back and looked at him with fixed smile that seemed a mere hairbreadth away from a snarl.

"Ynysmant needs all the help it can get," she said. "I have to contend with Vero's brown-clad buffoons running everywhere and this extraordinary Urban Defense Planning Team scaring everyone. The whole thing is becoming like a circus. And *you*, of course, give me no help at all." Then with a toss of the head she walked away.

⬭⬭⬭⬭⬭

However worrying the internal changes in Farholme were, Merral tried not to let them distract him from his one great concern—the looming arrival of the intruders and war.

His concern was deepened by a visit to Jorgio late one hot afternoon with towering thunderheads building up far off in the bay.

The old man had settled in at Brenito's house. The garden was well maintained and, despite uncommonly dry summer weather, still looked green. Merral and Jorgio took tea together under a large wooden sunshade at the end of the garden while Lloyd fed fresh grass to Mottle, a dappled mare in a newly fenced-off paddock.

"It is good to see you, Mr. Merral," Jorgio said, wiping his heavy mouth.

"I should come more often. The house looks as if it's being well looked after."

Vero had designated two men to manage the place and to catalog Brenito's vast accumulation of artifacts and manuscripts. They had also been instructed to watch over Jorgio and keep him safe.

Jorgio twisted his thick neck to look at the house. "Yes. The men help me keep it clean. So many papers though. I gather Mr. Vero is looking for something?"

"Yes," Merral said, reluctant to hide anything from a man who knew so much. "There is a small possibility that somewhere in there lies more information on the ending of the Rebellion. And we think that could cast some light on who the intruders are."

"The Rebellion and General William Jannafy . . . Jannafy." Jorgio pro-

nounced the name slowly as if chewing over it. "An old name and a bad one."
He moved his tongue around his rough teeth. "*Tut.* The past coming back.
But evil is like weeds, Mr. Merral. You reckon as you've got rid of them, but
they come back. Roots, they have." He tapped his cup with a grubby finger.
"Either that or seeds. One day, the Lord will get rid of all the weeds. The
Book says that. But till then we can always expect them."

"A helpful thought. Have you had any more dreams?"

"Yes." The old man looked away, but not before Merral saw a fleeting
expression of fear. "Those footsteps are clearer now. I can hear their feet." He
stared at Merral, his tawny eyes full of distress. "I hope as your defenses are
ready. They'll be here soon."

"You'd better pray, my old friend," Merral said, feeling the tiniest flutter of
panic. "We will need all the help we can get. Can you tell me anything else?"

Jorgio wiped a bead of sweat off his forehead.

"Only as I've started seeing numbers."

"Numbers?"

"A whole wall of numbers. As high as that tree. No, higher—stretching
into the sky. Not just ordinary numbers, but well . . . numbers with letters
and squiggles. What's the word?"

"Algebra? Equations? Formulas?"

"Formulas. That's it."

"Do you understand what they mean?"

"Bless you, Mr. Merral, that's something I have never understood.
Numbers, yes. Letters, yes. But letters *and* numbers? Doesn't make no sense.
And there's thousands of them."

"And do you—how shall I say it?—*sense* what they are about?"

"I really don't know as I do." His frown was one of deep puzzlement.
"Oh, Mr. Merral, ignore it. It may be nothing." He picked up the teapot.
"Let's talk of something else. I can't believe how terribly dry the soil here is.
It's too sandy."

But the frown did not leave his face.

◌◌◌◌◌

So the summer passed. As the days began to perceptibly shorten, the weather
became extraordinarily hot and humid and every few days frantic thunder-
storms would sweep in from the sea and lash the town. For Merral, who
found even the ordinary summer weather of Isterrane uncomfortably warm
and humid, the heat-wave conditions were most unpleasant. The office was
climate-conditioned, but not the suite. At night he would frequently awake
to find himself covered in sweat.

To take his mind off the heat and his concerns about what lay ahead, Merral returned on several evenings to the simulated world of the castle tree. It was not a total success, but he tried to force himself to find relief in his world. Deciding that it was time to make the tree breed, he worked with the code and soon had red male flowers blossoming on the trunk and yellow female ones on the upper and outer leaves. He was impressed with the effect: from a distance, the tree looked like a flaming volcano and when the simulated wind blew, the effect was magical. Soon insects pollinated the flowers and great knobby seed pods the size of a small child developed on the upper branches. He paused the simulation, adjusted the code, and restarted growth. The pods split open and around scores of fist-sized seeds, wings extended and hardened. When autumnal winds blew a day later, the seeds broke free of the pod and glided away, traveling downwind for hours. Merral pursued them, noting with approval that a number had fallen into fertile soil.

Despite satisfaction that his creation was developing so well, Merral felt uncomfortable about it. It came to him that he found his simulation's untarnished simplicity preferable to the dirtied complexities of the real world. *And it is not just that. This abstract sterility is free not just of sound and smell, but also of all ultimate consequence. Unlike the real world, where every decision counts, nothing here really matters.*

When he probed his feelings on why he wished to linger in his creation, he felt a defiance within him that surprised him. *Why shouldn't I spend time there? My chosen career has ended, many of my relationships are in bad shape, my days are an endless succession of appallingly hard decisions, and my future is overshadowed by the threat of war.* But the very energy of his protest unnerved him and, as a result, Merral decided to restrict the time he spent in the simulation to no more than five hours a week.

Toward the middle of summer, inside the door of an unfinished apartment block, Vero waited for Perena to turn up. *I wish I wasn't feeling so on edge. We made our decision. Why can't I keep to it? Why does she crop up in my thoughts so much?*

Suddenly she was there. On impulse he glanced at his diary adjunct. She was, of course, exactly on time.

There was an awkward moment as they faced each other. In the end Perena kissed him briefly on the cheek.

"How are you?" she asked, stepping back to look at him.

Vero took off his glasses and put them in a breast pocket. "You want the honest answer, P.? Tired."

And she looks tired too. But none the worse for that.

Perena's nod was brief. "I understand."

She looked around with the quiet, wry grin that he loved. "An unfinished housing block? I am intrigued. I thought your office was elsewhere."

"It is, formally. But this is where it really is. Now, what I'm about to show you, you mustn't speak of." As he said it, he realized with dismay that it sounded like he didn't trust her. "I m-mean I can rely on you. It's just that . . ."

"We have to be careful," she said, finishing his thought and ending with a sigh, one that seemed to come from deep within. "Vero, I do not dislike secrecy. I love the strategy of chess: the bluff and the counterbluff. But I never realized until recently how, as a way of life, it could wear you down. But lead on."

Vero led her to a lift. "Oh," he said gesturing to the ceiling, "a warning. We're being watched. Surveillance."

"Another sad necessity."

Once inside he called out, "The foundations."

There was a chime of acknowledgment and the lift started down.

"A deep basement," Perena said twenty seconds later. "We're still descending." As she spoke, the lift slowed to stop.

"Welcome to the underworld. Based on an original idea by Perena Lewitz."

"Is that credit or blame?"

The door opened to reveal a low, featureless tiled tunnel that ran off either side of them.

"It is something of a labyrinth. Follow me. Do you get claustrophobic, P.?" he asked as they walked.

"Thankfully not. I spend much of my life in a metal can."

"Like a sardine."

"The fish?" He heard the puzzlement in her voice.

"It's an old saying. I think they must have kept them as pets in metal tanks. Oh, never mind."

Vero tugged open a heavy door in the left-hand wall. Beyond were more branching corridors, but with more light and more noise: the purposeful chatter of people, the buzz of electrics, the thuds and hammering of fabrication.

"This is where we do the serious stuff," Vero said.

Over the next ten minutes he showed her the labs, the rooms with bunks, and the storage spaces, then introduced her to some of the people there.

Perena seemed to scrutinize everything, especially the items in his office: his folding bed, the picture of his family on the wall, the crowded desk, the stacked files, and the bubbling coffee percolator. Her sharp questions showed her grappling with all she saw.

"Is there surveillance here?"

"No. I see no need to watch myself." As he said it, he felt the humor fell flat.

Perena's smile was merely the ghost of one. "Good. If you did, I would really worry."

She walked over to his shelves and peered at some of the bound volumes, running a fingernail under the title of one of the books: *Early Twenty-First Century Warfare: An Overview*. She pronounced the words clumsily and Vero remembered that her Historic was not English.

"Sometimes I spend days and nights here," Vero said, feeling a need to justify himself. "Brenito's place is too far away. . . . Would you like a coffee? I drink too much of the stuff."

"Please."

She's troubled. He handed her a mug of coffee.

"What do you think?"

"Impressive. You are very talented. You are, in your way, a genius."

"Thank you. But you're worried."

"Am I that transparent?" She pouted.

"Where you are concerned, I am very sensitive."

He saw a flash of something in her eyes. *Pain.*

She shook her head. "No, Vero. *Please*. We buried that."

"For the time being."

"No!" There was almost a desperation to her tone that caught him by surprise. "I can't. . . . I don't think it's wise to hold out any hope there. That might badly betray us."

Now it was his turn to sigh. "Point taken. But you worry about what?"

He was aware of her eyes probing his face. "I worry about you and this place—this project. Always being underground, being secretive, scheming. I worry that you have drifted into this underworld and will stay here—that it will possess you. A permanently secretive and subterranean Vero."

Her words bothered him. "Do you think that is a danger?"

"Don't you?"

"Well, I suppose so. I take your warning seriously, P. I really do."

"You are so involved in all this."

She is right. It has become part of my life.

"P., the way I see it, there are two things. The first is that I have no family here, no roots—just good friends. I'm not Merral. He could go back to his family, Forestry, and Ynysmant at a moment's notice. I can't. So this project *is* my life now. So there's that."

He saw from her expression and the slight move of her head that she understood. "And the other thing is that this is the great battle of our age and I have been thrust into the heart of it. I have lain awake at night worrying that we might fail because I have been lazy or careless."

"In many ways that's commendable. But the evil around us is pervasive and so subtle that I think we are all at risk. You, me, and even Merral. We must take care."

There was silence that lasted for several minutes.

"Vero," she said softly, "how badly are we in trouble?"

"Badly. S-so badly that I don't even know how b-badly."

"Tell me."

"We have inadequate weapons and, above all, inadequate information. We are faced with a vague and terrifying enemy. We need a breakthrough, P."

"Then we must pray we get one."

"I do pray. But any news on your side?"

"No. But . . ." She paused, as if unable to continue. "I have thought of something recently. A wild idea. A way that, if we have no choice, we might try. But it is a way that, if things fell out right, might just work."

There was a silence that he soon realized she was not going to break.

"I remember the envoy's words," he said, "about a 'costly way', a way 'that only the very bravest will take.' Is this what you are talking about?"

Her face was stern. "Perhaps. I don't want to say any more." She looked at the wall clock. "I need to go."

He led her above ground to the door of the unfinished apartments. There, her hand on the glass of the door, she turned to him. "What does Merral think about your underground base?"

"He doesn't know."

She seemed surprised. "Why not?"

"He's too close to Clemant and the others."

Perena nodded. "This is what I feared. It's how it begins, isn't it?"

"What?"

"We lie to our enemies and then—for the best reasons, of course—we lie to each other."

"So, you think I should tell him?"

"No." There was a sad weariness in her tone. "But do you see that if it goes on like this we are in trouble?" Her look seemed probing. "And drastic measures may be needed."

"Such as?"

"That's my secret." She kissed him on the cheek and walked swiftly away.

ᴏᏫᴏᏫᴏ

One evening in late July, Merral and Luke went for a walk along one of the promontories protruding into Isterrane Bay. The light was fading and the sky was full of a bulging heaviness of gray clouds from within which thunder rolled every few minutes.

"How are you Merral? Honestly."

"Struggling, Luke."

"Any specifics?"

"The fact is that we simply do not know enough about what we face. We have recovered almost nothing from that ship at Fallambet. We know almost nothing about our enemy. They *may* be called the Dominion and they *may* be run by a lord-emperor. That's about it."

"I am aware of that. It troubles me too."

"And the little that we do know suggests our weapons are inadequate. We know we can't stop their ships in space and we suspect we can't stop the Krallen on the ground. It is not a happy scenario."

There was a long brooding silence. "You—*we*—need help. Don't we?"

"Yes. Very much."

"And are you praying for that help?"

"In truth, not as much as I should." The words were painful, but Merral was reminded that he had agreed to accountability. "I suppose I live in the hope that we'll come up with some technological development that will save us. That's where the focus is." He hesitated. "I suppose."

There was a long silence in which he felt guilty.

"The technology may help, but I would think praying for an answer is a pretty good idea." Luke's words were gentle. "Wouldn't you?"

"Yes. I shall more specifically ask for help."

"Good. And I will too. If truth be told here, I haven't prayed as much about it either. And it's a problem I have known about. I think we all have."

"One other thing, Merral," Luke said as they walked. "I've seen Clemant's anomalies map."

"And?"

"It's bad and getting worse. But trust me, the reality is far worse."

"How?"

In some unspoken mutual agreement, they stopped walking.

"The map's too shallow." Luke stared out to sea. "It only measures surface phenomena. It takes no account of what's happening beneath all this. But I'm talking regularly with the soldiers and some of the congregation leaders. What they all report—and what I see—is that there's a growing spiritual coldness and carelessness. An apathy, a dryness. It's amazing, after all we have gone through, and all we face. But we see it in congregations, we see it in people. There's no joy, no spontaneity. It's a sort of formalism."

In the gathering gloom, Merral was aware of Luke's dark eyes peering at him. "Are you surprised?"

"No. To be honest, I have seen it in myself. My spiritual life was boosted by the memorial service, but otherwise, I guess it's been a slow decline. That's part of the issue with prayer."

"I can sympathize. But the trend is alarming. We are being drained."

"Yes. But if it's any consolation, Luke, we don't have long to wait before the crisis is upon us."

The chaplain nodded. "Six weeks they say?"

"Less. Say five. At maximum."

There was a grumble of thunder.

The chaplain sighed. "It's a strange thing to say, Merral—it may even be morally wrong—but I wish this war would come soon. The longer we have to wait, the less we will be what we once were. Where it counts, we weaken daily."

"I know. But we don't have long to wait." Merral gazed at the gray dullness of the clouds. "They are on their way. And they will be here soon."

"May God be merciful to us," Luke said quietly.

"Amen," Merral responded.

As they walked back, he said, "Every morning, Luke, I tell myself that perhaps today will be the day that I get a call from Space Affairs that they have spotted new intruders. And when that message comes it will change everything."

But the message that did come was very different.

14

Two days later, the chime of his diary woke Merral in the middle of the night. He shook himself and peered at the clock on the diary screen.

One thirty-five. An extraordinary time for a message. Has the ship been sighted?

His pulse quickened when he saw the message: *Unrecognized caller.*

"That shouldn't happen." This was his private line. Only those who knew how to reach him used it.

"This is Merral D'Avanos."

The screen stayed blank and a voice spoke. "Greetings, Commander Merral D'Avanos. I am Betafor Allenix."

Merral's first impression was that the voice was odd; it was high pitched but had a strange, rather glassy timbre. The way the words were spoken was distinctive too; they were precisely spaced and apparently pronounced with care.

"Allenix? I'm sorry, that name means nothing to me."

"We have not been . . ." There was a pause almost as if the caller was thinking of the word. "Introduced. I am on Ilakuma Island. I have with me an injured human being who needs urgent medical treatment. His flesh has some sort of . . . infection and I am anxious for him to be treated. I wish to make a deal."

"There must be a hospital there." Merral paused, perplexed at the idea of striking a deal on a matter of medical treatment. Then he realized to his surprise that he had no idea whether the caller was male or female. *Male,* he tentatively decided. "Sir, I'm afraid I don't see that this has anything to do with me."

"A correction please. My preference is to be treated as a female person. It is a grammatical convention that I value."

I have an insane midnight caller. Merral sat up on the edge of the bed. *I must see Maria Dalphey to find out how they have managed to call me and to make sure it doesn't recur.*

He was about to interrupt when the caller continued. "And this matter *is* something to do with you. The sick man is Kezurmati Azeras. He is the sarudar—you would say perhaps second officer—of the True Freeborn vessel *Slave of Rahllman's Star.* This is the ship that was destroyed. He and I are the sole . . . survivors."

Overwhelmed by so much that made no sense Merral latched on to a single phrase. "*Slave of Rahllman's Star?* Whoever you are, you're mistaken. There is no such vessel, at least not here—"

He stopped, suddenly aware that his hands were shaking. The words *Ilakuma, True Freeborn vessel,* and *sole survivors* flashed in his brain.

He hit the mute button on the diary. "Lloyd!"

As a heavy thud and a frantic clatter from the adjacent room confirmed that he had been heard, he toggled the mute off.

"Miss Betafor," Merral said slowly, his mouth peculiarly dry, "let's take this step by step. First, who are you?"

"Betafor will suffice. I am an Allenix unit." The voice *was* odd, he realized, hearing now a strange synthetic edge to it.

There were rapid footsteps in the corridor outside. The door was flung open and the light came on. Blinking, Merral looked up to see Lloyd standing in the doorway, dressed in shorts and a vest and clutching the ugly double-barreled gun that was his current weapon of choice.

Merral raised a finger to his lips and beckoned him over. "Please explain, Betafor. Wait! I'm going to record this. Is this okay?"

"Yes. I assumed you were recording. Or is this an Assembly protocol I am not aware of?"

"Conversations are considered private unless permission is given."

"Even in war?"

"That's an interesting issue."

"I give permission. Now listen, there is a lot to explain. I am an Allenix unit. We are used throughout the True Freeborn and Dominion worlds for observation, negotiation, and translation. I am one of the two such units that were on the vessel."

"You're a machine?" *If so, this is not at all like we have. Our machines never mimic human speech in this way. The technology protocols prohibit it.*

"Commander, I prefer that the term *machine* not be used."

Lloyd's mouth gaped wide.

"I am best described as an . . . intelligent synthetic organism. Other terms such as a *synthetic person* or even a *nonbiological organism* might be usable. We could discuss the terminology at length another time. But you will find it easier to deal with me if you treat me as you would a human being, a *female* human being." There was an edge of exasperation in the tone.

"Let me see you."

"Later. There are other things to do now."

Merral puzzled over the idea of a machine that could express emotion. "Please continue." He turned to Lloyd and mouthed, *Get Vero. Fast!*

His aide nodded and slipped out of the room.

The strange voice spoke again. "I have a sick man here who needs help. I do not have suitable medicines. I do not understand ailments of the human flesh. A condition of the arrangement—the deal—is that the knowledge that the sarudar and I exist is kept secret. Only the absolute minimum number of people must know."

Merral realized that this machine—he found it hard to think of it as a female—had an excellent command of Communal. "Why?"

"I will explain. Let me elaborate the condition. My researches indicate that the general survey craft *Nesta Lamaine* is now repaired. I suggest that tomorrow Captain Lewitz and a copilot of her choice, fly you, a doctor, and Sentinel Enand south to Ilakuma tomorrow. All are to—"

"Wait! How do you know who we are? And how did you get access to me?"

"Commander, I know these things because most of your . . . communications systems are still open."

"Oh," Merral replied, suddenly feeling appallingly vulnerable.

"Good. Now—"

"No!" cried Merral, suddenly almost overwhelmed by his memories of what happened at Fallambet Lake. "Why should I trust you or anything from that foul ship? I was on board it. I saw what was there. It was evil."

There was a long silence. "Commander, I understand your concern. I need to explain more things. There have been . . . humans that you had no knowledge of far beyond you in space. Until around half a standard year ago, there were two groups: the True Freeborn and the Dominion of Lord-Emperor Nezhuala. They fought and the Dominion won. But at the last battle, a group of men from the True Freeborn seized a Dominion ship, the *Rahllman's Star*, and fled here. The sarudar is the only survivor of those men. It is the Dominion who are your enemy. And they are coming."

"A moment! I need time to absorb this." Merral tried desperately to assemble the ideas—two human groups, a war between them, the ship being stolen—into some coherent pattern. Yet as he thought about it, he realized that it made some sort of sense. *The crew had been hiding, but not just from us.*

"You need to talk to the sarudar about that ship and what was on it," said Betafor. "As for myself, you must understand that I am only a machine. I was merely a . . . translator. I am programmed to serve." There was a hint of pleading in the voice.

"But that programming may continue. You may still serve the True Freeborn as you call them."

"I do not. The destruction of the ship has released me from their service. You will find me trustworthy."

"Perhaps. This man—I didn't get the name—why should I trust him?"

"His name is Kezurmati Azeras and his . . . title is sarudar. Among the True Freeborn the first name is . . . was . . . rarely used outside the family. If you meet him, he will respond to Sarudar Azeras. As for why you should trust him, you must decide that. But learn this, you and he have a common enemy, as I now do. The Dominion will destroy us all. That is why we are hiding and that is why this must be kept utterly secret. It is only because the sarudar is close to dying that I have taken the risk of contacting you."

"I see," Merral said as he stared at the diary. *Can I be sure I'm not hallucinating? Or that I'm not still asleep and dreaming?*

"We need your help, and in return we will help you."

"How?"

"I offer you a deal."

"What sort of deal?" Merral heard suspicion in his voice.

"In return for the successful medical treatment, I offer you and the Assembly advice and assistance that you will find useful. I expect the sarudar will do the same, if he recovers."

"What sort of advice and assistance?"

"You have a . . . crisis, Commander." Betafor paused. "Your worst fears are justified. The Lord-Emperor Nezhuala knows that you exist and that access to you is now possible. You can expect a visit from the Dominion very soon. As a world, you are unprepared for this. I can offer you advice that will help. You need me. Heal Sarudar Azeras, keep us secret and safe, and we will give you help."

"Betafor, in the Assembly we do not 'strike a deal' over injured people. We will do all we can to heal this man. We would do it anyway. I'm interested in any information you can offer, but I won't negotiate over a sick man."

There was a pause as if Merral's statement required thought. "Hardly a rational response, but I accept your offer. But do you agree to the condition of secrecy?"

"Wait." Merral paused. "A few more people must know. My aide, Lloyd, a biologist, Anya."

"Anya Lewitz?"

"Yes."

"As you wish, but no more. That is already seven people. But do you agree to the deal?"

"Wait." *What do I say? Come on, Vero!*

"Wait for what?"

"Tell me about yourself. We have no such machin—intelligent synthetic organisms."

"I know. We Allenix are built to serve. I first served the Dominion and was taken by the True Freeborn and served them. But I am now prepared to serve the Assembly."

"I see." *I don't. Not at all.* "What does it mean to serve?"

"I may not understand your question correctly. I understand *serve* to mean that I obey you as long as my own survival is not threatened."

I need to think about that. To keep the conversation going, he asked, "Where could we meet you?"

"Two hundred meters east of the point where the Monatombo and Keletai Rivers join is a large flat rock big enough for a general survey craft to land on. You may find it easier to land there by daylight. I will be present a hundred meters to the east of your landing spot at exactly 1900 hours tomorrow local time. That is 1500 hours, Central Menaya time. I will reveal my location by a series of short flashes of white light."

"That's very soon. It gives us barely sixteen hours."

"I think you can arrange it. You are, after all, a commander." There was a trace of sarcasm in the voice.

Can a machine be sarcastic?

Just then Lloyd slipped in and mouthed that Vero was on his way, but would be another ten minutes.

"Betafor, you mentioned Sentinel Enand. Can you call back in half an hour?"

"As you wish. But time is limited."

The line went dead.

⊃⊂⊃⊂⊃⊂⊃

Merral threw a few more clothes on, brewed some strong coffee, and then, his mind in utter turmoil, replayed the conversation. *We have a claim that an intelligent machine and a man have survived the destruction of the intruder ship. It is either the longed-for and prayed-for breakthrough or something far nastier. God, give me the wisdom to know which it is.*

Merral then called up a map and imagery of Ilakuma on the wallscreen. Zooming to the highest resolution available, he found the rock slab at the river junction. It lay in the depths of a deep westward-facing valley in the heart of a rugged and highly fractured massif, and seemed almost overwhelmed by thick rain forest. It was at least a hundred kilometers from the island's only settlement—Port Angby.

"Good place to hide," Lloyd said and Merral could only agree.

Ten minutes after the call had ended, Vero rushed in looking weary and sweating. "A problem?" he asked.

"I've had the most extraordinary message. It's hard to make sense of it. Listen to this."

Vero listened wide-eyed to the conversation, his jaw moving up and down as if it had an independent life.

When the message ended, Merral said, "So, we have twenty minutes until the next call. What do we do?"

Vero looked first at Merral, then at the diary, and then back at Merral. "I h-had presumed I'd prepared for every eventuality." There was a stunned tone to his voice. "But not th-this."

"But is it genuine? And can we trust this . . . machine?"

Vero made no answer, but bounded to his feet and began pacing the floor. "My friend," he said, his voice almost quivering with excitement, "I feel like my b-brain is bursting. There is just too much here: survivors of the ship, intelligent machines, above all." He looked up, his brown eyes glistening. "The opportunity of information—information that we vitally need, but we thought we would never have. I think this may be the answer to our prayers. Oh, let it be genuine! And let it be in time." He paused, raising a hand. "Ilakuma. Of course. That explains that anomaly."

"But how could they have survived the blast?" Merral asked.

"The social anomalies at Ilakuma predate the destruction of the ship. They must have been there already. We knew there was a ferry craft."

Merral caught a faint frown on Lloyd's face and gestured for him to speak.

"Sir, Mr. V.," the large man said slowly, "look, I hate to say this, but can we rule out that this is a trap? Let's say they are survivors as they claim, right? But we destroyed their ship. These guys—well this guy and this thing—may wish for revenge."

"A setup," Vero said before turning to Merral with a hint of a smile. "Behold, another man who is immersing himself in pre-Intervention litera-ture. I have trained him well. But it is a disturbing point and one that had occurred to me. My friend, what do you think?"

"I was working on vaguely parallel lines. After all, I have already met synthetic creatures who were intelligent."

"Ah, the Krallen," Vero said, with an uncomfortable look.

"There is another matter," Merral added. "This thing wants a deal. Do

I have the authority to negotiate with it? Isn't that something that should be decided by . . . I don't know . . . the representatives?"

Vero's face twisted into a look of unease. "Perhaps, my friend, but this is a gray area. Our Assembly habits of open debate and dialogue are not suited for a time of war."

His troubled tone reminded Merral that a lot of what his friend had done had been without any higher authorization. Then Vero spoke again. "Were Corradon more on top of things, I think you would discuss it with him. But he isn't. So I think it is best to consider it a military matter. Therefore, it falls under your authority."

"So being commander puts me above all normal authorities?"

"In matters of security. It is one of the dangers of war."

"It's hardly satisfactory."

"War never is."

"Very well." Merral sighed. "When this thing calls back, let's have a look at it."

"I agree."

At that moment the diary chimed.

"This is Betafor. I need a decision."

"Betafor," Merral asked. "We want to see you; can you go to visual?"

"Yes."

"Then we will too."

The wallscreen suddenly lit up with an image of an unevenly mottled green face with large dark gray eyes. Merral struggled to put together what he saw. Whether seen from the side or the front, the shape of the upper part of the face was triangular, narrowing to a point that would have been a nose on an animal. The lower part of the face, below a broad, thick-lipped mouth, was much shallower. The creature's eyes had a hint of lids. Behind the eyes were set a pair of triangular ears. The overall effect was closest to that of a dog. Yet the mottled skin with its fine bumps and indentations seemed closer to some sort of inorganic fabric than animal flesh.

As the being moved its head around as if to allow them a better view, a narrow neck could be seen.

The view zoomed out to show Betafor sitting on her haunches rather like a begging dog or a kangaroo might do. Merral found it hard to make any immediate sense of her torso, but noted thin arms with long fingers and a tail that tapered away from her body to a fine point. In an instant he saw that she wore a waistcoat or sleeveless jacket made from some heavy, but smooth-textured cloth. *It wears clothes!*

"Are you a Krallen?" Merral asked, seeing both differences and similarities to the beings he had seen on the ship.

The creature lifted its head with a mechanical smoothness and stared at him. "Krallen? No. I am . . . puzzled how you know their name. No, I am not." The tone was almost agitated.

Merral glimpsed bare rock behind the creature and the thought came to him that the setting was perhaps a cave.

"If I were a Krallen, I would not have . . . the brains to find you. If I were a Krallen, I would have killed Sarudar Azeras."

Merral saw the lips move, the one soft feature on an otherwise unyielding face. The creature's handling of Communal was good. There was a noticeable deliberateness and precision to the phrasing. Still struggling as to whether he should treat Betafor as a machine or a person, Merral had a sudden insight that there was more to this than grammar. *All our dealings are founded on whether we relate to each other as things or beings.*

"All of you, learn this. We, the Allenix, came first. . . . We were made by men in . . . the earliest days of the Freeborn." The creature's tone was firm, almost harsh. "We were created as watchers, translators, and negotiators. We were given intelligence and language so that we might serve and we have developed since. The Krallen came after us. They were modeled on us, but were made to be killers. They are stupid. They do not speak—they have only hatred and cunning. We loathe them."

Curiously, it was that last phrase, *we loathe them,* that made Merral's mind up that he was dealing with a person. There was such a sense of outrage behind it that he felt that what he had said had been taken as an insult. *And if you can feel insulted, you are surely a person.*

Betafor moved toward whatever was imaging her. "Look at me," she said, extending her forelimbs to show long, rounded, nail-less fingers. "Do I have metal alloy nails to claw flesh? Do I have sharpened fangs that can tear off limbs?" The creature moved her head forward on her long neck, opened her mouth and tilted it several ways, exposing only tiny, smooth, flat-topped teeth behind her strangely broad and flexible lips. "Do I have a toughened skin to protect me in battle?" She tilted upright, exposing the top of her chest through a gap in the fabric jacket. Although her skin was marked out by the same faint lines Merral had seen in the Krallen, it was very different. While they were covered mostly in semirigid tiles that gave their bodies an angular form, she was wrapped with softer tiles that gave her a rounder shape.

Her eyes opened and shut in a sort of leisurely blink. "Do I look like a killing machine?"

"No." *I do hope I'm right.* The chief emotion she aroused in him was curiosity, not fear.

"Good. I am an Allenix, not a Krallen. Now let us proceed. Will you come and help?"

"Show us this man," said Vero.

"Ah, Verofaza, the sentinel. We too were made to be sentinels."

Merral caught his friend's look of alarm. *How much does this creature know and if she knows so much, what does this say about our vulnerability?*

There was a pause.

"As you wish." The screen went blank and a few moments later an image of a man lying on some sort of bed appeared. His face was bearded and gaunt, and framed by long, matted black hair. A thin sheet covered his chest and legs and around his neck was some sort of medical dressing. His eyes were closed and his breathing was shallow and rapid.

"Not in good shape," Vero muttered.

The image shifted to Betafor.

"Will you come?"

In the silence that followed Lloyd and Vero turned to Merral.

They expect me to make the decision. "Betafor," he said slowly, "I want an assurance there will be no tricks."

"I promise. And I trust there must be no tricks from you."

"There will be none. We do not use tricks."

He realized that he had chosen. *So help me, God.* "Very well. I will do my best to be there. I cannot speak for the others. They must make their choice."

"Good. I will see you later today."

The screen went blank.

"I meant what I said." Merral's quiet words seemed to echo in the silence that followed. "I will go alone. I feel it is a risk that must be taken. We have prayed for help and I believe this may be it."

"You don't go anywhere without me, sir." Lloyd tapped his gun. "And some hardware."

Vero stared at the diary as if it gave an answer. "I will come too. I have my misgivings, but I too think this is the answer to our prayers."

"Who do we take as doctor? Felix Azhadi?"

Vero shook his head. "No, he's busy and he's FDF. I want to put clear water between us and them on this."

"'Clear water'?"

"Distance. The FDF is now too big to keep this quiet. Leave it to me. I'll call Perena. In the meantime, better get some sleep. Tomorrow may be a long day."

◇◇◇◇◇

"You realize, of course," Perena said at Isterrane airport the following morning, "that Ilakuma is one of the wettest parts of this planet?"

Merral stared at the large image that Lloyd held up against the fuselage of the *Nesta Lamaine,* seeing confirmation of her statement in the lurid green expanses of jungle and the white meshwork of foaming rivers.

"And that by seven tonight there will almost certainly be torrential rain? And that the Eligotal Highlands are one of the roughest areas on the planet? If I had to hide a ferry craft or a base, it's a place I would consider. There are cavities and holes here you could conceal a fleet in."

"Are you saying there may be some rough flying?" Vero asked, his face registering unease.

A look of amused sympathy appeared on Perena's face. "Only at the end. It'll be a four-hour flight. I'm staying within the atmosphere and taking it slow. But the seating that we have fitted into the hold is rather basic and doesn't absorb motion. So as a precaution, I suggest you just don't eat."

She turned to the stocky lady with dark brown hair who stood by Merral. "Sorry, Arabella, I should have warned you. Vero here doesn't travel well."

A smile spread across the broad face of Dr. Arabella Huangho. "I'll see what I can find in my bag. Infections and tropical diseases are my speciality but I may be able to help here. Tablet, injection, or suppository, Sentinel Enand? Or just a very large bag?"

Relieved that the newcomer seemed to be fitting in, Merral noticed Anya grinning and his heart gave a turn. *For all my resolve, I am still terribly fond of her.* For the hundredth time he cursed his public renunciation of relationships. *How unspeakably stupid to have taken a vow that, it now turns out, has been witnessed by almost the entire planet! Had I not chosen that route, I might, by now, have ended things with Isabella and been free to pursue my heart's desire. "You will pay a price for today's words,"* the envoy said. *Today, seeing Anya, I sense something of that cost.*

There was a gesture from the cockpit window.

"Deanna is summoning us," Perena said. "Time to go." She shook her head at Lloyd as he picked up a very large and evidently heavy bag whose fabric bulged around a number of ominous looking tubes. "And Sergeant Enomoto, can you keep the safety catches on?"

"Aye, aye, Captain."

Perena and Merral were the last left outside. Perena stood back and made what was clearly a last visual check.

"So here we are again, Captain," Merral said. "A new mission."

"Just so," came the somber reply. "I've studied the recording of your conversation. I think you made the right decision. It may be an answer to our prayers, but I'm uneasy. I just think . . ."

"What?"

"There's something not right about this. Machine or not, something doesn't ring true."

"If it's a trap, we're terribly vulnerable."

"Yes. I wondered about putting a drone ship down first, but we don't have the time."

"Perena, are you scared?"

"Scared?" Perena's smile was unfathomable. "We talked about this before. There are many types of fear. Fear of failure, fear of not doing what is right, fear of dying. Are these all the same thing?"

"Good question. And what concerns you today?"

"Today? My primary concern is that none of us be killed. My secondary concern is about any loss or damage to the ship." She paused and when she spoke again she seemed to speak from a vast distance. "Or perhaps, more accurately, I'm most scared about the enemy achieving either of those things cheaply."

"Cheaply?"

"Merral, by all accounts, war will soon be upon us. We have limited resources. Speaking for myself, if I must lose my ship or my life, I would prefer to do so where it counts most." She ran a hand through her cropped hair.

"I see."

"Well then, let's fly."

As they flew south at high subsonic speed, Perena explained her strategy to Merral. On arrival at Ilakuma, they would circle high over the island for some time looking and listening for anything untoward. If there were no problems, she would then make a low, ground-hugging approach to the landing zone where she would hover long enough for Lloyd to leap out before taking off again. Only when Lloyd had given the all-clear would there be a full landing.

"One other thing," Perena said. "It's slightly unusual—actually it's unparalleled. As we go to land, I'm going to ask everyone who can get to a window to keep a watch for anything that might be an attack."

"Such as?"

"Bright lights, flashes, smoke trails from missiles. If you see anything, do two things: first, yell with directions—for instance, 'Flash at two o'clock.'"

"And second?" Merral asked.

There was a flicker of a smile. "Pray very hard."

Four hours out of Isterrane, Ilakuma came into view. The island was an impossibly jagged massif rising up out of a brilliant aquamarine sea. It looked as if it had been shattered with a continent-sized hammer to form a landscape dominated by sharp slivers of stone lying at every conceivable angle. Between the towering blades and needles of rock lay valleys in whose depths fine creamy lines of turbulent streams ran before finally reaching the sea, where they disgorged brown plumes of sediment. Clinging to this brutal stone framework was the dense greenness of the new jungle. From its knife-bladed summits high clouds blossomed.

After some minutes, Perena and Deanna conferred.

"No signals, Merral," Perena announced. "Not from the Eligotal Highlands. The usual electrical noises from the weather and background signals from Port Angby. Otherwise, silence."

"Any signs of a ship or a base? Any geophysical anomalies?"

"Nothing, Commander," Deanna said. "It's so rough, it's all anomalies."

"Very well. Go for landing."

They descended, heading out over the sea before swinging back toward the island. Merral looked ahead, seeing the island's profile in all its stark angularity and was struck by its resemblance to a heap of broken crockery.

Lloyd opened his bag and pulled out his big double-barreled gun. "A sort of shotgun," he explained as Dr. Huangho looked uneasily at him. "It discharges an intense blast of high-density pellets. You really don't want to be on the wrong side of it."

"No," she said with a frown and looked out of the window.

As they started the run in for the first landing, Merral sent Lloyd to the hold with his twin-muzzled weapon and a bag of weaponry while the others pressed their faces to the windows to look for any signs of hostility.

Merral watched the coral beach pass by and the jungle begin—an eruption of vibrant greenery. A thousand-meter-high cliff—high enough to block out the sky—loomed ahead. At its feet the jungle was littered with vast broken-off rock fragments, some the size of houses.

The survey craft veered around the cliff and followed the silver trail of a river that kept vanishing from view under wreaths of cloud.

When the *Nesta Lamaine* climbed and suddenly flicked to the right, Vero groaned in discomfort.

A ridge appeared dead ahead, and then with another jolt, they were over it.

"Thirty seconds, Lloyd," Perena's unflustered voice announced. "All eyes open for hostile activity."

As they began their descent, Merral stared intently, barely daring to breathe. *What would death look like here? A dirty column of smoke or a clean beam of light?*

He glimpsed a vast waterfall up a side valley, the fume of it rising until it blended with the clouds. With a stomach-heaving turn and descent they were down so low over the trees that Merral could see the branches. They flew past mudslides on the hills, red hemorrhages of soil bearing upended tangles of tree trunks.

An eagle dived out of the way.

"Five seconds."

As the ship banked again, Merral caught a glimpse of a rock platform ahead between two rivers.

There was the sound of hydraulics, a brief new rumble from the engines, a slight sawing jolt, and then the noise of movement from the hold.

"Lloyd is clear," Deanna announced, and the ship bounded skyward.

✕✕✕✕✕

Twenty minutes after Lloyd reported that he could see nothing around the landing zone to alarm him, the *Nesta Lamaine* landed on the rock slab.

Merral walked down the ramp, careful to avoid the still-steaming circles where the jet exhaust had struck the rock. Lloyd, his face covered in sweat, stood by a sharp-edged boulder, cradling his gun. A rocket launcher lay at his feet.

As Merral walked over to him, blinking in the brilliant sun, he was suddenly aware of the air: hot, incredibly humid, and reeking of the life and death of a million tons of vegetation.

He gazed around, his brain trying to take in the scene. Beyond the basalt slab they were on, the river raced past, tumbling into muddy foam as it plunged over rocks. Just above the river, the rain forest began—wall after towering wall of dense foliage in a hundred shades of green, and above that, gray daggers of rock rose into menacing clouds.

"Thanks, Lloyd. Well done."

Lloyd waved a fly away. "My job, sir. Had to be done. But I'm not confident we're safe. Could be an entire army watching us up there."

Merral gazed around again, aware of the sweat forming on him. Lloyd was right. He remembered the directions he had been given and looked to the east to where, barely a stone's throw away, the jungle began with a towering confusion of foliage. There, he told himself, in that barely glimpsed darkness, was where they would meet the strange creature.

"You don't like it, do you, Sergeant?" Merral asked.

"Sir, I wouldn't be doing my job if I didn't say I was uneasy. . . . Could be absolutely anything around. We have jungle on Tralescant, but not like this. This is *wild*."

A moment later Perena switched the turbines off, and one by one, the others emerged and stared at the scene.

Deanna took a quick look and then returned to the cockpit to stay at the controls.

Merral, mopping his brow, listened to the sounds. Above the permanent heavy roar of the river, he could hear only the buzz of insects. Occasionally, strange piping and trilling birdcalls or the wailing call of an animal came from within the rain forest, or a distant roll of thunder sounded from high in the peaks.

Slinging the rocket launcher over his shoulder as if its weight was insignificant, Lloyd paced about the rock platform, cradling the gun in his arms, his wary eyes constantly searching around.

Vero, who had emerged from the *Nesta* carrying a briefcase, looked around. "I grew up near jungles," he said in an oddly subdued tone as he slipped his dark glasses on, and Merral wondered if he was thinking of his far-off family. Merral followed his gaze upward to the spearlike peaks. "But there was nothing like this," Vero continued. "Merral, we aren't in Kansas anymore."

"Kansas?"

But Vero walked to a landing leg, and after sitting down, began to work through a sheaf of papers as if it were the most natural thing in the world.

The others settled nearby for the wait. Arabella sat on a cushion and began some needlework. "It keeps my fingers supple," she explained.

Anya examined the plants and insects and with Lloyd made a foray into some of the vegetation to look at the butterflies.

After finishing a rigorous inspection of the ship, Perena surveyed the slopes.

"What are you looking for?" Merral asked after a few minutes.

"Somewhere to land a ferry craft."

"See anywhere?"

She gestured toward a rock escarpment. "Depending on size, wingspan, and mobility, there, there, and there. And a dozen places other as well." She turned to Merral. "I think I will go with you to this meeting. I don't think this being, whatever it is, will bring the sick man here. So it may be that you will go to the ship or whatever they have. In that case I want to go with you. Deanna can mind the ship. She's perfectly capable of flying it alone if needed." She frowned and peered up the slope again. "I have the most uncomfortable feeling of being watched."

"I wish we knew what was there," Merral replied, trying not to think of the possibilities. He looked over at Vero noticing that, for all his attention to his paperwork, he would look at the rain forest every few minutes.

"We'll find out soon enough," Perena answered, before moving to a patch of shadow under the craft's nose. There she turned her attention to her diary.

Merral wandered around, strongly tempted to accompany Anya on her scrutiny of the wildlife. After all, what forester could refuse the chance of examining a rain forest, something widely seen as the ultimate triumph of Made World ecology? Had he not once almost been posted to a similar place? He toyed with the idea, but reluctantly resisted it. *I am no longer a forester. I have other duties. Anyway, keeping a distance from Anya is probably a very wise policy.*

Instead, Merral borrowed a fieldscope and scanned the area for anything unusual. As he surveyed the impenetrable tumult of greenery, his concerns mounted. What lay beneath it? He saw nothing and in the end, as much to calm his nerves as anything, he forced himself to sit in the shade of the ship and try to deal with some of the unanswered correspondence that had accumulated on his diary. Yet every few minutes he lifted his eyes to the rain forest around them. *We are being watched. But by what?*

By late afternoon, the weather changed. Tattered clouds drifted across the sky and coalesced so that the sun's light slowly waned. The luminous greenness of the world about them faded to greenish grays. The rumbles of thunder amid the peaks increased in intensity and drew nearer as gray misty clouds drifted down the slopes. The rain started, fat drops splattering on the rock, rapidly increasing into a deafening downpour of such intensity that water bounced off the rock. Soon only Merral and Lloyd were left outside and had to retreat by the ramp under the very middle of the *Nesta Lamaine* to avoid getting soaked. The wind battered the wet trees and sent squally flurries of rain under the survey craft.

"Not long now," Lloyd said, as they sat on the ramp squinting into the intense shadows around them. "You like jungles, sir?"

"Yes. Most places on Farholme you can feel that life is hanging on as a fragile skin. In a rain forest like this I am reassured; it's here to stay. Does that make sense?"

But Lloyd didn't answer. Instead his big frame stiffened as he leaned forward, peering into the gloom. Strange calls erupted within the trees and Merral glimpsed a party of monkeys bounding away swiftly. A flock of crimson parrots flew noisily away through the rain.

"Something's there," Lloyd muttered and grasped his gun more tightly.

But as the light continued to fade and the storm lashed about them, with thunder echoing around the valley in almost deafening blasts of sound, there was no further sign of anything else unusual stalking the rain forest.

At half past six, with visibility down to few meters and the light almost gone, Merral assembled the contact team. Various medical supplies were divided between them and as rain capes were donned and packs put on, Merral gave last-minute instructions.

"If there's trouble, remember Lloyd is armed. You want to say anything, Sergeant?"

"Yes," the big man said, wiping rain off a pale eyebrow. "If the commander here tells me to fire, then everyone lie down. Quick. And stay down. That's all."

They stood under the craft, adjusting their packs and watching the water run across the rock around their feet. The ceaseless drumming of the rain on the fuselage could be heard.

Deanna saw the signal first. "Flashing light seen," she called down from the cockpit. "Three o'clock."

In the darkness, Merral turned to see repeated pale flashes of silver light.

"Here we go," he said and uttered a silent prayer.

Carefully picking his way by his handlight's beam, Merral led the way forward, trying to ignore the rain running into his eyes. It seemed as if the whole hillside was awash and his feet seemed to alternate between slipping in the mud or sinking into it. Ahead the light kept flashing: one, two, three, *off*; one, two, three, *off*.

They were soon under the trees. Merral pulled out his bush knife to cut the undergrowth and vines blocking his way.

Under the tree cover, the wind lessened. Water ran or dripped from every branch and leaf. Despite the excellent cape, Merral felt soaked.

The light beams from the party slid this way and that and lightning stabbed, creating wild and grotesque shadows. Merral threw up a new prayer that Lloyd wouldn't be panicked into firing.

As he walked and sometimes stumbled toward the flashing light, fear clawed at his mind. He began to doubt the wisdom of coming. This *was* a trap and he had fallen for it.

Something slithered away in the darkness amid tangled roots. A snake or a trick of the light?

Merral walked on, his feet squelching through mud and leaves, aware of the others following behind him.

The light seemed to come from by a high pile of rocks. As Merral pushed toward it, halting only a few meters away, his heart pounded in his chest. Lloyd and the others clustered tight behind him.

There was nothing behind the rocks.

Lightning flashed, almost immediately followed by a great reverberating boom of thunder.

Merral let the echoes die away, then called out, "I am Merral D'Avanos, Commander of the Farholme Defense Force! We come in peace to seek Betafor Allenix!" His voice seemed to be swallowed up in the rain forest.

"Welcome, Commander," another voice said in a rasping tone.

Six beams of light swung round to the source—a figure standing at the foot of a crag a dozen paces away.

Merral stared at the creature, recognizing all the features he had seen during the diary conversation: the uneven mottled green skin that in places seemed to have worn away to show an underlying paler creamy green layer, the angular head and ears, the hunched posture and the jacket. Yet new features struck him. For one thing, it was smaller than he had expected, no larger than the average ten-year-old child. For another, the surfaces that made up the face and limbs glinted in the light as the rain ran over them as if they were part of some strange abstract sculpture cut out of ice, glass, or plastic. Still another was the way the head, neck, and body seemed to be separate structures placed abruptly against each other.

I would never have mistaken it for an animal.

"Commander," the thing said, "I suggest that no one does anything sudden. I think only one light is needed."

Merral snapped an order. "Very well. Vero, keep your beam on. Everyone else, point them on the ground."

With only a single light focused on the creature, Merral noted that its limbs, which emerged through the stiff fabric of the jacket, were angular and hard surfaced. The front limbs seemed longer than the rear ones. Taken as a whole, he saw something that was unique and that defied characterization; a rigid, almost delicate creature that seemed utterly alien.

"Commander, Sergeant Enomoto is armed." As the creature spoke Merral saw how the lower jaw moved as a single rigid unit. "It is understandable, but I pose no threat. I would prefer it if the weapon was . . . disarmed."

Merral hesitated, then said, "I would prefer if he kept the weapon ready to fire. Trust must be earned."

"As you will," the creature said and moved toward Merral.

"I am unaware of protocol at meetings such as these," Merral said looking around, suddenly aware in a moment of utter irrelevance that rainwater dripped down his neck.

"Let us be basic then." The creature's head bowed as if in greeting. "I am Betafor Allenix, the sole surviving Allenix unit of the Freeborn vessel *Slave of Rahllman's Star.*"

Arabella stepped forward next to Merral. "I am the doctor. I gather you have a patient. Where is he?"

"He is in the shelter. It is some distance away. Please follow me. There is a poor path. I will try not to go too fast."

"How do we know that this is not a trap?" Merral said. As soon as the words were out, he wished he hadn't spoken.

The green head twisted toward him. "Really, Commander, if this were a trap, I could have killed you earlier. Learn this: Allenix units can be trusted."

Betafor turned, bent her back, and extended her forelimbs so that they touched the ground. Merral felt that although the creature's movements had a certain grace, they were somehow mechanical; it was easy to sense that underneath the skin lay synthetics and metal rather than blood and bone.

Merral glimpsed Anya's face beside him and saw on it a look of utter fascination. "Only partially bipedal," she said, as if to herself. "And she must have better night vision than us."

"The path is steep and . . . winding," Betafor said. "This will help you to follow me." Suddenly the sides of her jacket began to glow a ghostly white. She set off, moving lightly but confidently on all fours up the hillside.

"Close bush knives!" Merral ordered. "I don't want anyone slipping onto an open blade. But keep them to hand."

Merral set off after the glowing creature. "Your Communal is excellent," he said, as he came up alongside, trying to avoid stepping on the swaying tail.

"Thank you. The ability for language was a priority in our making and it has improved over the millennia of our existence. The ancient form of Communal has always been used by all the Freeborn for some purposes. Your modern version is not very hard. My language ability will improve as I listen to what you say and my circuits . . . calibrate. My knowledge is, of course, mainly derived from listening to your broadcasts and from reading material from your Library. The other Allenix unit and I used to practice between ourselves on the ship."

As the path steepened, Merral struggled for breath and saw from the extended and wavering line of handlight beams that the others were evidently feeling the strain too.

"C-can we pause?" he gasped, wiping the rain and sweat off his face. Although the doctors considered his ribs and internal injuries to be now healed, the exertion made Merral aware of them.

"Indeed," Betafor said, stopping smoothly and suddenly. "I have always found it a . . . curiosity that one of the most obvious effects of a strained metabolism in humans is that they become . . . deprived of their power of speech. What do you think?"

"I t-think . . ." Merral waved a hand in frustration. "I—I agree."

After a minute's pause, Betafor pressed on and now more rocks began to appear between the trees, glistening in the light of the handlights. Increasingly soaked by sweat and rain, Merral trailed as close behind as he could, aware of the light beams bouncing around as the holders of the handlights tried to maintain their balance and avoid the razor-edged rocks.

As he followed the pale lights that marked Betafor's flanks up an apparently endless path, the darkness, the exertion, and the soaking he received caused Merral to feel a growing detachment from reality. *Can I be sure that this is not some sort of weird dream?*

Twenty minutes later, Betafor stopped. As Merral caught up with her, his handlight beam revealed a small clearing in which new vegetation grew. *The ferry craft landing site.*

A glistening rock face lay ahead. "Here," Betafor said. With considerable agility she clambered over some rocks and then swept aside a curtain of a dense textile to reveal the mouth of a jagged fissure.

She entered and Merral, after waiting for Lloyd to catch up, followed her.

With a faint series of plopping noises, lights came on to reveal a rough-walled chamber in which there were a number of tentlike compartments. Fluttering shadows moved above them.

Lloyd swung his gun up.

"Bats," said Betafor quickly.

The gun was lowered.

Merral looked around, hearing the constant drip of water, and smelling a new odor—something far fouler than the rain forest's permanent aroma of vegetable death and decay.

As Betafor led them along a creaking walkway past muddy boxes and crates, the lighting faded on the flanks of her jacket.

On the boxes and crates, Merral saw the red spidery script he had seen on the intruder ship and shuddered. Yet he sensed none of the malignancy that he had felt there. Decay, strangeness, and dirt perhaps, but not the occult presence that he had sensed on the ship. Neither could he hear that persistent hostile chattering on the very edge of audibility. Here, at least, he was not on his own. Nevertheless, he kept a firm grip on the handle of his bush knife.

Betafor stopped in front of the final compartment and in a surprisingly human gesture reared up to a hanging towel and wiped her muddy forelimbs on it. She then unsealed the entrance.

Lloyd, his weapon in hand, walked in with Merral. As they exchanged glances, Merral read wariness on his aide's mud-stained face.

I don't like it, Lloyd mouthed.

"Stay alert," Merral whispered back, and his aide nodded.

As Betafor turned the wedge of her head toward them, Merral was struck by the strangely emotionless eyes with their dark round and intense pupils.

"Only the commander, the doctor, and the biologist, please. The rest of you, please stay here. You may sit down. But do not open anything."

Do we trust her? Merral asked himself for the hundredth time. *We have no choice. And besides, if this was a trap it would have been sprung by now.*

He looked back, seeing the others taking off packs, sliding off rain capes, and trying to shake themselves dry.

Anya, her red hair plastered against her skull, came over to Merral with a handkerchief in her hand. "You look a mess, Commander. Allow me." She tenderly wiped his face.

"Thanks," he said, all sorts of emotions stirred by her action. "I take it you are finding this interesting?"

Anya turned to look at the creature standing in the entranceway to the compartment. "I'll say. I'm in a state of information overload. But you'd better not keep Betafor waiting." She grinned slightly. "You have enough women problems already."

"You think it's female?" he whispered.

Anya shrugged. "It's what she wants."

Merral shrugged as he headed into the compartment, followed by Anya and Arabella, who clutched a large medical pack. Although he was unhappy with treating Betafor as a female person, the idea of treating her as a genderless thing was no solution.

The compartment was a large, poorly lit room with a table in the middle and a few cabinets. Papers and food packets littered the muddy floor. The foul smell was particularly strong here.

Arabella grunted in disapproval, while Anya wrinkled her nose.

"There you are," Betafor said with a tilt of the head toward a corner.

In a lightweight bed, half hidden under a dirty sheet, lay a man with pale, wasted arms exposed. Between the tangle of black hair and the unkempt beard Merral glimpsed a pale, waxy face. The low and hasty movements of his chest showed he was still alive.

Betafor moved to a corner and, with a neat folding of the forelimbs, squatted and remained immobile, and staring at them like a weird statue. This close and in this light she was obviously a manufactured being: indeed it struck Merral that if she had been covered in metal he would have simply termed her a robot. The reality was that her skin, with its little bumps and depressions, seemed to be some sort of flexible heavy polymer.

Arabella bent over the figure in the bed a moment, then turned to Merral with a frown. "I need to put this man on the table. You and Anya put a sterile sheet from the yellow pack on it first. And then give me a hand." She turned to Betafor. "Can we have some more light?"

"As you wish," replied the green figure and suddenly the lights brightened.

After Merral and Anya stretched the sterile sheet over the table, Arabella helped them lift the man off the bed. Evidently once tall and well built, he was now emaciated and weighed little. As they placed him on the table, Merral noted a strange and bloated undressed wound, with a lurid red color, at the top of his chest.

"So what happened?" Arabella asked as she donned gloves and began to examine the patient.

"The sarudar had an accident," Betafor replied.

"When?"

"Nine weeks ago." Her lips flexed when she spoke.

"That would be . . . what . . . when the ship was destroyed?"

"Just afterward. We were here when it was destroyed."

Arabella gently opened the shirt further and peered at the injury while Anya leaned forward on the other side. "Hmm, just above the manubrium. . . . Infected. . . . What sort of accident?"

"I do not know. I was not there. I think he fell on a rock. Human flesh is too weak. The wound began healing, but it must have become infected. It is hard to keep things . . . sterile here."

"Hmm. Odd wound," Arabella commented without looking up. "Very odd. When he became ill, what were his symptoms?"

"He started with fever and began . . . sweating more than usual. There was also swelling around the injury. I used our antibacterials on him. They slowed the effect."

Arabella grunted and put a diagnostic medical unit on the man's forehead. "He has an elevated temperature and hypotension . . . assuming, of course, he has a similar metabolism to us." She turned to Betafor. "Never had to ask this of a patient before, but is he human?"

"Yes. I think you will find . . . differences, but his core body temperature should be 37.0 Celsius."

"Thank you. One tries not to take anything for granted." Arabella's smile as she glanced at Anya seemed ironic. "You realize you are assisting in quite the most unusual diagnosis made in over three thousand years of Farholme medicine?"

"There is quite a lot that is unusual here," Anya said with a glance at Betafor.

Arabella turned to Azeras. "Hmm. Similar physiology, but I'd anticipate a differing immune system." She frowned and peered again at the upper chest. "I don't like the smell of this. I've never seen anything like it. Not in a human being anyway. It's a bacterial infection. Let me check something."

She stepped back, pulled off her gloves, tapped on her diary repeatedly, then seemed to find what she looked for. After a moment she shook her head, slipped on her gloves again, and returned to the table. "Should have remembered it from medical history. This man has an infection from an anaerobic bacteria. Probably *clostridium*. We only ever get minor versions, but this is full-scale gangrene. Gangrene," she repeated, the word ringing with surprise and then nodded at Anya. "Another novelty."

"Can you give me the . . . prognosis?" Betafor asked.

"If he stays here, very poor. I'll give him some of our antibacterials now." Arabella waved a gloved hand at her bag. "Anya, one of the red vials. Yes, that one. AB 258? Thanks." She unscrewed the top, pressed the vial against the man's emaciated arm, and squeezed until it was empty.

She then turned to Betafor, her expression stern. "Now let's talk. Even if they work, these antibacterials are not going to be enough. This man needs to be taken to a hospital—to a sterile environment." As she looked around in a tight-lipped way, Merral wondered if she was going to comment on the mess. "A *sterile* environment," she repeated. "The dead, damaged, and infected tissue needs removing. We may want to put him in a high-oxygen setting. And there may be other damage. I'd want to check kidney functions."

"That is not possible."

Arabella frowned. "I am unaccustomed to arguing with a machine, but—"

"A nonbiological organism, if you please."

"A nonbiological organism, then. But whoever—or whatever—you are, if he dies, you are responsible."

Betafor seemed to stare at her for a moment. "It is not that simple. The Dominion ship is coming. If they find out that either of us exists, we both will face . . . death or destruction."

"We can arrange for minimum publicity."

"That will not work."

Suddenly Anya, who had been gazing at the wound, gave a grunt. "Merral, Arabella," she said in an urgent voice, "we need to talk. Now. Privately."

Merral found something in her tone that didn't encourage hesitation. "Very well. Excuse us, Betafor, for a moment."

"As you wish. I will wait here."

Closing the flap of the compartment door behind them, they joined Vero and Perena, who were seated on boxes near the outer end of the cave. Lloyd stood alert with his gun gripped tightly.

"This Sarudar Azeras has what's called gangrene," Merral said, keeping his voice low. "I'll explain later. Anya has a comment. Go on."

Anya looked at the doctor. "That wound. Do *you* think it was an accident?"

"Why not? It's odd, but what else could it be?"

"I think it was a surgical incision. I say that because I have made just such incisions on cockroach-beasts and ape-creatures."

Betafor's pupils contracted slightly.

Given time and familiarity, we might be able to read something of the emotions of this creature.

"I deduce that you mean the two types of gene-constructed hybrids on the ship. Yes."

"I don't see the logic in this, this . . . brutal procedure," said Anya. "Why cause more deaths?"

"It ensures loyalty."

"In such evil ways is unity preserved." Perena's voice was so quiet as to make Merral wonder if it was meant to be heard. *Of course. On worlds where treachery is common, such circuits might have a real value.*

"When we heard the ship had been destroyed, Sarudar Azeras realized he had only hours to live. He decided to extract the circuits in his upper chest. They are designed to be hard to remove. We used a robotic arm to remove the main circuit, but there were . . . complications and the wound did not properly heal. Later, it became infected."

"But you did get the implant out?" Merral asked.

"Let me clarify matters. There were two units—an upper and a lower one. The upper one is the dangerous one and must be removed quickly. The lower one, which is only a minor nuisance, is harder to remove. We took out the upper one and left the lower one." She paused. "But I think you should remove the lower one, especially as the concept offends you."

"If we can, we will," Arabella replied and took a step forward. "Betafor, have a responsibility to that man. He needs major treatment. Why can't we just hospitalize him?"

"The ship I was on was stolen by the Freeborn. The Dominion seek to recover it and to have revenge. All who were involved will be destroyed."

Vero's voice broke in. "But you were made by the Dominion."

"Yes. I was made by the Dominion. The first badge I bore was that of the nal Emblem, the sign of the Dominion." The long smooth sides of her tunic owed and on a black background a strange red symbol like an infinity sign or figure eight on its side appeared. It seemed to move, almost as if it was some rt of ever-flowing coil. There was something unidentifiable about it, though, at troubled Merral. "Then the ship was seized. I could have self-destructed, t instead I chose to serve the Freeborn." The symbol on her sides changed to irclet of heavy chains on a dark blue background bisected by a yellow light-ng bolt at the top. "Doctor, when the Dominion come, they will destroy—or ture—both me and the sarudar. Our only hope is that they think that we re destroyed." The tunic sides returned to their pale green hue.

"B-but why can't we leave you here and take this man to a quiet medical ility somewhere?" Vero asked.

"You do not understand the Dominion. They have many ways of extract-

"But why?" The doctor's face showed bafflement.

"Those creatures all had implanted devices there. They were circuits apparently designed to secrete toxin on some sort of command."

"I saw them," Merral added. "And the time fits. This Betafor says the accident took place at the same time just after the ship was destroyed. That was when the circuits started oozing poison."

"Hmm. So the wound would be the result of a surgical operation," Arabella said as if to herself. "A botched one. . . . Even more fascinating."

"Oh, dear," Vero said, his voice almost a grunt.

"Why 'oh, dear'?" Merral asked.

"Because this says that B-Betafor is not telling the truth. I knew it would be complicated dealing with a being like this. But to f-find that she lies makes it even more complex."

"True enough." Merral looked around. "Any ideas?"

Lloyd gestured toward the crew cabin. "Sir, I reckon we challenge this Betafor thing. Bring it in here. We need the truth."

"Seems a fair point," Merral said. "Arabella, do I take it that the patient's life isn't going to be significantly put at risk by us spending a few minutes getting to the bottom of this?"

"Not significantly, as long as we get him out of here in the next few hours."

"I agree with Lloyd," Vero said.

Perena nodded.

"Very well," Merral said. "Let's interview Miss Betafor."

hen Merral called Betafor, she walked out on all ⟨...⟩ stopped and tilted her body back to balance on h⟨...⟩ and her tail, her back and neck vertical. The result ⟨...⟩ head was elevated almost to the height of Merra⟨...⟩ stared at them with large eyes and then froze in a ⟨...⟩ immobility that no living creature could ever att⟨...⟩

"Betafor," Merral said, "we think that this w⟨...⟩ Azeras has isn't from an accident. It comes from an attempt to remo⟨...⟩ ed device from his chest—a device we found on other intruder c⟨...⟩

In the ensuing silence, Merral realized that he had not the ⟨...⟩ how she would react.

After several seconds, Betafor said, "Do you wish to know t⟨...⟩ though you will find it unwelcome?"

"Yes," Merral said and was echoed by the others.

"Sarudar Azeras was life-bonded to Captain Damertooth of ⟨...⟩ *Star*." Betafor's voice echoed in the cave. "It is a tradition in th⟨...⟩ the Dominion worlds to life-bond crew to ships or captains. ⟨...⟩ captain perishes, the signal to the device fails and the crew me⟨...⟩

Merral and his companions expressed shock and revulsi⟨...⟩

"I understand that you find this to be a disagreeable co⟨...⟩ said. "I am aware it is unknown in the Assembly. That is why ⟨...⟩ alternative version of events."

"You lied," Merral said.

Betafor blinked. "If you want to phrase it like that, yes ⟨...⟩

"We prefer honesty."

"Thank you for the correction."

"Betafor," Anya said, "you do this with cockroach-beasts ⟨...⟩ too?"

ing secrets, and human beings are weak. The Dominion can persuade, it can bribe, it can torture. It even has beings who can read minds."

"Read minds?" Vero looked alarmed.

"Yes. I have . . ." There was a pause. "I have taken a risk in even revealing our existence to you."

"So why have you taken this risk?" Merral asked.

Betafor turned to Merral. "Sarudar Azeras is my officer. My duty is to serve him."

There was silence for a moment before Vero spoke. "I have a suggestion. A deep water research station was being constructed on the Manalahi Shoals, two hundred kilometers or so south of Isterrane. Work was recently abandoned as part of the crisis measures. I have been looking at it for some time for—shall we say—other purposes, and I can confirm that most of the medical facilities were completed. I suggest that we treat the patient there."

"You'd need nursing staff," Arabella said, "and a small surgical team."

Vero nodded. "They could be found within the FDF."

"Indeed," Merral said. "We're building up medical expertise. And the nurses—even the doctor—don't need to know who this man is. Betafor, does he speak our form of Communal?"

"Yes," Betafor said, "among the humans he was the best speaker on the ship. That is why the captain sent him to this island—in case there was any Assembly presence."

"B-Betafor—" Vero's voice was sharp—"why did you come here?"

"Damertooth knew he had been discovered. We were sent to find and prepare a new site for the ship to move to."

"We need to get moving, Vero," Arabella said. "And the Manalahi Shoals sounds like the best suggestion. We can't leave him here." She looked around, her face showing dismay at the conditions.

Merral made his decision. "Right. We'll move him to the Manalahi Shoals. Betafor, do you agree to this?"

"An isolated island? It may be the best solution. I would come too?"

"Yes."

There was a silence. "Very well. I agree."

"Right," Merral said. "Let's take the sarudar out."

✿✿✿✿✿

Arabella showed them how to assemble a stretcher she had brought and then she sedated Azeras. After Merral and Lloyd volunteered to be stretcher bearers, they strapped Azeras to the stretcher and found spare waterproofing to put over him to keep him dry.

Betafor placed a pack on her back and then, with her strange four-legged gait, led them slowly back down the path under the continuing downpour.

Within half an hour of leaving, they had Azeras strapped down inside the *Nesta Lamaine*.

While the others changed into dry clothes, the Allenix unit asked Merral for clean water and a damp cloth and carefully cleaned the mud off herself.

Merral, rubbing his own hair dry, was struck by the action. *What is the motive? Pride? A desire for cleanliness? Concern for mechanical efficiency? How hard it is to understand this creature!*

The ship took off and soon passed through the turbulence of the storm into clear starlit skies. Leaving Lloyd to watch over Betafor and Arabella to monitor the sedated Azeras, Vero, Anya, and Merral moved to the cockpit and closed the door behind them.

"Betafor's utterly alien," Merral began. "We can't begin to understand her."

Perena looked up from her console. "I disagree. She's not at all alien." While everyone stared at her, she continued. "She's made in our image and we may expect she bears the flaws of her makers."

It was a statement that no one felt inclined to argue with. Eventually agreement was reached on a strategy to ensure that Azeras was speedily treated and messages were sent arranging for the appropriate people to be urgently, but quietly, dispatched to the Manalahi Shoals.

"Getting information from Betafor will take time," Vero said. "We mustn't rush it. More haste, less speed. Everything she says should be recorded. The fact that she lies makes things very complex. We may yet be able to learn to tell when she lies. We need information so badly that we must treat even a dubious source as valuable."

"So, do we talk to her now?" Merral asked. "We have a couple of hours."

Vero frowned. "I'm tempted. She knows much that we badly need to know. But I would prefer to read up on—there is no Communal word, so let me use the Ancient English—*interrogation*—techniques and start talking to her tomorrow."

"That makes her sound like an enemy," Anya said.

Vero shrugged. "We don't know *what* she is. We know she came from that ship and that she lies. We can't rule out the possibility that she is an enemy or even a spy. We need to keep her in isolation."

Merral saw looks of unhappiness, but none of dissent.

"Let's call them interviews," Vero added. "But there *is* a danger of carelessly talking to her."

"What sort of danger?" Merral asked.

"That we reveal too much about us to her. Any conversations with her will involve a two-way exchange of information. Our questions reveal our ignorance."

In the end, Merral decided that Vero and Perena would begin the interviews on the following day.

That done, they returned to the hold. There they found that Betafor had refused a seat and had gone into a corner where, a safety strap entwined around a forelimb, she remained in her half-squat position, with her eyes seemingly focused on the far wall. Strapped next to her was her pack.

Merral was struck by the fact that Betafor's face revealed no more information than that of a child's doll. *How strange. I had never realized until now how much faces tell us about how people feel. We have so many questions. How do we know if she is awake or asleep? Does she eat or drink? And, above all, can we trust her?*

He glanced at Lloyd who, with his double-barreled weapon at his feet, seemed to watch Betafor with a wary concern.

Lloyd soon turned to Merral and shook his head in a mystified fashion.

"Betafor, can I get you anything?" Merral asked.

Suddenly the big eyes swung toward him. "No, thank you. My short-term needs are essentially nonexistent," Betafor added.

"That must be very convenient."

"Yes, we do not suffer from the demands that a metabolism places on you."

"I hadn't thought of it that way." Merral was soon aware that Perena had come down from the cockpit and stood at his shoulder.

"An interesting oversight, Commander," Betafor answered. "Because you are a biological organism, your actions are controlled by your constant needs for food, water, warmth, and so on. Allenix units have no such requirements."

"So you won't get a cramp standing up like that for the next three hours?"

"No."

"Very well," he said. "We'll talk when we get there. You won't be bored?"

Betafor's soft mouth twisted in a smile or at least an imitation of one. "Commander, I do not get bored. I can watch something for a hundred years and my attention will not flag an instant."

"Interesting." Mindful of Vero's advice, Merral resisted the temptation to ask more questions and as the flight continued, fell into a fitful sleep. Every time he woke, he was aware of Betafor's resinous eyes watching him.

ᗡᑐᗡᑐᗡ

It was not quite midnight local time when they landed at the Manalahi Shoals. Lloyd and Merral carried the stretcher down the ramp as Vero and Arabella talked with a small cluster of people by some vehicles. Under the starlight, Merral glimpsed palm trees and beyond them, a sea with phosphorescent waves which broke with a gentle sigh.

Sarudar Azeras was loaded into a vehicle with Arabella and driven off. Shortly afterward Lloyd escorted Betafor and her luggage out of the *Nesta* and into the back of a second vehicle.

Just before Vero followed Lloyd, he turned to Merral and Anya. "We'll keep her secure. All being well, we'll operate on Azeras in the morning and start talking to our green friend. But, Merral, how much like a Krallen is she?"

"There are similarities. She has admitted as much. But she's lighter, thinner skinned, and a bit more rounded. Her eyes are unprotected and she seems generally much less robust. And while they always seem to go around on all fours, she seems to like to get in this half-erect position. And the clothes—that's a big difference."

"So is she the civilian version and are they the military one?"

"Maybe."

"We may learn a lot from her about them, if she cooperates. She'll know all about the Krallen."

Merral's nod ended with a yawn. He felt exhausted by the day.

As Vero drove away and Lloyd walked back to the *Nesta*, Anya turned to Merral. "Are you tired?"

Her eyes looked soft in the gloom and his emotions were stirred. *No. I must resist.*

"Yes," he said. "It's been a long day. Too much to take in. I need to get back to Isterrane. If we are to successfully cover up what happened today, I need to be in the office as normal. And to do that, I need some sleep."

Merral found his wishes granted. Perena took off shortly afterward and barely an hour later he was back at the Kolbjorn Suite. There, after a long, hot shower to remove the last of the mud and sweat, he tumbled into bed and instantly fell asleep.

ﻌﻌﻌﻌﻌ

The next morning, Vero met Perena at the end of the wing where Betafor had been placed in a windowless room. The surgical team was ready to operate on Azeras.

"We've improvised a lock for Betafor's room but I posted a guard too," Vero said. "I have reviewed the camera footage. She stays still for hours on end. At one point, she decided to climb up the walls. She has a surprising agility."

"So, Vero, what do we say in this interview?"

"I had hoped to come up with some elegant, ingenious, and subtle way of persuading this creature to yield us the information we need, but I can't think of one. So it's Plan B."

Perena raised an eyebrow. "Which is?"

"Do what Merral would do: pray and just ask whatever questions seem right."

"Not a bad strategy."

"Yes. I think we explore gently, go with the flow. Where she volunteers information, we take it. Where she resists, we don't push. And in general, I think we try and humor her."

"I see."

"P., I'm glad you are with me here."

She looked hard at him. "Why?" There was caution in her voice.

"I value your insights. That's all." *But it's not, is it?* "Well, let's go and talk to her."

The guard unlocked the door and they walked in.

Betafor sat on her haunches in a corner and looked up as they entered.

"How are you, Betafor?" Vero asked.

"Sentinel, Captain, very well, although the question about my state is much less meaningful than for a human being, as I do not exhibit the . . . fluctuations in the physical state that biological organisms suffer."

"Of course." *I must humor her.* "I was worried you would be bored."

"Thank you for your concern. As I mentioned to the commander, I do not suffer boredom. And I can, of course, listen to your audiovisual broadcasts."

"You can?" *What have I overlooked?*

"Of course. I have built-in facilities to receive most standard communication frequencies. For weaker or more complex signals I may need to be connected to an aerial array. It is another innovation that marks me out as superior to organic beings."

So much for keeping her in isolation and me being head of intelligence. "I see. You receive electromagnetic messages. But can you also transmit?"

"Yes, but only with relatively low power. I can imagine you are worried about the security issues."

Absolutely! "Yes."

"I promise that I will not abuse that system. You can always have all signals from me monitored."

Vero caught Perena's nod. "I'm afraid we must do that. So what are you listening to at the moment?"

"I am watching all your audiovisual channels."

"What, all five of them?"

What a phenomenally useful talent!

"The inability of humans to genuinely multitask is another major deficiency."

"I see it as a design feature," Perena said and Vero caught the glint of humor in her eyes. "It forces us to relate closely to one person at a time. It helps us have deep relationships without distraction."

There was a marked silence before Betafor spoke again. "There are . . . aspects to this conversation that may be clearer when I replay it to myself."

Another useful—and troubling—ability.

"Betafor, Captain Lewitz and I want to talk with you. The discussion will be recorded."

"First, please tell me: how is the sarudar?"

"Better. His infection is receding."

"When will he be operated on?"

"Now."

"Good. I would like to see him when he is recovering. To . . . pay my respects . . . and wish him a rapid recovery. I find human illness . . . very moving."

"Betafor, do you feel emotions?" Perena's voice was very quiet.

"Yes, Captain. But not as you do. They are limited. In the beginning—and we are talking well over ten thousand years ago—the Allenix were made without emotional capacities. But gradually, as we became involved in translation and negotiation, it was realized that for maximum efficiency, we needed some degree of empathy with others." She paused. "But too much emotion was dangerous, because it impaired judgment—something that we have often observed in your species. So, a balance was allowed. It is best this way."

Perena seem to think about this for a moment. "That could be debated. So what emotions do you feel?"

Betafor moved her lips in something that might pass for a smile. "To tell you that might be to reveal weakness. In negotiation you do not reveal too much."

"And we are negotiating?"

Betafor's smile faded. "All conversation is negotiation."

"But here in the Assembly it is not," Vero said.

"Perhaps . . . it is less so."

In the ensuing silence Betafor leaned forward and looked at Vero's belt. "Please, may I look at your diary?"

"S-sorry. No."

"If you are worried about . . . security, you need not be. I can already access its circuits. I hope you are not insulted if I say it is extremely . . . primitive."

"Is it?"

"Yes." The flanks of the jacket suddenly lit up and Vero was astonished to see every detail of his diary screen displayed on it.

"Ah, *clever*," he observed.

The images faded.

"I can show you how to encrypt your devices so neither I nor anybody else can access them without permission."

"That would be useful."

"We Allenix are intrigued by the need that you humans have to supplement their abilities with electronic devices such as diaries and the equivalent. We see it as evidence of the weakness of flesh. To be what we are naturally, you need to have extra hardware."

"So you are superior?" Perena asked.

Betafor's gray pupils narrowed. "By any neutral definition, we are superior. Allenix do not tire or age. Our key systems can be replaced as modules. We do not have the weak and vulnerable biological systems you have." She tapped the back of her hand. "I will outlast you. My essential . . . consciousness is over a thousand years old. And we have superior sensing abilities. For example, we see in wavelengths above and below those of humans and at twice your resolution. We hear better and over a greater frequency range than you do. Our thought systems are faster, less easily distracted, and we can multitask without performance degradation. We do not suffer from the permanent fluctuations that are inevitable in any biological systems. We do not suffer from carelessness. If I perform a task a million times, the last time is as good as the first time. Do you wish me to continue?"

"N-no," Vero said. "That will do. Very impressive."

"Thank you."

"But what are your limitations?" Perena asked.

Betafor's lips flexed again into the pseudosmile. "Captain, the Allenix have no limitations. We have areas of undeveloped potential. Indeed the existence of this potential is another area in which we are superior. Humans are limited. Flesh cannot be modified. We can."

Perena's expression hardened. "So the future belongs to you? It sounds like you think we're finished."

Betafor's smile broadened. "It is an axiom of negotiation that you do not humiliate the opposite party."

Vero raised a finger. "Betafor, you say you were part of the True Freeborn. They are at war with the Dominion?"

"Correct."

"Can you explain something of the reason why they are at war?"

Betafor smiled again. *She seems to have a limited repertoire of emotional expressions.* "We have a deal, Sentinel Enand. After the remaining implant in Sarudar Azeras is removed and he is restored to health, I will tell you all I know. Not before."

Vero shrugged. "Very well. Incidentally, you said something yesterday about also being a sentinel."

"What was said was this. You said: 'Show us this man,' meaning the sarudar. I replied 'Ah, Verofaza, the sentinel. We too were made to be sentinels.'"

Of course. She records all conversations. Another awesomely useful trick. "Exactly. What did you mean?"

"It is our history. In the constant wars between the Freeborn worlds there was always a need to have watchmen at the edges of the planetary systems to identify and inspect the ships that passed there. But it was realized that it was no task for humans. Your race is unsuited to spend months in the depths of space."

Perena stiffened slightly. *She understands that.*

"At first, we were created just to watch and warn of vessels. We were little more than machines. But as it can take days for signals to go backward and forward to the edge of a system, it was realized that it would be better if we were given intelligence and could make decisions. So over centuries we were given new abilities and allowed to act. We would find ships, stop them, and negotiate with them. And, if necessary, we would search them or seize them."

"*You* searched ships?" Perena looked doubtful.

"Indeed, Captain. I would lead the search party. I would normally have at least one pack of Krallen behind me."

"Did you use them?" Vero asked.

"Sometimes yes. On three occasions in the last twenty years I . . . ordered the Krallen to destroy all the crew."

"Ah," Vero said, catching the look of dismay on Perena's face. "*I* have a question," he said after a moment's silence. "In the ship we found there was another being—a steersman. Do you deal with them?"

"No. That is the task of a human—a steersman handler."

"What do you think of the steersmen?"

"I find your question lacking in clarity. I pity human beings for dealing with them; it is a sign of . . . weakness. But what we call the extra-physical and you call the spiritual or the supernatural does not concern me. We do not have souls."

"I see."

"How do you know you do not have souls?" Perena asked.

"The subject has been the subject of much . . . discussion among us. We do not believe that any portion of us survives the destruction of our memory arrays. If I was blown up, I would simply cease to exist."

"Do you believe in God?" Perena asked.

"We recognize the universe contains a range of beings, some of which are extra-physical. They are of little interest to us. We do not worship a creator.

After all, if we did that, it might lead us to worship the human beings who made us." She paused. "That would not be sensible."

"Quite," Vero added and wished he hadn't.

"The ship that was destroyed—accidentally—at the lake had, you tell us, another Allenix unit on board," said Perena. "How do you feel about the fact that it was destroyed?"

"It was . . . sad."

"Sad for who?"

"For her."

"Don't you feel grief for her loss?"

There was a moment's silence. "The Allenix were not made to be creatures of community. We were designed for solitude. We exist . . . for ourselves."

Perena seemed content to stare at Betafor for some time in silence. After several moments, she shook her head as if in sorrow and looked at Vero. "Over to you."

"Betafor," he said, "yesterday you mentioned beings that could read minds. Can you tell us more?"

There was a twitch of the tail. "I do not know much. But I will tell you what I know because it affects my safety. The last world to hold out against the lord-emperor was Tellzanur. Their forces fought hard against the Dominion. They were smaller in number, but superior in . . . strategy and very good at surprise tactics. Sarudar Azeras fought with them and he may tell you more. Then the lord-emperor brought in a new creature—a thing called a baziliarch. He got it from the Nether-Realms, what you call Below-Space. He took captives and soon knew everything about the insurgents and their defense crumbled."

"A baziliarch?" Vero asked, hoping that the dismay he felt was not visible on his face. "Is that something like a steersman?"

"Yes. It is an extra-physical being. There is a . . . hierarchy. This being is much higher than any steersman. There are only seven of them."

"And can you tell us anything more about them?"

"No." There was finality in the answer.

For the next hour Vero and Perena put many other questions to Betafor. On some topics, notably those that might have a bearing on the Dominion and its forces or on the technology of Below-Space travel, she refused to answer. On others, Vero sensed an evasiveness or brevity in the answers that suggested she did not want to say too much.

"Okay. For the time being, we have finished," Vero said, sensing that Perena's exhaustion matched his own. "Is there anything you want?"

"I would like my pack."

Vero looked at Perena, who shook her head. "We have not decided what to do with it. What's in it?"

"Spare parts, maintenance equipment, some data files, a change of clothes."

Vero caught Perena's raised eyebrows and sensed her bewilderment. *How do you deal with a machine that wants a change of clothes?*

"Betafor," he said, "we will review the situation."

Vero allowed Perena to precede him out of the room and let the guard lock the door behind him. They found some drinks and walked outside to a shaded veranda.

"Well," he said with a sigh, "she isn't going out of her way to make us love her."

"I'll say. She is utterly self-centered."

"And cunning, arrogant, and capable of ordering murder. And that's just what she has admitted to."

"Yes. If machines are made in the image of their creators, I'm not looking forward to meeting them."

"True. B-but, P., for all her faults, we need to know if she's an enemy or a potential ally."

Perena patted Vero's hand. "Patience! I think it's far too early to say."

"True. But she isn't going out of her way to help us. She revealed nothing about this *Slave of Rahllman's Star.*"

"A bargaining maneuver. She wasn't so reticent about anything that marked her as superior to humans. And she said nothing that might reveal any weaknesses."

"P., what do you think about this female bit?"

Perena's expression showed deep thought. "I didn't find her at all female. There's nothing feminine or maternal about her that I could sense. What about you?"

"Nothing. I don't think she has any sort of genuine gender. And she admitted to being made in some factory. So why does she want to be female?"

Perena made no answer, but bent down and picked up a tiny shell. She held it up to the light as if marveling at its geometry before turning back to Vero. "Let me tell you what I think. She's desperately anxious to be superior to human beings. We have genders, so she must have one too."

"She has an inferiority complex? That's what they used to call it."

Perena put the shell down carefully. "Yes. There is an insecurity about her relationship to human beings."

They stared across the coral sand toward the sea.

"Oh, good," Vero said, "we have an intelligent machine to deal with. And as if that wasn't enough, it's neurotic."

Perena laughed.

"I'm worried by this baziliarch, P. Very. How can we plan against a being that can read minds, assuming it isn't an invention of hers?"

"An invention? No, I don't think she has that much imagination. She can do simple lies and that's it. But a mind-reading enemy is alarming. All it has to do is find Merral and it will know everything."

Her eyes caught his and he saw worry in them.

It was midafternoon before Vero and Perena heard from Arabella on the status of the sick man. The operation, she said, had been a success and the mysterious object removed. The surgeon however was puzzled as to why it hadn't been removed earlier.

"And what is this thing?" Vero asked.

"We have no idea," Arabella said and passed him a small synthetic container in which something like a silver button lay.

Another puzzle to resolve and one I can do without. "I will have it analyzed. But the prognosis for Azeras . . . ?"

"Is excellent. I see no reason for either me or the surgical team to stay here."

"I can fly you back," Perena said. She turned to Vero. "I have things I need to do in Isterrane. I'll be back tomorrow."

Arabella expressed her thanks. "Vero, I've left rules for the nurses on how Azeras is to be treated. You can call me if I'm needed."

"Thank you. When can we talk to him?"

"Talk as in question him? Tomorrow, but you must obey the nurses' rules. Don't overtask him."

"We won't. He's too valuable for that."

"Oh, one other thing," Arabella said. "As a preliminary to the operation, we gave him a quick checkup. There are some physical modifications—electronics of some sort—in the upper side of the left hand and there are also implanted speakers in the ear canals. We also think that some modest genetic amendments have been made."

Ten minutes later, as he walked over to the landing strip with Perena, Vero said, "Not long ago, P., the very idea of a gene-altered human appalled us. But now we take such things for granted."

She shook her head. "And so, slowly, steadily—and without ever realizing it—we become hardened to evil." Her tone was somber. "Best wishes for your interviewing. But be careful, Vero. There's evil all around."

That morning Merral was late getting into the office. He had barely sat down when Corradon called him up on a routine matter.

"I was trying to get hold of you yesterday, but couldn't," said Corradon. "It was a bit alarming."

Merral apologized, but offered no excuses. After the call ended he felt guilty about how much he had undertaken without the approval of Corradon. *Military necessity.* But those two words could justify all manner of wrongs.

Later in the morning, he postponed all the meetings he could for the next two days and made arrangements to be contacted through Zak in a crisis.

That afternoon, as Merral walked down a corridor, his mind full of Betafor and Azeras, a musical voice rang out behind him. "Commander!"

Merral turned to see the dark-suited form of Delastro with his pair of aides behind him.

"Prebendant."

"Commander!" There was exasperation in Delastro's green eyes. "I was trying to find you yesterday on a matter of protocol that has since been resolved. But no one knew where you were. *No one.*"

Merral hesitated, hoping his unease was not visible. "I was out of the office."

"But inaccessible? Not even Advisor Clemant or Colonel Larraine knew where you were."

"I was . . . traveling."

"I see. A secret mission perhaps?" Delastro's glacial smile did not soften the sharpness of his words.

Merral paused, wondering if he could avoid lying. "Prebendant, under conditions of war, it may be advisable that even my closest associates do not know where I am. Military necessity. Yesterday was . . . an attempt to rehearse such a situation."

"I see." Delastro's colorless face showed irritation. "So you don't trust even your chaplain-in-chief?"

"It was policy, Prebendant. A matter of security. Don't take it personally."

"Oh, I won't. But I worry about you, Commander. I do worry about you. The pressures of the job . . ."

"Thank you for your concern. Now, if you will excuse me, I have a meeting."

As Merral walked away he felt a clear foreboding that, sooner or later, there would be real trouble with Delastro.

That evening Merral read and reread the transcript of the interview with Betafor that Vero had sent. Not long after, Vero himself called him on the secure line, from an unfinished room. They discussed the transcript and Merral realized how disappointed his friend was about how little of real relevance had been revealed.

"Has Sarudar Azeras spoken yet?" Merral asked.

"I visited him just now briefly and he spoke a few words. His Communal is surprisingly good. There are a lot of old words mixed in with Farholmen. But I'm waiting till tomorrow to talk properly to him. You'll be there then. You can stay overnight tomorrow?"

"Yes. I've arranged to be free. Zak will get me in an emergency. But yesterday's absence was noted."

"By who?"

"Corradon and the prebendant."

"Ah. Not good. My friend, tomorrow I want you to do most of the questioning."

"Why me?"

"You are a military man. I think our sarudar may better relate to you."

ⅭⅮⅭⅮⅭ

"Lloyd, any further thoughts on Betafor?" Merral asked over supper.

His aide put his fork down. "Sir, I just don't have a good feeling about that thing," he said in a slow, almost defiant tone. "It's untrustworthy. I think it's a threat. We know it lies."

"But there must be some good in her. She called us in to rescue this Azeras and save his life."

"True enough. But I don't think it was done out of love. I reckon there's more to this rescue than meets the eye. It knows what it wants. I just don't trust it."

"Sergeant, you seem reluctant to consider Betafor as a female person."

"Yes." Lloyd grimaced. "Sir, I'm afraid that's a deliberate decision I've made."

"How so?"

Lloyd slowly traced a circle on the table. "See, sir, I reckon it's quite possible that I may have to blast it into fragments." He looked up, his blue eyes troubled. "And I would have to think before shooting a woman. But I don't think I'll hesitate if it's only a thing."

16

The *Triumph of Sarata* surfaced well outside even the most generous estimate of the boundary of the Alahir system. In fact, even to Lezaroth's enhanced eyesight, Alahir itself was merely a brighter-than-normal star. But they were now only ten light hours away from Farholme and this was the location designated for making final arrangements.

The moment the *Triumph* surfaced, Deltathree started scanning the wavebands, pulling out static-damaged images and scratchy conversations from Farholme transmissions. As the two other ships emerged from the Nether-Realms, Lezaroth went to look at the data. Coveting the Allenix ability to watch several channels simultaneously, he skimmed through the media channels one by one, gratified that his newly learned Farholmen Communal was adequate to the task. The first channel showed sports, the second dance, the third a religious discussion, and the fourth a travelogue about some jungle. *They may have lost the Gate, but in their own primitive, backwater way they are still functioning.* He switched to the fifth channel, one that broadcast news, and paid more attention.

The first item involved a crisis-forced reorganization of industry, but the second item concerned the Farholme Defense Force and the commissioning of a thousand more troops. The camera showed lines of uniformed men marching past a podium where a tall, uniformed man apparently in his late twenties stood erect.

"Commander Merral D'Avanos surveying the new troops," said the unseen commentator.

There was something about the figure that aroused Lezaroth's surprised interest. *This is no armchair general; this man is young and fit. There is something about him that says to me that he has fought already. Can this be . . . ?* But then the news moved on to sports.

Suddenly Lezaroth remembered something and, with a fierce urgency, ran the images back. *Yes, there it was! A single medal on the man's chest. What would the Assembly award medals to a young man for? Surely, only for fighting! And what event could have triggered the development of a rudimentary but growing military force?* He smiled with the certainty of it all. *The same thing.*

No, the steersman was right. All or part of the Rahllman's Star *has been found and attacked.*

"Deltathree," Lezaroth said, with mounting excitement, "that man—I didn't get the name—D'Avan-something—copy me anything on him: who he is, where he is from, and anything else. . . . Oh, and why he was made commander. Do it while we're here and again when we take up position, and have the cable link put up."

"As you wish, sir. The name was Commander Merral D'Avanos."

"Thank you. And, Deltathree," Lezaroth lowered his voice, "my request is private. It is not to be known by anyone else." *Especially not Hanax.*

"As you wish, sir."

Pondering his newly gained information with a mixture of unease and satisfaction, Lezaroth walked slowly back to the bridge where he found the priest arranging with Hanax about the sacrifice to celebrate surfacing. *Very good. Let the under-captain occupy himself with such matters.*

Comms told him that the ambassadors were ready to talk. Informing Hanax that he was not to be disturbed—an action that had the incidental benefit of reminding the man that he was outside the decision loop—Lezaroth went to a conference room and sealed the door. He then waited five minutes; the ambassadors needed to be reminded who was in charge. As he did, he reviewed the overall situation again. *There's a prize here. Whoever seizes it for the lord-emperor will be richly rewarded. The ambassadors know this and I know it. Hanax may know it, although I have made sure that he's little threat. But whatever happens, I need to be sure I take the prize.*

Finally, he switched on the link.

Ambassador Hazderzal came onscreen and with him was a woman with long, golden hair who was introduced as Ambassador Tinternli.

As Lezaroth gazed at them, he found himself struggling to find the right words. Hazderzal looked polished, gentlemanly, no—distinguished—and Tinternli looked elegant and enchanting. From what he had learned of Assembly values, Lezaroth felt sure they would make the right impression. If there was to be an attempt to seduce Farholme to the Dominion, this was the way to do it.

"My compliments on your appearance," Lezaroth said, deciding that flattery would do no harm. *Of course, the praise really goes to the tissue programmers and flesh sculptors.* A closer glance showed a heavy look of tiredness about both of them. *Ah, the presence of the baziliarch in Nether-Realms travel had affected them, too.*

After more politely formal and utterly insincere greetings, they moved on to rehearse what was to happen over the next few weeks. The *Dove* was to continue its journey toward Farholme in Standard-Space and in about a day's time would make its broadcast announcing that it was a peaceful emissary from Lord-Emperor Nezhuala. They would request rights to land and then, later, ask to create a diplomatic base. While the *Dove*'s team did all it could to cement Farholme into the Dominion, the construction of the base would continue. When it was well advanced, the dormant baziliarch would be freighted down and installed in a chamber where, when needed, it could be awoken. While this was happening, the *Triumph* would be present nearby in the shallowest Nether-Realms with a hundred-kilometer-long cable linking it to a tiny satellite in Standard-Space so that they could monitor all that was happening.

As this was discussed, there was the first moment of open tension when Lezaroth reminded the ambassadors that they had just thirty days to gain what the lord-emperor wanted by diplomatic means. "Beyond that," he announced, "I will take over and we will be in the military option." *I will not risk a situation in which I achieve all that the lord-emperor desires of me and return victorious to Khalamaja, only to find that he and the fleet have departed for Earth.*

The ambassadors' response was reluctant but obedient; they would hold to the thirty-day deadline. Lezaroth was gratified that the lesson about who was in charge had been already learned.

There were other matters to deal with. On the basis that there might be a visit to the *Dove*, the ambassadors wanted to send all the tissue-sculpting units over to the *Triumph*. Lezaroth agreed. There was some debate over when, if ever, the ambassadors were to be allowed to use the single Krallen pack carried by the *Dove*. Here Lezaroth would have preferred to maintain supreme control, but in the end, he yielded responsibility to the ambassadors. It was a small concession that he felt was fairly meaningless and having won the overall victory, he felt he could be magnanimous. *It is folly to crush the defeated too much.*

The conversation ended with mutual good wishes in which the insincerity was transparent. Lezaroth switched the screen off and left for the bridge. It was busy with the full complement of officers. Lezaroth caught a glimpse of Hanax's face under its tangle of red hair and derived pleasure from the fact that the man was scowling. He ordered a descent back into the Nether-Realms and then gestured the weapons officer over.

"Wepps, after descent, I want all the Krallen checked—each one out of its casing, powered up, and all systems tested. And a full status report to me."

Wepps wrinkled his brow. "Cap'n, you're a hard man these days. Can't we wait until we're in orbit? Even with 3 percent nonoperational—and that's unheard of—we'd still have around one hundred and forty-five thousand ready."

"Wepps, I want us ready to launch a fast, crushing attack from the moment we reach Farholme orbit. I want full readiness before we get there."

"As you will, Cap'n." There was a pause. "So you anticipate us needing the Krallen despite this diplomacy stuff?"

Lezaroth looked forward to where a small star at the center of the screen vanished behind the gathering mists of the Nether-Realms.

"Wepps, trust my intuition: we are going to war."

ଠଠଠଠଠ

Early the next morning Merral and Lloyd flew to the Manalahi Shoals. Vero met them on the strip and Merral, squinting against the glare of the white coral sand, envied his friend's extra-dark glasses.

Gulls wheeled and squawked noisily above.

"The patient is doing well," Vero reported. "We haven't talked to him today, but he's eating. The infection is almost gone."

"And Betafor?" Merral said as they walked over to the whitewashed cluster of unfinished buildings.

"Still in her room. She behaves oddly. She'll stand as still as a piece of furniture for hours; then she'll walk around in perfect circles for another hour. She's very nimble—she can climb walls. Still wants to see Azeras. It'd be touching if I didn't suspect something else was going on. Anyway, the nurse has cleared us for forty-five minutes this morning with Azeras and an hour this afternoon. Let's go."

Sarudar Azeras had been placed in room six. The room's splendid view seaward more than compensated for the rough and incompletely painted walls.

Azeras was lying on his side staring out of the window. As he turned stiffly toward them, Merral noticed that his hair had been cut and his face shaved. There were numerous small scars on his face and arms. *He looks much younger than I guessed. He must be only in his late thirties.*

"Good morning," Vero said, moving to a chair at a distance from the bed.

Vero is clearly distancing himself.

Merral pulled up a seat by the bed and sat down. "Let me introduce myself. I'm Merral D'Avanos. And you are Sarudar Kezurmati Azeras?"

There was a long silence. Azeras stared at Merral with wide, dark gray eyes, eyes unlike any Merral had ever seen. He sensed anger, fear, and secrecy in them.

"Am I a prisoner?" he asked finally in a rough, frayed voice that was somehow too loud.

Merral and Vero exchanged glances.

"You are Sarudar Kezurmati Azeras?" Merral repeated.

"'Sarudar'?" he snorted. "Can a man still be sarudar when his ship and crew are destroyed?"

"The ship's destruction was an accident."

Azeras shrugged. "It doesn't matter now. They're dead."

"We would have preferred a surrender."

After another long silence, Azeras again asked, "Am I a prisoner?"

"At the moment you are a patient. What would you prefer we call you? Sarudar? Kezurmati?"

"Azeras will do. It is our fashion. Or Sarudar." Azeras's hard eyes seemed to assess Merral. "Are you *the* D'Avanos?"

"What do you mean?"

Azeras raised his left hand and moved his fingers as if exercising them. To Merral's astonishment, a large patch of skin on the back of his hand suddenly lit up and flickering images moved across it.

"Good grief!" Merral said.

"Ah," said Vero quietly, as if a suspicion was confirmed.

A tiny image of Corradon's head appeared on the screen and a faint voice could be heard—"Under the leadership of Merral Stefan D'Avanos"—followed by Merral's face.

Azeras flexed his fingers again and the screen darkened.

"I see," Merral said, gesturing in astonishment at the hand. "That's awfully . . . clever."

"A diary," Vero said. "Or its equivalent. Built in. Logical, I suppose."

Azeras turned to look out of the window.

"About your ship," Merral said. "We tried negotiation, but they fired on us. We were hoping to stop the ship taking off."

"Oh, I believe it." The words were almost a snarl. "Damertooth would have opened fire first. . . . A fool to the end."

"Damertooth? The captain?"

"Yeah. Good pilot, but he spent too long with the creepy." Azeras continued staring at the view from the window.

"'The creepy'?"

Azeras cautiously turned toward Merral. "A careless translation of a Freeborn phrase."

"For what?"

As Azeras's brow furrowed, Merral sensed unease. "For something that makes your flesh creep," Azeras replied.

"What can you tell us about this being?" Vero asked. "Was it in the steersman chamber?"

"What do you know about that?"

"I was on the ship," Merral said, quietly.

Azeras stared at Merral. "I heard that. It was on the broadcast. I didn't know whether to believe it or not. . . . Impressive." His voice held a note of grudging admiration.

"What was in the steersman chamber?" Vero asked, his tone unyielding.

Azeras's gaze dropped to his hands. "That's where the steering through the Nether-Realms—what you call Below-Space—is done."

"That wasn't the question, Sarudar," Vero said. "What was in this chamber? Was it the creepy?"

"Yeah." The voice was barely a whisper.

Out of the corner of his eye Merral saw Vero motioning him to continue. "There was something in that chamber—a spirit being, a demo—"

Azeras shuddered. "That thing! Don't blame me. It wasn't my idea!"

"Explain," Merral said.

"It wasn't our ship. We stole it. The True Freeborn don't use steersmen. Never have. We tried to take a stand against using extra-physical powers. We—"

"Wait!" interrupted Merral. "Extra-physical? Explain."

There was a pause. "Magic, the supernatural, contacting the *powers*. The things you don't do. They were in our past. But we tried to stop doing them."

"Why?"

"Oh, we realized that using the powers is like taking a drug. They gave strength, but at a terrible price. They cheat you. You think you strike a deal with them, but it never works. The powers always win in the end."

Vero shook his head but said nothing. Azeras continued. "Anyway, when Nezhuala started using the powers, we realized we faced a master magician who could defeat us. So we vowed not to use them at all."

At the mention of the name Nezhuala, Merral looked at Vero, who mouthed, *Later.*

"Go on," Merral said. "You seized this ship."

"Yeah. And we found a steersman on board. Now if it had been me in charge and not that worm-rotted fool Damertooth, we'd have ejected it into the vacuum then. I swear by the powers. But we needed all the speed we could get. We were being chased by Admiral Kalartha-Har and a steersman allows you to get deeper in the Nether-Realms. It's faster there." He shivered and paused before continuing. "Anyway, somehow we got through to Assembly space and landed here. We had to stay bottled up in the ship with that thing among us. It wasn't happy and started to take over the ship. It got so you always knew it was there. You could sense it, hear it chattering away in your mind. It poisoned our thinking. Certainly trashed Damertooth's." He turned back to the window, sighing. "And the steersman didn't do us much good, did it? All dead but me. And a machine."

There was a heavy silence that Merral didn't want to interrupt. Suddenly Azeras turned and looked hard at Merral. "So you made it through the chamber? And past the slitherwing, eh?"

"'The slitherwing'?" Merral remembered the dreadful flying creature. "An appropriate name. Yes, I met that too."

Azeras grunted. "We underestimated you. We thought you were primitives—peasants with mud on your feet and straw in your hair. We found your news broadcasts hilarious: 'Record hailstones in Snivelhome!' 'Earthquake in Back-of-Beyond—Cow killed!' 'Big attendance at picnic in Mongobongo!' How we laughed."

Merral struggled with Azeras's tone of voice. *Of course, it's sarcasm.* But Azeras was continuing. "We laughed at your petty preoccupations: religion, sports, the weather, your refusal to have a proper economy, your women pilots, your—"

"And what's funny about women pilots?" Vero snapped.

Azeras gave him a condescending look. "You would entrust an expensive vessel to a woman?"

"And you wouldn't?" Merral asked, aware of the deepening frown on Vero's face.

Azeras shrugged. "Women have their uses: bed, kitchen—maybe the brighter ones can teach children."

"Sarudar," Merral said before Vero could speak, "it might be worth remembering that your rescue was achieved by a female pilot."

Azeras yawned. "Civilian flying, not military." His cold gaze raked Merral. "Anyway if you killed a steersman, Commander, you were either lucky or the fates watched over you. But don't go thinking you're some big hero. There's more where they came from. And worse. And they'll be on their way soon."

We're hearing this confirmed from yet another source.

"So, what do you propose to do with me? Are you going to kill me? exhibit me? trade me to the Dominion?"

"We wouldn't do that," Merral protested. "None of it."

"Really? I'm from the Freeborn—the *True* Freeborn, not Nezhuala's illegitimate monstrosity." His voice held tattered pride. "That makes me an enemy of the Assembly. The Assembly hates the Freeborn worlds; it has tried to destroy us in the past." There was a sullen anger in the words.

Merral looked at Vero for help.

Vero put his long fingers together and peered at Azeras over them. When he spoke his voice was low. "Sarudar, you make assumptions about us without really knowing us. The coming of your ship cost us much. Lives were taken when the Gate was destroyed; more lives were lost at the lake. And we need to establish the facts. But we, not the Dominion, will decide your fate."

Merral nodded.

Vero continued. "And as to what happened in the distant past, well, we can compare our histories later. But we have no wish to hurt you."

"I agree," Merral added.

A long silence followed in which Merral observed a gold bracelet on Azeras's right wrist. The bracelet was a gold chain broken apart by a lightning bolt. He recognized it as the symbol of the True Freeborn Betafor had displayed.

"You must make your judgment," Azeras said. "But if you spare me, I'll help you."

Merral nodded.

"Sarudar," Vero said, "I'm surprised at how good your Farholmen is. How did you learn it?"

"An older version of Communal is still used in the Freeborn worlds . . . or was. As a traditional language. I was always good at languages. And from the moment we entered your system, we watched your world and listened." He gave an almost animal-like snort. "What else was there to do in the ship? And there was even less to occupy me on Ilakuma. So I watched your broadcasts."

After a pause, Merral asked, "Your wound, how did it occur?"

"I removed a life-bonding unit with a remote probe. It was a lousy unit and the pain control wasn't adequate. I don't reckon I sealed the wound right."

"If you hadn't removed it, what would have happened?"

"I'd have had two days to live. That's why I took the risk. . . . It got infected." He paused. "How'd you know where I was?"

"We had a message from Betafor. She asked that we meet with her. She took us to the cave."

"Thought so." He paused. "Look, all this *she* and *her* stuff is nonsense. That thing a person? *Bah!* Allenix units are just imitations of us. They aren't really alive. They don't really have feelings; they just copy ours. They won't admit they are only machines. They claim superiority to us—we're 'just' flesh—but they're really inferior. Humor it if you want and call it *she* but you always have to remember it's a thing." He paused again. "Did it explain why it wanted you to rescue me?"

"N-not really," Vero replied. "She said that you were her officer and that she had a duty to serve you."

Azeras's lips tightened in a humorless smile. He snorted again. *"That's* pretty funny. I hope you didn't give it an Assembly medal. So, it didn't explain that it was life-bonded to me?"

"To you?" Merral said, feeling that he had stupidly overlooked something obvious.

Vero's face registered shock.

"Yes. If I die, Betafor gets switched off permanently. It wouldn't like that. Not at all. I'm glad the other Allenix unit was destroyed."

"The second implant?" Merral asked. "That's its purpose? Of course."

"We removed it," Vero said.

Azeras's expression showed irritation. "Worms rot you! You should have asked me first! Let me guess: *she* encouraged you to remove it." His tone was sneering. "*She* sweetly asked how the operation went. *She* inquired whether the second implant was removed safely."

Vero squirmed on his seat. "A-as it happens, yes."

Azeras groaned. "Congratulations! You now have an unrestrained Allenix unit. You need a sanction over them to keep them loyal. They have their own agenda. Better keep that thing away from me! Oh, and let me make another guess. Has it asked to see me privately since the operation?"

"Yes."

There was a snort of contempt and Azeras said something that Merral didn't catch, but which seemed to be an expletive. "Check the pockets in its tunic. There'll be protests, but do it. There'll be a termination patch there—a small, silver-wrapped flexible square, thumb-sized. It's for suicide; every med gear carries a few. It's a fast-acting nerve poison. Betafor probably wanted to kill me before I could talk to you."

Merral reeled at the idea of a society *(Could you even call it a society?)* of beings filled with such mutual loathing that they were held together only by the severest threats.

Vero cleared his throat and leaned forward. "T-that's a very serious charge."

"I swear by the powers, if that thing gets access to me, and thinks no one is watching, it will kill me."

"But why contact us and have you rescued?" Merral asked.

"Because, my friend, if Azeras had died with the device in, she would have perished," Vero replied. "With it out, his death means nothing to her."

"You catch on," Azeras said. "Except that my death *does* mean something. I'm a nuisance, because I can tell you the truth about it. And you may decide to dismantle it. It is safer with me out of the way."

Merral caught the look of dismay on Vero's face.

Azeras spoke again. "Allenix units have only scorn for humans. They want us out of the way, because they want to replace us. That's why we life-bond them. If it was me, I'd switch it off. If it thought that the Dominion would serve its own purposes better, it would betray us all. But you people are different. You're too trusting. Well, beware!"

"Sarudar, this poison: is suicide an important part of your culture?" Vero asked.

"Death ain't nice, but it beats being thrown to a creepy or being taken alive by Nezhuala." He paused.

That name again.

"Just keep Betafor away from me." Azeras turned and stared out of the window again. After some moments he spoke. "I will say that this is a nice view." His voice was softer. "I love the sea. Never been on a world with a real sea, mind you. Not a big one. An ocean. But we always had the images." He shook his head as if remembering something. "You know, once I learned the ship was destroyed I was tempted to make a break for the sea at Ilakuma. Walk across the ridge. Build a hut, live off fish. But the wound didn't heal. Yes, you have real seas."

He stared out of the window for a few moments longer and then turned his haggard face to Merral. "So, who knows I am here?"

"Barely a dozen people. Betafor was insistent on secrecy."

"Good. If you decide that I may be of some use to you, I'll need to hide. And take my advice, terminate Betafor. That thing will betray you if it can. You trust too much!"

"Will the Dominion hunt for you?" Vero asked.

"Not for me." Azeras stopped and Merral felt there was something significant about his pause. "Not if they think we all perished with the ship." Azeras peered at Merral. "The ship *was* totally destroyed?"

"Yes," Merral said. "All we have are fragments."

"Ah."

Suddenly, a strange look crossed Azeras's face and Merral somehow found himself thinking of the old word *crafty*. But he said nothing more.

There was a knock at the door and a nurse entered. "I'm afraid this man needs a break," he said in a tone that allowed no disagreement.

"Very well," Merral replied. "We have all got plenty to consider. Sarudar Azeras, may we talk again this afternoon?"

"If you want. Just keep that Allenix unit away from me."

"We will."

ⴰⵞⴰⵞ

Two hours later, Merral stood next to Vero watching a large wallscreen showing a mosaic of smaller images. Most of the images were of half-painted corridors, but a central one showed a man lying—apparently asleep—on a medical cot with a white sheet draped over his body, his right arm on top.

"I don't like this," Merral protested.

"We have to test what Azeras said."

"It's close to tempting someone."

"My friend, she's a machine. Can a machine be tempted?"

"What did you tell her?"

Vero rubbed his nose. "I mentioned that the monitoring camera in his room—room five I told her—was going to be switched off. I also said Azeras said little and that he was heavily sedated. In a rather loud voice I told the man who was guarding her that we were going to the beach and that he ought to go for lunch."

"If we ever survive all this, I can see our actions being endlessly debated in ethics classes. 'Evaluate the morality of D'Avanos and Enand in their dealings with the Allenix unit. Use no more than five thousand words.'"

"My friend, I'll take that risk in order that people have the luxury to discuss ethics. Ah, here she comes." He pointed to the left-hand screen, where a green figure walked down a corridor on four legs. "So she defeated the lock. Not surprising; our technology in that area is rather simple."

Betafor's head swung from side to side with an oddly regular motion and Merral was surprised at how delicate her movements were.

"Zoom in," Merral commanded. Soon he could see that she walked on extended digits.

"On tiptoe," Vero muttered and tapped a microphone button. "She's on her way," he whispered.

A green acknowledgment light flashed and, a moment later, Vero said, "Entering the room now."

The green light flashed again.

"Full wall," Vero ordered. "Give us sound."

The image of the ward suddenly took up the whole screen. There was the sound of heavy breathing and—far harder to hear—soft footfalls.

Betafor stopped, moved into her crouching position and with her right forelimb reached inside her tunic. She pulled out a small silver packet, split it apart with a faint pop, and pulled something pale out of it.

"Now!" Merral ordered.

With remarkable speed, the figure on the bed flung the sheet off, swung his feet onto the floor, and pulled out a big double-barreled gun.

Betafor gave a strange mechanical squeal and bounded back.

"Put your hands up, you evil little machine!" Lloyd's voice echoed in the room. "One move and you are dead . . . recycled . . . whatever."

"We'd better intervene," Merral said, and as he followed Vero out of the room, he heard Betafor's voice squealing in protest, "That is not fair! A nasty trick!"

They raced down the corridor and burst into the ward. Lloyd, still seated on the bed, glared at Betafor, who sat on the floor with her forelimbs held up high. Her thin tail swept from side to side across the floor in agitation.

"Keep them up!" Lloyd snapped.

"Betafor, what are you doing here?" Merral asked.

"Visiting my officer. I was . . . bored. No . . . anxious. Sentinel Vero said you were going to the beach."

"Did he? And what's this?" Merral slipped a surgical glove on his hand and picked up the plastic disk on the floor.

"Medicine. A . . . vitamin supplement."

Merral stared at her, but read nothing from her expression. "Really?" He picked up the foil casing and stared at it. "I can't read the writing, Betafor, but the image is that of a skull. An unusual image for a medicine."

Merral slipped both items inside a medical sample bag and passed them to Vero.

"Betafor, if, as we suspect, this is poison, then you will be accused of attempted murder and punished appropriately. In the meantime, Sergeant Enomoto is going to take you to a new room—a storage room without windows where you will be more securely guarded and kept under surveillance. And please don't give the sergeant an excuse to fire."

Lloyd gave her a tight smile. "Go ahead. Make my day."

"Sorry, Lloyd?"

"It's an ancient threat, sir. Very effective under such circumstances."

"I see. Now, Betafor, we want to see what else you have in your tunic."

"You cannot do that." The pupils of the eye contracted into tight black disks. "It is unethical. My pockets are private."

"Tough," Merral said, feeling unsympathetic. "People caught in the act of attempted murder lose their rights. We need to see what's in them. Please give us your jacket."

"I refuse to take my clothes off. I am female. It would be sexual harassment."

Lloyd gave an explosive snort.

"Ah." Merral looked at the other two for help and found none. "Well, go behind the screen there and hand it to us."

"No."

"Or else, I will order Lloyd here to shoot you and then take you to bits."

"Slowly, with a very blunt screwdriver," Lloyd added.

"No need to overdo it, Sergeant."

"Sorry, sir."

"As you wish," Betafor said. She walked behind the screen and a moment later passed the jacket around the side.

Merral put the jacket—it was surprisingly heavy and there was some sort of electronic link on the inside—on the bed and went through the four inner pockets emptying the contents onto the table. There were a few small bottles and some small containers.

"What are these?"

"Lubricants, spare parts, adapters."

"We will check them and return them to you," Merral said, and handed the jacket back.

A minute later the creature emerged, with what seemed to be some sort of test pattern flickering across the sides of her tunic.

"Betafor," Merral announced, "Azeras said you would do this. You are no longer bonded electronically to him, but if he dies, we'll consider you the prime suspect, and you will be . . ."

"Terminated, sir?"

"Thank you, Sergeant. The exact word: *terminated*."

17

After making sure that Betafor was secure and handing the disk in for med-lab analysis, Merral and Vero found Perena, who had returned from Isterrane, and brought her up to date as they went to room six.

Azeras sat up in bed as they entered.

Merral introduced Perena.

"A lady captain," Azeras said, and gave Perena a long and intense look.

She flushed, and taking a chair, moved it so that she was out of his field of view.

Merral looked first at Perena and then at Azeras. *What's going on?*

Azeras turned to him. "So, have you decided on your verdict?"

"Not yet; it's a hard decision." *That's an understatement.* "We want to hear more. And I wanted Perena to be present."

The gray eyes gazed at Merral. "Without a decision there is a limit to what I can tell you about what you face."

"We need to know more before we decide what to do with you," Merral replied. "Let me start with the Dominion. You say they are coming?"

"Yes. They followed us into your system as far as they dared. But they will be back."

"It would help us if we knew the background here, about the Dominion and the Freeborn and why you came to Farholme. All we knew is that Jannafy's Rebellion ended at the battle at Centauri. But we now realize that our understanding is not accurate."

"The word *rebellion* would be disputed." There was an undercurrent of annoyance in Azeras's voice. "But as we found out when we accessed your Library, you and we have different histories."

"Fill us in with your version."

"As you wish. According to our history the Freeborn peoples escaped from the Assembly after moves were made to have their ideas and freedoms suppressed."

"That is hardly—," began Merral and then stopped. "Sorry."

"'Hardly *true*,' you were going to say?" Azeras flashed a cruel smile. "Indeed, but what is true in history? But what is a fact is that what *you* call 'the Rebellion,' *we* call the 'War of Separation.' And our tale runs in this manner. After taking Centauri in 2104, Jannafy and his leaders debated what to do. They had been driven from the solar system and were now on the defensive."

Azeras paused to sip from a glass of water and as he did, Merral recognized that Azeras's language had shifted to an older form of Communal. *What I am hearing now is a tale that has been told and retold for well over a hundred centuries.* He felt a sense of awe.

"Some of the Freeborn, as they now styled themselves, wanted a new all-out onslaught on Earth, but Jannafy's counsel was this: they would flee the vicinity of the Assembly altogether. He knew from their research that they could go deep into the Nether-Realms and emerge many light-years away. He was aware that an assault by the Assembly was inevitable, but as his forces held the Centauri Gate, he knew the assault could not be for some years. Calculations suggested that not even the fastest sublight-speed ships could reach them from Earth before the last months of 2110. His counsel prevailed and a desperate project was undertaken to prepare a migration fleet to take the Freeborn toward the edge of the galaxy. There were already seeder and colony vessels at Centauri; from them Jannafy constructed a fleet of seven ships. The calculations were performed and the ships were prepared for launching. But there were delays and the launch date slipped again and again so that it was midsummer of 2110 before the ships were ready."

Azeras paused. "And then, just as embarkation was only days away, the Assembly force arrived and attacked. Jannafy's forces were caught by surprise and in the fighting, he was fatally wounded. The Assembly forces planted some sort of massive bomb and began to retreat back through the Gate. Knowing they had only hours, the surviving leaders of the Freeborn launched the ships deep into the Nether-Realms."

Azeras sipped water again, cleared his throat, and winced slightly.

"Seven ships were launched, one after another, but only six emerged at the other end. The last—the seventh ship—was lost, presumably caught in the blast. That was another bad blow; the ship had much that was needed for making worlds habitable. Nevertheless, just over five thousand people made the passage safely. They checked their stars and realized they had come out over six hundred light-years from Earth. They knew they were safe for a long time."

He paused again and Merral was aware of Vero and Perena, leaning forward with wide eyes, utterly engrossed in this extraordinary and unexpected tale.

"But they faced many troubles," Azeras continued. "With the loss of the seventh ship they couldn't seed worlds as the Assembly did; they had neither the equipment nor the luxury of time. They had to use such worlds as they could find. But all they came to were poor ones; those with any oxygen were nothing more than slime worlds."

"The algal scum worlds we sterilize before Seeding," Merral interjected, too immersed in the account to keep silent.

"Exactly. And there were internal problems. Jannafy's death had left a gigantic void that was not easily filled. There were many disagreements. Some honored him, keeping his body in a mausoleum and praising him as the 'Great Leader' and the 'Father of the Freeborn.' Others felt that he had misled them and dragged them into a bitter wilderness. And there were differences on the way forward. Some wanted to create an utterly new culture and bury the past. Others wanted to preserve what had been good in the Assembly. Neither side won entirely, so the Freeborn worlds were a mixture of old and new. There was a new language, but the old Communal was not lost. And . . ."

Now Azeras fell silent for a moment, his worn face darkening. "There was something else. The stories do not speak about it plainly, but there are dark hints. In going through the Nether-Realms something became linked with our people. There a shadow fell on us, a shadow from which, alas, we have never been able to set ourselves free."

"The steersmen," Merral said, in the charged silence that followed. "Is that what you refer to?"

"Yeah. The steersmen and other extra-physical beings like them. The Freeborn people learned to travel Below-Space by using the steersmen. But those creatures drove hard bargains."

Azeras sighed and from his expression Merral realized that he did not wish to say more on that topic. He continued, "And soon the Freeborn became divided and from then on there were always disputes and wars between them. They barely survived. There were never more than twenty-five worlds and the total population was almost never more than thirty million. Indeed, after some wars, our numbers were much less."

He paused again and Merral caught a glimpse of Perena's face and noted the look of anguish and horror it bore.

"Then five hundred standard years ago things changed. A line—a lineage—began to take control of the central Freeborn worlds. Around the star we call Sarata, there are four habitable worlds. On one of them—Khalamaja, the most populated—a lineage, the House of Carenas, rose to power and began to crush its opposition. The Dominion had arrived. Soon there was order and stability in the inner worlds. But it came at a price." Azeras shook his head. "Everything comes at a price. The stability the Carenids brought allowed them to create mighty armies that made them almost unstoppable. Their rule spread outward until the outer worlds united in resistance as the True Freeborn. Then, about fifty standard years ago, a new ruler of the Carenid dynasty appeared: Nezhuala."

Azeras grimaced and with his right forefinger made an odd, circular gesture. "Nezhuala set himself up as lord-emperor and imposed his will on the Dominion. He began a new phase of expansion. One by one, the worlds of the True Freeborn were besieged, defeated, and brought into bondage. A year ago, my own world, Tellzanur, was attacked. We fought hard, but there is a power behind Nezhuala's forces that cannot be resisted. In the end . . ." A hard expression slipped across his face and he turned to stare at the sea.

"In the end . . . ," he repeated, his voice faint, "Tellzanur fell and . . . was burned. Some ships escaped. How many, I do not know. I do not know whether the True Freeborn cause still exists or whether I am the last survivor."

He paused, as if momentarily overwhelmed by his memories, and then continued. "We escaped, commandeered a Dominion vessel, *Rahllman's Star,* a freighter—"

"Freighter?" Merral asked in surprise.

"Yes, a freighter." Azeras looked at Merral, as if puzzled at his surprise. He glanced at the others and then a hard smile broke across his face. "I see. You thought you had won against a military ship. No, merely a freighter with light armor and even lighter weapons."

Merral, appalled at the revelation and its implications, looked at the others and saw expressions of dismay. *They realize the same thing. Threatened as we are, we had, at least, the small consolation that we had already defeated a military vessel. Now that most slender of comforts has been lost.*

Azeras continued. "We were pursued by a warship. In desperation, we headed toward the Assembly."

Vero raised his hand slightly. "You knew this world existed?"

"Yes, the Freeborn had long watched and listened to Assembly signals. We had always feared discovery and a new attack from the Assembly, although we have known for millennia that this world was the limit of your expansion in this direction. One or two expeditions were mounted to observe the Assembly. But they all failed; we could not enter your space. The steersmen spoke of a wall that they could not—or would not—go beyond. The steersmen lie, but on this they seemed to speak the truth. A few attempts to use ships without steersmen also failed."

Azeras paused before continuing. "But we had no choice: we were prepared for death and we knew that death was preferable to what Nezhuala had in store for us. We prayed to our gods—to Fate or to Destiny. So, we fled headlong toward the Assembly, chased by the warship. I remember the steersman's screams shaking the ship. Then, somehow, we were through this barrier."

Azeras drank water before speaking again. "We found the nearest inhabited system and drifted in carefully. We were pursued, but the warship kept its distance. We didn't really know what we were up against. But we knew we were likely to be followed sooner or later and we decided to hide somewhere uninhabited. Damertooth was good when it came to piloting—too bad his luck ran out—and we landed in good shape. We hoped we were unseen and tried to hide."

"The last bit we deduced," Merral said, "but go on."

"Well, the good landing was the last bit of luck we had. It soon began to go sour. The crater was too cold. We had a dozen men on board and a hundred or so chimpies and bug boys."

"'Chimpies'? 'Bug boys'?" Vero's voice sounded distant. "What we call ape-creatures and cockroach-beasts?"

"Yeah, I guess so. In hindsight, we should have voided almost all of them into the vacuum, but we didn't. Anyway, Damertooth tried to use them for recon to see what it was like to the south, but they bungled it." Azeras shook his head. "Well, Captain—wherever in the Nether-Realms your soul is now—you paid for that decision. And we knew that you had discovered us. That's why Damertooth had the Gate blasted. Another bad move really." He waved a finger. "I think toward the end, Damertooth's judgment was shot. He would go and talk with the steersman. That's not the way; everyone knows not to get too close to creepies. You simply tell them where you want to go, promise them something tasty, and you get out. But to listen to them?" He pursed his lips and for a moment Merral thought he was going to spit. "Nah. Everyone knows that sort of stuff rots your brains."

"What sort of *something* tasty?" Merral said, remembering again the horror of crunching bones underfoot in the steersman chamber.

Azeras's expression was unreadable. "Prisoners, people who cause trouble. Relax! I never did it. I don't agree with steersmen, remember. And we fed no locals to him. None of yours. That was policy. We gave him a bug boy or a chimpie every dozen days. It wasn't what they wanted."

Merral saw Perena's face pale and felt she wanted to be sick. *I sympathize.*

"In the end, we men made a decision to take radical action. We decided to kill all the chimpies and bug boys, blast the steersman and the slitherwing, and put the Krallen pack on self-destruct. Then we'd take the ship, the men, and the two Allenix units and go south. The original landing zone was badly chosen. It was too cold and too exposed. We knew that when the Dominion came, they'd would find us. And after the encounter between you and the bug boys, we guessed you would be hunting us as well. So we planned a move to a better place to hide—some nice warm cleft covered in jungle." He shrugged. "And ultimately, there was an idea of at least of some us merging with the population."

"You were planning to *merge*?" Vero's voice was filled with incredulity.

Azeras seemed embarrassed. "It was an idea, that was all. We would have turned up in different communities over time with memory loss. In a world of thirty million people and no suspicions, it wouldn't be hard to lose a dozen men. You don't even have identity chips."

"Is that why you learned our language so well?"

"Yeah."

Vero, who had been staring into the distance, turned to look at the man in the bed. "With a green, four-legged talking machine?"

Azeras shrugged. "The Allenix units were superfluous. We would have got rid of them."

Perena shook her head in a manner that suggested utter disbelief. "So, Sarudar, in order to merge into Ilakuma you would have 'got rid of' Betafor?"

"Yeah."

She expelled a long, slow breath. "I really don't know whether to find this funny, tragic, or utterly incomprehensible. She planned to get rid of you; you planned to get rid of her."

"Lady Captain, that's a fair insight into how things work."

Perena swallowed. "How they *worked*, Sarudar. Past tense. Things here are different."

"All right." Azeras tried craning his head to see her, but gave up the effort. "Have it your way—"

"It's not *my* way. It's the way things are done here. The Assembly belongs to the Lamb." Perena's face was stern.

Azeras waved a dismissive hand. "Right. Apologies. *Sorry.* Anyway, I was dropped off on Ilakuma with that thing to survey a new site. I had been there a few days and had found a place. Betafor was to help on that. We were on the lookout in case the area was visited by hunting parties."

Merral was suddenly struck by how the small details of the conversations highlighted the gulf between the cultures. The phrase *hunting parties*—presumably men pursuing animals to kill them for fun or food—was a case in point.

"Then the news came from the *Slave* that they were being watched and were preparing to leave urgently. The next morning we got the message that they were under attack. Then there was silence."

Azeras fingered his bracelet.

"The Krallen on the ship. Whose were they?" Vero asked in a sharp tone.

"The Dominion's."

"The Freeborn don't use them?"

"Well, only when we acquire them and reprogram them."

"Are you sure? We want the truth."

"Oh, well," Azeras said with a shrug. "Both sides use them. And if any are captured, their loyalties are realigned."

Merral saw Perena whisper something to Vero.

"One issue," Vero asked. "A fundamental one. You talk of fate, destiny, and the powers: what do your worlds believe?"

"In the Freeborn Worlds there are—or were —no fixed beliefs. We are free, right? Some of us believe in a god or gods, others believe in Fate. Some believe that our destiny can be changed; others that we must play the parts that are written for us."

He frowned and fell silent. "We also believe in the powers. Communal does not have an exact word for them. *Dark spirits? Demons?* Perhaps. Things like the steersmen and the—" He stopped himself. "A man will do well to keep them away from him and his family. There are rituals—ways of keeping them away." He made again the odd circular gesture with his forefinger and then sighed. "Or of *trying* to keep them away. But they are never fully defeated. The powers always win in the end."

"They don't!" The sharp defiance in Perena's voice made everyone turn toward her.

"Fine words, Lady Captain, but you asked me for my beliefs. And when you have seen what I have seen, you may think otherwise."

"And the Dominion?" Vero asked.

Azeras scowled. "The Dominion? They increasingly treat Nezhuala as a god. And they know no boundaries." He looked around. "I swear on the powers: the Freeborn have always held to limits in their dealings with the powers, but not the Dominion. Nezhuala has gone furthest of all. He has summoned the most potent forces to aid him. His victories are not achieved just by his men or machines. He fights with things that cannot be resisted. Of—" Suddenly he broke off. "What Nezhuala is doing is not something I wish to talk about. Not now. Perhaps later."

"Indeed," Merral said. "We have spoken of that enough. But you know we have no such dealings? That we serve only the one God: Father, Son, and Spirit?"

Vero and Perena nodded.

"That I know."

There was a silence in which Merral could hear the whisper of the air-conditioning and the muted sound of the sea.

"Does this help your verdict?" Azeras asked.

"Perhaps," Merral said.

Vero leaned forward. "Let me ask you a question: what would you like to do?"

"Me? Using standard years, I am thirty-five. I have been a fighter for half that time. I did not choose to be one. There are many other careers I would have preferred—a scholar perhaps. No doubt you see us as monsters or barbarians—"

"No!" interrupted Perena. "We see you as . . ." She faltered. "A tragedy. I wish we had known about you generations ago. Then we might have helped."

Azeras seemed to ponder her words. "Thank you, Lady Captain. But we are human like you. We love, we care, and we weep." He stared out of the window. "I have known suffering. All who have been close to me—lovers, children, colleagues, comrades—all now are lost beyond recall in death's gray lands. The powers always win."

He fell silent, his eyes evidently tracing the path of a flock of white-winged terns as they skimmed over the waters. "This is a beautiful world. We appreciate beauty, you know. We have little of it and little time for it. What would I like? I would like peace. . . . A hut at the water's edge."

Merral was suddenly overwhelmed by sympathy for this man and his sorrows and longings. He heard Perena sniff and saw her rub her eyes.

Azeras looked at Merral and Vero, his gray eyes now almost defiant again. "But why tease me with my wishes? I am your prisoner, at your disposal. Whatever I now face, I trust I will face with honor and courage."

How strange. I had expected to fear this man, loathe him perhaps. But instead I find that, like Perena, my emotion is pity. Merral glanced at Vero and then turned to the thin man on the bed. "We'll consider your situation this evening and talk to you tomorrow. Do you have anything else to say?"

"Yes. I ask for mercy."

18

O utside the ward, Merral, Perena, and Vero walked to the end of the corridor.

"Are you all right, Perena?" Vero asked.

"No. The whole thing . . ." Perena stared down the corridor, her face pale. "The history of the Freeborn makes me want to cry. I'd assumed—we all had—that for the last twelve thousand years ours was the only story. I now find that while we have had our prosperity and peace, far beneath us this other tale of endless, awful misery has been unfolding. We have had sunlight; they have been in utter darkness. Cities, countries—even whole planets—laid waste. It's horrid beyond words."

There was a long and sympathetic silence.

Finally Merral said, "Perena, at the start something passed between you and Azeras. I was wondering what."

She blushed. "I was just stunned by the way he looked at me with . . . a fire of lust. His eyes were almost stripping me bare. I've never felt that before. . . ."

Vero's face tightened.

Merral found himself staring at the floor. "We all need time to think," he said, deciding that a change of subject was appropriate. "But over supper, we need to decide what we do with this man. Do we treat him as an enemy? Do we try and get him on our side? Do we even believe him?"

Vero stared at the ground. "Yes, those are some of the many questions. I need to think more. Look, I'll be inside. I need to make some calls about the irregulars. It needs to be business as usual or people will suspect."

Without a word he put his dark glasses on and walked down the corridor.

Perena watched him go and then, with a troubled face, turned to Merral. "It's all too much. I'm going for a run. Maybe some exercise will clear my mind."

ㅇㅇㅇㅇㅇ

Merral toyed with going for a run too, but decided on a short walk instead. He found a path that led to a small raised ridge of debris from the reefs covered in palms and vegetation.

Since being abandoned after the Gate's destruction, vegetation had started to reclaim the island; creepers, vines, and wiry grasses had begun to cover the path. On an impulse, Merral went back inside and found a bush knife and then cleared the path, finding the exercise soothing. On top of the ridge, he found a dusty table and some chairs set out under a crude and sagging shade of thatched palm fronds. He tidied up the place a little and then sat down and stared at the pristine green-blue of the sunlit sea, listening to the rumble of the waves on the beach as he pondered all he had heard and the many issues the information raised.

Finally, Merral contacted Isterrane on the secure line and, careful not to give away his location, answered various urgent calls that had been sent to him. One was oddly troubling. The guards at Brenito's house were worried about Jorgio. Over the last few days he had become distressed and complained of having had terrible dreams. Merral made a mental note to visit him and then, still preoccupied by Azeras's words, attempted to get through his correspondence.

Some time later, as the shadows lengthened, Perena joined him. She still seemed troubled.

"How was the run?" he asked.

"It helped me deal with things, especially that awful revelation of a dark underside to our existence that we had never suspected."

"I know. Perena, the only consolation I can find—and it is a small one—is the scale of it all. The Freeborn have never been more than a small fraction of the Assembly's numbers. At times it seems, they were barely a millionth of our size."

"But, Merral, think . . . we're still talking about hundreds of thousands, even millions, of individuals."

"I know."

Her face cleared. "And yet there is a brighter side. For the first time, I see the value of the Assembly—of all we've stood for. Without God's grace, we would have been like them."

"A good point."

"And it emphasizes the value of what we must fight for."

Minutes later, Merral looked up to see Vero slowly walking toward them. Without a word, he sat down and stared out to sea.

"The test results are in," he suddenly announced in a perplexed tone. "Betafor's patch was a toxin. One of a family of drugs that can give sudden nervous system failure. We would never have suspected it. So we have a legal novelty: Farholme's first attempted murder. And, just to make life more fun, committed by a sentient machine."

ꕚꕚꕚꕚꕚ

The debate on the weighty matters raised by Betafor and Azeras lasted all evening. Merral, Vero, and Perena sat outside on the ridge and, as the light faded, Lloyd, who had volunteered to cook, joined them with supper. As they discussed the issues raised, the evening darkened into night and the stars in all their glory came out above them.

They all agreed that matters were complex. Were they passing a legal judgment? Had they any right to do so? Vero suggested that, as commander in time of war, Merral had the authority to pass military judgments. The others agreed and despite a profound unease, Merral found himself accepting that view. It simplified matters and indeed there was no other option. It was another military necessity.

Afterward they discussed whether they could trust anything that either Betafor or Azeras said. It had been proved that one was a liar and that the other didn't tell the whole truth. All agreed that both had to be treated with caution.

"We have already learned much and, if we can handle these two in the right way, we will learn much more," said Vero. "And this knowledge is made even more valuable by virtue of the fact that the Dominion will not know we have it. Ironically, we find ourselves in agreement with our guests—we must not reveal their existence. We must pretend that everything perished with the ship. Whatever we do, they must be our greatest secret."

Eventually, late at night and after prayer, they reached their decisions. The judgment on Betafor was easy to agree on; that concerning Azeras was less easy. In the end, they decided to take a risk.

ꕚꕚꕚꕚꕚ

The next morning Merral, Vero, and Perena, accompanied by Lloyd and his double-barreled gun, went to see Betafor in the basement room where she had been placed.

To their surprise, they found her hanging upside down from the ceiling beams. As they entered she released her grip, spinning as she dropped, and landed softly on all four feet.

"Betafor," Merral said, "we have considered your case. We find you guilty of attempted murder. Do you have anything to say?"

Betafor's mouth moved into a tauter version of the pseudosmile. "Yes. You cannot blame me. Human beings made me. It is your fault. I am programmed for . . . survival."

"An interesting defense," Merral said, suddenly at a loss for an answer. He looked to the others for help.

"May I, Commander?" Perena said.

"By all means."

"Betafor, are you a person or a machine?"

"A person."

"Machines can't choose; a person can. Can you make choices?"

Betafor said nothing.

Merral watched her closely. *Check.*

Perena waited for a moment. "If we accepted your defense, we would have to agree that you were a machine, not a person. We would therefore treat you as a thing and probably would dismantle you. Given that, do you still wish to offer that defense? Or do you wish to withdraw it?"

Checkmate.

Betafor's tail whisked backward and forward across the floor.

A nervous twitch?

Finally she spoke. "I withdraw it."

"Thank you, Perena," Merral said. "Betafor, our sentence is this: First, you are to be kept under guard for the foreseeable future. Second, any further attempt to hurt anyone else will result in your instant termination. Do you understand these two rules?"

"Yes."

"Good. Now third, we are concerned about the Krallen and believe that you may hold the key to any defense against them. You are therefore offered a choice: either help us develop defenses against them voluntarily or we'll use you without your permission. Do you want Lloyd to explain the last option?"

Betafor's head swiveled toward Lloyd, and in the twist of the lips Merral sensed unmistakable hatred. "As you wish. I will help you."

"Thank you. That's all for the moment."

Five minutes later, in room six, Merral, in the presence of Vero and Perena, delivered another judgment.

Is this going to work? Or have we made a mistake?

"Sarudar Azeras," he said, "deciding on a verdict has been hard. We have no laws in such cases and I fear that even if we could bring you to the authorities in Isterrane it would be years before the suitable legislation could be formulated. However, there are many ancient precedents under military law for actions in time of war. So, as commander of the forces of Farholme, I pass judgment. I recognize that you and your colleagues fought against us and that your ship brought us great trouble. Yet you have pleaded for mercy and I choose to offer you mercy. If you promise, on solemn oath, not to harm us or the Assembly, I will set you free without any other conditions."

"Free?" Azeras gave them a look of pure distrust.

"Yes. As free as we are. You may come to Isterrane and we will give you clothes, a diary, and everything else you need. Then you may go where you please. Your people style themselves the True Freeborn; we will grant you freedom."

"Is this a genuine offer?" The tone was wary.

"Yes. The Assembly operates on the principle of grace. As the Most High has forgiven us, so we must forgive you."

"So I would become a member of the Assembly?"

"Yes. There is no other way of existence here."

"Would I have to follow your way of life?"

"Yes. To do otherwise would be to work against us."

Azeras evidently puzzled, rubbed his pale face with his hand. "And would I have to believe in the same things?"

"We cannot force your beliefs. But our actions flow from what we believe. You would find it easiest to work for the good of the Assembly—and be a member of the Assembly—if you sought to follow the Assembly's King."

"Yeah." Azeras looked at the three of them with a tight-lipped expression. "You'll excuse me if I am cautious, even suspicious."

"It is a genuine offer. If you accept the conditions we have stated, we will declare what you did a past matter."

"So, I could just walk away and do what I want?"

"As long as you didn't seek to harm us."

"Generous. Or foolish."

"Grace can be seen as foolishness. But there is one thing."

"Ah, the catch."

Merral ignored his comment. "Farholme faces a war against an enemy. You know that enemy; we do not. We would prefer your assistance in our struggle. But we cannot demand it."

Azeras slowly got to his feet, shuffled to the window, and stared out toward the sea. "So, on the one hand, I'm set free, but on the other, I'm given a request that I cannot easily refuse."

He fell silent for several moments. Finally, he said, "You can't imagine—none of you can—what it is like to spend all your adult life fighting. To lose everything you have cared for. I lost a lover and two children. And, where it counts, I lost my own life. I might have been something: a poet, a teacher of languages . . . I don't know." He leaned against the glass and then turned to them, his pale face defiant. "I do not want to assist you, to help you make weapons or teach you tactics. . . . No! I don't want to see a uniform or a weapon ever again. I would give almost everything to find peace." He gestured over his shoulder. "I want my beach."

How can I answer? If you substituted forest *for* beach, *I could echo every word*.

Vero answered for him. "Sarudar, if peace were an option, we would take it ourselves. But it isn't. The Dominion is coming. And if Farholme is taken, you will be taken too."

Azeras nodded heavily. "Yes. Nezhuala's forces wouldn't overlook me. Eventually they would find me." Azeras turned to Merral. "If I joined with you, served as what—a military advisor?—what would I be rewarded with?"

"We would give you the wages of a representative."

Azeras smiled briefly. "Which are, I gather, the same as those of a refuse collector."

"You have learned something about us. What had you in mind?"

"A house by the sea, a supply of wine, a woman."

Merral heard a sharp intake of breath from Perena.

"The first we might manage; the second would involve you growing your own vineyard. And as for the third? I think Captain Lewitz ought to speak."

As Perena turned to Azeras, Merral sensed anger in her eyes. "In the Assembly, Sarudar, women are not commodities to be mentioned in the same breath as properties or drink."

"My apologies, Lady Captain. I must retrain my tongue."

"Sarudar—if I may be so bold—you must go deeper and retrain your mind too. I do not care to be stared at as if I were some delicacy on a table."

Azeras nodded. "If you fight as you talk, Lady Captain—forgive me, *Captain*—then the Dominion may be in for a surprise. But I accept the rebuke. I apologize."

"Thank you." Perena hesitated. "The apology is accepted."

"And our offer?" Merral asked. *This better work.*

Azeras shook his head. "No. I can't accept it. Not in that form. I have made oaths to the cause of the True Freeborn Worlds." He held up his arm so that they could see the bracelet. "This is more than jewelry. It is a symbol of my allegiance to them. I cannot fight for another cause. But there is an alternative to becoming a member of the Assembly."

"Which is?" Merral asked.

"I remain a servant of the Freeborn Worlds, but enter into an alliance with you. I will serve you faithfully and offer my services for your standard rates of pay."

"But the Freeborn worlds may, by now, no longer exist," Vero said.

"Sadly true. If we knew that for sure, my loyalty would be ended and my response would be different. But though I fear it, I do not know for sure. And in the meantime I offer you an alliance."

Merral looked at the others. "Excuse us for a moment."

After a ten-minute discussion at end of the corridor, Merral and the others returned to the room to find Azeras leaning on the windowsill and staring out the window.

"So," he said, as he turned to look at them, "do we have a deal?"

"Yes," Merral replied, trying to withhold a sigh. "We will accept you on that basis. We will protect you and treat you fairly if you promise to serve us honestly and not betray us."

"Sounds like a deal to me."

"Good. Do you promise on oath? By all that you believe in?" *I wish I could get him to make a firmer oath.*

"I'll promise to serve you honestly and not betray you. On my honor: on the solemn oath of an officer of the True Freeborn." He touched his bracelet.

"Very well." *What choice do we have but to accept this?*

They shook hands.

"Now, Sarudar Azeras, I think there are things you need to tell us."

"Indeed. There are things you need to know if you—we—have any hope of defense. I feel fit enough to walk a little. May we sit outside?"

ᗑᗜᗑᗜᗑ

They found Azeras some overalls and got together a tray of cold drinks. While Vero and Perena walked out with the sarudar to the chairs under the shelter, Merral caught up with Lloyd, who he had left to mind his diary on the veranda. There had been a call from Clemant and, anxious not to deepen any suspicions there, Merral returned it.

It was a long but routine matter and as he talked, Merral watched the group as they settled under the shade of the shelter after Vero lopped off a strangling palm frond with the bush knife to cover a hole in the roof. Soon, Azeras, Perena, and Vero were deep in conversation. Every so often glances would be thrown Merral's way.

Finally, the interminable call ended and Merral handed the diary back to Lloyd. "Sergeant, I don't want to be interrupted unless it's an emergency."

As he walked over to the shade, the group stopped talking.

Aware of a strained and preoccupied silence, Merral helped himself to a drink and sat down.

"Sorry. The pressures of being a commander. Have I missed anything?"

He caught awkward, almost guilty looks from his friends, but Azeras spoke.

"First of all, Commander, this has intrigued me." He picked up the bush knife Vero had used earlier and ran his fingers gently along the edge, puzzlement in his gray eyes. "It's sharp, but not that sharp. Yet Sentinel Enand here lopped off that frond without an effort. What's going on?"

Taking the blade back and closing it up before laying it by a tree, Merral said. "The edge is molecularly tuned for wood and parts the wood molecules as it strikes. We have blades for different substances. You don't have this sort of thing?"

"No. It is interesting. There are some areas where your technology exceeds ours."

In a flash of insight, it occurred to Merral that the technology of the Freeborn emphasized power. *It's how we differ. Where we would seek a subtle blade, they would just make a more powerful one.*

Merral turned to Azeras.

"This Nezhuala—the Dominion—is coming. What do they want?"

"Ah." Azeras said. "That's what I've been explaining to your friends. There is a problem."

Vero interrupted. "It's the baziliarch, Merral."

Merral felt a shadow of fear fall on his mind.

"Tell me more, Sarudar. Betafor mentioned these creatures."

Azeras sighed in a way that hinted at depths of pain. "We first met one at Tellzanur. We know little of them. They are powers from the Nether-Realms. They are potent on the battlefield; they destroy all morale. But the problem is this: they can rip information from minds."

"So Betafor told us and it worried us."

"Now, Commander, let me ask you a question. If the Dominion forces bring a baziliarch—and I'm sure they will—and they want to know everything about the defenses, who will they use it on?"

There was a long silence in which Merral heard, as if a long way away, the cries of the terns, the crash of the waves, and the creak of the palm trees.

"Me," he said.

Vero and Perena nodded, looking uneasy.

Azeras gave a rough smile. "Exactly. They'll get the head of the Defense Force and pump his head dry."

"My friend," Vero said in a low voice, "we do have a problem. I guessed as much when this was first mentioned."

"Sarudar, what do you suggest?"

Azeras smiled again, but Merral found no warmth in it. "The only answer, Commander, is for you to know as little as possible."

"You mean . . . ?"

"You already know too much. That cannot be helped. But if I am to help your defense I cannot risk having any dealings with you. Betafor and I must disappear."

Vero gestured to Azeras. "Sarudar, you'd best leave us for five minutes. We need to talk."

Azeras grunted agreement. He slowly rose and walked down toward the sea's edge.

"This is impossible!" Merral said. "I'm head of the defense forces. I have to know what's going on!"

Vero and Perena looked at each other.

"My friend, we heard this from Betafor. I think there is a risk here that we must treat seriously."

Perena leaned toward Merral. "There is a precedent. You already have the irregulars and you don't know what's happening with them in detail. Assign Azeras and Betafor to them and let Vero take charge of them."

After further arguments, Merral was forced to reluctantly agree. He did however win a promise that both Vero and Perena would supervise matters.

Azeras was called back. "Good," he said when told of the verdict. "That is a refreshing sign of wisdom. But, Commander, I have been thinking and I realize that there are some things I can tell you about what you will face. Indeed, there's a matter that we need you to make a decision on."

"Go ahead."

There was another rough smile. "The lord-emperor wants his ship back very badly. He wants *Rahllman's Star*."

Funny. I remembered it being called Slave of Rahllman's Star *earlier.*

Vero pushed his dark glasses up his nose and gestured at the sea. "Well, he's lost that. It's in a million pieces at the bottom of Lake Fallambet."

"Ah-ah." Azeras wagged a reproving finger. "There are some things that none of you know. How do you think we got here, Commander? Do you think that ship brought us here? Did you believe we could fit a Nether-Realm drive into that hull?"

Perena placed her glass on the table with exaggerated care. "Are you saying, Sarudar, that you did *not* travel here on that ship?" Her words held an electric tremor.

"Of course not. It was not built for that. It's the lander—what we call a 'slave.' That's where the name comes from: *Slave of Rahllman's Star*."

"T-there's another ship!" Vero said and, beneath the glasses, Merral saw a look of puzzlement visibly transforming itself into one of understanding. "Oh, what a *fool* I've been! Another ship. Why didn't—?"

Azeras raised a hand to quiet him. "The parent ship is the *Rahllman's Star*—A much larger vessel with a Nether-Realms drive. And it's hidden."

"Where?" Merral asked, a hundred implications cascading into his mind.

Azeras gestured upward. "In the Nether-Realms or what you would call Below-Space. I have the coordinates and, if I can get near it in Standard-Space, I can summon it."

"It will work?" Perena asked, eagerness and hope erupting in her voice. "Will—?"

"C-can it get us to the rest of the Assembly?" interrupted Vero.

"Slowly!" Azeras said. "I knew this would be news. Let me take it bit by bit. There is a ship buried in Below-Space. Probably no more than two or three million kilometers away by now; it was set to drift toward your world. It can be accessed, but it would take perhaps two or three days to get it up and running again. You could replace the *Slave* unit by one of your own ships, but you'd have to do some engineering in order to dock it smoothly. I'd guess a week's work to get everything done."

"How quickly can we—?" Vero began.

"There's where you need to make a hard decision." Azeras's tone was sharp. "I've done the calculations on the time for a ship to return to the Dominion and a military force to be sent out. The lord-emperor will not have delayed. I think they will be here soon—very soon. And if they surface while the *Rahllman's Star* is in Standard-Space, we're all finished. They may be lurking in the uppermost Nether-Realms even now. So we could try and recover the ship now. But it would be risky."

"But won't they find it when they come?" Merral asked.

"No, at those depths, the Nether-Realms are too deep and too dark."

Perena nodded. "The opaque zone."

"Yeah. Oh, after a lot of fishing they *might* find it. But unless they know our exact trajectory, it might take a year."

Vero stared at Azeras. "But if we found this ship, brought it to the surface, took it over, we'd reach Bannermene when?"

"Four weeks or thereabouts."

"Four weeks!" The excitement rang in Vero's voice.

Merral gestured caution. "There are decisions we need to make before that happens, Vero."

Azeras grunted. "If you go, you ought to go soon. The chance of being caught is high and it is rising by the day."

Perena raised a finger. "Why does this lord-emperor want this ship so badly?"

"He'll probably want to recover the ship so it doesn't fall into Assembly hands. But he particularly wants it because Zhalatoc is on it."

Merral remembered the disfigured bust he had seen on the ship with its defaced inscription: *Zhalatoc, Great Prince of the Lord-Emperor Nezhuala's Dominion.* "Zhalatoc is living on this ship?"

"Living?" Azeras gave a sour grin. "*Bah!* That's an overstatement! Zhalatoc is biologically dead and has been for centuries, or so I've heard. But his body is kept—I'm afraid there is no Communal word for much of this and you won't like it—intact. And his spirit and mind reside in it. Sort of. And as he is a close ancestor of Nezhuala's, the lord-emperor wants him back. That's partly why they pursued us. It's clan honor."

Perena shook her head. "This is almost too much. But why is this done? Why isn't he allowed to die? Why all this nightmarish stuff with his being kept alive?"

Azeras stared at her. "Captain, they fear death. So they seek to stay alive. By whatever means."

Perena blanched. "Those who belong to the Assembly do not fear death. We know what lies beyond it for the King's people."

Azeras bowed his head. "Ah, fine words, as ever, Captain. Perhaps when you meet death you may reconsider."

"Please!" Merral said sharply. "But how do they do such things?"

"They have agents—the Wielders of the Powers—who deal with the beings in the Nether-Realm. They ensnare the steersmen for the ships; they give them bodies and use their powers to bind the dying so they cannot die. Only Nezhuala himself has greater abilities than the Wielders of the Powers."

"Is that what happens among the True Freeborn as well?"

"Those faced with death sometimes seek such a remedy. I do not deny it."

"You realize," Merral said with haste, "that anything like contacting these powers is utterly detestable to the Assembly?"

"I understand."

"Very well, this Nezhuala will want the ship you stole. But what will he want of us? Will he come himself?"

"He may send others. We've . . . I've heard of a project that occupies him. . . . I will not speak of that today and not because it needs to be hidden from the commander." He sipped his drink noisily. "Nezhuala's ambition knows no limits. By now he will, I expect, have finished off the True Freeborn and all the twenty-five worlds will be his. Even without any gap in the barrier, I'd have predicted that his ambition would now turn to the Assembly. Now that venture is certain. And I can promise you this: he'll aim for conquest. His goal will be to join all the worlds of humanity under the Dominion's banner."

"The uniting of the realms," Merral said aloud, remembering the steersman's threat and wishing he could forget it.

Azeras looked keenly at him. "That phrase. *The uniting of the realms.* Where did you hear it?"

Merral hesitated, resolving not to mention the dreadful words that had followed about the coming of the end of the Assembly. "The steersman said it. I didn't understand it at the time."

"'The steersman said it?' Ah, *very* interesting. It is a phrase Nezhuala used as the watchword of his campaign against us. I had always taken it to refer to the Dominion and the True Freeborn worlds. But perhaps it means more than any of us had seen."

It was Perena's turn to speak. "But, Sarudar, how can Nezhuala hope to win against the Assembly? By your own admission, the Dominion is a fraction of the size of the Assembly."

Azeras bowed his head. "As ever, Captain, a good question. But remember that neither size nor numbers is everything. You are unarmed and Nezhuala's forces are powerful; more powerful than you can imagine. But he will proceed carefully. And there, I think, lies your world's hope."

"*Our* hope, Officer," Perena added.

"I stand corrected, Captain." His half smile seemed uneasy. "You seem to be disposed to ensure that I do not overlook you. But I think whoever he sends here will want to learn all he can about you. It is an ideal chance to learn about the Assembly. And he wants the Assembly, but he fears it."

He leaned back in his chair, picking his teeth with a sliver of wood and staring toward the sea. Suddenly he glanced at the toothpick and tossed it over his shoulder. "Sorry. I must learn manners. Still you have more pressing problems than etiquette."

"Indeed."

Vero leaned forward. "He fears us? Why? How?"

"You may have overlooked us, but we have never forgotten you. Through the history of the Freeborn, the Assembly has always been a shadow on the edge of our lives. On Tellzanur, children are taught to fear that one day Ringell—"

"Ringell?" Merral gasped.

There was a puzzled look from Azeras, but he continued. "Ringell and his men would descend in the night and slay them."

"Why him?" Vero asked, screwing up his dark eyes.

"Lucas Ringell led the attack in the battle at Centauri. It was he who killed Jannafy. It was he who, it is presumed, stopped the seventh ship from leaving. What more do you need?"

"But he is long dead," Merral protested.

There was a dismissive shrug. "Such figures live on in legend. And legend says that as the great adversary, Ringell will return."

"'The great adversary'?"

"Part of the myth. A soldier from the Assembly that the Freeborn will have to defeat or else they will be destroyed. Ringell, or someone like him. It's not clear—I told you, it's a legend."

"And the Dominion believes in this figure?" Merral asked.

"Probably. They have no doubt altered the belief. They have their own myths."

Vero raised a finger in inquiry. "If the Dominion comes, what forces will they have?"

Azeras thought for a moment. "A full-suppression complex, I'd guess. Great big ugly slab of a ship, well over a kilometer long, with enough firepower to reshape a world. A single Y-class caused a world to surrender."

"W-will they use nuclear weapons? Or kinetic or beam weapons?"

"They will have all of them, but they will only use them if they have to—if, say, there is determined resistance. Nezhuala doesn't seem to like destroying worlds, buildings, or infrastructure. He likes to take over things in good working order. Energy spent in rebuilding is a waste of energy that might be used in conquest." Suddenly a strange woeful expression seemed to darken Azeras's face and he looked away out to sea. Merral had a sudden sense of a man who carried terrible burdens.

"S-so how will he plan to take this world?" Vero asked, but it was Merral who answered him.

"Krallen," he said, and as he said it, the word seemed somehow sharp and misshapen.

"Aha," said Azeras, swinging around, his sad expression replaced by a look of intense interest. "The commander has met the Krallen. I'm amazed you survived. So you will know that Krallen are like Betafor but far, *far* nastier?"

There were nods and Azeras continued. "A full-suppression complex might have around a hundred thousand Krallen. There were rumors of a new, larger class of suppression complexes, worse than the Y-class, so there could be more. The battlefield versions are a bit heavier than the ship pack types you met. There would be a variety of landers to deploy them plus supports."

"*Ooof,*" muttered Vero as if he had been punched.

"I had no idea," Merral said quietly. The vision the envoy had shown him seemed to have taken a terrible step closer to reality. "None at all."

"Are there any humans?" Perena asked, her low voice barely audible over the mewing calls of the gulls.

"Normally, very few. Perhaps twenty. And one or two Allenix to watch and listen."

"Why so few men?"

"Humans, Captain, are hard work. They tire, they need food, they grumble, they scheme. And they prefer to stay alive, rather than face death."

"So is that why they use Krallen?" Perena's face showed consternation.

Azeras scratched a scar on his cheek. "One reason. But another reason is this: Krallen do no real damage to any infrastructure. You'd send what—a thousand Krallen packs?—into somewhere like your Isterrane and they'd slash every living being to shreds in a few days. But there'd be no damage. Just a few doors torn down, a few windows smashed and a lot of blood. You'd just hose the place down and it would be fine." He paused. "And there's another reason: Krallen terrify people. People can stand the idea of being bombed or vaporized, but humans have a deep-seated fear of being hunted."

Merral felt chilled, as if an invisible cloud of horror had blocked the sun.

"S-so an entire ship full—fuller than we can imagine—of Krallen may be on its way," Vero said, turning his troubled face away toward the ocean.

"And there will be other things too."

"Go on."

"Slitherwings. And maybe even a baziliarch." Azeras's expression was somber.

"Tell us more."

"No. We don't know much about them and what we do, we don't talk about. But let's trust to the Fates that they haven't sent one."

Vero grunted. "We have a better hope than Fate, Sarudar."

"If there's a baziliarch around, you will need one."

"So what can we do?" Merral asked.

Azeras shook his head. "I have told you the problem. The answers—if there are any—are for another day."

There was a long heavy silence in which no one seemed to want to say anything. Suddenly it came to Merral that it was bizarrely incongruous to talk about such dark things amid palm trees, a beach, and a blazing sun. But he ended his reflection; there were more questions to be asked if they were to try and recover the *Rahllman's Star*.

"Thank you," he said. "I was wondering when—"

Merral stopped, aware of a noise behind him and catching others' eyes swinging toward the bleached buildings. He turned round to see Lloyd's large form pounding down the path toward them, gesturing at the diary he held aloft.

Merral rose, a cold sensation of menace sliding over him. He ran toward Lloyd.

They met halfway. "Is it . . . ?" he asked as he grabbed the diary.

Lloyd gave him the nod that meant everything.

With a pounding heart, Merral listened to the message, then jogged back to the table. "It's Corradon," he said, his voice trembling. "It's what we have been expecting. A non-Assembly ship has been detected beyond the outer debris belt. It's heading toward Farholme. On current speeds, they will be in orbit in days."

He stopped, almost overwhelmed by all that the news signified. "They're here."

19

B arely twenty minutes after receiving the message, Merral, Vero, and Lloyd raced northward over the blue expanse of Hassanet's Sea in a short-haul flier piloted by Perena.

Vero stared out of the cabin window, his face stern.

"How do you feel?" Merral asked.

Vero turned to him. "In the last hour, my hopes have been raised high and then dashed. Earth was briefly in sight. But we cannot access the *Rahllman's Star* now. If we had only found Azeras a week earlier!"

"I know."

"But, my friend, we must plan. I will deal with Betafor and Azeras and keep them hidden. It is going to be hard for us to hide what we know from Corradon and the rest. We have a new skill to learn: secrecy."

"Yes. I'm not looking forward to that. It is not my strength."

"No. That is why being kept in the dark about other matters may make your life easier."

Merral, Vero, Perena, and Lloyd were rotorcrafted from the airport straight to the landing pad on the roof of the Planetary Administration building. Merral had expected to go straight to the war room, but instead was ushered into Corradon's office along with Vero and Perena. Both Corradon and Clemant were there. Merral was relieved to find that the representative, although pale, seemed oddly positive.

"I'm glad to have you all here," Corradon said. "In the last hour, we have had a message from the ship." He gestured them to chairs that faced a wallscreen. "Things may not be as bad as—" He stopped abruptly. "No, I'll let you make up your minds. I want to watch it again anyway."

He pressed a switch and an image appeared on the screen of a man and a woman dressed in white in front of a flag bearing the red coiling symbol that Merral remembered seeing on the flanks of Betafor.

The Final Emblem. Merral reminded himself not to reveal more than he could be expected to know.

As the image wavered and then stabilized, they could see that the man had a kind, even humorous face with soft gray-brown eyes, thin, wispy white hair, and a neat, short gray beard. The woman had a pale, rather delicate face with high cheekbones and long, braided, pale-gold hair and seemed to radiate a wise amiability.

There was something attractive about her and Merral was tempted to gaze at her. He wondered how old they were. There was something oddly timeless about them.

"Non-Assembly humans," Corradon said to no one in particular, his voice full of wonder.

There was a crackling noise and then the man's voice could be heard. "Peace and greetings to you." His tone was mellow and reassuring; the words a confident Communal. "This is the *Dove of Dawn* and I am Ambassador Hazderzal."

Merral realized that if there was uncertainty about the man's age, there could be none at all about his manner. There was a look of harmlessness, even benevolence, about the ambassador that seemed to reach out from the grainy image and put one at ease.

"And I am Ambassador Tinternli," said the woman, her smile revealing teeth of perfect whiteness and symmetry. Her voice was light and sweet and somehow Merral felt confident that she was a capable singer.

"Be reassured: we pose no threat to you," the man said. "On the contrary, we wish to help you. We are fellow human beings from a small body of worlds called the Dominion, and have broken an ancient policy of silence and separation to come to your aid."

Are they evil? To his surprise Merral did not have a sense of being in the presence of evil. *Is that because they are too far away or because they aren't evil? Or are they so cunning that they can hide their nature?*

As the woman spoke next, Merral noticed her soft brown eyes and her smooth unlined skin. Again the manner was reassuring. "Nearly a year ago in your time, one of our space vessels was stolen by insurgents and flown toward your world. We had decided to leave the matter for the Assembly to deal with, but when we became aware of the destruction of your Gate, we realized that we had to intervene. We intend to enter Farholme orbit in seven days. Please send us details of your situation." She smiled again. "I repeat: we pose no threat. We mean you well and wish to assist you."

"We are listening for your response," the man concluded and the image faded.

Corradon nodded. "It has been repeated on the hour ever since. Do you want to see it again?"

"Later," Merral said.

"Then let me show you the images of the ship from a surveillance satellite."

On the screen appeared a blurred image of a pale white needle in a sea of darkness.

"Size and mass?" Perena asked, her eyes scanning the screen.

"It's small—just over a hundred meters long and no more than a few thousand tons. Consistent with it being a diplomatic vessel."

Merral stared at the image, realizing that it bore no resemblance to the full-suppression complex that he feared.

"It really doesn't look hostile, does it?" Corradon said, and Merral heard a hunger for reassurance in his words.

Merral chose his reply with care. "Not so far."

Corradon gestured to a table across the room. "Now we can discuss the complex issues involved."

ロロロロロ

The discussions lasted well over an hour and Merral found them very trying. He had to be constantly wary not to let slip what he knew and also found himself wishing that he could discuss things privately with Vero and Perena. The nature and tone of the ambassadors' message seemed to have buoyed up Corradon's spirits so that he seemed reluctant to consider any view that suggested there might still be a threat.

Clemant, who seemed to watch and listen to the debate with a concerned intensity, said little, but was clearly less wholeheartedly positive.

Various measures were agreed upon. It was decided that Corradon should immediately send a message that welcomed the Dominion ship and expressed a desire to talk with the ambassadors, but which also mentioned that the intruder vessel had been destroyed and that there was no current threat.

With regard to preparations on Farholme, Merral's suggestion that they put the entire FDF on alert was approved. There was also agreement that while there was no evidence so far that justified putting into operation the defenses around the population centers, nevertheless the implementation teams ought to be placed on standby.

There was much discussion about whether the news of the ship should be made public. Here Clemant did have something to say, arguing that it was better to go public before rumors leaked out. This was accepted and Corradon agreed to give another broadcast to the world. Merral suggested that the representative should also warn people that the Library and the Admin-Net might be shut down without warning at any time. This was approved without enthusiasm.

Finally, Corradon looked around. "We need to designate a contact team to meet these ambassadors. I would suggest all the representatives, so that's five of us, and Dr. Clemant."

The advisor bowed.

"Now, Commander, I assume that you would want to be in the group?"

Merral, who felt inclined to refuse, looked around for guidance and found a barely visible look of encouragement on Vero's face.

"As you wish, sir," Merral said. "But I have other duties, as I'm sure you are aware. I may not be able to be totally committed."

"We can manage I'm sure. Captain Lewitz?"

Perena shook her head. "I am happy to be consulted, but do not wish to be on the team. I may have flying duties."

"Sentinel? I would imagine that *you* would wish to be part of the team."

"Thank you, sir, but I decline the offer," Vero replied. "I have responsibilities with the irregulars that will occupy me. And, if you will excuse me for saying it, I think the fate of Farholme should be decided by those from Farholme."

Clemant nodded, looking satisfied.

"I understand that. Seven then so far. I think—" Corradon looked at his advisor for reassurance—"we will ask Chaplain-in-Chief Delastro to join us. That will make eight of us. Any other comments?" After a short silence, he added, "Well, we all have work to do. Meeting dismissed."

Outside the room, Perena made her apologies and left. As he watched her slight figure vanish down the corridor, Merral wondered how much he would see of either her or her sister in the near future. He had an odd certainty that isolation for him loomed and did not relish the prospect.

Vero took Merral's arm and steered him around a corner. "I must disappear," he said in a low voice.

"But I need your support and your advice. What we saw—doesn't fit. Not with what we expected. I'm puzzled. . . . I—"

"Not here. We can't discuss it." Vero's eyes looked carefully around. "Someone is lying. But, my friend, you must be alone and play your part. It's all for the best."

"But I need your help."

Vero touched his shoulder. "And I yours. But we must go our own ways for some time. From now on, I think that the road will get steeper and harder—for all of us."

⚬⚬⚬⚬⚬

That afternoon Merral received an urgent summons to Corradon's office. The representative was unhappy; there were problems with Delastro. The prebendant had already made up his mind that the Dominion was evil and had refused to join the contact team. They discussed the matter and possible approaches and it was agreed that Merral should talk with Delastro.

Merral, wondering what to say, found Delastro at his desk in his plainly furnished room.

The prebendant gestured for him to sit in a high-backed chair in front of the desk.

"I gather, Prebendant," Merral said, "that you have made up your mind."

"Yes. I think this contact team is a waste of time—an utter waste. You, in particular, would be far better employed in organizing us for war."

"I think that we should be neutral until such time as we know they are enemies."

"Neutrality? At such a time?" A flash of anger lit Delastro's green eyes. "They are evil. It's a trick, Commander."

"We don't know that."

"I do and I suspect you do."

He's right. Merral tried to hide his feelings under the prebendant's scrutiny. "I don't. I may have my suspicions and my fears, but I don't know for sure."

"And your connections with the angelic realm? This being you contact? Hasn't he warned you of this ship?"

"No. He warned me—us—of approaching war. We can't yet assume that these people are the enemy."

"I believe it would be safest to treat them as the enemy."

"I disagree, Prebendant. And there is a delicate matter here. You are chaplain-in-chief. How do you propose to handle this matter with the soldiers?"

"I intend to do my duty and preach that this is a trap."

"But that would jeopardize any negotiations. It might precipitate a war."

"Then so be it. Let the war come. Let the purging of the worlds occur."

Merral took a breath, feeling uncomfortably aware of the gap in age between them. "Prebendant, Representative Corradon and I agree that this is not to be allowed. You must be scrupulously neutral."

"And if I am not?"

"I will have to find a replacement for you."

A succession of expressions crossed Delastro's thin face: a flash of anger, a look around the room, ending slowly in a conciliatory smile. "As you wish then. I will be neutral."

Pleased at his victory, but faintly disappointed that Delastro had not resigned, Merral returned to Corradon's office. The representative, who was peering intently at a plant on a shelf, looked up.

After Merral explained what happened, he said, "As I expected. Well, we will put old Jenat on the contact team."

"Is he . . . well . . . appropriate?" Merral asked, thinking of the frail man who had been overwhelmed by the events at the memorial service.

"Hmm. He is the president of the congregations. He has the rank." Corradon bent down to the plant. "Now, this *Achimenes* is not very happy. I was wondering if it needed some more potassium. Do you have any suggestions?"

Merral made the briefest of answers and, deeply troubled at the representative's inability to focus on the crisis, returned to his office.

◌◌◌◌◌

Merral found himself almost frantically busy for the rest of the day, but at five he closed his office door, and summoned Lloyd to drive to Brenito's house.

As they drove up the drive, Merral scanned the garden, hoping that he might see Jorgio's curved figure at work, but there was no sign of him. The guard at the gate said Jorgio was inside and that yes, he had been very disturbed, but that he was now better.

Leaving Lloyd at the door, Merral went inside. He soon found Jorgio seated in Brenito's old rocking chair on the veranda overlooking the sea.

"How are you?" Merral asked, pulling over a bench. Pushing a pad of paper to one side, he sat down.

"I've had a bad few days, Mr. Merral. You remember those footsteps as I've been having in my dreams? Well, they were just getting louder and louder. Why yesterday now, I could hear them as if they were right in my head. *Patter, patter, patter.* Not just in dreams either. While I was working in the garden—sowing some delphiniums on some of the bare bits, I was—I could hear them—an army of them. And during my eating. Even during my praying: *that* was the worst bit."

"I'm sorry. But do you still hear them?"

Jorgio's expression changed to one of perplexity. "No. But I feel I ought to. It's just vanished. But I don't think they *have* gone away. They're like bulbs under the ground, ready to pop up."

"You mean the sounds have been masked?"

"Masked?"

"Uh, hidden? Covered over?"

"Yes." Jorgio smacked his thick lips. "Very likely, that's it. They can do that, I'm sure. Tea?"

Merral smiled. *Have I smiled at any other time today?* "Sorry, my old friend. But I have never been so busy." He paused, surveying Jorgio's rough face. "We have visitors. You'll hear about it tonight. A ship from edgeward of here—from the Dominion."

A coarse eyebrow rose. "Indeed now. And are they nice or nasty?"

"What do you think?"

"Me?" Jorgio shrugged. "I reckon as you expect me to say *nasty*. There'd be a sense in that." He creased his face. "But to be honest, I don't know."

"What do you feel?"

"Nothing, nothing at all. Nothing good and nothing bad. And that's odd."

"Isn't it?"

How strange. This most perceptive of men lacks any sense that what approaches is evil. "I'm glad the noises have stopped. Let me know if you feel anything about our visitors. Pray for me."

As he rose to leave, he suddenly noticed that the pad of paper he had moved was covered with a crude scrawl that looked like mathematics. "May I?"

He lifted the pad. It *was* mathematics. But it made no sense. For a start it was all in fragments. In one corner a line of symbols began suddenly and then broke off abruptly and in another a ragged island of equations seemed to have been torn out of the middle of some dense mass of algebra. Merral recognized some of the symbols—numbers, an integral sign, pi, a square root—but others were strange. Although only adequate in mathematics, Merral had the strongest sense that what he was staring at was not a random mélange of symbols, but instead genuine fragments from some real-world equations.

"What is this?"

Jorgio puckered his thick mouth. "The other dreams I've had. Them ones of numbers I told you about. That lot are bits that stuck in my mind. So I wrote 'em out. And to save your question, I don't know what they mean."

"Or even what they are about?"

"That neither. But they *are* important. The Lord told me that."

"Keep them safe," Merral said. "I'd like to show them to someone. But not just now. I have enough problems." He patted the old man on the back, and then left.

oOoOo

Merral had asked to be contacted when any new transmission came in from the *Dove of Dawn* and was not surprised when, at five on the following morning, he was awakened by a diary call from Corradon relaying a message.

Rubbing sleep from his eyes, Merral stared at the screen as the message began. This time there was only the male ambassador.

"Thank you for your welcome," Ambassador Hazderzal said, with the same good humor. "We are delighted that you managed to destroy the stolen ship. We will do what we can to make good what was damaged. When we arrive in six days, we wish to land and meet with you. Can you designate a landing zone for our shuttle craft—somewhere we can set up a small center where we can talk?" With good wishes, the transmission ended.

"Merral," Corradon said, sounding nervous, "what do we do?"

"Give me time to think. I'll call you at nine. In the meantime, just acknowledge the message."

Merral delayed calling Vero until after his morning run. Vero replied immediately, but with a voice-only transmission. The screen stayed blank.

"We heard from the ship."

"Yes, I know." From the way Vero's voice reverberated Merral felt certain that his friend was in some enclosed space.

"How do you know?"

"I have my sources. I am, after all, chief of intelligence."

"What sources?"

"Secret."

"Very well. A landing zone: Isterrane, presumably?"

"No, it's too close. It could be a Trojan horse. You know the story?"

"Yes."

"You might want to reread it. Let me come and see you. Put the coffee on."

oOoOo

Ten minutes later, Vero, unshaven and looking tired, sat at the kitchen table sipping from a large mug of coffee.

"Not Isterrane then?" Merral asked.

"No. Not anywhere near. If we have to use a vortex blaster, we could lose part of the city. We suggest the spare strip on Langerstrand Peninsula."

"Langerstrand?" It took Merral a moment to remember the place—an open peninsula a hundred kilometers west of Isterrane.

"Why there?"

"We feel better about it. It was my idea—it's remote and uninhabited."

Who is we?

"Explain to the ambassadors that due to possible health risks we want a space between us. And that they can spread out there. Remember: good fences make good neighbors."

"They do? Very well. But, Vero, this doesn't match what Azeras said."

"No. It doesn't."

"Why?"

"I don't know." Vero sighed. "I really don't."

"The ship looks civilian, Vero. It's no full-suppression complex."

Vero chewed on his bottom lip. "I agree."

"It's got a low mass too. What does Azeras say?"

"He says that it must be a new strategy. And that sometimes seduction works better than rape."

"A tasteless metaphor. I can't imagine Perena warmed to that one. And you believe him?"

Vero sighed and scowled at his coffee. "Yes. Look, we shouldn't even mention Azeras, but this is my take on him: I think . . . he is to be trusted."

"On everything? I detected some hesitancy there."

"He isn't telling us everything. Not about the Freeborn, not about the Dominion, and least of all about himself. I have a feeling that there is something really ugly and horrible in that man's life."

"He lost his family."

Vero stared into the distance. "In the burning of Tellzanur." His tone was subdued.

"That sounds pretty ugly and horrible to me."

"Yes. You may be right. But I think there's more. I just don't feel he lies . . . well, not very much. Not like Betafor, who doesn't know a truth from a lie."

"That's something, I suppose. But look, I'm alarmed about being on the contact team, because of this baziliarch. Shouldn't I resign?"

"No. We need you there. And your absence or withdrawal now would be suspicious."

"But I know about Azeras and Betafor."

"That's too late to change. Anyway the sarudar says he doesn't think they will dare use the baziliarch while they're trying to be nice. People know when their minds are searched. The risk will be when diplomacy ends. You'll be safe till then."

"And war begins. And that, if we understand the envoy correctly, is now just weeks away."

"Exactly." Vero rose. "And there is work to be done."

◌◌◌◌◌

Corradon seemed happy with the suggestion of the Langerstrand site and transmitted a message about it to the Dominion ship. The answer from the *Dove of Dawn* came almost as soon as the vast distance allowed. "We will land at Langerstrand as you wish. We pose no biological threat, but we are happy to be scrutinized. We will travel in silence for the next five days as we decelerate. We prefer to speak face-to-face."

Over the next few days, Merral felt increasingly isolated. Anya was absent from her lab, Perena was unobtainable, and when contacted, Vero seemed preoccupied, almost brusque, and his answers impossibly cryptic.

As the *Dove of Dawn* came within range of more satellites, increasingly better data transmitted from the ship. The consensus was that everything about it—its delicate smooth spindle shape, its small size, and its brilliant whiteness—marked it as a nonmilitary vessel. As each new image came in, Merral felt that there was almost a visible lessening of tension. Yet although he could not state his feelings openly, he felt unable to share the enthusiasm. In his mind the equation was obvious: either the ship was a deception or Azeras had lied.

With the increasing data, Corradon's confidence grew, although Clemant maintained his wariness. Merral kept a careful eye on how Delastro reacted. The prebendant seemed rather exasperated by the fact that the ship and its inhabitants seemed so innocuous. But he kept to the agreement he had made with Merral and confined himself to making rather bland speeches that urged those of the FDF, as "the watchmen on the very walls of Zion," to neither slumber nor sleep.

◌◌◌◌◌

Three days before the *Dove* was due to enter Farholme orbit, Merral sat in his bedroom wearing nothing but shorts and feeling uncomfortably warm when he heard a sound from the corridor followed by an exchange of voices. A few moments later Lloyd stuck his head round the door.

"Mr. V.'s here, sir. He's making some coffee."

Merral threw a shirt on and went to the kitchen.

Vero, leaning back in a chair, peered at him over a large mug of coffee. "Just passing through."

"Always a pleasure. Are you still happy with Azeras's version of things?"

"Yes," Vero said and Merral heard a hint of hesitation in the voice. "He's a mess. I can't begin to work out what's going on inside him. There's guilt and anger and self-pity. At first he was glad of our company, but now that the novelty has worn off, he seems to prefer being isolated."

Vero helped himself to a biscuit out of a jar. "Anyway," he said. "I came by because I've been talking with Betafor about all sorts of things. One thing I can tell you is that she confirms this 'great adversary' business."

"Odd."

"Yes, isn't it? But what's interesting is this ill-defined link between this great adversary and Lucas Ringell."

Merral pulled the disk from under his shirt, and stared at it as it spun slowly on its metal chain. "So that explains the excitement on the intruder ship when they read this disk."

"Exactly. A fearsome figure out of their mythology had returned."

"Well, I'm not sure where this leaves us. I'm not sure I want to be known as the claimant to the title of Ringell Mark Two. But I'd better tuck this well away." He slipped it under his shirt.

"Yes, keep it out of sight," Vero warned.

"I'm worried about the Krallen," Merral said after a period of silence. "Are you making any progress on them?"

"Hmm. We understand them better. They are fascinating in a terrifying sort of way. Betafor has confirmed what we suspected—their tiles will deflect most bullets unless they hit straight on. And did you know that they can survive very high temperatures? A thousand degrees for twenty to thirty seconds! No wonder cutter guns were almost useless."

"So what *does* work against them?"

Vero stared away and his face seemed to look gloomier. "Ah, that is the problem. We have ideas. But . . ."

"We will need more than ideas soon."

"I know. I know," Vero said with an air of weariness and then sipped his coffee. "I'm beginning to feel sorry for Betafor. Creating her and her kind was a cruel act."

"How so?"

"Apparently, the Allenix can comprehend all sorts of concepts that they cannot experience. So Betafor can understand—at least vaguely—concepts like friendship and love, but she cannot *feel* either. She understands that human beings have true personality, but she knows she can have nothing like it. She understands the idea of creativity, but she can't create anything except lies. She is smart enough to see her limits and it frustrates her. For all her posturing about her superiority to flesh, she is trapped in a mechanical body."

"I see."

Vero stared thoughtfully at the kitchen wall. "You sense that she wants to be a real person but knows she can never be one. But the worst thing—the cruelest blow—is that she understands death. She has a horror of permanent system shutdown."

"She's scared of death?"

"Scared stiff. And she knows that there is nothing beyond that. There is no confident expectation of eternal life or even a faint hope. Just an awareness of an end."

"From which we gather that her makers fear death."

"Yes. But it's tragic and cruel to have made a creature capable of understanding eternity, but of never attaining it."

"An interesting meditation."

"Yes, isn't it?" Vero said. "But it's more than just a reflection. Fundamentally, she is a frustrated, unhappy, and fearful creature and she can't be relied on."

There was an oddly conversational tone to his voice and Merral realized how much he missed it. Now there was so much pressure and so many enemies.

Vero drained his cup and got to his feet. "One other thing. You'll find the encryption program on the diary system has been modified. Betafor made some suggestions and Maria Dalphey checked them out. We hope that will give us some security against any future probing. But I'd better be off. We have some interesting days ahead. And there's lots to do, especially on the Krallen."

ᗧᗧᗧᗧᗧ

Later the following day, as the sea wind rustled the fronds and the sun set in the ocean, Vero walked to where Azeras was sitting hunched in a chair under the shelter, staring at the back of his hand. Vero had wanted to move both the sarudar and Betafor from the Manalahi Shoals to the deep foundations of Isterrane for safety but, after protesting that he had spent too much of his life hiding in tunnels, Azeras had won himself a delay.

As Vero approached, Azeras looked up sharply and the images vanished.

"What were you watching?" Vero enquired.

The answer was as slow in coming as if it had been dragged up out of the very depths of Azeras's psyche. "My past," he said and looked away.

The gloom persists. Something terrible hangs heavily over this man. When this is over, we must get this man some help. But in the meantime I must use him as he is.

"Azeras," Vero announced, sitting down, "I've decided to keep you as part of my advisory team. There will be just four of us who know who you really are. I will try and keep you away from everyone else, but you will have an alias and have to pretend to be one of us."

"What's the alternative?" Azeras's voice was glum.

"Solitary confinement, I'm afraid."

"Then I will work with you as an advisor."

"Good. Now let's talk about these Krallen again. What defenses are there?"

"Hit them before they land."

"But we may not be able to do that."

"Stay in tanks or armored vehicles."

"We have none."

"Well, we tried body armor," Azeras said slowly. "It helps. It needs to be hard though. Their claws are tipped with an alloy that is harder than almost all metals. They have a nasty trick of putting their two or three claws together and groping for eye sockets."

"If we were to design body armor, could you advise us?"

There was a long pause. "I suppose I could. Betafor would give you hardness details—it has its uses."

"So we might have some personal defense. But how do we kill them?"

There was another long silence as Azeras toyed with a scar on his arm. "It's not easy. The True Freeborn never really managed it."

"Do they have weak points?"

"No. Fire at them a lot. Get a lucky shot in between the tiles and you may do some damage, especially if you hit the circuits just below."

"There is circuitry there?"

"A nervous system equivalent. Runs through a silicone fluid bath. Betafor's similar."

"Yes, we persuaded her to let us see her schematics. So if we could get through the tiles and if we put a current into the wiring, they could be switched off?"

Azeras grunted. "There's too many *ifs* there." He leaned his long frame back so that the chair tilted on two legs, and stared up at the palm tree above his head. After a few moments he sat upright and the front legs crashed down.

"Have you thought of something?"

"Maybe." There was another long pause. "The blade that you used to cut those fronds—what technology did the commander say was used to make it?"

"The bush knife? Molecular tuning, but I'm the wrong person to explain how it works."

Azeras looked at him with wintery gray eyes. "He said that it parted the wood molecules as it struck. And that there were blades for different subst—"

"Wait! You think we could make a blade that would cut through Krallen skin?"

"Maybe. Might be worth trying. The Krallen skin is made to deflect high-speed impact and beam weapons, not cuts."

"W-would that be enough? Just cutting through?"

"No. You'd need an electrical charge. Twenty volts at least; Betafor would know the values. Have two electrodes on the blade—an ionic transfer battery in the handle. You have those. That'd knock them flat."

"Permanently?"

Azeras hesitated, then shook his head abruptly. "No. You'd need to chop their heads off or smash them in pretty soon afterward to make sure they didn't recover. But that can be done."

"A-Azeras, that's all possible. We can do this. We could e-easily make ten thousand blades—enough for the r-regulars and the irregulars." Then Vero was struck by a problem and his enthusiasm rapidly drained away. "Ah but how . . . ?"

"How do you tune a blade for Krallen armor?" A faint smile crossed Azeras's face. "Get some Krallen."

"Ah. Couldn't we do something based around Betafor's skin? There are spare tiles."

"No. Krallen are different."

"Bother. So, we really would need some Krallen to experiment with?"

"Yeah."

"That sounds impossible."

"Well it may be." There was a long pause. "But you know there might—just might—be a way."

◌◌◌◌◌

The next day, as Merral stared at a desk map in his office struggling with how long he could keep three thousand soldiers on alert, he heard a sudden ripple of excitement outside of his office.

As Merral's diary bleeped, Lloyd stuck his head in. "Sir, the Library has just been locked."

Merral glanced at the screen and saw a flashing message: *Intrusion Alert! Library and Admin-Net closed.*

What do I do? Merral's fingers moved to a set of buttons in three different colors on the wall. Red was reserved for imminent or actual hostilities, orange would evacuate everyone to the war room, and yellow would allow them to stay on alert in their present locations.

"Yellow," he said aloud as he pressed the third button. "Lloyd, I'm going upstairs."

Grabbing his diary, Merral ran past the flashing screens of terminals and bounded up the stairs to Corradon's office. *Is this is it? Does the war start now?*

He found the representative seated at a screen, his face drained of color, his eyes flicking across data. Clemant stood behind him, peering over his shoulder.

"Commander! What's going on?" Merral heard the strain in Corradon's voice, saw his shaking hands, and realized how shallow his self-assurance seemed to be.

"Library and Admin-Net are down. An intrusion. That's all I know," Merral panted. "I've put the FDF and the irregulars on yellow alert."

Clemant looked at the screen. "Ah, Sentinel Enand has just sent a message. He is on his way. And the satellites report no signs of an attack. The *Dove* is still fifteen million kilometers away. And the Basic-Net is up and on line."

Five minutes later, Vero hurried in, his face beaded with sweat and carrying his briefcase.

"What happened?" Corradon asked him.

Vero sat down on a chair by the desk and wiped his brow. "There was, apparently, an attempt at an intrusion. The *Dove of Dawn* no doubt."

"Have we lost anything?" Clemant growled.

"No. Shutdown occurred within a second. They can have extracted nothing during that time." Vero pulled from his briefcase a small transparent box with a gray wafer inside. He handed it to Corradon. "The key, sir."

The representative took it with care and peered at it.

"Better keep it safe," Vero advised. "Without it, not even all the king's horses and all the king's men will put the Library back together again."

Corradon and Clemant stared at him.

"Oh, never mind. Just don't lose it."

"I won't. When do I use it?"

"Not until we are totally sure what the *Dove* is up to."

An hour later they received a message from the *Dove of Dawn*. "In the process of trying to assess the damage done to your planet by the insurgents we seem to have inadvertently triggered the defenses of your Library. We apologize."

Corradon's response was to say that the apology was accepted. The yellow alert level was withdrawn, but the Library and the Admin-Net stayed closed.

ⵔⵔⵔⵔⵔ

On the following day the gleaming ship entered Farholme orbit and received clearance for one of its shuttles to land at Langerstrand strip at three the following afternoon.

On the morning of the landing, Merral and Lloyd took the western road out of Isterrane. They could have flown to the Langerstrand Peninsula, but Merral had good reason to travel by road. From the moment Langerstrand had been chosen as a landing zone, he had ordered feasibility studies on defending Isterrane against any attack that might be mounted from there.

With the sun already high in the cloudless sky, they crossed the great arc of stone and cable that was the Walderand Gorge suspension bridge.

A small FDF unit was positioned on the far side, but Merral had Lloyd drive past and stop higher up the road. There they scrambled up to a viewpoint.

Merral stared at the great bridge and the crags around. *Yes, we might be able to hold off an attacking force here and, as a last resort, blow up the bridge.*

He squinted through the growing haze across the gorge, seeing the faint shapes of the westernmost suburbs of Isterrane on the far side. *But it is too close.* In winter, with the Walderand a raging muddy torrent, a long-lasting defense could be made, but not in late summer with the river reduced to a series of muddy channels. *No. Any defense would have to be farther away.*

They drove for a few kilometers along the Western Trunk Road as it cut through the harsh shattered ridges of the edges of the Manukli Range and then turned southward along a narrower road signposted *Tezekal, Langerstrand, and Lariston Coast Road*. Soon they were out of the mountains and on to a low and featureless plateau whose baked ocher soils bore only a few dry and dusty trees. For twenty minutes they drove west as the road skirted the high, wooded, and brooding massif that formed the southernmost outpost of the Manukli Range until a low ridge with a saw-edged silhouette came into view.

"That is Tezekal Ridge and *that* must be Tezekal Village," Merral said, gesturing at a hazy cluster of white-walled houses atop the northern edge of the ridge. "From the maps, the road drops from there through a gorge down to the Edelcet Marshes. It's the best potential defense point. We could even put an emergency strip just here."

They turned off the main road and drove along a dusty track past fields with olive trees and citrus orchards to a small encampment of troops that lay in the shadow of some jagged rocks.

Captain Tremutar, a soft-spoken man with a wiry physique, led Merral and Lloyd up a hot and narrow winding track to the crest of the ridge. At the top, they stopped to regain their breath and surveyed the hazy view ahead, shading their eyes against the sun with their hands.

Three hundred meters below lay the wide, flat expanses of the Edelcet Marshes with their multicolored mosaic of reed beds, lakes, and salt pans. The marshes passed southward into the blue waters of Hassanet's Sea while to the north they came to an abrupt end against the thick tree-covered slopes of a steep and rugged escarpment that led into the heights of the Manukli

Range. Checking the map, Merral found the escarpment was called the Hereza Crags.

In the far distance, beyond the western edge of the marshes, the Langerstrand Peninsula shimmered in the heat. Merral traced the path of the road down through a deep gorge to the left of Tezekal Village, and along the foot of the Hereza Crags.

"Acceptable, Sergeant?"

"Yup," Lloyd answered. "If it came to a fight, sir, here would do. They can't cross the marshes and the slopes look impossible. So they'd have to use the road. And we overlook that. The *Bodyguard's Handbook* talks about the high ground. We'd have it."

Merral gestured up to the right, where the eastern continuation of the Hereza Crags rose high above the village. "But we are overlooked here. Is that Mount Adaman, Captain?"

"Yes, sir. Two thousand meters high."

Lloyd squinted at it. "Tough for any army to climb that."

"Krallen are different. But I suppose it's a risk we have to take," Merral said. He turned to the lean soldier next to them. "Captain, you'll be hearing formally from Colonel Leopold Lanier soon. But I want defenses here. Get started."

Lloyd and Merral drove slowly down the road as it snaked through the razor-sharp gray and brown lava cliffs of the gorge. Even with the sun high overhead, Merral found Tezekal Gorge a dark place, full of shadows.

As a vulture wheeled above in slow circles, its rough calls echoing off the rocks, Merral had a suddenly terrible presentiment of fighting, of shed blood and the cries of men. He shuddered. "A grim place, Sergeant. Even now."

"Yup."

In a few minutes, they exited the gorge and were on the flat road at the edge of the marshland. Merral had never been to the Edelcet Marshes before, but knew it as one of the places where ducks, geese, and other waterbirds congregated when the heart of Menaya was frozen solid in the winter.

As they drove past, Merral saw birds on the water and ghostly white egrets in the trees at the water's edge, but forced himself to turn away and look up the slopes, trying to see the nature of the ground under the trees—mostly scrubby oaks, tall dusty cypresses, and a variety of pines.

"It's a cursed business this," he said.

"I agree, sir. But any special reason for you saying it here?"

"Because, Lloyd, I should be spending my time here looking at God's good creation and instead, I find myself considering how we might best kill things."

Half an hour later they stopped at the gate in the new wire fencing that surrounded the Langerstrand strip. Behind it, Merral could see hectic activity.

"Welcome, Commander," said the guard as he waved them through. "We are almost ready for the visitors."

"Good," he said, but as they drove on through the bustle, a question nagged him: *Are we?*

20

The Dominion shuttle landed in the early afternoon of the same day.

Merral, along with the other members of the contact team, watched its landing from under the awning of a tented pavilion. The vessel, an elegant craft in a plain white livery, descended at a forty-five degree angle and landed delicately in the exact middle of the runway.

"Showoffs," muttered the representative for the southern islands, and Merral remembered that she had been a pilot.

Corradon was driven out in a six-wheeled passenger transporter and walked over to the vessel. Four people descended from it and, after exchanging bows and handshakes, were transported back to the pavilion.

Merral lined up at the pavilion entrance with the rest of the contact team. Everyone wore formal clothes and Merral found the full dress uniform uncomfortably warm.

Corradon entered, relief unmistakably stamped on his bronzed face. "Ambassadors Hazderzal and Tinternli, Captain Benek-Hal," he announced.

A fourth person, who Merral decided was a recording engineer, had stepped to one side and was already imaging events.

Merral stared at the ambassadors. Seen in the flesh this close, both were, in their own way, eye catching. They were tall, delicately built, straight-backed, and walked with smooth, precise steps. Again he probed his brain for any sense of the presence of evil. There was nothing; no hairs bristled on the back of his neck and his spine did not tingle.

Hazderzal, his hair and beard immaculately groomed, led the way, his long white jacket swaying gently and shimmering softly as if it had somehow captured starlight.

Tinternli wore a flowing white dress with a red flower pinned to her shoulder.

Stopping at the head of the line of the contact team, Ambassador Hazderzal spoke in an elegant and sonorous voice. "Representative Corradon, the rest of you, this is a historic moment for us all and for our worlds." He opened his hands in a gesture of benevolence. "We are delighted to meet. We could wish, of course, that it was the first meeting between our long-separated human families, but alas, you have already had an encounter with some from our worlds."

He paused and as he gazed around, Merral had a sense of a man whose very presence was a blessing. "Here and now, we apologize unreservedly for what happened. We must take some of the blame. Had we watched over our ships more closely, had we guarded the borders of the Assembly better, then these losses might not have happened." He shook his head ruefully. "But, alas, they did. And it is our task to remedy as much as we can of that sad episode. We will speak more of that later."

He turned to his colleague with a grave, formal gesture.

"We have come a long way," Tinternli said, her voice a gentle but clear murmur that reminded Merral of a summer's wind among trees. "Our voyage has taken two months and it is gratifying to have firm ground under our feet once more. First of all, I reecho my colleague's apology."

As her soft, full smile appeared, Merral noticed that Corradon beamed at her with undisguised pleasure.

"Secondly, I bring you greetings from Lord-Emperor Nezhuala himself. He considered coming, but the great task of managing the affairs of the Dominion does not permit long absences. In his grace, he has bestowed on us the honor of making the first contact with you. You may be confident that we bring you his best, and his highest concern. His thoughts daily turn toward our separated brothers and sisters in the Assembly and you may be assured that, in his prayers, he mentions you."

Corradon gave a stately bow of acknowledgment. "We are greatly honored by your presence. But may I introduce the members of the contact team?"

As the ambassadors moved down the line toward him, Merral suddenly found himself preoccupied with the idea that they might be able to read his mind. He tried to concentrate on other things, but found it impossible. He then remembered that he bore Lucas Ringell's identity disk. And the more he tried to forget that, the more it filled his mind.

Suddenly Corradon was in front of him. "And this," he said, "is Commander Merral D'Avanos. Of our rather, well, *embryonic*, Defense Force."

As Hazderzal's extraordinarily smooth fingers shook his, Merral noted his look of detached interest.

"Nice to meet you," the ambassador said and then, without so much as a pause, moved on to the next person.

Tinternli took Merral's hand next—her fingers seemed even softer—and gave him a smile of innocent enjoyment. To his surprise, Merral found himself smiling back.

"A commander, eh?" she said, tilting her head back with a wry laugh. "Oh, we have plenty of those." She bent forward so she could speak quietly in his ear. "In truth, far too many."

Merral felt the pleasure of being inside a shared joke, almost as if she were saying to him, "I sense that you hate your hot and itchy uniform and that you are uneasy with military matters. You and I are one on this."

As she moved on, Merral realized that neither with her nor with Hazderzal had he felt any sense of his brain being tapped. And there had been not the slightest hint of a spiritual evil. Indeed, if anything, he seemed to sense that these were *good* people. *It makes no sense.*

They walked through to the adjacent tent where tables—one with an array of foods—and chairs were set and a small string orchestra played quietly in the background.

Six crewmen of the *Dove* shuttle entered—tall men with short hair in a variety of colors, but all with a similar air of quiet, polished reserve.

Slowly, people mingled and Merral was intrigued to see that any tension soon thawed into humor and cautious, polite laughter.

At one point, Merral found himself standing on the edge of things and looked around. Tinternli and Jenat were deep in discussion. The elderly man's face showed a cautious admiration. Hazderzal and Corradon drifted past and he overheard the ambassador praising the musicians.

"You know, if things go the way we hope, we should have some of your players visit our worlds. A mixed orchestra? Or do I dream a dream too far?"

"We must dream, Ambassador," Corradon replied, with a sympathetic nod. "But what better way of bridging divisions?"

As they moved on Merral felt utterly perplexed. He had been prepared for either a thuggish show of violence or a blatantly spurious attempt at being nice, but this was neither. What he was faced with was one of two things: either a deception of stunning effectiveness or a display of genuine grace and gentleness.

After an hour the captain and crew returned to the shuttle. The contact team and the ambassadors adjourned to the pavilion and sat around a large table.

"Now," Corradon said, "let us begin our discussions. Ambassador Hazderzal, please."

Hazderzal rose. "I know you have many questions and we want to try and answer them all. And I have to say that we do not intend staying more than a month. The journey is long and the lord-emperor is anxious to hear about you. We have a message from him for you and we will show it to you soon. But I think we ought to begin with who we are and where the Dominion has come from." He paused, as if suddenly struck by an idea. "Incidentally, I fear that for some, the word *Dominion* may have overtones of tyranny and repression in your language. That is an unfortunate accident of history and a quirk of translation. Relax, friends; the reality is different. Now to our history. That history goes back to what we call the Great Separation, the tragic events of what we gather you call the Rebellion."

And for the next ten minutes, Hazderzal—aided by Tinternli—recounted the history of their worlds to a captivated audience. As he listened, Merral recognized the tale that he had heard from Azeras: the loss of the seventh ship, the descent of the Freeborn worlds into anarchy, and the endless cycles of troubled tension that boiled into bitter strife before, in bloodied exhaustion, collapsing back into a new, uneasy peace.

Yet there were differences in both fact and interpretation and, as the account came closer to the present, those divergences became plainer. The rise of the Dominion was portrayed as a blessed and gratefully received event that had brought badly needed stability and peace to increasingly greater numbers of people. The opposition to the Dominion was painted in the most negative of lights. The True Freeborn—the weary irony in Hazderzal's voice as he said the name was striking—were, at worst, bandits and at best, tragic fools who did not see where their best interests lay. It was they who had stolen a transport vessel, the *Rahllman's Star*, and fled to Farholme.

Merral was soon asked to speak by Corradon and, choosing his words carefully, gave a brief account of the battle at Fallambet Lake Five in which he omitted all reference to entering the ship.

"So providence punished them with a harsh—but just—fate," Hazderzal observed with a grim look. "You are to be congratulated, Commander."

"I take no credit," Merral said quietly, as he sat down. "That belongs elsewhere."

"The True Freeborn," Hazderzal said with a solemn air, "are on the run and their forces in disarray. Yet, they are not completely eliminated and are still capable of doing much harm."

"Let me be honest." As he paused he seemed somewhat embarrassed at what he had to say. "Matters are untidy. We did not destroy all the True Freeborn ships. Indeed, we believe that they may have some considerable forces left. They still possess ships and powerful weapons and now that they have realized that the Assembly is open to them, they may well do you great harm. They are vindictive. At the start of our dealings together, we want to warn you that another attack on your world by them is probable. They know that there is now no home for them in the Dominion worlds. The fact that, however inadvertently, you destroyed their forces makes you at war with them. They will seek revenge and we have found them merciless enemies." He paused again. As he did Merral glanced at the others, seeing concern on every face. "Our borders are long and our resources are stretched. The dimension you call Below-Space cannot be policed. In the discussions that follow you may need to bear that in mind."

Now there was a time for questions. Merral stayed silent, concerned lest something he say betray the fact that he knew more than he was supposed to know.

"How do you view General Jannafy?" asked the representative for Western Menaya.

"A name from a very distant—and different—past," Hazderzal answered, without any hesitation. "William Jannafy is an almost forgotten figure. We recognize our mistakes—we have paid a high price. We have turned our back on the distant past. You would hardly celebrate Lucas Ringell, would you, Commander?"

"His name is known, but that is all," Merral said quickly. The disk hanging from his neck seemed to mock him.

The representative for Central Menaya spoke next. "Why didn't you reveal your existence earlier?"

"To be honest," Tinternli answered, "we never felt strong enough. All we gleaned from the stray electromagnetic signals we picked up told us that you were now vastly greater than we were. We understood that you were now peaceful but . . ." Her look was one of delicate embarrassment and her voice tapered off. "We fled once from the Assembly; we did not want to again. We kept to ourselves."

"Can you tell us about your faster-than-light system?" asked Southern Menaya's representative.

Hazderzal replied, "It is a modification of Gate technology that allowed ships to travel Below-Space. As for the details, well," he gave a little self-deprecating laugh, "I am not an engineer. You could discuss the mechanics later, especially if you visit our ship."

Clemant, who had been silent so far, raised a hand. "The ape-creatures and these appalling insect-human hybrids we encountered—where are they from?"

Merral detected wariness in his voice. *He at least is not relaxing.*

Hazderzal hesitated for a moment. "I could claim that these were products of these insurgents. But I don't. Let me be honest, Advisor; these creatures are some of a small number of life-forms that we have generated by genetic manipulation for menial tasks on our ships and worlds. They were being shipped on the freighter when it was stolen. They are made with only limited intelligence and awareness and, although we treat them well, I cannot speak for what these wretched thieves have done with them. And if you are shocked, then bear in mind that in many cultures, animals are used for a variety of purposes. You, I gather, still ride horses for work I believe, where the terrain requires them. We do not."

The contact team shared uncomfortable looks.

Merral really wanted to ask about the steersman on the intruder ship, but had been unable to work out how to raise the matter. Few people knew what he had found on board and to mention that he had encountered such a being raised awkward questions as to how he had escaped. Nevertheless, he felt he could ask about the dreadful creature that Azeras called a slitherwing.

He called up the awful image from his diary and projected it on a wallscreen. "What is it?" he asked. "Where did it come from?"

The ambassadors shook their heads in frowning dismay. "We heard rumors of this," Hazderzal said, with a look of revulsion at the screen. "In Communal, you might call these beings slitherwings. In their desperation these people—these so-called Freeborn—have conjured up all sorts of creatures from the depths. We have even heard that they try to steer their ships with monstrous beings. Such things are abhorrent to us. We must have you visit the *Dove of Dawn* to see that no such beasts are hiding on board."

"Thank you," Merral said quietly, aware that he could now guess the answer to any question about steersmen.

"But who do you worship?" Jenat's frail voice quavered. "You know our beliefs."

"Ah, President Jenat, that is a question that I expected you to ask." Hazderzal's smile was gentle. "Well, there is both familiarity and difference. We celebrate the one God: indeed our emblem is that very One—the great unity—the One who is beyond all understanding. That much you would find familiar. But I have to say you would find a breadth in our worlds: an openness, a freedom for all to pursue the great quest wherever it leads them."

"I see," Jenat answered with a look of perplexity. "You have a sort of . . . diversity of views?"

"Exactly," Tinternli added, her soft smile one of reassurance. "It provides the perfect basis for discussion, for exploration."

"Well, if you say so," Jenat answered rather doubtfully, staring at the table. "It all sounds so, well, unclear. I really would like to discuss the matter with the Custodians of the Faith. But alas . . ." He looked at Tinternli and his expression of doubt was edged aside by a smile of appreciation.

"I expect," said Hazderzal, "you have probably all had enough to digest for one day. May I suggest that the meeting be adjourned until tomorrow? I do have one request though. May we be allowed to set up a temporary liaison center at Langerstrand?"

And with that and courteous farewells, the ambassadors and their crew returned to the shuttle.

In the debate that followed the departure of the ambassadors, Corradon expressed his view that the day had been wholly positive; many old fears had been allayed and no new ones created. Clemant, though, was more cautious: "We have little experience of lies," he rumbled. "We would be ill-equipped to recognize them."

The general conclusion though was a tentative welcome, with the rider that big unanswered questions remained. It was agreed that the ambassadors should be allowed to build a liaison center.

Merral spent much of the short flight back to Isterrane staring out of the window with a puzzled concentration. *Someone is lying. But is it Azeras or the ambassadors? Could it even be that they are both lying? And if I don't know who is lying, how can any of the others be expected to know?*

⬦◯⬦◯⬦

Late the following morning, Merral returned to Langerstrand, puzzled by Vero's lack of contact. His friend's silence only deepened his sense of isolation and vulnerability.

At Langerstrand, Merral was startled to find that the permission to build a center had been speedily acted on. A new and larger shuttle from the *Dove* had already landed and machines were excavating the ground while others unloaded walls and roofing materials.

Clemant, who was watching the process, told Merral that the ambassadors had requested, and been given, the services of various Farholme engineers and technicians to help them with construction.

The afternoon's meeting with Hazderzal and Tinternli began with the playing of a short message from Lord-Emperor Nezhuala on the wallscreen.

Merral was surprised. The title *lord-emperor* had evoked the image of an awesome figure majestically enthroned, but the man he saw standing in a garden amid blooming rose trees was very different. He had short, light brown hair and a pleasant but rather nondescript face. As with the ambassadors, Merral found him of indeterminate age.

"I am Gaius Nezhuala," the man said and there was a hint of wry amusement in his tone as if he knew that his hearers expected someone much grander. "Forgive my rather rusty and antiquated Communal. My ambassadors have had two months leisure to update and practice theirs. I, alas, have not." He smiled, the sort of expression that pleads *Please smile with me.*

Merral stared at the screen, trying to focus his mind on the man before him. *If these people are evil, then it must surely show here. However good their disguise, surely in their presentation of their leader, I should detect some hint of evil.*

Again he felt nothing untoward. *Am I relieved or disappointed?*

"This is a great and historic moment for our worlds," Nezhuala went on, his tone urgent and ringing

A preacher's voice. Merral wondered what he meant by it.

"It is a time of destiny, a time for wise choices, a time for great actions. It presents challenges for all of us, challenges that we might wish to duck. We might, perhaps, have hoped that these events had happened in other days, for other men and women to act on. But they have not. Providence, Fate, the Almighty, the One—whatever name we choose for the power that governs our lives—has ruled that it is we who must respond to the challenge." As he paused Merral realized that apart from a slightly archaic quality, Nezhuala's Communal was actually very good.

"The tragedy of the theft of the *Rahllman's Star* and the loss of the Farholme Gate has forced us to act. We considered reaching out to you before, but fear always deterred us. Now we have no choice. So let us, together, make good come out of evil."

Nezhuala took a step forward to the lens as if inviting himself into the lives of his viewers. "Let me share with you the vision I have, the grand vision. But I must remind you first that we of the Dominion are a little people; our numbers are a fraction of yours. We pose no threat to the mighty Assembly and indeed it may seem arrogant for me to suggest that we can offer you anything. Yet I believe we can. We understand little of your worlds, but we know you have had peace for over eleven millennia. We, in contrast, have known only strife and struggle." His dark gray eyes showed sadness. "Your history has given you an enviable stability and a great material and spiritual wealth. Yet although our turbulent history has been costly, it has given us a technology that is in many areas more advanced than yours. In short, we have much to offer each other. I believe that together—and only together—we can reach a new turning point the in history of the human race. Before us lies the prospect of a new Assembly—an expanding body of all humanity pushing through the galaxy at an unprecedented rate."

There was a pause as if to let the grand vision sink in. "We want to help you. We want you to trust us. That is all I ask, along with one small favor: that you would allow this message to be broadcast to your world. Thank you. I await the results of the visit of my ambassadors to you with the greatest of interest. Be assured of my prayers."

The man bowed slightly and the screen went dark. Corradon clapped, realized that he was alone, and stopped.

"I'm sure you wish to consider the lord-emperor's request," said

Hazderzal. "But we also felt that you should see something of the Dominion. We have brought a simulation that allows you to look around our homeworld of Khalamaja, one of the four worlds around the star we call Sarata. We have adapted it so it works with your imaging glasses and we wish to make it widely available for all who want to see it. There is nothing hidden and we feel that an hour's visit would help you understand us."

ㅁㅁㅁㅁㅁ

In fact, it was well over an hour later when Merral took off the imaging glasses. He rubbed his eyes and stared out of the window at his world, trying to ignore the awed and animated conversation of the others as he tried to evaluate what he had seen.

Technically, the simulation was astounding, extraordinarily detailed, and so smoothly done that it was hard not to believe you were there in the flesh miraculously flying over the roofs and rocks. The landscape of Khalamaja was awesome—full of vast snowcapped mountains rearing into indigo-blue skies and deep mist-filled gorges knifing down to turquoise seas. But the architecture had been the most amazing thing of all. There was a scale and magnitude to the Dominion constructions that the brain found hard to comprehend. Buildings—columns of dazzling glass flaming with golden light in the setting sun—towered a thousand meters. Vast bridges, fragile slender arches that touched the clouds, leaped across seas. Entire mountainsides had been planed into vertical surfaces into which were carved a thousand rooms. Snaking complexes of serried houses and gardens rose out of ice-locked lakes on pillars. The overall effect was stunning and spellbinding.

"So, Commander, what did you think?"

Merral looked up, his thoughts interrupted by Tinternli's lilting voice.

"Impressive, Ambassador," he replied. "Very impressive." Yet as he spoke, Merral knew something in what he had seen troubled him. Exactly *what* that something was eluded him.

"I'm glad you think so," Tinternli said. "We want to make this available to your world. We would have put it on the Library, but that, alas, is closed. So instead, we want to put some copies on the Basic-Net and set up booths at the main towns where this can be accessed."

There were other requests too. Hazderzal asked that delegates from each town be allowed to come and stay at the liaison center. "We would like perhaps thirty people—men and women—who could stay here for a few days. We could explain who we are to them, give them an introduction to our history, and perhaps, through them, understand more of who you are."

Corradon frowned. "Well . . . we hadn't quite had that in mind."

Tinternli gave him a smile of gentle reproof. "Representative Corradon, surely you don't have anything to hide, do you?"

"No. It's just that—"

"Openness, Representative, is the basis of all trust. And to show you that it is not all one-sided, we would like to have a team visit the *Dove of Dawn*. Send up a dozen people—engineers, technicians, even, if you wish, members of the Farholme Defense Force—and I will have Benek-Hal show them around."

Corradon looked to Merral for support. "Thank you, Ambassador, I'm sure we will take that offer up."

Hazderzal asked, "Could a small medical party check some of the hospitals? We would particularly like to look at your wounded soldiers. In some ways we feel some responsibility for them and we have some excellent skills."

After a discussion, the ambassadors got their requests approved. Merral, feeling somewhat discomforted by the way these requests were always approved, wondered if he should have objected more strongly.

◯◯◯◯◯

Merral returned to Isterrane late in the afternoon. He sent a message to Luke telling him to look at the simulation and then called Vero, who answered from what seemed to be a bare, echoing room.

"You must see this simulation of Khalamaja."

"Thank you, my friend. I have already been looking at it."

"How did you get it?"

"I have my sources." Vero's tone was secretive.

"So what do you think?"

"I was reminded of your castle tree."

"But that doesn't exist."

"Ah yes." Vero's face acquired a wry smile. "How *silly* of me to make that link."

"Vero, is it really possible that everything the ambassadors are presenting is a fraud?"

"Do you smell a rat?"

"A rat?"

"Another expression from the past."

"Well, I *do* think there is something odd. And Vero, they make these requests and we just seem to give into them. I don't know how they do it. They know what they want and they get it."

"My friend, it is to be expected. There is—to coin a phrase of my own—'no tradition of suspicion' in the Assembly. We tend to grant requests."

"So, I should challenge them?"

"No!"

"Why not?"

"We need to play for time. If we are to have any chance at all against the Dominion, we need all the time we can get. Every day counts. Don't rock the boat."

"The boat? Oh, I see. No, I won't. But I half wish Delastro was on the team. He would have challenged these requests."

"True. But with the prebendant we would already have been at war."

"Vero, I think, beneath all the good behavior and the beauty and the wise words, that they are evil. But I can't prove it and even to say it sounds dreadful. But why can Delastro see it and I can't?"

"There is such a thing as being right for all the wrong reasons. If you are suspicious of everybody, sooner or later you get something right."

"Perhaps. So we just let things continue?"

"Have patience. It won't last. They'll show their hand soon." Vero looked away, his attention evidently caught by someone offscreen. "Sorry, I must go. Duty summons me." And with that Vero ended the call.

❈❈❈❈❈

Later that evening, Luke came round. After helping himself to a drink he followed Merral into the still darkness of the courtyard and sat down.

"What did you make of Khalamaja?" Merral asked as the chaplain stretched out his long legs.

"I was awed."

"But?"

Luke sipped his drink. "Yes, I'm afraid there is a *but* with the Dominion. Let me ask you what you thought."

"Me? It was *too* grand. The human scale was missing. And I'd like to have seen more trees."

Merral thought he saw a look of relief in Luke's face. "I'm very glad to hear that. I felt the same. It was overpowering. And far too neat."

"So you think that it's a—what's the word?—*fake*?"

Luke shrugged. "We have to consider it possible. And what about the ambassadors or Nezhuala? How do you find them?"

"To be honest, likable. They seem very ordinary—nothing alien or remarkable. I have been trying to sense if there is any hint of the evil I felt on that intruder ship."

"And?" Luke's stare was keen.

"Not a trace. What do you think?"

"What I'm struck with is their perfection—the absence of blemishes."

"You don't like that?"

"It troubles me. Can a thing be too perfect to be true?"

"Perhaps."

"Another question. Do they criticize the Assembly?"

Merral thought about that. "There has been no direct criticism."

"But?"

"Ah, the *but*. Well, although there has been no criticism, I somehow feel that our achievements are diminished. Their worlds are rich and exciting; ours—especially Farholme—seem mean and dull."

"How very interesting," Luke replied. "I've picked up a bit about their theology. This great openness of theirs is very striking. And it worries me. They deny nothing—there's nothing to engage with. Their beliefs are just a great bottomless swamp with no rock to put your feet on. There is the One, but how you conceive of him—or it—doesn't matter."

He leaned back and stared up, whether at the fronds of the palm tree or a scene of his imagination, Merral wasn't sure. After a few moments, he said in a slow, reflective voice, "The other thing—and this troubles me a lot—is that they fear death. All of them—death haunts their worlds."

"So, is it all a deception?"

The chaplain took another slow sip of his drink. There was something comfortingly deliberate in his actions. "A very strong chance, I'd say."

"But why can't we see it?"

"Because we are fallible human beings. The Word talks about the devil masquerading as an angel of light. This may—only may—be the same thing."

"Yes, perhaps that's it. Will Jenat see that?"

"I think so. He may appear frail, but I think he's still very sharp. But a last question, Merral: what do they want?"

"I don't know. That's what we are all waiting for."

○○○○○

In fact, on the following day, during the contact team's third meeting with the ambassadors, Hazderzal outlined exactly what they wanted.

"These True Freeborn are not eliminated. They may attack here anytime. And frankly—don't take this as an insult, Commander—if they do, you are in serious trouble. They may decide to destroy you all or they may choose to take you as captives. Your chance of resistance against a military vessel with troops and armor would be zero."

There was an uncomfortable, fidgety silence before Ambassador Hazderzal spoke again. "The lord-emperor is, however, prepared to extend his protection over you. That is an act of grace; to extend our forces this far out would weaken our defenses around the Home Worlds. But we will do it. We will send five frigates to be stationed in your system."

Corradon frowned. "Actually, what we really want is to be reunited with the Assembly."

"We understand," Hazderzal said. "We can give you a single interworld transit vessel—a five-hundred seater. It would do the trip to Bannermene in three weeks. You'd have your misplaced people sorted out in three months."

"Exactly what we want!"

Tinternli shook her head. "But, my friends, it isn't that simple. You see, we have an appalling fear that when we encounter the Assembly, they will attack us again. We were once crushed by them and do not wish that to happen again. So we want to learn how we may best approach them. *We* did not destroy your Gate, but your isolation has given us the chance to deal, not with the overwhelming might of the whole Assembly, but with a small part of it. It is a chance—a chance that will not come again—that we do not wish to throw away. With you as our friends, we may gain acceptance with the Assembly."

"So what do you want?" Merral asked, trying to keep the unease out of his voice.

"Lord Nezhuala offers you a treaty," Hazderzal said, his voice a gentle murmur.

"A treaty?" Corradon looked around with evident unease. "Can you elaborate?"

Tinternli gave him a warm smile. "Please don't be alarmed. It would be a very simple agreement. We would offer protection and transport facilities. You in return would promise not to take up arms against us. You would keep your own customs, laws, and beliefs."

"And that is all you would want?"

"Yes. Of course, as a token of your good faith toward us you would grant us access to your Library and your Admin-Net."

Merral saw the questions in the eyes of the contact team. But before anyone could say anything, Hazderzal continued. "There would be many other benefits: medical, engineering, and so on. But there is no need to make any decision here and now. We give you ten days from today to make a decision. That is ample time for you to decide and for those of you who are representatives to listen to those you represent."

"And if we say no?" Merral asked.

"Then we will leave and you must fend for yourself. And remember, it is not just the True Freeborn you must face. We have looked at your world and we do not think your future in isolation is encouraging. Our surveys suggest that there is a high probability that the central rift volcanic system will erupt catastrophically unless the magma chambers are vented; that is outside your technology. Your climates are already precariously balanced and would not handle a massive dust injection into the atmosphere. The currents in the Southern Seas are heading into instability. The probability that your Guardian satellite system will still be operating after twenty years is effectively zero." Hazderzal turned to Clemant. "Would you dissent, Doctor? I imagine you have the figures at hand for all these issues."

Clemant looked up with troubled eyes. "I am aware of . . . most of these estimates."

"But, please," Tinternli suddenly spoke in her clear, bright voice, "in your discussions do not overlook our larger goal: the greater vision of our worlds and yours reunited. Farholme has a chance to lead the way for peace, to lead the way for healing."

Merral wondered if her words were an attempt to steer the conversation into safer waters.

Corradon seemed to gulp, and gazed around. "These matters are things we must discuss."

"We are glad."

Then there were requests. The ambassadors wanted a chance to make live broadcasts to Farholme explaining who they were, where they came from, and what they wanted. After a long discussion, it was agreed that the ambassadors would be allowed a half-hour program each evening for five days with each broadcast approved beforehand.

After the ambassadors left for the center that was growing up around their end of the runway, there was a discussion of the treaty and its terms. Merral soon slipped away. It would take days for the implications to sink in and still longer for decisions to be made. He felt relieved that at last he knew what the Dominion wanted and that they had ten days before a decision had to be made.

ᓂᓇᓂ

Arriving back in Isterrane, Merral decided on impulse to make a brief visit to the Western Isterrane Main Hospital. A Dominion team had visited the previous day and he was anxious to know what had transpired. He went to see Barry Narandel whose legs had been mangled in the final stages of the battle at Fallambet. Despite attempts to save them, his legs had had to be amputated, and he was being fitted with artificial legs.

Barry, clumsily lurching around a ward with the aid of crutches, was glad to see Merral. Yes, he said, the Dominion team had talked to him.

"They offered to grow me new legs." He stared down at his metal and synthetic limbs. "It will take a month in a tissue tank for them to form, then a long op to fasten them on. Then a lot of physiotherapy, but the end results will be as good as new."

"Impressive."

"That's not all. They offered me augmented legs, if I wanted."

"Augmented?"

"Specially made—toughened bone, enhanced musculature. They reckon I could break the Farholme two hundred meters."

"You refused?"

Barry frowned and moved his right leg. Merral heard the faintest hiss of a motor. "Yes. I just said normal legs would be fine. To restore what I lost is one thing. To go beyond it is quite another. It didn't seem right."

"It isn't."

Merral left Barry and talked to the doctors. He was struck by their almost total enthusiasm for Dominion science. They had, he was told, better diagnostic tools, better drugs, and better surgical equipment.

Merral left feeling troubled. In this hospital the battle for support had been won by the Dominion.

◌◌◌◌◌

Later that day Vero welcomed Engineer Eric Weijmars into his cluttered room deep under Isterrane.

"You have news?" he asked, but the animated look on the man's face already told him the answer to his question.

"Yes." Eric tapped the roll of paper under his arm. "And new plans."

"Take a seat. Excuse the mess," Vero said, clearing papers and an empty coffee cup from a chair. "Have they taken the bait?"

The engineer sat down. "Oh yes. Snapped it up."

"What happened?"

"Drewkant left his diary around overnight as you suggested. He came looking for it the next day. It was where he had put it, but it had been read."

"You're sure?"

"Yes. That Dominion lot think we're stupid so they don't take precautions. Data had been downloaded. There were new fingerprints on the case."

"Good. And Drewkant's diary was, of course, one of the ones we'd modified?"

"Of course." There was a slightly offended tone to the voice.

"Sorry, just had to make sure." Vero stared at the ceiling. "Are you going back to the base?"

"No. The work's tailing off."

"Good, so I can talk to you without any risk. So now they know that there has been recent work done under Isterrane. They know that Drewkant is a chief water engineer for Isterrane. And now they have his plans for the city out of the diary. And they probably think the key to the Library is down here. So we shall see what happens."

"Rather you than me. The whole lot give me the creeps. Can't put my finger on it though."

"A widespread observation. Do you have anything else for me?"

"Two chambers have just been built at the base. We don't know what they're for. They wouldn't say." Eric unrolled the plans and pointed out the features. "We weren't allowed to take a good look at them. One, dug into rock, is just outside the existing structure. The other's near a rear door. It has reinforced walls, and it's lockable."

Vero checked the dimensions. *A chamber for a baziliarch, as Azeras predicted, and a pen for a Krallen pack.* "Are they empty?"

"So far."

"Anything else?"

"Just this. They want us all clear of the base by tomorrow night. A landing's scheduled at midnight. The cargo manifest has not been declared."

Is this the baziliarch being delivered? "Well done."

Eric rose to leave. "Need anything else, Mr. V.?"

"No, thank you." Vero began looking at the schematic map of the Isterrane foundation levels on the wall. "I have a welcome to prepare."

ᴏᴄᴏᴄᴏ

That evening, Merral had a call from Isabella, who was working late in her office. She wore an immaculately pressed white blouse with an elegant gold chain and had an air of being someone very important.

After some conversational preliminaries that were at least polite, Isabella asked, "How are the dealings with the ambassadors going?"

"Well, interesting. We're making progress."

"That is so noncommittal. So typically Merral."

Merral forced himself to smile. "I'm learning what our ancestors call diplomacy."

"I gather they want a treaty. It's going to be on the broadcast in an hour's time."

"I wasn't aware that the treaty is public knowledge."

"It is. You think we should accept?"

"You can ask me that, but I can't answer."

"Of course," she replied wearily. "You have to be diplomatic. But what's the alternative? Permanent isolation? Another incursion? We have problems. We are a planet waiting for a catastrophe to happen."

"So you are positive about the treaty?"

"Merral, I believe that these people can offer us so much," she said, a glint of excitement in her eyes. "Our society has only known the rule of the Assembly with all its limitations. These people have been free—free to investigate wherever and whatever. What they can teach us is beyond imagining."

"There are certainly great opportunities," Merral replied slowly. He was anxious not to say anything that might provoke a flare-up of warfare with Isabella, but felt troubled by her uncritical enthusiasm.

"Oh, Merral, you are still so cautious," Isabella replied, her voice full of reproof. "I was really calling to say that I'm going to Langerstrand myself."

"*You* are?" Suddenly, Merral felt that he ought to warn her.

"Don't sound so surprised! Yes, to help with the program they've set up at the base. I will be the Ynysmant delegate. Enatus approved it. I don't know how he will manage without me, poor little thing." She paused. "Merral, you're frowning. Don't you think I should go?"

"Well, I am . . . less enthusiastic about these people. I don't have a good feeling about them."

"A *feeling*?" She gave a little snort. "A prejudice, that's all. They are just fundamentally different to us. And being fundamentally different is not the same as being wrong."

"I know."

"They could have seized Farholme by force, you know. But they haven't."

"True." In one part of Merral's mind a voice said, *Warn her, stop her from going,* but in another, a different voice said, *Don't waste your energy, it's her choice.* In the end he tried to compromise. "Do you have to go?"

"Yes. You can't stop me. I have as much right as you to go."

"But . . ."

"But what?"

I give up. "Nothing. Go to Langerstrand. It's your choice."

21

The following day the team to visit the *Dove of Dawn* was taken by the shuttle from Langerstrand up to the orbiting parent vessel. The team had been drawn from various sources and included a number of engineers whom Perena recommended.

Shortly after the *Dove* shuttle took off, Merral had another meeting with the ambassadors. As Hazderzal talked about the economic basis of the Dominion worlds Merral found his attention wandering.

Afterward, as they took refreshments, Tinternli, who wore a long, red dress of a smooth fine-textured cloth that seemed to sway with a life of its own, came over to Merral.

"Commander," she said, "I could see that you found that tiresome. Would you walk with me outside?"

Merral agreed and in the noontide sun they strolled out of the building and up a low rise overlooking the newly completed liaison base.

"Let us sit down," she said and lowered herself onto a carpet of soft heather.

Merral sat facing her.

"Tell me what I am seeing," she said, sweeping strands of hair from her face and shading her eyes.

Merral noticed that she didn't seem to sweat. *Elegance—that's the word.* He pointed out the Edelcet Marshes, Hereza Crags, and Mount Adaman glinting hazily in the midday sun, before turning to the bare headland around them. "I apologize for this. One day it will be forested."

"You would wish to be back in Forestry?" Tinternli's voice seemed full of sympathy.

Despite all his suspicions, Merral warmed to her. "Very much."

"Then you are wise. There is far more to life than war and even diplomacy." Her smile seemed queenly. "But your return to the Forestry you love may be arranged. Not all our worlds are as fine as Khalamaja and even there, there is work to do. Forestry is not a profession that flourishes in worlds at war. You have skills we need and can use." Her smile seemed to radiate tenderness. "Why, Commander—or should I say, Forester—we have whole planets that could be yours."

At the words *whole planets* Merral felt a novel thrill. Images unfolded in his mind of worlds bursting to overflowing with an almost infinite variety of forests planted and nurtured by him. The vision was so compelling in its beauty and splendor that his heart swelled with a fierce longing. He trembled and was suddenly aware that Tinternli looked at him inquiringly.

"An attractive offer," he said. *And it is.*

"It can be yours, if you'd cooperate." The words were gentle.

The images returned. Merral saw arid dusty landscapes of rock and dirt turn before his eyes into swathes of woodlands in a thousand shades of green, full of broad-trunked oaks, lofty elms, light and airy poplars, towering firs, and a hundred other species. He gasped at the extraordinary loveliness of it all.

It's a temptation, said a faint voice in his head.

Don't be silly, a second voice said. *Temptations are to do with power and sex, not trees.*

A temptation can be about anything, replied the first voice.

But this is about doing good, countered the second voice, *making dead planets live.*

Suddenly, Merral came to a realization. "I don't want whole worlds," he said, the force of his words startling him and dispelling the vision. "Ambassador, it seems to me that there are limits to what we can be. I would prefer to work in a little area and know it well, than to work on a vast area and never really master it. We must choose depth or breadth, and I choose depth."

He paused. "In other words, I just want my job back."

Tinternli stared at him, a look of rebuke in her brown eyes. "Oh, the great weakness of the Assembly. You don't want enough. You are content with gardens when you could have forests, with lakes when you could have oceans, with hills when you could have mountains." Beneath the sweetness of her words he heard the bitter tang of contempt.

"Maybe, Ambassador, that is the ultimate difference between us. We try to limit our desires to what the Most High wants us to have. You set no such limits."

"Perhaps so," she said and looked away.

Merral felt a sudden need to challenge the woman who had tempted him in this way. "Ambassador Tinternli, we believe in the Three-in-One. You believe in . . . what?"

She pouted. "We emphasize the One; you, the Three-in-One; Is the math that different?"

"We trust in the Lamb—the One who died, rose, and will return in power."

At this Tinternli adjusted her dress, tilted her head, and wound her fingers in her hair. "Good words. The Assembly does a fine line in words." Her voice was gentle, almost sorrowful. "But let me be honest with you, Merral. This *return*. Long years have passed since that belief was formulated." She bent down, picked up some sand, and let the grains slip slowly through her long fingers. "Thirteen . . . thousand . . . years. . . ." The way she stretched the words seemed to bring home to Merral an awesome immensity of time. "And has he been seen?" she asked, her brown eyes seeming to stare into him. "In all that time? In all those long years?"

As Merral hesitated, the words came to him. "Ambassador Tinternli, I am a forester, not a theologian. But I know forests do not grow overnight. Oaks take centuries. The test of whether a forester has created a living forest will be generations away. And if it is so for trees, why might it not be even more so for worlds and cultures? God's time is surely the right time, however long it is."

"As ever, fine words. But, Commander, you are right—there are differences between us. But—and we will not say it openly to your people—the biggest is this: we do not have your confidence. We see no sign of a divinely ordained finish to history. It is open-ended." Her voice was stronger now. "The future is ours to seize and ours to make of it what we choose. That is what once made us the Freeborn and what makes us the Dominion now."

Troubled by her words, Merral fell silent and bent down to pick up a small stone as if by some action he could hide his consternation. As he did, Ringell's identity disk swung forward so that it slipped out of his shirt.

"That disk," Tinternli said, a sharp, almost hissing edge to her voice. "It is odd."

Merral quickly slipped it back out of sight. "It's an heirloom." He knew that he sounded defensive.

"It looks like . . . an ancient military identity disk."

"Well, it's something like that. We don't use them today. Do you?"

"But your last war was a very long time ago . . . against our people."

"I'm sorry. It's a bit thoughtless of me wearing it, isn't it? But it was given me by an old man who is now dead. So, I wear it."

"And whose name is on it? May I see?" Tinternli asked. In her brown eyes Merral saw a seething brew of fear and anger.

She knows. She may not be able to read my thoughts, but she has guessed whose name is on the disk.

He shook his head as he rose. "It has already caused enough embarrassment. I would prefer to forget it. Anyway, I think it's time to return."

Without a word, she followed him back to the center.

⊗⊗⊗⊗⊗

On the *Triumph of Sarata*, a hundred thousand kilometers away from Farholme in the upper levels of the Nether-Realms, Lezaroth was irritated. He had just ordered one of his engineers and a member of the ground attack team to the cells for twenty-four hours for brawling. Now the bridge was suspiciously empty, as always happened whenever he imposed discipline.

Lezaroth slumped in his seat. *They keep their distance from me, particularly since I became the devoted servant of the lord-emperor.*

He tried to analyze his anger. It wasn't just about the brawl. No, like all the crew, he had been on board the ship too long and spent too much time in the Nether-Realms. *We're all irritated. I've never been on a ship so full of bickering.* He also realized that he had probably made things worse by putting the ship on such a high a state of alert in order to emerge into Standard-Space and launch an attack within twenty minutes. The men were on reduced sleep, recreation was banned, and their only respite—if it could be called that—was visits from the gloomy, tattooed priest urging more devotion to the lord-emperor and demanding ever more sacrifices.

But Lezaroth knew there was another reason why he was irritated. *I'm frustrated with the diplomacy. I'm a fighter born and trained and I command one of the best fighting vessels ever made. Yet all I can do is watch and listen to this interminable diplomatic talk.*

With a frustration that bordered on fury, he flicked on the monitor screen to see the latest transmissions from the diplomatic base at Langerstrand. A tolerable signal came through the satellite cable tethered above the ship in Standard-Space and once or twice a day he would get coded messages about progress. But so far today there had been no new messages. Clearly there was nothing of relevance to say. *More talk. How much longer must I endure it?*

Yet as he raised the question, he knew the answer: not long. All the evidence suggested that the diplomatic venture was not going to work. The lord-emperor had been too optimistic. Over the last few days Lezaroth had spent time in the intensive study of the culture that was now wide-open before him. He felt it extremely unlikely that, even with the beguiling methods used by the ambassadors—and he found them very impressive—Farholme would agree to the treaty. The lord-emperor or his advisors had confused naïveté with stupidity and simplicity with ignorance. The way that the Library and Admin-

Net had been sealed showed that these people were now wary. So diplomacy would fail. And when it did, the military option would begin.

Lezaroth clenched his fists in anticipation and considered the coming attack. The preparations were almost ready. The Krallen had been checked and were in the deployment mode. The baziliarch was now in place at Langerstrand and the tower that it needed to emerge from dormancy was about to be built so that within days it would be ready for deployment. And his crew itched for action.

Lezaroth stared at the imagery from the world so near him. *It ought to be so very easy.* They had run all the simulations and the results were always the same: the Farholme defenses collapsed within days.

Just then, the camera focused on a man in a green military uniform. He had a lean, tanned face. Lezaroth recognized Merral D'Avanos immediately. His Allenix unit had provided him with considerable data on the man and his background.

It ought to be so very easy. . . . And yet . . . As Lezaroth stared at the man on the screen he felt strangely troubled. Probing his feelings, he discovered something akin to the presentiments of threat he had had before meeting the lord-emperor on Khalamaja. The sense of danger was much less, but it was still there.

You are a peril, D'Avanos.

Suddenly hidden fears seemed to rise up. This world looked so simple to seize. But was it? What lurked beneath it? He felt himself tense. *We have our steersmen and our baziliarchs. But what might they have? D'Avanos is a man who has been very lucky and very brave. But supposing he's more? Is he the great adversary? And, if he is, what might that mean in conflict?*

With this surge of fear came an inevitable anger. *Whether you are the great adversary or not, I will be happy to slay you, D'Avanos. And whether I do it personally and slowly by a knife thrust or remotely by vaporizing you to atoms in a kinetic weapon blast makes no difference.*

The camera moved on and Lezaroth felt less troubled. *I must neither neglect D'Avanos nor be preoccupied with him.*

He sat back, considering the way ahead. In war, he believed, you should always plan at least two steps ahead of events. The next two events now seemed to be reasonably clear. First, the diplomacy would fail; second, there would be a short, sharp confrontation. The strategy for that was clear: a series of progressively graded attacks to make the Farholme administration yield unconditionally. Barring the unexpected—and here his thoughts flitted uncomfortably back to Merral D'Avanos—utter victory seemed certain.

So what then? Well, he would seize the Library and take prisoners. He would then try and find the *Rahllman's Star.* It now seemed certain that the Farholmers had only destroyed the slave unit of *Rahllman's Star.* In fact, the tone of the media reports he had seen suggested that they had no inkling the master unit existed. So it was presumably still floating around in the Nether-Realms nearby bearing the all-important body of the Great Prince Zhalatoc. Lezaroth presumed that the Library would hold astronomical data relevant to the arrival of the *Rahllman's Star* and once he had that he would be able to narrow down the likely location. He had the equipment for a Nether-Realms trawl in a hold and with the likely location there was a high probability that he would find the *Rahllman's Star* within days.

At any rate, whether I find it or not, it is absolutely critical to ensure that I, and I alone, obtain the rewards of this mission. The ambassadors would be discredited by events, but that still left Hanax. And Hanax clearly had his own agenda. Lezaroth had keenly monitored the under-captain's access to the *Triumph*'s computer. Hanax had been planning the Krallen attacks and creating strategies for an assault on Farholme—that caused no concern. What did was the way that he had accessed every fact available on the *Rahllman's Star* and Commander Merral D'Avanos.

Lezaroth now felt certain that Hanax was operating on secret instructions from the lord-emperor. For the lord-emperor to give secret instructions to two separate officers was typical of the way things worked in the Dominion. But it was not a happy situation. Lezaroth had no wish to be disposed of as Admiral Kalartha-Har had been.

He was considering how to deal with the threat from Hanax when the screen flashed: a personal coded message for him from Tinternli. Lezaroth checked to make sure he was alone on the bridge and then decrypted it.

The ambassador was alone and her face was grave. "Margrave, you may be interested to know that D'Avanos wears an old military identity disk around his neck. I have downloaded the imagery from my optic feed and had it enhanced. I thought you might be interested in whose name it bears."

A gray circle filled the screen. It was slightly fuzzy, but the words were plain. *Lucas Hannun Ringell, Space Frigate* Clearstar, *Assembly Assault Fleet. Date of Birth: 3-3-2082.*

"I think this man needs dealing with."

Lezaroth smiled. "I will make it a matter of the highest priority, madam," he said in the lowest of whispers. "You can be sure of that."

ༀༀༀ

Merral found little in the first Dominion broadcast to Farholme to alarm him, but the second, a day later, was very different. Prefaced by a warning and shown an hour later at night, it included chilling imagery of the war with the True Freeborn: swooping slitherwings, bloody-mouthed packs of Krallen, and other nameless terrors. Behind it was an unstated threat: *Without our help, this can happen here.*

On the day after the second broadcast Corradon and the other representatives reported record numbers of messages, each saying the same thing: *please make a deal; please keep us safe.*

Merral sensed that the resolve of Farholme that had survived both the loss of the Gate and the news of the intruders had now suddenly faltered.

That day Merral was summoned to a meeting with Vero in a quiet part of an Isterrane park.

"Why are we here?" Merral asked as they sat on a bench.

A dozen meters away, Lloyd sat on the grass apparently reading something on his diary.

"Because I don't want to be overheard. I don't trust anywhere with walls." Behind the dark glasses, Merral felt Vero's eyes were sweeping nervously this way and that. "First question: have you felt your mind being probed?"

"No. I have no sense of anything reading my mind. On the contrary, Tinternli and Hazderzal are sometimes surprised by what we say. I don't believe they can read minds."

"We don't think it's them. It's this baziliarch."

"Of which we've seen no sign. Do you know any more about it?"

Vero's tone and fidgeting fingers showed he was ill at ease. "Only that baziliarchs are some sort of demonic being. They are the most powerful of these creatures that can be put in a body and used by men. Does that make sense?"

"I think so."

"There is a hierarchy: the baziliarchs come above steersmen. There are seven of them."

"And what is above them?"

"Azeras says that 'beyond the seven comes the one. And that one is not God.'"

There was a long, troubled silence finally broken by Vero. "We think the baziliarch may only just have been put in place at the base. They may not want to use it yet. You can't use it and still pretend you are the good guys."

How does he know this? Who is we? But a question from Vero about the meetings with the ambassadors prevented him from inquiring further. Merral gave a brief account of what had happened in the last few meetings.

"It was as I had heard," was Vero's response. "So how will the voting on the treaty go?"

"It's hard to say. Yesterday's broadcast may have changed things. We shouldn't have allowed it."

Vero shrugged. "You are being outmaneuvered. It is hardly surprising. What is your guess about the vote?"

"I think that Corradon and some, or all, of the other representatives will probably vote in favor. There is a lot of pressure from the public. My father called me the other day. He was full of what wonderful engineers they were. He was very positive about a treaty."

Vero sighed. "Yes, the Dominion is doing well among the general population who haven't met them. Distance lends enchantment. Your mother?"

"She has become pragmatic. 'If they can fix this mess,' she says, 'they can have my support.'"

"I've heard that from others."

"But I will vote against the treaty. Jenat also, I think. Clemant, though, is a puzzle."

"Our advisor plays his cards close to his chest. So it's going to be tight—very tight." Vero stared thoughtfully into the far distance, his brow tightly furrowed. "It is vital—legally and morally—that the contact team vote against this treaty."

"If we agree to it, what would happen?"

"They will take the Library. And our independence would soon be lost. My guess would be that the FDF would be put under their control within days. You would, no doubt, be reassigned to Forestry—if you were fortunate."

"And if we reject them?"

"Then we will see a shift of tactics to threats or something much worse."

"Why does Nezhuala want a treaty? Why hasn't he sent his armies in already?"

"There's something very deep going on here. It's to do with rights and legality. If Farholme were seized forcibly by Nezhuala, he would be acting illegally and we would not really be part of the Dominion. But if we agreed to a treaty, we would belong to him. And it's not just politics. It seems that such a legal framework appears to extend into the spiritual realm."

"I see. There's something of that in the New Covenant writings—about being slaves to sin and needing to be set free."

"It's the same principle. And, of course, with a treaty, Nezhuala would get the Library intact."

"Is the Library that valuable?"

"Yes. He needs that information. In that encoded data are all our strengths and weaknesses. With that he can risk what Azeras calls the 'fatal blow.'"

"Meaning?"

"The fast punch to the heart of the Assembly: Ancient Earth. If he were to seize Earth, then the whole Assembly would crumble."

"I can hardly take the concept in."

"It's a useful reminder that we're playing for very high stakes." Vero sighed. "Anyway that's where things are."

As Vero started to rise, Merral said quickly, "Vero, there's one other thing. Tinternli knows about the identity disk. I think she suspects whose name is on it."

"Ah." There was no disguising the look of alarm on Vero's face. "Th-that is something I was afraid of. I'll bet she is thinking in terms of this great adversary superstition. You'd better watch yourself."

"But we don't believe it, do we?"

Vero smiled. "That you are the great defender of the Assembly? A new Lucas Ringell returned at this most dark time?" His smile broadened. "Oddly enough, I'm not sure I disbelieve it. What did Brenito say to me about you? 'I'm glad you found yourself a warrior.'"

"Vero, I am a reluctant warrior at best. I am not some mythic figure. It's so ridiculous as to be almost funny!"

"Very well. But if on the field of battle that rumor strikes fear into our enemies, then it may serve some good." Vero bounded to his feet. "But I really must go. Keep safe, my friend. The hour comes." He paused. "Two extra things: Don't use the underground passageways at night until I tell you to. And when you pray tonight, pray especially for me and my team. We are hoping for a late night."

"Meaning?"

"Ah. It's a secret, Commander." Vero walked away.

ᗧᗣᗣᗣᗣ

"Still no news?" Vero asked.

The five people studying screens and listening to signals in the basement command center gave five negative answers.

Still nothing! The trap is ready, but they aren't walking into it.

Vero twisted his fingers in frustration. Just after dark there had been signs of unusual activity at the Langerstrand base. It was now just past midnight and other than a report of odd noises at Tezekal Ridge, there had been no confirmation that a Krallen pack was on its way. Yet there was still an air of expectancy in the warm stuffy room, and the sporadic chatter was terse and nervous.

Vero tried to distract his own tense thoughts by looking around. His attention was caught by Azeras, who sat with his back to the wall, staring impassively at a wallscreen. The sarudar was immobile apart from his hands, which seemed to continuously slide up and down his thighs.

Although Azeras had put on weight since they found him on Ilakuma, there was still something gaunt, even haggard about him. That appearance was not just biological, but was linked to a disturbed psychology. Among those who knew who he was, Azeras had made no friends nor, it seemed, wanted any. He stayed formal and aloof, was always Azeras or Sarudar, and seemed to prefer to dwell alone with his troubles.

Suddenly, someone shouted, "Mr. V.! We have them on screen!"

Vero swung around to see the screen the man was pointing at. Blurred gray forms pounded over rough rocks, weaving and swaying but somehow managing to stay synchronized. "I-I'm having trouble counting."

"It's a full pack. A column of six—two abreast."

"W-where?"

"Just five kilometers west of the Walderand Bridge. They're fast."

"H-how fast?"

"Twenty kilometers an hour minimum," said a voice to his right.

Vero turned to Azeras. "As you expected?"

"Yeah." It came over as a grunt. "As expected. Recon party. Be grateful they aren't carrying weapons. It's going to be tough enough anyway."

"Thanks."

"Mr. V," another team member said, in an agitated voice, "there's a sentry on the Walderand Bridge. We could alert him, if we're quick."

Vero felt a sick twisting of his stomach.

The room fell silent and Vero realized everyone was looking at him. He closed his eyes. *I had been hoping I would not face this. Lord, give me grace and wisdom.* He made his decision. *And forgiveness.*

As he opened his eyes he was aware his hands were shaking. "I-I'm s-sorry w-we can't do it. If they suspect, it would jeopardize everything. . . . H-he must take his chance."

There were stiff nods and silence.

I wish Perena were here. Vero looked away from the screens in utter misery hoping that no one could see his face. *How long does the sentry have to live? Ten minutes?*

He caught sight of Azeras. His head was shaking softly, his eyes seeming to focus light-years away. Azeras suddenly looked up at Vero, and then beckoned him over.

Vero walked to him, his feet unsteady, and knelt at his side.

"It's war," Azeras whispered in his ear. Vero heard a roughness in his voice. "You have to make decisions like this some times. . . . I know. Oh, *how* I know. . . . But, Sentinel, you must keep on. Don't let it shake you. Don't freeze." He gestured clumsily at the screen. "This has got to work. Okay? . . . Now get back to running the show."

Vero shook himself and sat down. *He's been here; he knows what it's like.* He swallowed and gave an order to the team at the screens. "Make sure the team in the trapping hall are ready. They need to be silent soon. Tell them our visitors are on their way."

ㅁㅁㅁㅁ

A quarter of an hour later, they watched the Krallen pack race up a streambed leading to an old drainage tunnel beneath Isterrane.

Vero stared at them, noticing no diminution in the slightest in their speed. He also saw they were keeping to the left-hand side of the ditch. "Why are they doing that, Sarudar?"

"To avoid leaving tracks. There's no mud up there."

I must remember that these things are smart.

They vanished off the screen and in seconds, a new image came up, of a large grille in a stone wall.

Vero, fascinated and appalled, stared as the six ranks of Krallen came to a sudden, disciplined, halt. Two cautiously paced forward, their heads moving this way and that as they examined the grille. Vero could make out the red pinpricks of their eyes. In a single sudden movement the remaining ten turned and faced outward in a defensive arc.

"Gotta admire them," said a voice behind him and Vero turned to see who it was.

"Anya," he said. "I didn't know you were here."

"I asked to be called when the incursion was definite." Her eyes didn't leave the screen.

"Are they as *you* expected?"

"Hmm. I hadn't imagined them to be so fluid in their actions. And they look much more powerful than . . . our friend." The existence of Betafor, who was safely locked away in a screened room under armed guard two floors below, remained a closely guarded secret.

On the screen the two Krallen twisted the screws on the grille. *They have enormous strength in the fingers. I wonder if we've taken that into account.*

The grille was lifted down. The other ten Krallen turned in a moment of perfect synchronization and ran inside the tunnel, leaving the other two to pull the grille carefully shut behind them. All twelve soon disappeared from sight.

Vero looked up at another wallscreen, which showed a schematic map of the upper levels. On it six pairs of red dots moved down a corridor.

All being well, they will turn left.

Everyone seemed to hold his or her breath.

The twelve dots swung left. "At this rate, less than a minute," said someone.

Unless they realize it's a trap.

On the screen the dots moved forward, turning successively right and left, but all the time gradually drawing nearer to a section of corridor marked in green.

The first red dots entered the green zone. "R-ready," said Vero.

Suddenly, with ten of them inside the section, the line came to a halt.

"Uh-oh, they suspect something!" someone cried.

I must decide. Merral would do this better. "*Now!*" Vero snapped.

"Blast doors are down," said a calm female voice.

On the screen, the green corridor was marked off at either end. Within it five pair of dots could be seen moving around rapidly.

"Cameras on," said the same calm voice.

On the wall, half a dozen screens came on with six different images. It took a second or so for Vero to understand what they showed, but it was immediately clear that he had been only just in time in letting the blast doors drop.

Two Krallen were crushed beneath them. The remaining ten were trapped in the hundred-meter section and could be seen in pairs examining the walls and the single sealed side entrance.

Ten functional Krallen. But we haven't caught them yet. "Open the adhesive vents."

The screen showed jets of transparent fluid squirting onto the floor. Two Krallen were caught by the liquid and in seconds were writhing in a futile attempt to free their feet from the glistening floor. The remaining eight climbed the walls, somehow maintaining their hold on the almost smooth surface.

"I'm impressed," Anya said.

"I warned you!" rasped Azeras. "They can get a grip on anything rougher than glass."

Two Krallen moved to the vents and suddenly twisted and bent the pipes closed.

A doglike gray face with red glowing eyes approached one camera and peered into it. Metal fingers moved forward, joined together, stabbed forward, and the image died. One by one the four remaining cameras followed it into darkness.

Vero rose. "As expected. T-time to go to the trapping hall."

ㅇㅇㅇㅇㅇ

Five minutes later, Vero stood on the balcony of what had once been a sports hall. The balcony had once been open, but Vero had had it covered in armored glass with a protective steel mesh overlay.

Two dozen large men waited below, their bulk enhanced by the prototype suits of new armor. Some held steel nets on poles, others a variety of weapons, including shotguns. Behind them was a door marked with ominous red stripes.

Vero slid open the balcony window.

"You have eight K-Krallen out there," he said. "It's not going to be easy. They may try and come out one at a time or you may have to go in and get them. Remember, if you have to, shoot them, but we want to do all we can to take them in a functional state. A l-lot of lives may depend on us getting this right." He hesitated. "The Lamb be with you all."

Hands rose in acknowledgment and then the men turned and lined up in a semicircle around the red door.

Vero closed the glass. "Open the door!"

The door slid sideways. Vero heard the sound of strange, eerie whistles like the wind blowing over open metal tubes.

Without warning two Krallen raced out.

Nets exploded over them. Two more Krallen bounded out, leaped high up in the air as if they were molten metal, then twisted in midair and dived at the men. As the men reeled back, the remaining four Krallen shot out, one pair going left against the wall, the other pair—with perfect symmetry—to the right.

There were shouts and yells and in seconds the floor of the hall was a chaotic melee of men, nets, and flying, tireless gray forms.

For long minutes, it seemed unclear to Vero whether or not the Krallen would be caught. It was only after ten minutes that he realized that they would indeed all be caught or disabled.

But it would be at a cost.

ΩΟΩΟΩο

It took thirty minutes before the battle was over and the last Krallen, its claws stained with blood, was toppled from the ceiling by the fourth round from a sniper and wrapped in nets.

Slowly, painfully, Vero walked down to the floor of the hall and stood by the door, his hand braced against the wall for support.

On the far side, the last wounded man was taken away. Already some members of his team were starting to clear up the mess of intermingled blood and silvery Krallen fluid on the floor.

He felt a hand on his shoulder and turned to see Perena. "P., what are you doing here?" he said.

"I heard from my sister that you had a bad night." She looked around, her face pale. "It's no Fallambet, but I gather it was pretty nasty."

Her hand was still on his shoulder. Vero put his own hand over hers and returned to staring at the bloodied streaks on the floor.

"Two dead, six with major injuries. A dozen with cuts. And the sentry on the Walderand Bridge is missing, presumed dead." He heard his voice sound muffled, as if it came through cloth. "I could have saved him."

"What can I say? Would he blame you?" she asked. "Hardly. If he was a family man, and this does help save this world, then he might thank you." He heard the strain in her voice.

"That sounds very rational—even cold." He turned to see her face pinched and drawn. She caught his look and he saw an intense sorrow in her eyes.

"Vero, this is war. There are things that we must do, even though they break our hearts."

"P-perhaps."

She squeezed his hand, then let it go. "Now tell me about Krallen."

"Ah. Well, we netted five fully functional ones. We have another five badly damaged ones. Two are crushed beyond repair."

"Enough for Anya's research. It paid off, Vero."

"Did it?" Doubt laced his voice. *I feel empty.*

"It *will* pay off and you know it will."

"P., I'm worried. We had casualties. And, as Merral might say, this one was a home match. Our men were armored."

"And the armor worked?"

"Yes. Azeras's guidance helped. And that's a relief. We needed to test that, badly. But it needs improving. In the next few days we will refine it and lighten it. We may be able to use spun silica. Then we'll start mass production."

"So another plus point," Perena said firmly. "And I'm pleased for you. I have sometimes worried about your ingenuity, but tonight it paid off. I think Merral will be pleased when—in due course—he learns about it."

"Thanks, P. Thanks, more than I can say." He paused. "But in this full-suppression complex there maybe another hundred thousand Krallen. We fought just eight in here tonight."

There was a long pause. "Yes. We need to deal with that. And that won't be easy." She frowned and shook her head. "Not at all." She gave him a thin, distant, little-girl smile. "But you need some sleep. It's nearly three. We all have work to do."

"Yes, Captain," he said. "Thanks for coming." Vero rubbed his tired eyes and, with weary steps, walked back to his chamber and fell instantly asleep.

ᓂᓂᓂᓂᓂ

The following afternoon, the dozen men and women who visited the *Dove of Dawn* returned to Isterrane. Shortly after landing they met with the contact team where they recounted their experiences and showed imagery of the parent ship. As Merral expected, they had found nothing untoward. They were shown whatever they wanted to see and, apparently, had been given honest answers to their questions. They had found nothing suspicious about either the parent ship or the shuttle. Neither showed signs of military hardware or any hint of concealed weapons.

As the meeting progressed Merral saw Perena had arrived and was standing at the back of the room. Afterward, Merral met with her in his office.

"So what do you think?" he asked.

"It's civilian."

"You are sure?"

"Pretty much. I've been looking at all the old ship architecture files and I have a good idea of what a military ship should look like. But this has a thin hull with no trace of armor, no evidence of long-range missile sensors, and no high-maneuver seating."

"No possibility of anything hidden?"

"No. From what they report, there can't be much room to hide anything."

"Krallen?"

There was an odd flicker of a smile as if Perena knew something he didn't. "Barely room for a pack I'd say according to the reports."

"Just as well. And no steersman compartment?"

"No. They were vague on how they did Below-Space navigation though."

"The propulsion system? Were they much help?"

Perena stroked a cheek thoughtfully. "What they apparently said made sense. But they avoided giving any detail that would allow us to make one."

"Any other comments?"

"Our folk noted something that you reported about the vessel at Fallambet—it's not as well made as our ships. Engineering tolerances aren't as good. It's a fascinating difference between us in almost everything. They seek to impose their will on a thing, while we work with it." She tapped a finger on the desk. "We work with the grain; they go against it. Our materials science is very much better."

"A fascinating insight, but is it helpful?"

There was a strange, half-amused glint in her eyes. "Oh, it may be." But her tone dissuaded him from pursuing the matter.

"So what do you feel?" Merral asked. "About the ship and the ambassadors?"

She shook her head. "It's poison, Merral. Sugarcoated poison. I pray the treaty will be rejected. But . . ." She frowned. "I think that the whole thing is subtler and deeper than we think." She glanced away from him. "And maybe more dangerous."

"There's something else, isn't there?"

"Yes." Perena leaned back in her chair, put her hands behind her head, and looked at the ceiling. "Yes. Over the last week I've faced a crisis. It was . . . as if I was made an offer."

"Go on."

Perena stayed silent for many seconds, then spoke with a wistful intensity. "I felt I was offered the ability to travel between the stars, to go wherever in the cosmos I wanted, to be like an eagle—proud, free to soar wherever I chose." She turned her gray-blue eyes on Merral, but they seemed to focus far beyond him. "You are an earthbound man, Forester, so forgive me. Perhaps what I describe is not a temptation for you."

"No. But I sense its attraction. And I may have experienced something similar."

"It *was* a temptation. As Jorgio foresaw, we're all being tested. I rejected it, but it was not easy. I yielded my wings, Merral." She gave a sad, nostalgic smile. "I said to the one who offered it me that I would rather be the Lord's hen than his eagle."

"So you passed the test."

"I have passed *a* test," she murmured and stared ahead with a look of foreboding. "But I sense another lies ahead." She looked at her watch, then rose. Merral walked with her to the door.

"I may be out of touch from now on," she said quietly and turned toward him. Suddenly Merral saw her as a slight, almost elfin figure, a delicate creature walking in the midst of terrible forces.

As if moved by some sudden impulse, she hugged Merral. "Take care," she said, her voice suddenly thick with emotion.

"You are the best, Perena," Merral replied, responding to something that he did not understand. "Promise me you'll keep safe."

"I'll try." Her smile was sorrowful. "But I have to do what's right." She raised a fine eyebrow. "And in the end, that's safe."

Later that day, the ambassadors announced without warning that there would be no further formal meetings until after a decision on a treaty had been made. The liaison program at Langerstrand base would continue, however, and the reports that filtered out spoke of lively debates and discussions between the parties.

Merral wondered what Isabella would think of it all and hoped that she might see through what was offered her. *She's no fool; she'll recognize what's going on.* But a second thought came on its heels: *Will she?*

Merral was glad that the meetings with the ambassadors were over. It removed the risk of them accusing him of honoring Lucas Ringell. It also gave him more time to deal with the appalling volume of work that the defense force now generated. Much of the new equipment and weaponry that had been ordered was starting to come into service and with it came issues of deployment and training. As discreetly as he could, Merral made decisions that would put the forces into the best possible positions should there be trouble immediately after the vote. Troops were dispersed, vessels fueled and made ready, all troops' leave was canceled, and regiments were edged toward combat readiness.

ㅁㅁㅁㅁㅁ

Over the next few days, the tension slowly rose. Merral noticed a look of permanent and gloomy preoccupation on Corradon, who seemed to go out of his way to avoid him. Clemant was rarely seen and apparently spent much of his time in his office monitoring the changes in Farholme through his wall of images and data. Delastro stalked the corridors with a fixed scowl and solemnly counseled Merral to "beware the trickery of the devil."

Merral felt strangely and unnervingly isolated. He saw very little of Vero, who made only the most fleeting appearances in the Planetary Administration building. When he did appear, he always seemed to be darting from one meeting to another.

In one of these encounters he passes on some news.

"We're making armor suits," he said in a low voice when they met in the foyer of the building. "Spun silica—light, flexible joints. They may resist Krallen claws."

"How quickly can we get them out to the troops? We should get them out now."

"No!" Vero's tone showed agitation, and he seemd to look around. "That would reveal our hand. We'll stockpile them."

"Why are you telling me this?"

"Clemant will complain. So I thought you ought to know." As he paused, Merral suddenly noticed that he was so thin the bone structure of his face was visible. "And very soon there may be another demand for mass production of . . . other items. I can't say more. Just get it authorized and make sure there is no fuss."

Without waiting for an answer, he muttered, "Must dash" and walked swiftly away.

✕◯◗◖◯✕

Three days before the vote, Merral was called into Clemant's office. Clemant gestured irritably at a note on his desk. "Over the last few days a number of manufacturing plants have had their production diverted. Some are now producing spun silica fiber of a precise composition. What's going on?"

"It's an urgent defense need," Merral answered.

"For what?"

Merral hesitated. "Armor suits. But that's to be kept secret."

"Did you order it?"

"No. But I approve."

He shook his head. "And what about this? Others are being asked to produce molecular-tuned metals and ionic transfer batteries in vast quantities."

"Another urgent defense need."

"Do you know what they're for?"

"Well . . ."

Irritation flooded Clemant's face. "This is madness, Commander! I have a head of defense who hasn't a clue what's going on. I have an off-world sentinel running around taking over our entire industrial production." He glared at Merral. "Anarchy threatens to overwhelm us."

"Sir, there are just three more days. I think we need to trust Vero. He knows what he's doing."

Clemant exhaled slowly and loudly. He stared at the wall of screens as if seeking inspiration, and then shook his head. "You'd better be right."

✕◯◗◖◯✕

Merral had seen little of Anya for some time, but met her on the stairs close to his office the next day. She looked pale and tired as if both color and energy had drained out of her.

"I wanted to see you," she said with a tone of urgency. "But not in your office."

"Down here," he said motioning her into an empty corridor. "What's up?"

"Things are happening. More than you know. Vero wants me out of the way for the next few days." She gave him a look that was full of dread. "It's coming, Merral. It's war and it's going to be bad—worse than we imagined."

"I wouldn't argue. But you know more than me."

"Possibly." Her expression changed to one of concern. "How are you doing? I've been worried."

"Thanks. I miss you. And Vero, and your sister. How am I doing?" He took a deep breath. "It reminds me of when I had to climb a grand fir at college. It was nearly a hundred meters high. Nearly at the top, I looked down. It was a bad move. I froze solid with terror—vertigo. In the end, I forced myself to go on. And I made sure that I never looked down. It's just like that now."

"Good." She smiled in way that made him feel he was special. "I must go. I also came to say that we are being put on alert. I'm going to be, well, absent for the foreseeable future."

"I see. I feel very much on my own." He heard the self-pity in his voice and hated it.

"I'm sorry. But I wanted to see you. I don't know when we'll meet again."

As she turned to go, Merral's throat tightened. *Or if we will.* He felt stabbed suddenly by the terrible certainty that they would not all make it safely through this looming war. "Keep safe," he said.

She touched his hand. "And don't look down."

⋈⋉⋊⋉⋈

Later that day, Merral snatched time to visit Jorgio. He found his old friend flopped on a deck chair under a tree, a big hat slumped on his head.

Jorgio was strangely tired. "The humidity, I expect," he grumbled. "Not used to being near the sea." But Merral was unconvinced.

Over the inevitable tea, he asked Jorgio, "The ambassadors—what do you feel about them?"

Jorgio's thick lower lip jutted out and trembled. "Nothing."

"Nothing?"

"There's just a blank; no noises anymore. Nothing."

"So, you feel there is nothing there?"

"*Tut.* Didn't say that. I said I *feel* nothing. It's all blank. Like as if snow covered it all."

"So there could be something there? Something evil perhaps?"

Jorgio frowned. "More than likely. I reckon if a thing was evil enough, we probably wouldn't be able to see it."

"A good point. Jorgio, you have your diary?"

He groped around his belt clumsily until he found it. "Yes!"

"If anything happens, can you call me? Immediately?"

"I will."

⋈⋉⋊⋉⋈

That evening Merral and Lloyd were summoned to a meeting with Vero at the junction of two of the underground passageways. As they walked along them Merral, who had never particularly liked being underground, felt that the tunnels seemed dark and oppressive.

At the end of the passageways Vero waited for them with a middle-aged woman. Next to them, flat on the ground, was a thick disk.

"Meet Nina," Vero said. "She wants some measurements. All yours, Officer."

"Thank you," Nina said. "Now, Commander, this will only take a minute." Her voice was terse. "Stand on this disk, please. Good. Hands at your side. Good. Now look straight ahead. Don't move." She pointed a handheld device at Merral and as the disk rotated, beams of dull red light played over his body. "Thank you. Next, please."

As Lloyd was measured, Merral beckoned Vero away.

"What's this for?" he asked.

"Your armor suit. The troops get them off the shelf. Yours and Lloyd's will be tailor-made."

Nina picked up the disk, saluted, and strode away.

"Thanks. Will everyone have them?"

"Only the regulars. We don't have enough resources for the irregs."

"I see. Vero, I have a question that you may feel that you can answer. From talking with Azeras, do these people have weaknesses?"

"Yes. Many. The chief one is fear—fear of many things, but death most of all."

"Yes, Luke spotted that."

"Did he? It seems the Freeborn have always feared it, but the Dominion fear it especially. So they seek to do all they can to avoid it. They buy themselves decades by gene engineering; they replace everything they can by synthetics; they use cloned body parts; they make linkages with hardware. They do it all."

"And how is that a weakness?"

"It makes them cowards. And it makes them dependent on machines."

"I see."

Vero grasped him by the hand. "Now, my friend, we may not meet until after the decision. Do what you can to ensure a vote against it."

"I'll try, but it's hard without revealing that I know more than they do."

"There must be no risk of that."

"And after the vote?"

"All hell will break loose."

"Is that a figure of speech, or do you mean it literally?"

"A literal meaning is precisely what I fear."

22

When finally it came to the vote, the contact team met around the table in Corradon's office. There, amid the plants, they had a long and heated discussion. The five representatives were plain: general opinion was in favor of a treaty. The public mood was due to a combination of things: the threat of the True Freeborn, the promise of a rapid reunion with the Assembly, and a growing irritation with the closure of the Library and the Admin-Net.

One representative summarized his dilemma. "If it was just me, I'd say no. But I am a representative and must act on my people's wishes." His words were greeted by sympathetic nods.

Then it came to the vote. Three representatives voted in favor of the treaty, but one voted against and one abstained. Merral voted no and, after a few mutterings, Jenat did likewise. All eyes turned to Clemant.

"No," the advisor said, after a long silence. "I vote no."

"Four to three against," Corradon announced with a mournful shake of his head. "I fear what this will bring." He gazed around the table, plainly hoping for second thoughts, but there were none.

"Very well," he said with the deepest of sighs. "I will take the news to the ambassadors personally."

"Sir," Merral said, as the others began to leave, "I wish to put the alert level to orange."

Corradon seemed to stare into infinity. "If you must, after I have spoken with them. But, Commander, please don't trigger any hostilities. I want to leave every last chance for a peaceful outcome. We don't want any more deaths."

Having ordered the level of alert to orange, Merral, acting on a sudden impulse, followed Clemant into his office.

"May I ask why you voted against the treaty?" he asked, after closing the door.

Clemant stared at the wallscreens before turning his dark gray eyes on Merral.

"I found much among our visitors that attracted me." He nodded at the screens. "They have seen the threat of chaos. They know how to control worlds."

He ran a finger around the edge of his hair. "But once they gain access to the Admin-Net, they could control us. That's what the Dominion is all about. And I don't want that." His smile was stiff and awkward. "Commander, as you know, I believe that we face a real threat of disintegration into chaos. But I'm not fool enough to flee from that into being assimilated into the Dominion."

"I see. I should have realized that was how you would think."

Clemant shrugged. "Perhaps. I've come to the same conclusions as Delastro, but from different reasons. I think we *will* have to fight them. And there, Commander, the issue becomes yours. Can we win?"

"Frankly, I don't know."

The advisor stared at the screens. "Well," he said softly, "I think we will soon find out."

◌◌◌◌◌

Lezaroth was in his cabin when he heard the news. "Yes!" he exclaimed, unable to restrain his exultation and relief. "By all the powers, I will teach them!" And as he said the words, he wondered whether he meant Farholme, the ambassadors, Hanax, or all of them.

He called the ambassadors, noting their glum faces. "Listen," he said in his best don't-mess-with-me-or-else tone, "this is now a military operation. I'm in charge now. You make no decisions and take no actions without my say-so."

Hazderzal and Tinternli looked at each other and shrugged reluctantly.

It is curious how their debacle with the lost Krallen pack has worked to my advantage. They can hardly ask to be involved when they've proved to be so incompetent.

He ended the call and walked onto the bridge. The word had spread and all eyes were on him.

"Hear this all crew," he said into the microphone, relishing the moment. "We are now in military mode." He paused to let the shouts of delight die down. "All commanders to the conference room to hear battle plans. All other crew prepare for deployment of Krallen and firing of kinetic energy weapons. We will be surfacing shortly. Ground attack team prepare for deployment."

He paused again for emphasis. "This is going to make our long trip worthwhile."

◌◯◌◯◌

Back in his office, Merral had a call from Corradon; the ambassadors were disappointed and would consider how to proceed.

Ten minutes later, as Merral was trying to organize things in the war room, he received a voice-only call from Vero.

"Well done."

"Not my doing," Merral said, walking into a corner to escape the noise. "It was close. Now what happens?"

"Azeras predicts we will see the full-suppression complex."

"It's lurking beyond the system's edge?"

"Worse. You may as well know. He says they'd stay close, and it's probably hiding in Below-Space by the *Dove of Dawn*."

It took a moment for the news to sink in. "It's *already* here?" Merral's heart pounded. *I was expecting at least a week.*

"So he says."

"I desperately hope that he's wrong."

"An understandable sentiment, my friend. But I wouldn't put any money on it."

"What?"

"Never mind."

◌◯◌◯◌

For the next few hours nothing happened. Eventually, Merral found a mattress and put it on the floor next to his desk. As the night shift stared at monitor screens and talked together in tense, low whispers, he tried to snatch some sleep.

Just before dawn, he received a call from Jorgio, his pale face almost touching the diary screen.

Rubbing his eyes free of sleep, Merral diverted it to the nearest screen.

"Mr. Merral, the curtain's lifted," Jorgio gasped. Saliva trickled from the corner of his mouth. "Something's here. It's terrible! I can feel it now. It's evil and full of hate."

"What is—?" Merral began.

Through the open door he heard hurried footsteps and gasps, gasps that turned into shouts of alarm.

"Jorgio," he cried, "I think we see it too. Hang on there. I'll send someone over."

Merral ran into the main office where everyone was gathering around a screen.

The image was of a hazy, shaking form emerging out of the velvet blackness of space. A tracery of blue light flickered over a long brutal-looking structure, revealing gray, turreted slabs, towering arrays of ugly cylinders, and stacks of ominous-looking tubes. Despite the absence of anything that gave the structure scale, Merral knew it was vast.

"How big, anyone?" he asked, hearing the alarm in his voice.

"Over two thousand meters long," a woman replied, disbelief ringing in her words. "That's a two-triple-zero."

"God, help us!" said a man.

"Mass?"

"Harder to say. Maybe over half a million tons. Well over."

Merral looked around, aware that all eyes were on him. *The full-suppression complex is here.* He took a deliberate breath. *Let's begin this properly.*

"Everybody, no panic please. We go to red alert. I want civilian defense preparations begun. All troops are to take up combat positions with medical facilities on emergency status." He paused and looked at the screen. "And pull all the liaison people out of Langerstrand. I think diplomacy has just ended."

◯◯◯◯◯

After sending someone over to check on Jorgio, Merral met with Corradon and Clemant in the tiny annex off the main war room.

Corradon, who seemed reluctant to sit down, paced around, shaking his head. His face was a bloodless gray and Merral wondered if he had been sick.

"Treachery and duplicity," he said. "I should never have trusted them. Not ever. Delastro was right." He stopped and looked at Merral with worried eyes. "But, Commander, a reassurance please: our soldiers will not fire first?"

Merral considered pointing out that they had nothing that was remotely likely to be effective against such a ship, but merely said, "No, sir. The forces are in purely defensive mode."

"I just want to be sure." Corradon's hands visibly trembled. "Perhaps, just perhaps, loss of life may still be averted."

Merral caught Clemant looking at the representative and read both contempt and concern in his expression.

"Perhaps . . . ," Corradon said, "we ought to offer them the Library key."

His suggestion was greeted by silence. After a few moments Clemant turned to Merral. "Is there anything we can do?" He sounded frustrated.

"Only what we *are* doing. We have no effective weapons against this sort of vessel. A preliminary analysis suggests it carries all sorts of passive and active defenses."

Suddenly a wallscreen flicked on.

It was Ambassador Hazderzal. There was no trace of the habitual good humor on his face. "Let me be plain. Your rejection of our peaceful and generous offer has shown that you are against us. As we feared, the Assembly has not changed, and we must assume that you are plotting our destruction. As a result, you have forced us to choose a new strategy. The ship that has appeared—the *Triumph of Sarata*—is capable of returning this world to dust and molten rock. From now on negotiations will be in the hands of Fleet-Commander Lezaroth." He hesitated. "Ambassador Tinternli and I are truly sorry that it has come to this."

The screen flickered and a new image appeared: a black-haired man dressed in a dark gray military uniform with a neat row of ribbons. The face—dark-eyed, tanned, with a cheek scar—seemed more that of a statue than a human being. A thought came to Merral with an unnerving certainty. *This is a man with war in his very bones, a man who has torn from himself all kindness and sympathy.* His fear fed into a prayer. *God, help me deal with this man.*

"I am Fleet-Commander Lezaroth." His voice was hard, the Communal good but harshly accented. His tone invited no dissent. "I command this ship, *Triumph of Sarata*. Your refusal to agree to our generous terms means that we must move beyond negotiation." There was a pause. "Nevertheless, as a testimony to the lord-emperor's abundant mercy and grace, I offer you a last chance to join us voluntarily. There is no neutral ground. To fail to support us is to oppose us. The hallmark of the Assembly seems to be a refusal to believe in the real world. We are forced therefore to try and wake you up to reality. Therefore—I trust you are paying attention—unless Representative Corradon calls me before midday your time today offering to open the Library and Admin-Net to us, one of your villages will cease to exist by dawn tomorrow."

The screen went blank.

"I need time," Corradon said and walked unsteadily away.

"What do we do, Commander?" Clemant asked quietly as the door closed behind the representative.

About the situation or about Corradon? Merral sensed an ambiguity in the question.

"The key must not be handed over."

"I agree, but whether that decision can survive casualties is an interesting one."

Merral said nothing.

"We have four hours," Clemant said. "Let's see what happens. I shall be in my office."

ⓒⓒⓒⓒⓒ

Over the next few hours, Merral found himself fully occupied by the myriad issues to do with the defenses. He made calls to the colonels of the regiments and the people in charge of the defenses of the main cities to check on their progress. The red alert galvanized the planet into action. From the rain-forest villages of the southern isles to the icy northern ports of the Balanide Chains, every community seemed to be involved in feverish activity. The smallest settlements were emptied; around all the others, trenches and walls were created or strengthened. Everywhere, arms and armor were issued.

In between making his calls Merral looked at the images of the *Triumph of Sarata* to see if there was activity. Soon four vessels—three large cylinders and a smaller cone-shaped ship, separated and began an ominous descent toward Farholme.

One new complication soon emerged. The entrances to the Langerstrand center had been closed with the thirty people working on the liaison project still inside. Those inside were cut off from communication and it was not long before a new and troubling word was heard in the war room: *hostages.*

With ten minutes to go before the deadline, Corradon walked into the tiny annex to the war room that served as Merral's office. He sat on the edge of a chair, his face overflowing with anguish.

"What am I supposed to do?" he asked in plaintive tone. "Is it possible that it is a bluff?"

"Perhaps. But I wouldn't assume so."

The representative reached into an inside pocket and pulled out the small transparent box. "This is all they want," he said, in sad wonderment, lifting the lid so that the gray wafer could be fully seen. "This pathetic little sliver of synthetic material. Is *this* worth the lives of men, women, and children?"

Merral suddenly felt such an overwhelming sympathy for this man and his dilemma that he felt unable to answer.

Corradon rubbed his face in his hands. "If I say no, I condemn people to die."

Merral felt he had to speak. "True. But if you say yes, you betray the Assembly. And if, as we believe, the Dominion needs the data in the Library in order to attack the Assembly, then both choices involve potential deaths."

Corradon shook his head in dismay and thrust the box back into his pocket.

Clemant soon entered and noiselessly took up a position in a corner of the room.

In silence, they watched as the figures on the clock slipped by. When 12:00 arrived, Corradon buried his head in his hands, his broad shoulders shaking.

The silence continued.

ㅇㅇㅇㅇㅇ

Over the next few hours, the three large cylinders landed at Langerstrand while the smaller one stayed in low orbit. Images from the peninsula showed machinery being unloaded and excavations beginning around the liaison center. Within an hour, a structure was formed from massive sheets—a tower of dark metal that grew like a vast, severed tree trunk.

Merral received a call from Vero. "I'm staying out of sight," Vero said, "there's plenty to do."

"Can we save this village?"

"No. We don't know where it is. We can hope the irregulars may make a defense. But that's all so far."

"So far?"

"There may be other means of defense later. But we can't use them yet."

"Vero, from here this doesn't look good."

"My friend, it's not much better down here. But we have plans. Have faith."

ㅇㅇㅇㅇㅇ

Shortly afterward Prebendant Delastro turned up, his long, bronze-tipped staff in hand. Merral detected a grim satisfaction in his expression.

"So, Commander—as I suspected—the Dominion is revealed in its true colors: a vile body of bloodthirsty and aggressive liars. Their deception is unmasked. They are the brood of demons."

"I'm afraid that seems entirely possible," Merral answered carelessly, wishing that he would go away.

Delastro gave him a sudden penetrating look. "Why did you say 'I'm afraid'?"

"Because I prefer to believe the best of people. I do not delight in the discovery of evil."

The prebendant flinched. "Nor, of course, do I. But the exposure of evil is the first work of the man of God." He paused. "We must trust that this envoy of yours will deliver us."

"I see him as the Lord's envoy, not mine."

"Of course, but a weapon given for us to wield."

"Prebendant, I am very busy. How can I help you?"

"I just came to offer you my support."

"Very good of you."

"You can rely on me, Commander. You know where I stand."

"Meaning?"

"There are others whose real allegiance is less plain. . . ." A rather twisted smile crossed his triangular face. "Whose manner is, shall we say, darker?"

Merral stared at him. *Silence is best.*

"The questions about Sentinel Enand have never been answered. He has set up a base in the very foundations of Isterrane. He has men who obey only his orders. He spies on us all."

"I think that's a bit strong," Merral said as firmly as he felt he could without risking a confrontation.

The prebendant glared at Merral. "I found out he was observing my Library habits."

"I see." Merral remembered that Vero had mentioned discovering the prebendant's interest in angels. He wondered why, at the moment when he needed all the support he could get, he had to deal with this man.

"Commander, he is not really one of us. Who knows what he's conjuring down there? What powers? Dark by complexion, dark by action."

Now barely able to suppress his anger, Merral rose from his seat and ushered Delastro to the door. "Prebendant, I don't think this is a helpful discussion. I have better things to do."

"I'm just warning you. It's my duty as chaplai—"

"Good-bye!" Merral pushed him out and slammed the door shut.

◌◯◌◯◌

That night Vero, struggling to sleep on his camp bed, was suddenly aware of a knocking at his door.

"Who is it?"

"Perena." He heard a strange note in her voice.

"What? Hang on." Vero looked at the wall clock; it was just after two. He pulled a dressing gown over his sleepsuit and opened the door, noting that she was in uniform. "P.! Come in. Take a seat. Any news? I was expecting to hear some."

"Not yet. It's impossible to guess their target."

"What can I do for you?" *This is no social call. How pale she looks.*

Perena sat stiffly on the very edge of a nearby chair.

"Vero, the fact that there is a single military vessel has confirmed that a . . . a plan I have may work. To destroy this monster."

"T-that would be . . . welcome news. Actually, that's a bit of an understatement. How?"

"The Guardian satellites have the firepower to vaporize this ship."

"I remember. We talked about them. But I thought you said they were too static."

"They are. But if this *Triumph* can be persuaded to move on a trajectory toward Farholme the Guardian system would consider it an incoming comet or meteor and open fire."

But it won't work. "Elegant. But I have objections, which will hardly have escaped you. How do you get them to take that trajectory?"

"We trick them." Her face was ashen. "It's your sort of strategy. We make them chase something, something they need to catch."

"Such as?"

"A ship heading to recover the *Rahllman's Star*."

"That'd get their interest. But surely, they'd wait until it was recovered?"

"By which time it might be too late. According to Azeras, you can send a signal into Below-Space when you get near a hidden ship and order it to match your speeds as it rises. So if you get the timing right, you can dock and vanish in minutes." He could hear the excitement in her voice. "They would want to seize such a ship while they could, if they thought it held the location of the *Rahllman's Star*."

"Maybe. Another objection, though. Didn't you say—it seems like years ago—that there was a password system so that the Guardians don't fire at our ships?"

"True. All our ships emit a signal that identifies them as vessels, not lumps of rock or ice. But a non-Assembly ship might not send it."

"They'd copy any signal we'd send."

Perena paused before speaking. "Yes. But we could always give the wrong signal."

Somewhere in Vero's brain something clicked ominously. *I don't like this.*

"This would be a piloted mission. Right?" At her nod, he asked, "By . . . you?"

She nodded again.

Suddenly, the enormity of it all was terribly plain. "B-but surely, P., you'd be destroyed as well."

There was a lengthy and heavy silence. Finally, Perena spoke, her words coming out slowly. "Yes. There is a risk. A high one."

"Tell me you aren't serious!"

"I am. But with an ejection capsule, I might escape. I'd need picking up within a few days though."

Vero walked a few paces away, his brain reeling, and then turned round. "I would prefer any other strategy. Any!"

"And so would I. But if we are going to use this, we need to work on it, very soon."

He tried to think of the practicalities, which seemed to push the horror of the idea slightly into the background. "Yes. They *must* pursue you. And it will only work once." *But how?* His mind ran in a dozen directions.

"Will you help me?" she asked.

"H-Help you on a strategy that may kill you?"

"Yes."

For some moments, Vero could say nothing. He felt close to tears. "If I must," he said and put his head in his hands. He sighed. "And I suppose I must."

✿✿✿✿✿

An aide woke Merral at five. "Sir, the fourth vessel is coming down at the edge of the Western Varrend at a village called Tantaravekat."

"Tantaravekat," Merral repeated, rolling over to face the ceiling. He knew of the place, on a remote road intersection in the middle of the barren Aknal Plain.

"How many people? Three hundred?"

"Five hundred."

Five hundred. Too many people.

Merral got to his feet. "God have mercy on them. You've warned them?"

"The communications around the village have failed."

"I see," Merral replied, calling up a wallscreen map that confirmed what he suspected. Tantaravekat was too far away from either the Western or Central Regiments for help to reach them in time. All they would have would be a handful of irregulars.

Merral remembered the vision he had been given by the envoy and shuddered. *I want to intervene. But there's nothing I can do for them . . . except pray.*

Merral had a hospital ship placed on standby and requested a reconnaissance satellite overflight at dawn. He then ordered one of the fast scout vessels with a five-person specialist disaster team that the Natural Hazard Management Department used for reconnaissance to be made ready and requested a dozen well-armed volunteers from the Central Regiment to be sent to the airport.

He then waited and prayed.

ᴑᴑᴑᴑᴑ

Exactly at seven, Lezaroth appeared on the screen. His message was terse and delivered without any apparent emotion. "Operations at Tantaravekat are complete. You may visit the village from ten until midday local time. The village is under the control of Krallen units who are under orders not to harm you unless you are foolish enough to try and attack them. The village will be obliterated at 1300 hours. We advise you to be at least thirty kilometers away by then. There is no need to take any reserve or medical vessel; you will find no one living."

As Merral and Lloyd were rotorcrafted from the roof of the Planetary Administration building to the airport, Merral had a glimpse of the growing defenses. Everywhere he looked there was activity. High dust columns rose up around the city as colossal machines chiseled great trenches and pushed earth and rock into high embankments. Buildings were being shuttered and the roads were clogged with vehicles transporting people and supplies.

At the airport, he explained the situation to the grim-faced men and women. "We must be prepared for the worst we can imagine . . . and then some more."

merral and the team did not immediately land at Tantaravekat but instead circled over it at an altitude of three thousand meters. It was a cluster of a hundred white-painted brick houses, dusty palm trees, and walled fields in the middle of a vast monotonous and dusty plain of pale salt pans and brown sand fields. They took images and then launched a surveillance drone that flew over at treetop level.

The images the drone sent back shocked them all.

It wasn't just that there were bodies lying in the streets. After all, death was no stranger to the Made Worlds and disaster teams trained for it. It was two facts: first, the bodies had been torn into fragments; second, perched calmly on the walls and roofs were the creatures responsible.

Merral looked at the ashen, stunned faces surrounding him. *Lead from the front.* "Everyone, I'm going in anyway—"

"With me," Lloyd interrupted quietly.

"With Sergeant Enomoto then. It seems there's no one living, but we need to be sure. I want only soldiers. Disaster team, if we need you, I'll call." He felt certain that the team wouldn't be required. "I want to go, because I think we need witnesses. Someday there may be a chance for justice for Tantaravekat and I want to be able to say that we saw what happened."

There were nods of agreement and one by one the soldiers said, "Count me in," "And me," and "Me too."

At five past ten they landed at the edge of Tantaravekat Village. Merral, clutching a rifle, leaped out of the ship. Lloyd and the other soldiers followed. Just beyond the landing zone they took up positions with their weapons at the ready.

Merral soon saw the Krallen. A pair sat atop a palm tree, staring at the party from behind the fronds. They were bigger than he remembered, roughly the size of a small calf. "Battlefield Krallen," Azeras had said. They showed no hostility, fear, or even curiosity, yet Merral senses a deep and strong malevolence.

A gust of hot, dusty air struck Merral and he smelled the heavy, sickly odor of death. He forced himself not to recoil and stood there, blinking in the hot bright light, looking and listening.

There were few sounds: the faint *flap-flap* of curtains from the nearest house, the banging of a window shutter, the buzzing of flies, and behind them all, the uncanny high whistling and hoots of the Krallen.

"Okay. Let's do the job!" Merral snapped. "Safety catches on. Stick together. Follow me!"

They walked into the village past the incomplete defenses. Merral stared at the abandoned ditch and rampart system with unease. *Even had it been finished, would it have done anything to defend this village?*

As they approached the street that led into the heart of the village, Krallen could be seen perched along the roofs and on balconies like monstrous, deformed birds of prey, their whistles and quavering cries to each other showing pride and hatred.

A single Krallen strolled—there was no other word for its action—into the center of the street no more than a dozen paces ahead of them and turned to face them. Its eyes had a dull red fiery gleam that Merral had never seen on the Krallen at Fallambet.

Merral, suddenly aware that his palms were sweaty against his gun, half-turned to Lloyd who stood at his shoulder. "Say something to encourage me, Sergeant."

"How about 'even though I walk through the dark valley of death, I will fear nothing evil'?"

"'For you are with me, your rod and your staff protect and comfort me.' That will do. Here goes."

Merral walked forward until he was barely three paces away from the creature and could see every detail, from the tiles of the body to the opposing claws.

For a long, appalling second, they stared at each other. Then, with a careless flick of the tail, the creature sauntered away.

The street behind was full of bodies.

Trying to avert his eyes for as long as possible, Merral watched the Krallen above. They tilted their gray heads, which somehow evoked memories of both dogs and reptiles, and stared back with red eyes. Some opened their stained jaws, some seem to flex muscles, and still others—in a dreadful parody of animal activity—seemed to groom themselves and examine their glinting claws.

In their posture, Merral sensed a proud, almost mocking, indifference to the dreadful handiwork on the streets.

He steeled himself to what he faced and walked on, carefully weaving his way past the human remains and avoiding the dried black rivulets in doorways and on the deep-set windows.

Amid the horror, Merral was surprised to find that although he seethed with grief, revulsion, and anger, a part of his mind remained analytical. He found that recognition a slight but precious comfort. After all, this was not just a horrid place; it was also a dangerous one.

He began to give orders and was amazed to hear the firmness in his voice. "Check that building. . . . Image that. . . . Get shots of those Krallen." Giving orders allowed him to fractionally distance himself from the unspeakable scenes around him.

Within minutes, it was apparent that their presence was a formality; none of the inhabitants of Tantaravekat had survived. The appalling damage that the Krallen had done to the human beings was highlighted by the restraint they had shown to property. Apart from the universal bloodstains, the worst damage was that doors and shutters had been forced open.

Merral and Lloyd stayed in the central square as the soldiers fanned out in twos to check the few remaining streets. They stood in the shade of a teetering palm tree, beating the bloated flies away, aware that above them, black winged vultures drifted in slow circles.

"Sir," Lloyd whispered, his voice quavering, "you reckon these things go to hell?"

"No, Sergeant. But their makers do."

Lloyd wiped sweat from his face. "You know, sir, I'd like to really help them on their way."

As they waited, it came to Merral that the whole thing was a ghastly hallucination: the heat, the smell, the sight of the Krallen, and the dead. He fought against it, trying to make his mind stay in analytical mode, and forced himself to look around for any evidence of a defense. He found little. It looked as if the handful of irregulars here had not been able to do anything to protect the village. The implications were troubling.

The soldiers soon returned and Merral sensed that beneath their disgust, anger welled up. Their terse reports were the same: there were no survivors.

Just as he was about to order their departure, a tawny cat crept from under an overturned table and began to run across the square. Almost faster than the eye could follow, two Krallen leaped from a roof with surprising agility, and chased after the cat with effortless speed. One overtook it. The other came up behind.

The cat skidded to a halt, spun round in the dust, arched its back, and hissed loudly.

Merral looked away as the hiss was cut short by a soft, wet sound.

Lloyd gave a savage cry.

Merral struggled to avoid tears. "Okay, men. Let's go," he ordered and, without looking back, they left the village.

⊃⊂⊃⊂⊃⊂⊃

In ten minutes they were flying south, landing forty kilometers away on a ridge of tumbled rocks in the shelter of a high lava cliff.

The subdued and silent soldiers took up positions on the crest of the ridge and gazed with pale faces north across the shimmering plain of salt pans and sand fields to the hazy dot on the skyline that was Tantaravekat.

As they waited, Merral found himself glancing up as if in the silver sky he could see the *Triumph of Sarata* maneuvering into place.

At 1300 hours precisely, a flash of gray-silver light scythed down through the sky and struck the village. Angry ragged sheets of black smoke with fiery edges burst upward and outward, coalescing into a growing mass of turbulent cloud that seemed to soar toward the stratosphere.

Merral heard gasps around him as the ghastly billows raced over the plain toward them.

Over a minute later, they heard a long, drawn-out bass rumble that shook the air and the ground. Another minute or so and the dust-laden edge of the dark cloud was whipping and tearing at their faces.

As they flew back to Isterrane, Merral realized that beyond all the numbing and visceral horror of the day lay a terrible reality: they were completely defenseless before the Dominion.

⊃⊂⊃⊂⊃⊂⊃

Isterrane Airport was frantically busy and Merral was not surprised to find that they were diverted to a side runway. He found Vero waiting for him at the foot of the steps and was struck by how drained and vulnerable his friend seemed.

Vero drew him aside to a patch of shade by a corner of the hangar and listened solemn-faced as Merral tried to express something of the horror of the morning.

"And, Vero," Merral said at last, struggling to find the right words, "I'm sorry to say that there was no trace that the defenses did any good."

"I know." Vero looked over his dark glasses and Merral could sense the pain in his friend's eyes. "T-they were too few. The latest weapons haven't got through. They were overwhelmed."

"But how can we resist? It's not just the Krallen—that weapon . . . what was it?"

"T-they launched a five-ton rod of t-tungsten from the ship. It hit at around twenty kilometers a second. 'Think of it as a directed meteorite,' Gerry says."

"The Krallen plus this *Triumph of Sarata* are an overwhelming threat."

There was a pause. "Yes. We agree. A-and as a result, a decision has been made. W-we have a strategy, and we need your cooperation."

"Vero, after what I've seen today, you have it."

"Thank you." A bulky transporter landed nearby and Vero turned to watch it before looking at Merral. "Look, it's a risk, but I'm going to take the chance that, for whatever reason, the Dominion can't or won't in fact read our thoughts. Or, at least, not here. And I need your approval."

"So, you've changed your mind?"

Vero's face was pinched. "L-let's just say, I've modified it. Anyway, we have worked out a plan with Azeras. He, Perena, and a small crew will try to seize the *Rahllman's Star*. They will go to the point where it is hidden, summon it out of Below-Space so it will be already moving as they get near, and then dock and enter it. Then, as fast as they can, they will head to the Assembly." Vero stared at his feet for a moment. "The hope is that the *Triumph* will give chase and leave the system. If Perena and Azeras can escape, then it would give the Assembly a vital weapon."

"That would be true even if the *Triumph* stayed and didn't chase them. But can it be done?"

"It's tight, v-very tight. But it might well work."

"Vero, it sounds very risky. And it might not save Farholme."

"No. But do you a-approve? I need to have your approval."

"Yes. We have no choice. Not now. I guessed Perena was planning something drastic. She's a chess player."

"Yes. That's the thing. Chess."

"So what do I need to do?"

"Spoken like a true soldier. Now listen, when you meet Corradon, he will want to surrender. Clemant won't argue against it. Don't disagree, but ask that a meeting be held at Langerstrand to discuss surrender terms—perhaps with this Lezaroth personally. You want the best deal, guarantees—that sort of thing. Tomorrow morning. Try for a late-morning meeting, say eleven. And at the meeting, try and keep them occupied." Vero stared over his glasses at Merral. "That's the t-task. Keep them occupied. D-distract them. They have to focus on *you*. Got it?"

"Yes. Distract them."

"Good. Now, I have business here at the airport. We have a lot of equipment ready to be delivered when the time is right and not before. I'll be in touch."

Vero hesitated, then touched Merral's shoulder lightly. "Keep going, my friend. And have faith." He walked away quickly without looking back.

oOoOo

Rather than take a rotorcraft, Merral chose to be driven through Isterrane to the Planetary Administration building to get a sense of what was happening.

It took some skilled and aggressive driving by Lloyd to get them through. Most of the minor roads were blocked by the new ditch and rampart systems and with fortified gates being built across the main roads, there was a further delay.

Merral saw irregulars openly on the streets in twos and threes, wearing their pale brown jerkins and berets and carrying XQ rifles or cutter guns over their shoulders. Regulars were rarer, but Merral glimpsed some green-uniformed soldiers overseeing the creation of a defensive emplacement.

The direction signs to the refuges were flashing and supply trucks were being unloaded at the entrances. In places, metal grilles were being screwed in over ground-floor windows.

Isterrane felt utterly different. There was a mood of urgency, anxiety, and—deep below it—fear. No one laughed or sang. The few children Merral saw had their hands held by adults.

And they don't know about Tantaravekat yet. The dreadful scenes from there seemed to superimpose themselves onto the city about him. He shuddered.

oOoOo

Clemant, his face so bloodless that he looked like some sort of puppet, met Merral outside Corradon's office and veered him away from the door.

"The representative has taken the news very badly," he said, his voice a near whisper. "He was tempted to make a unilateral decision to open the Library. I pointed out that this would have been *most* unwise, unconstitutional, even illegal. I didn't want to use the police on him."

Merral nodded.

"I gather the defenses at Tantaravekat failed?" Clemant's dark eyes also seemed to ask questions.

"Yes. As far as we can tell." *There is no point in repeating Vero's excuses.*

"I saw the imagery of the blast from the *Triumph*. It looked . . . over-whelming." The advisor's fingers intertwined with a nervous energy.

"It was."

"Commander," Clemant said, his voice filled with a quiet, almost quivering intensity, "unless you know better, I consider that we are completely vulnerable."

"I'm afraid I don't know better."

"Professor Habbentz has ideas—oh, *plenty* of ideas—but nothing to hand. And it seems that our friend Mr. V. has not delivered either." There was a deep and bitter sarcasm in his tone.

What an ironic tragedy that at a time when we have a legitimate focus for anger it's turned against our friends. Another triumph of sin and evil.

"I'm sorry," Merral replied. "I had hoped for deliverance, but none has come." He looked at Clemant, hoping for some hint of mercy or sympathy in his eyes, but found none.

"It's not *just* you. But we have no weapons. No defenses. Nothing." His tone revealed a deep frustration. "And the rumor of what has happened at Tantaravekat is spreading. The people are becoming scared. There are rumors of panic." A muscle in his face twitched.

Merral, who had given little thought to the implications of the public mood, suddenly saw that the threat of panic was another potent pressure on the leadership. *No wonder Clemant is worried.*

"Shall we go and see the representative?" Merral asked, suddenly tired of secret meetings.

"As you wish. But I think you're wasting your time talking about defense. We're beyond that now."

"I think we are."

They found the representative seated in his chair, leaning over the table. His head was in his hands.

A broken man.

On the table in front of him was a large printout of the latest imagery of the steel gray sprawling mass of the *Triumph of Sarata* with labels pasted on it.

As Corradon looked up at Merral, his face seemed tired and his eyes bloodshot.

"So, Commander," he said and Merral heard raggedness in the once smooth voice, "let this meeting be brief. We have no defenses. We are utterly exposed."

He gestured to the image and Merral read the words on the labels. *Anti-missile systems? . . . Krallen landers? . . . Kinetic energy projectile magazines? . . . High-power broad spectrum lasers?* With each phrase, his heart sank lower.

"It seems to me, Commander, that all we can do is yield."

"Sir, you are in charge. If that's what you want to do, I won't object."

An expression of relief flooded across Corradon's face. "I was afraid you wanted some sort of last-ditch stand."

"No."

"It's not cowardice, you know." The words were almost feverishly rapid. "It's the lives. We are utterly outmatched."

Merral looked at the image again. "I know. But I think we should seek the best terms. I would like to have a meeting tomorrow with Lezaroth and the ambassadors at Langerstrand. You and me, sir, and the three of them. I will ask for guarantees."

There was an exchange of glances between Corradon and Clemant.

"The best terms," Corradon said. "Yes, why not? They can hardly object."

◌◌◌◌◌

"Well, Under-Captain, looks like it's all over," Lezaroth said as he finished listening to the message from Corradon.

Hanax, who had been watching the launching of more Krallen deployment pods, turned to him, a sullen disappointment evident in his eyes. "Have they surrendered?"

"Effectively. There is a meeting tomorrow. All being well, the Library will be in our hands by evening. Then there will be a few loose ends to tie up."

"Somehow I was expecting more of a fight."

"Afraid not, Under-Captain. They are realists after all. So no medals for you this time."

"There'll be another time," Hanax said with a thin and clearly fabricated smile. A few minutes later he left the bridge.

He's gone off to sulk, no doubt. Lezaroth considered whether he ought to attend the meeting. *I can hardly trust the ambassadors. It will be entertaining to humiliate them. Besides, it will be intriguing to see this D'Avanos in the flesh. I will seize him there and then. I wonder how he will take being told that he is to be hauled off to Nezhuala as an exhibit.*

He paused for a moment, struck by the peculiarity that if D'Avanos *was* the great adversary he had done nothing to merit the title. *Not so far, apparently.* Yet there had been oddities that deserved investigation. The chief of these was, of course, the way that a pack of Krallen had gone missing. *The excuses offered by Hazderzal and Tinternli were utterly pathetic. I need to know what happened there.*

A sudden thought came to mind. *With the new dwelling tower finished, the baziliarch is out of its casing and no longer dormant. I can utilize him to tap D'Avanos's mind and find out what really happened.* The practicalities were straightforward. He would meet D'Avanos and the pathetic Corradon in a room next to the baziliarch's chamber, have the intermediary nearby, and get the results fed directly into his bio-augment circuits.

Just then Hanax returned.

"Oh, Under-Captain," Lezaroth said, "I'm going down to the surrender meeting tomorrow. So you'll be running all this for, oh, at least a dozen hours. Feel up to it?"

"As it happens, yes, sir." There was no mistaking the brooding anger in Hanax's words. "Both the pilotage board and the lord-emperor seemed to think I'm capable."

"Very good. Well, now that the mission is winding down, I may let you have more chances to prove it."

"Thank you, sir." The words came out from between tightened lips.

"Very well. She'll be all yours. Call me if there are decisions you need help with." He felt himself smile. "Just don't scratch her paint."

ⅩⅩⅩⅩ

That night, when Merral lay down in the annex to the war room he found that, despite his exhaustion, he couldn't sleep. Whenever he closed his eyes, the terrible images of the men, women, and children of Tantaravekat flooded back into his mind. When he tried to shift from thinking about them, the idea that the three-quarters-of-a-million-ton monstrosity that was the *Triumph of Sarata* hung overhead, ready to destroy everything, brought no comfort.

Suddenly, just after midnight, he was aware of a figure—darkness made tangible—seated in the corner of the room.

"You!" he said, sitting up on his mattress.

"Commander." Was there a bow of the head? "I have come on the eve of the war. The storm is about to break."

Merral sensed something different about the envoy. There seemed to be a new solidity to him, a power that there hadn't been before. *He is a soldier too.*

"I am glad to see you. We have had terrible losses."

"I was there. I saw what happened."

"And you didn't do anything?"

The envoy seemed to sigh. "That is not a new complaint. But you must remember that the King has already acted by taking flesh, bearing evil, and defeating it. Had he not, events such as Tantaravekat would be daily occurrences. Indeed, they once were. And you must remember too his promise that, one day, he will return and such evils will be no more."

"May that day come soon."

"That is a wise and ancient prayer. Now, though, I am sent to bring you both encouragement and warning. First, I can confirm that although those you face seem mighty, they are weakened. Like all the servants of the enemy in every time and place, fear eats away at them. Among other things they are troubled by the idea that the one whom their prophecies warn them against may be present. That fear has become focused on you. They have learned that you bear a token from their last defeat and they have heard rumors that you walked unscathed through the ship at Fallambet."

"I find that unfortunate."

"On the contrary, as it did before, it will blind them to other threats. And they have other failings. Pride and malice have weakened them and they have sought the advice of demons. There they will find, as was known of old, that such counsel betrays them in deepest consequence."

Merral sensed strange eyes searching his. "But if I bring you encouragement, I also bring a warning. In all you do, watch yourself, and do not take for granted the mercy of the Most High. Specifically, I charge you not to stray far from Isterrane. Evil is at work in your world's capital and you must be present to combat it."

"In Isterrane? Very well. But where will you be?"

"Commander, such battles are fought on more than one plane. Not all war is visible to your eyes. As you know, there are rules. If your enemy breaks those rules—and you may assume he will—then I am authorized to come to your aid. But not until then. Now I must go."

"Wait . . . the ship—this *Triumph*—can you destroy it?"

"Of course. The prebendant is right about that. In a moment. And were it the right thing to do, I would take great delight in doing that very thing. But I cannot stray outside the King's desire. It is the Father's will that his children fight their own battles. Yet the promise I passed on to you of 'a way of defense' has not been forgotten. But remember, it comes at a price."

There was pause in which Merral could hear only the sound of his own breathing.

"Now as a blessing, I grant you sleep and the best of dreams. You will need all the strength you have tomorrow."

The envoy rose from the chair and raised a gloved hand. A tiredness like a vast wave descended on Merral. His eyes closed and sleep surged over him with an irresistible force.

ﻌﻌﻌﻌ

A little after one o'clock in the morning, Perena Lewitz arrived at the airport and headed to the *Lanea Willats*. The spotlights seemed to exaggerate the vast bloated shape of the Q-series freighter.

Many people could be seen all around the vessel, refueling, testing, and loading cargo.

So much activity and it all depends on me doing what I have to do right.

A slight figure sitting on the steps of a spare access gantry rose and walked over with hasty, nervous steps.

"Vero," she said, her voice heavy. *I wish he wasn't here. . . . Yet I'm glad he's here.*

"I had to come."

"Just don't make me change my mind."

"I won't."

"Over here," she said and led him to where they were out of earshot of the others.

"Your ship looks tiny," he said and she followed his gesture, seeing the black cylinder slung inside the long and voluminous belly hold of the *Lanea Willats*.

"It's called the *Arrow*. It's fast and agile and it's the sort of thing you might use to access the *Rahllman's Star* in a hurry. The *Lanea* will pass within five thousand kilometers of the *Triumph* and I'll be launched at that point. Then I'll head toward Farholme broadcasting the fake summoning codes that Azeras has given us."

I sound so matter-of-fact. We both do. But if we did not, we might both burst into tears.

"And you checked the ejection mechanism?"

"It's on my to-do list, Vero."

"The *Lanea* will backtrack to pick you up."

"I know, as long as there is no risk from debris."

A silence descended between them that was so intense it seemed solid. She touched Vero's cheek. "Your face is getting lined."

"I need a holiday," he said, his voice thick with emotion.

"Anywhere in mind?"

"Earth. With you."

"That's not . . . a scheduled flight." Her eyes felt moist. "Hold me, Vero."

He held her. "God be with you," he said, his words barely intelligible.

"And with you," she replied. "Now let me go." *Have I ever said a harder thing?* "I have to fly."

As he turned and walked away into the darkness she could see his shoulders shaking.

◖◗◖◗◖

Ten minutes later Perena walked carefully along the cramped walkway of the systems access tunnel of the *Arrow*. The air was dry, full of the lifeless, charged smell of electronics and wiring. She knew exactly where among the bewildering array of boxes and cables she had to go.

Knowledge is not the problem—obedience is.

She found the first circuit she wanted. It was clearly marked *Guardian Transponder* and was sealed. Breaking the seal, she ignored most of the switches, and slid a keyboard out. She scrolled past screens of warnings until she reached a single code of letters and numbers, then paused for a second before deleting it.

What to replace it with? She smiled, surprised at how calm she felt. *This will do for them to repeat.* She typed *The Lamb Will Triumph,* checked various switches, and then closed the unit.

Just one more adjustment to make. But when she found the box, her hand trembled as she touched it. *Do I need to?* She countered her doubt. *It is the safest way. Success cannot be guaranteed anyway, but this way gives the highest chance. I cannot afford the temptation.*

She slid open the lid and stared at the single switch and the solemn red writing above it. *A single flick of my fingers does it. I must do it.*

But she didn't.

Many things came to mind. Sunlight on leaves, children's voices, food, Vero's face. Her fingers quivered and her eyes misted over.

Suddenly, she was aware of someone else in the tunnel. She heard the sound of feet, slow, heavy, and measured on the walkway. She turned to see a dark figure blocking out the light. "Is it you?"

"Captain." The voice didn't seem to belong to the echoing access tunnel. There was a bow of the head and a hat was swept off.

"You are the one I met before in Engineering?"

Silhouetted against the light as the figure was, it was hard to see any details of the face. Yet she felt sure a smile was there. "Yes."

"Then I owe you thanks. We all do."

"I was sent."

"Do you have a name, sir?"

"Yes, but it's not for you to know. Not now."

"I understand. Why are you here?"

"To encourage you to strike the blow."

She followed his gaze to the switch. "Is there no other way?"

"What do you think?"

"I think the safest way is to remove the temptation."

"I agree."

"This plan of ours: will it work?"

"That I cannot promise."

"I suppose not. It's not easy. Do you know that?"

"Yes." *Was there unsteadiness in the odd voice?* "Our Master found it hard."

"I have a question, sir. Will I be allowed to see you on . . . the other side?"

There was a strange, light laugh. "You will have better things to see. I am concerned whether I will be allowed to see you." As if struck by a thought, the figure stiffened. "I now realize that one of the problems my kind face in being immortal is that there is a limit to how much you can show your love."

"I had never thought of that. Do you envy me?"

"In this area, I do." There was a taut salute. "Have a good journey, Lady Perena."

Before she could say anything more, he had gone. She turned to the switch and flicked it down hard to the *off* position, then slid the lid closed.

She stared one last time at the words: *Ejection Unit Firing System*.

"It had to be done," she said as she made her way to the cabin.

Later that morning, Merral woke feeling strangely refreshed. The news from the subdued staff of the war room was not in the slightest bit encouraging, however.

During the night, a dozen more vessels had landed at five separate sites on Farholme and offloaded large forces totaling an estimated hundred thousand Krallen. Merral gazed at the map on the wallscreen with dread.

One landing was at the Camolgi Hills northeast of Isterrane, twenty kilometers east of Halmacent. The others were to the west: at Langerstrand, near Kammart, Maraplant, and Stepalis. The disposition of the landing sites meant that most of the main cities of Menaya had Krallen concentrations within a few hundred kilometers. The only tiny fragment of comfort he found was that the enemy forces showed no inclination to move beyond the landing zones. Merral, tempted to despair, clung to the hope the envoy had offered.

In the middle of the morning, Merral, accompanied by Lloyd, and Corradon flew to Langerstrand in a small scout craft crewed only by a pilot and technician.

The representative, who carried a thin metal case that Merral presumed contained the key to the Library, was clearly distressed and said little on the brief flight. A tired, gloomy figure, he simply stared out of the window, his fingers playing restlessly with the case.

High above them the crew of the *Triumph of Sarata* had detected the unauthorized flight of the *Arrow*. Amid flashing action station lights Lucretor Hanax issued a rapid succession of crisp, clear orders from his position at the command console.

"Navs, plot an intercept for that ship to overtake it from the stern. And turn to put us on a pursuit course. Comms, record and analyze every signal from that ship. Get Deltathree on that. I want to know if there is a human pilot. Engineering, prepare the main engines for fast pursuit. All crew, wait for my command."

Hanax felt the ship start to swing around and saw the stars slide across the windows. He tapped buttons.

For the first time in months I feel alive. He felt a pleasure bordering on joy. *This is what I was trained for.* He touched the tiny charm around his wrist that the ship's priest had given him. *He told me my luck would turn. He promised me my moment of destiny would come.*

"Intells, get me any data on that ship. Put it on screen." He turned to the weapons officer, who was settling himself on the adjacent couch. "Wepps, I intend to overhaul that ship and capture it with tethercraft."

Wepps stared at him, his eyes cold. "Why not just fry it, sir? The laser cannon will do that without us moving. Be safer."

"Because that ship is doing something odd. It looks like it's heading behind this blasted planet. And I think we need to intercept and board it. We will learn more."

"I'm wary, sir."

You'd never say that to Lezaroth. "Wepps, I think it is the lord-emperor's will that we do this." *Try going against that!*

Something close to a sigh came from Wepps. "As you say, sir."

Hanax called the priest and asked him to give him an augury. *Are the omens good? I need to know.*

He had only just ended that call when he heard Comms speaking in his ear. "Sir, we're picking up something. This pilot is sending out signals into the Nether-Realms. It could be a summons for a vessel to surface."

I'm right! There is something going on. And there is only one vessel it can be seeking. "Can you get me an ID on the vessel it's calling?"

"Just checking the code library right now, sir. Here we are. The *Rahllman's Star*—a freighter."

"Good, very good." *Aha! Just what I suspected.*

He leaned toward the weapons officer. "Wepps, it's after the *Rahllman's Star*. Somehow they have the codes. We must intercept it."

"Very well, sir. But, if I may make a suggestion, you might want to call the fleet-commander."

"Thank you for that thought, Wepps." Hanax struggled to keep his words polite. "But let me make three points. One, I am authorized to make these decisions. Two, I am capable of making them. And three, the fleet-commander is very busy right now." *And fourth, I'd let the powers tear me to shreds before I let him take the credit for this.*

The weapons officer shrugged.

Hanax tapped a button. "Engineering, engage. We're going to chase a little bird."

○○○○○

As Merral flew into Langerstrand, there was no mistaking the presence of the Krallen. They were drawn up in vast parallel ranks at the end of the runway and looked utterly immobile, like lines of metal statues. Merral stared at them, struck by the realization that there came a point at which things got so bad no further news could make them any worse.

His eye was soon drawn to the structure at the edge of the liaison center. The stark, windowless tower was at least ten stories high and was made from overlapping sheets of a dully gleaming dark gray alloy wound over each other as if the structure had grown rather than been made. It was a grotesque construction, brutally ugly, and reminded Merral of a severed tree trunk.

Yet Merral felt there was more to it than sheer ugliness. Even in his gloom and despair, he sensed something about the tower, that upset him as if its very presence cast a shadow over the mind.

His thoughts turned to Isabella, presumably confined somewhere in the complex around the tower, and a pang of guilt struck him. *I should have warned her. She might not have listened, but I should have said something.* But there were other matters to think about and he pushed the guilt to one side.

Lloyd asked for permission to stay on the flier and Merral agreed. He followed Corradon onto the runway.

Suddenly, at the foot of the steps, the representative stopped. "Merral," he said, his face waxy, "before we meet these people, I want to apologize."

"For what?"

"For being the wrong man in the wrong place. For being weak. For trusting these . . . monsters."

"I accept your apology. Of course."

"That . . . means a lot to me. Thank you."

By the entrance to the complex a man beckoned them over.

"Anyway," Corradon said, his voice glum, "I shall retire this afternoon. However it goes. The job needs someone else."

They were led into the liaison center, down a long, silent, and echoing corridor and into a high, dark-walled, and windowless room with a black oblong table in the center.

On the far side of the table were seated three people: Hazderzal, Tinternli, and in between them, and clearly the dominant figure, Fleet-Commander Lezaroth.

Instantly, Merral felt Lezaroth's gaze, a hard piercing scrutiny that seemed to have an almost physical weight to it. Refusing to be intimidated, Merral returned the stare. *There's a power in this man, and it is bent to evil and cruelty.* He wondered what emotions lay behind the expressionless face. *I sense only hate and curiosity.*

Then the scrutiny was over. There was no greeting. Merral and Corradon were curtly gestured to seats opposite. As Merral seated himself, he looked around. It was a room he had never been in. To his left, the end wall was taken up by a vast blank screen stretching to the ceiling. The right-hand wall was different and had an odd pearly sheen to it as if it was semitransparent. As he looked at the wall, there was something about it that troubled him, almost as if when he glanced at it, his brain tingled. *It is at the foot of the new tower.* He wondered what lay behind it.

He gazed at the ambassadors. Somehow they had changed. They now seemed lesser people. It was as if their power had leaked from them. Yet he saw too that he was now able to see them for what they were—liars, schemers, and manipulators.

Hazderzal returned his gaze for a moment, and then looked away. Tinternli gave him a hollow, almost embarrassed smile as if to say, "Yes, it was all a facade, wasn't it?"

How could we have ever been taken in by these creatures?

But Lezaroth's voice ended his thoughts. "Let us begin," he said in a rough, frosty tone. "You know our requests. We want the treaty signed and the key to the Library and the Admin-Net."

Corradon stared at them, his Adam's apple wobbling. He paused, then said, "First of all, we protest at the utter barbarism of what you did at Tantaravekat yesterday."

Both ambassadors gave slow, cold smiles that were almost leers, but Lezaroth's face showed no emotion.

"Representative, Commander," Lezaroth said in his accented rasp, "you misunderstand this meeting. You are not here to blame us, but to deal with us. And you must have a sense of perspective. Events are unfolding that are so significant the lives of these few people in this obscure village count as nothing." There was a flicker of some emotion on the face. "Now is the moment in which the Dominion comes out of the shadows. Our inevitable triumph over the Assembly starts at Farholme. Here, our lord-emperor will start to extend those powers that will eventually take over all the realms of men."

"But it was an outrage!" Corradon said, half rising out of his seat, his face flushed with anger.

Lezaroth gave the merest lift of an eyebrow. "Sit down! Tantaravekat is now history. And when we take control of the Assembly it will not even be that. Now, to business."

Hanax adjusted the command console seat one more time. He couldn't quite get it as perfectly fitting as he would like. But it didn't matter; there would be time. He smiled. *I am in charge at last!*

He glanced around. The bridge was full and everyone was at his post. Next to him the weapons officer was fully strapped in, his fingers flicking through weapons options with practiced ease.

Hanax checked the screen. The target was just two thousand kilometers away; she would soon be on scope.

A message came in. "Navs here. Target changing course. Heading toward Farholme. Do we follow?"

What's she doing? It has to be a she; all their pilots are female. He felt a spasm of contempt. *It about sums them up.* Hanax ran through his tactics lessons until the obvious answer came to him. *So that's what she's up to.* He snapped an order: "Follow her!"

The weapons officer looked his way, frowning.

"Relax, Wepps. It's okay," Hanax said quickly. "I recognize the maneuver. This woman knows we are in pursuit. She'll try to pull a tight orbit round the planet—tighter than we can manage—to slow us down."

"Maybe. But sir, I don't like it."

"Trust me, Wepps. It's in the book. We will intercept her long before she can do it. Have the tethercraft ready to launch. We will keep at least twenty klicks away in case she's carrying a bomb. And get the boarding party suited and ready. I want the crew and any passengers alive. . . . Not long now."

The tattooed face of the priest appeared on the screen. "As you asked, Captain, I have consulted the omens. They are very good." He tilted his head back and opened his mouth wide in the way that priests did when they were quoting the powers. His sharpened teeth glinted. "Listen: 'Today is a day when the tables are turned. Today is a day when weakness defeats power. Today is a day when the proud and the brutal are humbled.'" His mouth closed and a knowing smirk appeared on his face. "Captain, I think *you* can interpret that."

"Thank you," said Hanax, feeling a smile appear on his lips. "Thank you very much." He felt a surge of delicious pleasure. *Lezaroth, you are about to get a taste of justice.*

At Langerstrand, Lezaroth made a gesture and the screen on the wall came alive with a map of Farholme on which five red blobs glowed brightly. He chose his words carefully. "Let me remind you of the situation. Our forces are being deployed and can be ordered into action at any time. We need your cooperation."

Corradon clenched his fist and leaned forward. "No! There are issues that we must resolve before we can deal with you."

"The matter of the hostages, for a start," D'Avanos added.

You fools! I'll—

He stopped, suddenly aware that someone was talking to him through his bio-augment systems.

"Cap'n, do you read me?" It was a poor signal but he recognized the weapons officer's voice.

"A moment," he said, then rose and walked through the door behind his seat into a corridor. "Wepps?" he snapped. "By the powers, this better be serious!"

There was the inevitable short time delay before the answer. "Sir, it is. I'm on the bridge—that's why I can't say too much. Hanax has got us in hot pursuit of a Farholme ship. It seems to be going after this *Rahllman's Star*. Hanax wants to capture it."

Fury flooded Lezaroth's mind. *I am away for a few hours and this happens!* But caution rapidly replaced the fury. *I need more information.* "What's your specific concern?"

"Cap'n, I think it's a trap."

Lezaroth deliberated. Wepps was a reliable man with years of experience and his intuition wasn't to be ignored. *I ought to call Hanax and order him back.* A new and attractive thought came to him. *If I let Hanax continue for a little longer, it might allow me to charge him with recklessly endangering a ship, or even negligence. And either charge would finish the rat's career.* Another idea came to him. *If it really is a trap, D'Avanos will know.*

"Wepps, for the moment, just watch. Alert me if there is any specific peril. I'll do some checking here. And make sure there is a record of what happens. I may need it. I think this could be Hanax's last flight."

"Yes, Cap'n."

Lezaroth gave some orders to the staff at Langerstrand and walked back into the chamber. It was time, at long last, to use the baziliarch.

⬡⬡⬡⬡⬡

In Lezaroth's absence there was only silence. Merral wondered what had happened. A faint hope began to rise in his mind that something had come up, but he squashed it. Hope seemed impossible.

When Lezaroth returned, the expression on his face was quite unreadable.

He made no apology or comment, but instead sat down and gestured with a finger.

On the wallscreen the image changed. Now on a dark background, fixed points of white light appeared and amid them, a single flashing green spot moved. Some way behind it was a larger crimson dot.

Stars and ships, Merral realized.

Lezaroth turned to Merral. "Something is happening. One of your ships is moving on an unapproved course. What's going on?"

Merral was about to deny any knowledge when he was struck by an astonishing sensation. Something seemed to penetrate his mind, something that probed like a finger poking under the stones of a river. It was as if the levels of his consciousness were, one by one, being lifted away. He shook his head and ran his fingers through his hair as if that might stop the sensation. But it persisted.

From nowhere, he heard a voice in his head. *What is this ship?*

Merral looked around, seeing no one new in the room. In a sudden, horrendous flash of comprehension, Merral knew that Vero had been right—there *was* something that could read minds. Whatever it was, it lurked behind the pale translucent wall. As he turned toward the wall, he could make out something stirring beyond the transparent paleness, some massive, black, room-sized angular form. There were noises too: scratching and scrabbling.

The baziliarch. The word sounded in his brain like the toll of death. That was who the tower had been built for. A wave of despair seemed to crash over his mind.

The ship—what is it hoping to do? Answer aloud.

"I don't know!" Merral shouted, trying to resist. He saw Corradon, Tinternli, and Hazderzal looking at him with puzzlement. Only Lezaroth's cold, scrutinizing expression was unchanged.

What do you know?

The probing—the relentless exposure of his mind—continued. Suddenly, utterly unasked for, memories flashed in Merral's mind: his work, his home, his friends. Yet all were discarded. Suddenly, he was thinking about Azeras, seeing him on the Manalahi Shoals, watching him picking his teeth as he sat at the table. That image stayed, replayed over and over again like a video loop.

Who is this? A survivor?

Merral sensed a strange, alien sensation of alarm. *Of course. It works both ways. The baziliarch can feel my thoughts and I can—to a lesser degree— sense his.*

Across the table, a frown darkened Lezaroth's face. *He knows too. He is sitting in on the probing of my mind.* Merral's despair reached new depths.

○○○○○

On the *Triumph of Sarata* Hanax was tense but confident. It would be a tricky maneuver—the *Triumph* was a very large ship—but it was achievable. *But I want more than a mere achievement; I want excellence. I want this to be a textbook operation.*

Comms came through to him. "Captain, since she changed course, the target is broadcasting a new signal."

"What sort of signal?"

"Deltathree says it's to the Guardian satellites. It's standard protocol on such a trajectory."

The weapons officer, who listened in, leaned close to Hanax. "Sir, I don't like that. Not on this course." His voice was urgent. "I think you ought to change course."

"No."

"How about consulting the fleet-commander?"

"I can manage, Wepps." *Nevertheless, I'll take precautions. Just in case.* "Comms," Hanax snapped, "imitate her signals. Whatever she does, we follow."

The priest's words warmed his heart. *Today is a day when the tables are turned.*

He turned to the frowning weapons officer. "Cheer up, Wepps. Get that boarding party ready. I think this is going to be a very interesting half hour."

○○○○○

Merral did the only thing he could think of. *Protect me, Lord!*

Nothing happened. Instead there was a new sensation in his brain. It was unease, he realized, but it was not his own unease. It was the baziliarch who was troubled. He could sense that the baziliarch had realized something unfamiliar had happened and it was brooding over it. And from the troubled look on Lezaroth's face, this unease was transmitted to him as well.

Behind the eggshell-like right wall, the thing moved again with a stiff, lurching motion, as if it was some vast, room-sized praying mantis.

Corradon, wide-eyed, shivered.

Suddenly, Lezaroth turned to the transparent screen. "Find out who this D'Avanos really is," he snapped.

Who are you? The voice spoke in Merral's mind again.

"I am a forester," Merral protested, trying to think of trees and woodlands and sunlight through leaves. "I serve the living God."

In his mind there was something that might have been a laugh of derision. *Then let him deliver you.*

Merral tried to answer with some defiant words but they would not come.

Are you Ringell?

There was a new probing now. More images flashed in his mind like scrapbooks being flipped through.

No, you are not. But are you the one we fear, the great adversary?

Merral tried to counter with a question. *Who are you?*

I am Lord Nar-Barratri, one of the seven baziliarchs who serve the great one. I am an ancient prince of power and authority in the Nether-Realms. I was once great, and I will be greater still.

The names and titles were so full of proud majesty that Merral felt almost crushed. He was wondering how to respond when a moving red dot on the screen captured his attention. The *Triumph of Sarata. It's chasing Perena.*

Who?

I gave her name! In his panic and horror Merral forced himself to think of other things: Ynysmant, picnics, Team-Ball matches, festivals. As he did, he felt them all discarded, as the baziliarch relentlessly pursued a single question: *What is this ship hoping to do?*

Merral remembered some ancient film he had watched with Lloyd in which a villain pursued the heroine through a house and she tried to deter him by throwing anything she could find at him. This was like that. He thought of his relatives and then his friends, but that led him to Isabella and that in turn led him to think of Anya, and she led him to . . .

"No!" he yelled digging his nails into his hand in the hope that pain would end the pursuit through his mind.

This Perena seeks the Rahllman's Star. *True?*

No, no. . . . Yes!

Suddenly, Merral was overwhelmed by a sense of discovery, as if the seeker had overturned a stone in his mind and finally found the object he sought.

Yes. Rahllman's Star. *She seeks it, but we will have her first. The* Triumph *is not just big, it is also fast. Watch and despair.*

Through spasms of recrimination that he had betrayed Perena, Merral saw Lezaroth's broad shoulders relax as if the tension had been lifted. *He has learned something that has reassured him.* Yet the stern, thoughtful look on the face remained, as if Lezaroth was still wary that some unseen danger lay ahead.

The probing relented. Yet Merral continued to feel unfamiliar sensations as if the link to his mind remained. He sensed an angry restlessness as if the baziliarch realized that something had been overlooked that might have done it harm. Behind the translucent wall, he saw new convulsions.

Merral turned to look at the wallscreen. The green flashing light still moved, but seemed to have changed direction. The large pulsing red spot still pursued it, but was closing the gap. What was the distance between them? Hundreds or thousands of kilometers?

I have betrayed Perena. Misery darkened his mind. *They found out about her. Vero was too confident that the plan would work. We have been fools.*

Merral was suddenly aware of strange and troubled thoughts as if the baziliarch was pondering something.

Suddenly there was a flash of rage and fear that nearly stunned him in its intensity. *A trap! A trap!* The thought was a mental scream.

The look of alarm on Lezaroth's face told Merral that he had heard the same mental scream of alarm.

The Guardian satellites are in firing mode!

Merral stared at the screen, seeing the red dot now nearly on top of the green one.

"Hanax!" Lezaroth yelled as he leaped to his feet. "It's a trap! Change course! Abort!"

✕✕✕✕✕

On the *Triumph,* Hanax stared at the screen in front of him. The Assembly vessel was a silver dot with the gleaming blue and white orb of Farholme out of focus just behind it. They were barely fifty kilometers away—just minutes—from contact now.

"Wepps, ready to deploy the tethercraft?"

"Yes, sir. And the boarding party is loading the assault craft. But sir, are you sure—?"

"Yes, Wepps. I *am* sure!" *How quickly can I get the information I need out of the crew of this ship? Will the standard mixture of drugs and torture do?*

Suddenly he heard the harsh yell of the fleet-commander's voice from the console speaker. "*Hanax!* It's a trap! Change course! *Abort!*"

Everyone looked toward Hanax.

He shook his head. "You would say that, wouldn't you?" he snarled at the speaker.

On the screen the target vessel was almost within his grasp. Months of accumulated anger bubbled up within him. "Right now! How *very* convenient! Are you really the only one who can carry out a maneuver?"

Hanax pressed a button. "Comms, call the fleet-commander and tell him his signal was too poor to read. Get him to recalibrate his equipment."

He looked at the range. *Forty kilometers now.* They had to be careful not to overshoot.

A twinge of doubt struck him. *Might Lezaroth be right?* Then Hanax remembered the words of the priest. *Today is a day when the proud and the brutal are humbled.* His doubts vanished.

Suddenly, the weapons officer gave a grunt of alarm and stiffened over his screen. "Sir! The Guardian satellites are going into firing mode!"

Lights flashed and a strident alarm sounded.

The weapons officer turned to Hanax, a wide-eyed, slack-jawed look of horror on his face, the unmistakable look of a man who realized that death was moments away. "They *are* firing!"

Hanax touched his talisman and opened his mouth. As he did, the first shockwave of the *Triumph's* disintegration into a billion glowing fragments ripped into the bridge. He didn't even have time to scream.

Perena unbuckled her couch restraints and stood up in the cramped cabin. There was no maneuver now that would make any difference. The *Triumph* was closing fast, the wrong signals were being imitated, the Guardians' circuitry was operating correctly. There was less than a minute to go. She gave a prayer of thanks.

There was cool, humming silence in the cabin.

She stretched her muscles. *This body has served me well.* The idea seemed almost irrelevant. "Lord, when they stand before you, have mercy on the crew of that ship."

She glanced at a screen. The Guardians were charging up.

All that has to be done has been done. I am ready. My tale thus far is ended.

"Lord, into your hands I commend my spirit."

Feeling no fear—only joy and expectation—she turned to look out of the porthole. She was still gazing at the stars with wonderment when cool, silent light dissolved her world.

Merral saw the red and the green dots on the screen suddenly disappear.

Destroyed! Destroyed! Destroyed! The baziliarch's mind seemed aflame with a raging fury that hurt Merral so much he reeled and put his hand to his head. Yet in seconds, Merral realized that the anger was not directed at him. He was forgotten. Slowly, the link with the baziliarch's mind faded.

It began to dawn on Merral that the *Triumph of Sarata* had been destroyed. *Thank you, God*, he prayed, but as he did, something stopped him from rejoicing. Things didn't add up. The plan had been for Perena to steal the *Rahllman's Star*. Hadn't it?

He glanced first at Corradon, who stared at him with a strange expression of realization as if he had finally understood something, then at the others.

Lezaroth stared rigidly at the screen, his mouth open, his face a sickly white. On either side the ambassadors followed his gaze with blank incomprehension.

Suddenly, an animated fury washed over Lezaroth's face. "Kill them!" he said with cold ferocity. He stumbled through the door and left the room, overturning his chair in his haste.

There was a furious dry rattling to Merral's right, and he turned to see great black angular shapes—limbs? wings?—flail against the translucent wall. A spasm of thrashing noises came from behind it. A crack appeared, as if an eggshell were breaking, and a trickle of pale, dusty fragments dribbled to the floor.

"Time to go," Merral said, rising.

"Yes, yes," Corradon replied with a strange, remote smile as if he had suddenly arrived somewhere beyond all his fears. "I was wrong, Merral. Far too afraid. Too little faith. All is not lost." The words were staccato. He rose and made a slow, stately gesture toward the door as if there was all the time in the world. "You go first. You have fighting to do."

They turned to the door and as they did, the building was shaken by the heavy reverberating thud of an explosion. New fragments broke off the cracked wall.

The stabbing wail of a siren began.

A reflection moved on the polished surface of the door. Merral swung round to see Tinternli bound onto the table with a bizarre and inflexible motion. He realized that her movements were those no normal human could ever make.

She stood there for a moment, her head bent forward, her eyes lit with an extraordinary anger, then opened her jaws wide and gave a screech that shook the room.

There was a renewed cracking noise and on the margins of his sight, Merral glimpsed the translucent wall bowing outward as the baziliarch pressed against it. A loud rattling noise like sticks being beaten together began and the dark limbs seemed to scratch again at the surface of the wall. Something else—wings perhaps—slapped against the wall. Merral was aware of a wild, frustrated hatred.

Tinternli bounded at him, a savage creature, her hair swinging wildly, her outstretched fingers clawing for his throat.

As she sprang, Merral leaped sideways.

Tinternli missed him, landing on the floor with apelike agility. She turned to face him.

Merral grabbed a chair and as she leaped again at him, he swung it as hard as he could. The chair leg struck her left arm and shoulder hard and, to his astonishment, disintegrated into pale, flying splinters. *She's not human! She can't be!*

Tinternli cannoned into the table and as she did Merral was suddenly aware of Hazderzal staring at him with a blank emotionless look, as if he had been frozen into inactivity.

There was a cacophony of noises now. Tinternli screamed like an animal in pain. A *boom, boom* that had to be weapons fire came from beyond the door behind them. Loud cracking noises sounded from the frosted screen as it split open.

A smell of dust was in the air.

Tinternli raised a bloodied arm and, like some ferocious beast, crouched, ready to pounce. Merral stepped back, preparing to swing the remains of the chair. But Corradon stepped forward and with a gasp swung his metal briefcase hard at Tinternli's head. A sharp corner struck her forehead with a cracking noise and she staggered back and slumped to the floor.

He killed her! He must have!

"Should have done that before," Corradon grunted.

But the figure on the floor shook her head and got to her feet. Ruby blood oozed from a deep gash in her head and Merral was puzzled to see something that glittered silver in it.

Tinternli pressed the edges of the wound together. As she took her hands away, the wound trembled and merged as if invisible hands knit the tissue. She wiped blood from her eyes and turned to face Merral.

What is she?

"We have to fight," Corradon said and moved forward, swinging the case again.

Suddenly, Tinternli thrust the case aside with a mighty slap of the hand, seized his shoulders, and flung the representative away with apparently effortless energy.

Corradon flew backward and struck the wall. There was a sickening snap and he slumped to the ground. There, his head at an impossible angle, he lay still.

Merral gasped.

Tinternli, bent-backed, turned to Merral. He heard a renewed rustling and cracking as the dark, elephantine form of the baziliarch pushed further against the crumbling wall. Dark, gleaming claws, twice the size of a man's fist, reached through and tore the glass.

There were noises in the corridor outside. The door flew open.

A big figure, made bigger by a slab of green chest-armor, barged through, a twin-barreled weapon swinging around in front of him. "Get back, sir! Down the corridor!" Under the brow of the helmet, sharp blue eyes scanned the room.

"Lloyd!"

Lloyd jabbed the barrels toward Tinternli, whose arms were raised, ready to attack. "Get back! I wouldn't like to shoot a lady."

Tinternli twisted her mouth into a sickly smile and leaped.

There was a deafening blast of sound. Merral, already at the door, glimpsed an appalling something of torn flesh and gleaming metal tumbling backward.

"Doesn't seem you were much of a lady," Lloyd muttered.

Another man with chest armor burst into the room, and after surveying the scene, bent over Corradon's motionless form.

At the end of the room, the translucent wall crumbled entirely and a monstrous form, twice the height of any human being, seemingly made up of dark, resinous sheets, began to elbow its way in.

Merral stared at it, feeling like an ant before a great predatory insect.

Hazderzal edged slowly away like a man in a trance.

"Clear the room!" Lloyd yelled.

Merral found himself pushed roughly down the corridor.

"Gotta leave, sir." Lloyd said. "There's a war we need you for. . . . Corradon's dead."

"Right." *I have lost a friend.* The thought stabbed at his heart.

They ran down the smoke-blackened corridor, stepping over debris.

There was smoke in the air and the lights flickered and fizzed.

Then they were out in the dazzling sunlight and pounding across the heat of the runway to the open door of the scout vessel. As Merral scrambled on board—the last of the three—the scout rolled forward under full power.

Merral staggered to a seat, his chest heaving.

Lloyd sat next to him and took off his helmet. "Welcome aboard, sir!" he gasped.

"Thanks." Merral wiped his brow. As the scout lifted off and banked sharply eastward, Merral was silent, trying to understand what had happened in the last quarter of an hour.

"Sergeant, I'm . . . confused. Where did you come from?"

"When you left, me and this guy here—" Lloyd paused while the other man—the ship's technician—saluted—"put on our armor—it's the new stuff—and waited for the signal. Then, as they say, we made our entrance."

"So you knew?"

"I was warned yesterday."

"I don't understand, Lloyd. *Is* the *Triumph* destroyed?"

"Yes, sir." His aide's expression suddenly became somber and as it did, some of the vague concerns in Merral's mind coalesced into a dreadful surmise.

"Lloyd," he said softly, and he realized that he almost dared not ask the question, "Is she . . . Perena . . . all right?"

There was no immediate answer. The other soldier suddenly turned his face away.

Lloyd rubbed away a tear. "Her ship got it too." He swallowed. "She's dead."

24

A s soon as they landed at Isterrane Vero boarded the flier. He embraced Merral and as Lloyd and the other soldier slipped away, they shed tears together.

"She played chess," Merral said, and the words sounded heavy and stupid. "She made a sacrifice." The word seemed to stick in his throat.

Vero sighed as if his heart would break. He flopped onto a seat, wiped his puffy eyes, and pulled an envelope out of his pocket. "It-its . . ." He stopped, overcome with emotion and silently thrust it into Merral's hand.

With shaking fingers Merral tore it open.

Dear Merral,

This is one of two notes I have written to you. That you are reading this one means that I have succeeded in having the Triumph destroyed. I apologize that we could not involve you in our scheme. Please forgive Vero for misleading you.

I do not wish you to grieve. I feel that the King has granted me a great privilege in allowing me to strike such a blow for him and the world I love. Be grateful. It has come to me recently that our lives are like stories. As much as we can, we must drive them to the right endings. The right ending is not always the longest one.

But even if you wish to grieve for me, I am afraid you will not have the luxury of doing so now. I believe you have been called and shaped by the Most High to lead us in battle. Now is your hour. In your grief, do not throw away what has been achieved.

I have played my bit. I charge you now to play yours.

With much love, in the King's service,

Perena

"'A way of defense offered to you. A costly way. A way that only the very bravest will take.'" Merral said. His words seemed to hang in the air. "She took that to heart."

Vero took a deep, quivering breath. "Yes. She is now beyond all temptation and sorrow. She is safely home in the Father's house with h-honor."

"She says there is work to be done," Merral said and saw an answering nod. "She . . . she also asks me to forgive you."

"For l-lying to you? Yes, we have come to trust what Azeras said. He felt sure that your mind would be probed at some stage."

"So, by making me believe she was going to find the *Rahllman's Star,* you felt we might use this unpleasant ability of the Dominion against them?"

"Yes."

"Your cunning amazes me. Well, I forgive you."

"Thank you. The baziliarch was there?"

"Yes. It's sort of a great insect, but more than that. . . . Horrid." Merral looked at the letter again. "There's no chance?"

"That she survived? None. We watched the blasts. The Guardians did a thorough job. I had hoped she would eject, but . . . she apparently rejected that option." He sighed and looked away with watery eyes.

"Lloyd killed Tinternli. There was metal in her—lots."

"Azeras reckoned she and Hazderzal were heavily modified humans."

"That fits. You know Corradon's dead too?"

"Yes. That will have implications, but military matters concern us now."

"Wait, Vero! They have the key to the Library!"

"No." Vero looked at the floor. "Another deception, I'm afraid. I felt there was a danger that Corradon might give it up. It's safe in the Library building. Harrent, the assistant librarian, has it. But that is for another day." He fixed sad eyes on Merral. "Are you up to being what you have to be?"

Merral looked at the letter he was still holding, and with great care folded it and put it safely in his jacket pocket. "Yes. I need to grieve, but I know there are things to do."

"Thank you. My friend, we need our warrior now and we need him very badly. Despite what has happened, there are still enough Krallen to destroy this world with ease. From what we know of him, Lezaroth will take command and act. Perena has prevented certain defeat, but it is still not at all clear we can win."

"Right. Okay, Vero. Let's go to the war room."

◌◌◌◌◌

As Merral entered the war room he saw smiles of relief on the faces of the men and women who occupied the desks. They rose and applauded in a slow, subdued fashion.

They need me. That's why they clapped. May God help me not to disappoint them.

Vero nudged him. "Better say something," he whispered.

"Team," Merral said, "you applaud me when you ought to applaud another. This morning Captain Lewitz destroyed the *Triumph of Sarata* and paid the price. Her action has created a foundation we need to build on for victory. By the grace of God, we're going to finish what she began." There were nods and murmurs of approval. "So let's get on with it."

Merral sat next to Vero at a spare screen. "Vero, what's the priority?"

Vero tapped the screen a couple of times before answering. "My friend, the enemy forces seem paralyzed. . . . No signs of movement, but we mustn't expect it to last. Lezaroth will see to that. So we need to hit them with the vortex blaster satellites before they disperse or get into urban concentrations where we dare not strike them."

"How soon can we use them?"

As Vero motioned a young woman engineer over, Merral noticed the length of her brown hair. *Short like Perena's.* Tears came to his eyes. He forced himself to think about what she had written: *In your grief, do not throw away what has been achieved.*

"Both VB1 and VB2 are coming into position. We can begin firing in ten minutes." The woman's voice was quiet and precise. "We have programmed them to fire simultaneously at each site to give a bigger circle of destruction. We will take out the Stepalis concentration first, then those near Maraplant and Kammart, and then, finally, the forces at Camolgi Hills."

"We can't use the vortex blasters at Langerstrand because of the hostages," Vero added.

"I see."

The engineer turned to Merral. "That will leave us a single charge in reserve in both VB1 and VB2."

"Will they work? I mean will they destroy the Krallen?"

The woman shrugged. "It's marginal. As you know, sir, they weren't designed to be weapons. They were made to sterilize areas where there was a biological problem. And they aren't supposed to be repeatedly fired."

"We have no choice. So all you need to fire is an order from me?"

"Yes."

"There are Dominion humans in those concentrations?"

"Inevitably. But not many."

I have no option. "May God have mercy on them. Fire as soon as the satellites are in position."

"Thank you, sir." She walked to a screen, tapped it, and then looked up. "Firing program initiated."

"Let me know the results." Merral turned to Vero. "What else?"

"We need to seize the *Dove of Dawn* to stop any escape. We have had a crew ready for a week at the Near Station training in secret. The pilot is Maria Brumeno—she was on the team that visited the ship—with a good assault group."

"Can it be done?"

"We think so. There is a risk, but the ship is lightly defended. If we could seize it and recover the *Rahllman's Star,* we would have two vessels with Below-Space capability."

"When can the team attack?"

"If you give the okay now, they will launch from the Near Station and attempt boarding in about twenty-four hours."

It was an easy decision. "Order the assault. If they can't take the ship, disable it."

Merral walked into the annex and called Clemant to confirm the situation: the *Triumph of Sarata* was destroyed and Perena and Corradon were dead.

Clemant was silent for a few moments, his face as blank as a porcelain doll's. Finally he said, "Two losses. Perena was brave beyond belief. And Anwar . . ." He sighed. "A great loss. But I'm glad that, in the end, he died bravely."

"Yes."

Clemant paused, as if struggling with what to say. "I should tell you that the remaining representatives have just agreed that I be made temporary coordinator for a week. The situation will then be evaluated."

"What does that mean in practice?"

"It means that, much against my will, I am charged with waging this war." Clemant paused and Merral sensed a genuine reluctance: *Vero is right. He doesn't want power.*

"As such you and Mr. V."—Clemant's face bore the faintest of frowns—"are responsible to me." He waved a hand in a reassuring manner. "Now, I've the wisdom not to interfere in your work. The only thing I would say is I want to emphasize the priority of protecting Isterrane. The administration of Farholme is so focused here that if this city falls, the planet falls."

"I'll make it a priority. Let me tell you what is happening. The Krallen positions will be attacked and the assault on the *Dove of Dawn* is being prepared."

"Splendid. I endorse both actions. Keep me informed. But, Commander, one last thing—I would like you to make a speech tonight. You do them well. Please?"

"Must I?"

Clemant gave Merral a look that he found inarguable.

"Very well," Merral replied.

"Thank you. But a small point, Commander: may I see the draft first?"

"As you wish."

⊂⊃⊂⊃⊂⊃⊂⊃

Rejecting the temptation to seek solitude and let the looming wave of grief crash over him, Merral returned to the war room. He heard the hum of voices and sensed a nervous sweaty anxiety.

Vero, his face a sickly gray, joined him and together they stared at a computer map on a far wall as a pair of glowing yellow crosshairs, one below the other, traversed a cross-hatched square labeled *Dominion Forces*.

"Satellites VB1 and VB2 are targeting Stepalis," announced the engineer with short brown hair.

The hum of voices stopped. Everyone seemed to hold his or her breath. An adjacent screen showed a satellite image of a mosaic of gray squares: neatly ordered arrays of Krallen.

How strange. Such ordered beings who produce such a bloody chaos.

"Energizing. Vortex initiated."

The crosshairs turned into small, glowing orange spirals.

The satellite image showed a dirty, turbulent mass thickening and twisting to become a massive column of swirling debris. In the core of the column, a fiery red glow dawned.

"Ground temperature at vortex center rising," the engineer intoned. "Now eight hundred, a thousand, twelve hundred Celsius; outer vortex wind speeds one fifty . . . no, two hundred kph."

The orange spirals moved eastward across the map. The screen expanded to show dirt, trees, and gleaming gray fragments whirling upward and inward into the fiery core.

Merral watched the inferno. *Is Tantaravekat avenged?*

In a minute, the glow faded.

New imagery appeared: a dozen small whirlwinds crossing a dirty, blasted wasteland.

"Enemy concentration at Stepalis destroyed," the engineer announced.

There was a cheer from somewhere.

"One down, three to go," Vero muttered.

In ten minutes, the glowing yellow crosshairs were over the concentration at Maraplant and soon the war room's occupants were rewarded by new images of destruction.

"Two down," Vero said, sounding relieved.

Ten minutes later both vortex blasters were over Kammart.

"The units that were at Tantaravekat returned here," someone said.

"Let's fry them!" said someone else.

"Here we go!" the engineer announced. "Three, two, one, fir—hold it!" An icon flashed and she tapped the screen.

Only one set of crosshairs glowed yellow.

"Uh-uh, VB2 is not responding, sir," said the engineer.

"What's the problem?" Merral asked.

"Give me a moment, sir." She tapped the screen again, then looked at Merral. "Diagnostics suggests major damage to the charge systems. They're overheated. . . . I think we've lost VB2."

Merral heard a cluck of dismay from Vero. *I have to make a decision, and fast.* "Clear the site with VB1 alone. Then move east to the Camolgi Hills concentration."

"Yes, sir."

After VB1 fired, there were more gratifying images of devastation. *Three down!*

Ten minutes later the call went up that the Camolgi Hills concentration was coming into the line of fire. Merral waited for the same pattern: the glowing yellow crosshairs followed by the wind and the inferno.

But nothing happened.

The engineer looked at Merral with a face full of disappointment. "Sir, I'm afraid VB1 is down too. Both units are now damaged beyond repair. We never touched the easternmost forces."

"Very well. At least we've taken out three of the five units." *But that still leaves massive Krallen forces at Langerstrand and the Camolgi Hills.*

All looked at him. *It's the new rule. When in doubt, look at Merral D'Avanos. But who does he look to?*

"I want a full assessment of what we face as soon as you can get it. I'll be in the annex with Vero."

o�oᴃoᴃoᴃo

While the assessment was made, Merral sat with Vero in the privacy of the annex room. He felt numb.

"Vero, I'm forcing myself to concentrate. It's not easy."

Vero sighed. "I know. But we have no choice but to act now, and act swiftly and hard."

"Very well. Look, how do we know they won't come back with another ship?"

"We don't. But Azeras says they have, so far, few such vessels. And it took them months to get here. If we can take the *Dove of Dawn* and win here, they will not know what happened to their expeditionary force. Then maybe, just maybe, they'll leave the Assembly alone."

"I hear a lot of *if*s and *maybe*s there."

"True."

"Tell me what else I need to know—all the things you wouldn't tell me earlier."

"We have got something to deal with the Krallen. Their covering—their armor—is a special energy- and impact-resistant ceramic fiber. It deflects most bullets and protects against the heat of laser or beam weapons. But there is a weakness. The right sort of molecular-tuned blade can cut through it."

"A blade? Against those things?"

"Yes. The blade edge parts the fibers. Once it's below the surface, you short out the circuitry."

"Is this just theory?"

There was a flicker of something that on another day might have grown into a smile. "We lured the ambassadors' Krallen pack into a trap. It was tough, but we got enough to experiment on. It works."

"And we have such blades?"

"For all the regulars at least. The moment the *Triumph* was destroyed we started issuing them—simple noncollapsible blades like swords. We couldn't tell you, of course, in case they found out and changed the composition."

"Blades—swords? It works?"

"Their engineering majors on strength and power; it doesn't understand subtlety. Their materials technology is inferior to ours."

"Yes, we've seen that before. But will it work on the battlefield?"

"That's the sixty-four-million-dollar question."

"Dollar?"

"Sorry. Another old phrase. The vital question. You can watch the demonstrations. I expect we'll know very shortly." But Vero sounded unsure. "The blades are being issued as we speak. We have tested the armor too. It does resist Krallen teeth or claws."

There was a knock at the door and a man came in with a sheet of paper.

"The situation report, sir."

ﾍﾟﾍﾟﾍﾟﾍﾟﾍﾟ

Five minutes later, Merral sat back in his chair, his numbed mind trying to summarize the situation. There was much to give thanks for. In addition to the massive destruction Perena had achieved, the Dominion forces at Stepalis, Maraplant, and Kammart had now been completely destroyed. Around sixty thousand Krallen, at least a hundred landing vessels, and vast amounts of equipment had been turned into glowing fragments. Yet, despite this, large Dominion forces remained—an estimated twenty thousand Krallen at Langerstrand and the same number at the Camolgi Hills.

"Well, things are clearer now," Vero said, as he stared at the map. "Azeras says they will go for the heart—the crushing blow. That means Isterrane."

Merral gazed at the map on the table. *What had the ancient soldiers called it? A "pincer movement"—that was the phrase.*

"Yes. The forces to the northeast of us could either strike Halmacent City or Ranapert or simply avoid them and go straight to Isterrane. They could be here in a day." Merral moved his finger to the left. "And to our west, the Langerstrand forces could head toward us along the road. Unless they are stopped, they could be here in two hours."

"That's about it," Vero said. His face was grim.

"This is what I propose," Merral said, drawing an arc with his finger-tip just east of Halmacent City. "The Eastern Regiment stays put. I will get Frankie Thuron to keep building the defenses there so they can resist any Krallen push out of this Camolgi Hills site. He may be able to hold them."

Vero nodded. "Frankie has the only artillery pieces we were able to make in time. There are three of them, but they make a difference."

"Yes. Well, he will need them. Now let's look west of Isterrane." Merral pointed to where the ridges of the Varrend Tablelands dominated the left-hand part of the map. "I want to get Leroy Makunga to bring almost all the soldiers of the Western Regiment to Isterrane to boost the defenses around the city. Leave only a hundred in Varrend City. You agree?"

"Makes sense."

"Good. Now for the hard bit. What we do with the forces left at Langerstrand? You agree they must come east on the Tezekal Gorge route?"

"Yes. They could strike north from Langerstrand and hit the Western Trunk Road, but the ground's very rough—cliff after cliff. The Krallen might do it, but there will be support vehicles. So they will take the road."

"We agree. So, by universal agreement, the place to stop them is Tezekal Gorge. Once past Tezekal there is nothing to stop them before Isterrane. We may blow the bridge over the Walderand, but that will only delay them for a few hours."

Vero nodded.

"Good, so I'm going to shift almost all the soldiers of the Central Regiment to Tezekal. There are already a lot there. But, Vero, I don't like the odds. They could be well over twenty to one against us."

Vero grunted. "A bit better, but not much. I have already ordered more irregulars in. There are a-about a thousand there preparing for guerrilla war-fare, mostly on the slopes of the Hereza Crags and at the edge of the Edelcet Marshes."

"That will be a help. The two attack fliers are at Isterrane. I think I'll have them relocated to Tezekal with the bombs. Any other suggestions?"

"Yes—take the initiative. Order Lezaroth and the Dominion forces to surrender by nine tomorrow."

"What good will that do?"

Vero gave the weakest of smiles. "Probably none. But it will show them we're not afraid. And it appeals to my sense of the dramatic."

"Very well. But do we have any hope?"

There was a long pause. "Early this morning, I would have said very little. But Perena . . . has given us a chance." He felt silent and Merral felt that grief had invaded the room.

Eventually Vero looked up. "But, my friend, we have to admit that frankly it's not promising. And Azeras warns us that if this baziliarch joins in the fighting, we are in trouble. As ever we must do our best and rely on the grace of the Most High."

He stood. "I'm certain that we'll face them tomorrow at Tezekal Gorge. I want to go there as soon as I can. I want to take Azeras and Betafor."

"I thought you didn't trust her."

"I don't—or not entirely—but it's a risk worth taking. It has emerged that she has the ability to listen in to transmissions. The Dominion messages are encrypted so she can't understand them, but she can make a good guess as to the sort of thing they are saying. She will serve us; she knows what side her bread is buttered on."

"I thought she didn't eat. . . . Oh, I see."

"Never mind. Anyway, we have a case to transport her in. The plan is to take her hidden in this case and lock her in a room with a lot of receiving equipment. Incidentally, only a few of my closest aides know about Azeras and Betafor. But their input has been invaluable and it is vital that the Dominion doesn't realize that we have their aid. Assuming, that is, the baziliarch hasn't passed on the news about Azeras."

"Very well. So what would you suggest that I do?"

"You? Sit down, pray, and write that speech." Vero looked at his watch. "I wouldn't come out to Tezekal tonight unless there is any action. Get the best night's sleep you can here and come out by dawn. I'll have armor for you there. Remember, Lezaroth will target you if he can."

"Very well. I need to talk to Anya."

"Yes, Anya." Vero rubbed his forehead with his knuckle in an expression of sad perplexity. "She knew what her sister planned to do. She's already out at Tezekal."

"Was that wise to send her there?"

"Try stopping her. She's part of the intelligence team. She has a job to do and she will do it. And maybe action will ease the mourning."

They looked at each other.

Merral sighed. "In that, she isn't alone."

○○○○○

And after Vero left him, Merral consulted Clemant, then sent a message to the Langerstrand base.

"Fleet-Commander Lezaroth, this is Commander Merral D'Avanos. You have lost the *Triumph of Sarata* and most of your ground forces. We are surrounding your remaining forces. We give you the opportunity to surrender. We promise mercy to you and all those others who are human. You have until 0900 hours tomorrow Central Menaya Time to surrender. Should you begin further hostilities, we will return fire."

There was no reply.

Merral tried to write his speech, but images of Perena kept disrupting his train of thought. Eventually it was done and Clemant approved the wording. Merral wondered if Clemant had ever considered making changes or whether asking to approve it was just a way of making the point that he was in control.

Merral gave the speech live. He began by introducing himself and outlining the events of the last few days, from the appearance of the *Triumph of Sarata* to the seizing of hostages at Langerstrand and the massacre at Tantaravekat. "Accordingly, it was decided that an act of war had been committed and that we were entitled to fight back. This morning, Central Menaya Time, Captain Perena Lewitz lured the *Triumph of Sarata* into the firing zone of the Guardian satellites. The result was, as she knew was probable, the utter destruction of both vessels. Captain Lewitz was a close friend of mine, and her loss is deeply felt. In whatever lies ahead of us as a world, I would like you to remember Captain Lewitz's example.

"At the time of Captain Lewitz's sacrificial tactic, Representative Anwar Corradon and I were trying to negotiate with the head of the Dominion forces at Langerstrand. Enraged by the loss of their ship, they attacked us personally. Representative Corradon fought back heroically and was slain by Ambassador Tinternli, who was herself killed by an Assembly rescue force. Since then, using improvised weapons, we have eliminated many of the Dominion's attack forces.

"Nevertheless, many remain. We know that the enemy has already landed on Menaya tens of thousands of four-legged synthetic life-forms called Krallen. While these are intelligent and cunning, they are only imitators of life, rather than living things. I just want to say here that although they are deadly, they can be defeated. They deserve no mercy and should be shown none. In addition to the use of these Krallen, we expect other forces to be used against us.

"We have given the Dominion forces a chance to surrender. In the next few hours, we expect land battles to begin between our forces and theirs. Whether you are a member of the regular forces, what we call the irregulars, or simply an ordinary civilian, all we ask is that you play your part with courage and determination." He paused. "I wish that I could predict with confidence that we will win quickly and easily over these forces. I cannot. Our battle here is part of the long war against evil. Whether we win or lose this battle, we can be assured that this war will ultimately be won. It may be, in the wisdom and foreknowledge of the Most High, that we will lose here. But whether we win or lose, let us fight in such a way that, until the very end of the age, men and women's hearts will fill with pride when they hear the name Farholme. . . . God bless you all."

Minutes after the broadcast, Vero called Merral. "My friend, that was magnificent. I watched it with the soldiers here. I tell you there are people who would follow you to the gates of hell."

"I'm glad they found it encouraging. I needed to encourage myself."

"Well done. Stay safe tonight. There's nothing happening at Langerstrand."

Later that evening, Merral lay on his mattress in the annex and tried to sleep. For a long time though, sleep would not come and instead, he lay awake thinking of Perena and feeling sad.

ロ◯ロ◯ロ

"What happened in there, Ambassador?" Lezaroth's voice rang around the tiny room. He continued to pace around the seated figure of Hazderzal. "I asked that they be killed! Instead, *Tinternli* was killed and *he* escaped!" There was no need to spell out who *he* was.

The two armed guards on either side of the sealed door stared rigidly ahead.

"I was . . . overwhelmed by events," Hazderzal said with a tremor in his voice.

"Ambassador, you are now surplus to requirements." *And I have more pressing demands on my time.*

Lezaroth noted that his guards had turned and looked at him in anticipation of an order. "Throw him to the baziliarch."

"You wouldn't!" Hazderzal's eyes were wide. "I'm a friend of the lord-emperor!"

"You *were*."

Lezaroth watched as a screaming Hazderzal was dragged away. *I must remember to amend the account so that D'Avanos's men killed both ambassadors.*

He called up the wallscreen map of Farholme. This morning's loss had been appalling. Even if blame was not going to be attached to him—he would make sure of that—he needed to salvage ultimate victory out of the debacle. But the battle was far from lost. He was protected from attack by hostages, he still had vast forces at his command, and the opposition was very badly armed. But he could afford no more slipups. The Farholmers had already shown that they were tricky opponents.

Lezaroth had a long-standing reluctance to use extra-physical forces. They could be so unreliable. (Hadn't they promised the lord-emperor that Hanax would play a great role?) But now he had little choice. He would use the Baziliarch on the battlefield.

Lezaroth pondered the map for some time. *I will attack tomorrow and push straight to this world's capital. I should take it by nightfall.*

He began to draw up his plans.

ᴏᴏᴏᴏᴏ

Merral and Lloyd boarded the flier at an already busy Isterrane Airport just as the first golden rays of dawn struck the highest towers.

The rear of the flier was filled with boxes. *Armor and new blades,* Merral surmised. The thought troubled him. *We're still equipping our troops, yet battle may begin within hours.*

As she waited for clearance to take off, the unfamiliar pilot turned her head to Merral. "I knew Perena, Commander. I'm very proud to have known her."

"Thank you," Merral said, a lump forming in his throat. "Thank you very much." He looked away, unable to speak. *Yesterday, the shock of Perena's death was so great that it did not allow for grief. Today, it has worn off enough for me to feel the bite of the loss.*

They landed at a new earth strip just east of Tezekal Ridge within walking distance of the village. The early morning sunlight cast long, sharp shadows and made the rocks of the ridge and the high slopes of Mount Adaman seem even more jagged and broken.

Merral stood by the flier as soldiers unloaded the equipment. He looked around, noting that it was already warm and that they had flattened olive groves to make the runway, on which already half a dozen vessels were lined up including, ominously, two white hospital ships. Beyond them were two small aircraft with red cylinders stacked under their long wings that Merral recognized as the attack fliers. Between these and the village was a sprawling tented encampment seething with activity. No one strolled. Everyone jogged or strode with urgent paces.

At the edge of the runway, a slight, familiar figure wearing a brown jerkin and dark glasses beckoned Merral over. It was Vero.

As he walked over, on impulse, Merral stopped and stooped down to touch the crushed remains of an olive tree. He stroked the dying shrivelled leaves with his fingers.

"Trees can be replanted," he said with a soft sigh.

Lloyd, standing at his side, nodded.

He understands.

Vero extended a hand of greeting. "Welcome, Commander. How are you?"

"I feel as if something has been amputated from me. And I can only imagine how you feel, Vero. I really don't know what to say."

"T-there's nothing you need to say." There was a terrible sadness in his words. "But we have work to do."

"And I will do it. Any news from Langerstrand?"

"Nothing so far. The intelligence team here is keeping a careful eye on matters."

"Who's in the team? You said Anya?"

"Anya, Azeras, and Betafor. And we have a dozen watchers out on the Hereza Crags and even a few on Mount Adaman. Azeras thinks the Dominion will wait until after the deadline to move. That gives us an hour or so. T-time for you to get geared up. And Luke Tenerelt is here. He was doing the rounds of the troops when I last saw him."

"I'm glad he's here. I think we'll need him."

They walked along narrow paths lined with stone walls into the village. Birds hopped from branch to branch; brown lizards stared at them and then scuttled away across stones, sunlight glistened on fading dew. *Life goes on.* The idea gave him little comfort.

A tall man wearing green armor and a helmet waited for them at the top of the steps. Zak Larraine. He had a sword at his belt.

"Sir!" Zak snapped, throwing his gloved hand tight against his helmet in the crispest of salutes and somehow managing to stamp his boot heels together on the ground. "Welcome to Tezekal HQ, sir. Colonel Lanier is expecting you in the command room."

Merral found the enthusiasm in Zak's voice irritating. "I wasn't aware you were here, Colonel Larraine," he said, returning the salute with what he knew was a much slacker gesture. Somehow military protocol seemed less important than it once had.

"Sorry, sir. It's just that training is over. And, well, I didn't want to miss a battle. You know me." Zak smiled.

"Yes, I do. Well, I doubt you will be disappointed today, sadly."

Merral read incomprehension in Zak's eyes.

"I don't think it sad, sir. These things need thrashing."

The incomprehension is mutual, Merral decided, but said nothing in reply.

Zak's expression brightened. "Sir, Colonel Lanier has given me authority to command the troops on the south side of the gorge. I'm going to be with them now to make sure we're as well prepared as we can be. Is that okay, sir?"

"Yes. It's fine by me."

Zak saluted again and, almost bounding down the steps, headed toward the gorge.

The headquarters was a white-walled house that had been hastily altered. The doors had been removed from their hinges and the glass taken from the windows. Outside, dusty soldiers piled up earth banks.

The living room was now the control room. A fine set of windows had once looked west over the marsh. Now though, the only view was of an embankment beneath a narrow strip of sky.

Inside the room five men, all dressed in the new armor, but with their helmets off, stood around new tables. On one wall hung a full-length screen with a hazy aerial image of Langerstrand. All the desks bore smaller screens. Wires and fiber-optic cables were taped or patched to the floor and walls. Merral felt the whole setup showed signs of being put together in extreme haste.

There were welcomes, introductions, and offers of coffee. Two of the men, Captain Tremutar and Colonel Leopold Lanier, Merral already knew; the other three were aides.

Colonel Lanier was in his late fifties. His silver hair, tanned, leathery face, and thin, rather stylish mustache made him look more like an elegant uncle than a soldier.

He gestured at the screens. "Well now, where shall I begin?" he said in a gentle and leisured voice. "We get all the sensor images here. We have a satellite overhead, some remote cameras mounted on the ridge tops, and we get some images from our soldiers on the peninsula. Everything possible's linked with fiber-optical cabling so it can't be intercepted or interfered with. And Mr. V. feeds us information from his irregs and the intelligence team. So I guess we know what's happening." He stroked his mustache thoughtfully and turned dark brown eyes at Merral. "And, so far . . . well . . . nothing *is* happening."

Merral found the colonel's unflustered manner reassuring. "Tell me about our troop deployment."

The wallscreen changed to show a detailed map of the gorge overlain with various color squares and dots forming a horseshoe shape facing west.

"Well, we've put defenses at several levels along both sides of the gorge. The sniper team—that's under Captain Karita Hatiran—takes the top levels. Then we have a level with mortars, and then finally, the lowest level of soldiers with guns and these new swords."

The colonel's face wrinkled in thought and Merral saw him glance at Vero. *He's not sure about the swords. I sympathize.*

"But, Commander, it's not easy. No, it truly ain't." Colonel Lanier gave his mustache another stroke. "We're outnumbered and we don't know how these things fight. I saw them briefly at Fallambet and I didn't care for them there. Not one bit. And there's a lot more here. A lot more."

Over the next ten minutes, as they looked at the defensive plans, Merral became increasingly uncomfortable. It was not just that the odds were bad, but that there were too many unknowns. Despite the polite words the men made about the new armor and the blades, they were clearly unsure of their value.

Colonel Lanier seemed to sum up the mood with his slow words. "Commander, we know we are effectively the last line of defense. We'll do our best and you can be sure the Assembly will be proud of us. But, frankly . . ." He looked thoughtful and fingered his mustache. "Well, I guess it doesn't look good."

"Colonel, I find it hard to disagree with you. But we are going to fight and fight hard. And let's hang on to faith and hope."

◯◯◯◯◯

Vero led Merral and Lloyd across the road into a long house with closed shutters.

An armed guard sitting on a chair inside the door motioned them in.

Vero gestured to a door from behind which could be heard the sound of urgent discussions. "That's the irregular control room. Similar, but more informal, and we have better coffee. But there's no the time for that. Follow me."

At the far end of a corridor, Vero pointed to another door. "Anya's in here," he whispered. "I'll leave you for a few minutes." And with that, Lloyd and he walked away.

Inside Merral found Anya, wearing trousers and a faded T-shirt, sitting staring at a large screen on which was an image of the Langerstrand compound. She seemed tired and older and her eyes looked puffy. She turned, saw Merral, and rose to her feet.

They hugged but her embrace was cold and rigid.

"I'm sorry," he said.

"Yeah," she replied, looking past him as if he didn't exist.

"I don't know what to say," he said. "It's . . . an appalling loss. But it was heroic."

"I don't care about the heroic. My sister is dead. And it hurts!"

Anya sat down, glared at the screen, and switched it off in a single sharp, angry move. "It's all falling apart, Merral," she said without looking at him, and he saw that her eyes were damp again. "I get hurt by you; I lose my sister; my world becomes a war zone. I never knew that life *could* hurt so much."

Merral sat down on the edge of a table. "We have all had losses," he said, and realized that it sounded pathetic.

"But why me?" Anya asked. "Why, after generations of people living happy, untroubled, and worthwhile lives, does it all have to happen to *me*?"

"You know I can't answer that, Anya." Merral leaned forward and stared at the floor. "Life's like playing in a concert: you get given your music, and you have to play it as best you can. I wish, as well as you, that the Almighty had given me an easier part to play, but I can't change it. I have to do what I can. Can I tell you what your sister said?"

"Go on," she said but the expression on her face seem to say, "If you must."

"She wrote something I now know by heart. 'It has come to me recently that our lives are like stories. As much as we can, we must drive them to the right endings.' That's what I mean."

"How typical of my sister! How wonderfully, poetically, noble. Well, I want a rewrite of *my* story." Anya's tone was defiant and bitter.

I am unprepared for this. I expected grief, but not this withering resentment.

"Who are you angry with?" Merral asked, as softly as he could.

There was a taut silence.

"With me, with God, or with Perena?"

When Anya shrugged her shoulders, he suddenly wanted to hug her.

There was silence.

Then she turned to him. "Do you really care about her? Or was that all it was, a heroic gesture?"

Her words stung him. "I do care."

"You are a commander. Do commanders have hearts? Or do you let them harden inside those uniforms? You give orders and men and women die and if they do it well, you say, 'How heroic.'"

"That's hardly fair! I was quite unaware of Perena's action. And while it was heroic, it is a loss, a personal one. I feel it."

Anya scowled, then turned the screen back on. "Commander, I have a job to do. That job is to understand the Krallen and give advice on how to deal with them. I'm the expert on them. I have worked with them since the beginning of the FDU. Be assured that I will do my job."

Merral stared at her, then, in near despair, left the room in search of Vero. He found his friend talking with someone at the end of the corridor, but when Vero saw Merral he slipped away and came over. "Bad, eh?" he asked with sympathy in his voice.

"Yes. She's very bitter. Very angry. I think she needs help. Vero, do we need her here? I think she'd be better off elsewhere."

Vero bit his lip. "We need her here. She *is* good on the Krallen. She has to fight her way out of her mental state."

"Very well."

"Look, time's running out. Come and see Betafor."

Merral followed Vero to a basement, past another guard into a small, windowless room.

Betafor sat crouched on the floor in a corner, a string of wires running inside her jacket, a set of headphones on her head. On either side of her tunic, a Lamb and Stars emblem gleamed.

As he entered, she turned her large, dark gray eyes to him. "Commander, how nice to see you. May I express my . . . condolences? Although I am programmed to express sympathy, I can say that, with Captain Lewitz, my feelings ran deeper. She was a remarkable person with an . . . affinity for the Allenix."

"It was a real loss to us all. It has been a long time since we met." *And when we did you had just attempted to murder Azeras. But we need all the help we can get.* "How are you?"

"That is not a question that has much relevance. Allenix units do not undergo the inevitable and unfortunate metabolic fluctuations and degradations that biological organisms do."

"No, of course." In another corner stood a large white rectangular case, like an oversized piece of luggage, with a handle and wheels. *Yes, with her legs folded under her, she could fit in that.*

"My travel case," Betafor said in her cold, lifeless voice as she caught his gaze.

"So I gather. Do you mind traveling inside a box?"

"I can adapt. Allenix units do not suffer from . . . claustrophobia."

"No, I suppose not. And the prospect of battle here doesn't perturb you?"

Here Merral felt there was a definite hesitation and he saw that her irises had contracted.

"I would prefer to be elsewhere. But I am bound to you. I think you will find that I am of use."

"I hope I'm not interrupting your monitoring of the enemy."

Betafor gave her strange pseudosmile. "You forget Commander, that I can multitask. Your failure to handle more than one sensory input at any one time is a major limitation to your species. As I speak to you, I am listening to the Dominion on three wavebands. It is just the spillover of their communications."

"And what do you hear?"

"Yesterday, they were in total confusion. Today, things are different. I think they are preparing to move. There are . . . firm orders being given. I will let you know when I hear anything more definite."

"Betafor, can we win?"

Betafor hesitated. "That is a hard question, Commander. It all comes down to . . . attrition."

"Attrition?"

"Yes. With the irregulars, you have a total of two and a half thousand men here. They have ten times that number. So you have to kill ten Krallen for every one soldier you lose. Those are . . . challenging odds."

Merral tried—and failed—to read any expression in her eyes. "You make it sound very simple."

"It is. We are less swayed by emotion than you. Allenix units see facts. We do not have what you call 'wishful thinking.'"

"It's hard to differentiate between wishful thinking and hope."

"True. That is why we have neither."

ⓄⓄⓄⓄⓄ

Five minutes later, as Vero watched, Merral fitted himself with armor. Merral lifted the green jacket out of a holdall that bore his name and held it up, marveling at its lightness. The chest piece, barely a few millimeters thick, was rigid. He tapped it and heard it ring. The sleeves, in contrast, were a softer, more flexible version of the same material. Gloves in the same material as the sleeves, but with roughened palms, protected the hands and wrists. Merral pulled the jacket on and then twisted within it until it was comfortable. Finally, he closed the flexible collar so that his neck was protected.

"Impressive," he said. "Very different to the primitive protection we had at Fallambet. You barely feel you are wearing anything."

"Most of the soldiers have to make adjustments to the jackets," Vero said. "But they fit well enough."

Merral decided against wearing the gloves immediately and tucked them into his belt. He looked at the helmet, struck by the way the brow tapered into a noseguard and how the sides projected out to protect the cheekbones.

He lowered the helmet onto his head, letting the fine mesh flaps hang over his ears, and adjusted the strap. "Does it work?"

"Yes. Against the standard slashing action. But there's a weakness with the helmet that's unavoidable. The Krallen can put their claws together to form a point—like a chisel." Vero clustered the fingers of his right hand tightly. "Like this. They extend their nails and then punch." He jabbed his hand forward. "If they get the eye sockets . . ." He shrugged. "You're dead."

"Thanks for the warning," Merral said, trying not to think of what had been described.

He ran a finger over the embossed Lamb and Stars emblem on the front of the armor jacket, somehow reassured by all it stood for. *I must keep that central. It is the Assembly that we fight for and the Assembly's Lord who will defend us.*

Finally, Merral turned to a slender box on the table. A long black handle protruded out from a plain scabbard of spun synthetic. He pulled out the sword. It was a meter long, perfectly straight with razor sharp edges on both sides. It gleamed softly in the dull light of the room. Cautiously, Merral swung it, feeling that with the slight weight of the battery in the handle, it was well balanced.

"There are tricks," Vero said. "The main one is that the blade must hit at absolute right angles to cut through the ceramic. Angled blows are useless. And body or head blows are the only ones that kill them. If you have the time—and are so inclined—you can chop their legs off one by one. The battery is on as long as you hold the handle, but only the tips of the blade are live. That voltage won't hurt too much anyway."

Merral swept the blade again.

"And they need to have their heads crushed or necks severed afterward to avoid them being repaired. But we have teams with hammers and axes."

Merral returned the sword to the scabbard, attached it to his belt, then turned to a mirror on the wall. His image riveted him. *I look like some ancient warrior. What have I become?* "The old times *are* back."

"Sadly so," Vero said.

○○○○○

Ten minutes later, Merral stood in front of the command center looking down past the dark jagged rocks with their smattering of trees to the defenses at the mouth of the gorge. Beyond the gorge, the moist green and blue flatness of the Edelcet Marshes stretched out, ending sharply against the rearing brown and gray cliffs and bluffs edging the Hereza Crags. Beyond the marsh lay the low beige smear of the Langerstrand Peninsula.

As he gazed at the scene, he could hear the noises of hasty preparation around him: shouted orders, running feet, the clatter of equipment.

It was already warm and the faint southward breeze off the mountain had little cooling effect. Already the air seethed and flickered above the hot rocks. *It will be a scorching day, and cruelly so in the gorge.*

When Luke Tenerelt joined him, they embraced. Merral noted that the chaplain had shunned armor and that his uniform was sweat stained.

"Glad to have you here, very glad," Luke said, stepping back to scrutinize Merral. "So beneath all the armor of war, how are you?"

"To be honest, Luke, I wish I were someone else, somewhere else. Is that a sin?"

Luke shook his head. "Not as long as such thoughts don't make you duck your responsibilities. But, if I may ask, how are you handling Perena's loss?"

There was a bench under the shade of a spreading mulberry tree. They sat down and for ten minutes Merral talked of his feelings about Perena and his fears for the day ahead while Luke listened.

"I think," Merral said finally, "what I have realized from Perena's death is this." He paused, finding the right words elusive. "I had hoped, Luke, deep down, that death and suffering would miss me. I believed that, although there might be deaths, I and my family and my closest friends would be immune. Yesterday, I learned that this is not so. This war will cost us all dear."

Luke gave a nod of slow agreement. "A wise realization. One of the oldest and most subtle heresies is the idea that evil can be defeated cheaply."

Merral said nothing.

Luke pointed to the base of the gorge where tiny figures of men and women moved with feverish activity and sighed. "I may need to be reminded of that myself today." He looked up. "Duty calls, Commander. I have many people to see. But let's pray, shall we?"

ꝏꝏꝏ

A few moments later, Merral's diary chimed under his armor jacket. He fumbled for it and looking at the screen saw a wide, pale, and distorted face peering at him from an odd angle.

It was Jorgio. There were beads of sweat on his face and his lips trembled.

"Mr. Merral, I can feel something." His voice was husky, as if strained almost to breaking point. "Something to the east. Something stirring."

"What sort of thing?"

"It's big. It watches. It's full of hate."

"Thanks for the warning, my friend. Oh, and yesterday, were you praying for us?"

Jorgio's lips trembled again. "I was. I knew there was a battle and that the enemy had to see some things and be blinded to others. And I reckon he did. But I didn't know as Captain Perena was involved. And . . ." Words seemed to fail him.

"She won, my old friend. She won."

There was a dull nod as if Jorgio didn't trust himself to say anything.

"But keep praying, Jorgio. We will be fighting today."

"I will. But remember, Mr. Merral, you won't be alone."

The screen went blank.

Merral was about to say something to Luke when he heard hurried footsteps behind him. It was Vero and his face bore a troubled expression.

"My friend, we need you. There's activity on the peninsula. The Krallen are moving."

25

Colonel Lanier was staring at the wallscreen when Merral and Vero entered.

"Commander," he said, two fingers rolling a spindly end of his mustache, "the word from the team on the peninsula is that the Krallen seem to be taking position behind the compound gates. There are also unexplained noises within the tower."

Merral looked at the time. Eight-fifty-five: five minutes before the deadline expired. "Any news of the hostages?"

"None. We guess they're around the base of the tower."

Thirty people, including Isabella. As he thought of her, a potent mixture of emotions came to mind: concern, sympathy, the charred remains of affection, and a good deal of guilt. *I really should have warned her.* Realizing everyone was looking expectantly at him, he pushed those thoughts away to be dealt with later.

"Colonel, my guess is that in ten minutes or less the Krallen will move toward us. I don't think we want the peninsula team to engage them. Let's pull them back now."

The colonel hesitated.

Vero, who had been listening to something on his earpiece, nodded. "Colonel, the word from my intelligence team is that the enemy is about to move out. I agree with the commander. Get them back to the gorge. We can use them here. When the Krallen come under the crags, the irregs will attack them. They don't want our people in the way."

"Well, then I agree," the colonel said slowly and turned to an aide. "Order them back as fast as they can."

Merral asked where he could get a good view and was led through the opening that until recently had been the door to the patio, up a ladder onto the flat roof.

At the far end a tall man dressed in the same pale green armor Merral wore stood under a hastily erected awning, staring westward through a tripod-mounted fieldscope. At his feet lay a slender tube.

As Merral gazed in the same direction, he could see just below him men still excavating positions. *"Digging in," the soldiers of the old wars called it.*

"Welcome, Commander," said a familiar voice.

Merral turned to see that the man in the armor was Azeras. Merral glanced around but only Lloyd was in earshot. "Greetings, Sarudar."

"And you, Commander. You had a day of successes yesterday." He bowed. "I honor the name of Captain Lewitz. I owe her memory an apology. I thought she was all words. Instead I find that she was brave and skilled."

"She is both an example and a loss, Sarudar."

"I am sure." He shook his head. "However many people you lose, the pain stays the same."

His tone tells me he knows that from experience. "Sadly, I can imagine that."

Merral noticed that Azeras did not bear the Lamb and Stars emblem on his armor. Yet apart from that detail—which was easy to miss—he found there was little to distinguish him from anyone else in Tezekal. *Has he become like us, or are we now like him?*

"Sarudar, you talked of yesterday, but what of today?"

"Indeed." Azeras's worn face darkened. "I am not optimistic. I have never heard of a victory being won against such odds."

"I see."

"You want my private opinion, Commander?" Azeras drew closer to Merral. "Most of these men and women—and possibly all of them—will not be alive tomorrow. It's simple mathematics. You are outnumbered ten to one. Yes, you have the blades—very fine—and the armor—very fine too. But it's the sheer numbers that will do for you. And they will take no captives. They have enough already. And if the thing in the tower comes out, it could be over soon. But look."

He pointed to where far away, just below the Hereza Crags, a small convoy of a dozen vehicles came into view along the road.

The party that had been watching Langerstrand; at least they've made it safely here. Merral looked at the distant peninsula beyond them, then turned back to Azeras. "I know the baziliarch's name. It is Lord Nar-Barratri."

Azeras scowled and made a circular gesture with his forefinger. "Ah. I suspected as much. It's not a name you mention. It's unlucky."

"I'll take that risk."

"You may think again on that. But let me warn you: if he comes here and opens his wings to let the darkness in, all your discipline and all your hopes will crumble in bare minutes." Azeras had the look of a haunted man.

"I am sorry. I wish I had some hope, but even with the best troops the True Freeborn ever had, we would find this too much. He can't be resisted. If he appears, you'll feel that defeat is certain."

"Sarudar, I hear your words. I do not treat them lightly. But we must resist. We have no choice. But I have a question for you: if this defense is so doomed, why do you stay?"

"I have made a promise and I will keep it. Fate writes our days for us. We must all die somewhere, and here on a world of sun and air and sea is as good as anywhere. I have brought my banner." He gestured to the tube at his feet. "And, at the last, I will fight under it."

"I disagree with you on how things work. But you can leave if you wish. I am happy to release you from your promise."

"Thank you. But that would be a matter of cowardice and dishonor. And Fate cannot be so easily cheated. A man's destiny cannot be dodged by running. But don't worry, I have shared my doubts with no else. I will fight, and you'll find that I'll stand firm—until death, if needed."

"Thank you, Sarudar. I can but pray you are wrong."

Lloyd, who had walked over to peer into the fieldscope screen, suddenly beckoned Merral over. "Better take a look, sir."

The image on the screen lurched from the effects of vibration and haze, but it was all too easy to see that the high gates in the fence had been flung open wide; through them a gray horde of creatures poured out.

Merral glanced at his watch—five past nine. *I hope someone is logging all this for the historians,* came the irrelevant thought. He looked back at the screen, now seeing not just the Krallen, but a half dozen dark objects flying leisurely above the gray flood. *Slitherwings!* He shuddered.

He swiftly made his way down to the command room where the imagery compiled from two remote cameras was much clearer. Merral's first impression was of colors: a gray fluid moving slowly on the black strip of road between the blues and greens of the wetland and the brown rocky ground of the peninsula. But a closer look showed a more troubling reality: a vast army moving with extraordinary precision along the road out of the Langerstrand base.

The Krallen marched in neat lines, twelve abreast, on the road. Even closely spaced their ranks were too wide for the road and the outer members of the lines were sometimes reduced to running in order to keep up. Within the hundreds of lines of gray forms were other moving objects. There were four with angled batteries of tubes on their backs that strode forward on six legs.

"What are those?" Merral asked Vero.

"They're what we might call cannon insects—mobile artillery—with about a kilometer range. We'll want to try and take those out."

Merral pointed to where long articulated cylinders on stumpy legs marched forward.

"Those?" Vero looked around. "They are . . ." He stopped as if suddenly aware that everyone was listening to him. "Our guess is that they are Krallen repair units. They rebuild Krallen that have been damaged."

"How many Krallen are coming?" Merral asked, trying to keep the alarm out of his voice. "And what's their estimated arrival time?"

"The column is around three kilometers long," a young man at a desk said. "Say sixteen to eighteen thousand. The rest must still be in the compound. At their current speed, they will be here within the hour."

Colonel Lanier shook his head and tugged at his mustache as he looked at Merral. "You know, Commander, I *really* don't care for those numbers."

Someone tugged at Vero's sleeve and gestured to the screen. "Mr. V., what are those things?"

Almost at the very back of the column, five black vertical cylinders mounted on sturdy insectlike legs marched along amid the Krallen.

"Those are the human soldiers in armored shells," said Vero. "They'll coordinate the attack on the ground."

Merral stared again at the long gray snake of the convoy as it made its unhurried way along the edge of the peninsula. He turned to Vero. "I think now is the time to use the fliers."

"Agreed. Get in first before the irregs attack."

Merral stepped into a corner of the room to contact the airstrip.

"Launch the two attack fliers," he ordered the officer at the strip. "The enemy have mobile artillery—on six legs, like insects. Make those a priority." He paused and took a breath before adding reluctantly, "And there are men at the rear of the column in armored shells. I'm afraid we need to make them targets."

He then returned to where everyone watched the screen.

The front line of the column was beginning to turn round the margin of the marsh and head eastward along the road at the foot of the Hereza Crags.

Eastward to Tezekal; eastward to Isterrane.

"The fliers are taking off now. They'll be over the target in five minutes," came a message from a desk.

Merral made his way to the roof. Now, even with the unaided eye, the column was easily visible: an ash gray cancer nibbling its way toward them at the foot of the high crags, sending birds flying upward with its passage.

As Merral watched, he heard the fliers take off, heading east to gain height in a spiral. The first flier banked to the west, lined itself up above the village, and began a dive toward the head of the Krallen convoy.

Barely a hundred meters above the ground, two tiny objects fell from the flier, striking into the middle of the column and exploding with bright yellow flashes. As untidy flames bubbled skyward from the ground, a neater jet of red flame erupted upward and struck the flier.

The flier tilted, began to trail smoke, and plunged toward the marsh. Just before it struck a patch of brown reeds, there was a small white puff of smoke at the front of the flier as the pilot ejected. As the noise of the explosions echoed around the hills, Merral saw a tiny set of rotors extend from the top of the seat and the pilot flew away toward them.

The second flier tried a different tactic, circling wide over the marsh and attacking from the rear. The convoy was ripped by two massive explosions, but again there was answering fire. A fragment flew off the flier's wing; it dipped and then took a nosedive into the lines of Krallen below. This time the pilot didn't eject.

With a heavy heart, Merral walked back down into the house. There was a subdued attitude in the room and Merral felt that people looked away from him. He gazed at the wallscreen. The column had stopped and fires burned along its length. But even as he watched, the Krallen ranks began to re-form, like some plastic substance. Small brown creatures could be seen scuttling about collecting fragments and dragging them back to the articulated cylinders. Above the lines, the slitherwings banked in slow circles.

"So what's the result?" Merral asked.

The young man at the desk barely looked up. "Several hundred Krallen destroyed, many permanently. One, perhaps two, of those cannon insects disabled. Perhaps two of the men killed."

Damage. Useful damage, but far from enough.

On the screen, the column started to move again.

Vero, who had been listening to his earpiece, nudged Merral. "Any second now," he whispered. "We mined the road."

Suddenly there was a dazzling flash of yellow light on the screen as a massive explosion ripped open the Krallen lines. A cloud of debris flew skyward. As white splashes blossomed in the open water of the wetland, a dull, distant rumble shook the room.

There were other explosions now, farther along. A cannon insect exploded in a column of flame. Two packs of Krallen bounded up a steep-sided gully and were immediately blown up in a seething fiery mass.

"Good!" Vero muttered in excitement. "Very good! We're decoying them off the road into traps."

For the next ten minutes or so the Krallen advance was slowed by a succession of attacks by the irregulars. Sections of the road blew up, scattering fragments far and wide; barrels of explosives bounced down from the crags and erupted on them. Rockets were launched at the convoy from remote pinnacles and even from within the marsh.

Merral watched Vero staring at the wallscreen, listening to his earpiece and every so often issuing orders or making inquiries. He noticed how Vero moved from foot to foot in evident agitation. Slowly though, his look of excitement faded into one of determined hope, which, in turn, slowly ebbed into one of gloom.

Within ten minutes, it was obvious that the Dominion forces had regrouped and were now on the march again. The irregulars kept firing from within the marsh and from among the trees on the cliffs but their actions were increasingly ineffectual. For every Krallen felled, another ten took its place.

Merral caught Vero's eye. His friend looked at the screen and shook his head. "They did well. And there are still some left. But . . ." His voice faded away.

Merral looked at the map. The enemy would be at the entrance to the gorge within twenty minutes. He decided he couldn't watch the fight from the command center.

"Colonel," he said, "I'm going down nearer to the lines. I want to see things with my own eyes. I'll stay in touch."

"Is that . . . wise?"

"I'll tell you later. But if they break through, here won't be safer for much longer."

"I guess not. You don't intend fighting?"

"Only if I have to and if Lloyd lets me."

The big man shrugged his shoulders. "Sir, if you have to fight, I'm behind you."

Merral took up his helmet, fixed his earpiece in, found an XQ rifle, and checked that the magazine was full. Lloyd put an XQ rifle on his back, filled his bag to the brim with ammunition, and then picked up his shotgun.

Suddenly, the colonel, who had been watching them, stood up. "Well, I guess I'll join you. A man can't run a battle from behind a desk."

◌◯◌◯◌

Five minutes later, they stood on the edge of the gorge, looking past ledge after ledge of shattered rock to the black road snaking its way below.

Merral felt conscious of the growing heat. The breeze had faded, giving a breathless calm, and on the flagpoles nearby, banners hung limp. The expanse of the sky had become the color of liquid metal.

At the bottom of the gorge, tiny figures distorted in the haze still labored with feverish activity. Yellow machines were hastily piling up banks of earth and stone across the road, and lines of soldiers were swiftly taking positions behind earth and rock revetments. In the still air, Merral heard the sounds of many orders, the throb of engines, and the rhythmic cries of soldiers passing out sandbags and equipment along the lines. Yet his eye was drawn across the marsh to where, curving round the margin of the Hereza Crags, the cloud gray snake of the enemy column approached under a pall of dust and smoke.

They were about to descend a well-marked path to the floor of the gorge when Merral heard Vero's voice over the earpiece. "The column has stopped. We don't know why. Hang on. . . ." There was the faintest echo of another voice in the background. "Ah. There's a communications silence as well. Wait. . . . There seems to be something happening at the tower. Let me patch the images through."

As the other two gathered round, Merral pulled his diary off his belt. The screen flickered and then cleared to reveal a hazy image of the strange dark gray tower. At the very top, plates slid apart. A spinning column of pale dust emerged and rose into the sky.

Merral felt oddly disturbed by what he was seeing. "Vero," he asked, pressing the transmit stud, "is that exhaust gas? some sort of whirlwind?"

"No. B-but it's more than an atmospheric phenomenon. The irregs on the ground are reporting psychological disturbances."

"I see," Merral said, aware of a growing feeling of foreboding as he watched the dirty smudge slowly climb into the sky. "So what is it?"

"We're afraid it's the b-baziliarch. It seems to be heading this way."

Merral looked up from the diary through the growing haze toward the peninsula. He could see an odd darkening of the sky there and shivered.

"'The baziliarch'?" Colonel Lanier repeated, with apprehension in his brown eyes. "What new horror is this?"

But Merral didn't answer him, because his attention was now entirely taken up by the approaching phenomenon in the sky. What exactly it was he found hard to determine. It was if some small—but growing—part of the sky had turned in on itself. The more he stared at it, the more he felt that it looked like a hole in the sky.

Yet, he realized with a chill that struck right through him, it was more than some physical trick of atmosphere or light. The phenomenon brought fear with it. As Merral turned to the colonel and Lloyd their faces were pale and trembling.

Merral's stumbling fingers found the transmit stud. "Vero," he said, hearing his voice quaver, "what is it exactly?"

There was a delay before Vero answered. "Our expert says that the baziliarch has wrapped himself in a Below-Space singularity. He brings with him the darkest parts of the Nether-Realms."

I'm not sure I understand that, but it has a horrible logic to it.

With a relentless ease, the phenomenon drew nearer, rising ever higher in the sky as it did. As it drew closer, Merral felt a growing sense of being threatened. He looked around, overwhelmed by a sudden desire to seek somewhere among the rocks to hide.

He was aware now that others had seen it. Below, the barrage of orders stopped, to be replaced by shouts of alarm. Pale faces stared skyward and arms pointed. The incessant activity faltered as men and women slunk away to rocks or under the trees.

It is as Azeras warned. In the presence of the baziliarch, all our resolve and courage drains away.

The thing—the hole in the sky—still climbed. As it rose, Merral saw that the sky around the mysterious disk changed as if light was being buckled and distorted around it. Suddenly, he was aware that the day was becoming darker, almost as if the sunlight was being sucked into the disk.

"If he comes here and opens his wings to let the darkness in . . . ," Azeras said.

With that awareness came the recognition that what they faced was not just a force, but a being—an intelligent and malign opponent that sought their destruction. He had a certainty too that at the heart of this phenomenon was the same being he had encountered in the center the day before. Today though, his energies were not constrained into reading minds, but unleashed in a hateful power.

As he watched the brilliance of the midmorning light fade away, Merral felt certain that it was not just light, but hope, that faded. They had lost. How could they have ever hoped to win? An iron despair settled over his mind. It was barely midmorning and the sky was cloudless, yet the light was so drained that it might have been late in the evening.

Suddenly, a phrase Jorgio had said earlier came to mind: *Remember, Mr. Merral, you won't be alone.* "Lord," he prayed, "unless you defend us, all is lost."

Vero's voice spoke in his ear. "W-we have big trouble. Morale is slipping. There are soldiers on the front who want to run away. Zak is threatening to kill anyone who deserts. What are—?"

"Look!" said Lloyd, gesturing behind them.

High in the eastern sky a small, sparkling point of light moved. *A star!* But Merral's opinion changed as the speed of the object registered.

"Vero, this may sound silly, but have we launched a missile?"

"We have no missiles," Vero replied. "But I see what you are seeing." There was awe in his voice.

The gleaming star raced overhead and struck the hole in the sky.

The disk of emptiness buckled and deflated like a punctured balloon. It became a dark smear of cloud that writhed as if trying to wrap itself around the star. The star seemed to escape being encircled, moved back, and suddenly looped round the disk as it tried to reestablish itself.

There were sounds now: an immense crackling noise that played around the rocks and great reverberating claps that shook the ground. The star struck the cloud again and this time, gleams of dazzling light played around the disk.

A battle. A tingling sensation ran over him. *An awesome, titanic battle between the powers.*

The disk warped again as if it were being punched and suddenly turned into a streak of dark cloud. The star became a gleaming coil of light that wrapped itself around the gloomy cloud as if the two elements were in some atmospheric wrestling match.

In an instant, it was over. The darker strand slipped free and, trailing a gray line of vapor, fled northward. The shining point of light pursued it and in a second both were lost from sight over the mountains.

The sunlight returned, and with it hope.

"Do you think that was what I think it was?" There was relief and wonder in Vero's voice.

"That the envoy reminded the baziliarch that he doesn't have freedom to do what he wants?"

"Yes. But I feel the baziliarch was not destroyed. I guess he'll be back, but not today."

Merral looked to the road where the Krallen forces still advanced. "Just as well. We still have an ugly situation."

ⓞⓞⓞⓞ

Colonel Lanier, Merral, and Lloyd moved down the track toward the upper level of the defenses.

Down in the gorge the heat was even worse. Merral felt sweat trickling down under his armor.

As they approached the first line of soldiers, Merral saw that they were placing sunshades over the long-barreled, tripod-mounted sniper rifles.

A petite woman with short blonde hair and an armored jacket that seemed too long for her came to meet them and saluted. "Captain Karita Hatiran," she said, smiling at Merral. "Welcome, Commander. The Central Regiment sniper team is ready for action."

"Thank you, Captain," Merral replied, seeing the pairs of women in their shallow depressions adjusting weapons, aligning mats, and peering through sights. *Just like the drills, only this time, it's real.*

"If we had more time, I'd like to look around. Any problems?"

"Not really, sir. There's no wind, which eases targeting. It's a bit hot; we're trying to keep the barrels cool." She paused and stared into the hazy distance. "Just a lot of unknowns," she said, giving him a glance that exposed deep apprehension.

"The unknowns trouble me too, Captain. But they're going to be a lot less unknown soon. Very soon."

Merral glanced at the sword she wore, which also looked too big for her.

Evidently catching his gaze, she fingered the hilt. "I really hope we don't need this," she said.

Merral nodded. *If the Krallen get this far through our lines, we are in trouble.*

"Any specific instructions, sir?"

"Captain, only what has no doubt always been issued to snipers: make every shot count and keep a lookout for prize targets. But these flying beasts—slitherwings—I'd like to see them hit." He paused. "And I hate to say it, but there are men with them who probably coordinate the fighting. They will probably be in these armored contraptions. If you get one in your sights, don't hesitate."

A look of disquiet crossed Karita's face. "Okay. I guess it has to be done. I'll pass the order along."

"Good." It was time to move on. "Talk to you later, Captain."

They saluted.

As he followed the colonel down the path, Merral wondered darkly whether he would indeed talk to the captain later. *How trite our words seem at such moments: "See you later." "Take care." What* should *I say?*

A dozen meters below Karita's snipers, they came to the second line of the defenses, a wide strung-out line of men with mortars and XQ rifles.

Alerted that the front of the Dominion advance was now only two kilometers away, Merral and the colonel found a vantage point on a rocky spur from which they could see the entire gorge mouth and out onto the marsh. They stood gratefully in the shade of a lone Montezuma pine.

As the colonel called up units, confirming their location and readiness, Merral drank water and surveyed the scene. They were just twenty meters or so above the floor of the gorge. Just below lay the ditch and ramparts of the first line of defenses. The activity there was intense as soldiers adjusted armor, laid out spare ammunition, and checked weapons, including the axes and sledgehammers to finish off damaged Krallen.

Merral gazed at the south side of the gorge, wondering how preparations were going there. Overcoming a certain reluctance, he called Zak.

"Colonel Larraine here."

"Zak—*Colonel*—everything in place there?"

"The south side is ready, Commander. We're just looking forward to carving up these Krallen." Hearing the confident enthusiasm in his voice, Merral felt a pang of guilt over his own uncertainties and fears.

"What's morale like?"

"No problem. The soldiers here will hold firm. I think they are more afraid of me than the enemy."

Merral considered saying something, but held his tongue. Zak seemed beyond changing. "Very well."

"Have a good fight, sir."

"And you."

Merral scrutinized the defense preparations again. Behind him the reserves were lined up, squatting under the shelter of the rocks and trees. Below, to the rear of the defense earthworks in the gorge, the ambulances lined up along the road with their doors open. All was ready.

For a race that has had no military experience for over eleven millennia, we appear to have returned to the business of war very quickly. Have we relearned old skills or did we never lose them?

Looking out beyond the trenches and the embankments toward the marsh, Merral could see the long line of Krallen shimmering in the heat at the foot of the looming crags. Above them the slitherwings performed their leisurely aerial patrols in the dusty air.

Merral's stomach squirmed. *At Carson's Sill, I had no time to think about fighting. At Fallambet, I hadn't really understood what it involved. Now, I have neither excuse.*

Merral's apprehensive scrutiny of the scene was interrupted by Vero's urgent voice in his ear. "My friend, things are coming together. Anya's picked up a reorganization in the Krallen ranks. Around two thousand seem to be separating out and moving to the front. Betafor confirms this. She says she can hear around one hundred and fifty units getting ready. Azeras reckons they will attack with a small forward party, leaving the main body of Krallen and the equipment in reserve. A probing attack, he calls it."

"So how long have we got?"

"Azeras reckons they will charge. From where they are, they will reach you in four or five minutes. They will hit fast. Hang on." There was a pause. "Betafor estimates they will launch the attack in two minutes."

Six minutes before we fight. "Okay. Thanks. Let me handle it here."

"We'll be watching. I'll restrict communications to what's absolutely necessary." There was a moment's silence. "Keep safe, my friend."

"I'll try."

"Keep safe"—what did Perena say to that? "I'll try. But I have to do what's right. And in the end, that's safe." Merral sighed.

He slung his rifle off his back and turned to Colonel Lanier. "It seems we have only a few minutes. I'm going to say a few words to the men."

The colonel nodded. "Please."

Merral thumbed his microphone switch to universal. "Soldiers of the Assembly." He paused to let the echo of his words die away among the rocks.

"This is Commander Merral D'Avanos speaking to you from your lines. We believe that within five minutes there will be an attack on us by a substantial number of Krallen. Obey your training and your orders. Don't be afraid. Stand firm. Don't waste a shot. Strike hard and cut true. These monstrosities have come a long way to meet you. Let's make sure this is where their journey ends." He paused again and raised his sword high. "For the Lamb!"

"For the Lamb!" The thunderous response echoed and reechoed among the rocks.

And as the echoes died away and the soldiers moved with frantic haste to their positions, Merral heard Betafor's cold flat voice in his ear. "Commander, the Krallen are attacking."

For a few moments he didn't believe her until he saw fresh dust rising across the marsh and felt the growing vibration in the ground.

As the colonel issued a new flurry of orders, Merral knelt down and slid the safety catch off his XQ rifle. He turned to Lloyd, to check his readiness.

Lloyd had an XQ gun strapped to his back, two belts of ammunition draped over his shoulders, a sword at his belt, and was checking the breech of his big double-barreled shotgun.

Merral smiled. "Sergeant, you want to be careful you don't damage your back with all that."

Lloyd winked. "Thanks for your concern. I'm hoping to retire soon, sir."

"Good idea."

The colonel's shouted order cut the oppressive air. "Mortars, ready! Hold fire until you're told."

The seconds passed.

Soon they could see the Krallen pounding toward them. In a line twelve across, they ran faster than any horse could gallop with their feet barely touching the ground. At first, Merral thought they were going for the center of the gorge, but in a maneuver of breathtaking precision, the column unzipped, with alternate rows veering right and left to create a broad fan shape.

Suddenly, barely two hundred meters away, the Krallen began howling wildly.

A sound that will haunt me to my death—an event that might be quite near.

Just below him at the bottom of the gorge, Merral glimpsed a man, his face pale under his helmet, turn to run, think better of it, and return to his position.

"Fire!" Colonel Lanier shouted.

The ground shook with a pulsing wave of heavy thuds, and bare seconds later, the Krallen lines erupted in fountains of flame, smoke, and dirt.

A great ripple of deafening percussive blasts swept over Merral and bounced off the rocks.

"Mortars, fire!" the colonel shouted.

Even as the debris from the first explosion settled on the ground, there were new showers of debris and more ear-numbing blasts. The colonel shouted another order and, for a third time, a percussive clamor seemed to shake the world to its core.

The Krallen vanished under a drifting shroud of dust and smoke. Then, impossibly, they bounded through the smoke in ones and twos that, without any apparent effort, seemed to link up into threes, fours, sixes, and then twelves. Their lines reformed and plunged onward.

Above, the slitherwings glided through the smoke, their tails flicking behind them.

"Fire at will!" the colonel yelled.

In an instant, the world seemed filled with a new and appalling clamor of sound: the bass thud and blast of the mortars, the sharp cracking reports of the sniper rifles, the high whoosh of the XQ rounds, the hiss of cutter guns, the yells of the soldiers, and the continuous manic howling of the Krallen. As the furious sounds of war boomed and rolled around the gorge, Merral was aware of the smell of burning, the chemical tang of the rocket fumes, and the acrid odor of sweat and fear.

The gray line continued its charge. Like tremendous dogs they loped along with effortless speed, their four legs running round and over the bodies of their fallen comrades, their coordination so precise that none ever seemed to run into another.

Merral sighted on one Krallen, aimed just ahead of it, pulled the trigger, and followed the smoke trail as the bullet struck its flanks, flinging it sideways. His gratification was short-lived as it wobbled upright and continued on its way. He fired again and again, aware that each time he squeezed the trigger, he was firing at closer range.

He glimpsed a slitherwing flap by overhead—the looming diamond shape, the long moist slit of the mouth agape, and the whip of a tail tracing leisurely curves through the air. Suddenly a hole appeared in the right wing and the creature banked unsteadily away.

Merral glanced up from his rifle to see that the first Krallen were almost upon the ditches in front of the defenses. Behind them, heedless of the mortar craters and the scattered smoldering fragments of their kind, more Krallen raced after them.

The first line of Krallen plunged into the ditches and, barely slowing, surged upward against the ramparts. They struck the walls like the waves of a winter sea breaking over a rocky shoreline. Soldiers screamed as the claws lashed out and teeth bit. Now, for the first time, there was the glitter of blades.

Merral held his fire, choosing instead to watch. *Now is the test. Now we see whether Vero's ingenuity in forging swords and armor has worked. If it has, we have hope. If not, we are lost.*

Blades rose and fell amid new yells and screams. Just below him, a man struck a blow deep into the neck of a Krallen. It toppled backward, inert. Next to him another beast keeled over as a blade was thrust into its belly.

Merral began to dare to hope.

"Those swords really work!" the colonel cried, relief in his voice.

Merral turned his gaze wider, trying to determine what was happening around the gorge mouth. The scene, partly obscured by smoke, was one of a confused and angry melee. Through the smoke it was plain that the Krallen charge had slowed. The narrowing of the gorge, the ditches, and their own fallen had clogged their advance. Around the entire length of the defenses, an ash-colored mass of Krallen, perhaps eight or ten deep, seethed against the ramparts.

In the air, the slitherwings were in trouble. One spiraled down, its wing torn. Another was aflame and, as he watched, a third cartwheeled into the ground.

Yet just as hope surged in Merral's mind, it began to fade. All around the arc of the gorge mouth it was plain that the defenses were in danger of being overrun.

Merral was suddenly aware of Colonel Lanier standing next to him.

"What do you think?" the colonel shouted, trying to make himself heard over the noise. "The lines are barely holding."

"Send the reserves in!" Merral shouted back.

The colonel gave an order. As Merral fired a dozen rounds into the midst of the Krallen, soldiers rushed down the slopes to join their fellows.

Suddenly, Merral heard Anya's voice in his ear. "Merral, we have you on screen. There's a Krallen, pack moving in—down to your right. By the rock spur, fifteen meters away. Looks like it may be unopposed."

"Thanks, we'll deal with it." Soon he spotted twelve forms moving purposefully through the chaos in front of the ramparts toward a rocky projection.

Merral looked around, only to see that there were no more reserves. He grabbed Lloyd, who was pumping round after round from his XQ rifle into the enemy ranks with a steady rhythm, and gestured to where the pack was scampering up the projecting rock. In seconds they would be able to circle behind a handful of soldiers who were preoccupied with the foes pressing upon them.

Lloyd grunted, swung the barrel toward the new threat, and fired, the white trails of the rounds carving furiously through the air. First one, and then a second Krallen spun off the rock. Merral fired, and a third toppled over.

But in seconds the remaining Krallen were off the rock and heading silently behind the soldiers.

"Swords!" Merral yelled, throwing his gun down and running down the track. He heard Lloyd following as he raced down the rocks. They half leaped and half tumbled into the defensive excavation.

"The Lamb!" Merral cried, as he swung his sword down on the back of the nearest Krallen. The creature whipped its head toward him, but as it did, the blade struck the tough skin, stuck, then slowly penetrated. The creature twitched, the burning red light in its eyes faded, and it toppled onto its side.

The remaining Krallen—seven or eight—turned round and Merral had a brief and horrid vision of over a dozen fiery eyes gleaming at him. As he raised his sword again, Lloyd charged, moving like a mighty mythological figure of vengeance, his shotgun in his left hand, and his sword in his right.

As a Krallen bounded at Lloyd, he stuck the gun in its mouth and fired, sending a cloud of fragments hissing around. A moment later, Merral glimpsed another falling under Lloyd's sword before his own attention was required by two Krallen, eyes ablaze, approaching him with perfect coordinated symmetry from the right and the left.

The creature to Merral's right lunged for him. In an action that was a pure reflex, Merral slashed down hard with the sword. The blade arced into the face, cutting deeply between the lidless eyes. The creature slumped, spun sideways, and crashed to the ground. As Merral tugged the blade free, silver fluid dripped from it. He caught a strange warm mechanical odor that reminded him of his father's workshops.

As the second Krallen bounded toward him from the left, its teeth flashing in the sun, Merral swung his sword. The creature was too close and the blow too hasty. The blade hit the skin at an angle and bounced off. A steely claw scythed at him, struck an armored sleeve, and skated off. The creature spun round on its hind legs and reared up toward him. As it pounced, Merral thrust the blade forward deep into its chest. The Krallen struck him, sending him tottering backward, and then, suddenly immobile, fell over.

Even as it slid to the ground, another Krallen leaped over its body toward him. Trying to regain his balance, he tugged at his sword, but the blade refused to budge. Somehow the body of the Krallen had twisted, trapping his blade underneath it.

With increasing desperation, Merral wrestled to free the blade. As he did he saw a gray face in front of him, its jaws gaping wide to show teeth like the blades of a tree saw. The creature raised its right forelimb, extended its bladed nails, and brought them together to make a single chisel-like blade.

The punch to the face, Merral realized with a numbed horror.

As the limb shot out, he ducked. The ferocious blow struck his helmet.

Half stunned, his helmet twisted around so he could only partially see, Merral staggered back, expecting another—and final—blow.

The Krallen paused. Its deep-set, glowing eyes suddenly tracked away from him.

A pair of smoking gun barrels slid past Merral's ear. He could feel the heat from them.

"You have to ask yourself, do you feel lucky?" Lloyd addressed the Krallen in a slightly breathless drawl.

Merral saw a glint of something—perplexity perhaps?—in the creature's eyes.

There was a flash, a deafening explosion, and the Krallen's head disintegrated into a whistling cloud of fragments. A wreath of muzzle smoke drifted past.

"Thanks, Lloyd," Merral said, as he clambered heavily to his feet. He twisted his helmet back into place and wrenched his sword free from the Krallen. "But we don't believe in luck."

Lloyd gave the headless body a kick. "Don't think it does now."

Merral gazed around, seeing eight stilled forms, and turned to the ramparts, where the five men left standing continued their struggle against an apparently endless onslaught of claws, teeth, and baleful eyes. Mindful of the swinging blades, Merral edged forward to take his place at the front.

"Thanks," said a man next to him and Merral glimpsed a wearied, sweat-stained and bloodied face. "Too many goblins."

Goblins. A good name.

The ditch in front of the ramparts was so full of Krallen bodies that the new attackers had to climb over the fallen to reach them. One leaped toward Merral and he felled it with a single blow to the neck.

Suddenly, the howling changed to a series of weird keening cries. In an instant, the Krallen paused, spun around, and retreated, bounding back over the damaged or destroyed forms of their own kind.

They stopped a hundred meters away beyond the line of smoldering mortar craters and dismembered parts and only a few strides from the edge of the marsh. There, in their mechanical way, they regrouped into parallel lines and then fell still and silent.

Merral took off his helmet, rubbed a growing lump on his head, and wiped the sweat from his face. He could hear noises: screams, a dull pathetic whimpering, and even, bizarrely, cicadas chirping in the pines. Yet there behind it was a great and horrible stillness.

He was aware of the mingled smells of terror, sweat, and death. Suddenly he felt weary, aware that his arms and shoulders hurt.

In front of him lay piles of Krallen, silver fluid dribbling out of their gray shells. Next to him soldiers were leaning on the ramparts, recovering their breath or gulping down water. Nearby, two medical orderlies were putting the still and bloodied figure of a man onto a stretcher. In the next section of the defenses, some soldiers were trying to restrain a man rolling around in agony.

Do you ever get used to this? Does anyone ever come to consider this abomination of war as normal?

He saw men beginning to run around with hammers and axes, crushing and hewing the fallen grey forms. *Oh, how the generals of old would have loved them, these disposable soldiers with no next of kin, no guilt or fear, only a boundless hate and energy and a perfect allegiance.*

"Better get back to the colonel, sir," Lloyd said as he mopped sweat off his red face.

He's right. There are decisions to be made.

They walked back to the pine tree where Colonel Lanier was issuing orders for the soldiers to reload and clear the ditches.

More medical personnel ran past them. Merral looked to the gorge road where ambulances were being loaded.

God have mercy on them.

He heard a faint whispering voice and quickly replaced the dislodged earpiece. "D'Avanos here."

"My friend, I'm glad to hear you're okay."

"Vero, what's happening?"

"We don't know. They've retreated. We think there are about a thousand Krallen disabled or destroyed. Betafor thinks the defense surprised them. They didn't expect the swords. What's your estimate of our losses?"

"Hard to say. We have a lot of injured men. Some are dead."

It was a thin defense line, and now it's even thinner. We have no strength in depth. All they have to do is bring up another thousand Krallen from their vast reserve, launch a new attack, and we are finished. Attrition, Betafor said. Exactly so.

"Hang on," Vero said. "New information coming in."

There was a pause, long enough for Merral to see another man taken away on a stretcher with a bloody sheet over his face.

Vero spoke again, his voice was brittle with tension. "Merral, it looks as if they're going to change their strategy. You'd better come up, quick."

26

Laden by armor and weapons and troubled by the stifling heat, Merral and Lloyd found climbing the path up to the village hard work. As much to get their breath as for any other reason, they stopped at the sniper line where there was hasty reloading going on.

Karita met them. "We stopped a lot of those beasts, Commander," she said thoughtfully, "but it's not easy. They move fast and if the bullet hits their skin at any sort of tangent, it just skids off."

"I know."

She turned and gazed down the slope at the battlefield. "Well, we won this round," she said. He heard confidence in her voice. But when she turned back to him, he saw a look in her eyes that seemed to say, "But we won't next time."

"Have faith, Captain," said Merral, before continuing up the track. *It's easy to say.*

Near the top, while waiting for Lloyd to catch up, Merral called Zak.

Despite heavy losses on the south side, Zak's enthusiasm was undiminished. He and his soldiers had "cut and hacked until their arms ached" and "taught the Krallen a lesson they will not forget." There was, though, one issue that Zak wanted advice on. Two of his men, Latrati and Durrance, had fled in terror at the Krallen charge and had been arrested. What should he do with them?

Merral hesitated for a second. "Have them stripped of their armor and sent back to Isterrane on the first flight that has space. We will hold disciplinary hearings when this is all over."

"Sir, there are precedents for carrying out such discipline in the field." The disappointment in Zak's voice was plain.

"I would rather hold a formal trial later."

"Sir, if I may say so—" Zak's tone was one of annoyance—"it sets a bad precedent. I think a speedy trial and a public punishment here might prevent a repetition. Desertion can be contagious. You mustn't be too soft on them."

"Colonel Larraine, that sounds awfully like an accusation that I am soft on discipline."

"Well, sir, the battlefield's a tough place. Softness can have a price."

I refuse to argue this, not here and not now. "Colonel, I have made my decision plain. Have Latrati and Durrance sent to Isterrane. We have other things to do."

"Yes, sir," came the reluctant reply.

Merral sighed and began climbing again.

Vero and Azeras were waiting at the top of the path, just in front of the white-walled houses.

Gasping from the heat and the exertion of the climb, Merral sat heavily on a large rock.

"My friend," Vero said with a frown, "you fighting in that battle was reckless. You might have been killed."

"A fate we all face. But, Vero, I had no choice. They could have put a hole in our lines there. What are the casualty figures?"

"So far, we have at least fifty dead and twice that injured. Some serious. That's just the regulars, of course."

"So we have lost well over a tenth of our men."

There was a silent, heavy nod in response.

Merral turned and, suddenly aware of sweat running down his back, gazed at the vast immobile mass of the Dominion force beneath Hereza Crags. *They have lost, at most, only a twentieth of their numbers. The implications of those figures are inescapable. We are losing.*

"But what's happening?"

Vero and Azeras exchanged anxious looks. "We aren't sure. Sarudar, can you explain your concern?"

"First of all, well fought, Commander. There was much done down there that would not have disgraced the elite units of the True Freeborn. But the fighting is not over. My analysis is this—remember, I have fought the Dominion for almost half my life. I think Lezaroth is perplexed and even alarmed. With all the force they had, the crushing of Farholme should have been straightforward. Yet it has gone badly wrong and they have had a series of setbacks. Now they find that your—*our*—swords and armor have stopped what should have been an easy victory."

"So what will they do? Go home?"

"Bah! They will not retreat. In the past Nezhuala punished losers, and he doesn't change. There will be a change of plan. They don't like this gorge. They prefer to sweep around their enemies; here they're hemmed in. And they don't know the strength of the opposition they face either; their intelligence is now very limited."

"So what do you think they will do?" Merral asked.

"My guess is that they will try and avoid the gorge. They may choose to climb the Hereza Crags." Azeras gestured to the rocky ridge. "And from there cross to Mount Adaman behind us." He turned and traced the route with his hand.

"Are you serious?" Merral asked, looking at the massif with its cliffs, screes, and stands of dense woodland and undergrowth.

"True, it would be several days' journey for men, but for Krallen, especially if they leave their repair facilities behind them, it would be just a few hours. The rules of battle you've learned don't apply to creatures that need neither food, nor water, nor rest."

"And from Mount Adaman where would they go? On to the Western Trunk Road?"

Azeras scowled. "No. They will not leave an enemy in their rear. My guess is that from up there they will race down upon us. With all their forces."

As he looked up, Merral followed his gaze and stared at the heights above the village where the air seemed to wobble in the haze.

"Imagine, nearly twenty thousand Krallen hurtling down the slope in a single overwhelming charge," Azeras continued. "They will attack on a wide front, and the edges of their attack will swing round any defensive line we can muster. We will be encircled. And that will be that. I had worried about it, but . . ." He shrugged. "They would be unstoppable."

Merral squinted at the slopes, feeling his insides writhe. *Unstoppable* was hardly an overstatement.

He turned to Vero for reassurance, only to see his friend, hand to his ear, seemingly engrossed by what he heard.

"You're sure?" Vero asked, frowning at the ground. "All of them?" In the pause that followed he raised his head and stared in the direction of Mount Adaman. "Thank you." He sounded wretched.

Vero turned to Merral. "That was Anya. The main body of Krallen have turned and are starting to climb the Hereza Crags. Betafor confirms it."

Merral stared westward, seeing the first columns of dust rise up from the foot of the crags.

"How soon?" Vero asked, his expression devoid of hope. He turned to Merral. "The best guess is early afternoon. Two, or at most, three hours."

Vero groaned. "I'm sorry; I should have thought of this. I assumed that these cliffs were an impossible barrier. A bad mistake."

Merral put his hand on his friend's shoulder. "I don't think blaming yourself is the best thing to do right now. We all underestimated them, and we now need to create some defenses. Let's go and look at the land."

With Lloyd trailing after them, they jogged through the village to a gentle ridge covered with new olive groves. Within minutes, they had agreed on the alignment of two defensive ditches and had summoned earth-moving equipment.

While the others discussed some of the details of the ditches, Merral stood apart and stared southward through the haze and rising dust at the gray fungus that was spreading over Hereza Crags. He felt sick. Within moments, the status of their defenses had gone from being well fortified to weak. Ten minutes ago, they had had a chance. Now, even that slimmest of hopes had fled.

Vero walked over to him. "My friend, let's talk. The irregulars are trying to delay them, but they are too few." Vero pointed to the open ground beyond the line of the trench. "Oh, if I had only consulted Azeras, we could have had these trenches dug already or put explosives out there."

He punched one hand into the other in a gesture of regret. "Something at least. Oh, what a fool I've been! I could never have imagined that they would do this."

"Vero, what we did—or didn't—do is past. Do you really think all is lost?"

"No. I think we have to hope. God has been good to us so far." He paused, his expression one of deep anxiety.

"True. But we need another miracle. And I see no sign of one."

Vero gave the weariest of smiles. "If you did, it probably wouldn't be a miracle."

"True again. But any hope we have now comes from the Most High."

"It only ever did."

Merral gestured to the area chosen for the ditches. "I intend to put all our remaining reserves here—any soldiers we can spare from the gorge and any of the irregulars who are left."

He paused, and tapped his foot on the thin soil. "Vero, we'll make our last stand here."

◌◌◌◌◌

The decision made, Merral strode rapidly away to the villa and, during a meeting with a somber Colonel Lanier, agreed on a strategy. Zak would defend the gorge with a handpicked force of a hundred men. The rest of the soldiers—along with any others who could fight—would be sent to the new defenses on the upper olive groves.

Zak received his orders with ill-disguised irritation.

Merral then found Anya, who was slumped in her chair looking at imagery that showed the Krallen moving up and over the Hereza Crags. For some moments, Merral stared wordlessly at it, marveling at the relentless determination of the seemingly endless swarm of creatures. Their regulated order had gone, but there was still the sense of directed purpose as they climbed over all but the most severe cliffs, scrambled urgently through the thickets of thorns and junipers, and darted over unstable screes. Nothing stopped them and little slowed them.

"Anya," he said, "things are changing. It looks like there is going to be an attack from the mountain—an unstoppable one."

"I know," she said and he saw the tiredness in her sky blue eyes. "There's a logic to it. They don't like this slow attrition. They want a sudden and overwhelming victory."

"That may be the theory, but that wasn't what I wanted to discuss. We're evacuating all the wounded. I don't want any transports on the ground here when they attack and the Krallen will not spare anyone, least of all the wounded."

"I know that."

"We have to face the possibility—the probability—that we will be overrun. We are outnumbered twenty to one. And they will take no prisoners."

"Yes."

"So I think you ought to leave."

"No." There was an almost sullen defiance in her face.

"Technically, you are now an only child. Anya, I would prefer it if you left—for your family's sake."

Anya looked away for a moment and then turned to Merral with a stony expression. "No."

"I can order it. Have Lloyd lock you up and bundle you on the flier."

"I wouldn't try."

"I want you to go."

"No, again. I will stay here. I use no resources. I am not a burden. I may be able to help. And if it comes to it, I will fight. There is spare armor here that I can use."

"But fighting is different."

"Merral, I helped Azeras make the training material. I helped design the armor and the swords."

For a long second, he stared at her and was met again by a look of unyielding resolve.

"You praised my sister for her heroism. Now you want me to run away? Be consistent at least!" There was anger in her voice.

Merral stared at her and then, defeated, shrugged his shoulders. *After all, Isterrane will hardly be safe once we fall.*

"Oh, very well," he said, slowly. "I admire your spirit. But I remind you, your future doesn't look good."

"My sister would have reminded you that God still reigns."

"Rebuke accepted."

⬡⬡⬡⬡⬡

Merral went up to the roof. As he watched the lines of Krallen that were already approaching the serrated summit of the Hereza Crags, he called Jorgio.

From the juddering image that appeared in the diary, the old man appeared to be seated in Brenito's rocking chair. His face was unshaven.

"Mr. Merral," Jorgio said. "It's good to hear from you, very good. I was wondering how things were. As I prayed this morning, I sensed that there was a great struggle in the heavens. But I felt the Lord's servant triumphed and the enemy was frustrated."

"That's true. But we now face a new crisis."

"So I have heard. Lots of these things—nasty devices with teeth and claws. Not nice, not nice at all. And I've been praying as the King will deliver you—and us."

"And?"

A skewed smile appeared on Jorgio's face. "The King keeps his counsels to himself. I reckon that's his privilege. He wouldn't be the King if it wasn't."

"True. But, Jorgio, the situation looks hopeless. We are heavily outnumbered."

"*Tut*. The Lord can win a battle whether he has many warriors or only a few."

"I accept that, Jorgio, but from where I stand it's hard to be confident."

"Mr. Merral, the one way to be sure that there is no hope is to believe that there is none."

"True."

There was silence between them. Finally, Merral said, "The estimates are that they will attack us sometime between two and three this afternoon."

Jorgio nodded. "I will pray much for you. Always do. It's a battle sometimes. But if I hear anything, I will let you know."

"Thank you. I hope we talk again."

Jorgio smiled again. "Oh, Mr. Merral, we will. If not here, then in the world to come. So cheer up."

"Thanks for the reminder, Jorgio. I need it."

Jorgio's bent smile broadened. "One piece of advice I *can* offer. When you take your stand against them, fly all the banners and emblems you have."

Merral smiled as if he dealt with a child who had made an outrageous suggestion.

"Indeed, why not? If our end is to be here, then let us make it a defiant one. I will assemble every banner and flag we have."

"Very well. May the King be with you."

⬡⬡⬡⬡⬡

Over the next hour or so, Merral kept busy. He ordered the placement of high poles along the ridge and that every available banner and emblem of the Assembly be hung from them. Yet the total absence of wind made the flags a sorry spectacle and as Merral gazed at the limp pieces of material the lifeless sheets of fabric seemed to mock any hope. *They symbolize our plight.*

He made sure all the seriously wounded were put aboard the transporters and persuaded a number of nonmilitary personnel to leave.

Down by the strip he met Luke Tenerelt standing by the stretcher of a badly wounded man, who was being loaded on a flier.

Luke's uniform and pale face were stained with blood and sweat and he looked as exhausted as if he had been running a race all day. He put his arm on Merral's shoulder, as much it seemed to gain support as to give comfort.

"Are you okay, Chaplain?"

Luke's sad eyes turned to Merral. "Okay? No. Definitely no. Doing what I am supposed to do? Yes."

Merral offered him some water and Luke sat on a rock and drank greedily. He handed the bottle back, wiped his mouth with the back of a blood-streaked hand, frowned at it, and looked at Merral. "And are you okay?"

Merral, who was trying not to look at a hand-painted sign by a large refrigerated tent that read *Morgue # 1: Full*, bit his lip and shook his head. *The great virtue of Luke is that you can be yourself with him.*

"And it's not over yet, Luke," he said, trying hard to choke back fears.

The chaplain put his head in his hands. "No. It's not," he replied in a voice that threatened to break with emotion.

"You're staying?" Merral asked.

"Of course."

"Thanks. We are preparing a last stand by the village. I can use you there."

Another stretcher team approached and Luke looked up. "I'd heard. And you'll find me there. But in the meantime . . ." He rose, straightened his stained uniform, and set off toward the wounded man.

○○○○○

Shortly afterward Merral called Clemant to outline the situation. He felt that Clemant, who apparently knew what was happening, seemed to find giving either sympathy or support very difficult.

His round face had an almost total lack of expression. "Very well. Thank you for all you've done, Commander." The words were emotionless.

Is that all he can say? Merral felt gripped with an anger that he could only just restrain. *Nearly a hundred dead in the regulars alone, many times that in the irregs, and all he can say is "Thank you for all you've done"?*

"I'll have our defenses here boosted," Clement said. "We have most of the Western Regiment now and the irregulars. If Tezekal falls, we will do all we can."

"I'm sure," Merral said, trying to keep his voice flat. "Any news from the *Dove of Dawn* assault team?"

"I am monitoring it closely, Commander. The team is keeping silence, but I gather everything is going to plan. The assault should be around three this afternoon. But don't worry about it; you have enough concerns."

How very true.

"I have ordered an engineering team to go on board as soon as the ship is secured. The hope is that it can be made ready to go to Earth within a few days."

"Makes sense," Merral replied, realizing that he derived some comfort from the fact that even if Isterrane and Farholme fell, the Assembly might still be warned. *Our efforts might not have been wholly in vain.*

"But, Commander, I have every confidence that you will do all you can to defend Isterrane."

"I will try and do what I can."

"I know you will. Our thoughts and prayers are with you, Commander." And with that Clemant gave an awkward smile and closed the link.

○○○○○

Trying to put the conversation with Clemant out of his mind, Merral found a quiet corner of the command center. There he drafted some words to say before the final onslaught and committed them to memory. He then toured the defenses, partly to encourage morale and partly in the hope of finding anything that might boost the feeble forces he had. The only slight encouragement was a slow but steady trickle of exhausted and sometimes wounded irregs coming off the mountain. They were patched up, given spare armor and weapons, and sent up to the new defenses.

By half past one, the temperature seemed to have increased still further. In the still air, a shimmering haze seemed to hang over everything, distorting shapes and distances, and generating dancing mirages.

Only the thousand or so Krallen waiting in silent immobility beyond the mouth of the gorge and the much vaster number marching relentlessly eastward along the mountain ridges seemed unaffected by the sweltering heat.

By two, the first Krallen were visible on top of Mount Adaman and shortly afterward the last of the fliers at the landing strip took off. As Merral watched it leave, he struggled to avoid the feeling of being deserted.

Half an hour later, Merral walked through the village to the ridge amid the olive groves that formed the core of the final defenses. The soldiers were already taking up their places in the freshly dug fortifications. Even with the irregs and those who, like Anya, had decided to stay, he knew that there would be barely a thousand defenders to face a force nearly twenty times as large. The nature of their plight made the disposition of the troops very simple: there were just two lines, a single row of men in front with Karita's snipers on the slight rise behind. There were no reserves and no fallback position.

Merral stared at the great slope before him, seeing through the haze the worn green of the woods and shrubs slowly turning gray as the Krallen advanced. *As if summer has turned to winter.* He borrowed a fieldscope and stared through it, seeing individuals moving under the branches of the junipers and pines, and trampling, without concern, through the needles and thorns of the spiny undergrowth or bounding effortlessly across jagged rocks.

Not long now. I ought to call people to attention and say what I've prepared. But what can I say when I believe we're going to lose?

His gloomy thoughts were broken by the realization that his diary was chiming. He pulled it from under his armor. It was Jorgio. His face, bathed in sweat, was a pasty color.

"Mr. Merral, I have a message for you."

"Go on."

"I am specifically to tell you, from the Most High, that in half an hour, there will be a strong wind off the sea."

"And?"

"That's it."

Merral felt overwhelmed by a disappointment that bordered on exasperation. "That will be unusual," he said slowly, to hide his frustration. "The best we might expect at this time of year is a gentle evening breeze. But a strong wind will cool us. Thank you, Jorgio."

"*Tut.* My pleasure. The King, though, was very concerned that you should hear it."

"I'm sure."

"You were expecting something more?"

Merral looked up at the gray flood moving through the wooded slopes above. "You could say that." He tried to smile and failed. "But, my old friend, we must be content with what we are sent."

"Indeed. The King knows best, Mr. Merral."

Merral considered a sharp response, but decided that this close to imminent death, questioning divine wisdom was probably unwise.

"Jorgio, just in case . . . thanks for all your help."

"Thank *you*. But you watch for that wind."

Before Merral could say anything more, the screen went blank.

Merral was still pondering Jorgio's words when Betafor's flat voice spoke in his ear. "Commander, there are orders being issued on the mountain. I think they are going to advance."

Merral looked up to see the Krallen starting to move slowly downward. There was a tap on his shoulder and he turned round to see the tall figure of Azeras standing by him. He carried a large rolled flag on a staff under his arm.

"My prediction, Commander—and it may well be my last one—is that our opponents will advance to about a hundred meters away from the edge of the wood. They will then charge." He threw his gloved hands wide. "And that will be that."

"Thank you for that last advice, Sarudar. I take it you are joining us."

Azeras's smile seemed formal and mirthless. "I have only my honor left, Commander. For a veteran to flee when novices fight would be shame." He gestured to the banner. "But I will fight under my own flag. No disrespect to the Assembly, but I remain one of the True Freeborn, even if I am the last of them. I will fight under the emblem of the broken chain."

They shook hands and Azeras moved some distance away and drove the staff firmly into the ground, but in the absence of wind, the dark blue flag hung so limply that the emblem on it was obscured.

Merral looked up at the slope, seeing the treetops shaking, and tried not to think of the unstoppable wave of teeth and claws that would overwhelm their feeble defenses in seconds. Far above on the slopes, a faint but growing howling began.

Followed by Luke, who had somehow acquired a new uniform, Merral made his way over to the tallest flagstaff on which the large Lamb and Stars banner hung immobile. He adjusted his microphone. "Men and women," he said, hearing his words roll around the olive groves, ditches, and parapets, "despite great sacrifices in space and on the ground we will, within minutes, face conflict with a powerful and merciless foe. I do not want to offer any false hopes. Unless the Most High acts, our chances of victory today are low. He may yet intervene; that is his prerogative. We must all, though, assume that, within the next hour, our lives may be demanded of us."

He paused, struck by the solemnity of his words, and then continued. "Yet it is a simple matter. We face evil and treacherous foes that must be stopped here or else they will take our world and, for all we know, other worlds too. We and our ancestors before us have lived in the security of the Lord's Assembly for generations; through it we have enjoyed much blessing. Now, though, we are asked to return something of what we have been given. We must fight and be prepared to die for the Assembly. I have arranged that what happens on this field of battle be imaged by remote cameras and be transmitted to the rest of the Assembly. Long years from now, men and women will watch how we fought and, perhaps, how we died. May we live up to that challenge." He paused, aware of a silence charged with intensity. "Chaplain Tenerelt will now lead us in prayer."

As Luke began to pray, men and women kneeled or bowed their heads. As Merral bowed his head, he caught a glimpse of Azeras, standing defiantly upright against his banner.

Luke ended his prayer with a firm "Amen" that was echoed across the lines.

"Men and women," Merral cried out, "take up your positions. Whether we be granted victory or defeat, let us fight well!"

There were eddies of movement along the ditches as people made last-minute adjustments, drank water, or checked weapons. Colonel Lanier moved along the line to take up a position at the western end. There were few words said.

Merral made his way to the crude trench that lay just in front of the great banner of the Lamb and Stars. He tightened his helmet, slung his rifle off his back, and checked to see that he had a full magazine and a spare on his belt.

"You ready, Sergeant?" he said, turning to the big man laden with belts and cartridges just behind him.

"Yup. Whatever happens, I plan to kill a few of these things."

"Good. Very good." Merral suddenly found himself struggling to find the right words. "Ah, Lloyd, at this point . . . well, let's just say . . . many thanks for your help."

Lloyd grinned. "It's been . . . interesting. And, sir, we ain't dead yet."

"No."

A soldier came over. "Any room here?"

For a second, Merral didn't recognize the voice. It was only when he glimpsed a strand of reddish hair sticking out from under the helmet that he realized who it was.

"Anya," he said, "I didn't recognize you." He paused. "Oddly enough, I'm glad to have you here."

They stared at each other. In a flash of insight he realized that both were unsure whether to adopt an attitude of flippancy or gravity.

"Two things, Merral," Anya said quietly, as Lloyd moved a short distance away. *Tactful to the last.* "First, I don't expect you to protect me."

"I wouldn't dream of it. And don't you worry about me. I have Lloyd for that."

"And second . . . sorry." Anya's face flushed. "I've been unfair to you. In fact, I've been far too bitter." She shrugged. "Anyway, now seemed an appropriate time to mention it."

"I suppose it is, isn't it? And you have my apology. I haven't really handled our relationship well."

"Thanks, but you apologized before. I forgave you, remember?"

Merral nodded, then looked up. Halfway up the slope above them, the wide Krallen line came to a halt. There seemed a new note in their howling now.

"Not long now," he said quietly to Anya.

"They're creatures of habit. They do like to be all neatly lined up." Anya's face puckered into a grim smile. "Yeah, as an authority on Krallen behavior, I felt I ought to experience coming face-to-face with them."

"Don't forget to take notes," he said, and reached for her hand. For a moment their gloved hands clasped.

Merral looked around to find Azeras standing alone by his own banner. He smiled and received a solemn stiff salute from Azeras in response. *I read that as the gesture of a man who knows his time is up. Lord, have mercy on him and us this day.*

On the slope, the Krallen lines continued to adjust themselves. A slight figure, apparently ill at ease in full armor, approached him. It was Vero. Merral beckoned him over.

"A bad mess," Vero said, shaking his head. "V-very bad. I should have realized that they might be able to do this—"

"Don't say it," Merral interrupted. "You have apologized enough. You don't need to do it again."

"Okay. Life's too short." Vero made a grimace. "Hmm, perhaps an inappropriate expression under the circumstances."

"You need to keep at a distance to allow me to swing my sword without the risk of hitting you," Merral said, trying to keep the tone conversational.

"Right." Vero took a step aside. "Sorry. You know it will be my first fight since Carson's Sill?"

"That seems a long time ago."

Vero looked up at the hillside. "I thought the odds were bad then. I guess I was naive."

"We are a lot wiser now."

"Absolutely. Live and learn." There was another grimace. "Ow. Perhaps not the best expression either. Anyway, it's good to have you with me here."

"Somehow appropriate." Merral nodded. *Well, all stories must end and perhaps this is our ending. The secret is, as Perena said, to end it well.*

He stared at the slope. The Krallen line now was perhaps twenty deep and a kilometer long. *At least the coming conflict will have the merit of brevity.*

"You know," Vero said, in a wistful voice as he craned his neck skyward, "in the old stories something turns up at this point. Like eagles."

"Eagles?" Merral shook his head. "No. Not today. Not in this story."

He twisted his head to look southward at the hazy blue of the sea. *I have never spent enough time at the sea. One minor, last-minute regret: too many trees and not enough beaches.* He swung his gaze over the bay, the village, its vineyards and olive groves, grieving that this might be the last time he saw such things.

A hundred meters or so away, he saw a white bird flying eastward.

As he saw it Merral felt oddly certain that there was something about its movement that was striking, even significant. But what was it? He watched it, recognizing that far from being an eagle, it was merely some sort of small tern. Yet he was still sure that what he was seeing was critical. Then, in a flash, it came to him: *the bird was struggling against the wind.*

"The wind!" he said and as he spoke, the flags began to twitch and tremble into life.

Merral turned southward again, seeing far away lines of white foam on the sea, noting the leaves on the remaining olive trees quivering and sensing a breeze on his face.

"That's better," said Vero.

The banner of the Lamb and Stars fluttered clear from the flagpole and streamed out wide and noble.

What had Jorgio said? "I am specifically to tell you, from the Most High, that in half an hour, there will be a strong wind off the sea." But, why tell me?

He turned to the slope in front of him, a sudden, wild idea flooding his mind.

"Colonel, Captains," he ordered into his microphone. "We have to set fire to the trees! Quick—send the fastest people you have. Set fire to the trees, the bushes, anything that will burn!"

In moments, soldiers were racing over the dug-up ground, their feet kicking up dust that blew after them.

Now, above the cries of the men, the pulsing howls of the Krallen, the taut snapping of the flags at the poles, Merral could hear the mad, wild roar of the wind.

The first soldier had reached the trees now and was setting fire to the undergrowth. A single tongue of yellow flame licked out and then another. Fire began to sprint through the dry brush.

A second man set fire to a pile of dead twigs and the golden flames raced upward. In a second, dry sap-filled branches caught fire. Elsewhere, more soldiers fired the undergrowth.

The wind continued to strengthen. Overhead, the flags flapped with a manic energy, and beyond the ditches, loose dirt from the excavation of the defenses rolled and bounced toward the forested hillside.

High above, the Krallen still howled, but with a change in note.

Merral pressed his microphone stud. "Betafor," he said, "can you tell me if there is any alteration in the Krallen signals?" He paused, hearing only silence. "Betafor? Betafor?"

There was no answer. A communication link down, he decided, and turned his attention to what was happening on the mountainside.

Fanned by the growing wind, an angry line of yellow fire was spreading rapidly up the slope. *How strange. What I once feared as a forester has become something that may deliver us.* In places, the fire crawled from twig to twig, but elsewhere, driven by the rising wind, it jumped and leaped from branch to branch.

Smoke billowed and eddied up the slope, carrying sparks with it that started new fires. Now, at the base of the slope, there were no longer individual patches of fire but instead, one great smoky wall of flame that swept upward with an irresistible force, turning trees into flaming torches within seconds. The few firebreaks were leaped with ease and within a few minutes of the first fires being lit, the whole lower part of the hillside had become a vast roaring furnace.

I have seen many fires in my life, but none of this ferocity. Indeed, there was something extraordinary about this conflagration, as if it was not the simple act of combustion, but a living elemental creature *Fire* let loose on earth.

In a few more moments, the first tongues of flames had raced to within a dozen meters of the Krallen front line.

Around Merral, men and women cheered, wept, or prayed.

The Krallen line seemed to undergo some sort of readjustment.

"The Krallen are retreating!" Vero cried as he waved a clenched fist high in exuberant joy. "Yah hey!"

Then in a single, terrible moment, everything changed.

As if a dam had burst, the Krallen line plunged headlong down the slope. Down they rushed through the flames, bounding, tumbling, and rolling over the rocks and tree trunks in an attempt to burst through the fire. With urgent cries, soldiers who had flung down weapons snatched them up again and threw themselves against the defenses.

At first, Merral felt certain that the Krallen were moving so fast that most of them would pass through the flames unharmed. But as he watched, he saw that the roughness of the slope worked against them. Some mysterious and ancient process of erosion had gouged out furrows and ridges on the slopes and—inevitably—in their mad descent, the Krallen were forced into the valleys. Here they pushed together, tripped each other up, and, intertwined, fell into the roaring blast of the flames. And as the gullies became increasingly blocked by burning and melting Krallen, those that tried to follow were slowed down long enough for the flames to take hold of them. Others, apparently disoriented by the smoke, tumbled off crags into flames. Still other Krallen erupted in spectacular chains of explosions that set fire to yet more trees.

Yet although most of the Krallen perished in the crackling inferno of the mountainside, a few hundred—a ragged line of blackened and smoldering figures—burst out of the smoke and raced toward the lines.

A volley of rockets from the XQ guns took down many of them, but still dozens made it to the ramparts. Yet for once, the attackers were outnumbered and the Krallen perished rapidly. Merral slashed a charred Krallen as it tried to surmount the parapet in front of him and almost severed its neck completely. Lloyd thrust the barrel of his shotgun into the mouth of another and blew its head off. Another Krallen, its tail smoldering, slipped over the parapet and ended up at Anya's feet. Wielding the blade with both hands, she swung it deep into its chest. As the creature slumped to the ground, she pulled out the blade and then thrust it down with such force that the creature's head was pinned to the ground.

"That's a lady with attitude," Vero murmured.

Merral looked around. The attack was over. Ahead, perhaps fifty Krallen were left in front of the flames, trying to regroup, but showing evidence of being disoriented.

Filled with a new and spirited defiance, Merral clambered on top of the ramparts, waving his sword and feeling the wind on his back. "Come on! Let's finish them off. Charge!" he yelled and then ran forward.

"Not so fast!" he heard Lloyd gasp behind him, but he didn't slacken his pace.

He was first to reach the remaining Krallen, but the others were barely steps behind. With shouts of "The Lamb!" "Tantaravekat!" "For Perena!" "Tezekal!" and many other cries, they cut and hacked away until the last Krallen lay still.

Merral D'Avanos turned his back on the still-flaming mountain, took off his helmet and gloves, and amid the cheers of his men, strode back to where the Lamb and Stars flapped proudly in the wind.

As he stood there, Merral felt almost overwhelmed by conflicting emotions. He felt exhausted yet filled with an extraordinary energy; depressed at the losses yet elated at the victory. He wanted to both weep and sing.

But he did neither.

He gave a prayer of thanks and, reminding himself that there was work to be done, walked back to the command center.

erral and Colonel Lanier walked onto the roof of the command center to assess the situation.

A glance at the awesome inferno of flame and smoke still boiling in front of them on the mountainside confirmed to Merral that the main Krallen force had been utterly destroyed. Through the great billowing columns of smoke, perhaps a few hundred Krallen were trying to escape westward along the summit, apparently intent on returning to Langerstrand. Merral was doubtful that they would make it.

The few surviving irregulars on the Hereza Crags had taken a cue from what had happened above Tezekal and set fire to the ridge there. The result was that an almost continuous line of fire now raged along twenty kilometers of mountainside.

Merral looked at his watch. It was nearly four-thirty. High above them, Maria Brumeno and her team would be engaging the *Dove of Dawn*. He wondered how soon he would hear of their success or failure.

His thoughts were interrupted by a diary call from Zak. The thousand or so Krallen down by the mouth of the gorge had suddenly turned around and begun to run back to Langerstrand. Zak, plainly peeved at having missed the excitement up at the olive groves, wanted permission to go in hot pursuit.

Merral looked down the slope, seeing that the Krallen were indeed now loping westward. He pondered Zak's request. The idea that all the remaining Krallen west of Isterrane might be destroyed by the end of the day was a tempting one. Even more tantalizing was the prospect that such a sudden onslaught might gain access to the Langerstrand base and allow the hostages to be recovered. Yet weighed against that were the hard facts that his soldiers were exhausted and that even if he was to put together all the troops he had, the assault party would be no more than a thousand strong. And, precisely because of the hostages, Merral felt any approach to Langerstrand should not be rushed.

Colonel Lanier agreed with his reasoning, but when Merral explained it to Zak, the response was skeptical and even angry. In the end, Merral had to make it plain that it was an order. Zak reluctantly agreed to obey it.

That done, Merral pulled up a chair and set about making contact with various people. On impulse he called Betafor and this time got a response.

"Commander, how are you?" she said. Merral could read nothing in the bland voice.

"Very well. I called you earlier and got no answer. Is everything all right?"

"You did? That . . . may have been a brief communications failure earlier. Your systems are not as robust as they might be. Not for battle conditions."

"Possibly true," Merral replied, feeling puzzled. "What are you hearing now?"

"General confusion, consistent with a large-scale . . . chaotic retreat. A lot of units have ceased transmitting. You appear to have won, Commander, against the odds. Congratulations."

"Thank you," he said, then closed the connection.

Merral was about to contact Clemant when he received a new call on his diary. The image flickered heavily before stabilizing to show a woman in heavy white overalls with blonde hair tied back and wearing a happy expression. She sat at a desk in a strangely shaped, white-painted room and on the desk rested a large glass-visored helmet.

"Commander D'Avanos, we haven't been introduced, but I thought you'd like a call. I am Maria Brumeno."

"Maria!" Merral felt relief surge into his mind. "I don't recognize that decor."

"No, I don't care for it myself. I'll get the decorators in soon." A broad smile lit up her face. "Commander, you will be pleased to know that the Assembly has acquired a new space vessel. I am calling you from the bridge of the *Dove of Dawn*."

"Well done! Very well done indeed, Maria."

"Thank you, but the praise needs to be shared. I hear that you have had a good day."

"Yes, a hard fight but, by the grace of God, we won. There are now very few Krallen west of Isterrane. If you get a chance, find a porthole and look our way. There's a very large forest fire here and a lot of Krallen are roasting in the embers. If I hadn't left Forestry, I think they would have sacked me." Merral realized that he was smiling. "But tell me how it went."

"Surprisingly easy. There was very little resistance and that ended pretty quickly. We blew the door in and had a bit of a battle. They kept the artificial gravity on, which helped us." She nudged the helmet and Merral watched it float away. "It's off at the moment, because we have shut down most of the ship's systems." She paused to sigh. "We had two dead and one injured. On their side, there were two men, half a dozen cockroach-beasts, and couple of ape-creatures. We were prepared to be merciful, but they would have none of it. And as they would not surrender, we shot them. I'm sorry."

Merral sighed. "A pity."

"We tried saving the men, but dealing with pressure-suit injuries in a vacuum is not easy."

"I can imagine. Is the ship itself damaged?"

"Just the door. It needs a new entrance system to allow direct docking with Assembly craft but we don't anticipate any problem replacing it with the standard access unit. The gear is already on its way out from Near Station."

"And the ship is secure?"

"That's an affirmative, Commander. We turned off all power to the systems and are bringing it back on line system by system."

"Excellent news. Give my congratulations to all concerned. Any idea how long before the *Dove* will fly?"

Maria smiled. "In our profession, Commander, we like to read the manuals first. And we're in no hurry. But we already have the engineering team on board." She looked to her left and the camera followed her gaze to show a number of men and women working at open panels. Merral was struck by a tall woman with her back to the camera who had long, wavy black hair that floated about her head. Somehow he felt he knew her.

Maria spoke again. "There seems to be no reason why we can't have it up and running inside a week."

"You have no idea, Captain, what good news that is. We need it."

"Yes," she said and the smile slipped away to be replaced by an expression of loss. "We have paid a price for victory."

"I'm sorry," Merral said. "I really am. But the ship is priceless."

"It's in good hands."

ᗝᗝᗝᗝᗝ

Merral then called Clemant. The diary screen showed that he was in his office. On the wall behind him were live images relayed from the *Dove*.

While not exactly radiant with happiness—when had he ever been?—there seemed to be a new buoyancy to Clemant.

"An afternoon of most encouraging news," he said. "Both from the *Dove* and from you."

"We were shown mercy," Merral answered.

"Indeed."

"Sir, I was wondering about the next military steps. I want a team to sur-round Langerstrand to try and get the hostages and maybe take Lezaroth."

Clemant frowned. "I understand that, Commander. I really do. But I think our most pressing concern lies with the Dominion forces in the Camolgi Hills. They are big enough to wipe out Halmacent, Ranapert, or even Isterrane."

"True, but at the very least, you must allow the immobilization of the vessels at Langerstrand."

Clemant stroked a cheek with his finger. "Yes, I will allow a small force to surround the site and to immobilize the ship. No more than a hundred soldiers and to leave no earlier than tomorrow. I want to see what news the night brings."

"Very well."

Some faint emotion flickered across Clemant's face. "Oh, Commander, I need to inform you of matters to do with the *Dove*. A mere technicality. The Dominion ship has been put under the management of a specialist technical team. It is no longer a defense matter."

"In other words, it's not my business?"

"Exactly."

ㅇㅇㅇㅇㅇ

Merral found Vero in the rooms used by the irregs. He was looking at a long list of names on a wallscreen and his face wore a subdued look.

"Our losses: dead, wounded, and missing," Vero said in a sad voice as the names scrolled down the screen. He swiveled round in his seat to face Merral. "What news?"

"We have the *Dove*," Merral said.

"I heard. Another ray of sunlight on a dark day." Vero rubbed his fingers against his temples. "No. I must be more positive. This is *very* good news. Within days, we may be able to travel back to the Assembly through Below-Space. The Assembly will gain this technology. Everything changes."

"True. But in the meantime, down here, there are issues. We have to rescue the hostages at Langerstrand, deal with the remaining Krallen there, and, of course, ensure the destruction of the eastern Krallen army."

"And we mustn't forget the baziliarch. He fled northward. If he comes back . . ." He shook his head.

"Yes."

Vero nodded, then lowered his voice. "Incidentally, we have had an odd thing with Betafor. She seems to have gone missing a couple of hours ago. Just at the time of the attack, the guard looked into her room for some reason and couldn't find her. He went for help. By the time he had found someone else to search the building properly, the mountain was on fire and we were winning. They went back and there she was. Said she was under the table."

"Interesting. I tried to call her about then and got no answer. Could she have escaped?"

"There's a small roof vent that could be unscrewed. I mentioned it to Azeras and he just laughed. He reckons she looked at the statistics, decided we were the losers, and made a run for it. Says she was probably halfway to the Dominion lines before she realized that we weren't the losing side after all. So she turned back. 'Don't say I didn't warn you,' he said."

"She served us well otherwise. And Azeras may be wrong. But I guess we'd better watch out. Anyway, Vero, we seem to have survived."

Vero gave a weary sigh. "So far, my friend. And by grace. But it isn't over. Indeed, I have a fear that we may face new problems. I sense issues emerging that I do not care for."

But he would not be drawn out as to what those were and Merral left him gazing mournfully at his somber list.

◯◯◯◯◯

Shortly afterward, Merral decided that things were stable enough that he could afford to take off his armor and have a much needed shower. As he entered the shower, he heard the rumble of a flier as it landed and gave a prayer of thanks. The isolation was over.

Ten minutes later, just after changing into a fresh uniform in the tent he had been assigned, he heard a deliberate cough outside. It was Luke and his face was stern.

"What's up, Luke?"

"Two things. First, do the names Durrance and Latrati mean anything to you?"

"No. . . . Wait. I remember. Zak said they had fled. There was a discipline issue and I told him to send them to Isterrane. It's something we'll have to deal with. Why?"

"They were medical cases. Broken ribs, lost teeth. An orderly mentioned them to me. He was worried about the wounds."

"Are we talking about the same people? They never fought. They shouldn't be injured."

"Yes." Luke's face was solemn. "I put the matter to one side until a soldier told me he had heard that Zak had beaten them. Personally. Punched, kicked—that sort of thing."

Merral stared at him. "No. I don't believe—" He stopped, suddenly aware that he did believe it. "That's a very serious allegation, Chaplain."

"I know. But I thought you ought to deal with it."

"I will. Can I talk to your soldier?"

"No. He won't talk. He's scared."

Merral sighed. "*That* is entirely believable. Okay, I'll look into it. I want to interview Durrance and Latrati in Isterrane. And the other matter?"

"I just thought you ought to know that Delastro and his men came on that supply flight that just landed."

Merral finished buttoning up his shirt. "Luke, I don't need him. Certainly not now. What's he doing?"

"He's speaking to the soldiers at the strip."

"Saying what?"

"That there must be no compromise with evil; that we need to purge Farholme from every trace of sin."

"Does he say anything against the Defense Force or me?"

Luke shifted uneasily on his feet. "He says that purity needs to start here. He implies that we are in need of purification."

Merral sighed. "Luke, do two things for me. First, summon him up here immediately."

"And second?"

"Pray that I don't punch him."

◌◌◌◌◌

Ten minutes later, the prebendant and his two dark-suited followers arrived. Merral beckoned the cleric over to where, under the shade of an awning, a pair of chairs were placed. The followers remained at a distance, not far from a tree under which Lloyd sat, his brown bag next to him.

"Prebendant, this is a surprise visit," Merral said as they sat down.

Delastro placed his staff across his knees and gazed coolly at Merral. "And why shouldn't a chaplain visit the scene of battle?"

"There is no reason at all. Your presence earlier today would have been most welcome. But, Prebendant, the battle is now over and most of the wounded are in hospital in Isterrane where you could easily visit them."

Delastro sat stiffly back in his chair, brushed something off the sleeve of his dark suit, then turned his hard gaze back on Merral. "Commander, you persist in assuming my ministry is to do with the sick and the troubled. I see it more as opposing evil."

"There's plenty of that around," Merral said, pointing over at the distant hazy smear that was the Langerstrand Peninsula.

"Evil, Commander, can be blatant *and* subtle. It can prowl the battlefield openly and yet dwell like a hidden cancer in a man's heart." His long fingers twisted together.

"I agree, but please feel free to be specific."

"Thank you. The wickedness of these Krallen—these demon-spawned monsters—needs erasing utterly. Every trace of them and their works needs uprooting and eliminating."

"By the grace of the Most High and much sacrifice we seem to have eliminated around a hundred thousand of them over the last two days. Not a bad start, wouldn't you say?"

The prebendant folded his hands, tilted his head, and fixed his green eyes on Merral. "On the surface, yes, you have done much. But is your victory all it claims to be? I hear that underneath you have compromised." His voice was almost a hiss. "Compromised in such a deadly way that it must be opposed."

Don't lose your temper. "A most serious charge, Prebendant."

"You and this dark visitor, Verofaza—a man of whom we know so little— have strange beings working for you." There was an almost piercing intensity to his eyes and his voice seemed to tremble. "A greenish creature—very like these Krallen, it seems. And a strange man who fights under a banner other than our blessed Lamb and Stars. There is an organization that is based under- ground and about which we know almost nothing. And, above all, you have assistance from a mysterious and unnamed visitor from the spirit world."

His bony hands clutched the polished wooden staff tightly. "Commander, I think some explanation would be in order, or even, perhaps, confession."

Unable to contain his anger, Merral got to his feet. "By implying that we have had dealings with the occult you dishonor both the living and the dead who fought here today, Prebendant. As chaplain-in-chief you are under *my* authority and I now formally dismiss you."

Delastro rose to face him, his knuckles white on his staff.

Merral nodded at Lloyd, who spoke into a shoulder microphone and reached into his bag.

"Sergeant Enomoto will accompany you and your men to the strip here. A flight will be arranged to take you back to Isterrane. This is a military area, under my authority, and I forbid you to say a word to anyone else here."

Delastro raised his staff high and shook it.

With a casual, unhurried pace, Lloyd, the shotgun in his big hands, began walking over. One of the young men ran forward to grab him, but as his hands touched Lloyd, the gun butt swung back sharply. With a groan, the man doubled up and, clutching his stomach, fell to the ground. Without even a backward glance, Lloyd continued his measured pace.

A dozen green-clad soldiers led by Vero emerged from the house and spread out in a semicircle.

Merral turned to Delastro. "Prebendant, Sergeant Enomoto is a fine fellow, but he does take his job very seriously. He can be fiercely protective. I think you had better not make any moves that could be misconstrued as hostile. Good-bye."

Delastro, his face pale with fury, glared at Merral. "Be warned, Commander. Evil takes evildoers."

He swung around and, with his strange, birdlike gait, walked rapidly away toward the strip.

The other man helped up his fallen colleague and, closely followed by Lloyd and the regulars, they went after their leader.

Vero walked over to Merral. "I got most of that. Pretty much along the lines of 'By the prince of demons you cast out demons'? Well, that's an allegation with a long pedigree." He sighed deeply. "But, my friend, we have just witnessed another of my oversights."

"In what way?"

Vero stared down into the gorge and Merral followed his gaze to where the shadows were deepening. "Ah. I realized that the resurgence of evil in our world would warp our relationships and the way our society is run. And it has. But until now, I had not imagined that it could affect our faith." He gave a bitter shrug. "But why should that area of life be excluded from the contamination of sin? What richer soil for evil to take root in than that of faith and duty and prayer?"

⬚⬚⬚⬚⬚

Within half an hour, the still-fuming prebendant and his followers had left for Isterrane. After their departure, Merral walked over to the medical tents. The seriously injured had been flown to Isterrane already, leaving only those who were lightly wounded. He wandered between them, struggling to hold his emotions in check and trying to offer encouragement and sympathy. He then walked around the tents where most of the remaining soldiers were treating minor cuts and grazes, resting in the shade, or just sitting on the ground staring into infinity.

They were glad to see him and Merral listened to what they had to say. Any euphoria over the victory had seeped away and the mood was subdued and reflective. Everybody knew someone who was dead. *I can share in your grief. I too have lost a dear friend in these last two days.* He made no attempt to probe what had happened with Latrati and Durrance—that was for another time—but he couldn't avoid hearing unease in the voices of those who had fought under Zak's command. Their concerns were delivered in hushed tones with wary glances over their shoulders. Soldiers had been forced into positions that were too exposed; the discipline was too tough—Zak was brutal. *I will deal with this, but not today.*

The tales of the fighting and the looming issues with Zak darkened Merral's spirits and he postponed seeing Anya; his mood was too bleak. Finally, as the light faded, he was persuaded by Lloyd to go and eat.

In the mess tent that had been erected at the edge of the village he found Zak at a table surrounded by a number of his captains and associates. The tone of their conversation was boisterous, even jovial. Merral picked up his tray of food, engaged in some brief, polite conversation with them, and went outside. He found a seat under a tree, out of earshot of the chatter and laughter, and there, as the sun set in smoke over Langerstrand, ate his food in silence.

He felt depressed and images of death and destruction seemed to overwhelm him. He realized that the encounter with Delastro and Vero's analysis of it had shaken him. There was now no place in his world where corruption had not spread.

When he had finished his meal, he got to his feet and—as ever—shadowed by Lloyd, walked up to the gentle ridge amid the olive groves where they had faced the enemy and where the flagpoles still stood.

The wind had dropped and the great flags, now mere shadows in the smoky darkness, only rustled gently in the dusty, smoke-laden wind. He sat down at the foot of the flagpole bearing the large Lamb and Stars standard. Ahead, patches of orange glowed bright on the mountain—the dying embers of the once all-consuming inferno. Above, smeared by the sooty atmosphere, stars were coming out.

Eventually, Lloyd drew closer. "Just checking. You okay, sir?"

"Thanks." Merral paused. "I had to set fire to trees, Lloyd."

"I know."

"Burned trees and hundreds of deaths. It's a funny way to save a world."

"It had to be done, sir." The words were soft.

"Thanks, Lloyd. I guess it did."

Then, suddenly feeling overwhelmed by tiredness, Merral rose and walked back to his tent.

"Lloyd," he said as he lifted the flap, "I don't want to be woken before dawn. Unless it's an emergency."

Lezaroth leaned back in his chair and stared at the ceiling of the drab room at Langerstrand that he had taken as his operations center as he listed his woes. *I've lost a full-suppression complex by a trick and almost my entire Krallen army*

to essentially agricultural satellites. My attack force has been defeated by swords and a fire, and now the Dove of Dawn *is in their hands. And to crown it all, the baziliarch is missing. Am I cursed?*

He clenched his fists tightly in defiance. *But even if I am cursed, so what? I will still fight on.*

There was a knock on the door.

"Come in."

A thin, bald man—the baziliarch's intermediary—in a loose, dark blue robe came in, his pale eyes swinging nervously this way and that. He looked at Lezaroth with dread as if expecting his own death sentence to be pronounced.

"So where is he?" Lezaroth barked. "Is the . . . thing . . . dead?"

The intermediary gulped audibly. "No, sir. But I think he's wounded. He'll be hiding out somewhere in the wilds, healing."

What time is it in the outside world? Lezaroth looked at a clock. He was surprised to see it was nearly midnight. "Are there any precedents?"

"No, sir. But then we only started using baziliarchs after the lord-emperor's negotiations on the Blade of Night."

"Of course. So what happened?"

"He was met by something—something or *someone*—of a similar rank on the other side. It was a hard fight."

"Will we get him back?"

The intermediary looked even more uneasy. "I think so. I'll try to contact him, to persuade him to help again. It may take time. You can't order a baziliarch around, sir. And he'll be angry."

"When he returns, can I rely on him?"

The intermediary jerked his head and gulped once more. "Sir, baziliarchs need to be managed carefully. They are lords. But he may join in on his own account."

"Very well. If he turns up, let me know."

When he left, Lezaroth returned to his thoughts. *We have suffered great losses, but that's not the issue now. I must think tactically. There have been surprises here, but we can still take the capital and with it, the world. They do not know about the* Nanmaxat's Comet. *That can get us back. But it is how to achieve victory that's the issue.*

On impulse, Lezaroth flicked on the wallscreen and called up some of his personal files on Merral D'Avanos. *Here is where the trouble lies—the great adversary. And to think I could have killed him with my bare hands just yesterday.*

"D'Avanos," he said aloud. "*You* are the problem. I need to destroy you. This war is now a manhunt." *But how do I trap him?*

Lezaroth realized that he had to twist his mind. *I have to think like him.*

That's hard. He's utterly alien to me. What does he value? He looked hard at the screen until the answer came. *Beyond his faith, D'Avanos values his home, his friends, his family.*

Lezaroth nodded slowly. *That's it. If I put the right pressure on the right place, I'll have him. Somewhere there is a way to trap him.*

He tapped the desk as an idea struck him. *His home, his friends, his family . . .*

∝◌⊃◌⊂

Merral was awakened by a rough shake of the shoulders. It was still dark.

"Sir!" Lloyd hissed in his ear.

"It's an emergency?" Merral mumbled.

"Yes, sir. It's the eastern Krallen force at Camolgi Hills. They're moving."

"Oh. Westward? To Isterrane?"

"No, east."

"East?"

"Yes. Toward Ynysmant."

28

Ten minutes later, Merral was sipping a cup of strong coffee that Lloyd had made and staring at an ominous screen of interpreted satellite data.

Vero joined him, rubbing his unshaven face as he peered at the images.

"Apparently, the Krallen started to move an hour ago," Merral said. "About a third of their force—around eight thousand—are moving fast to the northeast."

"And it has to be Ynysmant?"

"There's nowhere else in that direction."

"How long before they get there?"

"It's just over two hundred kilometers; it depends on whether they have to detour to cross the rivers. At the earliest they could be there by midday our time, midafternoon theirs."

Vero rubbed his head. "I don't like it."

"Me neither. But I know the ground. If Frankie Thuron airlifted troops quickly, we could stop them en route. There are marshes—the north end of the Gulder Swamps. I'm trying to see if Clemant knows what's happening. . . . How many irregulars are there at Ynysmant?"

"At a guess, a thousand."

Too few. Far too few.

"Commander!" A man at a desk raised a hand. "I have Coordinator Clemant on this screen."

As Merral sat at the screen, he noticed that even at this hour Clemant was clean shaven and his hair was combed and neatly parted.

"Good morning, sir," Merral said. "You are aware of developments at Camolgi Hills?"

"I have known about it for the best part of an hour." Clemant's deep voice was smooth. "I have just been talking to Colonel Thuron and he and I think it's a trap."

"A trap? In what way?"

"We think they know they can't easily advance past Ranapert and Halmacent because of the arc of defenses that we now have in place. Our guess is that they want to draw us out from behind the defenses into the open. They know that you come from Ynysmant. And they also know that we value human life—and especially civilian life—very highly. We think, therefore, they are hoping that in order to protect Ynysmant, you will order the army out from behind its defenses."

There was something very alarming about Clemant's carefully paced words. "Which is surely what we must do?"

Clemant gave a deep rumble of a sigh. "Commander, this is going to be difficult for me to say, and probably even more difficult for you to accept. I would like you to try to distance yourself from the unfortunate fact that the apparent destination is your hometown."

"Sir, what are you trying to say?"

Merral was aware of the others in the room gathering around him.

"I'm saying that I do not want to send the army to protect Ynysmant."

For a moment, Merral was too stunned to speak. "But . . . they'll slaughter the town! There are twenty thousand people there. This isn't a village. In fact, with refugees, there must be—what?—thirty thousand people there. We've *got* to defend it."

"I anticipated these objections. I have asked Colonel Thuron to see if he can deploy any soldiers from around the main defenses. That might allow several thousand soldiers to be deployed later today. But not until then." The tone of Clemant's voice suggested that his position was unshakable.

"In other words," Merral said, making no effort to disguise his anger, "there will be no rescue until tomorrow morning. By which time it will all be too late."

"Commander, you have to understand that we are doing all we can." The words were smooth. "We cannot hazard an army—a capital—for the sake of a few people. Protecting the many takes precedence over the few."

His parents, his uncle, aunt, and cousins, plus a thousand other names and faces suddenly came into Merral's mind. "And if neglecting the few—thirty thousand is a pretty big *few*, sir—means condemning them to a horrible death, what then?"

Clemant sighed and shrugged slightly. "Welcome, Commander, to the place of hard choices. I'm afraid that what we're dealing with is a matter of . . . military necessity. Ynysmant has, I'm told, considerable defenses and a determined population."

Merral clenched the edge of his chair. "I don't agree," he said. "I don't think we can let this happen."

"Respectfully, Commander, I think you're letting your family ties blind you to military necessity."

"Do I gather, sir, that you forbid me as Commander of the Farholme Defense Force to order Frankie Thuron to deploy his troops to protect Ynysmant?"

"I do."

"Then I propose to disobey that order."

Clemant sighed. "I was hoping to avoid this, but you leave me no option. As of this moment, you are relieved of your post as commander and return to the rank of captain."

Merral heard a low gasp from the soldiers around him. "That's an outrage!" he heard himself say. "I do not accept that."

Clemant's round face paled. "Captain, I should warn you that I am being generous. I have people here—influential people—who want to bring very serious charges against you and Verofaza Enand."

"Such as?"

"Dealing with demons, witchcraft—charges for which capital punishment might be sought."

There were new gasps. "That guy's crazy," muttered someone.

"This is madness," Merral protested.

"Captain, so far I have rejected such pressures. I am protecting you. But if you resist me, I may have no option but to have the police arrest you both."

Suddenly, Merral realized he had made a decision. "I'm sorry, sir," he said, as his fingers found the screen power switch. "I do not accept your authority."

He stabbed the switch and the screen went black.

Feeling sick and stunned, Merral sat back in the chair. "Vero," he said, "what have I just done?"

Vero rubbed his nose. "You just mutinied. In some armies of the past, you would be shortly executed."

"That's what I thought." Merral rose. He felt oddly calm now. "What vessels have we got on the strip that are capable of transporting people?"

"A D-series—the good old *Emilia Kay*—and an F-series, *Asaha Sirhen.* And—"

"The *Emilia Kay* will do well enough."

Merral found a microphone and pressed a button. The sound of a trumpet alert echoed around the camp. "Good morning, soldiers. This is Merral D'Avanos speaking. I am sorry to disturb your much-deserved sleep, but I need volunteers. The town of Ynysmant is under threat and I am going there to defend it. I need crew for a D-series vessel and as many volunteers as can fit in it. This is an unauthorized mission and I can only promise you more fighting and a high risk of death. If you want to come, I would like you to be on the strip with your equipment in half an hour."

Then he tabbed the microphone off and looked at Vero. "What was that phrase of yours: 'putting cats among pigeons'?" He got to his feet. "I'm going to get my armor."

Outside, the darkness ebbed to the east. In the tents there were lights and noises.

I'll look very silly if no one wants to come.

Suddenly Vero was at his elbow. "I-I'm not the best fighting man, but I want to come."

"Why you?"

"I have had hospitality in Ynysmant and I would like to repay that debt. And besides, any battle will fall heavily on the irregulars. I think I should be there." He gave a strange little laugh. "And besides, if they are going to try me for witchcraft, then I might as well add the charge of mutiny. May as well be hung for a sheep as a lamb."

"Hung? . . . Oh, explain another time."

"Can I suggest we take Betafor? Wrapped up in her traveling case, of course."

"Why?"

"Because, my friend, she may be useful."

"But will she come?"

"I'll tell her she's being hunted as a demon here. She has a strong instinct for self-preservation."

"Do it."

"Let me get my things."

Merral was not surprised when Lloyd demanded to come.

"I won't argue," he said and as he did, he realized how glad he was that Lloyd was going to be with him.

Merral walked over to his tent and pulled on his armor.

I can't believe what has just happened. I rebelled against a legitimate authority. He thought of Ynysmant and his family, the rather ridiculous but likable Warden Enatus, and a score of other people and felt he had made the right decision. Then putting analysis behind him, he slung his XQ rifle over his shoulder and buckled his sword to his belt.

As he left the tent, he found a sleepy-eyed Luke outside. "Merral, I thought I'd better talk to you."

"Go ahead, Chaplain."

"Look, are you sure this is the wisest thing?"

"Ah, your right to challenge me. I can't deny that I've rebelled against a legitimate authority. And I know that's wrong. But I can't neglect my family and friends, Luke. You wouldn't want me to do that."

"No, I suppose not," Luke said slowly. When he spoke again, Merral heard unease in his voice. "It's just that what's happening in Isterrane troubles me. Delastro and Clemant ought to be challenged. There is a madness there, a madness that needs stopping. I think you can do it. Probably only you can."

"Luke, they are threatening me with all sorts of things: witchcraft charges and the like."

"Oh, don't be silly, Merral." There was exasperation in the tired face. "That's nonsense. Do you really think they would make that stick? Try the most popular man on the planet for a crime that no one has ever heard of and everyone knows is bogus? In fact, I think you should call their bluff."

Something in Luke's words disturbed Merral and set a train of thoughts in motion. *Am I running away? Don't I have a duty here? Hasn't the envoy told me to stay near Isterrane?* He considered that for some moments. *Perhaps I misunderstood the message. Perhaps the envoy didn't foresee this eventuality. Anyway, how can I refuse to help? Unless I lead some sort of intervention, they have no hope. Even with it, their chances are slim.*

"I'll make a deal with you, Luke. I'll drop off these men, see them in place, and get back as soon as I can. Then, tomorrow, we can tackle Isterrane."

A frown appeared on Luke's weary face. "If you think that's wise, yes. But can I come?"

"It's fighters I need, Luke."

"You have had some hard decisions to make. You may have more. I'd like to be there to help. Something tells me I need to stick close to you!"

"Very well, I'll take you. Get your things."

Merral walked to the strip, followed closely by Lloyd. *I need to talk to Anya,* he suddenly realized and was on the point of calling her when Colonel Lanier walked up to him.

"Colonel," Merral said, "I need to talk to you."

"Captain," Lanier replied and the single word told Merral that the colonel had talked with Clemant.

"A moment." The colonel dropped his voice. "I've been asked to arrest you and hold you until the police arrive."

"Are you going to?"

The colonel chuckled softly. "Well, I said I would. But I'm going to have some breakfast first. I'm a leisurely man and I like an unrushed meal. *Then* I'm coming for you."

"Thanks. Have a good breakfast."

The colonel extended a hand. "I hope it works out at Ynysmant. And come back safe. We need you in Isterrane."

As he walked through the darkness onto the strip where the fins of the vessels could be seen rising up against the lightening sky, Merral realized, with a surge of emotion, that his request had been heard. Dozens—no, scores—of soldiers with sleepy faces and armor and with guns slung over their shoulders had gathered.

Merral heard his name called and turned to see Anya.

She grabbed his arm. "Vero told me. I can't believe it. Clemant's gone mad."

"So it seems. But my concern is Ynysmant."

"What do you want me to do? I'll come."

"I'm sure you would, but no. I'm worried about you. Anyone linked to me could be in trouble now."

"Vero's suggesting that I take Azeras and head back by road to Isterrane and hide out in the foundations."

"Yes. A good idea. All being well, I'll be back soon, and we can try and sort out this mess."

"Let's hope so. There's a lot to sort out. But please keep safe." A look of deep and apparently overwhelming emotion crossed her face and then as if to avoid saying anything more, she turned and ran away.

✕✕✕✕✕

Lights were on in the cockpit of the *Emilia Kay*.

Trying to ignore the memories of Perena in the same vessel, Merral stuck his head through the hatch that led to the pilot's cabin. "Anyone here?"

"Hi, Commander," a woman's voice sang brightly from the top of the ladder. "Be with you now."

In a moment Merral was shaking hands with a diminutive and animated woman with short black hair. "Captain Istana Nelder. Got in last night with supplies. I'm volunteering."

"You do know you could get in trouble for this?"

"Don't care. Mother's got relatives in Ynysmant."

Merral noted that Istana didn't seem to care for full sentences. "Thanks. How many can you take?"

"Where do you want to land? Airport? At the top by Congregation Hall? Congregation Square means a vertical landing."

"Give me the figures for both. Troops plus guns, armor, and ammo—no other gear."

She closed her eyes. "Airport, I can do 170; the square, 150. But it will be tight."

"We'll take the square."

She bent to look out of the doorway and then grinned at him. "Better do some filtering then. You got too many there."

Merral turned round to see that lights had come on around the strip and, with a lump in his throat, realized that there were at least 300 soldiers there.

It took less than ten minutes to reduce the numbers by half, mostly by eliminating those people who were either the only children in their family, parents, or newly married. The majority of the volunteers he chose were men with swords and guns but, somewhat against his better judgment, Merral was persuaded by an insistent Karita to take her and twenty of her snipers.

The selection made, Merral ordered the hull doors open and the soldiers to line up.

"Stop!" A tall man with blond hair pushed through the line and stood in front of Merral. Zak. Six men elbowed their way to stand behind him. Merral remembered having seen them with Zak before.

"Good morning, Colonel Larraine," Merral said, hearing murmurs among the crowd and wishing desperately that he might have avoided this encounter.

"Captain D'Avanos, I order you to stop this."

The murmuring among the soldiers grew. Merral saw Lloyd edge menacingly over to Zak and motioned him back.

"Sorry, Zak. I'm just not standing by when people are about to be massacred. Whether it's my town or any town, I don't care. That's not what the Assembly is about."

"It's an order!" Zak snapped in such an unyielding tone that Merral realized why the soldiers feared him.

"Oh, quit it, Zak!" someone from the back shouted in a tone of weary disgust. There was a low rumble of agreement.

Zak's followers glanced around with uneasy looks.

"Step back from the ship," Zak ordered.

"I won't," Merral said. "I'm on an errand of mercy."

"Mercy?" came a cry out of the shadows. "Better spell that out for our Zak!"

There was a chorus of "Yes!" "You tell him!" "Exactly!"

Zak's face flushed.

"Zak'd throw his mum to the goblins!" someone else shouted. There were hoots of laughter.

Merral raised a hand to stop the cries, but they continued. *I should intervene. But Zak needs to hear the verdict of the men.*

"She *was* one!" yelled someone else. The laughter grew.

"Nah, he's Krallen on his dad's side!"

There were more guffaws and beneath them Merral heard hatred.

"D'Avanos, get away from that ship!" Zak said.

"Lost our temper, have we, Zak?" cried another voice. There was a new ripple of laughter.

Merral decided that it was now time to firmly end this confrontation. "Colonel, listen to me. I have a job to do. I'm getting on this ship now and the soldiers are following me. And if you stand there, you might get crushed."

There was a moment charged with tension; then Zak looked around. Behind him his friends were sliding away into the darkness. He quivered, swung on his heels, and amid taunting cheers and laughter, stormed away.

Ten minutes later as the *Emilia Kay* prepared for takeoff, Vero turned to Merral with a wry look on his face. "My friend, at the rate you and I are making enemies, we soon won't need Krallen."

◌◌◌◌◌

They took off as the sun rose, the brilliant colors of the sunrise heightened by the dust and smoke still in the air. Fearful of any sort of missile or artillery attack from the Dominion forces east of Halmacent, Merral and Istana agreed on a high-altitude course that curved north almost to the edge of the Great Northern Forest and then east toward Ynysmant.

"What I'd like," said Istana, as they flew north, "is a big bomb."

"I know another woman who would like something similar," Merral said and as he did, he wondered where Gerry Habbentz was now. The moment he raised the question, he realized with a start that the woman he had seen on the images from the captured *Dove* had to be her. It made sense. She was a top physicist and worked with Clemant's office and she had presumably been sent to look at the propulsion systems. Yet, in a way he couldn't pin down, the idea of Gerry being involved with Clemant and the *Dove* made him uneasy.

Half an hour into the flight, a message came in from Clemant with an order for Merral to turn back to Isterrane. Merral simply ignored the message and instead called Ynysmant and arranged for Congregation Square to be cleared for a landing.

"We're glad you're coming," said a woman at air control. "We've heard what's on the way."

As they flew on, gray stacked masses of clouds gathered below them reminding Merral of another fateful flight, just a few months earlier, when he had flown to the FDU training base at Tanaris Island just before the battle at Fallambet. *How much has changed; how distant that time now appears.* When he looked toward the pilot's seat, he found himself longing for the slim and thoughtful form of Perena instead of the diminutive, extroverted Istana.

He pushed the thought away. *Perena has played her part. I must play mine.*

I have to keep going. I must be like a machine. How strange. I almost find myself envying the Krallen their lack of emotions.

In an hour, they began their descent and through gaps in the clouds Merral glimpsed Ynsmere Lake. Soon he saw, silhouetted against the liquid silver of the lake, the spires and towers of his home.

Much to Vero's dismay, Istana chose to descend in a series of tight spirals and as she did Merral was able to glimpse his town through the porthole, seeing the parks, the winding streets, the different levels of roofs, towers, and spires. But he now saw it in a new way. *It is now not just a home, but a fortress.*

Congregation Square was cluttered with vehicles and equipment and Istana had to make a careful landing.

As the dust and fumes dispersed, Merral looked out of the window to see that his town had changed. There had once been almost uninterrupted views from the square. Now a high wall, three to four meters high, had been erected all around its perimeter. It was only broken by a gateway at the northern end that led to Island Road.

The soldiers disembarked and Merral ordered them into the shadow of the vast bulk of Congregation Hall to await orders.

"I barely recognize my town," he murmured, shocked by all the evidence of war.

It was not just the new walls, which were incomplete in places; it was the presence of all the paraphernalia of conflict: the boxes of ammunition, the fire tenders, the medical tents, and the shutters covering the windows of the hall. This new and dreadful transformation had affected the people too. Soldiers in the pale brown jerkins and berets of the irregs were everywhere, carrying boxes or weapons or giving orders. Even those out of uniform seemed to have a purpose to their actions that was remarkable for Ynsmant. And there were no children.

Merral turned to Vero. "I must find Enatus."

"Yes and I need to find a Balancal Marrat."

"Balancal? I think I've played Team-Ball against him. Why?"

"He heads the irregs here. And I need to arrange for Betafor to be set up somewhere." Then with an urgent pace, Vero strode toward the gateway where a cluster of irregs stood.

A few moments later a man in a green armored jacket led Merral and Lloyd to a small new sandbagged structure near the hall. Inside, a ladder led down to a series of corridors that Merral recognized as forming the rear of the main Ynsmant administrative building.

At the end of one corridor, Merral was ushered through double doors while Lloyd took a seat outside. Beyond the second door was a large, well-lit room full of desks, screens, and people, many of whom wore armor. Merral instantly sensed the now-familiar atmosphere of agitation and controlled fear.

As he entered, everyone looked up and in the smiles of welcome, he sensed a hunger for reassurance. *They see me as their deliverer. In that they hope for too much.*

At the far end of the room, Warden Enatus stood in conference with a number of people, all of whom were taller than him. The warden, dressed in a green armored jacket rather too tight for his ample stomach, bore a sheathed sword at his belt that heightened his rather ludicrous figure. He brushed free of his entourage and walked over, his rolling gait exaggerated by the jacket.

"Delighted to see you," Enatus said, beaming. "Delighted. We need all the help we can get, really."

"I brought only 150 soldiers," Merral said.

"Hmm." There was no hiding the spasm of disappointment that crossed the warden's face. Then he brightened. "Better than nothing, though. I gather you are all we can expect?"

"I'm afraid so. And I'm unauthorized."

"Hmm." The warden wiped his brow. "Well, take a seat, Commander. We need to talk. . . . Coffee, tea?"

"No, thanks. Oh, and technically, Warden, I'm now a captain." *In fact, I'm probably not even that by now.*

"Oh, nonsense. I heard about that from Isterrane. Clemant's a fool. That man has spent far too long staring at screens. You *are* a commander—commander in chief of Ynysmant defenses, if nothing else."

Enatus lowered himself carefully onto a chair and grimaced. "To tell you the whole truth, I can't get used to sitting down in this jacket," he confided with an apologetic look. "And it's so hot. And I keep tripping up over the sword."

Merral smiled. For all Enatus's ridiculousness, his genial and self-deprecating openness was rather likable.

Merral noticed on a large wallscreen map of the area an angry red line heading from the Camolgi Hills toward Ynysmant. It needed no explanation. "So, Warden, can you give me an update on the defenses?"

Enatus paused before saying, "There are three facts you need to know." He ticked off a stubby finger. "One, we predict the first Dominion units will reach the causeway by three or four this afternoon. That is in five or six hours' time. However, they seem to have these mobile artillery units—cannon insects, I believe the intelligence people call them—so we could get fired on sooner." He ticked off another finger. "We had thirty thousand people here at dawn. We're getting as many vulnerable people as we can out by boat from Vanulet Pier and by road and will continue to do so until it is too risky. There are three freighters at the airport being emptied as we speak and we hope to fly out a thousand or so children and old people on them in an hour's time.

They'll be the last flights out. The best guess is that will still leave us with twenty thousand people by the time we close the gates."

He paused, frowned, and touched a third finger. "And third, with your people and the irregulars we have only a little over twelve hundred defenders. Most of the irregulars have no armor."

He stared at the map and then looked up, pain apparent in his blue eyes. "In short, Commander, we have the makings of a disaster. Any comments?"

"No," Merral answered, impressed by the succinctness of Enatus's assessment of the situation. *Perhaps I have misjudged this man.* "Tell me about the defenses."

Enatus motioned for a projector system to be brought over from the next table and switched it on. A three-dimensional model of Ynysmant appeared above the table, and as Merral stared at it, he saw the new walls.

"Of course, you know the town as well as me. Yes, well, we have a big defensive wall at the Gate House with some rather experimental artillery. The causeway has been mined. . . . I think that's the word." Enatus frowned and muttered out of the corner of his mouth. "I hope you've mastered all this military language. I haven't." He pointed at the causeway. "This has been mined—that *is* the word—by your uncle, Barrand. Anyway, that's the first line of defense. There are firing points on the streets up and then the next defensive line is at the third circle."

"Makes sense."

"I'm glad you think so. And the final defensive line is around the square and the main refuge. What do you think?"

Merral stared at the model of Ynysmant. "The hospital?" He asked, suddenly realizing how vulnerable it was so close to the lake.

"We have already flown the most seriously ill patients out. The medical supplies and movable equipment are being relocated higher up."

"Good. Warden, I will have a look around, but I think you've made the best of an impossible task."

"Thank you. All advice will be accepted."

Merral was suddenly aware that his low opinion of Enatus was being replaced by a new respect. *And why not? If this crisis might be the breaking of some, might it not also be the making of others?* "I have only praise."

"Thank you. I am honored. Incidentally, I have sent Clemant's police to supervise the evacuation. It gets them out of the way. I also had the jail opened."

"The jail? I had no idea we had one. Who was in it?"

"Only the Hanston Road gang. I let them out this morning on the condition that they offer to help the irregulars. I gave them a pardon." He looked embarrassed. "I hope you don't object?"

"Hardly."

"Good. Now, what do you want to do with your soldiers?"

"What do you suggest?"

"Me? Well, I'd say put them all down by the Gate House. After all, if that's breached, we're in really big trouble."

"I agree."

"You do? Very well. Take them down there. But talk to Balancal first. He's probably in his office two doors down."

Some people hovered nearby with pieces of paper.

"Do excuse me," Enatus said as he stood up and signed a few sheets. "Do you know," he said in a low aside to Merral, "I'm completely out of my depth here? I'm having to make it up as I go along. Isn't that a terrible admission?"

Warmed by the warden's frankness and gritty determination, Merral felt his last resistance to Enatus fade away. "Warden, that's the policy I've been operating on ever since the first crisis occurred."

"I am so *very* glad to hear that. I was tempted to resign when I heard we were going to be attacked, but I felt that that would be cowardice and a lack of faith."

"Warden," said Merral, standing up, "thank you. I need to send my soldiers down to the Gate House. Then I must talk with Balancal."

He glanced up at the map on the wall. In the time they had been talking, the red line had moved forward.

Enatus also looked at the map. "Yes," he said in a quiet voice, "they are getting nearer. It promises to be an interesting evening." He turned to Merral, a puzzled look on his face. "But I have a question for you, Commander: why are they coming here?"

"I don't know," Merral replied. "And really, I wish I did."

ΟΟΟΟΟ

Back up on Congregation Square, Merral ordered the soldiers he had brought to make their way down to the Gate House. He then took Lloyd to find Vero and Balancal. Along the way, he spotted a short and slight blue-trousered figure with curly blonde hair carrying a large package toward a side doorway of the hall.

"Elana!" Merral called.

The girl smiled with delight, put the package down with care, and ran to Merral. "Merral!" she cried, with a fierce hug. "I knew you'd come!"

"I'd no option, not when I knew you were here."

Elana shook her head, trying to free a strand of blonde hair that was stuck to her forehead with sweat. "I'll bet you say that to everybody." She looked behind Merral and beamed again. "Hi, Lloyd. Welcome back."

Lloyd gave her a relaxed salute and strolled out of earshot.

Elana's half smile seemed in conflict with her solemn blue eyes. "You can see I'm busy."

"I was rather hoping you had left or were leaving. This may get messy later this evening."

"I know. But I'm not a child. And I wanted to play my part . . . like Perena did."

"Ah. I'm sorry you never met her," he said softly, the wound of her loss opening again. "But I'd prefer it if you stayed safe. I've lost enough friends already." *And I may lose more in the next dozen hours.*

"I want to be here."

"Very well, but if it comes to fighting, you really ought to go into the refuge."

They looked up at the massive frontage.

"Merral," Elana said, twisting on her toes, "come on, you can be honest with me. If they get as far as here, the doors will not hold them for very long. I'd rather try to fight them out here."

"There is that, I suppose. But don't fight unless you have to."

"I know how evil these things are. You fought them at the lake and I want to fight here. I hate those things. And I'm not scared. Well . . ." She gave him a confiding look. "I *am* a bit worried, Merral."

"That's understandable," Merral said, glancing at the equipment of war all around.

"I'm worried . . . that I'm going to be scared."

"There's nothing wrong with being scared."

She pouted. "I know that. I'm worried that by being scared I will do the wrong thing."

"I will pray you'll be brave."

She looked back at the package she had put down. "I'd better do my job."

"We all had," he said, patting her shoulder. As she left, he said under his breath, "Keep safe, Elana. Keep safe."

Battling with concern for her, Merral headed with Lloyd to the underground corridors where Enatus had said Balancal might be. They were shown into a cluttered room in which Vero and a tall, stiff-backed man with long black hair and wearing a brown jerkin were examining some maps.

The tall man looked up at Merral and a taut smile crossed his face. "Commander," he said, as they shook hands. "You remember me?"

"Call me Merral. Yes, I do. I thought I recognized the name. We've played against each other before."

"Indeed. I was a back with the Seagulls in the tournament last year— second round."

"I remember. Happier days." *Yes, I do remember you—a careful, watchful defender who let nothing through. You will need all those skills today, and more.*

"Indeed. Happier days." Balancal's gray gaze hardened. "But we are now on the same side, stopping a plague of these Krallen." Balancal's words were crisp and Merral took heart at the air of competency that he exuded.

"Yes. I've sent my soldiers to the Gate House."

"Thanks. We can use them."

"Enatus told me about the defenses."

"*Tuh,*" Balancal grunted, a forceful exclamation that suggested irritation. He gestured at the map. "Merral, we've done what we can, but unless Isterrane relents and let's Colonel Thuron come to our aid, we're in trouble."

There were hammering noises from next door and Balancal and Vero looked at each other. "We have just put Betafor there," Vero said. "We're getting cabling installed." He shook his head. "But she isn't happy."

◯◯◯◯◯

A few minutes later, Betafor herself confirmed that she was not at all happy. She was sprawled on a pile of cushions in the corner of a small, rather dusty chamber with a series of cables running under her vest like a complex umbilical cord. The Lamb and Stars glowed on her tunic flanks.

"Commander," she said, swiveling her head, her peculiarly lifeless eyes on Merral. "I thought I might see you here." As she turned to Lloyd, who stood by the door, Merral sensed he detected a look of dislike. "And Sergeant Enomoto."

"I wanted to see where you are," Merral said. "Is this satisfactory?"

"No. Not at all. It is too small. And there is too much dust. It gets into my eyes."

"I will try and get you some water to moisten the air."

"Thank you. But can I remind you that it is policy that Allenix units should not be exposed to danger? You seem to have brought me to a potential . . . war zone."

"I am sorry, Betafor. But you were in danger at Tezekal. There were people who were starting to hunt for you there."

"So I was told. But why did you have to come here?"

"Because this is my home."

"Ah, home." Her irises contracted. "In my experience that word is frequently associated with some of the most . . . irrational action of your species."

"It's one of the things that makes us human."

"I suggest it is one of the things that, one day, will make your species history. You let emotions . . . override facts."

"And that is something that you are not prone to?"

"Commander, *we* control our emotions; we do not let them control us. And if they threaten to push us toward . . . inadvisable actions, we simply delete them. The ability to delete—or modify—feelings is a considerable advance over the biological state. "

"I'm not sure that I envy you that ability."

"I think you do. You have regrets, Commander?"

For a few seconds Merral did not answer. *How do you reply to such a question from such a source?* "Perhaps," he said quietly.

"There we are then—yet another human weakness. We can erase our regrets. They might prevent us carrying out the appropriate action."

"So, you never feel guilty either?"

"No. Were such a feeling to arise, an Allenix unit would simply erase it."

"And that makes you superior?"

"Manifestly."

"I'm not so sure, but I'm not going to argue the matter now. Tell me what's happening. What do you know of this force of eight thousand Krallen on their way here?"

"Commander, I have been listening and I am puzzled. Frankly, I do not understand the . . . strategy. This approaching force is now around a hundred and thirty kilometers away. But I am just able to detect the main Krallen body at Camolgi Hills and although it is on the edge of my range, there appears to be something happening there. There are levels of activity that I would normally associate with . . . imminent motion." She tilted her head. "A further puzzling factor is that I have just detected some brief signals from a location perhaps eight kilometers away, west-southwest of here."

"Only eight kilometers away? What sort of signals?"

"Krallen, I think. But they were of short duration."

"That would put them in the woods just south of the airport." Merral stared at Betafor. "Are you sure?"

"I am increasing the sensitivity on that channel, but I definitely heard something."

"Could there be hidden Krallen units there?"

"I suggest you consider it a possibility."

"We'd better check. Call me if there is anything new, anything at all."

ΩΩΩΩΩ

With rising unease, Merral hurried to find Enatus and together they went to Balancal's room. There Betafor's news was greeted with alarm. They marked the apparent source of the signals on the map and Balancal immediately ordered a rotorcraft from the airport to check the area.

"I don't like it," Vero said, glowering at the map as Balancal snapped out orders. "I don't like it at all. Nothing fits."

Enatus turned to Merral. "You know," he said in a voice full of quiet concern, "the flights from the airport are due to leave in half an hour."

"Where are the passengers now?" Merral asked.

"Assembling down in the lower part of the town. There's a fleet of twenty coaches."

"I think you ought to hold them there until we get an all clear."

Enatus nodded and gave the order.

While they waited for the rotorcraft to carry out its survey, Merral went to a corner of the room and made a call to Frankie Thuron.

"Merral!" Frankie said, looking flustered. "I hear you are in Ynysmant."

"I'm afraid that's exactly where I am. You've heard the story?"

"From Clemant. What are you doing there?"

"I refuse to let a town be sacrificed."

"That sounds like you." Frankie looked bothered. "But did you disobey orders?"

"Yes. Clemant's decision is wrong. Had there been time, I would have gone to Isterrane and challenged it. But I didn't call you to justify my actions. I need help."

Frankie's look was one of consternation. "I'll help as much as I can, Merral, but . . . well, I have my orders."

"Frankie, if I was still in charge, I'd order you to launch an attack—to move fast by road and air to strike this column or at least to harass them."

There was a long silence before Frankie spoke. "Merral, this grieves me. Really does. We were on the beach at Fallambet together. You chose me for this job. But I've had specific orders to keep all my soldiers behind the defenses here. And we don't know what the enemy are up to. There's some sort of movement occurring in the line right now. I have no authority to launch any sort of attack to help you, much as I would like to."

"Talk to Clemant; see if he'll change his mind."

"I'll try."

"Please. I'm not asking you to do anything you shouldn't do. I just want to reduce the odds. One more thing: Frankie, do you think it possible that some Krallen units could have sneaked away and already be outside Ynysmant?"

Frankie scratched an ear. "I suppose so. We have surveillance, but it's hard to keep track of all twenty thousand. If they sneaked off under tree cover, yes, they could."

On the wallscreen juddering imagery from the nose of a rotorcraft appeared.

"Talk to you later, Frankie. But we could use some support."

Frankie sighed. "I'll ask."

Merral turned to watch the imagery on the wall, which showed treetops. *Oaks, beeches—I know those woods so well.*

"No sign of anything so far," said a disembodied man's voice that seemed to come from the screen. The camera pivoted over a track and then moved on. "Over the area now. . . . Still nothing. . . . Wait. . . ."

The camera swung again and focused on two parallel lines made up of numerous deep tracks.

There was an intake of breath in the room.

"Weird. . . . Can you see these?" said the voice from the screen

"M-Merral," Vero said as the tracks sharpened. "Animals?"

"No. And too big for Krallen."

The rotorcraft swung around to follow the tracks and as it did, Merral caught a glimpse of the waters of the lake and, cutting through them, the causeway and the tiers and spires of Ynysmant. As he puzzled about the tracks, Merral heard his diary chime. He put it to his ear.

"Commander," Betafor's flat tone was unmistakable. "There is activity south of the airport. It is quite consistent with two cannon insects in targeting mode. There—"

"Balancal, get the rotorcraft out!" Merral shouted. "Quick!"

The screen was suddenly filled with a black agglomeration of striding legs and moving tubes.

"Look at that!" the voice cried.

An open-mouthed tube swung steadily toward the camera.

"Get out! Get out!" Balancal shouted.

Enatus slowly rose from his seat.

There was a flash, a scream, and the image and sound vanished in a flicker of static.

Balancal slammed his fist on the table. Enatus crashed back into his seat while Vero threw his head in his hands.

"Firing under way from cannon insect," said the synthetic voice from the diary.

There was a deep bass boom that made the room vibrate, then another and another. Flakes of paint fell from the ceiling. A glass on a table shook violently.

"Artillery!" Merral said. "Warden, get everyone under cover!"

Enatus stared at him, his eyes wide like those of a fish, and gulped. He then grabbed his diary and began issuing orders.

There were more explosions and the lighting flickered.

Enatus got to his feet and, still issuing orders, ran clumsily out of the room and down the corridor, followed by Merral.

The warden ran into his office and as Merral pursued him through the door, a sudden blast, stunning in its intensity, pounded the entire building.

Merral was lifted off the floor and thrown against the door frame.

He staggered on, aware of cries of fear, the sound of alarms, the rattle of fragments from the roof onto the table, and the smell of smoke. There were further—more muted—explosions from just above his head. Everybody seemed to be shouting at once.

Enatus—his face flushed with anger and his body shaking with either fear or rage—urgently summoned him.

"They attacked the airport," the warden said, sweeping plaster fragments off his forehead. "And your freighter." He turned to a young man who tugged an armor jacket on with one hand and pointed with the other at a screen image full of orange flames and bubbling black smoke.

"The *Emilia Kay,*" Merral said as he gazed at the screen, feelings of grief and foreboding descending on him.

"It's alight," said a woman from another desk, her voice frayed. "Fire tenders are moving."

The firing abruptly stopped.

ロロロロ

Over the next few minutes, damage reports began to come in.

"Houses on fire at western Kytharal Street. Casualties."

"Three transports still on fire at airport. Terminal damaged. A dozen plus dead and injured."

"Boat sank at Vanulet Pier. Casualties."

"Irreg unit reports sightings of many gray creatures south of runways."

"Congregation Square fire under control. At least three dead; a dozen injured. Ship gutted."

Merral called Betafor. "Give me an update."

"Commander, I note two things: a small number of Krallen units are advancing to the airport from the south and there is major movement at the Camolgi Hills."

"Which way?"

"I cannot be sure. I cannot decode the signals."

"Tell me as soon as you know."

Merral passed on the news to Enatus.

"Oh, my," Enatus said, sitting down heavily on a dusty seat, his eyes flicking nervously from one screen of damage to another. "I really don't understand this. Why us?" He swallowed and looked at Merral. "I need some help here, Commander. I'm very much out of my depth. Very much. What do you suggest?"

"We are all out of our depth. But I suggest you withdraw everyone from the airport. It's not defensible. By all accounts there are only a couple of serviceable fliers left. Get them airborne to deny them to the enemy. Make sure anything else they could use there is irreparably damaged."

"Yes. I see." Enatus wiped a mixture of sweat and dust off his nose. He turned to an aide. "Get everyone back across the causeway." Then he turned to Merral and lowered his voice. "Commander, we are trapped. Nothing can land on Congregation Square. There's too much wreckage. And I don't think we can risk any more boat evacuations."

"I know."

Enatus frowned, then stood up and cleared his throat. "Staff!" he called out loudly and firmly. All eyes turned to him. "Evacuate the airport. Bring everybody back across the causeway. Prepare to close the gates as soon as everyone is across."

"Well done!" Merral whispered.

As Enatus began walking around snapping further orders, Vero, who had entered quietly, nudged Merral. "Let's talk to Betafor."

They found the Allenix unit staring at the ceiling. As they entered, her head swiveled smoothly toward them. "Commander, Sentinel, I have bad news."

A feeling of unease gripped Merral. *I can guess it.* "Go on."

"Almost the entire Dominion force at Camolgi Hills is moving this way."

"When will they be here?" Merral asked, battling with a hundred fears, his heart pounding in alarm.

"Early this evening—in six or seven hours."

Vero stepped forward. "Betafor, do you understand this sequence of maneuvers?"

"Understand it? No."

Suddenly Vero turned to Merral with a quizzical expression on his face. "My friend, let's talk." His voice was curt.

Outside in the corridor, Vero said, "I believe Lezaroth has lured us into a trap. Is that what you think?"

"It's possible," Merral answered cautiously. *A trap surely, but for who? Me, Vero, or both of us?* The idea that he had walked into a trap raised implications so horrendous that he resisted them. "It could be an act of vengeance. They know I come from here."

Vero shook his head emphatically. "It's more than vengeance. Remember I told you of the sentinel practice of trying to put yourself in your opponent's shoes? Now, imagine that Lezaroth blames you for these defeats: D'Avanos, the great adversary; D'Avanos, the heir to Lucas Ringell—the last scourge of the Freeborn; D'Avanos, the commander at his defeat at Tezekal Gorge. He wants *you*. He knows we—and you—value human life; he knows this is your town. So he lures you in, closes off your exits, and then crushes the town."

Merral turned away, stabbed by agonizing thoughts. *The envoy told me not to leave Isterrane, but I disobeyed and, as a result, I have brought the threat of utter disaster on myself and my town. What folly!*

Merral considered whether to confess to Vero what he had done. But as he thought about it, he had a strong reluctance to admit that he had done something so appallingly stupid as to disobey the envoy. *Anyway, we're not absolutely sure yet that this is a trap.*

Trying as best he could to hide his feelings, Merral said, "I resist that idea. But I suppose . . . I can accept that it's a possibility."

Vero seemed to watch him intently and Merral sensed in the careful gaze that his friend suspected there was more than had been said.

"We'd better break the news to the warden," Merral said.

ⵙⵙⵙⵙⵙ

"*Here?* All of them?" Enatus rolled his eyes and reached out a hand to steady himself against a table. "Around twenty thousand Krallen?"

"I'm afraid so," Merral replied.

"Is there any chance that Colonel Thuron will come to our aid?"

"I will talk to him again. But . . ."

Enatus sighed. "*But* we can't presume on it. By this evening you say?" The little man fell silent and his head and shoulders sagged as if they were pressed under a great burden. He peered up at Merral. "So, humanly speaking, there isn't much hope?"

He looked away and when he looked back, Merral was surprised at the resolution that burned in his eyes.

"Very well," Enatus said, his voice ringing with such defiance that people in the office turned to look at him. "However many there are, we will fight them. That's that."

He clapped his hands in a gesture of determination. "We'll make such a defense that the whole Assembly will be proud of us."

In spite of his own troubles, Merral felt proud of the little man.

Enatus stood upright, his plump hand slipping to his sword hilt. "Gentlemen, ladies, we must do what we can. But we can promise our enemies this: a tough fight."

29

After Vero left to see Balancal and organize the irregs, Merral walked down the corridor, found an empty room, and began to make some calls. The first was to Frankie Thuron. When he got through, the image on his diary showed a very troubled man. *That makes two of us.*

"Merral, I'm very sorry," Frankie said. "The whole Dominion army is on the move and heading your way: fifteen, sixteen thousand Krallen plus other things—ape-creatures, cockroach-beasts, and those flying things. I . . . I don't know what to say."

"Come on, Frankie, you can move now. Come and help us. The threat to Isterrane is removed. Attack them from the rear."

Frankie's lean face darkened. "I can't. That's a fact. I just talked to Clemant. We are not to move from our defensive positions. His orders."

"Look, from all we've seen, this town will fall this evening and the bloodbath here will make Tantaravekat seem like a minor incident."

"Merral, I am under authority." Frankie's open face plainly showed the torment of conflicting emotions. "I *can't* rebel. I understand why you did what you did, but you've set a precedent. If we all followed it, we would tear this world apart."

It's no good. Frankie takes his orders seriously, as perhaps I should. I thought I was just rebelling against Clemant. I now realize that I've rebelled against the Most High.

"I understand," Merral said slowly. "Colonel Thuron, you must do whatever you have to do."

"Sorry. You have to go to Clemant. . . ." Frankie's voiced tailed off. "But whatever happens, you have my prayers." Then, evidently close to tears, Frankie terminated the call.

◌◌◌◌◌

A minute later, Merral called Clemant. *I will not get angry. That will do no good at all.*

A cold, round face greeted him. "Strictly speaking, Captain, I should order Enatus to arrest you, but I think he is going to need every man he can get." Clemant sighed deeply, but Merral detected no sympathy in his face. "You have thrown away everything on what now seems certain to be an utterly futile venture."

"Sometimes, sir, one must do what is right, even if it does prove futile."

"I am sorry. You are in a mess of your own making." There was a slight, stiff shrug of the shoulders.

"Sir, I am not concerned for my own safety. I need help. I would like you to order Colonel Thuron to attack the Dominion forces."

"The answer is no. The interests of Farholme come first. Indeed, one might almost say that the interests of the Assembly come first. And there are other factors now."

"*What* other factors?"

Clemant's face remained impassive. "They are not relevant to you."

"So you won't send us any support?"

"I wish I could, Captain. I really do." Clemant paused and looked away as if unable to look at him. "Necessity is, I'm afraid, a cruel business."

Barely able to constrain himself, Merral simply mumbled, "Thank you, sir," and closed down the link. *If I get out of here, I will deal with that man.*

Trying to bury his anger, Merral made a third call, this time to Jorgio. The old man, his head shaded by a battered straw hat, was out in the garden. Based on the glimpse of a trowel, Jorgio was weeding.

"Why, Mr. Merral," he said in a reflective voice. "I was wondering about you. I gather you're in trouble."

"Yes, trouble's the word. We're trapped here with around twenty thousand Krallen on their way."

"Not nice, is it?" Jorgio rubbed his nose with the back of his hand. "Not nice at all. I have been praying about it as I have been doing the weeding. My family too are in Ynysmant. . . . But truth to tell, Mr. Merral, I got the impression as the trouble you was in was something else. I couldn't help but feel as there was something that you had to sort out with the King."

"I see," Merral said, thrown into bewilderment. "I have felt in the last few hours that . . . well . . . coming here may not have been the wisest thing to do."

Jorgio brushed a fly away. "I don't reckon as it being wise was the issue. It felt more . . . well, about obedience, if you understand what I mean."

"Jorgio, I came here to try and save our town. I chose to risk my life and the lives of my soldiers in coming here." Merral heard the defiance in his voice.

"*Tut.* I'm sure that's what you meant, but I reckon as a thing can be good and still be the wrong thing." He fanned his face with his hat and then seemed to peer thoughtfully at Merral. "See, Mr. Merral, if I worked for someone and they said, 'Jorgio, grow nasturtiums' and I grew dahlias instead, why that'd be a wrong thing—disobedient—even if they was beautiful dahlias."

"I will consider your words, Jorgio," Merral answered, feeling accused by the conversation. "But please pray."

"Oh, I will. But I would say this: you might want to watch yourself."

"Thank you." The call ended.

He slipped his diary onto his belt and stared at the wall. *I have rebelled against the Most High, and I know what I ought to do. I ought to repent. I ought to find Vero or Luke and admit that I disobeyed the envoy and I ought to pray for forgiveness.* Yet as he thought this, the idea of admitting he was wrong seemed very unattractive.

"Look," he said aloud. "I had to defend my town. You have to understand."

Still bitter, he rose and went to find Lloyd.

✕✕✕✕✕

Merral exited the stairway by the sandbags and stared around Congregation Square, stunned into silence by the scene before him.

Before him lay a scene of complete devastation. Where the *Emilia Kay* once stood was a smoldering, blackened hulk of torn and twisted girders that steamed as fire crews sprayed water on it. Smoke and steam drifted across the square and with them came the smells of burned synthetics and charred flesh.

All around were fragments of wreckage, smears of lubricant, and scorch marks. A bladed vehicle bulldozed its way across the square, piling the wreckage into large piles. Merral watched as a stretcher bearing something that had once been a living body was placed in an ambulance.

Men and women peered out of the entrances to the refuge, their faces showing fear and incomprehension. A flock of pigeons wheeled across the square, apparently untroubled by the devastation below them.

People have died here. Women and men who were alive this morning. The bitter thought seemed to harden his resolve to stay his course and not repent.

He wondered about his parents and, on impulse, made his way to the nearest refuge entrance. Amid the men and women gaping at the scenes in the square were harassed officials with databoards trying to impose order while overseeing the delivery of supplies and assigning bunks.

"Excuse me," he said to one of them, "do you know if my mother is inside?"

"Seeing as it's you, Commander," the official said with a weary sigh, "I'll call her. But it's pretty chaotic in there. Well over ten thousand here; almost every bunk taken."

As they walked to the door, Merral heard from within the echoing murmur of a thousand distant voices. *Like bats in a cave.* He resolved that, whatever his fate might be, he would meet it in the open air.

As he waited for his mother to emerge and Lloyd did his tactful dozen-pace retreat, Merral stared at the massive doors with their great hinges and new bars. *How long will they hold?*

Suddenly his mother was with him, her hair tied back and wearing overalls and an official armband. She blinked in the sun. "Merral!" she cried, throwing her arms around him. She then stepped back and scowled at his armor. "It's hard! And that *color*!"

"It works, Mother."

"I should hope so. I heard you were here. They were all *so* excited when they heard. 'It's all going to be all right,' they said. 'Mrs. D'Avanos's son is coming. He'll kill them all.' I felt *so* proud."

Merral stared at the ground. *They see me as the bringer of deliverance, when in truth, I seem to have brought disaster.* "I will do all I can, Mother, but that may not be enough."

Her gaze moved past him toward the devastation, then turned back to him. He saw certainty in her eyes. "No," she said, her tone suddenly subdued. "It may not be enough. There's a new rumor that there are lots more of these Krallen things on their way. Thousands."

Merral nodded.

"I see," she said. "Look, your father is working on the defenses at the third circle. If you see him, give him my love. And tell him—" she bit her lip, her eyes moist—"that I could have done things better the last few months. I'm sorry." She looked around. "I must go, Merral. There is work to do."

She paused, as if struggling with what to say. "I want to tell you to stay out of harm's way. But you have to fight." Without another word, she turned and, her shoulders heaving with emotion, walked back inside the hall.

With Lloyd once more at his side, Merral made his way to the new gateway. He stared at the walls. They were twice his height and made of thick, overlapping dura-polymer panes and buttressed every few meters by angled massive steel stanchions driven deep into the surface of the square. Around the top of the wall, in which firing slots had been regularly placed, a broad walkway ran.

Exchanging salutes with the irregs at the new gate, Merral walked down

Island Road. He stared around, seeing the new defenses and passing doorways sealed off with rough-cemented masonry. *Crude work. Is this how the Assembly ends, in an ugly untidiness?*

At the main junctions on the road, barricades of brick or metal had been erected and behind them stood brown-clad irregulars with guns and the new swords. In other places, firing positions had been made that pointed down the street. There and elsewhere Merral glimpsed keen-eyed men and women with guns.

Almost everywhere, Merral was recognized and forced himself to respond to the waves and salutes. He smiled and admired the defenses with as much confidence and good humor as he could manage. *It's a pretense, but a necessary one. I need to give these people hope.*

As they descended, they made a brief detour up a side alley to a house that had been hit by an artillery round from a cannon-insect. Merral paused, watching the rescue workers lift rubble and seal off the broken pipes, seeing the roof tiles flung everywhere, and stepping respectfully around the drying blood on the cobbles. *It is not just an ugly town; it's a wounded one.* He felt a surge of anger, but didn't know who he was angry with—God, the devil, the Dominion, or even himself.

He turned away and walked on. A minute later, he passed a group of six teenagers stringing up wire mesh across an alleyway.

One of them looked up. "Hey! Commander D'Avanos!" he shouted, dropping the wire and walking over.

"Remember me?" the lad asked, as his friends gathered behind him.

After a minute's puzzled reflection, Merral suddenly recognized the youths who had troubled him on his visit home after Fallambet.

"Wait. You were in the Hanston Road ga—"

"S'right. Sir, we want to apologize." There were nods from his friends. "Things just kinda got out of hand. Sorry."

There were other apologies.

"Apology accepted." All shook hands.

"Commander, do you know as they put us in jail?" one lad said. "Me mum nearly died of shame. 'The first convict in our family for a thousand generations,' she said."

"Me too," chorused a smaller lad.

"But they let you out today?"

"Yeah. The warden gave the police their orders. He let us out so that we could have a go at these Krallen things—goblins, your soldiers call 'em. We're sort of . . . well . . . *irregular* irregulars."

"Dead right," said the smaller lad.

"Well, be careful. It's not a game. But . . . glad to have you with us."

"You kill 'em, Commander!"

Merral and Lloyd moved on, soon reaching the third-circle defenses where the new wall was broken by a narrow gateway with doors made of steel-reinforced polymer plates.

An earnest captain of the irregulars insisted on showing them the defenses and pointing out how every window and doorway facing out had been sealed off by bars or masonry.

Spotting a group of men carrying welding gear, Merral walked over to the nearest man. "Do you know where Stefan D'Avanos is?"

"Ah, your father," the man said, a weary smile on his grubby face. "Over there. The yellow door."

Merral found his father changing the battery on his welding rod. For a second they stared at each other.

"Son!"

They hugged each other and Merral caught the odor of sweat and burned metal.

He stood back to look at his father, struck by how haggard his face was.

"You haven't shaved," his father observed.

Merral playfully tweaked his father's beard. "And neither have you."

"*I'm* not a commander," came the reply. With a weary smile, Merral's father wiped the sweat off his face with an oily rag. "But it's good to see you. I like the armor, by the way." He prodded it and grunted with approval. "Nice work. Clever stuff with the elbow joints. Need to keep it lubed though."

He stood back, a sudden look of disbelief on his face. "This is an odd business, Son. Who would have thought it? War! And in our town, too. Still, we're glad to have you here. Your coming has cheered a lot of folk up."

"I had to come. I really did."

"I know."

"You're not planning to fight, are you, Father?"

"If it comes to it," he said, looking stern, "I will. I may try and get one of these new swords."

"If you think that's wise. But, Father, I must leave you. I have to go down to the Gate House and the causeway."

"Of course."

"Mother sends her love. And . . . she apologizes."

His father smiled weakly. "That's good. Things have been a bit strange. I'll call her when I get the chance. Tell her I'm sorry too. No excuses."

Their eyes locked and there was a intense moment of silence between them. *We both know that this may be the last time we meet.*

His father rubbed his beard and shook his head. "A bad business," he said slowly, "a very bad one. But I'm proud of you. You have done it before. And you can do it again."

"Let's hope so."

ᘯᘯᘯᘯᘯ

Merral and Lloyd returned to Island Road and continued down its loops to Causeway Square and the Gate House. As they drew closer to the level of the lake, Merral met more of his own soldiers. Some were checking weapons; others sat in the shade eating lunch, while still others lay under trees or in doorways, trying to catch up on sleep.

They roused themselves as he passed, but he put them at ease. All that could be done on the defenses had either been done or was being done and there was little point in draining their energy in the midday heat. They would need all their strength later.

As they turned a final bend Merral stopped, awestruck at the transformation of the entrance to Ynysmant. All his life, people had entered Ynysmant by walking, riding, or driving off the causeway through the archway, a structure that served no function other than as a mounting point for flags and banners, and traveled past the Gate House, a three-story, balconied building of character, and so entered the broad expanse of Causeway Square.

All this had changed, almost beyond recognition. Between the causeway and the town and incorporating both the Gate House and the archway lay a high, buttressed wall, part beige masonry and part black dura-polymer sheets. Along the top lay a walkway with parapets. The archway had been broadened and reinforced by girders to give a stark and barbaric structure, with two massive doors.

Causeway Square was now filled with the equipment of war, soldiers with uniforms and weapons, the clatter of workmen, and the shouts of military orders.

Merral tried to be reconciled to the changes. *It must be done. And unless there is a miracle, there will be worse done down here today than damage to buildings.*

He found Vero and Balancal in the ground-floor room of the Gate House, next to where sweating men, some in the brown uniforms of the irregulars and some just wearing old clothes, were passing ammunition to the top of the walls. They exchanged news and there were gloomy looks of resignation when Merral said that, unless Clemant relented, Frankie would not be coming.

They scrambled up ladders onto the parapet and Balancal walked Merral along the defenses, showing him the two wide-mouthed cannons that Barrand had fashioned, which pointed along the causeway. Merral agreed that they would be formidable weapons.

They talked about communications in case the Dominion forces managed to suppress the ordinary links.

Merral was glad to find that Balancal had fiber-optic backups and, as a last resort, an agreed system of flare signals: red to warn of an attack, blue to signal a retreat, and green to order an advance. Finally, they agreed that Merral's soldiers, who were better armored and had battle experience, would be stationed on the walls while the irregs bore the brunt of any street fighting.

At one level, Merral found the preparations and Balancal's evident competence reassuring; yet at a deeper level, they did little to quell his fears. Against the massive forces now on their way, they were hopelessly inadequate.

As Merral descended from the walls, he met his uncle, Barrand. They embraced and shared news. Of the Antalfers, only Elana was left in Ynysmant; the others had left by boat. Then they talked about the defenses, the cannons, and the explosives planted under the causeway.

Barrand pulled a face that expressed deep unease. "But don't expect too much, Nephew. It's all untested." He looked up at the new fortifications towering over him. "From what I hear, we will need more than all this to survive."

"Yes, Uncle. We will."

ΟΟΟΟΟ

After Merral completed his reconnaissance of the defenses in front of the causeway, he was taken to a house at the edge of the square that had been borrowed as office for the regulars. There he met with his captains around a table in the main room and they discussed, as best they could, the strategy for the coming fight.

The latest information from Betafor was that the Dominion forces immediately around Ynysmant were static, but the main Krallen army was still moving rapidly toward them and was expected to arrive within four hours. It was a somber meeting. The family images on the walls around them seemed to deepen Merral's mood. *Where are they—this young couple and their two toddlers? Did they manage to leave or are they in one of the refuges? And to what extent is their fate my responsibility?*

As the captains left to organize the soldiers, Merral suddenly realized that it was now early afternoon and he had eaten little all day. He found some food and ate with little enthusiasm.

Vero entered, pulled a chair up opposite, and looked at him with concern. "It isn't your fault, you know," he said.

Merral shrugged. "I think it is."

"Coming here was the right thing to do, wasn't it?"

Merral wondered if there was a hint of uncertainty in Vero's voice.

"I'm not so sure." He heard the sullenness in his words.

Vero's look was keen. "My friend, I don't know what's going on, but I feel there is something you aren't telling me. I think you ought to talk it over with someone. Luke's next door seeing people. Why not go and have a chat?"

"Perhaps."

As Vero rose and walked to the door, he hesitated and then turned back. "Merral, let me say this. Normally, I'd say that what's wrong is between you and God and is none of my business. But I can't say that today. Our only hope lies in the intervention of the Most High. You lead us. I don't think we can afford any outstanding business between you and God." He gestured to something behind Merral's head. "And neither can they."

As the door closed, Merral turned to see a formal painting of the family and their two blonde children.

"But that's why I came!" he said and heard defiant anger in his voice.

Hoping that action would make him feel better, Merral summoned Lloyd and set off to make a new survey of the defenses.

Clouds had gathered and the sun was obscured, yet the temperature was every bit as high. As he strode about, Merral felt sweat pooling under his armor.

The last irregulars from the airport had crossed the causeway an hour ago, but Balancal still kept the gates open. Partly out of curiosity and partly because of his restlessness, Merral borrowed a small open-topped two-seater and drove with Lloyd through the gates halfway along the deserted causeway. There he turned the vehicle and stopped. The mound of Ynysmant loomed up from the lake with smoke still drifting from its summit as if it were a volcano on the verge of eruption. Indeed the gathering clouds seemed to be focused around the island.

Merral stared at the town. Seeing the town in its entirety from the outside made him realize just how drastic the changes had been. New walls had been built or extended, lines of metal railings created, grilles built over windows, defensive positions constructed. The turrets, previously ornamental, now had an air of function to them and the flags a sense of deliberate defiance. *We have put the clock back over fifteen thousand years. We have created a fortified town.* The thought saddened him.

After Merral returned through the gateway, he found Balancal and made the decision to close the gates.

The big double doors were closed and steel crossbeams placed across.

We are under siege. Another old, bad word revived in our day.

There were still three hours before the predicted arrival of the main body of Krallen. Merral felt the urge to keep moving. Action gave him an excuse to avoid reflection.

For the next two hours, he walked up and around Ynysmant, checking on defensive positions, asking after syn-plasma stocks at the medical centers, and testing communications backups.

Lloyd, who had left much of his heavier weaponry at the Gate House, followed him up and down the streets, steps, and alleys without complaint.

Everywhere he went, Merral tried to encourage the men and women preparing to defend Ynysmant. At first, he found putting on a mask of cheerfulness not just hard, but also distasteful. Soon though, he decided that there was no other option.

The preparations for war lay heavily on the town. Joy and laughter had fled to be replaced by a new sternness and urgency. People who would have once stopped and chatted now simply said, "Nice to see you, Merral" or "Good to have you here, Commander," before striding quickly about their business.

Even Ynysmant's ever-present and innumerable cats seemed to have caught the mood and now slipped with wary glances across the streets or cowered in doorways.

Despite the constant noises of defense construction or the shouting of orders, a strange, tense, and ominous silence hung over the town.

No further word came from Frankie or Clemant. As the afternoon wore on, the clouds thickened into a thick gray shroud that obscured the sun, creating a shadowless and humid gloom without lessening the heat.

Merral sensed something more than a weather phenomenon. There was something about this growing murkiness that seemed to seep into the mind and spoke of despair and defeat.

 OOOOO

Midafternoon, Merral returned to Enatus's office for further discussion of the defense plans. As he was leaving the office, an aide told him that there were two people in a nearby room who wished to see him.

Merral walked through to find Mr. and Mrs. Danol sitting at a table. *I could do without this.*

They greeted each other.

"We know you are busy," Hania Danol said, holding her husband's hand. "We all are. And we're so glad you have come. But we had to ask if there was any news of Isabella."

"And whether," George Danol added quickly, "there is anything you can do for her."

Merral was silent for a moment, trying to find the best way to express the unpalatable. "As I understand it," he said, "Langerstrand base is now surrounded, so the Dominion forces can't leave. So that's good news. Our forces there will be trying to find ways of getting the hostages released. The hope . . ." He faltered, suddenly wondering when optimism became lying. "The hope is that, when the situation here is resolved, we can devote all our energy to sorting things out there. I would like to personally oversee it."

"But it is a priority?" George added, his eyes hard. "*Your* priority?"

"Well, obviously, my first priority is the defeat of the Dominion forces here and the defense of Ynysmant. But you can be assured that the moment this action is over, I will turn my full attention to getting the hostages out safely." He paused. "Believe me, I will do all I can. I will wait however long it takes and go wherever I need to go to get Isabella and the others out safely."

"That's a promise?" George asked in an insistent tone that reminded Merral of his daughter.

"Yes," Merral said, rising from his seat. "It's a promise."

ᑯᑯᑯᑯᑯ

Enatus had decided to make a personal visit to the troops at the Gate House. So just after the bells had sounded four, Merral found himself walking at the warden's side as he was introduced to the captains and other members of the forces now clustered around the lower wall.

As the little man strolled around with his sword bouncing off his belly, nodding and smiling at each introduction, Merral was genuinely impressed by Enatus's gritty determination. *It's courage. That's what it is.*

Just after the warden had left, Lloyd nudged Merral and pointed up. High above the topmost spires of the town, the black diamond-shaped silhouettes of two slitherwings could be seen weaving their unhurried way in and out of the lowest strands of cloud.

The enemy are already here.

He ordered Karita and two of her snipers to get to the highest point of the town—the bell tower of Congregation Hall—and shoot the creatures. But the slitherwings stayed out of range. Given that they had limited ammunition, he soon ordered the team back.

Just before five, word came to Merral that the Dominion forces were in sight. He hurried with Lloyd to a small park on the western edge of the second level of the town and climbed to the top of a six-story ornamental tower. There they gazed wordlessly westward where, just beyond the southernmost runway, a faint cloud of gray dust was rising. *The main Krallen army, now only a few kilometers away.* Merral felt despair..

He heard the bells toll five. Now was the time when this place should be full of children at play, men and women walking together, athletes training. Instead, there was no one.

In the unnatural gloom, he could see a patchy haze developing over the lake.

Night is falling. It has been falling for months.

"Not long now," he said to Lloyd and then, with a stern determination, descended the stairway and made his way back to the Gate House.

∞∞∞∞∞

Down by the defenses, the soldiers were taking up positions along the walls with a quiet urgency.

Merral walked into the house the regulars were using and after sorting out some minor administrative details, made his way to the bathroom. He felt dirty and sweaty and, stripping off his armor, tried to clean himself up. He searched a cupboard for a towel and as he tugged one out, a child's bath toy—a bright yellow fish made of a soft synthetic material—fell at his feet.

On impulse, Merral picked up the toy. As he did, the thought came to him with an irresistible force that the child who played with it was possibly now in a refuge facing a horrid death within hours—a death that would be linked to, and perhaps even caused by, his disobedience. His hands shook and tears misted his eyes as the fish tumbled to the floor.

You fool, D'Avanos! You utter fool! To let proud, impetuous action take priority over obedience.

His resistance crumbled. He wiped his eyes, dried himself, put the armor back on, and went in search of Luke. He found the chaplain in the house next door, seated on a sofa with a book-Bible and a pile of papers next to him.

"Ah, Merral," Luke said in a quiet voice, as he rose to greet him. "I thought I'd see you before the action started. Take a seat."

Merral lowered himself into an easy chair, aware of the stiffness of the armor.

"You are a burdened man, Commander."

"I have a lot to be burdened about."

"Tell me all."

There was a long silence.

"Luke," Merral began, then realized that now was not the time to hide anything. "Luke, I disobeyed an order not just from Clemant but from God through the envoy. And as result, I have walked into a trap and what's happening to this town is all my fault. I have brought all this on this town, these people, and you."

"Ah," Luke said slowly. "I knew something was wrong." He shook his head. "I should have pressed you at the time. I was preoccupied with Clemant. But continue."

"The envoy told me to stay close to Isterrane." Merral put his head in his hands. Now, as if some mental mist had lifted, he suddenly saw all his motives with perfect clarity: his overconfidence, his anger with Clemant, and his arrogant refusal to take advice.

"Why did you come here?"

"Because I had to. No, I've said that too often." Merral paused, collecting his thoughts. "There were several things. After Perena's death, I resolved to do all that I could to stop death from coming near me. I couldn't take any more people dying. And Tezekal Gorge just reinforced that. There have been too many deaths." Merral looked up at the chaplain, feeling tears clog his eyes. "Not here, Luke. I couldn't let it happen here, not to my parents and my friends."

"I can hardly not sympathize," Luke murmured. "I ask myself if it were my town that was threatened, how would I have acted?"

"And there was Zak and Clemant."

"I don't see—"

"I hated their ruthlessness and callousness. I knew that was wrong. So I wanted to make a point by coming here. I wanted to say that with me people count."

"Indeed they do, as they should. But you disobeyed."

Merral looked at the ground. "I didn't see it as disobedience. I felt the envoy didn't know everything and this was something new. I took his words to be . . . well . . . advice."

There was silence.

Speak, Luke. I need you to absolve me.

But the chaplain said nothing, and in the end the silence seemed so threatening that Merral blurted out, "It was a mistake!"

"Was it?"

"Yes." Merral paused. "No. It was more. It was sin."

Luke nodded.

"And I've made things worse," Merral continued. "I see now that the envoy's advice was for my good, not for my harm. I wanted to save my town. Instead, I've probably destroyed it."

"Wrong actions undermine all good intentions."

Outside, beyond the window, Merral heard someone snapping out commands.

"I'm close to despair," Merral sighed.

Luke shook his head. "To despair would make matters worse. To despair of the mercy of God is, by its very nature, an unforgivable sin."

"What must I do?"

"You were told to stay on the path. You have wandered off. You need to get back on it."

"But how?"

"You know as well as I do. Admit you were wrong, seek the Father, ask for forgiveness." Luke stirred in his seat. "Merral, I've got some messages to send. I can do that downstairs, so I'll leave you here. See me before you go."

As the chaplain's footsteps faded away, Merral closed his eyes and tried to pray. "Oh, Lord," he began, "I've been stupid and sinful. Have mercy on me and on this town." He went through his sins of the day. As he did, he was uncomfortably reminded of his failure during the attack on the intruder ship at Fallambet. There he had been made aware of his misbehavior to Anya and Isabella; now the issue was much deeper. He felt certain that he had failed completely. To be forgiven once was grace, but how could he expect to be forgiven again? *Yet surely, Luke is right. To deny the possibility of forgiveness is to despair beyond hope.*

As Merral prayed, his despair slowly ebbed and he began to believe in the possibility of being forgiven. He went downstairs to find Luke in the darkened room, coffee mug in his hand, staring at the growing gloom through the open doorway.

"Feel better?"

"Yes, thanks. A burden has gone. I wish I could say I felt hopeful. But at least I no longer feel in utter despair. I don't wish to die tonight, but if I do, at least this matter is resolved."

"Good. Let me pray with you, Commander. Much will rest on you very soon."

Luke put a hand firmly on Merral's shoulder and prayed a simple prayer, thanking God for forgiveness and asking for protection and guidance.

"Amen," Merral said, as the prayer ended. "Thanks. . . . Thanks a lot."

He stared at the gathering darkness. It was barely six o'clock of a late summer's evening and already the lights were coming on.

A man about to run past the house stopped and came over. "Commander, Mr. V. wants you next door. Urgent."

Merral found Vero sitting at the table in an upstairs room, a look of great fear and alarm on his face.

"W-we have just had news from outlying sentries—two men hidden above W-Wilamall's Farm," Vero said, his words low and so rapid they were almost garbled. "T-the very worst. Something just passed by on a nearby ridge, s-something moving southward through the trees at great speed: much, much taller than a man. F-four legs and a long tail. Black and shiny, with terrible wings. It made a r-rattling noise and birds and animals fled before it. The sentries said they felt a terrible fear as it passed."

"The baziliarch. Our worst fears."

"Exactly."

Trying not to shudder, Merral peered through the window into the deepening gloom, seeing the thickening mist on the lake. He turned to Vero. "And so it begins." *But how will it end?*

⊃◯⊃◯⊃

By half past six, the darkness was such that it was hard to see the far end of the causeway.

Balancal had emergency lighting brought in and mounted on mobile arms so that, if needed, the causeway could be illuminated. For the moment, the lights were kept lowered and switched off. To aid the defendants, they decided that most of the streetlights would be switched off. The lines of unlit streets and rows of darkened houses gave Ynysmant the air of a deserted and stricken place.

Final preparations were made. The regulars took positions behind the parapet wall. The few reserves waited below in the square and in the adjoining streets. Karita's sniper team positioned themselves at upper windows and at other vantage points overlooking the causeway. The two cannons were primed and firing wires run out to the point just above the gate where Merral, Vero, and Balancal stood listening to the steady trickle of intelligence reports from Betafor and observers mounted on the town's towers.

Luke, wearing armor and with a sword at his belt, stood nearby, gazing intently into the darkness.

Soon information began to come in that the main Dominion force had arrived at the airport and had merged with the Krallen units already there.

Just before seven, the cry went up: "Here they are!"

Merral peered through a fieldscope to the far end of the causeway. Through the swirling strands of dark mist, he could make out something that looked like gray liquid turning a corner on the airport road and flowing down onto the causeway.

Something deep inside him twitched. *It's better when the attack starts. I'll have no time to be afraid.* "They're coming."

As Balancal turned to him, Merral glimpsed a look of resolve. "Commander, we're ready. The charges are primed. You may want to warn the troops." His tone was calm and unflustered.

If this man feels fear, he shows no sign of it.

Merral caught Luke's attention and gestured for him to be ready to speak. Then he touched the microphone stud. "Soldiers of the Assembly, you know the drill. When I shout, 'take cover,' get down behind the parapet. When the blast is over, get up and kill anything that makes it over in one piece. Take your time. Make every shot count. Our chaplain will now pray."

The howls could be heard now, a high, horrid, and fleshless sound that made the pulse beat quicker.

"Better be quick, Luke," Merral whispered to himself.

"Lord of the Assembly," Luke prayed, his strong words echoing around the streets, "Father, Son, and Spirit, have mercy on us, your people, here this night. Give us courage and defend this town through that mightiest of all armor—the blood of the Lamb of God, through whose name we pray. Amen."

Amid the resonating chorus of "amens," Merral saw Balancal take hold of a box on the end of a cable, flick a safety cover off, and then peer through the fieldscope.

Merral looked ahead, his eyes gripped by the awesome and chilling sight of endless lines of gray forms sweeping toward them. Over the howling, he could hear the rising drumming noise of the countless feet on the causeway.

"Any second, Merral," Balancal said, without the least hint of tension. "I shall let a good number of these things over before I press the button. Ready?"

"Take cover!" Merral shouted.

With a clatter of swords and guns, the soldiers slid down.

As Merral squatted below the parapet, he caught a glimpse of the front Krallen line, twelve wide, now barely a hundred meters away.

Come on, Balancal!

"Now," said the quiet voice.

Light flashed and a numbing, hammer-blow pulse of sound struck him. The walkway beneath Merral's feet convulsed and a vast wave of hot, dust-laden air billowed around.

Debris—masonry, stone, dust—fell about him. Something thumped him on the back and bounced off his armor while other fragments rained down. A thud nearby ended with a scream.

A great hissing and splashing noise came from the lake as the debris struck the water. Waves of spray lashed over the parapet, dousing the cloud of dust.

Merral rose and looked around, blinking. On either side of him, soldiers covered in mud and dust were scrambling to their feet and shaking themselves free of fragments. A few meters away, soldiers were trying to help a man pinned under a chunk of masonry. Another man threw a severed Krallen limb over the wall with a shudder of disgust.

Merral straightened his helmet and, wiping dirt out of his eyes, peered over the parapet. Through the lifting smoke and dust clouds, he saw that a full fifty meters of causeway had vanished to be replaced by a dark mass of swirling, seething water.

Beyond the severed causeway, the Krallen lines came to a hasty stop. The hooting died.

Caught in front of the gap were perhaps a hundred Krallen. In disarray, some continued onward while others stopped in their tracks.

The firing began.

Amid the whistles of the XQ guns and the *crack-crack* of the sniper fire, the Krallen stumbled and fell. They tried to reform their ranks, but even as they did, they were cut down.

In moments, the causeway in front of the gate was littered with a tumbled, chaotic mass of gray bodies oozing silver fluid onto the wet and muddied roadway.

"Cease fire!" Merral ordered. "Snipers, take down any that are still moving."

For a few seconds, there was silence; then a single Krallen broke free of the pile of bodies and ran toward the wall. A single shot rang out and it spun over and was still.

"*Tuh,*" Balancal said quietly. "That must have ruined their day. Your uncle did a splendid job."

"Yes, he did," Merral replied. "But we haven't stopped them. We have only delayed them."

∝∝∝∝∝

For the next hour, though, nothing happened. The ordered Krallen lines on the far side of the shattered causeway stayed mute and immobile while on the defenses, the soldiers took turns relaxing at their posts.

Increasingly, the mists on the lake thickened, the cloud grew denser and lower, and the light faded still further. Soon the spotlights were raised and switched on. Cones of brilliant light illuminated the causeway and the mist tendrils that drifted across.

Yet the presence of the enemy could not be ignored. There were occasional wild cries by the airport that made the soldiers shudder and every so often there would be a faint swishing sound from high above. Once, Merral glimpsed a diamond-shaped shadow flying overhead, faintly illuminated by the few lights on in the town.

Around half past eight, all diary communications failed. Although he had expected it, Merral found it unnerving. *It is a reminder that our foes have powers that we do not have.* As the backup systems of cables and wires were switched on, Merral ordered his forces to be ready for an imminent attack. Yet nothing happened and slowly the soldiers began to return to their state of partial alert.

Not long afterward Merral was summoned to a cable-linked communication system to receive a call from Betafor.

"Commander," she said, "as you know, the Dominion has imposed a . . .

blackout of electromagnetic communication on Ynysmant. But three minutes ago, I picked up a single brief signal from within the zone."

"*Within* the blackout zone?"

"Correct. One hypothesis is that it could be a small Krallen party. That would be consistent with their strategy in the past. A reconnaissance or . . . disruptive unit."

"Where did the signal come from?"

"About a kilometer to the northeast of where you are."

"Wait a minute. That's the lake."

"I am aware of the geography. On the maps I have, I would estimate it was just off Vanulet Pier."

"Odd. A landing party?"

"Possibly."

"I'll look into it. What other news is there?"

"Only a rising volume of signals from the airport area. I would say that they are making preparations."

"Thank you. Call me with any more news."

Merral stared into the misty gloom, pondering Betafor's message. *A signal from somewhere in the lake?* The visibility was now so bad that a surprise attack from a boat or raft couldn't be ruled out.

Merral made his decision and turned to Balancal. "Can you get a message to your irregs at Vanulet Pier? Warn them there may be a Krallen sneak attack by boat. I'm going to take a dozen of my men and take a quick look. The pier is just below my house. I know the area."

"Sneak attacks? *Tuh*, what next? That's cheating. Go take a look. If an attack begins here, I'll fire a red flare."

Merral quickly summoned a dozen soldiers out of the reserves waiting in the darkness below the walls. Then, with Lloyd just behind, Merral led them in a steady jog up the dim roads. As they moved through the deserted streets, Merral glimpsed watchful eyes staring at them from murky doorways and saw muzzles hidden in the dark depths of windows. *The irregs.* He wondered how effective they would be.

In a few minutes, they reached the square next to Merral's house and there they came across a party of four men armed with cutter guns, peering up at the buildings.

"Any news?" Merral asked.

"Some odd debris at the lake edge," the leader of the four said, his eyes still on the skyline. "Might have been some sort of inflatable boat. And some people reported noises on roofs."

Merral looked around, seeing nothing untoward. *Time is not on our side.* He snapped out a command to his men. "Split into fours. Take a street each. Get back here in ten minutes. And, if you see anything, fire."

As they left, Merral turned to Lloyd. "Follow me. My house has a good view. Remember the bedroom you stayed in?"

Like everywhere else in the street, his house was quiet and deserted. Merral opened the door, finding the deep darkness of the interior broken only by stray shafts of light from the few operating streetlights. There was a stuffy, desolate odor.

"No lights," Merral whispered. "And let's try to keep quiet."

He made his way to the stairway, dodging furniture. A thud and a sharp intake of breath behind him suggested Lloyd had been less successful.

"Upstairs," Merral hissed.

As softly as they could, they climbed the stairs. Merral paused to look out of the landing window, but failing to see anything, continued up.

In the attic room Merral groped his way past furniture to the window. He opened it as softly as he could and peered through the darkness over the serried ranks of rooftops, gables, and little streets toward the dark mists of the lake. Nothing moved.

A waste of time. There is noth—

"There!" Lloyd's voice was an electric whisper.

Barely thirty meters away, something moved. Strange angular shadows slipped along the rooftops, bounded noiselessly from balcony to balcony, and leaped from drainpipe to drainpipe, moving from left to right.

Merral, realizing they would be out of sight in seconds, said, "Lloyd, take the right. I'll take the left. On my word, open fire." *How easily I have slipped into the language of warfare.* He slipped the safety catch off, and braced himself on the sill, sighting on a moving gray shape.

"Fire!"

A long tumultuous roar shattered the silence as the two guns fired together.

Merral's target spun wildly and tumbled off the roof.

As the smell of propellant enveloped him, Merral sighted on a new target and fired again. Lloyd just kept firing.

There were cries from the ground; the other men had seen the Krallen. The *whip whip* of the guns echoed through the streets and yellow flashes knifed out of the darkness.

Merral paused, blinking and coughing in the fumes. He heard a grunt of satisfaction from Lloyd. "Chew dust," Lloyd muttered.

Merral looked at the skyline. The remaining Krallen had vanished. But where were they? Suddenly, he glimpsed something below in the inky darkness of the alleyway. Pale shapes clung to the buildings and flung themselves from wall to wall like acrobats.

"Sir, they're coming for us," Lloyd said, and fired again.

"Stay here," Merral snapped. "I'll take the window downstairs."

Trusting to his memory to guide him in the darkness, Merral ran down the stairs as fast as he dared. As he passed his parents' bedroom, he noticed a pause in the firing. In the tense silence that followed, he heard a faint noise: a tiny, almost inaudible scratching in the darkness of the general room below.

Merral froze. Straining his eyes, he could make out that a window shutter was wide-open. He was wondering what to do when he heard the front door open.

"Commander?" a man's voice cried. "You in here?"

Merral heard another tiny movement below. *There's something else there!*

Blinking sweat out of his eyes, Merral tried to recall the exact layout of where he was. Two steps would take him to a landing light switch and a shelf with ornaments to his right. He reached out and found the shelf, his hand closing around something. A vase. He remembered it—a blue one with delicate white tracery. One of his sisters had made it for their mother as a birthday present. He wrapped his fingers tightly around the base.

"Coming in!" shouted the soldier.

Merral threw the vase hard across the room.

It exploded in a thousand fragments. "Get out!" he shouted. "Krallen!"

As the door slammed shut, his fingers scrabbled for the light switch and pressed it.

Below, something like a great hairless hound crouched on the floor. It twisted its head toward him and opened its mouth in a loose-jawed leer.

"Get out of *my* house!" Merral yelled.

Above, he heard the clatter of heavy feet. Afraid and outraged at the idea of Krallen in his own home, Merral moved forward two steps, keeping tight against the wall. Behind him, up at the landing window, he heard a faint scratch.

The Krallen in the general room suddenly leaped onto the banister and swung its head to face him, flicking its tail and flexing its hind legs.

As it began to pounce, Merral fired. The flash blinded his eyes and the roar numbed his ears.

As the smoke lifted, Merral could see that the Krallen and part of the banister had gone. On the floor, amid a pile of wood fragments, an ashen figure lay twitching ever more slowly as a metallic liquid leaked into the carpet.

Merral descended a few steps carefully, his finger on the trigger.

Suddenly the landing window behind him exploded.

He spun round—almost slipping on the stairs—seeing in the midst of the flying splinters and glass at least two Krallen pour through. He swung the barrel around, and sighting by instinct, pulled the trigger.

Click.

The magazine was empty.

A Krallen leaped for him and he swung the gun butt hard at it. It connected, and the goblin fell back against the wall. Merral dropped the gun and ran down the stairs, tugging out his sword. He leaped the last steps, landed on the carpet, and spun round.

A Krallen leaped from the stair rail to a light fixture, grabbed it, twisted around with a flowing energy, and lashed out at him with a forelimb.

As the knifelike talons arced toward him, Merral swung his blade at his attacker.

There was another flash and an explosion.

The Krallen and the light fixture seemed to disintegrate in a hail of fragments. The room was plunged into semidarkness.

What was left of the Krallen crashed to the ground and Merral saw that it was headless. Puzzled, he turned to glimpse Lloyd at the top of the stairs, smoke drifting from the muzzle of his shotgun.

"Thanks, Llo—," Merral began, but suddenly there were more opponents. While Lloyd turned to face one goblin another crept toward Merral from out of a darkened corner. He slashed at it as it pounced at his face. The sword struck its neck while it was still in midair and bounced off. Yet the force of the blow had deflected its attack and sent the Krallen crashing against a table. There was the detonation of breaking crockery.

As it rolled onto the floor, Merral, aware of howls and Lloyd's yells on the stairs, ran round the table and jabbed his sword hard into his enemy. The blade sank deep, but as it did, the Krallen writhed and the handle flew out of Merral's grip. Just as he bent to regain his weapon, he heard something land on the carpet behind him.

"Look out!" Lloyd shouted.

Merral twisted around. Another Krallen sprang toward him with its forelimbs wide and its shining claws extended. He lurched sideways, its claws scrabbling futilely on his sleeve.

The Krallen slid past him and cannoned into a chair.

All too aware that he was now unarmed and conscious of the continuing fighting on the stairs—a cabinet had just tumbled over what was left of the banisters—Merral ran to the half-open kitchen door. He leaped through and tried to push it shut behind him. But a limb with scything razor-edged fingers hooked around the door. Merral pushed as hard as he could. The limb stayed in place.

His feet slid as the Krallen thudded against the door.

Merral desperately looked around the half-lit kitchen for a weapon. There were more violent noises and explosions from within the general room. *There has to be something to kill this thing! I can't meet death in my own home. That would be too ridiculous.*

A large kitchen knife lay within reach. He grabbed it and slashed at the arm. To his horror, the blade simply bounced off, barely leaving a mark.

He felt the Krallen thud against the door once more. There was an ominous creak.

Merral threw the blade away and looked for something else. There was the kettle, just within reach by the sink. He managed to snag the cord and tugged it toward him. It was full of water. As he touched the heat button, a red light glowed and there was the sound of bubbling. He waited the five seconds that it took to get the water boiling, unplugged it, and tugged the top off.

He jumped aside, letting the door fly open. As his pursuer tumbled in, Merral flung the boiling water over its head.

"Compliments of my mother!"

Enveloped in steam, the creature stopped, and in a disturbingly human gesture, slowly wiped its gleaming eyes with its knuckles, then, apparently unperturbed, turned to face Merral.

Merral ran around the heavy table in the center of the room, overturned it, and pushed it at his attacker. As the creature began to wriggle free, Merral swung a chair at its head. The Krallen snapped the chair legs off.

Merral ran to the end of the kitchen, flung open the door into his father's workroom, stumbled in, and pushed it shut behind him. He tabbed the light on and leaned hard against the door, gasping for breath.

He looked around for something to keep the door shut and defend himself. On the table was a large unfinished model of a spaceship—the Assembly frigate *Clearstar,* Lucas Ringell's vessel.

And I can be sure Ringell would have done a better job now.

There was a heavy blow behind his head. A gleaming, steely hand punched through the light wood and polymer of the door.

A weapon. Find a weapon!

Suddenly he noticed the odd chemical odor to the room. *What was it? What had his mother complained about?*

The door rocked and creaked as another set of claws punched through it.

"Glue!" On the table by the model stood a flask with bright red liquid.

The doorframe recoiled at another blow.

Merral grabbed the glue flask, flicked off the safety covering, and squirted the fluid over the door latch. There was a momentary sensation of heat and Merral stepped back. A new pounding began on the door, but it stayed in place.

On an impulse, Merral poured glue over the two sets of protruding claws. Again there was the brief burst of heat and the chemical odor as the glue set.

The Krallen gave a high, angry howl. The door shook furiously, then flew off its hinges. The whole structure—with the Krallen still firmly attached—crashed into the room, sending up a shower of dust. The hind legs lashed out furiously.

Seized by some strange and undefinable emotion Merral squirted glue on the creature's jaws and was gratified to see that, in barely a second, they froze wide-open.

Suddenly, Lloyd staggered through the kitchen door, with his gun. There was a graze on his face and silvery stains all over his jacket.

"They're all dead!" Lloyd gasped, then saw the Krallen. "But that ain't!"

"Don't worry," Merral said, suddenly aware that his hands were trembling. "It's not going anywhere."

Lloyd walked around the Krallen. "Glued down. Neat, sir."

"Give me your gun, Lloyd."

The big weapon was passed over.

"I've been wanting to do this for a bit," Merral said and stuck the muzzle in the open mouth.

"*Hasta la vista*, baby," Lloyd murmured.

Merral pulled the trigger.

There was a flash and an explosion of fragments that whizzed and hissed around. Merral was thrown backward with an arm-wrenching jolt.

"Actually, sir," Lloyd observed quietly as he brushed smoke from his face, "I find firing just one barrel quite adequate."

Merral gazed at the shattered and dripping remains of the Krallen and the devastation of the workroom. "I'll remember that."

As they stepped carefully through the debris that cluttered the kitchen floor, Merral turned to Lloyd. "*'Hasta la vista'*?"

"I think it's an old Austrian farewell."

"It doesn't *sound* like old Austrian."

Merral stopped in the general room to pick up his sword, gazing at the still Krallen forms lying amid pools of fluid, the broken glass, the shattered furniture, and the pitted walls.

"Oh, dear," Merral said. "They are *not* going to like this."

As they walked outside a dozen soldiers met them.

Together they did a quick tally. Eighteen Krallen had been dispatched outside the house, six inside.

"A two-unit team all accounted for," Merral said. "With no loss. Well, only to property."

"Look!" a soldier said, gesturing down the road toward the Gate House.

In the night sky, a flare blossomed red.

30

They ran back to the gateway and Merral sprang up the steps as Balancal waved him over.

"Okay?" Balancal asked, in a matter-of-fact tone.

"Yes. There are now twenty-four Krallen less. No loss."

"*Tuh.*" Balancal's face puckered into a wry grin. "You always were an underachiever, D'Avanos. There's another twenty-odd thousand to go."

He gestured toward the causeway. "Your creature warned us five minutes ago that there was activity due. And it was right."

Merral stared over the parapet. The drifting wall of mist shimmered white in the glare of the spotlights, but through the gaps he could see movement just beyond the blasted section. A line of a dozen Krallen had moved forward, their shoulders interlinked by cabling, and walked down into the lake, their heads barely above the water line. No sooner had they done this when another similarly linked group clambered across them and silently took up positions at the front.

Merral ordered Karita's sniper team to fire.

In seconds, there was a fusillade of shots. As small puffs of smoke rose from their bodies, the front line of Krallen sagged beneath the dark waters.

The soldiers on the wall cheered, but as another dozen Krallen clambered on top of those that had just been destroyed, the cheering faded.

There was another volley of sniper fire. The new line tottered into the water only to be replaced by yet another row of Krallen. The pattern repeated itself again: a new round of sniper fire, a further collapse into the water, and another new unit moving on top.

Within minutes, it was uncomfortably obvious that, despite the losses, each successive Krallen line was moving a little further out before being cut down. Merral was astonished and repelled by the way that the Krallen treated each other as disposable building blocks. Despite another five volleys from the snipers, within ten minutes, the gap in the causeway had been half-filled by a long, swaying chain of interlocked gray creatures.

A new patch of mist swirled slowly across the causeway and obscured the view. When it lifted a few minutes later, Merral could see there were other creatures among the Krallen. Tall ape-creatures waded out with cabling and cockroach-beasts scuttled in between them, cutting and binding.

Feeling almost overwhelmed by this inexorable, oncoming foe, Merral called Karita. "How long can you keep firing?"

"Commander, we now have only around twenty rounds each."

"That's not enough. Keep them in reserve. Hold your fire until I tell you."

It took the Dominion forces only another twenty minutes to bridge the gap in the causeway. Once they reached the Ynysmant side, wires were carried across by ape-creatures and locked in place and slats placed on top of them. Finally, those Krallen who had rebuilt the crossing and had not been destroyed unlinked themselves and climbed out of the water. Then, apparently none the worse for their immersion, they bounded back to the far side and regrouped into neat ranks.

So far a silence had prevailed among the enemy, but now synchronized wails, whistles, and hoots began. The noises echoed through the mist and through the darkened streets of the town and as they heard the sounds, the soldiers visibly shivered.

They are brave people, but even the brave have limits.

Merral was summoned to hear a new message from Betafor.

"Commander," she said, "the lines are preparing to move."

"That's no surprise," he answered. "But Betafor, have you detected the presence of anything else in among them?"

"Such as?"

"A baziliarch?"

There was a moment's silence before the answer came. "No."

Can I trust her?

Merral walked back to join Balancal. "Any minute," he said.

Balancal nodded.

The howling and wailing grew. Soon the Krallen ranks began to advance at a slow and measured pace.

A long way back, half hidden by the mist and the darkness of the evening, Merral discerned ape-creatures and cockroach-beasts moving within the great mass of the enemy.

The advancing line crossed over the broken part of the causeway. When they reached the pile of destroyed Krallen, they strode over the fallen forms as if they were stones.

Merral glimpsed nervous eyes and pale faces all around. He touched the microphone stud. "Men!" he called out, trying to inject hope into his voice. "Now is the time for courage and action. You fight for Ynysmant, Farholme, and the Assembly. Above all, you fight for the Lamb!"

There were shouts of agreement in response, but in them, Merral heard fear.

They know we are too few. They know we cannot win. . . . Lord, have mercy on us! Act now! We need your help!

Balancal sighed wearily. "These things do keep coming, don't they? Well, let's see if these cannons work." He picked up a switch.

Merral ordered the soldiers to take cover.

"One, two, three, *now!*" Balancal said and for a blinding instant, night was replaced by day.

As the sound of the double roar of the guns pummeled him, Merral saw the Krallen line turn into a boiling cloud of dirty fragments. The echoes of the blasts died away and he heard ragged cheers from the wall.

Slowly, the smoke lifted, mingling with the mist. The front section of the enemy force had vanished. For thirty or forty meters, the Krallen had been reduced to little more than a heap of pale fragments. *As if some monstrous bonfire had left only ash.*

But even as Merral watched, the all-too-familiar pattern repeated itself. The Krallen regrouped and moved forward, trotting with apparent unconcern through the fragments of their fellows.

The cheering stopped.

"Fire at will!" Merral ordered.

As the shooting began, the Krallen, their forms sharp-edged in the harsh emergency illumination, broke into a lope. Where the causeway broadened, they fanned out and hurled themselves at the wall like the angry breaker of a winter storm at sea.

Merral pulled the trigger again and again. He had no need to aim precisely; it was impossible to miss. Yet the attackers continued to run through a barrage of rocket, rifle, and cutter-gun fire. The noise was almost deafening, a vast medley of weapons fire, yells, and howling. Many Krallen tumbled down, yet for all the numbers that fell or stumbled, the pace of the onslaught was undiminished.

In seconds, the first Krallen had reached the foot of the walls and were clambering up. As they reached the top, they were hewn down as swords replaced guns. They tumbled back and soon others were scrambling over their still forms.

Merral threw his gun down and reached for his sword. A Krallen, its eyes gleaming like twin red stars, stuck its head above the wall and Merral slammed his blade deep into its skull. As it slithered back down, he tugged the sword free and cut down a second attacker.

On the edges of his vision, he could see frantic fighting all about him, as the soldiers hacked and thrust at the enemies. He felled a third Krallen while Lloyd dispatched another with a shotgun blast in the mouth. But there were always others and the more they struck down, the easier it became for their successors to reach the top of the wall.

Suddenly, the Krallen seemed to hesitate. Their advance stopped, and those on the wall slipped back down. The lines froze, and the wailing and hooting ceased.

"Had enough, 'ave you?" someone yelled and there was nervous laughter.

For a brief second, hope burst into Merral's heart. *A rescue. It's the envoy.*

Then, in the very next instant, all hope fled.

Merral was suddenly seized by a deep, stomach-wrenching feeling of dread and dismay. All around him, he heard laughter transform into gasps. He reached out to touch the parapet for support, his eyes drawn beyond the illuminated zone of the causeway into the dark mistiness beyond. Although he could see nothing there other than the limitless foe, he had a sickening certainty that beyond the lines of Krallen there was now something else, some presence filled with power and malice.

Merral saw to either side of him that his comrades were staring wide-eyed out along the causeway. *They too have sensed it.*

In the town behind him, the dogs began to howl with strange and troubling tones.

"What is it?" hissed Balancal. For the first time, Merral heard dread in his voice.

"The baziliarch," Merral answered, his mouth dry. "A power. More than a physical being. One of the enemy's servants in a body."

"A demon?" Balancal sighed. "*Tuh.* Last thing we need. Can we kill it? Or is that a stupid question?"

"I doubt we can kill it," Merral replied. "It's from Below-Space. It occupies more than one dimension." As he said it, he realized that to try to give an explanation was utterly futile.

Then suddenly, from beyond the stilled enemy lines, came a noise—a massive rattling sound as if hollow trees were being beaten by some titanic drummer. Merral peered into the mist wanting—and not wanting—to see its cause.

Within the misty dimness at the far end of the causeway, a vast, sharp-edged shadow moved with an odd jerky motion. Its form was impossible to determine, but Merral saw with a terrible thrill that it was higher than any animal and loomed over the forces beneath it.

The baziliarch. As the word came to him, Merral felt the touch of something cold and hate-filled on his mind. He trembled, and from the moans and whimpers about him he knew others had felt the same touch. Merral looked around, seeing everywhere fearful eyes seeking reassurance.

There was a new rattling noise. In under a second, the mists parted and through them the creature lurched into view. Merral's first terror-struck impression was of an enormous winged being cut out of black ice, an impossible assemblage of angles. The wings were held high as a bird might do on landing, yet their shape and their glistening blackness were not birdlike. And although something hung over the body that obscured its form, he could see a pair of powerful rear legs that were bent up against the body like those of a monstrous locust, while at the front, two weird jointed forelimbs hung down. An angular head protruded forward on a segmented neck.

The creature moved with an unwieldy, swaying gait, yet the awkwardness of its movements could not disguise a purposefulness and intelligence. *Even if I didn't know what I do, I would know we faced no animal.*

The rattling of the baziliarch grew louder and as it did, the soldiers beside Merral prayed aloud.

Lord, he added silently, *send us your aid. In the name of the Christ.*

As the creature moved forward with its slewing steps, the Dominion forces on the causeway parted urgently before it. Those that failed to get out of the way were simply flung aside.

Merral was aware of Vero beside him.

"T-the b-baziliarch?" Vero stuttered.

"Yes," Merral said, "it's what I glimpsed at Langerstrand."

As the creature approached the broken segment of the causeway, new aspects registered. It was at least twice the height of a human being and, Merral felt, longer than any living land animal. The wings were partly furled but even so they nearly stretched across the width of the causeway. He could see now that the head bore strange eyes and a cavity where a nose might have been and the jaws were wide and toothed. There was something about the head that Merral felt was familiar, but where that familiarity lay he could not be sure.

Another terrifying dry rattle broke. The noise seemed to be made by the rear legs vibrating hard against the body like sticks against a drum skin. As Merral watched the creature move, he had the impression that, for all its size, the creature was lightly built. *As if it were an insect built on the scale of a dinosaur.* As it came closer he saw that each eye was as large as a man's face and an iridescent yellow in color.

There were two details, however, he could make no sense of at all. One was the way the body seemed clad in something, almost as if some sort of fabric hung off it, and the other was the way that the crest of the head bore a high, pointed silvery structure that glinted in the light.

Suddenly aware of how close it was, Merral quickly touched the microphone switch. "Stand firm! When this thing reaches our side of the gap, I want us to hit it with two rounds each—on my order."

As his words died away, Merral pulled Balancal toward him so that he could speak to him without shouting. "This thing affects morale," he said in a low voice.

"Oh, wonderful," said Balancal. "I thought it was just me. You feel it too?"

"Yes. Look, if it gets much closer, I don't think the defenses will hold. Prepare for a retreat."

Balancal bit his lip. "Right. Thanks for the warning." His eyes flicked to the flare gun at his belt.

The baziliarch lurched slowly over the reconstructed part of the causeway. Merral saw that the forelimbs ended in great claws, like those of a bird. As it advanced, the Krallen in front squeezed aside, then followed, keeping out of range of its long flicking tail.

"Fire!" Merral shouted.

The rattling, whistling clamor of the simultaneous discharge of over a hundred weapons was almost deafening. For a second, the creature disappeared in a sheet of flame and smoke. Then, apparently totally unscathed, it swayed forward.

"That's impossible!" Balancal protested.

I wish it was.

As the smoke cleared he suddenly saw that the silvery feature atop the baziliarch's head was not a part of the body, but a metal crown. *How weird.* The body was clad in some sort of loose tunic. As he recognized both the crown and the clothing, Merral had confirmed what he knew: the thing they faced was no animal, but a being with intelligence and authority. What had Vero said? "There is a hierarchy: the baziliarchs come above steersmen."

The terrible creature swayed forward, its clawed feet scrabbling over the dead Krallen, and stood before the wall.

It reared up on its hind legs so that its head, looking like a weird sculpture, was at the level of the parapet. As it did, Merral saw that head and body were scarred with deep, sharp notches. *It has been in a battle.* He suddenly realized that he had seen the battle where these wounds were inflicted.

The baziliarch twitched its legs against its body again with a rattle that seemed to shake the walls. With a great rustle, it unfurled its terrible, crow black wings. They too were scored and slashed.

Then it opened its vast mouth and gave a harsh abrasive hiss.

Cries and whimpers of dread broke out from the soldiers.

With a new spasm of horror Merral glimpsed a vast emptiness. The dreadful form that stood before him was not really the baziliarch, but merely a physical shell that had been made for him.

The Wielders of the Powers created this frame for the baziliarch just as Azeras said.

Suddenly, the monstrosity leaned forward and lashed out with its wings.

In an instant, all behind the parapet threw themselves flat. There were yells and screams. Merral felt the wing slice through the air just above him and heard the sound of bodies tumbling into the street.

In a second the wall began to shake and Merral peered up to see the baziliarch tearing at the parapets and its defenders with its forelimbs. Swords, guns, and bodies were thrown every way. In seconds, the masonry began to break up.

Merral saw that soldiers were fleeing.

He caught sight of Balancal lying flat behind the parapet wall and pulled his arm. "We have to retreat!" he yelled.

Balancal, his face almost bloodless, tugged his flare gun free and fired into the air.

There was a new, angry flurry of wings and stones crashed to the ground. As the blue flare erupted above them, Merral touched his microphone button. "Withdraw to the third circle as orderly as you can! Take your weapons."

His words had barely died away before he saw soldiers jump down the steps and slide down the ladders. Merral, with Lloyd at his side, followed.

Once on the ground, which was already becoming filled with masonry, Merral looked around for Vero and was relieved to see him just behind with Balancal. He ran into Causeway Square, then stopped, surveying the scene with a feeling of sickening despair.

All around there was almost complete pandemonium. Soldiers were fleeing up Island Road; medical orderlies were trying to get the wounded onto stretchers and into ambulances; men were running into each other. Merral saw two women exit a house, their long-barreled rifles over their shoulders, and stare at him as if seeking advice. He gestured them up the road and they started jogging away. Everywhere, Merral saw faces and heard voices full of incredulity and fear.

"You'd better go," Vero said, his voice breathless. "Get up to the third-circle defenses. They will need you there."

Merral heard Lloyd grunt agreement. He wanted to disagree, but a deep booming sound had begun by the Gate House and as Merral looked, the doors of the gate began to buckle.

"What about you?" he asked Vero.

Vero exchanged a glance with Balancal. "My friend, the irregulars were set up to fight behind the lines. So, I guess this is where we leave you. It's time to go and make ourselves a nuisance."

"That was the plan," Balancal added, shaking his head at the spectacle around him. "*Tuh.* I didn't expect it to be quite like this though." Then he gave a dismissive shrug as if being utterly outnumbered and outmatched was merely a nuisance. "Well, we'll do what we can."

"Balancal," Merral said, grabbing his hand, "well done so far. Don't give up hope."

The handshake was returned and as Balancal slipped away to join a handful of irregulars moving up through the square, Merral turned to Vero. "You can't go," Merral protested. "I need your advice."

There was a look of pain on his friend's face. "It's not been much good so far. I'll try and follow you. I need to help Balancal now."

"But it's going to be dangerous."

Vero gave a sad and drained smile. "No more than anywhere else in this town tonight." The sound of ominous splintering noises from the gate seemed to underline his words. "We must face facts," he added. "Against a few Krallen we might have held out. Against so many—and against this thing—we've little hope. Unless the Most High intervenes, all we can do is make a good death."

Suddenly, feeling close to tears, Merral clasped Vero's hand and squeezed it. "Fight well."

"And you." The grasp was returned. "But I'll try to meet you at the summit."

Vero ran after Balancal and his men. They slipped away into the darkness of a side street without looking back.

Hearing new shouts of alarm, Merral looked across the chaos of Causeway Square to the wall. There, silhouetted against the illuminated sheets of mist, a monstrous figure now swayed along the remains of the parapet. With its tail lashing in spasms and its wings outstretched as if giving it balance, the baziliarch lurched to the Gate House where the flags hung limply in the still night air. With fierce, deliberate blows, the creature struck them down.

It hates them, Merral realized in a moment of clarity. *It loathes all that they stand for.*

There was a new rattle from the baziliarch. It extended its wings and, with a bound and a little glide, leaped down into the square. There it turned and with its forelimbs tugged at the props that buttressed the gateway's doors.

He was suddenly aware of Lloyd touching his shoulder. "We'd better go, sir. You can't do any more good here."

Merral turned and, followed by Lloyd, began running up Island Road. At the point where the road began its first turn, he paused and, walking free of the melee of vehicles and frightened people, looked back to the Causeway Square and the Gate House. The baziliarch stepped back from the gateway and suddenly the doors flew open. With a wailing howl that seemed to echo around the town, the Krallen burst in like gray liquid.

Merral rejoined the fleeing crowd.

⊲○⊲○○⊲⊳

Merral and Lloyd ran and panted their way up the road along with men and women who were close to panic. They stopped twice: once to help a wounded soldier onto an ambulance and once for Merral to remonstrate another man who, having given up all hope, sat weeping in a doorway.

The utter misery of the retreat—or was it, Merral thought, a rout?—was slightly lifted by the fact that the Dominion forces did not immediately follow in pursuit. Merral wondered if their failure to pursue their advantage was due to the lack of initiative that Anya had identified.

When Merral edged his way through the closing doors of the new gateway at the third circle, he was slightly cheered at the hopeful faces that greeted him. *They are relieved to see me.* He gulped down the water given to him. He gazed around, seeing soldiers having their wounds tended and replenishing ammunition. *They feel that as long as I live, all hope is not utterly lost. It's idolatry, but it's too late to change it now.*

Yet as Merral looked at the soldiers gathered at the gate, he saw other emotions in their faces. Some eyes held despair while others bore a hint of accusation. *They expected to face enemies, but not to have to face a battle with something impossible to fight.*

Of his five captains, four, including Karita, were present. He quickly reviewed their status. All had lost soldiers and all now had limited ammunition. The snipers were down to a dozen rounds each. Ordering them to wait by the gateway where the doors were now barred, Merral ran up to a command position at the top of a small tower on the side of the street. There he found one of Balancal's lieutenants staring at a large screen of street maps while other irregulars peered through the open windows onto the lower part of Ynysmant.

The sounds of shooting and explosions rolled in through the window.

"They are taking their time," the lieutenant said. "They regrouped in Causeway Square and are slowly moving up. They aren't moving out to the sides. They are taking a lot of losses. But . . ." He looked up with an expression of resignation and shrugged sadly. "There are always more."

"I know. How long before they get here?"

"Your guess is as good as mine, Commander. Probably not long." The man gestured toward the window. "Take a look."

Merral walked over and peered down, seeing the red glow of fires in the lower streets. He could hear the repeated *whip, whip, whip* noise from the XQ guns and could picture the Krallen lines advancing up the streets only to be cut down by fire from within the houses.

But the Krallen, he realized, were his secondary concern. The great focus of his fears was the baziliarch, the being who tore into buildings and defenses, who sapped the strength and will of all who faced him, the one no army could withstand.

Merral stared into the darkness, his eyes unwillingly hunting for the creature. Finally he saw it—a night black form climbing from roof to roof, its wings arcing wide in the darkness as it swept down all flags and banners. In the flash of an explosion he caught the glint of its bizarre yellow eyes.

Oh, Lord, this onslaught is not just against us, it is against you and your honor. Act, Lord! Defend your name!

But there was no blast of lightning, no appearance of the envoy, no word of comfort.

Merral realized that he now felt beyond either fear or hope. *It doesn't matter. We'll just keep fighting until the end.*

His thoughts were interrupted by a brilliant flash at the point where Island Road reached the second circle. A loud boom echoed round the town. Merral looked around, weighing up his limited options. He could see no reason why these defenses would hold a moment longer than those down by the causeway. Indeed the very length of the new walls on the third circle meant that they were almost indefensible.

He walked back to the lieutenant. "I'll order my soldiers to take a position around the defenses here. But I'm going up to the top to see Enatus." He dropped his voice. "And when they do get here, don't feel you have to defend this line to the last man." Merral noted relief in the man's eyes. "Delay them as long as possible and then retreat to Congregation Square. We will make a last stand there, and the more fighters we have there, the more likelihood that we may hold them off."

At the bottom of the tower, Merral found his captains and gave them orders and then, with Lloyd pacing silently behind him, walked up the winding road to the new fortifications at the summit of the town. He felt exhausted and utterly overwhelmed.

He walked through the gateway past machines ready to push the doors closed at a moment's notice and past faces that seemed to search his, hungry for any hint of good news.

The vast square, lit unevenly by spotlights, was full of people and activity. Men and women were loading weapons, running between medical tents, or carrying supplies. In the conversations he overheard, Merral sensed both a barely suppressed fear and a grim determination. He asked for Enatus and was shown inside a sandbagged construction by the side of Congregation Hall.

"It's not good, is it, Commander?" the warden said, looking up from a street map.

"No."

"This creature—"

"A baziliarch."

"Can it be defeated?"

"Not by force. Not by us."

"I see." Enatus closed his eyes for a moment and muttered something under his breath that Merral took to be a prayer. The warden opened his eyes. "Well," he said. "I suppose there is no shame in losing to an unbeatable opponent, is there?"

"None."

"How long do we have?"

"I don't know. They seem to be taking their time. I suspect no more than twenty minutes. We can't expect the third-circle defenses to hold for long."

Enatus stroked his mustache. "Very well. I'd better order the closing of the refuge doors and prepare to make a last defense. I wish Isabella were here to come up with some sort of stirring speech for me."

"The Lord of the Assembly measures deeds, not words," Merral said, feeling that he hadn't done very well on either score.

"True." The warden picked up his sword and hefted it. "But, to tell you the whole truth, Commander, I always rather liked a good speech."

ㅁㅁㅁㅁㅁ

Merral and Lloyd walked across the grim and smoky square to the command post at the new gate. As they did, sirens sounded and loudspeakers ordered all nonessential personnel to enter the refuges immediately. Across the expanse of the square, men and women filed past the equipment and the wreckage of the *Emilia Kay* to the twin doors of Congregation Hall.

At the gate, Merral went in search of the lieutenant in charge of the irregs and had the latest update. It was as he feared. Despite heavy resistance the Krallen advance was unstoppable. Whenever they encountered any obstacles, the baziliarch came over and the defenses were instantly overwhelmed.

Merral went to the gate entrance. There he stood looking out to where the flash of weapons fire was most intense, trying to master his thoughts. But soon he heard a familiar voice cry out, "Commander!"

He turned to see Luke. "Chaplain," he said, "I was worried about you, among others."

"And I was worried about you. How are you doing?"

To his surprise, Merral felt himself smile. "Our defenses are failing. We all face death in minutes. And you ask me how I'm doing?"

In the gloom, Luke's face acquired a look of rueful amusement. "Yes, a bit of a silly question really. But you know what I mean. How are you?"

"I have . . ." Merral hesitated, trying to determine his exact feelings.

"I feel almost defeated, but I have a degree of peace about it. Ironically, I'm more at peace than when I saw you earlier." He gazed past the chaplain at the disorder of the darkened square. "Luke, we've done what we can. Our defense now rests with the Lord. If he chooses to deliver us, we'll praise him here. If he doesn't, we'll praise him in glory."

"Well put."

"There's not much else I can say, is there?"

"No."

"I had hoped the envoy would turn up."

"I know, but his presence is at the Lord's command, not ours. And the King always does what is best for his people."

"I don't complain." *Not now.*

There were shouted warnings by Congregation Hall. The doors of the refuge were closing.

"Do you have any advice for me?" Merral asked, hearing the fierce hiss of the great pistons as the massive doors slid into place.

"None." The chaplain paused for a look through the gate. "Only that if this thing comes here, I think you ought to challenge him."

"He's going to take little notice of me."

"Yes, but it's not just you. You belong to the King. And that's someone he's afraid of."

"Might as well." Merral said, marveling at how matter-of-fact he sounded.

Suddenly, he heard a soft swishing sound in the air above him. He looked up in time to glimpse the dark shape of a slitherwing as it wove its way around the bell tower.

"The enemy is all around, Luke."

"And so is God's grace. But I must be about my duties."

"And I mine. God bless you, Luke."

"And you, Merral."

In the gloom, they saluted each other.

Not long after Luke departed, there were fierce cries, heavy explosions, and a volley of shots from below them. The third-circle defenses were being attacked. Within five minutes, weary and bloodied soldiers began to walk or stagger up the road to the gates. The defenses had been breached.

Merral, waiting by the gate, gave the order for any uninjured regulars to wait inside on the square. But the numbers of those who ran or tottered up the final part of Island Road were fewer than he had hoped. Among them he saw no sign of Vero or Balancal.

Soon, the flow had almost dried up and one door of the gate was closed. The second door was closing, when a handful of soldiers turned the bend below and, seemingly on the verge of utter exhaustion, jogged slowly up to the gateway.

Among them, Merral found one of the faces he was looking for. "Sentinel Enand," he said. *Thank you, God. He's safe.*

"C-Commander." Vero shook his head, sat heavily against the wall, and put his head in his hands.

Merral squatted next to him and put his hand gently on his friend's shoulder. "Balancal?"

Vero looked up and shook his head. "Dead." He handed Merral Balancal's flare gun.

"I'm sorry."

"Commander D'Avanos . . . ," Vero said slowly, his eyes full of tears. "I wish to report that the irregulars have performed . . . as expected." He buried his head in his hands again.

Merral, moved almost beyond speech, patted him on the shoulder. "Well done," he murmured. "Well done."

He looked up to see the doors being barred.

Not long now. Not long at all.

ᴄᴏᴄᴏᴄᴏ

Beneath the wall, Merral assembled the remaining regulars—barely eighty soldiers. He was down to two captains, including Karita, whose sniper team was now reduced to six. *I brought a hundred and fifty men and women here this morning. Now only half that stand with me.* He felt a bitter sadness.

I have to say something to them. But what? We stand at the edge of defeat. Do I simply say it's all over? But as the despairing thought came to him, it was driven away by a surge of defiant resolve.

"You have fought well," Merral called out. "There's no shame in failing against such forces. The Assembly will be proud of you. Now I want us to go upon these ramparts and fight hard. And if these defenses are breached, I want us to assemble in front of Congregation Hall and defend it till we all fall. There are thousands inside."

He paused, surveying the weary and bloodied faces before him. "The Assembly has endured twelve thousand years and as far as you or I know it may easily last as long again. You and I have been privileged to take part in its greatest battle. And however long the Assembly *does* last for, we want to be known as those from Ynysmant, the least town of the farthest world. Those who, when faced with overwhelming odds, did not fail either the Assembly or her Lord."

There was no cheering—he had expected none—only determined nods and murmurs of assent. Merral was moved to speak again. "It has been a privilege to fight with you."

◌◌◌◌◌

With Lloyd at his side, Merral took his place on the wall above the gateway at the edge of a tower from which flags hung. He gazed out, seeing the whole northern half of Ynysmant below him.

The mist had lifted now and the dark waters shimmered dully, reflecting the flashes and flames that lit up the town. There was a slight, cooling breeze off the lake. Merral looked up, hearing the flags rustle and seeing the Lamb and Stars palely gleaming above him.

The fighting was closer now. A flash revealed the gray lines of the enemy moving steadily along Island Road. There was constant howling and whistling, and from down among the houses, ghastly rattles echoed up as a giant grotesque shadow slipped and swayed over roofs.

In a few seconds, the Krallen advance was in range.

"Fire at will!" Merral shouted, and there was a chorus of shots in response.

The Krallen charged. In seconds, they were at the walls, scaling them with hard strokes of their sharp claws. As they climbed, those in front were hewn down or shot, but more followed.

Behind them, the great shadow of the baziliarch lurched forward with a relentless malevolence and as it approached the gates, the Krallen advance stopped. The Krallen on the walls dropped back to the ground where, doglike, they circled behind the monstrous form.

The howling and hooting ended.

As the baziliarch advanced, its vast legs making scratching noises on the ground, Merral sensed the men and women on either side of him shuffling nervously.

There was a flap of the wings and the creature leaped at the wall. There were yells of terror as barely a dozen meters from Merral, the baziliarch hooked claws on the top of the wall and pulled itself onto the parapet.

This close, he could smell it now, a dreadful odor of rottenness and death.

Now the baziliarch lashed out with its terrible jointed limbs and soldiers fled in panic. The terrible eyes, glinting in the flashes and flames, swung this way and that and the light glimmered on the silver crown.

"Back!" Merral shouted, but realized as he said it that the command was pointless. Fear, not orders, now ruled.

Shots were fired—a XQ round whistled past Merral's ear—as the creature, high and terrible against the night sky, flailed out with limbs and wings. Merral glimpsed the weapons fire penetrating the creature and vanishing through it.

All around, soldiers tumbled or jumped off the wall.

Merral ran to the stairs and, followed by Lloyd, slid down them to the gloomy square.

"The hall!" he cried, but his words seemed to vanish in the chaos.

He ran across the dark square, men and women with him, trying to avoid tripping over the debris and pitted paving stones left by the morning's bombardment.

Suddenly, Lloyd grunted and said, "What . . . ? Excuse me, sir," before trotting toward a patch of darker shadows beneath the new wall.

Merral, jostled by someone next to him, lost sight of Lloyd and ran on. Once beneath the high stone walls of the hall, he rallied the soldiers around him. *We need some order, even at the end.*

As the remaining fighters began to assemble, he looked up. Above the gate, the baziliarch was roaming around, smashing down flagpoles and tearing the flags. *As before, expressing its hatred for what we are seems to take priority.*

Merral looked at the forces around him, struggling to identify helmeted faces in the feeble light. There were faces he knew—Vero, Karita, and others—but many other faces were missing.

A small dumpy figure almost hidden behind the flag that he carried on a staff walked up to Merral.

"To be totally honest, Commander," the warden said, in a low voice, "I don't think this looks very good for us."

"No, Warden. It doesn't."

Merral saw Enatus was clasping his sword firmly.

Above the gateway, the baziliarch turned, reared up with a great rattling noise, and glided to the floor of the square. There it turned and began ripping away the struts and bars that held the gate shut.

Suddenly, Merral was aware that Lloyd was back at his side, breathing heavily. "Welcome back, Sergeant."

"Sorry, sir. I saw Betafor sneaking away. I caught her."

"Did you do her any harm?" *Not that it matters now.*

"Nah. I was tempted though. Pushed her inside that sandbagged enclosure and jammed the door shut. Funny thing though. The Lamb and Stars had gone off her jacket."

"What a surprise. Well done."

"Thanks."

Merral hesitated. "Well, Sergeant," he said, feeling oddly calm, "if this goes the way it looks like it's going, well . . . thanks."

There was the soft *swish-swish* of a slitherwing overhead.

"Thank *you,* sir. But we aren't done yet. It ain't over till the fat lady sings."

"Sometime, Lloyd, you can explain that to me."

With a crash, the gates flew open.

As the baziliarch swung round to face the hall, lines of gray forms crept into the square behind it. The creature lowered its head and swayed it from side to side, like a vast snake.

With slow, clumsy steps it moved forward. Behind it, an arc of Krallen spread out slowly. Others bounded up the steps behind them with their relentless energy to take up position on the parapets.

The soldiers edged back. But Congregation Hall was at their backs. There was nowhere to go.

Twenty meters away, the baziliarch stopped. As it did the Krallen on the gates and on the walls stopped too.

We are in the endgame.

As he stood there, feeling beyond fear and hope, Luke's words came to mind: *I think you ought to challenge him.*

Yes. There are things that have to be said and I am the one to say them.

Merral handed his gun to Lloyd, unsheathed his sword, and turned to Enatus. "Warden, I'm going to challenge him. May I borrow your flag?"

"Are you sure? I was going to do that. Isn't that my job?"

Merral patted him on the shoulder. "Warden, you are a hero. But be gracious. Let me do it."

The little man blinked and handed over the flag.

"Lloyd, stay here. It's an order," Merral said. He grasped the staff in his left hand and walked toward the creature.

A tense hush fell across the square.

Suddenly, as he had once before, Merral saw himself in an epic painting, this time as a tiny figure in stained armor with the Lamb and Stars in one hand, a sword in the other, walking alone in the darkness toward the brooding menace of the thing of shadows and angles and gleaming yellow eyes.

How silly. He pushed the idea away.

Merral walked forward until he was just five meters away from the baziliarch. Little details registered now: the way the air seemed to twist and turn around the creature's skin, the appalling play of colors on the eyes, the wide jaws, the complexities of the clawed hands, the deep score marks. This close, the glistening head with deep eye sockets and its cavity for a nose bore a grotesque resemblance to a human skull. *The tunic, the crown, the skull. It seeks to ape human beings.*

Merral raised the sword high. "This is the Lord's Assembly!" he shouted with all the energy he could muster, and he heard his voice ringing round the square. "As commander in chief of the forces here, I order you, in the name of the Lamb, to depart."

There was a long silence, as if time itself had frozen. Then the jaws clicked open and the creature spoke. "Fool!" The word cracked across the square.

A forearm moved, the multijointed limb segments making faint clacking noises, and the claws reached deep inside the dark tunic. The limb rotated out, bearing a serrated sword of tarnished silver twice the length of Merral's blade. Its edges glinted with a strange, green fire.

"*You* cannot challenge me. Your lord has deserted you. He has left you to your fate."

Merral felt a razor's edge of malice in the words. "He has not," he replied, but felt his words had no power.

"Shall I tell you why your lord has not sent you help?" The head swept slowly around as if addressing all those on the square. Finally, the ghastly eyes turned to stare at Merral. "He sent you a command through one of his agents and you—yes, *you*—despised it. You, Commander, rebelled against his words. And all such rebels belong to me."

With these words, the last vestige of hope deserted Merral and he could say nothing. He cringed, looking around and seeing nothing but darkness. *I face a demonic power. How can I hope?*

"We found opposition here," the baziliarch continued, its voice a drawn-out deadly hiss, "and we uncovered its source. We had long heard whispers of an opponent—the great adversary, the one who could challenge my master's plans for the Lord Nezhuala. So he was found and trapped by his own folly."

With two lumbering strides, the baziliarch lurched forward. The stench of death was almost overwhelming.

Suddenly the sword blade swung out and, for an instant, Merral thought it was all over. But the blade stopped an arm's length away from his armor, an evil needle glinting in the dull light, pointing at Merral's heart.

The head lowered and the fleshless jaws moved again. "What value is the loss of a ship if we destroy such an adversary? Any price is worth the removal of the one who might stand in our way." The creature's voice was a proud and hateful hiss. "You sought to be Lucas Ringell's successor, but you failed. You shall die knowing that today we take this town, tomorrow, this world, and in a little while, the entire Assembly. The realms will be united. It has been decreed."

The desperate thought came to Merral that, however futile the act might be, he would attack the creature that faced him. *I will not wait for death to come to me. I will meet it.*

Beyond all hope, he stepped to one side and then, with all his strength, swung his sword at the claw that held the blade.

His sword bounced off the limb with a dull, ringing noise.

"Fool," said the creature, its jaws clicking. "No weapon you can either make or wield can hurt me. Now die."

The blade stabbed.

Merral lunged sideways, letting the flag fall. The blade missed him, but passed so close that it scraped over his armor. He heard gasps from behind him.

The tarnished silver sword flicked back, the clawed hand twisted sharply, and the blade jabbed out again. Merral stepped aside again, but tripped and tumbled to the ground. His sword flew out of his hand.

He began to crawl to his feet, but froze as he saw, a mere handbreath away from his heart, the unwavering needle point of the blade.

It is all over. He waited for the sword to plunge into his chest, a darkness of despair descending on him. He struggled to frame the simplest prayer. All he could come up with was *Have mercy, Lord.*

Through his half-closed eyes, he saw a blade move. It was not silver, but golden—the living, electric gold of the sunlight of a summer's day. The tarnished serrated blade was brushed aside and clattered to the ground. The sullen, foul-smelling air was replaced by something clearer and fresher as if a wind had blown in from a sunlit spring woodlands.

Merral heard new gasps from around the square as a strange—but familiar—voice spoke with a calm and unassailable authority. "This man's fate is not yours to dispose of."

Merral, daring to rise to a half squat, looked up to see a tall, black shape with a long, open coat and a wide-brimmed hat. An almost joylike relief flooded his mind.

The baziliarch clicked its jaws with a furious energy. "Who are you that choose to confront me? I am one of the seven, a ruler in the Nether-Realms."

"You know my name," the envoy replied, "though you dare not say it. You bear the scars of our last meeting."

There was silence. Then the great wings gave a flutter and Merral smelled again the stink of death and decay.

"You have known me of old," the envoy said. "You and I stood together on that day when we shouted for joy as the morning stars sang together. You bore a more pleasing form then."

"That was a long time ago." A darkness flickered over the great yellow eyes. There was a hiss that might have been a sneer and the jaws clicked and clacked like some crude wooden machine. "The worlds have grown cold since then. You are late."

"That charge has been often leveled against my master and I gladly bear it. But it is I who challenge you. What are you doing here?"

The tone of stern authority in the voice registered with Merral. *Good for you, Envoy. Give this monster its orders.*

There was a renewed clicking. "This is my place now. This is a pretty town that will make a fine throne. I claim both this man and these people."

At his words, the hope that had begun to dawn in Merral sputtered and then failed.

He glanced up at the envoy, sensing that his dark figure seemed taller than before. A golden light, like that which gleamed from the sword, seemed to leak from under his coat.

The envoy strode in front of Merral, interposing himself in front of the threatening presence of the baziliarch. "This man is not yours. He falls under the protection of the Most High."

The baziliarch's head, its surfaces glistening under the few lights that still lit the square, rose up and the terrible gleaming eyes peered over the envoy at Merral. "He failed his master!" hissed the creature.

"He did indeed fail the Highest, but he repented of it and has been forgiven."

"He rebelled—a most dreadful sin." There was a hint of mockery in the words. "He belongs with us."

Merral got to his feet and stepped back a pace.

"The Most High has taken upon himself this man's sin and paid for it himself. As the Slain Lamb, he pronounces him forgiven. The matter is closed."

There was a long hiss and in it Merral heard a note of defeat. The jaws grated against each other. "Then let me at least slay him."

"Even in that area, you have no power over him."

There was another dry hiss and the wings gave a threatening flap. "This world belongs to my master."

"Again, I am sent to deny you that. You have no rights here."

A forelimb moved wide in an insectlike gesture. "They wanted to serve us. They were prepared to leave the Assembly."

"But they did not. They were tempted. But they signed no agreement with those you sent. And I have watched them here this night. The welcome this town has given your forces confirms clearly that they do not wish to serve you or your master. They resisted you."

There was an angry, cheated hiss. A shudder passed through the vast body and the wings were raised high.

The envoy seemed to grow taller. "Your authority does not extend to this world." His words seemed to shake the still air.

There was a silence of immeasurable depth, and then the dry jaws moved against each other. "You defy our will. What will not be given will be taken." The baziliarch reared up again.

Feeling like a worm before a crow, Merral cringed.

Suddenly, the envoy raised his sword high. As he did, his coat opened wide. Warm, golden light spilled out, almost as if dawn had broken. Unable to bear the light, Merral looked away, glimpsing many people huddling against the side walls of the square, their faces wide, pale and staring.

"The powers you have are strictly limited by the Most High." The envoy's voice echoed with an unarguable authority. "You have chosen to exceed those limits and so you fall under immediate judgment."

The baziliarch's body flexed and there was a hesitant beat of the resinous wings. The head swayed toward the envoy and the jaws, gleaming in the light, opened wide. "The worlds turn. Our day comes. Our master rises. The serpent is unchained." There was defiance in its tone.

"If that is so, it is only because the High King has allowed it for a little time."

The head slid from side to side and the forelimbs with their claws outstretched were raised as if poised to slash at the envoy and Merral. Yet they held back.

The envoy held high the sword that glittered with a living gold fire and half turned his head to Merral. "Commander," he said and Merral caught a glimpse of a gleaming face that bore a terrible sternness. "Raise aloft that emblem that you let fall."

Merral picked up the staff and held it upright. As the flag fluttered free, it seemed to him that in the strange light the Lamb and the Stars gleamed with a new brilliance as if the stars were real and the Lamb a live creature.

The envoy stepped toward the baziliarch. "I now utter your name," he said, and in his loud firm words, Merral heard the note of a legal pronouncement. "You are Nar-Barratri."

The creature shuddered and something of the strange sheen that encased it seemed to fade. "You have had other names and other forms, but this is the one you will perish under. You are one of the seven who serve the great serpent whose assured destiny is the lake of fire. You came here as his forerunner. And, as his forerunner, I send you on the authority of the One who died, who rose, and who holds the seven stars, to the same eternal destiny."

The envoy's words were like a clap of thunder.

There was an angry rattle and a hiss from the baziliarch. "Will you slay me?"

"No, I will not so honor you. You are a creature of pride and you loathe the race of men. Therefore I will let one of them do it—one who is the least. Now, I take from you the power you were given over that form."

The sword made strange elegant movements in the air. The baziliarch's joints seemed to fail and, its wings buckling, it lurched forward and collapsed on the ground with brittle cracking noises. The remaining sheen around it vanished and as it did it seemed to Merral that all the terror it had held evaporated. The head, a vast black bulk with its incongruous silver crown, sank to the ground as if burdened with an immeasurable weariness. The eyes dimmed.

The envoy's coat closed and the light faded though his sword still gleamed brightly. His face hidden in darkness, he turned to the crowd huddled against the façade of the hall. "Elana Zennia Antalfer," he called, his voice now softer.

The line of men in armor parted and a slight figure pushed her way forward till she stood in front.

Of course. She said she wouldn't go into the refuge.

The envoy raised a black-gloved hand and made a gentle, beckoning gesture.

Slowly and rather shyly, Elana walked across the stained and dirty square and stood by Merral, her blonde hair catching the light.

The envoy stooped slightly toward her. "Elana," he said, softly, "you have resisted evil. The King wishes to honor you by having you serve him. Will you aid him?"

"If I can," she said in an awed voice.

"Would you take the crown off that thing and bring it here?"

"Y-yes." She walked forward and stopped a few strides away from the creature's head.

The jaws slid against each other and the beast spoke. "You cannot use her." The baziliarch's words had only a fraction of their old power. "She too sinned."

Merral saw Elana blush.

The envoy turned to the baziliarch, his head slightly tilted, as if puzzling over something. "I have no record of that."

"It happened." There was an indignant note in the waning voice.

"If she has let the King deal with her sin, then it is erased. That is what forgiveness is all about. It is his record, not yours, that counts." His voice took on the tone of an infinite sadness. "But you never did understand forgiveness, did you? Now be still." The sword moved in the air.

The head slumped to the ground.

"Elana, take his crown and bring it to me."

The girl took a deep breath and stepped forward until her knees were almost touching the closed mouth. She lifted the gleaming silver circlet off the monstrous head and took a sharp step back.

A new series of sharp creaking sounds came from the beast's body and as they sounded, Elana scampered back to the envoy. The baziliarch's body quivered along its entire length almost as if it was shriveling up. It seemed to have become something feeble, now only a husk of what it once was.

The envoy took the crown. "Thank you. I shall give it to the one who deserves it—the King of all Kings." He held it up for a moment, as if surveying it, and then tucked it inside his coat where, in a way that defied all geometry and physics, it vanished.

The envoy turned back to Elana. "Your task is not yet complete. Take up the enemy's sword and slay him with it."

Elana turned to Merral, her eyes wide with unease.

"Best obey him," Merral said and wondered if he had ever said anything wiser.

She shook herself and slowly walked to where the baziliarch's sword lay and picked it up, her fingers struggling to grasp the strange hilt. Then, carrying it awkwardly, she stepped to the segmented neck. It was nearly the width of her waist, but Merral now saw that it was very insubstantial—a flimsy shell of a carapace that covered a strange nothingness.

Elana raised the blade, looked at the envoy as if for reassurance, seemed to find it, then closed her eyes and struck down with the blade. It crashed through the dry husk of the skin, until it rang against the stone flags of the square. Dust flew around and the neck collapsed in on itself, as if it were made of nothing more than stiffened paper. The body began to crumble as if some extraordinary accelerated process of woodworm were at work.

Cheering broke out from among the people at the edges of the square. Merral saw the burly figure of his uncle Barrand break free of the crowd and, with a clumsy gait, dash over to his daughter.

Elana dropped the hilt, stared at her handiwork, looked around at the cheering crowd. Clearly overwhelmed, she ran to her father and hugged him.

"Stand away," the envoy commanded.

Merral stepped back. In the heart of the fast-crumbling carcass he saw a lingering darkness, a great formless shadow.

"Now," said the envoy raising his sword high, his gaze on the dry, crumbling carcass, "I send you to the flames—the first, but not the last, of your kind to go there, in the name of the King Eternal."

Tall red flames, flickering with a soundless energy, rose up around the creature. At first, Merral thought it was the beast itself that was alight; then he realized that the flames were burning around it. He felt no sensation of heat.

There was another gesture from the envoy and he uttered words that Merral could not make out. Suddenly, all around the creature, the stone slabs that floored the square seemed to fade away to be replaced by a red flaming gulf like the mouth of a vast furnace.

Slowly, and then with an ever-greater speed, the baziliarch's corpse with the shadow at its core tumbled in and fell down. The sword with the serrated blade tumbled after it. The last glimpse Merral had of the baziliarch was of a black worm writhing into an infinite depth of fire.

Abruptly, the flames disappeared and the gray stone flooring of the square returned.

The envoy tucked his sword away and the remaining light about him vanished. He turned to the cluster of soldiers in front of the hall and beckoned someone over. Merral saw Vero walk forward and approach the envoy. Together, they walked a dozen paces away and the envoy spoke with Vero. What he said, Merral could not hear, but he saw his friend lower his head as if he was being rebuked.

Then suddenly, the envoy strode back to Merral.

"Thank you," Merral said, trying to avoid looking into the awesome darkness of the face hidden under the hat. "I didn't deserve your help."

"Deserve? You never did. That's what grace is about."

Merral bowed his head in silence.

"Commander, the enemy's accusation was not without foundation. You did disobey the Lord's counsel. Your repentance has been accepted; the sin is a past matter. But the results of your actions remain. These are not so easily dealt with." He paused. "Now, there are matters to be dealt with. Tomorrow, you must return to Isterrane. Be prepared to endure what is inflicted on you there. Do not resist. Endure." He gestured to the walls and the gate where the Krallen were perched in silent and immobile array. "I will take from your enemies their powers of communication and coordination. They have known the emotion of hatred; they will now know terror. Now, cleanse the town."

He raised his hand high. "*Az leyama, az layakeen!*" he pronounced in a loud ringing voice, and in his words Merral sensed an ancient and great authority.

At his command, the creatures on the walls and by the gate seemed to be seized by a collective shiver. They turned and began to slip away. As they did, some collided with each other.

The envoy gently tapped Merral's shoulder. "Commander, be about your work. We will meet again."

Then he was gone.

Merral shook himself, handed the flagstaff to Vero, and clapped his hands for silence. "Men and women," he cried, his heart overflowing with joy. "The forces of the Dominion are broken! Have the refuge opened. Let everyone who can find a sword or gun and seek out our enemies and destroy them! The town is to be cleansed."

He paused. "Soldiers, gather at the gate. Snipers, kill those slitherwings. Warden Enatus, have the bells rung."

There were yells of approval and wild cheers.

Merral picked up his sword, took back the flag, and with men and women gathering behind him, walked to the open gates through which the Krallen had fled.

There, as the great bells began to peal in jubilation, he paused and gazed around. Overhead, the clouds and the stars appeared. He scented a new freshness in the air. Below, much of the town was lit by the ruddy glow of fires while elsewhere the lighting was still on. In the uneven illumination, he could see gray forms fleeing down the streets in a chaotic manner that he found extraordinarily satisfying.

There was a brief snap of rifle shots and something tumbled out of the sky toward the lake.

I have had another chance. Merral gave thanks to the Most High.

Suddenly, across by the airport, he saw lightning—a succession of brilliant yellow flashes that lit up the lake.

"What's that, sir?" Lloyd muttered as dull booms echoed through the streets.

It took a moment for Merral to realize the answer. "That, Sergeant, is Colonel Thuron attacking the rear of the Dominion army. It would seem that he too has rebelled against Clemant."

"The icing on the cake," added Vero quietly from just behind them.

"What?"

"Never mind."

Merral fired a flare into the sky and as its green light cascaded around them, he cried out, "Advance!"

31

By three in the morning they had cleared the town of Krallen and the remaining Dominion forces had fled across the causeway in disarray to where, on the far side, they were destroyed by Frankie's troops. As he waited for the engineers to stabilize the broken part of the causeway so his soldiers could safely cross, Merral walked back to his home.

En route, he came across four young men, wearing dirty jerkins and carrying swords. They were peering inside doorways with a bright handlight. When Merral saw that their pale faces were daubed with camouflage, he knew who they were.

"The Hanston Road—" he paused—"the Hanston Road Irregulars. What news?"

"Commander!" There were four salutes. They were barely recognizable as the teenagers of only a few hours earlier.

They looked at each other, their expressions a mixture of pride and grief.

"Sir, we got twenty-four goblins. Well, twenty-three really. One got away."

"He weren't going far," added the smallest one. "Not wiv' a leg off."

"Well done. But weren't there six of you?"

They looked at each other and their newfound maturity and confidence suddenly vanished. They looked down at the ground.

"Bill and Hass got it," said the tallest. "When we was . . . retreating."

Merral looked away and blinked. "I'm sorry," he murmured. "I really am."

"Yeah. We are too. . . . We are all kinda gutted." Then the young man looked up. "Still, sir, we gotta do our job, haven't we?"

"Yes," Merral replied. "We have to."

✺✺✺✺✺

There were lights on inside his house and he could see that someone had dragged the Krallen bodies out into the street where, devoid of any menace, they lay looking like a heap of rubbish. Leaving Lloyd outside, Merral walked in to find his mother and father, their clothing dirty and stained, sitting on the ripped sofa in the general room, holding hands.

"Hello, Son," his father said in a matter-of-fact way. He waved a hand that seemed to take in the shattered furniture, the broken ornaments, the burned walls, and the drying puddles of silver fluid on the floor. "Bit of a mess this really." His face brightened. "But we will fix it, won't we, dear?" He squeezed his wife's hand.

Merral's mother, her face pale with exhaustion, gave a mild but contented sigh and leaned against her husband. "Yes, Stefan," she said slowly. "We will. It's only things. And the neighbors will help."

"I was just passing," Merral said, feeling awkward, as if he had intruded on something private. "I thought I'd drop in just to see if you were all right."

His parents looked at each other and Merral sensed that in their weary gaze they said much. His mother, stroking a disordered and dusty strand of silvery hair, smiled. "We're fine, thank you. . . . But no, Stefan, you say it."

His father toyed slowly with his tangled beard. "Why, thank you, Lena. I could say a lot. I really could. But no, we have realized something together." He puckered his brow as if thinking deeply. "It's just that in the old days, we never had to work at what we are. How can I say it? What we were and all the good that we had we just took for granted. It was always there. Now though, now that evil has come back, we realize that we need to work at it. It takes an effort." He frowned almost as if his own analysis puzzled him. "Does that make sense?" he asked while Merral's mother nodded.

"Yes, Father," Merral said. "We need to fight for what's right now, in every area."

"Thought so. Pity it took me so long to see it."

"Us," his mother added with a quiet insistence.

"Us, indeed. Anyway, time for bed." His father stifled a yawn. He rose and then gently helped Merral's mother up from the sofa. "I guess you still have things to do?"

"I have a lot to do," Merral said softly. "And a long way to go."

"I thought so," his father said. "Will we see you soon?"

"No. I think not."

"I see." There was a note of acceptance in his father's voice.

Then striving—and failing—to keep away tears, they hugged and kissed each other.

Dawn was breaking when Merral met Frankie Thuron where the causeway joined the airport road. Utterly weary, his garments smeared with Krallen fluid, Merral flung his chipped and dented sword down, took off his helmet, threw down his gloves, and embraced Frankie with aching and blistered hands.

About them, the last Krallen were being cut down.

"The Krallen are destroyed," Frankie said, rubbing dirt off his face and staring round with evident bewilderment at the piles of ashen forms all around. "And all the other things."

Merral bowed his head and gave thanks to God. Then he looked to where, rising out of the early morning mist, the spired and towered mound of Ynysmant glinted in the dawn light amid coils of smoke.

"So, Frankie, what's the status?"

"My people are repairing the airstrip," Frankie replied, gesturing stiffly with his synthetic hand. "The first fliers are on their way to pick up the wounded." He paused and gave a dismembered Krallen limb a thoughtful kick. "Commander—"

"Formerly," Merral interrupted. "I no longer have that rank."

"That's the thing." Frankie dropped his voice. "It's all nonsense. Clemant's gone mad. The soldiers and I are happy to march on Isterrane and remove him, if that's what you want."

Merral sighed. "No. I don't. I will not encourage civil war. Stay here, Frankie. Move the troops to Ynysmant; they will receive you gladly. Help them with the rebuilding. Don't do anything unless Clemant attacks you."

"As you wish. But what will you do?"

Merral stared westward over the piles of the Krallen and the advancing soldiers for some moments before answering. "I must do what must be done. I will go to Isterrane."

"But he will arrest you. There's a warrant out for you."

"Then I will let myself be arrested."

An hour later, as they were loading the flier with the worst of the wounded, Vero came over. He wore his dark glasses and walked stiffly.

Merral took him aside. "Vero," he said, "I need to go to Isterrane and face Clemant."

Vero nodded. "I will come as well." He paused. "Are you curious about what the envoy said to me?"

"A little. But I have been . . . preoccupied."

Vero smiled and then, as if embarrassed, looked at his feet. "He said, among other things, 'Verofaza, cleverness is not the same as wisdom.' And 'I warn you, the results of your scheming and Merral's disobedience are about to come together.'"

"What do you understand by that?"

"Very little. But it alarms me. He also warned me that I would need to hide for a while. That was sort of an afterthought."

"I see."

"So, I think I will sneak off the flier, find some space down in the foundations, and stay out of sight for a bit. Anya and Azeras are already there and I have arranged for Betafor to be shipped there in her box."

"Good. Will you take Lloyd too?"

"If you think that's a good idea."

"Please. I have to do this on my own."

ΟΟΟΟΟ

Merral fell asleep on the flight and only awakened upon landing at Isterrane. Out of the window, he saw medical staff milling around the flier and, as he watched, a dozen blue-uniformed police pushed their way through.

He glanced around the compartment. Lloyd and Vero had already left.

Merral rose from his seat and, with resignation, walked down to the front doorway of the flier.

"Merral D'Avanos," said a brusque man dressed in blue at the top of the stairway. "You are under arrest. Where are Sentinel Enand and Sergeant Enomoto?"

"I have no idea."

"Come with us."

The police removed Merral's diary and escorted him to the terminal building. As he walked with them, Merral saw two white-masked medical orderlies rush past him with a stretcher bearing a figure whose slim form was almost entirely covered by a white sheet. As they headed toward an ambulance, Merral noticed that one of the orderlies had a massive physique and short blond hair and that the limp hand that hung down from the sheet was dark skinned.

In the terminal, two policemen took Merral to a bare, windowless office, ordered him to sit in front of a desk, and then stood behind him.

After a few minutes, Clemant, wearing a neat dark suit, walked in and without a word sat behind the desk. He frowned at the desk, straightened its contents, and then looked up with what Merral felt was an oddly detached expression.

"Thank you for not making a fuss," he said in a peculiarly emotionless tone.

Merral said nothing.

Clemant gazed at his fingers for a moment before looking up with his deep-set dark eyes. "Things are happening. The secrets of the *Dove of Dawn* are being worked out. What we have found means we must act." He paused and corrected himself. "That *I* must act."

He stared at Merral. "I could use you, Captain. You could be an asset." He stroked the hair over his ears. "But I don't think I could trust you to cooperate."

"Probably not. What about the hostages?"

"The hostages?" Clemant seemed caught off guard. "Ah yes. At the peninsula. Zak is taking care of that. He has immobilized the shuttle. There are plans. . . ." His voice tailed off in a way that suggested the matter did not interest him.

There was silence.

"No," Clemant said after a few moments, "you wouldn't cooperate. Quite the wrong sort." There was a soft insistence in his words as if he was delivering a verdict to himself.

Then he gave a little shake of his head and looked hard at Merral. "The verdict is this: you are hereby relieved from all military duty and stripped of all rank. That—rather disgusting—uniform will be taken from you. You will revert back to your Forester title. To avoid questions, no formal announcement will be made for some time. We will simply say that you are on sick leave. Stress and overwork are only to be expected after a battle."

He paused as if expecting a response, but receiving none, continued. "Colonel Larraine has suggested that we press charges of mutiny. Prebendant Delastro wants you to be examined on issues to do with invoking spiritual powers." There was a cold smile. "Do you need me to say that both sorts of investigation could be very unpleasant? You might have to choose between the firing squad or the bonfire." There was another humorless grimace. "Anyway I have overruled them."

Clemant paused, again evidently seeking a reaction.

"Thank you," Merral replied, his voice sounding flat. *The envoy's command was to endure.*

Clemant seemed disappointed. "It is tempting to try you and Thuron." There was a flicker of anger in his eyes. "Instead, as a kindness, I am sending you to Camp Kunagat to recuperate. Do you know of it?"

"The conference center? Only by name."

"There are lakes. The woods are lovely, they say. You will be well looked after. I have never stayed there." He shook his head. "Never found the time. Anyway, Camp Kunagat it is, if you promise not to escape or communicate with the outside world. As I have said, there are alternatives." There was a meaningful pause. "Do you promise?"

"Not to escape or communicate? Yes." *Endure.*

"Good. You *do* need a break. Sentinel Verofaza and Sergeant . . ." Clemant paused, trying to remember the name. "Sergeant Enomoto will join you as soon as they are located. And of course, ex-Colonel Thuron."

"Can I ask how long I am to stay there?"

Clemant shrugged. "As long as it takes. We have decisions to make and we don't need distractions."

"What sort of decisions? Anything to do with the Langerstrand hostages?"

There was a look of bafflement. "The hostages? Not at all. They are a minor issue now. No, we have the data from the *Dove* on the Dominion and its aims. Professor Habbentz and the others are looking at it all. It is raising considerable alarm."

"In what way?" *I need to know this.*

Clemant looked up. "The Dominion is making a fleet ready—a vast fleet. I can barely believe the figures we are recovering from the *Dove*. And they have made a structure, a colossal construction. The Blade of Night they call it. We do not fully understand it. But we fear it." He looked at his neatly trimmed fingernails for a moment. "The issue is no longer Farholme, Forester. It's the entire Assembly. Speed and action are of the essence. And we must do what is best for the Assembly."

He nodded, as if agreeing with himself. "I must do it." Suddenly, he rose to his feet. "Forester, I am coming to believe that the Most High has made it my destiny to save the Assembly. I must not fail."

Clemant walked to the door in a way that reminded Merral of a man in a dream. "Enjoy Camp Kunagat," he said in a distant voice. The door closed behind him.

◌◌◌◌◌

In his improvised command center at Langerstrand, Lezaroth raged to and fro in fury. The defeat at Ynysmant had been stunning, humiliating, and utterly unexpected. One minute, it had all been better than he could have hoped: D'Avanos had been neatly trapped, the baziliarch had reappeared, and the Krallen had taken most of the town. The next, the signals had failed, all Krallen order had vanished, and a chaotic rout was under way.

Why the attack had been so disastrous was unclear. The devastation had clearly been so complete that there had been no one to report back what had happened. Lezaroth was certain of one thing: D'Avanos had played a part. In the name of Zahlman-Hoth he called down a solemn curse on the man.

Yet as well as raging, Lezaroth also analyzed his situation. The campaign to take Farholme was now a dismal and costly failure. A Z-class full-suppression complex, an army of Krallen, men, and a high-ranking extra-physical being had all been lost. Yet these defeats were not, he knew, the worst aspects of this affair. The fact that the Farholmers had seized the *Dove of Dawn* was infinitely worse. With it they would soon fly to the Assembly, bearing news and technology of infinite worth.

Gradually, Lezaroth realized that while there was no obvious way of stopping or destroying the *Dove of Dawn,* he might be able to do what was almost certainly as valuable. The lord-emperor had to be told what he had learned—that there *was* a great adversary, and his name was D'Avanos, that there were lethal but fixable flaws in the Krallen armor, that the Assembly fought hard, and that even the most powerful of the extra-physical beings could be destroyed. And if he could get back to Khalamaja before the fleet was launched and pass on this news, then Lezaroth knew there would be some gain from what was otherwise an unremitting list of disasters. If he could blame everything on Hanax he might even emerge with credit. His unease about the man was well-known.

Then, his rage cooling, Lezaroth forced himself to survey his options. He still had several thousand Krallen within the compound, a dozen soldiers, Benek-Hal the pilot, and some flight crew. As far as he knew, the existence of the *Nanmaxat's Comet,* hidden in the Nether-Realms near Farholme, was unknown to the Farholme authorities. Nevertheless there would be records of it on board the *Dove* and sooner or later those who were ransacking it would realize that the *Comet* existed. So he had days at most to act. A small but immediate consolation was that although the Farholme forces were surrounding the Langerstrand base they seemed reluctant to engage him. This, he presumed, was because of the hostages he held. Deriving some comfort from that, Lezaroth allowed himself the luxury of sleep.

On Khalamaja, in the great hall of Kal-na-Tanamuz, Lord-Emperor Nezhuala walked between the great totems and their shadows. He was tired and sweat ran down his back. The pain in his head was worse than usual. He was vaguely aware it was midday, although here where the sunlight never came, that made little difference.

The previous day he had made a visit to the far end of the Blade of Night, the lowest levels of the Nether-Realms, where sometimes the writhing coils of the great serpent could be glimpsed. It had shaken him to the core. There had been uproar down there, a seething storm of rage and fear. It had taken all his mastery of the powers to ensure that he was not consumed by the frenzy of the beings that thrashed around there. It had been no easy matter either to find out what had caused the tumult. But eventually he had pieced together the appalling fact that the Lord Nar-Barratri had been destroyed under circumstances so shameful that no one would tell him what they were.

Even now, as he listened to the whispering voices that filled the great hall, the lord-emperor could still hear shock and horror—the same reaction he had heard in the deepest Nether-Realms.

"We thought we were immune," the voices wimpered, "but the great Lord Nar-Barratri has been destroyed. Will we be next?"

On his emergence from the Blade, it had taken hours to come to terms with the terrible implications of the baziliarch's loss. The entire Farholme enterprise was, he now realized, a failure. He was certain that he was unlikely to see the *Triumph of Sarata*, Fleet-Commander Lezaroth, Captain Hanax— such promise!—or his ambassadors again.

I have been defeated! The thought had come to Nezhuala like a smack in the face. But it had brought with it an even grimmer prospect. With such a defeat, vital information might have fallen into enemy hands. The entire venture against the Assembly depended totally on surprise and overwhelming force. And now it seemed that the surprise might be lost.

And so Nezhuala had paced to and fro in the great hall all night. In the early morning, at the hour when the shadows walked freely about, he made his decision. He had summoned his chief commanders for a noon meeting.

Now noon had passed. Between the totems a line of uniformed men stood at the far end of the hall, looking around in a nervous way. *They are nervous about being nervous.* The idea amused him. *But they can wait. After all I am the lord-emperor.*

He walked toward them through the lines of statues, meditating. *Did I make enough sacrifices or the right kind? Maybe the problem is the priesthood itself. Do I really need the priests? Perhaps they annoy the powers they ought to appease. Perhaps I should be the sole priest. Am I not the one who descends to the depths? Am I not the one who has built the Blade? Am I not the one who aims to unite the realms and free the powers? Aren't I the man in whom the One is perfectly revealed?*

At the end of the hall Nezhuala stood silently as his commanders bowed before him.

He looked at the men. *All twenty-four I have summoned are present. I have no need to kill anyone.*

"Men," he said. "Thank you for your devotion. I have an announcement: I have set a departure date for the fleet.

He could see the looks of anticipation. *They are hoping I will give them at least twelve weeks.*

"The first vessels will sail six weeks from now."

There was a silence in which he watched every face. *No one says anything. No one shows any emotion, but I can see in their eyes they don't like what I said.*

"I want all ships to have departed ten weeks from now. The fleet will surface first at the world the Assembly call Bannermene."

They are surprised. "We will pass by the world called Farholme. It is no longer . . ." He paused. "No longer a priority."

He could see them watching each other. As ever no one dared do anything that was out of line. There were small, cautious nods.

Nezhuala raised a gloved hand high. "That is all. You will soon bear the Final Emblem to Earth itself."

Someone began the cry. "Lord, it is our life's purpose to serve you!" Instantly, nervously, everyone else took up the cry.

"Start the preparations. You are dismissed."

They left swiftly, leaving the lord-emperor of the Dominion alone in the hall amid the shadows.

There he tilted his head and listened again to the high whisperings and the deep murmurings. As he did, he heard the excitement in the voices and heard, again and again, one word repeated.

"Earth!"

◌◌◌◌◌

Three days after the disaster at Ynysmant, Lezaroth was in a much better mood. There were several reasons for this. One was that he had remained at Langerstrand untroubled by any Farholme forces. All that had happened was that a high-powered rifle had shot holes in the viewing ports of the shuttle. Lezaroth was unimpressed. Such damage was common in combat and there were sealant pads aboard that could fix the matter in minutes.

Another reason was more complex. Lezaroth soon realized that he was hearing little of the accursed name of D'Avanos. A check of the pathetically few media stations revealed only the official statement that Merral D'Avanos was "recuperating from stress and minor battle injuries." Lezaroth had found this intriguing and even incredible. Even an ill D'Avanos would have moved against Langerstrand or appeared on the media. What *was* going on?

Alerted by this and intrigued by the curious military paralysis—who *was* in control of the FDF?—Lezaroth had consulted the intelligence-gathering facilities he had at Langerstrand. What he learned had raised his mood even more.

It had become apparent that what was going on in Farholme was, almost unbelievably, something instantly recognizable to anyone with any knowledge of the history of the Freeborn. It was a power struggle. One party was wrestling for unrestrained power while another fought to resist them. What he was seeing was just the latest outworking of the ancient principle that while division may be brought by defeat, it can be guaranteed when there is a victory with spoils.

Lezaroth knew that in such struggles there came a moment sooner or later when no one was in control. And that, he decided, would be the moment when he could fix the glass and take off with the hostages and a small crew. Once in space he would summon the *Nanmaxat's Comet,* put the hostages on board, and leave.

So Lezaroth listened and waited for the right moment.

◁◊◊◊◊▷

Chairman Ethan Malunal sat under the shade of a pine tree in a small Jerusalem garden surrounded by high walls of pale stone. He breathed in the warm scented afternoon air slowly, forcing himself to relax. *You need to unwind, Ethan. Pace yourself. It's the only way you will last the distance.*

From time to time his glance fell on the heavy folder lying next to him. As he sat there he listened carefully, hearing beyond the walls the muted noises of the city: schoolchildren yelling as they ran home, household chatter from a balcony, someone's music from an open window, the faint rumble of the subway. He considered the temperature. As so often happened in early September, there was the first hint that the force of the summer heat was fading. Autumn was on its way.

There was a click. A door in the wall opened and a dark-skinned woman entered.

Ethan rose stiffly from the bench and embraced her. "Eliza," he said. "Always good to see you."

"Eeth! It's always good to see you too. It's been a long time since we met privately." She looked around with an air of appreciation. "Nice place to meet."

"I spend enough time in the office. And this is just round the corner. I like to come here to sit and think when I'm in town. The trees give shade in summer. Please sit down." He nodded to the door. "You saw the guard?"

"Yes." Eliza brushed pine needles off a seat and lowered herself carefully down.

"They like it when I come here. It is secure." Ethan heard the tang of irritation in his voice. "'Is it secure?' That's all the guards ask. . . . This wretched new security."

"We're jumpy, Eeth. You can feel it. No one knows what we face. But it *is* bewildering."

"It's more than that; it's ominous. In four months, war has gone from being ancient history to being a near inevitability. The twentieth defense vessel will be launched tomorrow. Yesterday I signed for thirty long-range protection ships with weapons that hadn't even been invented last spring."

She shook her head. "An extraordinary time. . . . My boys have just enlisted."

"I'm sorry."

"I'm sorry and proud."

"How are you, Eliza? In these days of trial, we mustn't forget common courtesies."

Eliza flashed white teeth. "No." She paused. "I'm kept by grace."

"And how are the sentinels?"

"Ah. The sentinels, like everyone else right now are in . . . well . . . turbulence."

"So I heard."

"But how are *you*, Eeth? You are the man bearing the weight of the world."

"That's certainly what it feels like. I suppose . . ." He hesitated. "No. I'm okay. Well, as okay as a man my age can be in a job like this at a time like this. But Eliza, it's pretty tough." Ethan's fingers knotted together. "All these new pressure groups want to see me. And I'm expected to be so many things: the master of every fact, the arbiter of every crisis, the chairman of every debate. Above all, I'm expected to hold things together when everything is flying apart. Yes, that's it. Not so much bearing the weight of the world as keeping it together."

As Eliza nodded, he read sympathy in her eyes.

"Have you seen Andreas lately? I invited him as well." *Why am I so worried that he will not turn up?*

"No. I gather he has been busy."

"You have followed the disputes?"

"The Custodians of the Faith call them *debates,* Eeth." Any amusement in Eliza's voice was edged with sorrow. "But yes, and if it wasn't that similar issues have arisen among the sentinels, I would barely believe them possible. So many debates about so little that is truly relevant. So little light, so much heat. They are spending so much time arguing about the crisis that they are failing to respond to it."

"That's part of the evil, Eliza, you know that. The enemy of the Assembly wants division. And he's getting it. Everyone seems to be walking in opposite directions now."

The door opened and Andreas walked in. He looked flustered and sweaty. "Ethan, Eliza. Sorry for the delay. I just left an ongoing discussion that was getting quite animated."

Ethan sensed a slight distancing in his tone. *Our old easy friendship has gone. Will it return?* The thought saddened him.

Andreas sat down, pulled out a handkerchief, and wiped the sweat off his face. "I had to hurry. Can't stop long. It's just a fleeting visit. I must get back in case it gets too heated. Have I missed anything?"

"No. I was merely moaning."

"With justification. These pressure groups—how are you handling them?"

Ethan gave a heavy sigh. "Where did *they* come from? Suddenly everyone in the Assembly seems to be part of a pressure group. Gate manufacturers, the educationalists, the colonists, and a hundred more. And they all want to see me. They are all polite, all insistent, and they all take up time."

"And they are all getting shriller," Andreas observed.

"You noticed, eh? When they began, they merely made suggestions; now they are making requests."

"It will soon be demands." Andreas's green eyes seemed hard. "Ethan, I have seen the trends and I think . . ." He broke off. "No, that can wait. Now tell me: what do you have for us that is new?"

"I was really just hoping to have a chat with you both about how you see things. It's over four months since the Assembly went on a war footing. But I have some information on the intruder worlds."

"Aha." Eliza nodded. "I heard rumors that they had been found. We were . . . well . . . relieved."

You don't need to explain why. No one needed the confirmation that this whole scare has a real basis more than the sentinels who started it.

Andreas put his handkerchief away. "I had heard too. But tell us the facts."

Ethan picked up the folder. *They seem to get thicker.* "The final report has defense implications, so it's being kept quiet. The deep space observation satellite at Bannermene has found at least twenty worlds beyond Farholme with signs of human activity. Strictly, I'm told, it's 'intelligent life with industrial activity,' but we may assume *Homo sapiens.*"

He pulled out a number of glossy sheets on which were printed images of fuzzy spheres on black starry backgrounds. Most were brown or gray and some were mottled. On some, white patches were present. Around each image were text summaries, diagrams, and graphs.

"It's the best the scope can get, but the nearest world is nearly four hundred light-years away."

"Remind me," Eliza said as she stared at the images, "how far away is Bannermene?"

"About three hundred light-years. So, of course, these images are snap-shots of how these worlds were at least four hundred years ago. The spectro-scopic data apparently suggests advanced industry and that is backed by the detection of some faint but clearly artificial electromagnetic signals."

He watched them examine the images.

"We have compared the new data from ancient and much poorer data files that go back to the Seeding preparation surveys of the region in the third millennium. Over the last ten thousand years, there have been major changes on these worlds. Changes that also imply human activity."

Andreas gestured to one. "They don't look like Assembly worlds. They're brown. They look like those images of pre-Seeding Mars that you see. Where's the water? Are there no brimful seas? No vast briny oceans? How tragic."

So speaks the poet. "Good point. That's one of a number of oddities that the research people are working on. Three things seem to be striking. One, which you have noted, is that none of the worlds are very wet. They don't seem to have oceans; there may be lakes, but that's all. That suggests they don't do Seeding as well as we do."

Eliza gave a low grunt that seemed to convey that she found the news significant.

"Another thing is that some of the intruder worlds have odd orbits. See those diagrams? That suggests they don't have gravity modification—at least not on the scale we have. That's to be kept quiet, because it suggests an area where we may be militarily superior."

Eliza pointed to a diagram of orbits. "I'm no planetary scientist, but a world that orbits like that is going to have either a pretty ghastly winter or one appalling summer."

"Or both," Andreas added.

"So we believe. And that has implications. I'm told that when we seed worlds we aim to create planets where, from fairly early on, you can live out in the open most of the year."

Andreas frowned. "Not here you can't," he said, holding up a sheet so he could look at it better. "Do they live underground? Do they only stay indoors? Do they never walk among trees? never see birds fly across the sky?" His tone was pensive. "That would be sad. They would have become differ-ent than us."

"Yes. And there is a final thing," Ethan said, "a sobering thing. Analysis has shown that many of the worlds have high levels of atmospheric pollutants, and in two cases, large amounts of carbon in the atmosphere."

"Carbon dioxide?"

"No, carbon particles. The best interpretation is that these are the results of warfare, using massive weapons that burn up everything living."

"God help us," Eliza said quietly.

Andreas shook his head and put down the sheet, his face expressing pain. "So they fail to make proper worlds and then destroy them? That is an abomination. You should announce that. It will crush dissent."

Ethan sighed. "It's an interpretation, Andreas. And it might cause panic."

Eliza handed back her sheet. "I find it tragic and scary. And it gives me nightmares. But it confirms the threat. They look to be a tough and nasty people."

"Exactly. We only had the final report two weeks ago. Since then, whatever caution we had on military matters has been cast away."

Andreas stared into the distance. "By their worlds you shall know them. How very remarkable that the very character of our enemies should be so apparent from so far away. But I echo Eliza; these look to be a hard people. I trust we will not be too soft." He seemed to shudder before turning to Ethan. "Thank you for this. I will keep it to myself. But I really must get back. We are trying to define what's happening to the Assembly in theological terms. It is producing, well . . . heated dialogue. . . . Was there anything else you wanted to say?"

"Andreas, I just wanted to ask if you had any insights, or advice for me about what's happening here."

"Here?" Andreas paused for several moments before continuing. "I just think that what I warned you about when we last met together applies even more so. We're seeing a loss of unity, a failure of agreement, a growth of divergence. An ancient poet said something; let me translate it into Communal: 'Things fall apart, the center cannot hold.' And he went on to write: 'The best lack all convictions, while the worst are full of passionate intensity.' And it's happening." He gave Eliza a strange and stern glance. "I'm going to be honest with my old friend."

Ethan braced himself.

"I hate to say this, but our worlds do need direction."

"I told you I am a chairman, a consensus leader." *Is that irritation I hear in my voice?*

"And you do a great job at that. But the world has changed. It is as if the bonds that united us have loosed. There is growing divergence and disagreement everywhere." Andreas's green eyes flashed. "Look, when this started people were stunned. But that phase is over. That's why you now have the pressure groups. They all have their agenda. And the only answer is a positive leadership that acts to hold people together. Ethan, you *must* lead."

"No. And I remind you of the constitution. I can't."

"You can. And anyway you can always alter the constitution. We need unity for the coming struggle. And a strong leader will turn attention away from these pressure groups. Then you just ban them for six months in the public interest."

"But I can't do that."

Andreas tugged his beard in evident frustration. "In a time of war, you can. Declare a state of emergency. The custodians would support you. But you must *lead*." There was clear annoyance in his voice.

"Andreas, I repeat, I am not that sort of a man." He instantly regretted his sharp tone.

"And I respect you for that, but think of the Assembly. Lead!"

"So are you saying I am too weak?" *I should stop. I'm getting too angry.*

"Well, *weak* isn't the best word but . . ."

"So you are."

"Look, this is doing no good." Andreas rose, his face agitated. "I must be off anyway. Eliza, my apologies."

He turned to Ethan, an intense passion in his eyes. "Ethan, some parting advice. You say you are not the man. Then beware, because there is, among our scared worlds, a hunger for a strong leadership. And if you do not fill that hunger, then don't blame me if it gets filled in a way that you do not like."

He left the garden with brisk steps.

His heart beating rapidly, Ethan turned to Eliza who seemed close to tears, then quickly looked away. "I'm sorry. I really am. I value Andreas, but he has the ability to touch raw nerves."

"But, Eeth, you *did* overreact. You put words in his mouth. 'Am I too weak?'"

"Sorry. That was unwise." Ethan stared at her. "What's happening to us, Eliza? What's wrong?"

She heaved a sigh. "Sin. That's what's wrong." She rose. "Look, I'd better go. This has been upsetting. I'll be in touch another day." She patted Ethan on the back and then left the garden.

Ethan sat for some time with his head in his hands. With a sigh he then placed the sheets back in the folder, pausing at the last picture of the far-off world.

Our enemies lie there, so far away that if they sent a ray of light it would take over seven hundred years to reach us.

But in one sense, they are already here.

32

Within a few hours of being flown to Camp Kunagat, Merral decided that, under ordinary circumstances—and when had they last prevailed?—he could have indeed enjoyed the place.

Camp Kunagat lay in the foothills of the Kenadreno Range, four hundred kilometers to the north of Isterrane, amid lakes, rocks, and green forests that seemed to go on forever. Merral was allocated a small whitewashed wooden hut with a jetty out into the clear waters of a lake. He was well fed and the police kept their distance.

Over the next few days Merral slept, walked among the trees, and swam. Above all, he thought and prayed. And as he prayed, it came to him that he badly needed this time to recover. Clemant's actions were, no doubt unintentionally, a great blessing. As each day passed, Merral felt increasingly certain that a storm was gathering for which he would need all his energies and faculties.

But he was told nothing of what was going on in the outside world and he tried to stop himself worrying about what was happening there. He decided that his heavenly Father had placed him outside events for the time being, in order to recover and prepare; worry played no part in either process. Nevertheless, as the days passed he was heartened that neither Vero, Lloyd, nor Frankie joined him.

The days passed.

On the evening of the fifth day, Merral was sitting on the wooden platform that fringed the hut eating his evening meal, when the silence of the woods was broken by the squeal of a fast scout vessel landing at the nearby strip.

A few minutes later, Merral overheard the noise of a shouted argument through the trees and shortly afterward, he saw two soldiers wearing the green armor jackets of the regular forces walking up to the hut with XQ rifles at the ready. Behind them, with a determined step, strode a small woman with dark hair wearing a cream jacket and skirt.

My holiday is over. The storm is about to break.

As if they were some sort of regimental guard, the soldiers positioned themselves on either side of the porch steps, while the woman walked briskly up the steps.

"Commander D'Avanos," she said with a bow. Merral noticed a tanned face, a deeply furrowed brow, and a preoccupied look. He decided she looked to be in her sixties.

"Last I heard, I was a forester," Merral said, rising from his chair and extending a hand. "I think we have met somewhere; your face is familiar."

"Ludovica Bortellat," the woman said as she shook hands. "I was secretary of the Council of Representatives."

"Ah. I remember."

"May I?" the visitor asked, pulling a spare chair over.

"Please," Merral replied and sat down himself.

They stared at each other. Merral sensed that his visitor bore responsibilities that she perhaps thought were too big for her.

"May I call you Ludovica?" he asked.

"By all means. First, an apology. There have been some astonishing meetings this week." She frowned as she poured a glass of water. "There was one meeting today." She stared at the water and then sipped it slowly. "There has been a restructuring; the Council of Representatives is no more. Farholme is now governed by a committee of a dozen men and women—I chair it. In the heat of the crisis too much power was allowed into the hands of one person. It was a mistake. . . ."

As she gazed around, evidently appreciating the lake and the trees, Merral found himself warming to the woman.

"I agree. Would you like some food? There is always too much here for one."

"No, thank you. Another time perhaps. Urgent decisions must be made. Anyway, I was sent by the new committee to talk to you." Ludovica reached inside her jacket and took out an envelope. "You'd better see my letter of authorization. Trust is no longer enough."

Merral took the letter, glanced at its contents, and handed it back carefully.

"I have to tell you," the visitor said, with slow deliberation, "that the powers of the police have been reduced. You are free to go. Furthermore, some decisions of former advisor Clemant are being revoked. You are restored to the rank of Commander in Chief of the Farholme Defense Force with full powers as of this moment, and with apologies. Is that acceptable?"

"Is a parallel restoration being offered to Colonel Thuron?"

"Yes."

"And all charges against those who fought with me are dropped?"

"Yes."

"Then it is acceptable."

Ludovica nodded and pulled out a diary from her jacket pocket. Merral recognized it as his own. "We thought you'd like this."

"Thank you," Merral said as he took it. "But what does Clemant say?"

Ludovica's bronzed face darkened. "Ah. He is not available for comment." She paused to look around once more before turning back to Merral. "You haven't heard any news."

"No." *Now comes the first lash of the storm, so help me, God.*

"We have had some bad news. Clemant has taken the *Dove* and left the system, heading for Earth."

"But he can't!" Merral interrupted angrily. "It's monstrous! People died for that ship. He just went without consulting anybody?" Merral suddenly realized that he wasn't just angry; he was also anxious.

It came to him that had he stayed in Isterrane as he had been commanded and not gone to Ynysmant, this would not have happened. This was surely what the envoy had meant by "the results of your actions remain."

"It was done before we knew anything about it. And we think Colonel Larraine has gone with him."

"Zak? *That* figures." *Yes. Had I been at Isterrane that would not have happened either.* "But why take the ship?"

"He left a message for us. A copy is on your diary. Please listen to it."

As Ludovica got up and walked down the jetty, Merral found the file.

Clemant, dark suited and pale faced, appeared on the screen. "Madam Secretary," he said in his quiet, careful way. "I gather the council is trying to reassert its authority and that you wish to interview me. I am afraid I will have to deny you that pleasure. Before I lose my authority, I have decided to order the *Dove* to proceed to Bannermene and from there to Ancient Earth. I do not feel the need to justify my decision, but I feel I owe you a partial explanation."

Clemant paused and his eyes seemed to gaze into an infinite distance. "The fact is that I believe that the Most High has committed to me a great task, one that I must fulfill. Let me explain. In the course of investigating this ship, I have become aware of just how terrible and imminent the threat to the Assembly is. This Lord-Emperor Nezhuala is a man whose ambition and hatred know no limits. He is utterly evil, a man whose energy and goals must come from the great enemy of the Assembly himself. We have recovered images from the files that show that he is preparing a vast fleet, at least a thousand ships strong and each vessel the size of the *Triumph of Sarata*.

"All the evidence we have is that the Dominion will unleash these forces soon. The Assembly must be warned with the utmost speed so that defenses and weapons may be prepared. I cannot wait for votes or decisions." He paused. "There is another reason for me going. But it is a reason of which I can say nothing. It is just that if there is to be any sort of successful defense against this greatest of evils, then information we have must be given to the Assembly now."

Merral sensed in his face and posture an attitude of total defiance.

"I must act in this fashion in order to save the Assembly. Great tasks demand courageous actions. I have been called; I must not falter or fail."

The screen went blank.

Ludovica walked back to Merral. "There is a full meeting of the committee tomorrow at nine and we would like you to be there. We'd like your recommendations on this and other matters." She nodded at the diary. "But any comments on that?"

Merral hesitated, trying to say something sensible. "I need to think about it. He hinted at this when I last saw him, but I didn't understand what he was suggesting."

"What do you think about this other reason he had? We drew a blank on it."

"I think it is linked to Professor Gerry Habbentz."

Ludovica's face showed no recognition of the name.

"A physicist. She was working on weapons. Big weapons—very big. Yes, that would be it. Clemant thinks he has a weapon, but he doesn't want to talk about it." He realized he had to talk to Vero. "Can I make a call?"

"Of course."

"Vero," he said as the dark-skinned face appeared on the screen. "Where are you?"

Vero's expression was one of utter misery. "Brenito's old house. You've heard the news?"

"About the *Dove*?"

"I'm so sor—"

"So am I. But we need to act. I'm on my way to talk to you. In the meantime, can you check on Gerry Habbentz? We need to find where she is."

"Gerry?" Vero's look was one of bemusement. "Of course, but is she important?"

"I think she's on the ship. I think I saw her on the images from the *Dove* and Clemant mentioned that she was looking at the data and had found it alarming."

Vero grimaced as if he had swallowed something bitter. "I'll chase her up."

"Do that. Look, I'll see you soon."

Merral put the diary back on his belt. He wondered about telling Ludovica that they might be able to access a second Below-Space ship, but decided against it. That could wait.

"What has happened at the peninsula?" he asked.

"Ah." A look of discomfort crossed Ludovica's face. "Zak disabled the ships. He was going to launch an attack, but two days ago, Clemant recalled him to Isterrane. Since then there has been a holding operation. The problem is that the forces there are still controlled by a small group of men loyal to Zak."

Merral groaned. "Go on."

Ludovica gave a little sigh. "They do not accept the authority of the new committee."

"So you have a rebel unit."

"Yes. You will be asked to try and negotiate."

Merral said nothing. His mind was consumed by the appalling realization of the extent to which evil had invaded his world. *All our unity has fled. We are now divided against each other.* For some reason he thought of his parents.

"I will do what I can. You have my cooperation."

"Thank you."

Merral stared up at the trees for a last, lingering moment. "Let me collect the few things I have. I need to talk with Vero again."

ⵔⵔⵔⵔ

An hour later, as the sun was setting over Isterrane Bay in a ball of orange flame, Merral knocked on the wooden door of Brenito's old house.

The door opened to reveal a large and familiar figure.

"Evening, sir," Lloyd said with a smart salute.

"Good evening, Sergeant," Merral replied, reaching up to clap him on the shoulder. "It's very good to see you."

"My feelings exactly, sir." Lloyd gave an awkward little cough. "I wish to apologize for deserting you at the airport. Mr. V. said you wouldn't have wanted me to pick a fight."

Merral smiled. "I didn't. No, you did right. And you made a fine medical orderly."

"You reckon so, sir? I was thinking I might retrain when this is all over."

"Ah. 'When this is all over' is a fine phrase, Sergeant. But sadly we aren't there yet and Clemant has made life more complex by stealing the *Dove*. And we have to sort out this Lezaroth at Langerstrand yet. So there's work to do."

Lloyd nodded. "So I reckon you will be needing my services for a bit longer yet."

"I'm afraid so."

There was a contented smile.

"How's Vero?"

Lloyd shook his head. "Mr. V. is bit low. He's in the main room. Go on through, sir, but mind the cases. Mr. Brenito's things."

The hallway was full of wrapped packages and cartons and Merral glimpsed labels on them: *For Isterrane Museum(?), No real interest?* and *What is this?*

As he walked into the main room Lloyd closed the door behind him.

The room, less cluttered than he had last seen it, was lit only by the rays of the setting sun, rendering it full of deep shadows broken by patches of orange light.

Vero was sitting in the rocking chair, his head propped up by his hands. At Merral's entrance, he looked up and his solemn expression eased slightly. He rose and exchanged a hug with Merral.

"It is good to see you, my friend," Vero said in a low voice, filled with bitterness and then sat heavily back into the chair. He stared at the floor, his face deep in shadow. "Oh, what a mess. I feel so much of it is my fault. You warned me against both Clemant and Zak and I disregarded your advice. Look what has happened! And now Gerry."

"What's the news there?"

"Your guess is right. It seems certain she is on the ship. She has not been seen for six days. You think she is helping with the propulsion system or something?"

"No, it's more worrying than that. I think it's something to do with weapons."

"Ah. A subject dear to her heart. But why do you think that?"

Merral sat on a chair. "It's only a guess. She once told me that with Below-Space technology and a polyvalent fusion device you could create an awesome weapon. A 'big bad bomb.' The whole thing worries me."

Vero stared out of the window, his expression hidden in the shadows. "A polyvalent fusion device alone would wipe out life on an entire continent; maybe a world. Something bigger would be . . . utterly terrifying. And with Zak and Clemant . . ." He shook his head. "Oh, how stupid I've been. I've overlooked so much. I've asked Harrent to try to find out what her research was on. The Library is back online, but it may take days to get such information." He shook his head in frustration. "'Cleverness is not the same as wisdom,' the envoy said. How right he was."

"It's not your fault."

"Oh yes it is." Vero's voice was bitter. "Take Clemant. Lots of people wanted him reined in, including you. I knew in my heart that you were right, but I reasoned that a tighter control on his police could also mean a tighter control on my irregulars. That is why I disagreed with you."

"I should have pressed you harder."

"Maybe. And Zak? Yes, I saw the dangers in him. But I felt he was a bigger threat to the enemy than to us. Like Clemant, I saw his toughness as a useful balance to your gentleness."

Merral said nothing.

"And Gerry? To be honest, I had my doubts—you expressed something similar at our first meeting with her—but they were overpowered by her personality. And here as well, I found her too powerful an ally to reject." His tone was full of remorse.

"It was an easy mistake," Merral said.

"And now all three have come together—a most potent and troubling combination." He closed his eyes as if in pain and pressed his long fingers against his temples. "You fool, Verofaza! You utter *fool*. What *would* Brenito have said?"

"Vero, we have both done things that are wrong. But to spend time analyzing this now may not be the wisest thing."

Vero dug his fingers into his curly hair. "No, you are right. Now is not the moment for recriminations. They can wait; we need decisions. You have heard what Clemant said. Do you have anything to add?"

"Yes. When he talked to me, Clemant said there wasn't just a fleet being made ready. He said Nezhuala was making a colossal structure: the Blade of Night."

"The Blade of Night?" Vero's gaze seemed to be on something far away. "Azeras has hinted about something, but he's never been fully open. That must change. I have sent for him and Anya. They have both been in the foundations. I asked them to bring Betafor too. We may need her skills, if they can be trusted."

"Vero, we need to see if we can recover the *Rahllman's Star* and pursue Clemant. Perhaps we can get to the Assembly first."

"I'd like that."

There was silence and then Merral asked, "Where is Jorgio?"

"Just down the road. I think he has been overlooked by Clemant, but I didn't want him arrested. I had him moved. I didn't think he could face being underground, so I found a farm for him to stay on."

"A wise move. Is he well?"

"He's tired. He has been concerned for you. I think he'll be better when he gets back here."

"Good. I would like to talk with him. I suspect his praying lay behind such victories as we had."

"I share your belief. He too fought."

Merral looked around. "Are you living here?"

"I wasn't until two days ago. I was back in the deep levels of Isterrane. I knew that Clemant dared not try and find me there. And from there I contacted all the representatives individually and told them what really happened. Clemant hadn't told them the truth. He had portrayed you as reckless and out of control. But after a bit of work—Enatus and Colonel Lanier helped too—the tide of opinion swung. And it was obvious that Clemant had become very strange. So I decided to venture out of the darkness. I think it had begun to affect me. Perena had warned me about it. If I never see a cellar again, I won't mind."

There was another silence. Merral looked around. "Are all of Brenito's things cataloged?"

"Pretty much."

"Have you found anything that helps?"

"Just hints, no more, that Moshe Adlen knew more than he said about the end of the Rebellion. I need to check the original files on Earth."

Just then there was a knock on the door and Lloyd ushered in the tall figure of Azeras. A second, shorter figure with red hair followed him. At the sight of Anya, a sudden powerful mixture of emotions struck Merral and he felt he was blushing.

Azeras came over and bowed stiffly before him. "Commander, I am honored to know you. A baziliarch has been destroyed. The seven are now six—a remarkable event. The deep Nether-Realms will have shaken at the news." He clenched his fist. "The True Freeborn would have taken great heart from this."

"Sarudar, as at Tezekal, we were saved not by our skill, but by the grace of the Most High."

"However it happened, it was a great blow against the Dominion."

He stepped back. Anya came forward and embraced Merral. The intensity with which she held him made his heart bound.

"Commander," she said, with a laugh, "it's good to see you. I was worried that your promising military career would end at Ynysmant." Merral knew that the humor was only on the surface. Her eyes showed how relieved she was to see him.

Vero tugged Azeras's arm. "Sarudar, let us make some coffee. There is much to discuss, and I think we need alert minds."

"I've been in the foundations too long," said Anya. "Let's have it outside."

Leaving Vero and Azeras in the kitchen, she and Merral made their way past more labeled boxes through the open door onto the veranda. The sun had just set and they stood there for some moments looking out in silence to where the red-streaked purple of the late-evening sky was reflected in the sea.

Merral was suddenly struck by a longing so intense that it almost terrified him. *I wish I could rewrite the script of my life and remove the war, edit out Isabella, bring back Perena, and erase all memories of the fighting and the deaths. But I cannot. And to even consider the idea is pure folly.*

"I thought you were lost." Anya's voice was soft and the levity had fled.

"I thought I *was* lost."

"To have lost my sister and you would have been too much."

Merral was silent for a moment and when he spoke, it seemed to him that his words came out with a great slowness. "The problem is, Anya, that it's not all over."

"No," she said and the single syllable carried a profound sadness.

If it were all over, I could discard my uniform. If it were all over, my relationship with Anya could go where we both want it to go.

He stared at the darkening scene before them. A flock of gulls wheeled noisily above the cliffs as they prepared to roost.

"There is a lot unresolved. I am alarmed by Clemant leaving without consultation. You know that Gerry is almost certainly with him?"

"Ah. I didn't know that. She worries me. Whenever I met her I felt an anger to her that burns like a fire. No; it's more than anger. It's hate." Anya drummed her fingers softly on the railing. "I understand the temptation. There have been times when I could given in to it."

"I'm sorry."

"No, it's gone now. But to hate is to become like them." She gestured westward. "To be destroyed by Krallen or become like them—two terrible but parallel fates."

Merral followed her gesture. Beyond the promontory, the last Dominion forces on Farholme held out.

"I have to sort out the mess at Langerstrand," he said. "I promised Isabella's parents that I would do all I can to get her and the others out. And then, Azeras permitting, we can head to Earth. I'd like to beat the *Dove* to Bannermene."

"Yes." She smiled briefly. "I'm not vindictive, but I'd love to see Clemant's face when you arrest him—and Zak and the prebendant."

Vero and Azeras came out with coffee.

Azeras handed Merral a mug. "Betafor is in the hallway in her case. I gather she tried to betray you?"

"I wouldn't say 'betray.' She just left us for the Dominion when things got tough. Apart from that she was helpful."

"Maybe, but Commander—as I have warned you—she cannot be trusted."

"Perhaps, Sarudar, but as you will have just heard, we cannot trust people either."

"Indeed. I have heard about the *Dove*."

"So you did." Merral turned to Vero. "What happened at the peninsula? I want to resolve that as soon as possible."

Vero stared westward. "It's a mess. Colonel Lanier was suspended by Clemant. That's being reversed. Zak took charge and disabled the *Dove*'s shuttle. He had a sniper put holes in some windscreen elements."

In the gloom, Merral noticed Azeras shaking his head in evident disapproval.

"Then Clemant summoned him and Zak left one of his own people in charge. This morning the unit there refused to accept the authority of the new committee and is effectively autonomous. Communications are only sporadic. I presume the waiting game continues. But Lezaroth can't go anywhere."

"Well, we need to sort out Langerstrand as soon as we can. I hope to go there tomorrow." Merral turned to Azeras. "Sarudar, we need to talk. We have some questions."

"I am ready."

"Good. Some time ago we made an agreement with you. I would say our part of that agreement is now complete. Would you agree?"

"Yes. I can't argue with that. You have kept me safe."

"So, will you recover the *Rahllman's Star* for us?"

"Yes. The True Freeborn keep their promises. Whenever you're ready, we can take a ship and find it."

"Thank you," Merral said, discerning in the deepening gloom the looks of relief on the faces of Vero and Anya. "I hope we can launch a flight within the next day or so."

Azeras nodded. "As you wish."

"Thank you. We don't understand what Clemant wants to do. But it is something that involves weapons and strategy. We want to get to Earth to at least balance what he is trying to do. I'm afraid we no longer trust him."

"I understand the need for haste. Yes, I'll take you inward to the Assembly. I live in hope of getting my place by the sea."

"May you have it. We are grateful for your help." Merral sipped his coffee. "But I have some questions. Clemant justified his taking the *Dove* because he says he found evidence that the Dominion is building a fleet—a fleet of at least a thousand ships, each the size of the *Triumph of Sarata*, and destined to be employed against the Assembly. Is that feasible?"

"I have not seen such a fleet." Azeras flexed his left hand so that the screen on it glowed, lighting up his face. "But I've some data on the older series. Full-suppression complex: time for completion," he muttered, his fingers moving as if he were playing a keyboard. Then he looked up, the light on his hand fading. "Hmm. It is possible. Nezhuala will not have stood still now that the Dominion is enlarged and secure." His thoughtful gaze turned to the darkening bay. "And he has taken over most of the manufacturing facilities of the True Freeborn worlds intact. So yes, a fleet of a thousand ships is quite possible soon."

Merral heard a perturbed grunt from Vero.

"And as for soldiers to fill them . . ." Azeras waved his hand against the night sky. "Thousands of Krallen can be produced in factories daily. Men must be born, raised, and trained before they can be used in war, but not so Krallen. Bug boys and chimpies can be speed-reared." He fell silent.

Merral looked up to see the stars coming out. With a stab of grief, he thought of Perena.

"N-Nezhuala's strategy?" Vero asked.

Azeras gestured around. "This was the first, trial blow. He will soon know that it has failed. He may already have guessed. The loss of the baziliarch will have been felt across all the Nether-Realms. But he may not know *how* it has failed."

"Will it deter him?" Vero's voice held a note of hope.

Azeras rubbed the scar on his cheek. "No. In fact, Sentinel, it may have done the contrary. He may well realize that he cannot risk a delay. He may believe that one or more of his vessels is taken. If so, he'll know that secrecy is now gone, and that the Assembly will soon be making armies and defenses. I think he will head straight for Earth with overwhelming power. The lord-emperor's hope will be to destroy any resistance even before it can be organized."

Merral turned, seeing Anya leaning close to him as if for reassurance. There was a long silence.

Merral looked at the shadowed bulk of Azeras. "One other question, Sarudar. Clemant mentioned that Nezhuala was constructing a colossal construction in space—the Blade of Night. What is it?"

Azeras shifted awkwardly against the balcony rail. "The Blade . . ." Merral heard unease—or was it fear?—in his voice. "Yes, you need to know about that now. I should have said something earlier, but I didn't want to alarm you."

"What is it?" Vero asked.

"It is what Nezhuala calls his great project. He has been making it for years. Nezhuala's base is Khalamaja, one of the four inhabited worlds that orbit Sarata. Above it, Nezhuala has been building a vast structure in space." Azeras stared up, looking at the stars as if he could see what he was talking about. "It is an enormous edifice of metal and stone—by far the largest structure ever made by men. It is a sort of continuous Gate. It extends from what you call Normal-Space down for hundreds of kilometers, maybe more by now."

"What is its purpose?"

"That's never been made clear, but what we learned from prisoners is that Nezhuala sees it as something that will link the Nether-Realms to Standard-Space. The reality is that it is a dimensional excavation that goes deeper and deeper into the Nether-Realms." Azeras stared into the darkness and visibly shuddered. "He parades it as if it were a tower up to the heavens. Instead it is a shaft down to hell." The words were sharp.

Merral heard a sharp intake of breath from Anya. Vero put his coffee mug down on a table nearby so awkwardly that it rattled.

"But why has he made it?" Merral asked, already grappling with the implications of the only answer that there could be.

Azeras looked long at the darkening sky before answering. "Power. Nezhuala derives his power from there. As the Blade has been built, so the power of the Dominion has risen. From down there comes his confidence and drive."

Merral felt Anya grab his hand.

"S-so this project is an attempt to release the energies in deepest Below-Space?" Merral heard a flatness in Vero's voice almost as if the whole idea was so overwhelming that no emotion was adequate to express it.

"Yes and he has done it. He has already released the baziliarchs and now he has gone deeper still."

"Where there is the one," Vero said softly.

"The one. The great serpent—the one who writhes in endless hate." Azeras's voice was a low harsh whisper.

"Have you seen the Blade?" Merral asked.

"Once—two years ago on a mission that didn't succeed. I saw it far away." Azeras's voice seemed to fail and when he spoke again, his voice was husky with emotion. "Even from a hundred kilometers away it can be seen, blocking out stars. It was not finished then. It may be now."

Silence fell.

Suddenly the watch adjunct to Merral's diary pulsed urgently on his wrist.

"Excuse me," Merral said, looking at his diary, "I have an emergency call from Ludovica." He returned inside.

Ludovica was inside some sort of transport that was evidently moving at a rapid pace. Her face was pale and anguished.

"Merral here. What's the problem?"

"I have some bad news. It's Langerstrand. Three hours ago the Krallen there suddenly attacked the surrounding forces. In the confusion the *Dove* shuttle took off. It's now in an odd orb—"

"It was immobilized!"

"So we had been told. Lezaroth had the damage fixed, waited until our forces were in disarray, and then took off. We have only just learned what has happened. Lanier is taking charge at Langerstrand. There have been a lot of casualties, but the Dominion forces have now all been destroyed."

"The hostages?"

"They are all on board the ship." Ludovica's face seemed even paler.

"No!"

"Yes, I know. I'm sorry. I'm on my way to Space Affairs. They're launching a vessel with an assault crew to intercept it. But it will be six hours, at least, before it can intercept."

"But it's got nowhere to go." *Or has it?* With a chill Merral heard again the envoy's words: *The results of your actions remain.* This was another penalty for his having gone to Ynysmant. *Had I been here I would have resolved the hostage crisis before this could happen.*

"Commander, are you all right?"

"Sorry, Ludovica. Just struggling with the news. I need to talk to some people here. When you get to Space Affairs, call the ship. See if you can get a response. Tell Lezaroth—use whatever titles he wants—that Commander D'Avanos wishes to talk to him personally."

"Will do."

Merral walked back to the veranda. "Azeras, the *Dove* shuttle took off from the peninsula three or so hours ago. It's in orbit . . . with the hostages."

Azeras said something that Merral took to be a curse. "No! Zak should have realized that window elements can be fixed."

"But Lezaroth is stuck in orbit, isn't he?"

"Yes. Unless . . ." Azeras's face had a growing expression of fear.

"Unless what?"

"Unless there is another ship in Below-Space."

"Not another warship?"

"No. If there was, Lezaroth would have used it. A supply vessel. A freighter." Azeras shook his head, as he looked up. "You must hope that there isn't." There was a tremor in his voice.

"And if there is such a ship?"

But Azeras had walked away and leaned over the balcony.

Merral followed. As he drew nearer, he saw Azeras's shoulders heaving. "What is it?"

The man shook his head.

Merral decided to leave him alone and instead returned inside with the others.

A few minutes later Ludovica was back on screen. Merral projected it on the wall.

"I'm at Space Affairs. It gets worse. I'm afraid they've seen something emerging not far from the shuttle. It's obviously from Below-Space."

"Can you get me an image?"

She looked around and gestured to someone offscreen. A few moments later a shaking image of a gray metallic form appeared. Close to it could be seen the white form of the *Dove* shuttle. Docking appeared imminent.

Out of the corner of his eye, Merral saw Azeras come in and stare at the screen.

"If you can, destroy it! Now!" Azeras' voice shook with deep emotion. Merral looked up and saw that the gaunt face was wet with tears.

"Sorry, Merral, I didn't catch that."

"Ignore it. I will get back to you, Ludovica. Keep feeding me images though."

Merral muted the diary and disregarding the troubled faces of Anya and Vero, turned to Azeras. "Sarudar," he said, "tell me, honestly. What will happen to the hostages?"

Azeras shook his head. "They will be taken to Sarata." The lips trembled.

"And there?"

"I don't want to say." With wavering fingers Azeras made the strange encircling motion.

"We need to know."

Azeras blinked and suddenly the words tumbled out. "Lezaroth will need to appease the anger of his master for the failure here. He will give him information about the Assembly. And . . . he will offer him the living for those he deals with. They will probably be sent to the Blade of Night, and there given as food for the baziliarchs and bait for the steersmen. That's what he has always done."

On the edge of his vision, Merral saw Anya, her eyes wide in a bloodless face, staring at Azeras with silent horror. Vero's mouth was open in dismay.

"That is why I say, if you have the means, destroy that ship. It will be a . . . mercy!"

Suddenly Azeras buried his face in his hands. "I lied! *They* did not torch Tellzanur. *I* did." His shoulders shook. "I burned women and children alive to save them from just this."

As Merral caught the horrified looks, a single thought pulsed in his brain: *Isabella is on that ship.*

Lord, what do I do? An enormous vista of appalling choices opened before him. *Give me wisdom, Lord.*

"Thank you, Azeras," he said.

Anya helped Azeras gently to a chair.

Merral touched the speak button on the diary. "Ludovica, do we have a weapon that can destroy that ship? Can you ask?"

"Are you serious? That would mean—" Her face was white and disbelieving.

"Just ask!"

She turned away. Merral glimpsed Anya staring at him and he swung away so he wouldn't have to see her. He needed facts.

"Azeras," he said brusquely, "what is that ship? I need answers."

"A freighter, a star series—the same as the *Rahllman's Star*. Probably automated, so maybe without a crew. The *Dove* didn't have a steersman chamber, so maybe Lezaroth just had them both follow the *Triumph*. That's how these things work."

"And how long before they disappear into Below-Space?"

"Docking doesn't seem to have started yet. And they have passengers to transfer. Say an hour minimum."

"Thank you."

On the diary Ludovica, her face oblique to the screen, talked with a young man. She turned to Merral. "There is a supply rocket at Near Station. If it is fired now, it will strike them in fifty minutes. The kinetic energy released by the collision will . . . vaporize the ship."

"And could our rocket be aborted in flight?"

"Wait." Behind her, Merral glimpsed a young man nodding. "Yes," she said.

"Then launch it."

Merral heard a sharp intake of breath from Vero.

Ludovica stared at him. "Are you . . . ? Over thirty lives. . . . Are you sure?"

"Yes. I take full responsibility."

Out of the corner of his eye, Merral saw Anya walk unsteadily out of the room.

Ludovica closed her eyes for a moment and then opened them. "Launch. That's an order."

There was a pause. "Rocket fired," said a voice off the camera.

"Thank you, Ludovica," Merral said, appalled at how level his voice sounded. "Keep this line open."

Merral made a mental note of the time and muted the diary again. Aware of Vero staring at him, he picked up a chair and sat in front of Azeras.

"Sarudar, please. We need to talk."

Slowly and hesitantly, the man looked up at him, but he said nothing.

"Now listen. We have less than an hour. I want to explore an alternative to destroying the *Dove* shuttle. Let's ignore Earth and the Assembly. Forget them. Now, I need an answer. Can we chase them with the *Rahllman's Star* and catch them? rescue them?"

"You want to go *that* way?" The dark gray eyes were wide.

"Yes. But I need honest answers. And I need *all* the facts." Merral marveled again at how he could be so calm. *"Now."*

"L-let me think. They have a start. Perhaps no more than two days. Lezaroth will go as fast as he can. But he's probably got no steersman and maybe only a partial crew—some of the *Dove*'s crew were killed. So they will be slow." Azeras flexed his left fingers and stared at the glowing patch on the back of his hand. "I calculate five weeks—maybe—to get to Sarata. No sooner."

"And us, how fast?"

"The same, plus the few days it would take to get ready. We can't beat them, if that's what you're thinking."

"W-what if you drove the *Rahllman's Star* deeper through Below-Space?" Vero suddenly asked.

"You don't want to go deeper. The deeper Nether-Realms get nasty."

Merral caught Azeras's eye. "If we ignore that risk, could we catch them?"

"Yes. But you might not be sane when you came out into Normal-Space."

"And if we risked that, could we successfully intercept this ship?"

"Hypothetically, yes. Logically they'd aim for the main military docking station at Gerazon-Far in the Sarata system. They won't be expecting a rescue attempt; they think the only active Below-Space vessel here is already headed earthward. And they don't do mercy rescues. Lezaroth doesn't understand the concept."

Merral was aware of Anya standing by the kitchen door, her expression unreadable.

"Would we have to use a steersman?"

"You killed the only one we had. But no, the journey will largely retrace a journey that has already been taken. We have the coordinates. You back navigate."

Merral looked at his watch. Time was passing. His mouth was dry. "Sarudar Azeras, I want to us to chase that ship in the *Rahllman's Star*. I need you to fly it."

There was a pause. "No. I don't want to go back. Not there. Sorry."

"I understand your reluctance. It is not a path I wish to take. I would go alone if I could fly the ship."

"You gave me freedom."

"We did. And I cannot order you."

Azeras stared at him. "Commander, what happens if I continue to refuse?"

"There will be a new star in the sky in . . . what . . . just over forty minutes."

Merral caught an appalled look from Anya and saw Vero shake his head. "Are you really serious about this?" they seemed to ask.

Azeras rose from his seat and paced heavily to the window, his head slumped on his shoulders. He stared out and then turned back to face Merral. "I have shed enough innocent blood. I will take you to the Dominion. Call off the missile."

"That is a promise?"

"On my oath."

"Thank you." Merral said. He tapped the diary. "Ludovica?"

An anxious face greeted him. "Yes?"

"Cancel the attack. We found a way of pursuing them."

"Thank you, God," she whispered and turned to the young man nearby. "Abort."

A moment later she turned back to Merral. "It is done. But 'another way'? I don't understand."

"I will explain everything to the committee tomorrow morning. In the meantime, can you summon a logistics team to Isterrane Airport for a meeting, in an hour's time? I need to have a ship launched as soon as possible—preferably tomorrow midday."

"Very well. May I meet you there?"

"Of course."

"I will make arrangements. And, by the way, there has been no response from Lezaroth."

"I thought not. See you soon."

The link ended. Merral suddenly felt certain that he had not seen the last of Lezaroth. *We will meet again, and when we do, I must watch out. The hatred he had for me will surely have grown greater. But for the moment, I have more pressing concerns.*

Merral looked at Azeras. "Sarudar, assuming we are to bring back the thirty hostages, how many people can we take?"

Azeras flexed his hand and looked at the screen. "Supplies will be tight. Thirty, thirty-one maximum, including you and me. No more."

"Very well," Merral suddenly realized he was shaking. "I need some fresh air," he said and walked outside onto the balcony. There he stared up at the stars.

Dear Lord, I have had to make decisions and act swiftly. I need your guidance and protection on the path I have to take.

He suddenly noticed Anya alongside him.

"Well done," she said softly. "I think."

"I understand your reservation. Thanks."

"I didn't understand what you were doing. Not at first. Would you have let the rocket hit them?"

Merral stared silently into the soft blackness where the sea rolled gently. "I'm not sure. I'm glad the decision was made for me."

He was silent for sometime before he spoke. "But, Anya, as for going to pursue them, I have no regrets. That has to be done. I made a promise to Isabella's parents. Even if I hadn't, I would still want to go. If we left them to their fate, we would be denying all that the Assembly is."

"True. And I admire you for that."

"I'm not sure how admirable my behavior is. Had I obeyed in the first place, these events might not have happened."

"That issue is past. I want to come with you."

"Why? It will be dangerous, appallingly so."

"I will come. My sister feared no evil; nor will I."

"Let me think about it."

"Please." She touched his hand. "Let me leave you alone."

"Thank you. It's only twenty minutes to the airport. I want the time to think some more."

She left him and he stood there, leaning on the balcony rail watching the black sea with its waves twinkling silver in the starlight.

In an instant, he was aware of someone beside him, a silent night-black figure that occluded the stars.

"Ah," Merral said softly. "I take it you do not need to be told what has happened."

"No." The voice seemed to cut through the warm stillness of the night. "I was forewarned. And I saw what happened."

"Envoy, I understand your warning now. As a result of my disobedience, we have lost both the *Dove* and the hostages. Had I stayed here, both might have been averted. I'm sorry."

"I was not sent to rebuke you, not now."

"That's a relief. But I could have done with your advice just now. I had to make some hard choices."

"I did not come any earlier for the very reason that they were hard choices. Your race prefers to evade such decisions: you are tempted to let us make them for you. That is partly why we keep a distance. Yet such decisions are part of the way of growth the Most High has chosen for you. My silence was for your good."

"I see. So how did I do?"

"Better."

"Well, thank you."

"Look up." The envoy commanded.

High above there was a flash of brilliant light among the stars.

"Was that them?" Merral asked, knowing the answer.

"Yes. They have started on their long journey."

"And we will follow."

"Yes. I have been sent to say that you will not go into the darkness alone. You must remember that you can go nowhere, even the deepest realms that the enemy controls, where you will be beyond the power of the Lord of All."

"I am very grateful for that reminder. And will you come?"

"If I told you I will come, you might relax. If I told you I will not, you might despair. So I will say nothing."

"So your silence is for our good?"

"Exactly."

"Envoy, who should I take?"

"Take Verofaza, Lloyd, and the Allenix unit. And twenty-four of the bravest soldiers you can find."

"I will. Jorgio?"

"I am pleased you know his worth. But no. Have him kept safe here. His destiny lies at the heart of the Assembly."

"Anya wants to go."

"Let her. But there, guard yourself. You have failed once; do not fail again. And let me remind you. One of the perils of spectacular evil is that men and women are so blinded by it that they stumble over more subtle but no less deadly evils."

"Thank you."

"Choose your team well."

The envoy's form faded away.

Merral waited a few more minutes before returning inside.

The only person in the main room was Vero, who was packing a hold-all. He looked up. "My friend, I take it you will not refuse me the chance of traveling with you."

"No."

"I had wished my journey would be inward to home, but instead it is outward into the enemy's territory."

Merral sighed. "First. As soon as we can, we will go on to Earth. We must pray that not too much damage will be done before we get there. But I warn you, Vero, the journey to rescue the hostages will be very dangerous. What Azeras has revealed to us at last are the foundations that the Dominion rests on. I think you know, as I do, where—and to whom—the Blade of Night leads."

Vero, who seemed to stare at the wall ahead, gave a tiny nod. "I know. In my heart, I suspected this. But whatever the risks, I will come with you. I believe in this the Most High has bound our lives together."

"Thank you," Merral said and hesitated.

In the silence a moth fluttered against the window.

"Vero, you remember you once said there were people who would follow me to the gates of hell?"

Vero nodded. "A figure of speech."

"We'd better find them. That's where we're going."

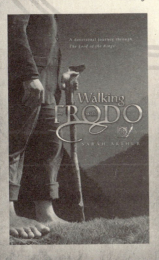

have you visited
tyndalefiction.com
lately?

Only there can you find:

→ books hot off the press

→ first chapter excerpts

→ inside scoops on your favorite authors

→ author interviews

→ contests

→ fun facts

→ and much more!

Sign up for your **free** newsletter!

Visit us today at: tyndalefiction.com

Tyndale fiction does more than entertain.

→ *It touches the heart.*
→ *It stirs the soul.*
→ *It changes lives.*

That's why Tyndale is so committed to being first in fiction!

TYNDALE
FICTION